The tall spire of the Sanctum, high over head, had started to sway. The Gargoyles that squatted around it reacted slowly, their wings shuddering uncertainly as they unfolded them from their hunched positions and prepared to take flight. Inside the building, all the soldiers and both mind mages were probably already dead; if not, they would die within moments.

The massive spire toppled and fell. The Sanctum of the Stars completely collapsed. It seemed to happen with a horrific slowness. The immense weight of cracking, falling stone created a terrifying roar. People in the streets were screaming in panic, and fleeing to safety. Chandra turned and fled, too.

The enormous impact of the Sanctum collapsing on itself hurled rocks, flames, ashes, dust, and debris across the main square and down the length of every surrounding street. Chandra was knocked off her feet when the ground shook and a wave of rock and ash hurled her forward. Someone trampled her prone body as they ran headlong from the disaster. Winded and in pain, Chandra was lying face down in the street, debris still showering down on her as the dust of pulverized stone filled her lungs.

Coughing and bleeding, she lay there in a daze.

Fire above, the whole thing! The whole building! I didn't mean to do that.

To Abel Gance

Acknowledgments

A book of this sort cannot be the work of one person; it depends on a great deal of cooperation and generosity. My fond hopes of a definitive history of the silent film were dashed when I realized the immensity of the task. What I have aimed at is a re-creation of the atmosphere and achievements of the period, through the memories of those who created it. I have checked and cross-checked the facts, but I am enough of a realist to know that absolute accuracy is a myth. Realism is only one's view of it. From scores of interviews with silent-film personalities, a picture of the era emerged which I believe to be true. Wherever possible, I have quoted original interviews rather than impose my own opinions and phraseology. For their assistance, generosity, and hospitality I am profoundly grateful to the stars, directors, producers, and cameramen listed below:

Minta Durfee ARBUCKLE
Dorothy ARZNER
Nils ASTHER
Olga BACLANOVA
Enid BENNETT
Ouida BERGERE
Raymond BERNARD
Constance BINNEY
Frank BLOUNT
Betty BLYTHE
Margaret BOOTH
Monte BRICE
Clive BROOK
Louise BROOKS
Clarence BROWN
Francis X. BUSHMAN
Alberto CAVALCANTI
Mary CARR
Nancy CARROLL
Charles CHAPLIN
Lenore COFFEE
Betty COMPSON
Chester CONKLIN
Marc CONNELLY
Merian C. COOPER
Ricardo CORTEZ
William Joyce COWEN
Henri D'ABBADIE D'ARRAST
Bebe DANIELS
Priscilla DEAN
Reginald DENNY
Marlene DIETRICH
Albert DIEUDONNÉ

Beulah Marie DIX
Louise DRESSER
Vivian DUNCAN
Allan DWAN
Douglas FAIRBANKS, Jr.
Geraldine FARRAR
Robert FLOREY
Sidney FRANKLIN
Abel GANCE
Marco de GASTYNE
Dorothy GISH
Lillian GISH
Dagmar GODOWSKY
Albert HACKETT
Hope HAMPTON
Howard HAWKS
Alfred HITCHCOCK
William HORNBECK
James Wong HOWE
Gareth HUGHES
Sam JAFFE
Leatrice JOY
Boris KARLOFF
Buster KEATON
Henry KING
Louise LAGRANGE
Fritz LANG
Jesse L. LASKY, Jr.
Marcel L'HERBIER
Anatole LITVAK
Harold LLOYD
Anita LOOS
Bessie LOVE

Ben LYON
Francis McDONALD
William McGANN
Don MALKAMES
Enid MARKEY
Percy MARMONT
Leon MATHOT
Lothar MENDES
Arthur MILLER
Patsy Ruth MILLER
Virgil MILLER
Karin MOLANDER
Colleen MOORE
James MORRISON
Carmel MYERS
Conrad NAGEL
Pola NEGRI
Al PARKER
Mary PICKFORD
Aileen PRINGLE
Jean RENOIR
Hal ROACH
Charles Buddy ROGERS
Charles ROSHER
Hal ROSSON
Henrik SARTOV
Mrs. B. P. SCHULBERG
John F. SEITZ

David O. SELZNICK
Irene Mayer SELZNICK
Edward SLOMAN
Josef von STERNBERG
Andrew L. STONE
Doris STONE
Mrs. Al ST. JOHN
Adela Rogers ST. JOHNS
Donald Ogden STEWART
Eddie SUTHERLAND
Gloria SWANSON
Blanche SWEET
Phil TANNURA
Lowell THOMAS
Richard THORPE
Jacques TOURNEUR
James Van TREES
Frank TUTTLE
King VIDOR
George WALSH
Raoul WALSH
Walter WANGER
William WELLMAN
Irvin WILLAT
Lois WILSON
William WYLER
Adolph ZUKOR

A Note of Thanks

THE PARADE'S GONE BY . . . took shape after my first visit to America; for this Sloane Shelton must take responsibility. She provided both incentive and inspiration. I am also indebted to J. M. Burgoyne-Johnson, who started my collection of films; William K. Everson and Bert Langdon, who opened up their collections and their knowledge; and Liam O'Leary, Philip Jenkinson, the British Film Institute, Eastman House, Filmhistoriska Samlingarna, and the Cinémathèque Française. In America, George Pratt, David Bradley, Tom Webster, Elinor and Tom Jones, George Mitchell, Jr., Agnes de Mille, Alan Brock, James Card, Robert Florey, Gilbert Seldes, and Maurice Schaded rendered vital assistance. I owe an especial debt to Louise Brooks for acting as a prime mover in this book's publication. Others who have contributed more than they realize and for whose kindness I am deeply grateful: John and Anne Krish, Peter and Carole Smith, Bernard Eisenschitz, Peter and Johanna Suschitzky, Dick and Pauline Jobson, Andrew Mollo, Mamoun Hassan, Harold Dunham, John Gillett, Leslie Flint, Thomasina Jones, Mr. and Mrs. George Ornstein, Oscar Lewenstein, and John Kobal, who tracked down many of the rare stills used in this book. And finally special thanks are due to Janet Reder. This book could not have been produced without her.

PUBLICATIONS ACKNOWLEDGMENTS

In addition to the books and magazines credited in footnotes, the following publications were used for research:

Austin G. Lescaboura: Behind the Motion Picture Screen. *New York: Scientific American Publishing Company; 1919.*

Homer Croy: How Motion Pictures Are Made. *New York: Harper & Brothers; 1918.*

Carl Louis Gregory: Motion Picture Photography. *New York: New York Institute of Photography; 1920.*

Maurice Bardèche and Robert Brassilach: The History of the Film. *London: George Allen & Unwin; 1938.*

Virgil Miller: Splinters from Hollywood Tripods. *New York: Exposition Press; 1964.*

Modern Authorship, Representative Photoplays Analyzed. *Hollywood: Palmer Institute of Authorship; 1924.*

The Moving Picture World *(trade paper)*

American Cinematographer

Film Daily Year Books *1919–29*

Films in Review

Variety

Close-Up

Movie Monthly

Photo Play Journal

Picture Show

Kine Weekly

Bioscope

Cine-Cinea

STILL-PICTURE ACKNOWLEDGMENTS *(by page number)*

Minta Durfee Arbuckle: 38, 357 *(above)*, 475
Betty Blythe: 327, 383
David Bradley: 241 *(above)*
Louise Brooks: 357, 373 *(above)*
Clarence Brown: 139, 143, 148, 151, 329
Kevin Brownlow Collection: 7, 15, 17 *(below)*, 27, 28, 33, 37, 55 *(below)*, 69, 79, 99, 121, 181 *(below)*, 214 *(above)*, 221–3, 240 *(above)*, 243, 265, 268–9, 274 *(above)*, 292 *(below)*, 306, 310 *(left)*, 313, 321 *(above)*, 336–7, 418, 419, 423, 429, 431, 440 *(above)*, 441 *(above)*, 452–3, 461, 467, 475, 488, 497, 500 *(below)*, 502, 512, 513 *(right)*, 549, 555, 560–1
Bebe Daniels: 461 *(below)*
Agnes de Mille: 340
Aubrey Dewar: 208, 209 *(above)*
Louise Elliott: 121
William Everson: 332 *(below)*

Contents

1 / *INTRODUCTION*

The title of this book sprang from an interview with Monte Brice. Brice, who had been a writer and director of silent comedies, told me of the time he watched the shooting of *The Buster Keaton Story,* a 1957 Paramount film loosely based on Keaton's life.

"They had it all wrong," said Brice. "I tried to tell them that things weren't like that in the twenties, but they wouldn't listen. I remember the assistant, a young guy. He said to me, 'Look, why don't you go away? Times have changed. You're an old man. The parade's gone by . . .' "

The silent era is regarded as prehistoric, even by those who work in motion pictures. Crude, fumbling, naïve, the films exist only to be chuckled at—quaint reminders of a simple-minded past, like Victorian samplers.

This book attempts to correct these distortions, for the silent era was the richest in the cinema's history. I have tried to recapture the spirit of the era through the words of those who created it. Linking chapters provide a context for the interviews, in the way that establishing shots precede closeups. But the use of direct material has led to gaps, and I cannot claim that this book is definitive. I regret omitting a chapter on Erich von Stroheim, for example, but I never met him and could throw no more light on his work than the many other writers whose books and articles have already been published. I regret still more the exclusion of other personalities whom I *did* meet, and who gave me so much fascinating material. The silent era is far too rich and complex a period to be covered in one book; I hope eventually to publish all these interviews.

I have tried to see the films I write about, rather than depending on secondhand reports. Certainly, many have disappeared, but I had access to private collections, company vaults, and national archives, and can claim to have seen a representative cross section of the films of the time. I have also built up my own collection of silent features. William K. Everson, the film historian who has done more than anyone to rescue and to document the silent era, also did more than anyone to help me, by making available both his knowledge and his collection.

Throughout the book I have quoted frequently from *Photoplay* magazine. Fan magazines are not noted for their accuracy or wit, but *Photoplay* had nothing in common with its present-day counterparts. It was a forthright, hard-hitting, well-balanced, and highly entertaining publication, and it was a gold mine of information about the making of pictures. *Photoplay's* success was engineered by James Quirk, former editor of *Popular Mechanics.* He gave it a sort of clinical accuracy which none of the other magazines shared. Quirk knew the film business and seldom fell for press-agent stories. Occasionally, he would brighten an issue by publishing the more outrageous publicity stunts; he printed a picture of Dorothy Mackaill, having her lips tattooed, and captioned it "pure bunk." *Photoplay* set the standard for film journalism, publishing work by Robert E. Sherwood, H. L. Mencken, George Jean Nathan, and Donald Ogden Stewart.

As a film technician in the modern industry, I have a deep admiration for my counterparts of forty years ago. Carried away by the novelty of the new medium by the lack of conventions and rules, by their newly acquired wealth and by the glamour, excitement, and risk of motion-picture production, the film makers of silent-era Hollywood created something valuable enough to be called art.

The beginnings of this newest art are so recent that many of those who developed it are still alive. Commercial interests, however, have destroyed their work.

When the money-making life of a film is over, prints are generally incinerated. The average existence of a motion picture is five years. Thanks to archives, and the enlightened carelessness of certain members of the film business, many silent films still survive. But not enough to satisfy those who saw silents originally, and who remember the great ones which have now completely vanished.

The secret of the silent film lay in its unique ability to conjure up a situation that closely involved an audience, because demands were made on its imagination. The audience responded to suggestion, supplied the missing sounds and voices, and became a creative contributor to the process of projection. A high degree of technical skill was required to make such demands effective; what the audience saw it had to believe in.

When sound arrived, it not only brought the silent era to a close. It wrecked the careers of many stars and of many directors, who, while expert with silent pictures, were lost when it came to dialogue. Like sculptors forced suddenly to take up painting, they found themselves working in the same studios, in the same business, but in a completely different medium.

The golden era was the period from 1916 to 1928. It is a neglected period, forgotten often by the very men who enriched it. They have seen their films reissued on television; bad prints shown at the wrong speed have distorted their memory. Perhaps the ballyhoo meant nothing. Perhaps their much-praised pictures *were* as jerky and as primitive as they appear today.

They were not. Even at their worst, American silent pictures were technically competent. At their best, the photography glistened and gleamed, lights and gauzes fused with magical effect until the art of lighting reached its zenith. It was not merely the stories or the stars that gave magic to the silent screen. It was the patience, hard work, tenacity, and skill of the silent-film technician—the man who, in less than ten years, had developed a craft and perfected an art.

The story, so beloved of film historians, in which audiences scream, faint or stampede at the first glimpse of Lumière's train may arouse suspicions of fantasy. For the public was not completely unprepared for the motion picture. Attempts to represent movement are as old as cave paintings. Shadowplays, images thrown in silhouette upon a white screen, preceded the theater itself. During the eighteenth and nineteenth centuries, various optical toys created an astonishingly convincing illusion of movement, depicting birds flying, figures leaping, and horses galloping. The magic-lantern show was generally a static display, but some elaborate slides were fitted with the mechanism of motion. When a small handle was turned, wheels revolved, trees waved, and chimneys smoked.

But these movements were lateral. They usually occurred on one plane. The Zoetrope bird flapped energetically, and appeared to be traveling from right to left. The smoke in the lantern slide drifted upward. When Lumière's train arrived at La Ciotat station in 1895, it made history. For it was photographed as it came toward, and past, the camera. The motion picture had at last made it possible to show an object *approaching* an audience.

Lumière selected this head-on view in order to get the whole train into the picture; a side angle would have been inadequate. By doing this, he unconsciously added the one element missing from other attempts at simulating movement: dynamism.

Although it was peacefully steaming to a halt, a sight familiar to every member of the audience, Lumière's train appeared to be hurtling out of the screen. Had they had time to think, the spectators' common sense would have preserved their dignity. As it was, they scarcely had time to duck. According to original reports, some women screamed, others fainted. And Lumière's train was not the only film to arouse alarm.

In America, in April 1896, at Koster and Bial's Music Hall, Edison's Vitascope was presented. Operating the projection equipment on this historic occasion was pioneer Thomas Armat. Interviewed by *The New York Times* on the fiftieth anniversary of this event, Armat recalled that one of the items, *Sea Waves,* "started a panicky commotion among those up front" as the sea came rushing toward them. And he remembered how the audience went wild and cheered when the dancer Annabelle appeared life-size on the screen.

Some of the reports from this time were undoubtedly colored by journalistic excitement, but the basic truth remains: adults, with normal reactions and intelligence, reacted like children. The fact that this occurred in 1896 makes little difference. As late as 1931, when Georovesti, Rumania, was treated to its first motion-picture show, twelve peasants were hurt in the rush for the exit. In the mid-1950's, when the huge Cinerama screen was unveiled, the audience found itself enduring the sudden lurches and sickening plunges of a roller-coaster ride. Screams, gasps and groans filled the theater; years of moviegoing counted for nothing. The audience was caught off guard; the startling dynamism of the sequence shattered its barriers of defense. A roller coaster, a train—what is recorded is immaterial. For it is not the movement itself that is magical, but how that movement is used.

During the primitive years, the emphasis was on movement for movement's sake. Film manufacturers exploited only the most basic characteristic of the motion picture. The public's interest flagged as the novelty wore thin. The little one-shot

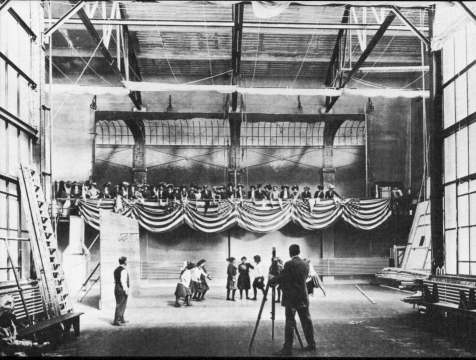

Edison Studios, 1908: Henry Cronjager filming A Country Girl's Seminary Life and Experiences.

G. W. Bitzer filming U.S. Artillery maneuvers, 1904.

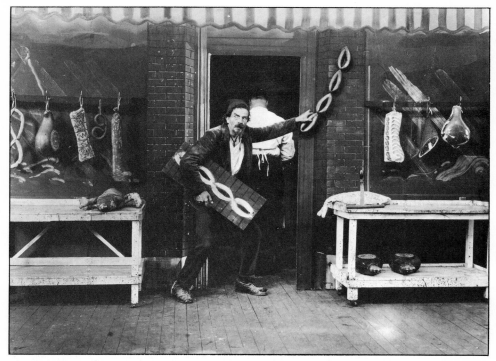

The primitive motion picture: **The Starving Artist** *(Vitagraph, 1907).*

films like Lumière's *Demolition of a Wall* and *Launching of a Boat* continued to be shown for many years at fairgrounds and by traveling showmen, but their theatrical attraction was diminishing by the turn of the century. In America, the big vaudeville houses decided that the living-picture craze was over. They dispensed with their equipment. The cheaper theaters continued to use films—but only as chasers, clearing the houses, like the advertising intermissions of today.

Vaudeville, however, supplied entertainment mainly for the middle classes. America's working classes, its immigrant population, continued to find living pictures exciting, even if they had to peer into hand-cranked machines to see them. Owners of Kinetoscopes and Mutoscopes, aware of the money they were making from their penny arcades, quickly realized the money they *could* make. They acquired projection machines and converted their arcades into picture theaters. Before long, the penny arcades became nickelodeons. Vacant stores were bought up and converted by entrepreneurs, working feverishly against the time they feared the craze would cease.

The middle classes regarded such exhibitions as "penny claptrap." Homer Dunne, writing in *Motion Picture Magazine* in 1916, vividly recalled his disillusionment at a "moving photograph" show in Philadelphia in the late 1890s. Dunne was attracted to a store window, blazing with the light of two arc lamps, in which a young man cranked the handle of "an odd looking boxlike contrivance upon a tripod." A barker harangued a knot of curious bystanders. Dunne parted with five cents and went inside.

"At the far end of the store a small sheet, obviously dirty, was hung loosely from a wire. It was biliously yellow, and had a seam down the center. A rope was stretched from one wall to the other, about three feet in front of the sheet. There were no seats; the half-dozen spectators smoked vigorously and mopped their fevered foreheads. Presently there sounded a noisy sputtering and spitting in the window. Upon the sheet appeared the silhouette of the head of the perspiring young man who officiated at the clothes-wringer handle. The shadow moved here and there, as though he were dodging a crowd of angry hornets. If this were a "moving photograph" I decided I preferred the shadowgraphs of donkeys and rabbits I had learned to throw upon the wall in my youth.

"I was on the point of leaving when the voice of the barker took on a new thrill of urgency. The sputtering and the spitting became louder and sharper. The silhouette of the young man's head disappeared and the sheet suddenly glowed with an exaggerated phosphorescence. A noise like the grinding of a coffee-mill became audible. Clickety-clack! Click! Sputter! Spit and click! Then the sheet broke into a rash of magnified measles. Great blobs of pearl-colored light danced from one side to the other. These were interspersed with flashes of zigzag lightning and punctuated with soft and mellow glows like a summer sunset. As an exhibition of a "light fantasy" it was an unqualified success. But as yet nothing even remotely resembling a picture, moving or still, had appeared.

"After a few minutes of this luminous orgy, however, a man's face popped out from between two brilliant splotches of light. Soon, another face appeared in the northwest corner of the sheet. Later, a human torso flashed into view; then its arms popped into place, then its legs; its head arrived soon after, and it stood revealed in its entirety—a perfect man. Eventually, he was joined by his pal. For nearly a minute they gestured and gesticulated at each other. Finally Number One lost his temper. Without warning he launched a vicious blow at Number Two.

"Whether the blow was a knockout I shall never know. Before it landed, the sheet was plunged into pitchy darkness—and the show was over.

"I have often wondered what would have happened if I had predicted to those who witnessed with me that weird performance that the day would come when that same moving photograph would be developed and perfected . . . For no one took that exhibition seriously. How could we, when not one of us knew what it was all about?"[1]

In Europe, several forces were transforming the watching of films from an optical assault into a magical experience. One of these was a genuine magician, Georges Méliès. Among the first to tell a story with film, Méliès invariably provided a full-scale pantomime—with trimmings no stage manager could achieve. He and his staff produced trick effects which at the time seemed stupendous, and which even today appear remarkable. Méliès, however, was not a true *cinéaste*. He was a dedicated showman; he regarded the camera as an invaluable prop which improved beyond measure many of his stage effects. With films he could reach a far wider audience. Although he employed new effects, such as a form of dissolve, Méliès's camera recorded the customary theatrical mid-long-shot—from the front seat of the stalls.

[1] Motion Picture Magazine, *Aug. 1916, p. 81.*

Whatever his methods, however, he told a story and was the most influential of the pioneers. Deeply impressed by his work was Edwin S. Porter, cameraman and director for the Edison Company in America. Porter once said that it was the Méliès pictures that led him to a significant conclusion: since the attraction of the one-shot films was beginning to pall, perhaps the straightforward telling of a story might draw the customers back to the theaters.

Porter took some of the Edison Company's one-shot films, fifty-foot lengths with the common subject of fire. He had them joined together; the result lasted four hundred and twenty-five feet and was titled *The Life of an American Fireman*. The scenes were purely informative, showing the firehouse and crew, and the fire engines racing to a call. To make these stock shots more exciting, Porter photographed extra scenes—the fireman thinking of his wife and baby, and the final rescue from the burning building. The Edison Company, in their publicity, glossed over the fact that the stock shots showed different fire departments by claiming: "We were compelled to enlist the services of the fire departments of four different cities. It will be difficult for the exhibitor to conceive the amount of work involved and the number of rehearsals necessary to turn out a film of this kind."[2]

Porter's epoch-making editing of this film and the more elaborate *Great Train Robbery* (1903) has been the subject of much analysis and supposition. Actually, like so many other important events in motion pictures, it was casual and intuitive.

Yet few other film makers followed this compelling style—not even Porter, whose later films were conservative and theatrical. For dramatic subjects of this period were invariably reproductions of stage plays. The players conducted themselves as though on the stage—from which most of them had come. The scenery was generally painted, and the camera was rigid. Titles announced the content of the scene. Little was left to the imagination.

But some of those crouched in the scented darkness of the nickelodeon had never seen a play, and these films were a revelation. Some, poorly paid workers, were illiterate. Others, penniless immigrants, did not speak English. But the titles were read from the screen aloud and translated into a dozen languages. It was Babel, but there were few who did not benefit. The commotion encouraged the stranger; here was one place where he was accepted and where he felt at ease. Gradually the little films taught him customs and ways of life which had previously baffled him; they began to extend his outlook and enlarge his interests. America's immigrant population learned from the movies in a way denied them by the spoken theater.

Others, for whom the theater had been the principal diversion, discovered new advantages in the movies. Accustomed to the cheapest seats, they found the camera giving them the view from the best seats in the house. The scenes, though lengthy, were much shorter than those of theatrical productions. The titles that separated them were swifter than a curtain. When two scenes were joined together without a title, the impact on audiences used to the tedious delays of scene shifting was understandably startling.

But for all these advantages, the middle-class patrons of vaudeville, and of the legitimate stage, had yet to be won over to the movies. The main deterrent

[2] *George Pratt:* Spellbound in Darkness *(Rochester, N.Y.: University of Rochester; 1966), p. 27. This is the most important reference work on the silent era.*

was the movie houses themselves. Owners protested that their houses were clean and free from vermin; they had sprayed the disinfectant themselves. Somehow, the middle classes remained unconvinced. Certain exhibitors opened luxurious new theaters and were gratified by the response. But the prosperous classes demanded more than colored lights and plush. Motion pictures remained the common language of the poor.

A vast number of short films were churned out during this period. Most of them were sold outright, and so many have survived—unlike the silent films of later years, which were returned to the distributor for destruction. When seen today these early films are interesting historically, academically, and sociologically —but seldom cinematically. Apart from the occasional breakthrough, such as the experiments of Méliès and Porter, films of this very early period were not films at all. Shots were joined together but not edited. Scenes were illuminated but not lit.

Yet the foundations for a new industry were being laid. And by laying the foundations for industry, these pioneers were providing the groundwork of an art.

3 / EARLY DAYS AT VITAGRAPH

Although the American film industry is associated exclusively with Hollywood, it was born in the East. James Morrison, one of the earliest names to be known by the public, was an actor with the Vitagraph Company in Flatbush, Brooklyn. He now lives in New York City and retains warm memories of the industry as it existed in the early years of the century.

Vitagraph was one of the leading pioneer companies; so many important personalities received their training there that it became known as the Vitagraph High School. In the last years of its existence, before it was taken over by Warner Brothers, Vitagraph was a shadow of its former glory. Referred to as the Morgue of the Movies, it still succeeded in producing pictures of high quality: *Black Beauty; Pampered Youth,* the silent version of *The Magnificent Ambersons; Captain Blood; The Beloved Brute,* Victor McLaglen's first American film.

James Morrison knew Vitagraph at all its stages, and while he had no illusions about the crudity of the very early productions, he had great admiration for what was achieved later. When I met him in New York in 1964 he was in his seventies but retained his boyish good looks. A recent hip operation had forced him to use crutches. He blamed his disability—indirectly, at least—on a picture called *The Nth Commandment.* "I'm sure it's due to us actors doing all our own stunts in those early days," he said. "I did a skating scene in that picture, and the assistant counted thirty-eight falls!"

Morrison retired from pictures in 1926 and returned to the stage, with which he was still in close contact. He had no sentimentality about the past, but displayed a warm nostalgia for the people he worked with. As he talked, it became clear that this journey to the past was a significant experience for him. "Why," he exclaimed at one point, "you're bringing up names I haven't thought of for forty years!"

JAMES MORRISON: My career began at the American Academy of Dramatic Arts, where I specialized in pantomime. We had a tremendous teacher there called Madame Alberti; her great theory was that pantomime had to be the basis of all acting. If your pantomime wasn't correct, you didn't read your line correctly. I still agree with her. She taught us the inner-thought business, which is really the basis of Stanislavsky.

Well, films were coming along, and one summer I went down to the Vitagraph Company at Flatbush to see if I could put what I'd been studying with her to use. I told them that perhaps I might fit in, since I had been working on pantomime. They thought that was very nice, but they felt I should have more experience.

Quite frankly, I didn't know what to do. I knew you had to have a job in order to get a job, so I went to Chicago—my home's in Illinois—to Ravinia Park, which was a summer theater. I didn't play in anything, but I saw several stock-company performances.

Then I returned to town, and thought I'd try Vitagraph again. I told them I'd been to Ravinia Park. "That's fine," they said. "Now you've got some professional experience, let's see what you can do."

So I was in. At this time—1911—Carlyle Blackwell, a leading juvenile man, was leaving, and they thought they'd try me out in the things that he'd been doing. We weren't at all alike—but that's how I started.

The first thing I did was *A Tale of Two Cities*—and this was one of Norma

James Morrison and Jean Paige (Mrs. Albert E. Smith) in Vitagraph's **Black Beauty** *(1921), directed by David Smith.*

Talmadge's first appearances, too. I played the peasant brother, and Lillian Walker played my sister. In one scene I had to leap a balustrade and attack the Marquis, while a big ball was going on. I went back as far as I could to get momentum— about twenty-five feet against the back wall—then I ran forward, and as I leaped the balcony I let out a loud yell.

Afterward, Julia Swayne Gordon told me: "When I heard that cry, it really struck truth to me. I was in the toilet at the time, but I had to come out to see who on earth had done it." So my training had not been in vain! . . .

Within another week, Mabel Normand arrived, so all of us stuck together because we didn't know a thing. We were raw beginners. I knew a bit more than Norma or Mabel, because I'd done some acting.

We had no contracts. I never had a written contract with the Vitagraph until after I'd left them. We all started at about twenty-five dollars a week. You used to get a raise in an odd sort of a way. It usually came through either the English or the French office, who would write the American office and say: "So-and-so was very good in such-and-such a picture." That was worth a five-dollar raise.

But it created some confusion. We always got our money in cash, never by check, so when we got a raise we thought we'd been miscounted. You'd look at your money and you'd think: "Oh, my. That's wrong. I must have counted twice." So if we got a raise we'd always have to get one of the others to count our salary.

And even some of the older people there would encounter the same trouble. I remember Julia Swayne Gordon saying one time, "Jim, I hate to do this, but would you mind counting my money?" She had a fifteen-dollar raise for something special she'd done. They never said anything about it—they just gave it to her.

The Vitagraph Corporation really was a great big happy family. Two young men from England, Albert E. Smith and J. Stuart Blackton, had started it with a man called Pop Rock. Pop had the money. That was what Pop had . . .

Blackton and Smith had their separate companies. I was taken in by Blackton's side, and for a while Smith's side didn't have anything to do with me. There was quite a difference between the two camps. In the Smith group I think it was, just for a short time, they tried out the most pitiful method of direction. The director would call "Number five!" and the leading woman would pull expression number five. That was all there was to it—one two three four five. Luckily it didn't last very long.

We were doing a job in those days. There was no feeling about starting anything new. It was a job and we did it. Nevertheless, there were experiments. In 1911, Larry Trimble made a whole story using only hands and feet. Not until the very end did he reveal the two people.

But in the same year, just to show you how primitive it all was, I had to lie on the floor for three hours without moving. They had a number of scenes on this set, and they'd placed the camera solidly in one position. They never thought of moving the camera, and they didn't want a jump, so they had to have me in that one spot. I didn't have any lunch . . .

This was for *A Tale of Two Cities;* very soon after that they discovered that they could break the shot, go to a title or another shot, and then come back without the audience noticing any jump. But I actually lay on that floor for three hours. When you're young and that interested, you don't care about things like that.

We were the first to use the nine-foot line. When I started, they would frame the scene as in a theater, a long shot with everyone shown full length. We were the first ones to bring people up to within nine feet of the camera. The nine-foot line was a line of tape on the floor; if you came any nearer you'd go out of focus. The next innovation in the movies was when Griffith did the close-up. We thought of the nine-foot line, but we didn't think of the close-up.

We did all our own stunts. The third time I ever rode on a horse I had to be shot off it . . . in full gallop. This was for *The Seepore Rebellion,* in which Wallace Reid was an extra man. In *The Redemption of Dave Darcey* I had to climb up the side of a house. The director, Paul Scardon, pointed to a spouting. "Grab that," be said, "and get over on the roof. Do you think you can do it?"

"I don't know," I said. "I might make it . . ." There was nothing but a cement sidewalk underneath. No mattress had been provided—nothing. And like a fool I started up. In those days, when you were told to do something, you tried to do it.

I got along pretty well until I was about my own height up. Then my feet started slipping because there was cement on the bricks. My nails were going too by this time. I struggled to keep climbing—and the cameraman announced that he was going to change the angle.

J. Stuart Blackton directing The Life Drama of Napoleon Bonaparte and Empress Josephin of France *for Vitagraph, 1909.*

David Smith directing Captain Blood *(1924); J. Warren Kerrigan, center, James Morrison behind Smith.*

"You keep right on with what you're doing!" I snapped between clenched teeth. Then I grabbed the spouting—and it was rusty and it began to give. How I did that last heave on the roof I'll never know, but I got there.

And when I saw the film at the Vitagraph Theatre, I heard some people behind me say: "You know what they do? That's all laid out on the floor, and all they have to do is crawl along it."

There was another incident which wasn't amusing at the time, but is amusing to look back on. Julia Swayne Gordon was a vamp, and I played her young lover. She had a tiger, in this picture, as a pet, and it had been in captivity for just six months. We got it from Coney Island, and we had to work with it on the same set. No double exposure or anything. The carpenters had built a great fence around us, and everyone was standing around with guns. Not that they would have been much help; the damage would have been done before they could fire—and they probably wouldn't have dared to shoot for fear of killing us.

Julia and I felt like a couple of Christians . . . I was supposed to be afraid of the tiger, that's what worried me. I expect the tiger could smell my natural fear, on top of which I had to act frightened—I had to back away from it.

In between shots, Julia was stroking the tiger's head, trying to keep him quiet. And she just happened to touch its ear. The tiger raised its head and took her arm in its mouth. We didn't breathe. We were frozen absolutely still.

The tiger held her arm for just a little while, then it looked at her as if to say "Don't do that again" and opened its jaws and let her go.

There was a man called Nick Dunaew, who was Russian—we called him Nick the Dime-Bender. He was probably of peasant stock, but he knew enough about Russia and its aristocracy to help us a lot as adviser when we did Russian pictures. When Earle Williams and Clara Kimball Young did *My Official Wife* [1914] he brought in a fellow called Leon Trotsky. He was unknown then, of course—it was only afterward that everyone realized he'd been with us.[1]

John Bunny, Mary Charleson, and I opened the Vitagraph Theatre. It was the first time they'd ever charged a dollar for a movie. We opened in a pantomime written by J. Stuart Blackton called *The Honeymooners;* we appeared in person, and they followed that with a dramatic film. We'd taken the Criterion Theatre, on the site of the present Criterion.

Everyone said we'd fail. We were scared out of our wits—here we were invading Broadway. But we had a packed house at the opening—just packed. Diamond Jim Brady was down front, and we got thirteen curtain calls. We played close to four months, with the same show, and after that the Vitagraph used it as a first-run theater for their pictures. They only tried one other show— a comedy with Flora Finch—but it didn't work too well.

I was the first one at Vitagraph to have a tuxedo. Maurice Costello had one, and I had one. Then Earle Williams came in with a wardrobe. That set us back on our heels . . .

At the beginning we would be cast as extras as well as leading players. Somebody would be shooting a banquet scene, and they'd say, "Get into your dress suit, and come in here." We had quite a battle to get to the point where we were leading players only, and weren't used as extra people.

[1] *Trotsky had been one of the principal leaders of the 1905 revolution in Russia, but his name was little known in America.*

We had artificial light all the time at the Vitagraph. Mercury-vapor tubes—the light was sort of greenish. We had to wear a blue shirt if we wanted it to photograph white; real white was too glaring. All our dress clothes had to be dyed—even our tan would take white. Klieg lights were coming in,[2] but they used them without any protective glass. The arc throws off a burning carbon dust for several feet around. It gets into your eyes, and they'd swell up and go pink—this was called Klieg eyes. It would take two or three days before they'd be normal. It was agony. Out on the Coast, they had constant sunlight, so it was some time before they began using artificial light.

In *The Battle Hymn of the Republic,* directed by J. Stuart Blackton, I remember one marvelous effect. There were some huge columns flanking a great stairway built into the Vitagraph tank. They were supposed to come crashing down into the water. Well, everybody held their breath. Down came the columns—but the damn things floated, because they'd been made of wood. It broke their hearts.

I left the Vitagraph in 1918 when they brought in efficiency experts. When that happened, the art of the company disappeared. Here were three people dividing two million dollars a year—and yet they brought in efficiency experts. These experts limited the amount of film that directors could shoot . . . and they even had people straightening nails.

I left, and took the first vacation I'd ever had—in Bermuda. After a period with producer Ivan Abramson I came back to town and one of the Fort Lee studios offered me eighty-five dollars a week. I wrote to Albert Smith: "Dear Mr. Smith: I'm back in town. Eclair have offered me eighty-five dollars a week."

He wrote back, at the bottom of my letter: "If Eclair want you for eighty-five, then Vitagraph certainly does. Come back and go to work." And I found myself back with the Vitagraph Corporation.

---

[2] *Klieg lights were designed for theatrical use.*

4 / THE EXPERIMENTERS

Like a Jules Verne fantasy, the twentieth century burst forth in a riot of speed. Communications, transport, pictures—all miraculously acquired wings. Everything was on the move. In America, the automobile industry was in ascendancy, closely paced by the moving-picture business. Modifications and alterations were improving the product all the time, but the earlier, cruder models remained for all to see. In these young, vigorous industries, improvements were astonishingly rapid, and one week's output could make obsolete the work of a decade.

The great changes that took place in the motion picture industry have been attributed to the influence of one man: David Wark Griffith.

Griffith had been an unsuccessful playwright. He wrote under the name of Lawrence Griffith, keeping his real name for more successful ventures in the future. When one of his plays closed prematurely, crushing his hopes, he tried to sell stories to the galloping tintypes.

At the Edison Studios, he encountered Edwin S. Porter. Porter did not buy his stories, but he hired him as an actor. Griffith was chagrined; only failures allowed themselves to appear in moving pictures. However, he needed the money. Then he was offered the opportunity to direct, but was afraid that he would make mistakes and lose his acting job as well. He was persuaded that his job would be safe, and realizing that directing was more remunerative, and more anonymous, he began work on *The Adventures of Dollie*.

Griffith was the son of a Kentucky colonel, and he regarded himself as a member of the aristocracy. This affair of moving pictures, he felt, was degrading. To show his lack of respect he broke all the existing rules of film making. But there was more to it than mere perversity. Griffith also regarded himself as an artist of potential genius. As Lloyd Morris has profoundly put it: "He had no respect for the medium in which he was working, but his temperament compelled him to treat it as if it were an art. The result was that he made it one."[1]

The Adventures of Dollie, made in 1908, contained none of the significant advances claimed for it by historians. But, as William K. Everson says, "one can point to the overall construction and the stress on suspense and melodramatic chase as being a kind of blueprint for all the great Griffith material that was to follow."[2]

Many of the later Griffith films *were* great. Ground out at an astonishing rate —he directed more than four hundred one- and two-reelers before *The Birth of a Nation*—these little stories ranged from the pedantic to the brilliant. But in practically all of them there was some experiment, however insignificant. It may have been a silhouette shot against a window, or an unusual bit of business. In the bolder films—*An Unseen Enemy, The Musketeers of Pig Alley, The Massacre*—the innovations went beyond mere experiment. These were confident, expert productions, well paced and cut, with striking close-ups, amazing long shots taken from hundreds of yards away, and countless small touches which, for their date (1911–12), are remarkable.

Billy Bitzer, Griffith's cameraman, resented these departures from convention, claiming, like so many cameramen since, that they were impossible.

"That's why you have to do it," Griffith would reply cheerfully. Bitzer, grumbling, would achieve miracles. Eventually he grew to accept Griffith's ideas; when-

---

[1] *Lloyd Morris:* Not So Long Ago (*New York: Random House;* 1949), *p. 59.*
[2] *Notes of the Theodore Huff Memorial Film Society, Sept. 20, 1960.*

ever he was skeptical, Griffith's enthusiasm restored his morale—"Well, come on, let's do it anyway. I don't give a damn what anybody thinks about it."

In 1913, the Biograph Company took an advertisement in the New York *Dramatic Mirror* to make known the achievements of their director:

D. W. GRIFFITH: *Producer of all the great Biograph successes, revolutionizing the Motion Picture Drama, and founding the modern technique of the art.*

Included in the innovations which he introduced and which are now generally followed by the most advanced producers are: the use of large close-up figures, distant views as reproduced first in Ramona, *the "switchback," sustained suspense, the "fade-out," and restraint in expression, raising motion picture acting which has won for it recognition as a genuine art.*[3]

Griffith took ideas from other directors and other countries, of course—few creators work in a vacuum, and this early part of the silent era was particularly rich in the interchange of ideas. Others called it stealing; a number of pioneer film makers countered Griffith's extravagant claims with wry comments. J. Stuart Blackton pointed out that he had taken close shots in his newsreel work as early as 1898, ten years before Griffith had begun directing. And in 1889, long before anybody had entered the business, W. K. L. Dickson and his colleagues at the Edison plant were producing motion pictures in close shot; *Fred Ott's Sneeze* is a famous example. But the actual invention, or discovery, of such devices is comparatively unimportant. What is significant is to find out who first put them to creative use.

Griffith's films changed the whole course of the American cinema. Some directors, imitating him, discovered that they were breaking new ground themselves. Phillips Smalley, making a story similar to *An Unseen Enemy* with *Suspense* (Rex, 1913), included all the Griffith effects—close-ups, traveling shots, high angles— and he went further and introduced a triptych. *Sheridan's Ride* (Universal, 1912) was made by Otis Turner, known as the Dean of Directors. The majority of this production is conventionally handled, but when the famous ride begins, Turner breaks triumphantly through the theatrical confines of the earlier scenes and cuts from furious tracking shots of Sheridan's cavalry to scenes of the U. S. Army being routed by Confederate onslaughts. The shots are held longer than is necessary, even for the uninitiated audiences of 1912. But since Turner employed the unprecedented number of five hundred extras for the battle scenes, his self-indulgence is forgivable.

On the whole, however, film makers at this period felt that if they could tell their stories simply and directly, without recourse to mechanical tricks, they should do so. Apart from anything else, a traveling shot took a great deal of time to prepare. It was difficult to keep the camera in focus, and the delays cost money. Nevertheless, some technicians were fascinated by the untapped resources of motion-picture gadgetry. William F. Alder, cameraman on *The Second-in-Command* (directed by William Bowman for Fred Balshofer in 1915), enlivened a theatrical and mediocre production with several beautifully executed and surprisingly intricate traveling shots. The movement was absolutely smooth, even when

---

[3] *New York* Dramatic Mirror, *Dec. 3, 1913.*

Frame enlargements from Suspense *(Rex, 1913); the prowler's view through a keyhole.*

The beginning of the triptych. The camera masks all but the central triangle.

The triptych complete; the wife chatting unsuspectingly to her husband as the prowler advances.

G. W. Bitzer with Mae Marsh and Pathé camera, 1915.

the camera, mounted on two dollies, slid backward and then sideways. *The Second-in-Command* appeared a full ten years before *The Last Laugh,* acknowledged by historians as the first film to exploit the moving camera, but two years after *Cabiria,* the Italian epic that gave its name to the trucking shot (Cabiria movement).

"Suppose I had patented the fade-out," said Griffith mournfully in 1926. "I would be drawing at least a million a year in royalties. The fade-out is absolutely necessary to the smooth telling of a story. Try counting the number of times it is used in a single picture. To eliminate it would make necessary the abrupt beginning and ending of scenes. It would jar and distort the whole observation of a film drama. Yes, I might have patented it. You can patent anything derived from a mechanical device. I just didn't realize its significance then. We were all beginners —and I wanted to help the business."[4]

The early cinema depended upon interaction; Griffith no more invented the fade-out than he did the close-up. He and Bitzer arrived at some of these effects independently, and often accidentally. Others he consciously or unconsciously took from American and European pictures. But he used these devices with intelligence, sometimes with genius, and film makers were happy to take their improved ideas back again. Artistic and technical progress at this time was thus astonishingly fast.

It is a fact, and a disturbing one in many ways, that every basic device of cinematic storytelling had been established by 1912. The close-up, the tracking shot, the high angle, the flashback, the insert, effect lighting, masking, fades, dissolves —the whole gamut was there. But it was as though the components of a steam train had been assembled, and no one knew how to light the boiler. For while all the components of the narrative film had been devised, no one was fully exploiting them.

The first match was struck by Griffith, and it led to an explosion, the effects of which the industry is still feeling. *The Birth of a Nation* was cinematic revolution —it was responsible for revolutions in every field affected by motion pictures. Riots and demonstrations were living proof of the power of the film. No well-informed person could allow himself to ignore it. The intelligentsia, who had regarded movies much as the jukebox is regarded today, conceded at last that the film had value. With critics and writers embroiled in controversy, the middle classes went to see for themselves. And more important still, the men who controlled the business grew ambitious again.

The Birth of a Nation was the first feature to be made in the same fluid way as pictures are made today. It was the most widely seen production of the time and it had the strongest influence. It is still being shown—but now it looks like an actor who has been on the stage for half a century. A pale, worn shadow, its original glory is a memory rather than an actuality. The film has been reprinted and cut frequently; it is also shown at the speed of sound films—twenty-four frames a second—instead of the sixteen frames more suitable for it. But, as with the actor, it is good to have it with us after all this time.

With the success of *The Birth of a Nation,* three major producers, Griffith, Thomas Ince and Mack Sennett, were joined together to form the Triangle Corporation. As the strongest rivals to Famous Players, a company formed to exploit

4 Photoplay, *Dec. 1926, p. 30.*

Frame enlargements from Sheridan's Ride *(Universal, 1912); William Clifford as General Sheridan.*

U.S. Army troops in flight.

Confederate troops routing U.S. soldiers.

theatrical success, Triangle attracted a cluster of Broadway stars. With De Wolf Hopper, William Collier, Beerbohm Tree, and Constance Collier appearing in pictures, theater people were at last forced to take the cinema seriously.

Griffith merely supervised his apex at Triangle.[5] His energies were being devoted to his next production, *Intolerance*. This amazing picture was a commercial failure. It lost a great deal of money, but it telescoped what might otherwise have been years of slow, patient technical progress—and it sparked off one of the most exciting and concentrated creative eras in the history of art.

[5] *He later denied producing anything at Triangle, saying that his name was used for its prestige value. His influence, however, is indelibly stamped on many of the films, some of which were made from his own stories.*

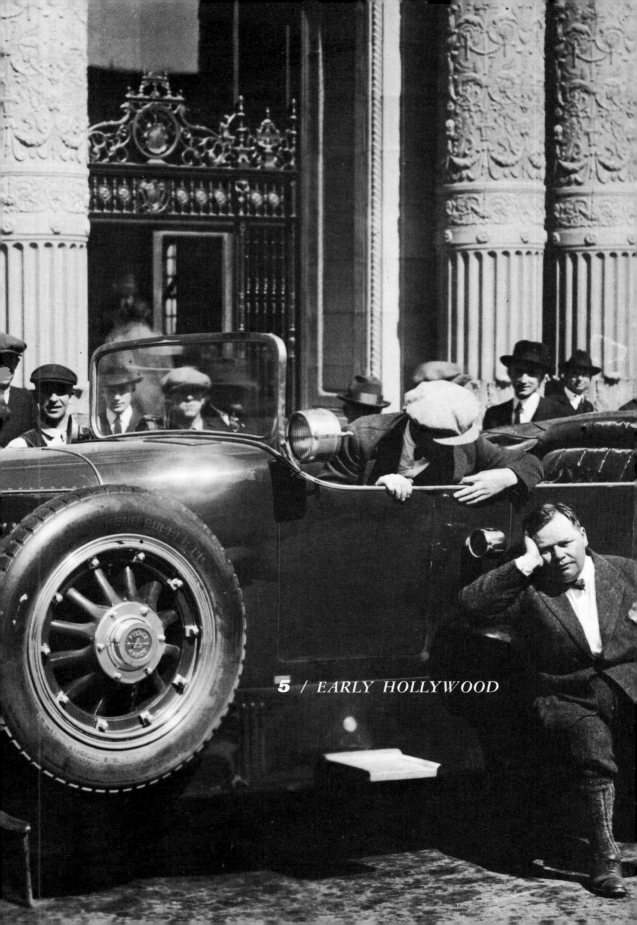

5 / EARLY HOLLYWOOD

Sunny and somnolent, aglow with orange groves, fruit trees, palms, and poinsettias, Hollywood in its early years was an ideal place for retirement. In 1894, Horace Henderson Wilcox, a Kansas prohibitionist, bought 120 acres near Los Angeles for his country home. His wife named the place Hollywood.

By the turn of the century, only a few hundred people had settled there, for lush as it was, Hollywood had once been a barren cactus thicket, and the encroaching desert waited only for drought to re-establish itself. In 1910, lack of water forced the town to seek protection from Los Angeles, and Hollywood became a suburb, separated from the city by eight miles of rough country road.

The arrival of motion pictures took the form more of a gradual infiltration than an open invasion. The studio of the American Biograph and Mutoscope Company was established in Los Angeles in 1906, and in 1907 director Francis Boggs arrived in the city with a handful of players from Chicago's Selig Company. Colonel Selig had been attracted by the Chamber of Commerce claim that Los Angeles enjoyed 350 sunny days a year.

Boggs and his group had been making a trip through the whole country, filming single-reel dramas on the way. In Los Angeles, one of the actors decided to leave. Boggs replaced him with a stage director named Hobart Bosworth, a former Broadway actor who had lost his voice, and his acting career, after an attack of consumption. Boggs had little trouble persuading Bosworth that since his voice would not be heard in pictures, he could resume his acting career.

With Bosworth in the lead, Boggs directed *The Power of the Sultan,* believed to be the first dramatic film made entirely in California, on a vacant lot next to a Chinese laundry at Olive and Seventh.[1] Because he was working in the open air, Bosworth began to recover from the aftereffects of his illness. He was therefore appalled when Colonel Selig wrote from Chicago to recall the company. "I couldn't go to Chicago," he protested to Francis Boggs. "I'd be dead in a year."[2]

Boggs suggested that he write to Selig, explaining that California was the best possible place in which to make motion pictures. Bosworth was so eloquent in describing the unvarying sunshine and the ideal conditions that instead of insisting that the company take the next train back East, Selig took a train West.

The Los Angeles Chamber of Commerce echoed Bosworth's letter in their advertising:

Environment certainly affects creative workers. You realize surely the importance in such essentially sensitive production as the making of Motion Pictures the vital importance of having every member of an organization awake in the morning and start to work in a flood of happy sunshine.

Cold rain and slushy snow do not tend to the proper mental condition for the best creative work.[3]

Selig built a small studio at 1845 Alessandro Street. In 1909, Adam Kessel and Charles Baumann arrived from the East and erected an open stage at 1712 Alessandro Street, later to be the headquarters of the Mack Sennett Keystone

---

[1] *Also in the cast were Stella Adams, Tom Santschi, Frank Montgomery, and a future director, Robert Leonard.*
[2] Motion Picture Classic, *Aug. 1927, p. 49.*
[3] *WID's Year Book, 1919 (ed. Wid Gunning), p. 127.*

Company. D. W. Griffith came West in the same year to make use of the authentic western backgrounds.

The first studio in Hollywood itself, however, was not opened until October 1911, when the Centaur company, owned by two Englishmen, William and David Horsley, established a West Coast branch, Nestor. Centaur's chief director, Al Christie had been making westerns in the East, in Bayonne, New Jersey, and he had begun to tire of the inaccurate local backgrounds. He was anxious to try shooting in California, but David Horsley felt that Florida would offer better climate and terrain. Christie tossed a coin, and California won.

On the train out West, Horsley and Christie met a theatrical producer who advised them to see Frank Hoover, owner of a photographic business at Hollywood Boulevard and Gower Street. Hoover persuaded them to set up business in California.

The real-estate man who drove the motion-picture men to possible sites felt that Edendale or Santa Monica would prove the most suitable areas. He left Hollywood until last. But on dusty Sunset Boulevard, Christie spotted some property he liked. Nearby was a decrepit building, a roadhouse, which they leased for forty dollars a month.[4]

"Behind this building," recalled Nestor cameraman Charles Rosher, "there was a barn in the garden where we developed all the film. We made one-reel pictures like *Indian Raiders,* directed by Tom Ricketts, with real Indians brought in from New Mexico by Jack Parsons, who later started the Western Costume Company.

"Although we had a developing room, we had no printing machinery. The picture was cut directly from the negative, and we thought nothing of running original negative through the projector. Scratches and abrasions were mere details. When the negative was cut, the completed reel was sent to New York or Chicago for printing.

"Today, the huge building of the Columbia Broadcasting System stands on the site of the roadhouse."[5]

The Nestor company soon discovered that they could churn out picture after picture, with few delays from bad weather. Other companies, enduring the erratic climate of the East, marveled at Nestor's steady output and improved photographic quality and came out to Hollywood to learn the secret. Within months, fifteen companies were shooting in and around Hollywood.

The fine weather was certainly a major incentive for many companies to move their entire organizations to the West Coast, but Hollywood offered another advantage. An industrial dispute, known as the Patents War and fought with weapons and violence enough to justify the term, had forced several producers to flee from New York to Chicago—and even to Cuba. These producers had infringed the Edison patents by making equipment built from pirated designs. An immediate cause of the dispute was the Latham Loop, a patented mechanism incorporated in the camera. Hollywood offered an ideal sanctuary for refugees of the Patents War, for should trouble appear, the Mexican border was a mere hundred-mile drive away.

---

[4] *The building was owned by Louis Blondeau, who was, for a time, Hollywood's only barber. He bought up several such sites in the area and became very wealthy very quickly.*
[5] *Charles Rosher to author, London, July 1966.*

Motion Pictures East and West. East Coast production: George D. Baker directing Marion Davies in The Cinema Murder, *1919.*

"Horsley was the leader in the fight against the Edison Trust," said Rosher, "and we had to keep our eyes open for spies. We never dared open our cameras outside, in case someone saw the Latham Loop. So to load or unload them, or simply to clean them, we took them inside houses."

The atmosphere of the wild West was re-created not only on film. The bitter rivalry between these early barnstorming producers led to armed clashes on several occasions. Charles Rosher remembered one of these:

"In May 1912, the Nestor company was taken over by Universal. Universal was also supposed to have taken over Kay-Bee [Kessel and Baumann], but there was some dispute between the two factions. The general manager of Universal, William Swanson, asked me to go and seize control of Kay-Bee. I was armed with power of attorney and I took a bunch of cowboys armed with guns. I remember Fred Mace, the comedian, and a group of them were sitting there playing cards when we marched in and seized control. That was quite a thing to do . . . I was told to search the place, and I came across private papers showing just who was out for a fast buck. They were pretty wild guys in those days."

Griffith, Sennett, Ince, Zukor, Lasky, De Mille—by 1914, Hollywood had become the center of a major industry. Its advantages, however, were not apparent to everyone. When the newly formed Metro company sent Francis X. Bushman to make one picture a month in California, he found it extremely difficult. The blight of Los Angeles today is smog; at that time it was ordinary fog. A spate of foggy

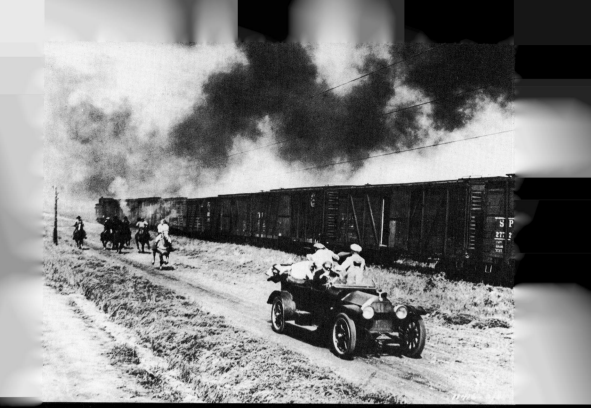

West Coast production: shooting a serial, about 1915. (This photograph, so authentic that i *has deceived several historians, is actually a still from* The Perils of Pauline, *an otherwise anachronistic reconstruction of 1946.)*

The Lasky Feature Play Company assembled during the making of The Squaw Man, *directed by C.B. De Mille and Oscar Apfel in 1913. Half of this structure was still in use as a barn. The barn stands today on the present Paramount lot.*

mornings put paid to the company's plans. Often it was not possible to begin shooting until two in the afternoon, when the fog had cleared.

"And it wasn't just the fog," said Bushman. "This is semitropical country, and the people we were using weren't accustomed to working hard in this weather. As soon as we were out of sight they'd all loaf, start playing billiards or something. I did four pictures out there, and then I went back to New York, where we had studios with artificial light."[6]

During World War I, however, power and coal shortages in the East sent many more companies scurrying across country to the sun. By 1919, eighty per cent of the motion pictures of the world were being produced in southern California.

Some citizens of Hollywood regarded the activities of the motion-picture people with dismay, feeling as though their respectable town had been overrun by gypsies. Others were indifferent, displaying no more interest in the film makers' antics than in the games of the neighborhood children. Film people were called "movies" by Hollywood residents, who were unaware that the term referred to the product, not to the personnel. The word conjured up the right sort of vision; it was vaguely suggestive of irritating insects.

The more influential citizens took a firm stand against the "movies," and for many years it was as hard for a motion-picture person to join a country club as it was for a Jew or a Negro. For this was the West; its respectability was a thin and brittle veneer that inadequately concealed California's explosive past. Anything out of the ordinary was shunned. As late as 1918, the exclusive Garden Court Apartments were holding out against picture people, and only the dignified, conservative, and English J. Stuart Blackton was allowed residence there.

Ostracized by Los Angeles society, the motion-picture colony enjoyed a healthy democracy. The casual atmosphere lasted until Douglas Fairbanks and Mary Pickford were married and began entertaining visiting dignitaries. Class distinctions than began to consolidate.

The lower orders were extras, cowboys, stagehands, and people who worked at Universal. Blue blood was generally established by green currency. Later, it was deemed necessary to marry into the foreign aristocracy; a number of penniless immigrants added a title to their names and received warm welcomes in Hollywood. Whenever royalty arrived, the motion-picture aristocrats fought for invitations. The Princess Beatriz de Ortego y Braganza of Alhambre Granada, Spain, was given the red-carpet treatment until she was unmasked as a typist from San Francisco.

Said Herbert Howe: "Ever since Doug and Mary lowered the drawbridge of Pickfair to the Duke d'Alba and Lord and Lady Mountbatten all Hollywood has been rushing royalty. The social columns teem with notices of entertainments for such guests as Beatrice Lillie (Lady Peel) and Peggy Joyce (Countess Morner). It's not what you are that counts in Hollywood, but what you are in parentheses."[7]

Titled people came to Hollywood not so much to be entertained at social functions as to see the industry at work, to meet their favorite players, and, if possible, to play in pictures themselves. Both Beatrice Lillie and Peggy Hopkins Joyce were starred; Miss Lillie was a fine comedienne in her own right, while Peggy Hopkins Joyce was the subject of numerous scandal stories.

[6] *Francis X. Bushman to author, Hollywood, Dec. 1964.*
[7] Photoplay, *Aug. 1926, p. 42.*

The Mack Sennett studios, Edendale, 1915.

Thomas H. Ince, one of the most important and one of the most colorful characters of early Hollywood.

Some of the aristocrats, refugees from Russia, genuinely needed work; General Lodijenski, who did bit parts and ran a Russian restaurant, and whose story inspired *The Last Command*, was a celebrated example. Others took part in pictures for the fun of it. Viscount Glerawly was cast by Cecil B. De Mille, an inveterate title hound, in *The Ten Commandments*. Sir Gerald Maxwell-Wilshire made his debut with Constance Binney, and Baron Henri Arnous de Rivière appeared in pictures with Strongheart, the dog. The Duke of Ducal, a cousin of the King of Spain, was given a bit in Fairbanks's *The Thief of Bagdad*. Count Mario Caracciolo, a former military attaché, shortened his name to Mario Carillo and appeared with Norma Talmadge in *Dust of Desire*. Archduke Leopold of Austria appeared in a number of films, including John Ford's *Four Sons*.

Encouraged by these noble examples, American social leaders consented to perform in motion pictures. Mrs. Morgan Belmont, a prominent member of the New York Four Hundred, played the part of a Boston society lady in Griffith's *Way Down East*. Mrs. Lydig Hoyt, leader of New York's younger set, announced that she had tired of the butterfly life and longed to do something worthwhile, so she went to do her bit in pictures.

Elinor Glyn was incontestably the Dowager Duchess of Hollywood, but during a visit to London she betrayed her amusement at the colony's lack of breeding. "Where else in the world," she asked, "will you find a colored cook bursting into a drawing room to say 'You folks better hustle to dinner if you don't want the stuff to get cold.'?"[8]

Protocol spread from seating arrangements at private dinners to strategy and marshaling in restaurants. Headwaiters knew the social status of each of their patrons, and they would seat them accordingly. If one of them was placed in the outside room, gossip would flare instantly.

This struggle for recognition, this love of protocol, betrays a naïveté which today seems faintly sad. It has been left to posterity to decide the true aristocracy of Hollywood—the aristocracy of merit. Is it significant that those inveterate social-whirlers Mary Pickford and Douglas Fairbanks should be leading here again?

Scandals and wild nightlife gave Hollywood the lure of a modern Babylon; the area's film-making activities were merely a colorful background. Hollywood gained worldwide renown because of its excesses and the startling behavior of some of its occupants, not because it was a center of motion-picture production.

More exhibitionists were attracted to this town than to any other in history, and their behavior, provided it made suitable newspaper copy, was subject to public analysis and dissection. For Hollywood was an occupied area. Newspapermen were everywhere. You never knew whom you could trust. Neighbors might betray any sort of confidence to the press. Your closest friend could not tell whether disclosures would appear as useful publicity or as a smear.

The truth behind the fantasy world of journalism was less lurid, and sensation seekers on safari for wildlife in the motion-picture jungle seldom had their thirst for blood fully gratified. "The joint is as dead as a New York nightclub," complained Wilson Mizner. "I thought it was going to be like a delightful trip through a sewer in a glass-bottomed boat."[9]

While the nation scowled reproachfully at this juvenile playground, distin-

[8] Photoplay, *May 1924, p. 58.*
[9] Photoplay, *Oct. 1927, p. 78.*

Douglas Fairbanks and Charlie Chaplin.

Archduke Leopold of Austria (second from right) takes part in a scene from Four Sons *(1927), with Earle Foxe and Francis X. Bushman, Jr. John Ford directs; George Schneiderman a the camera.*

guished observers tried to improve its reputation. H. L. Mencken, editor of *The American Mercury,* said in 1927 that the wildest nightlife he encountered was at Aimee Semple McPherson's tabernacle. "I saw no wildness among the movie folk. They seemed to me, in the main, to be very serious and even somber people. And no wonder, for they are worked like Pullman porters or magazine editors. When they finish their day's labors they are far too tired for any recreation requiring stamina. Immorality? Oh, my God! Hollywood seemed to me to be one of the most respectable towns in America. Even Baltimore can't beat it."[1]

Generalizations about Hollywood are also generalizations about Los Angeles, Glendale, Burbank, Culver City, Malibu, and Santa Monica. Hollywood is a generic term as well as a specific place. When you arrive in Hollywood itself, you are still miles away from several major Hollywood studios and six miles from the homes of the stars in Beverly Hills. It is for this reason that the sprawling city of Los Angeles has been called "six suburbs in search of a city."

Hollywood was transformed from a paradise for retired Iowan farmers into a seventh heaven for youth. Catering to the two extremes, the town did not provide those links with the past that give stability to the present; there were no art galleries, very few bookshops, no proper theaters or museums, and, until the Hollywood Bowl was built, no concert halls. Europeans could find no point of reference, and they were made uneasy by the all-pervading atmosphere of impermanence. It was a cultural vacuum. In this respect it was little different from other American country towns. But as the capital of an industry, outsiders ex-

[1] Photoplay, *April 1927, p. 37.*

Roscoe Arbuckle with his new Pierce-Arrow, allegedly photographed on the day the scandal broke.

pected Hollywood to offer them the amenities and tradition of the capital of a nation.

Entertainment was what Hollywood and its environs offered, and they offered it in the widest possible variety. While motion-picture people were highly circumspect during the week, retiring at ten in order to get up at five in the morning, the weekends were different.

Prohibition did little to dampen the attractions of Hollywood nightlife; the colony was near enough to the coast to receive plentiful supplies, and when drink was required, curtains were discreetly drawn.

From the earliest days, the underworld took a firm grip; petty racketeers, drug peddlers, blackmailers, and phony agents found Hollywood a paradise. One of the most dangerous men was a charming, apparently inoffensive actor on the Sennett lot.

"Everyone who took drugs in the industry was started by this man," said Eddie Sutherland. "He was one of the quietest, nicest actors I've ever known. He put Mabel Normand on the junk, Wallie Reid, Alma Rubens. All three died as a direct result. Somebody would have a hangover, and he'd say, 'I'll fix it for you,' and that was that."

Divorces and illicit affairs provided the newspapers with a solid core of gasp-producing features. Whenever sales began to slip, newspapermen managed to uncover fresh scandal. Roscoe Arbuckle was among the first victims of these campaigns. Next to Chaplin, Arbuckle was the world's most popular comedian. A weekend party at the St. Francis Hotel in San Francisco grew slightly riotous, and a young actress called Virginia Rappé became ill and later died. Arbuckle was charged with rape. The newspapers managed to keep his case blazing on front pages throughout three trials. At two of them, the jury was unable to agree. The third was an acquittal, but Arbuckle's career was finished.

Minta Durfee, Arbuckle's ex-wife, stood by him during the case. "Rappé," she said, "was the girl friend of Henry "Pathe" Lehrman. She worked at Sennett; I knew her well. She was very sweet, but she was suffering from several diseases, one of which so shocked Sennett that he closed down the studio and had it fumigated."[2] And according to Eddie Sutherland, "Roscoe was destroyed by ambitious lawyers and some renegade people from Hollywood who gave him the worst of it when he'd given them the best of it." Hollywood was seriously affected by the scandal, and many people who remember the case are still bitter about it.

Hollywood's golden era was for many the most desperate time of their lives. Thousands of girls poured into the town, pathetically anxious to work in pictures. There were chances for less than one in a hundred. The unlucky girls faced poverty, starvation, and sometimes suicide. They arrived without money or contacts. Their first shock was the discovery that the studios they continually had to visit to seek work were scattered over a fifty-mile radius.

Infrequent and overcrowded trolley cars and buses served certain routes; at other times the girls had to beg lifts. This was always risky, sometimes downright dangerous, for few men would allow a girl to refuse their hospitality once they had her in the car. The other extra girls would offer no help. Their position was every bit as desperate.

[2] *Minta Durfee Arbuckle to author, Hollywood, Dec. 1964.*

The movie czar Will Hays, who had been made supreme arbiter in 1922 after Hollywood's scandals had shaken box-office receipts, tried to stem the flow. He ensured that all extras were obtained through Central Casting. But the flow did not stop; the misery merely increased. Studio casting offices were the scenes of daily emotional outbursts.

Photoplay writer Ruth Waterbury tried to beat the new casting system and break into movies on her own merit. She failed, and her reminiscences remain a terrifying account of what Hollywood offered an extra girl. On one occasion, after a series of exhausting experiences, Miss Waterbury was waiting in a casting office. An actor asked some girls if they had worked recently. They hadn't. Instead of a job, he produced a handful of mints.

"I'm big-hearted. I just made three-fifty. So I'm going to treat you girls. Every girl gets one."

Ruth Waterbury continued: "I had noticed a gaunt woman next to me. Now she rushed forward and clutched at the man's hands, grabbing the little packages.

" 'No you don't,' he cried. 'Give those back. You can only have one.'

"She paid no attention to him. She was already stuffing those candies in her mouth. To her, plainly, they were food. I was trembling a little as I left . . ."[3]

Time eventually erodes the sharpness from memory, and the past becomes suffused with the rosy glow of nostalgia. Nevertheless, to ignore this grim background to the golden age would be as dishonest and misleading as discounting the casualties of a great victory. For these people, directly or indirectly, were the casualties of a great period.

[3] Photoplay, *Jan. 1927, p. 107.*

From the solid training of the D. W. Griffith studios spread the backbone of the American film industry. Like most great artists, Griffith was besieged by people eager to work with him and be taught by him. For a while it was enough to mention Griffith's name as a former employer to secure the best jobs in the business. Gradually the privilege became abused, and eventually something more was required than a day's extra work on a Griffith picture.

The directors, cameramen, and players who had been carefully nurtured and developed within the Griffith family carried his teaching with them when they joined other companies. The films of this period often show unmistakable signs of the Griffith influence. Erich von Stroheim, Sidney Franklin, Elmer Clifton, Donald Crisp, Raoul Walsh, Lloyd Ingraham, Paul Powell, Allan Dwan, Tod Browning, Edward Dillon, Joseph Henabery . . . these are a few of the directors whose careers were shaped by Griffith.

Joseph Henabery's career demonstrates clearly the benefits of working for this extraordinary man. As he points out, Griffith did not systematically instruct his employees in the art of making pictures. His influence was applied unconsciously. He demanded a great deal from those who worked with him, and his associates were forced to learn their job quickly—or lose it. These young men, initiated in the deep end, found the experience an immense advantage when they began to work on their own.

Joseph Henabery quickly became one of America's top directors. He worked with Douglas Fairbanks and made one of the best of his early pictures, *His Majesty the American*. He directed Mary Miles Minter, Roscoe Arbuckle, and Rudolph Valentino (*A Sainted Devil*), and he made Douglas Fairbanks, Jr.'s, first, *Stephen Steps Out*.

Even when he had slipped from his position among the premier directors, Henabery continued to demonstrate his artistic integrity and his visual flair. His *River Woman*, photographed by Ray June, was made for Gotham, a poverty-row company, in 1928. It achieved the miracle of transforming an ordinary story with no production or entertainment value into a work of fine observation, sensitive playing, and intricate camera movement.

Henabery played Abraham Lincoln in *The Birth of a Nation* and was an assistant director and actor on *Intolerance*. His description of the early days of the industry throw new light on a forgotten era.

JOSEPH HENABERY:[1] When I was seventeen, my family and I moved to southern California. I started work for a railroad—a link in a transcontinental system. This was in 1905. I worked for the railroad for eight years, starting in the correspondence-filing section. Here I handled a great deal of highly confidential information.

One day the man in charge of this section fell victim to a nervous breakdown and I was asked to dig out some urgently needed information. The correspondence interested me, and I could remember a lot of it. So I came up with what they wanted. After several weeks, the boss decided that nobody knew the work as well as I did and, despite the problem of my youth, he gave me the job—at eighty-five dollars per month! In 1907, that was tremendous, and it created quite a storm.

[1] *Interviewed in Hollywood, Dec. 1964.*

This pay hassle developed problems. I was promoted during the ensuing years, but they never allowed me the pay rise my new jobs merited. Finally the situation got under my skin. I began to wonder what to do next.

About this time, motion pictures were being shown in hole-in-the-wall movie houses. I often dropped in for half an hour at noontime. Most of the pictures were pretty bad. Comparing their quality with the plays I had seen in the legitimate theater, I found it hard to believe that the movies could really be considered entertainment.

By the time I was twenty-five, in 1913, I had seen about four hundred legitimate performances. Sometimes I got a kick out of suping [being a supernumerary] with a grand opera or a spectacle company. I enjoyed the backstage action and atmosphere, and the contact with theatrical people.

Another of my after-work activities was membership in clubs or groups for young people. Before there was any acceptable entertainment apart from the theater, many of these groups presented amateur plays. I was in a number of them, and I couldn't help comparing our mediocre things with professional shows. The club people accepted the old-fashioned declamatory methods directed by the coach, a professional actor of the old school. Finally I could take it no longer. An upheaval took place and the coach quit. Now the club had a date to fulfill, but no director. They asked me to take over. I continued to produce and direct amateur shows for some time afterward.

During my later days at the railroad, I bought a motion-picture trade journal, which had departments covering all phases of production. I studied the ads and got to be able to judge the size and importance of the various companies. At this time, they were all out East.

Then, in one issue, I was thrilled to read of a company moving out to California. It wasn't long before others followed. I started thinking about the movies as an occupation. But I could not figure, though, that it would be smart to give up my good job for an uncertain future.

Like most of the older residents of Hollywood, I was annoyed by the invasion of the movies. I remember coming home to Hollywood on vacation. I was walking down the street when I saw a crowd of people ahead of me. A fellow stuck out his arm and said, "Hold it. We're shooting."

It was a comedy outfit. The actors wore comic clothes and the make-up was very exaggerated—a vivid pink, much heavier than most stage make-ups I had seen.

I watched them work. The action was very broad—pratfalls—and the scenes were so short and unrelated that I couldn't make head nor tail of what was going on. I was not impressed.

These first, noisy, uninhibited movie people were soon joined by other picture companies. On the whole, these were quieter. They were also affluent. They rented some of the fine homes, they owned cars, they dressed well, and they spent money like water. And, quite obviously, they enjoyed their work.

The movies steadily improved in quality. Now there could be no doubt; they really were going to amount to something. Again I gave real thought to my problem. I balanced the value of a secure job against the haphazard life of the movies.

I said to myself that this was a developing business. "And it's here, right here in Hollywood. Now if I was back East, and the least bit adventurous, I'd probably get on my bicycle and race off to Hollywood. But here it is on my doorstep—and on the doorstep of everyone else in southern California—yet we're doing nothing about it."

I resolved to give the movies a try.

When I announced that I was quitting, my boss at the railroad was amazed. "What do you plan to do?" he asked.

I was too embarrassed to tell him. I simply said that I didn't know.

He gave me a puzzled look. "Why don't you think things over for a few days?"

"No," I said quickly. "My mind is made up." I knew that if I started to think things over, I would back out.

So, at twenty-six, I made the break. I went down and mingled with the extras at Universal's open lot on Gower and Sunset—these lots were called bullpens. I found out that as a rule the lot was empty by noon because the extra people they needed had been engaged earlier in the day. But I just had a feeling that eventually somebody might need someone in the afternoon . . .

And that's what happened. I was out there at noon, all by myself, and I saw a wide-eyed, frantic casting director stick his head out of his office door. There was nobody there but me. He started back into his office and I guess he had an afterthought.

"Hey you—have you got a dress suit?"

"I sure have."

"How long would it take you to get it?"

"About fifteen minutes."

"Go get it."

I ran. I lived up the hill a ways, and I ran up there, got my dress clothes, and ran back. I had cracked the ice.

Joseph Henabery.

This rare still, showing Joseph Henabery as Lincoln, his knees raised by planks, was rejected on photographic grounds from the publicity material of **The Birth of a Nation**.

Magnificent art direction with no art director; the gates of Babylon constructed by Huck Wortman for **Intolerance**.

A few days later, he came up to me again and said, "I can use you." I went along to a set where an old guy who was known as the Dean of Directors—Otis Turner—was working. At that time he was very badly crippled with arthritis. He was a little hunched-up guy, a short fellow, and he was directing a thing about Italian peasants.

In those days, around 1913, no one would tell you what you were doing. They just shoved some clothes at you and said, "Put these on." You were a piece of scenery, that was all. You didn't have to have any talent. All you had to be able to do was to move if you were asked to.

They gave me an Italian peasant's outfit. I had my make-up with me, so I thought I'd put on a big mustache like the Italian peasants I'd seen on the stage and in paintings. Strangely enough, this seemed to get over all right. As a matter of fact, I was pulled up from way in the back to way up front. I had no part to play, but I was in with all the principals, and I followed one of my fundamental rules: when anyone's talking, pay them a little attention. Follow the conversation around. And I had the satisfaction of hearing Otis Turner say to his assistant, "Who is that guy?"

After that, whenever Otis Turner started a picture, I was on the list. In those days, of course, a picture started every week, maybe more often than that. And everybody said, "You're in. This guy is the king bee of the lot."

One afternoon when I wasn't working, I went down to the city and saw a picture that D. W. Griffith had made—*The Avenging Conscience*. I had very little idea who Griffith was—but the picture knocked me right out of my seat. It was the most wonderful movie I had ever seen. Compared to all the pictures I had seen previously—and I'd seen many one- and two-reelers—I thought this was it.

When I was next at Universal, I was talking about this picture and its director. And one of the fellows said, "He's out in Hollywood now—just came out to start work here."

I went down the next afternoon to make sure, and there it was—the Griffith lot. I reasoned that if you use extras one place you use them another, so I went back to Universal to pick up the stuff I had at the studio. One of the fellows said, "Why, you're nuts. You've got a start here. You're in."

"I don't care," I said. "I'm interested in working for that studio."

About this time, Griffith was making preparations to shoot *The Clansman*—later *The Birth of a Nation*—and he had a lot of his stock people tied up in the picture. That meant that the other directors making one- and two-reelers on the lot had to kind of grope around to get their players.

So it was only two or three days after I'd been out there that a director came into the bullpen and said, "Hey you! Have you ever worked in pictures?"

I didn't tell him my whole life story. I said, "Yeah, sure."

"Whereabouts?"

"Universal."

"Come on in with me. I think we can use you."

I followed him to where the fellow in charge of production had his office. The director said, "He looks the type to me."

It turned out they thought I had an Irish grin—and they wanted me to play a young Irish policeman. And that was the lead in the picture!

The first fellow I worked for was Fred Kelsey. Then I did pictures for directors like Eddie Dillon, Christy Cabanne, Frank Powell, and a man we called Sheriff Maclay, who always did the westerns—he'd played the sheriff with Broncho Billy.

If you'd had two or three years of motion pictures you were a pioneer, a veteran. You'd really been through the mill. You might have made a hundred and some pictures in that time—a one-reeler could be made in a day.

One day I saw a fellow going around the lot wearing a Lincoln make-up. I said to myself, "My, that is a *horrible* make-up."

Somebody said to me, "Griffith's looking for someone to play Abraham Lincoln in *The Clansman.*" I thought to myself, get him to look for me, too!

I had got to know the fellow in charge of production, Frank Woods, and I said, "Mr. Woods, I've seen some people going around here in Lincoln make-up. Is Mr. Griffith looking for someone to play the part? If so, I think I can put on a better make-up than any I've seen around here . . ."

He said that he'd speak to Mr. Griffith about it. In the meantime, I went down to the public library, looked up several books on Lincoln, and I studied his pictures. At home, I tried out a Lincoln make-up.

I heard nothing from Frank Woods, so I tackled him again. He'd forgotten—but he went in to see Griffith immediately, and then came out and called to me: "Come on over—I want him to see you."

Griffith had seen me at rehearsals, and he knew that I'd had some experience. He looked me over from head to foot. I was taller than average, thinner in those days than I am now, and I had a long face. Everybody seems to think that Lincoln had a very long face—which he hadn't. His cheekbones were very wide.

Griffith looked at me and said: "Have you ever made up for Lincoln?"[2]

I said: "Yes, sir." I didn't tell him I'd only made up in private! He called his assistant over. "Get the Lincoln outfit and let this fellow make up."

I worked most all of the afternoon, putting on the make-up. When I came out, people stared at me in amazement; it was the dead come to life. I went over to the open stage where Griffith was working, and got into a position where he could see me.

In those days, a stage was a large platform open to the sky. Overhead were muslin diffusers, which could be drawn across the set to soften the direct glare of the sun.

I just stood on this stage, waiting. Every so often, as Griffith worked with people, he would turn, study me in great detail, and then go back to his work. He did this four or five times. Meanwhile, I was standing there in the boiling hot sun, with heavy clothes and padding in certain places, with a wig, a false nose, spirit gum, hair—I was just roasting.

But he didn't say anything to me, so I thought he didn't care much about it and I left the stage and took off the make-up. Next day, I was out on the lot again and the assistant came up and said, "Where were you yesterday?"

"I was on the stage there."

"Mr. Griffith wanted to see you!"

"He saw me half a dozen times."

"Well, go and put that make-up on again."

I didn't mind; they were paying me five dollars every time I put it on. Once

---

[2] *Griffith had himself played the part on the stage.*

more I went down to where Griffith was working, and darn me if the same thing didn't happen *again*. I said to myself, "I don't understand this man. He looks at me and says nothing, and the day is almost gone." What could I do for him, just standing there? I decided I couldn't do anything so I left the stage and took the make-up off once more.

Oh, did I get a bawling out for that! Oh, boy. Well, he didn't ask me to put it on again. I didn't hear any more about it; I guessed I'd queered that one.

About two weeks later I heard they were erecting a set—the Ford's Theater scene. I felt kind of bad about it because I'd have very much liked to have done the part. I didn't know how much of a part it was going to be—I knew it wasn't very large, but it was an important part. When the set was finished an assistant came to me and said, "Put on the Lincoln make-up tomorrow morning and be ready at eight o'clock."

Oh, boy! That was great—but it meant murder, for one reason. In those days the dressing rooms were little sheds, with no protection against cold. At this time of year it was awful cold in the morning, and it was very difficult to work putty with ice-cold hands. I allowed myself plenty of time; I got there at five a.m.

You know the distorted mirrors they have in fairgrounds? Well, the only mirror in this little shed was like one of those. When you look at yourself one way, your nose is nice and straight. Go over this way, and the nose is crooked. Now which one is right?

But worst of all was the cold. I had a candle, and a spoon to heat the putty, but it still took a very long time to put the make-up on. Eight o'clock came and I wasn't anywhere near ready.

Assistants came bawling me out, but I said, "I can't help this—I've been working on it for hours." Finally, around eight thirty, Griffith himself appeared at the door of the shed.

"I thought," he said, "that you were to be ready at eight o'clock."

"I'd like to have been," I said.

"You were supposed to be ready at eight o'clock," he repeated.

"Mr. Griffith," I said, "I got here at five o'clock. Feel my hands. Do you think you could melt putty with those hands?"

I was sore. I felt imposed upon. I didn't give a damn whether he told me to get off the lot or not. Griffith was surprised; he looked at me with a little understanding, and he said, "Make it as soon as you can."

So I came out onto the stage as soon as I could. The first scenes were not on the Ford's Theater set but in an office of the White House where I was to do a scene with Ralph Lewis, who played Senator Stoneman.

I had no instructions, no script, no idea what I was supposed to do. By this time I was full of the Lincoln story. I had read many books about him, and I knew his physical characteristics, his habits and everything else. And I sat in the chair on my tailbone, sort of hunchbacked. Griffith looked at me with a frown.

"Don't sit like that," he said.

Now at this time Griffith was such an outstanding figure in the motion-picture business that he was surrounded by a great many yes men. Everything he did, it was: "Yes Mr. Griffith, yes Mr. Griffith." No one was contradictory. By nature, I'm a little combative. I've a lot of Irish in me, and if I'm right I don't mind speaking my piece.

So I said, "Mr. Griffith, I'm sitting in the most frequently mentioned position that Abraham Lincoln sat in. They say that he sat down on his tailbone, with his knees up, like this . . ."

Now Griffith couldn't soak himself in details about every one of his characters, as I could with Lincoln. And he realized that I knew my facts.

"Get a board," he ordered. "Get a board and put it under his feet. Get two boards—make his knees come up high . . ."

He knew that you have to exaggerate sometimes in order to convey an idea.

His attitude changed. He began to relax. He looked a little happier. I think he felt maybe he hadn't picked as much of a lemon as he'd thought. Now he described a part of the scene in which I was supposed to sign some papers on the desk.

"May I say something, Mr. Griffith?" I said. "The books on Lincoln say that when he wrote, or read, it was customary for him to wear glasses."

"Well, have you got them?"

"Yes, sir." I'd dug up an old-fashioned pair of steel-rimmed specs. I showed them to him.

"Use them," he said.

So when the paper was put down I made it part of my business to fish around for my glasses, to take my time putting them on, and then to sign the paper.

Well, now he's happy. He realizes that I have studied the character, and that I know something about the period. When it came to the Ford's Theater scenes, he'd tell me what he was going to do in the long shots, and I'd tell him what I'd read that Lincoln would be doing.

Griffith's attitude was simple: "If somebody has made an effort to study his part, then I'm going to make use of what knowledge he has acquired."

When the Lincoln part was finished, I did thirteen bit parts. In one sequence I played in a group of renegade colored people, being pursued by white people— and I was in both groups, chasing myself through the whole sequence.

When the picture was finished, they put me in stock. That was a promotion. They didn't have much money in those days—they were darn near skidding along on their bottoms, that's what the truth of it was, until the big showing here. And you know the history of that.

I'll never forget that first big showing. It was here in Los Angeles, and the picture was still called *The Clansman*. The audience was made up largely of professional people and it was our first big showing—the whole industry's first big showing.

I have never heard at any exhibition—play, concert, or anything—an audience react at the finish as they did at the end of *The Clansman*. They literally tore the place apart. Why were they so wildly enthusiastic? Because they felt in their inner souls that something had really grown and developed—and this was a kind of fulfillment. From that time on the picture had tremendously long runs at high seat prices.

I shudder when I see bits of that film shown at twenty-four frames a second with people hopping around because they're fifty per cent overspeed.[3] It really shocks me. I admit some people are able to make adjustments in their mind, especially those in the business, but young audiences have no conception that there

---

[3] The Birth of a Nation *was shot at camera speeds ranging from twelve to eighteen frames a second.*

was ever a difference in film speed. They just think it's comic. They cannot conceive that the picture has any merit at all.

When Griffith came back from his big opening in New York, the whole plan for making feature pictures through the Triangle Corporation was in his mind. He started immediately setting up companies to make them.

I was rehearsing with Douglas Fairbanks at Fine Arts—the Griffith apex of Triangle—when I got word that Mr. Griffith wanted to see me. I went over, and he began talking about an idea for improving a picture that he'd made earlier as a sort of potboiler. It was called *The Mother and the Law* and it was a little, cheap, quickie picture.

One of his ideas for improvement was to incorporate a grand reception scene, such as our New York Four Hundred used to have. In those days the Four Hundred was made up of people of great wealth, such as railroad tycoons, and they spent enormous sums on their receptions. Griffith wanted one of these as a prologue to *The Mother and the Law*.

Knowing that I could dig in and find things, he wanted me to do some research on how to conduct an affair of this sort. He wanted a lot of footmen, powdered wigs, knee breeches, and all that sort of thing. I left the rehearsals and started trying to get the data—but found I'd hit a really tough snag.

I found out about the lavish expenditure, and about the clowns who attended these affairs. But I couldn't get much idea about how it was conducted. Then I had a brainwave. A lot of very wealthy people came out from New York to spend the winter in Pasadena, and many of them spent their time at one of the big hotels—the Green or the Maryland. I found a lady, the hostess at the Maryland, who had been a secretary for some of these people, and she gave me the most perfect outline.

"To start with," she said, "you're off on the wrong foot. They don't have flunkies in powdered wigs. They wear uniforms, knee breeches, and tails, maybe with some silver lace, but no fluffy frills—and their hair is trimmed."

I wrote down pages of notes for Mr. Griffith, and drew designs of the uniforms she'd described. We figured they would cost forty dollars apiece—that would be a hundred and fifty today. Griffith told me to order them and to find some boys that they'd fit. And that's how I started to do research for the film that was amplified into *Intolerance*.

No sooner had I returned to my rehearsals with Fairbanks than somebody came over and said: "You're not going to play in the Fairbanks picture—stay with Griffith." He wanted some more research.

One Sunday, some of Griffith's key people were called to the projection room, where he was to screen the old *Mother and the Law*. I'll never forget that day. He had about eight people there, including Frank Woods, head of the scenario department, George Siegmann, and George (later Andre) Beranger, who were both assistants. The projection room was a little flat-roofed place, and I remember the rain poured on the roof. Thank heaven we didn't have to worry about sound, because we'd never have heard anything the way it rained that day.

I'd never seen the picture before. Some of the others had. When it was finished, the usual thing: "Oh, Mr. Griffith, it's marvelous! It's wonderful!" It's this, it's that. Gradually, they left the place and went off in the rain. I sort of hung back, because I didn't want to air my feelings in front of all those people. It wouldn't be a very nice thing to do, and it would only serve to make him resist an idea. Anyway, I didn't want to put myself in the humiliating position of trying to tell him something, because he knew so much more than I did that there was just no comparison.

When they'd all gone, he said, "Well? Now what about you?"

The Mother and the Law was a tearjerker. The principal characters were very appealing, but some of the settings were shoddy. I told him that there were four or five things that bothered me.

"To begin with, when Bobby Harron is taken to be executed, he is accompanied by a chaplain, and the outfit they've provided for him is not an outfit that any American priest ever wears. You have the tabs of a French curé. It would get a laugh from all the Catholics in the country."

He was startled. He didn't know the difference. "Do you think we could get the right outfit?" he asked.

I was lucky. In Los Angeles I found a Catholic priest who had been a chaplain at San Quentin. I told him the whole story.

"Why, I'd be glad to help you," he said. "I'll come out and I'll stand by and tell you how certain things are done. I'd like to see it done right. You can use my vestments if it would help."

I told Mr. Griffith and he was delighted. We brought the priest up and reshot all that part of the picture. And there were a few other details I mentioned, and he fixed those. So I felt I had played quite an important part. Most people in the studio were unaware of how these changes came about, and I wasn't likely to blab my mouth off—I'm waiting until this day and age to do that!

Griffith then began to enlarge his ideas. He began to get more and more grandiose notions. He got involved with the idea of Babylon and the St. Bartholomew Massacre and the Crucifixion. These eras provided a contrast between the activities of the rich and powerful, and the intolerance practiced on the poor and helpless. Finally, he asked me for material on each of these epochs.

You wouldn't think you could find as many books on Babylon and Assyria as I found. I ended up with a shelf about fifteen feet long, crammed with books. Griffith would ask me, "Now what kind of a chariot would we use for the year of Belshazzar's Feast?"

And I'd have to go through book after book and put stickers in. There were so many plates and illustrations and descriptions that I couldn't keep it straight. I decided to buy two more copies of each book, so that where there were pictures on both sides of a page, I would be able to cut them up and arrange them in a scrapbook. There would be sections for armor, chariots, cooking utensils, and so on.

But when the business manager of the studio found out that I was buying two more sets of books and spending all this money—oh, he blew his top.

"Listen," I said. "This is the cheapest way to do it. If I had those illustrations photographed, the cost would be a great deal higher."

He wasn't satisfied, and he went to Griffith about it. So I told Griffith the same thing—I told him it was the only way we could assemble the stuff in its proper order.

"Go ahead and get them," he said. "Don't pay any attention to him."

The scrapbook was a mammoth affair. At first, Griffith didn't think it was too good, but as he began to ask for things I'd consult it and say: "You can make a choice on some of these things here." He'd flip through and say: "No—these pages here . . ." It got to the point where he was carrying the scrapbook around under his arm. I often wonder what happened to it. I would love to own that scrapbook now. . . .

I would contact anybody I thought would be able to help me. A rabbi who helped on the Jewish period was the father of Carmel Myers, who came out to Triangle as a result.

The greatest authority on the backgrounds and costumes of the Jewish period was a French artist called Tissot. He published a set of four beautiful books, in color, of paintings and drawings that he'd made in the Holy Land. We followed carefully the garments that he painted in his *Life of Christ*. I had many books relating to the period, and I couldn't find any equal to his. He went into details about what a phylactery looked like. He'd paint close-ups of it, and of all the things that were part of the Jewish faith. Strangely enough, this artist had been known in France as a great painter of the nude figure, until something happened in his life and he became religious, and the great authority on the life of Christ.

All the time the picture's being shot, I'm not only researching—I'm working as an assistant and playing Admiral Coligny in the French period, or one of the old Pharisees in the Jewish period. I was in the parts that were remade of *The Mother and the Law*. No one else worked with me on research until the last month, when I was working day and night, and a man by the name of R. Ellis Wales came in. I was on the set all the time and couldn't cope with the research any more. Most of the basic material was assembled, however.

As I saw what Griffith was shooting, I began to ask myself some questions: Where do we go from here? How can we make a picture with all this stuff we've been shooting? How are we going to fit all these sets we've built into the little *Mother and the Law*?

I couldn't see it. I thought it was a great waste of effort, talent, and money to try to squeeze everything into the one picture. I hinted to Griffith something about what was bothering me—and handed him several novels set in Babylon.

Well, he's a pretty wise guy. One Monday morning, with everyone ready for rehearsals in the special room built for rehearsing, he came in. "Well," he said, "I thought until yesterday that maybe Hanabery was right." He called me Hanabery. "But now I know he's all wrong."

That, I thought, is a nice way to tell me to shut my mouth. But that, in effect, was what he wanted me to do now—keep quiet. The others in the room had no idea what he meant—only I knew. He had a habit of speaking indirectly. This was his way of telling me he was going ahead with his ideas.

But I'll say this. When the picture was finished, and he was in the throes of cutting, he came out of the projection room one night. He had his old hat pulled down over his eyes. He said, "Well, I wish I'd made a Babylonian picture."

Frank "Huck" Wortman was our chief carpenter, set builder, and stage mechanic. He'd do something for forty cents that today would cost four million. I can remember the streets of Jerusalem, with the archways. Huck would take thin boards, put a rope on the scantlings and bend them down, then plasterers would get in and plaster it—and there you had your archway, beautifully shaped.

The backgrounds of *Intolerance* were probably the finest job of set building that has ever been done in motion pictures. But we had one problem. The boys we had could paint a set, but they couldn't age it or do anything to give it character.

So one day Griffith came up to me and said: "You know about the San Francisco Exposition?"

"Yes," I said. "I was up there."

"Do you remember the interior of the Doge's Palace in the Italian section?"

"Yes, I remember it very well."

"I want you to go up to San Francisco—see if you can find any of the people who worked on it. See if you can get them down here."

The exposition was long since over, and the people who worked on it had left. I noticed a number of plaster shops around town—shops which made art objects in plaster of Paris—and here I got most of my leads. The shops were run by Italians, and eventually I tracked down three of the craftsmen who had worked on the Italian section. I made a deal with them: "You're going to come to Hollywood," I said. "I'll pay you so much a week, I'll pay your fare, and I'll guarantee you so many months' work."

I brought down two sculptors and a painter. I was warned before I left that the painter was an awful lush—but, boy, what an artist! He was the man who had done some of the beautiful aging work that Griffith had noticed. He wasn't an Italian; he was actually a Frenchman and became known as Frenchie.

He was like a fine scene painter, except that he was working on a different canvas—a plaster wall. We built big scaffolds so that he could get up high and make the walls of Babylon looked aged. He was so proficient that some of the other painters, who had been around for years, used to sneak over to the lot, and I'd see them peeking through, watching this fellow. They had never realized what a man could do with a brush.

But I had quite a time with this character. Every so often he'd go off on a bat and wouldn't show up at all. When he finally appeared, I would tackle him. "Frenchie," I'd say, "you're putting me in one awful spot. They spent a great deal of money to send me up to San Francisco to bring you down here— and they want you to do the job. You're letting me down. They're blaming me for this . . ." They weren't, of course, but I had to lay it on pretty thick.

"Oh, Meester Joe," he'd say, "it no happen again. So sorry."

He'd go back up and do some marvelous work, but pretty soon he'd be off on a bender again. The reason he got drunk so often was because we paid him more than he was used to.

One of the other guys I brought down from San Francisco was put in charge of our plaster workshop. We didn't have a plaster shop when he arrived, but he developed one, and he developed lots of people to work in it. He was a wonderful sculptor, and he used to make models in clay to show Griffith what he had in mind. All those things in Babylon—the lions, the elephants, and all the other statuary—were the work of these men.

Griffith was very keen on those elephants. He wanted one on top of each of the eight pedestals in Belshazzar's palace. I searched through all my books. "I'm sorry," I said, "I can't find any excuse for elephants. I don't care what Doré or any other Biblical artist has drawn—I can find no reason for putting elephants up there. To begin with, elephants were not native to this country. They may have known about them, but I can't find any references."

Finally, this fellow Wales found someplace a comment about the elephants on the walls of Babylon, and Griffith, delighted, just grabbed it. He very much wanted elephants up there!

An important part of research is logical deduction. Should you have great timbered halls in Babylon? No. Why not? Because there is no place in the area where such timbers could be found.

The only time I really got stuck was when Griffith asked me for a Babylonian beerhall. "I don't think I've ever seen an illustration of one," I said. "I've seen the equivalent of an Egyptian beerhall, but not a Babylonian one." I had to research into Egyptian history in order to correlate my facts—to see where something might have spread from one country to the other. Finally, I told Griffith I could make one that would be acceptable. "We'll cut up great palms, and they'll be the pedestals for the tables . . ."

"That'll be fine," he said. There was little authentic justification, but you might say it would have been appropriate.

One of the many things I admired about Griffith was his appreciation of realism. "Tomorrow," he used to say, "I want to shoot on such-and-such a set. See that they get it ready." So I'd go over and look at it, and try and make it look natural. I'd get the boys to plant weeds and vegetation in certain places, to make it look as though the building had been there for years.

It delighted me to have Griffith look with approval on it. He never said anything—but I could tell when he was satisfied. When anybody did something on their own initiative, he would really enjoy it.

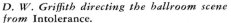
D. W. Griffith directing the ballroom scene from Intolerance.

Carpenters sweep the floor before shooting starts on the massive Babylon set.

From the Crucifixion episode of Intolerance; *Howard Gaye as Christ, Bessie Love as the Bride of Cana, and George Walsh as her Bridegroom (right).*

I remember one time in the Babylonian episode I was playing a soldier. I was up in front of a judge of the Babylonian court because a man had charged me with molesting his wife. And so I was telling the judge, in pantomime, how I had been walking along the street when I heard a whistle; I looked around and here was this woman up at a window, and she gave me the wink . . . I was doing the little gestures all the time, improvising as I went along. And then I caught sight of Griffith. You'd think he'd lost his gut. He was *loving* it. So I kept building it up, elaborating it. Now I don't like to use the word "pantomime," because I don't care for classic pantomime. I prefer the subtler form of acting—the glance and the wink are much more effective than going overboard with a lot of hand stuff. And Griffith was a man who had a great appreciation of these details.

That's the reason Griffith was an inspiration to me. Not because of his innovations—but because he was the first man to realize that a good story depends upon characters who are well developed and interesting. Our early pictures were crude and elementary; two people would meet and you knew nothing whatsoever about them as people—where they came from, what they were, whether they liked Limburger cheese or ladyfingers. They were just impersonal puppets.

But Griffith made sure you knew his characters. He'd begin by saying, "Now what does a woman do who takes care of a home for a family?" And he might show her on the porch, and she'd be husking corn, and with little details he would get you to feel the character—"That's my mother," you'd think.

He had great insight, and a great feeling for contrasts. I can remember in *The Battle of Elderbush Gulch,* the scene where Mae Marsh is hidden from the Indians in a flour barrel. When that little comedy figure pops up and peeps over the top of the barrel, it acts as an amusing contrast to a tense and highly melodramatic situation.

In *The Birth of a Nation,* the Negro soldiers are about to break into the little log cabin where some of the refugee whites have hidden, and one faithful household servant stands at the window. As these fellows try to come through she biffs them, one at a time, with a rifle butt. Well, people were so tense by the time this developed that every time she struck one of them they'd go into roars of laughter. That wasn't laughter, really. It was a release. And you enjoyed it all the more because you became involved in the battle. You weren't just a by-stander, you were emotionally involved. That's our side getting along there!

This man Griffith worked without any of the aides we consider necessary today. Look at a present-day motion picture or TV show, for instance. Look at all the credits for the people involved. Griffith had a cameraman, a prop man, a stage carpenter, an assistant director, and someone on research. Most of these men had their own assistants, but Griffith had no art director, no character make-up men, no hairdressers, no special-effects department, no scriptwriter— no script!

He was a very appreciative man. He didn't come up, clap you on the back, and say: "Swell, boy, that was a swell job." But something would happen in your favor, and that's how he would show his appreciation.

Many times we would shoot at night. Electrical illumination was not in full use in California, so we used flares. In those days we had no loud-speakers to direct crowds, some of which could be two blocks away, so we used megaphones. A great many people found their voices tiring after a few hours with one of these, but I learned to breathe differently. I guess it was like opera singing; I used my diaphragm. I would call out to people slowly—I didn't speak so fast the words were jumbled—and I'd be right there on the stand beside Mr. Griffith.

We had one of the grand shots of all time in *Intolerance*. We built a tower facing the Babylonian set, with an elevator in it, a studio-constructed elevator. The camera platform was mounted on top of this device. As it descended vertically, the tower moved forward on wheeled trucks which rode on railroad tracks. These trucks had cast-iron wheels, eighteen inches across; they were the kind of platform trucks used by railroad maintenance men.

Four people rode on the camera platform: Griffith; Bitzer; Karl Brown, his assistant; and myself. The scene opened on a full, high setup of the palace with thousands of people in the scene. Without any cut or break, it gradually descended to a medium shot which included just the principals. The shot was repeated a number of times. During the rehearsal, Griffith would call attention to background action he wanted corrected. At the end of the rehearsal move, I would run back into the set and tell the group captains about the changes. Griffith made corrections to the foreground action himself. Then we would return to the camera platform and ride up to the top. We rehearsed for about one and a half hours. Now we had to begin shooting to catch the light at the proper angle. The scene itself was made three or four times. As I recall it, each shot appeared to be okay. However, as retakes would have cost a fortune, the shot was repeated for protection with some minor changes in exposure.

I never put a tape measure to the camera platform, but one figure is firmly fixed in my mind, a figure which can be used to scale most of the sets. The walls of Babylon were ninety feet high. The walls were about the same height as the columns on which the elephants were erected; it is safe to estimate the overall height at one hundred and forty feet. The camera platform was between a hundred and a hundred and fifteen feet; as I recall it, we were in a line horizontally with the elephant platforms, and the camera was slightly below them. At its widest point, the tower structure was forty feet.

Altogether we spent little more than a couple of hours on the scene. We had to shoot with the light. If we wanted the full effect of the settings, we had to take the scene when the lighting was appropriate. We couldn't take it in backlight, for instance. We'd have to take it in maybe a nice crosslight, or half-backlight. So we were limited to a period between ten a.m. and eleven a.m.

I found the locations for the battle scenes which were supposed to be along the rivers Euphrates and Tigris. They were shot a little below what we call the Baldwin Hills. Historically, it was about the same type of land. Acres and acres of swampy plain. I got permission from the heirs to the Dominguez Estate and arranged with the Pacific Electric Railroad to take special electric cars, hauling our extras, to within a short distance of where we wanted to work.

Assisting Griffith meant that I also had to cope with the mobs of people. Let's say we were going to have two thousand people; how do you get two thousand people costumed and ready, early in the morning, unless you break it down some way? I figured that I would give each man a card. This would indicate which booth he would get his costume from—and he would be one of, say, one

Joseph Henabery's orgy scene for Intolerance.

The army of Cyrus the Great.

hundred and fifty people who would get their costume from that booth. I had the backs of the Babylon sets divided into booths, and labeled, and had the costumes placed as I wanted them, so they'd be orderly. And I had two thousand ready by eight a.m.

Technically speaking, George Siegmann was the principal assistant director. He was a grand fellow, but he didn't care too much about either organization or research, and lots of times he'd come to me when they were making a scene and say, "Which way should they go? Left or right?" But he did more for me than any human being would ever do for someone working in a similar capacity. He was a wonderful guy.[4]

Lunches were ordered the night before. I had to take a gamble on the weather. Many a time I've boiled in oil when the fog didn't break until way late, and we had a couple of thousand extras standing by.

A cafeteria in the city would work all night to prepare these lunches, and I was very strict about leftovers. I'd tell them to make up just the right number, and I insisted that the food be fresh because the lunches were a great psychological help. Extras got their carfare, their lunch, and a dollar and a quarter a day. They only got a dollar and ten cents a day when they worked on *Birth of a Nation;* this wasn't much of a raise, but it was more than other companies paid their mobs.

I could get two thousand boxed lunches on two trucks. And they were nice lunches. They cost thirty-five cents apiece, which in those days meant a darn good deal. I would arrange for them to be distributed from the same places that I had for the costumes, and I could feed the whole mob in no time at all. When

[4] *Siegmann and George (Andre) Beranger were also actors.*

D. W. Griffith and G. W. Bitzer prepare a running shot for Intolerance.

the trucks came on, they'd make a run for it, yelling "Hey! L-u-n-c-h! L-u-n-c-h!" and you couldn't control them. They'd grab their lunches and their milk, and oh boy, they were very happy with that.

I had noticed one old guy who always seemed to get away from the rest, after he'd got his box lunch. He'd go over to where we had kind of a canvas fence surrounding the property, the barrier that kept the public out, and he'd sit on the ground. I couldn't figure what was going on over there—until one day I strolled over to a point where I could see both sides of the fence. And there, on the other side, was his poor old wife. He was passing part of his lunch to her, under the fence.

When you work with people, you learn much more about them than you can from distant observation. My experiences during the making of this picture changed my whole outlook. I began to think very differently about certain human beings.

We used to get a lot of extras from Skid Row, a slum area of Los Angeles. Skid Row had what the term implies—a great many people who were booze hounds, and down-and-outers. Unfortunately, as I soon learned, there were many, many people who were physically unable to work, or to hold a steady job.

We'd bring the "mob" people up to the studio in electric cars, and herd them to these different places to be dressed. They would take off their clothes, or roll them up, and you'd see what a terrible condition they were in. Malnutrition . . . some of them with severe varicose veins . . . the sort of things that men without money cannot cope with. If you're broke, and down and out, you go from bad to worse and end up on Skid Row. You're not a drunkard at all, just a poor, worn-out, worthless human being as far as the public is concerned. Someone they cast aside and label "bum"—and that's your lot until you're fortunate enough to die.

Another surprise for me was to find out how sadistic some people can be. We put part of the mobs up on the walls of Babylon. The Persian army would flood across the ground below, attacking, shooting their arrows, and all that sort of thing. We gave the boys above bows and arrows, spears, and what we called magnesium bombs, which were historically accurate. We'd take a roll of chicken wire, cover it with canvas, and coat it with magnesium. The men above would light their bombs and hurl them on the Persians below. How delighted they were when they could hit a guy who was supposed to be dead! When you saw a dead guy leap to his feet and run you knew someone was throwing bombs or plugging arrows at him.

One time, a guy came into the first-aid tent; an arrow had pierced the side of his head and come out on top of his scalp. . . . The injuries were mostly of a minor nature, but we once had as many as sixty-seven in that first-aid tent in one day. There was no excuse for many of these accidents. Most of them were malicious—caused by people who took delight in making their fellow men uncomfortable. The battle scenes gave them the time of their lives.

In those days we had a group called the IWW's—the Industrial Workers of the World. We used to call them the I Won't Works, the Wobblies. These Wobblies thought that we were a kind of lemon they could squeeze.

We were shooting the Crucifixion, and we wanted to do it at dusk, when we didn't have strong sunlight, and we could get certain effects with lights and flares. These guys started to insist on another day's pay if they were going to stay on.

"I told you this morning," I said, "that we would pay you seventy-five cents for two extra hours—and that you'd be through by seven thirty this evening."

"We won't work."

The haranguing went on for quite a time. Finally I told them they would get seventy-five cents—take it or leave it.

"We leave it."

They started up the hill to the gate, which would be two hundred yards away, around through sets. I beat them to it. I ran around another way, and as I went past a carpenter I saw that he had a hammer in his overalls. I grabbed it and got to the gate just before the Wobblies.

There was a box there. I climbed onto it and yelled; "The first son of a bitch who tries to get out of this gate is going to get this hammer right in the head."

You've always got ringleaders you watch for. That's how you lick these mobs. "Now you—come on through! Come on through!"

Of course, I wouldn't have hit him. I don't know what I would have done, to tell you the truth.

Luckily, the first ringleader folded. As soon as he folded, so did the second leader, and I had them back in no time at all.

Some of the exterior sets had platforms in back of the set to give the effect of a floor of a room. Some of the IWW's would get under the platforms and hide. They didn't want to work; they'd find a good cool spot under there and they'd lay out for a sleep. It was some time before I got wise to this.

I went up to one of the cowboys who patrolled the area on horseback—Jim Kidd, a very famous Wild West and circus star.

"Jim," I said, "there are guys under those sets over there, and I want to roust them out. Get on your horse and give them a spin."

He rode up onto the platforms, the horse spun around, making a noise with its hoofs, and Jim put on a terrible show. He pulled out his revolver and fired off his blanks, yelling "Come out, goddammit, or I'll kill you!"

The noise must have been terrible under there. You should have seen the guys come out—ten or fifteen of them scrambled out, panic-stricken.

"All right, boys," I said. "Come on over and give me your tickets." I took their tickets away. "Now go on over there, get rid of your costumes, and get the hell off the lot."

Well, they protested. They were only fooling, they were just this, they were just that . . .

"Get off the lot."

Next morning, around five thirty, I watched the men coming in, and sure enough some of these guys were in line, hiding behind other people.

"You!" I'd say. "You were kicked off yesterday. Out! *Out!*"

I had one poor little old guy beg me and beg me: "Oh, please!" I relented, and gave him and a few others a second chance. I had my thumb on them now. Boy, did they perform thereafter! They were in everything. They worked their heads off.

We had battle scenes on the walls of Babylon in which people were supposed to be thrown off. For some of the close-ups, stunt men were used. We placed nets underneath. One man, who was highly experienced in falling into nets, having done circus and carnival work, was Leo Noomis—afterward a leading Hollywood stunt man. Then we dug up some fellows who had had some experience in doing high dives—into water.

Noomis got hold of these boys and said, "Look, when you land in the net, land on your back. Don't forget. Never land on your feet."

I can remember the scene distinctly. We framed the shot just above the net, so they wouldn't bounce back into the shot. Noomis came off fine, but he was followed by the others, who landed on their feet. Their feet jammed right back, their knees shot up, and we had three broken noses about *that* fast. I guess they'd decided Noomis just didn't know what he was talking about, even though he'd done hundreds of successful stunts for us.

We had tried dummies for the long shots. I thought they were putrid. They'd flop this way and flop that way, and they looked like what they really were— stuffed long johns.

"We ought to be able to build something better than that," I said to Griffith.

"Why don't you?" he asked.

As soon as the day's work was over, I went into the prop department. With several prop men helping, I worked until one a.m. I had in mind a figure with joints which could not bend the wrong way. I arranged threads so that as the body fell, the threads would snap and release an arm or a leg, and thus give body movements that were natural.

Around nine o'clock, who should walk into the shop but Griffith. He didn't say anything. He just looked at me with a kind of a grin and walked out again.

I had the thing working beautifully. The only disadvantage was the amount of work involved in getting the thread triggered for every shot. But it was a vast improvement over the sloppy falls you usually see with ordinary dummies.

The time came when the picture was to be taken over to Pomona for its first showing. I had never seen any rushes, let alone any completed cuts of the picture. That was always Griffith's privilege. I'd stand outside the projection room and wait for him. I could recall that near the end of *The Birth of a Nation* he said to me: "Well, how do you like yourself?"

"What do you mean?"

"As Lincoln."

"How do you suppose I'd ever get to see Lincoln?"

He laughed. . . .

I rode to Pomona in Griffith's Fiat with Bobby Harron, Mae Marsh, Lillian Gish, Mr. Griffith, and his chauffeur. In those days it was a terrible thirty-mile ride to Pomona; there were no paved highways then. We plowed through to Pomona because it was an out-of-the-way place where we could be sure of an unprejudiced reaction.

We had the showing—and I was utterly confused by the picture. I was so discouraged and disappointed. On the way home, everyone was raving, raving, raving—"Oh, it's wonderful."

Sure, it had wonderful scenes in it, wonderful settings and many wonderful ideas. But to me it was a very disconnected story. I knew that Griffith had had a problem trying to utilize all this material in a sensible way. But he had ended up with cuts a foot long. He had switched from period to period and he had it all chopped up. He just had too much material.

A modern audience might be able to grasp it, because they follow such techniques more often. But in those days people expected continuity.

The thing that disturbed me more than anything else was the subtitles. I was the last one to be dropped off, and as the chauffeur drove me home I gave the picture a lot of thought.

At ten next morning, I met Griffith in the little open area between his office and the scenario department. He stopped and said, "Well, what did you think about last night?"

I was very hesitant to say anything. Finally, I came out with: "Well, I was disappointed. The worst feature, as I see it, is that you have many titles in there that mean absolutely nothing to the audience. You and I, and a few people around here, have been close to the subject. We know the relationship between certain characters and certain events. But you're asking an audience, some of whom are almost illiterate, to absorb points beyond their grasp. It's impossible. It's—"

Griffith suddenly got very angry, something he very seldom did. "You don't know what you're talking about," he snapped. He left me and walked up to the scenario department.

I didn't feel bad about what I had said. I had it off my chest; at least that was one thing. I would have felt very remiss if I hadn't expressed my opinion.

Several hours later, I was standing on the stage, not far from where he was working, waiting till he came out. He might want to order something for the next day; I could never tell. Eventually, he emerged from the scenario department and began to walk to his office across the stage when he noticed me.

"Hey, Hanabery!" he said, and came over to meet me. "What was this you were saying this morning about titles?"

I started to recite some of the points once more. Then Frank Woods came from the scenario department, and Griffith called him over.

"Frank," he said, "Hanabery's right. How *do* they know that Cyrus the Great was related to so-and-so? How *could* they know?" He turned to me. "Come into the office after lunch."

I sat in there for about three hours. I hit the titles I particularly objected to. I made suggestions and they worked my ideas over and revamped the titles. In a way, this was very flattering to me. I'm human and I'm susceptible to flattery.

I had worked very hard on this picture. Many times I had worked far into the night making arrangements for the next day's work. I had often slept on the benches in the costume department so that I could be there at five the next morning, when the people started arriving.

I remember, after all the shooting was finished, George Siegmann and I went to see an outstanding picture that had just been made by Tom Ince—*Civilization*. We went in the afternoon. I'd see the start of a scene, I'd fall asleep, and I'd wake up again before the scene was over. I just couldn't concentrate any more. I was washed out. I felt terrible.

Finally, Griffith took the picture back East and apparently some of the powers that be said, "You ought to have more sex in it." As usual, the guys that sell to the public figured that the public all think in a certain way.

So Griffith wired Woods: "Have Hanabery shoot scenes of Belshazzar's Feast." And he described what he wanted—naked women and all this and that.

"He can't shoot naked women," I said. "You can't get away with that sort of thing."

"That's what he says," replied Woods, "and that's what I want you to do."

Gosh, I felt terrible about it. I talked to Billy Bitzer.

"I'm in a spot here. This stuff is going to be terrible."

"You do what you think is right," said Bitzer. "Whatever you do, I'll shoot it."

So I got a bunch of people together, and as a basic shot I developed a section from an old painting known as Belshazzar's Feast. It was a wild party, I can tell you. A real orgy. I had people lying around so that they weren't stark naked —almost, but not quite. Nevertheless, Frank Woods was sore because I hadn't followed orders—and there was no time to make new scenes.

I didn't know it at the time, but Griffith back East was shooting some naked women he'd dug up from the red-light district. Horrible-looking creatures. He made five or six close shots that were eventually injected into the sequence.

I didn't hear anything more about the matter until Griffith's return. Again he spoke in his indirect way. "You know," he said, "it's a strange thing when your assistant shoots better scenes than you do." Some minutes passed before I connected the remark with what I'd done.

Griffith went back East, and one day I was rehearsing with a company when Frank Woods called me. "Hey, Henabery. Do you think you could make a motion picture? Before Mr. Griffith left, he said that the first opportunity for a director was to be given to you."

I must have been silent for almost fifteen seconds, thinking of all the experienced people who had asked him, unsuccessfully, for a similar chance. Then I said: "Yes, I can do it."

And that's how I became a motion-picture director.

Popular illusion sees the role of the motion-picture director as the very essence of glamour and romance—and the nearest equivalent to a Divine Power yet achieved by mankind. People behave as he tells them to, events occur when he wants them to. He has the ability to freeze time and to reshape history—not just on paper but in actuality. And when he has committed his creation to film, he can play God all over again and rearrange events and characters in the cutting room.

Directors, however, are human. While creating their motion-picture events they are at the mercy of real ones. They may be able to part the Red Sea, but they're helpless if the sun goes down while they're shooting it.

In order to get a story on film, a director has to combine the organizational abilities of an army general with the patience and insight of a psychoanalyst. He has to have energy and stamina enough to give full rein to his talents as an artist and as a craftsman. He is answerable for his work on every level—financial, artistic, and administrative—and his job carries enormous responsibility. But his compensations can be equally great. For when the director has transformed his imaginings into reality, and when he has preserved that reality on motion-picture film, he has experienced something no other artist can know.

When the movies began there were just two technicians—one to photograph the film, the other to direct it. The cameraman had to prove he could thread a camera, but the director did not need to prove anything. All he had to do was shout. And since those days no one has ever determined just what qualifications a director needs, apart from lung power.

"When they ask me what elements are necessary for a director," said Josef von Sternberg, "I propose some absolutely horrible qualifications. I tell them he must know all the languages, he must know the history of the theater from its beginnings, he must be an expert at psychoanalysis and must have had some psychiatric training. He must know every emotion. And they ask me, 'Did you know all this?' And I say, 'No—but I never asked anyone how to become a director.' "[1]

The motion picture was a new industry, staffed by new people. There was no backlog of old hands awaiting promotion. If you were twenty and thought you could direct, one company or another would probably give you the chance. It didn't matter that you had just come from working on the railroad and had no impressive references. The man hiring you was probably a European immigrant who had been cutting cloth on the Lower East Side. He would have no illusions about education or position; if your pictures were good your pay would be good.

There is an old Hollywood story about an actor who got off a streetcar and insisted on shaking hands with the conductor. "That man," he explained, "might be my director tomorrow." Outsiders were baffled that so important a job as direction could be so casually assigned. One literary figure wrote indignantly: "I have seen writers, men with education, dramatic training, and a human share of common sense fail miserably. I have seen cameramen, ham actors, engineers, and men with no special training become big directors . . . ."[2]

[1] *Josef von Sternberg to author, Hollywood, Dec. 1964.*
[2] Photoplay, *June 1923, p. 27.*

Cameraman Al Gilks and director Irvin Willat on **North of 36** *(1924).*

And that was the secret of the silent era. Men unhampered by a literary education had a greater facility for visual narrative than men trained all their lives to use words; they may have been inarticulate in speech, but they were often superbly eloquent with pictures. And they had *lived*. Silent-film directors were mostly young men, but in those barnstorming days youth did not mean inexperience. Recruited from all branches of the industry, they came from every conceivable background. Sam Wood had worked on pipelines for an oil company. Edwin Carewe had been a tramp. James Cruze had worked in a medicine show. George Melford had started out with a blacksmith. Clarence Brown had been an auto salesman. W. S. Van Dyke had been a lumberjack, gold miner, railroader, and mercenary. They had no qualifications but their experiences—but these were often ideal training for the job, preparing them for rough assignments, tough personality problems, and uncomfortable location trips.

"They were marvelous men, these silent-picture makers," said David O. Selznick. "They had no affectation, they were full of adventure and the desire to do things. They were fast-moving and impatient and made their pictures very quickly. They were extremely imaginative and extremely knowledgeable. They were a wonderful breed."[3]

The silent era was the era of the director, the halcyon period before producers assumed creative control. In the twenties, one often saw the name of a director billed larger than that of the star. Since the public had responded so enthusi-

[3] *David O. Selznick to author, New York, Dec. 1964.*

astically to the star system, producers tried to extend the system to include directors. Not everyone approved.

"There seems to be a general movement to put the name of the director before the public eye," wrote a fan to *Photoplay* in 1923, "attempting to belittle the drawing power of a star. The only thing that matters in a picture *is* the star. I don't go to see a picture because I note it is directed by so-and-so. I go if the star appeals to me. In my opinion, the value of the star cannot be overestimated."[4]

"Who is the average 'star-director' of the hour?" asked James Quirk in 1921. "What sort of man is he? What has been his training—what are his special gifts? He is, as a rule, a very young man with the impatient assurance of youth. Usually he has been made by one or two phenomenally successful pictures, pictures which may have been phenomenons at the box office because of their highly interesting subjects, possibly selected by some obscure, unrewarded person. What happens next is not his fault, for he is starched out of all human semblance, blown up like a balloon and cranially inflated by a series of wild competitive offers from managers who seek anyone or anything that has a tang of success.

"Let us hasten to add that the young director is more sinned against than sinning. If he shows a flash of talent, his situation is more dangerous than that of a friendless, pretty girl against the world. The careless autocrats put him, without education, without maturity, astride the optic Bucephalus, and hand him not only the reins but a whip and spurs."[5]

In 1925, Paramount announced that the policy of the company was to hand the reins to the director. The director even had the power to ban the producer from the projection room while rushes were being shown. This idyllic state was short-lived, for 1925 was the year in which Thalberg revitalized the supervisor system. Nevertheless, such a statement demonstrates that directors mattered a great deal more than they do now—even if they were favored only by a temporary phase of the industry's development.

Photoplay decided, in 1921, that they would satisfy a long-felt want by answering a question that, they said, had puzzled film audiences, producers, actors, extras, and even assistant directors: what is a director?[6]

King Vidor said simply that a director was the channel through which a motion picture reaches a screen. Rex Ingram considered that a director was the best illustration of the term "fall-guy" that he could think of. "He is the one upon whose shoulders *all* of the blame invariably falls if the picture is not good—and if it is good, he is not always the one to get the thanks." Ingram added a grim foretaste of the future: "My sympathies are all with those directors who stand or fall on their own merits. I have too often seen a good picture, and the career of a promising director, ruined by so-called *supervision.*" Thomas Ince described the role of a director as being the same as a conductor in music: both are interpreters of artistic creations. "But just as the virtuosos often extend their work into the field of composing, so the director becomes a creator by originating supplementary ideas to enhance the values of the photoplay."

Jesse Lasky replied with facility: "A director, to be successful, must combine efficiency with artistry, blending the two by the exercise of judgment and finesse,

[4] Photoplay, *April 1923, p. 14.*
[5] Photoplay, *Feb. 1921, p. 49.*
[6] Photoplay, *Aug. 1921, p. 54.*

Rex Ingram directing The Four Horsemen of the Apocalypse *(1921). John Seitz at camera.*

Twenty-eight-year-old Mervyn Le Roy directing Harold Teen *(1928).*

and knowing instinctively when to cease exercising one quality and when to begin employing the other. He should at once possess the qualifications of a dramatist, of an actor; should be a good executive and have a sympathetic understanding of human nature."

Betty Blythe, star of *The Queen of Sheba,* defined a director as "the only man besides your husband who can tell you how many of your clothes to take off."

Cecil B. De Mille emphasized the administrative aspects of a director's job. He described him as a man who never sleeps. "Because if he superintends a staff of brilliant and infallible scenario writers, temperamental stars and untemperamental actors, helpless extra people, nut cameramen, artistic artists, impractical technical directors, excitable designers, varied electricians and carpenters, strange title writers, the financial department and the check signers; if he endeavors ultimately to please the exhibitors, the critics, the censors, the exchange men, and the public, it's a perfect cinch he won't have time to sleep."

Frank Lloyd, however, gave the most enlightening definition: "The director is essentially an interpreter. To him is given the task of making logical and understandable, pictorially, what the author and the continuity writer have set down. He must understand how to make the public understand. He must be as fluent with his camera as the author is with his pen. He must possess a sound sense of the mechanics of the motion picture, of composition, of continuity, of sequence. He must be a barometer of public opinion."

The director as an interpreter is a concept few critics or historians will accept —they feel the director is all-important, the true author of the work. They give credit for everything—even the photography—to the director. This oversimplification has a danger: while some reputations will be deserved, others become grossly inflated, and important contributions from less famous technicians are completely overlooked. Names that deserve to be remembered are erased from film history. And these technicians are not like Renaissance painters, whose reputations are only of academic interest. Many of them are still alive, and their careers have suffered from this wanton neglect.

The trouble is, of course, that there are too many people connected with film production. You cannot follow every title with a string of names, and you cannot hope to find out who was responsible for certain effects—whether it was really the director, or whether it was the cameraman, scenarist, editor, art director, assistant, or second-unit man.

The confusions surrounding credits are endless; even if you manage to contact the people who worked on a picture, they may twist history to their own advantage, as is human nature. The most common phrase I heard in Hollywood was: "I practically directed that myself." I heard it from actors, producers, cameramen, and assistants. In some cases it might have been true. But without substantiation it suggests wishful thinking. The statement indicates, however, that everyone thinks of the director as being the logical representative of a creative team; he is the man in authority, the field commander who accepts responsibility. And while lieutenants may get decorated, it is the commander who gets remembered.

The concept of a director as an author is a European idea. It can be applied in relatively few cases to American directors. D. W. Griffith was generally responsible for both idea and direction, as were Erich von Stroheim, Charles Chaplin, and such writers-turned-directors as Edmund Goulding. But there the list ends.

Even such great men as King Vidor, Rex Ingram, Ernst Lubitsch, and F. W. Murnau worked from other people's scenarios. They frequently contributed to the writing, but that hardly entitles them to be considered authors.

Most of these men were too busy shooting or editing or setting up production to work full-time on the script. The writer-directors, who involved themselves in all stages of their films' production, had to be satisfied with a much lower output. But they concentrated on quality, and thus greatly enhanced their reputations. Equally deserving of admiration were those journeyman directors who took what they were given, and, although restricted by budget and schedule, still achieved excellent results.

As the same crews worked together on picture after picture, creative teams developed. Several directors formed partnerships with cameramen: Herbert Brenon and the young Chinese James Wong Howe, Rex Ingram and John Seitz, James Cruze and Karl Brown, Griffith and Bitzer. Then there were equally rewarding partnerships between writer and director; Rex Ingram and June Mathis, Ouida Bergere and George Fitzmaurice—who were a husband-and-wife team, as were Josephine Lovett and John S. Robertson and, later, Clara Beranger and William de Mille. The partnership which survived the longest was that between Jeanie McPherson and Cecil B. De Mille.

The old directors are ready to discuss anything, except the way they actually directed. Not that they feel unwilling to disclose closely guarded secrets; they just cannot find the right words to explain what they mean. Asked to describe how they directed performances, they usually seize the most obvious anecdote: "I tell this girl that she's useless, that she's costing us a hell of a lot of money, and that we're going to get this scene if it takes us all night. She bursts into tears. The cameras are turning and we get it. Perfect. 'Okay,' I says, 'you were great. I'm sorry kid, I knew you had it in you. Let's go home.' "

The silent-film director is remembered as a figure in breeches and puttees or riding boots, swaggering around with the bravado of a Prussian cavalry officer, displaying the subtlety of a circus trainer. Certainly, distinctive dress was important to the militaristic director, the man who demanded obedience rather than interpretation. And many players declared that they preferred working for these authoritative directors, who seemed to know exactly what they wanted, rather than for men who looked to them for ideas and suggestions.

There was one badge of rank which almost every director carried: the megaphone. They came in every size—tiny models for intimate studio work, huge loud speakers for mob scenes. The director's name was usually stenciled along the side. Megaphones were vital because in silent pictures directors were dependent upon sound—the sound of music, the hypnotic, grinding sound of the camera, and above all the sound of the director's voice, given a greater volume and a greater urgency by the megaphone.

The director would whisper through it, his voice taking on the color of the scene. The musicians would swing softly into "Moonlight and Roses," the cameras would begin cranking, and the director would caress the actress with his voice: "Now remember, dear, remember that you've just lost your mother . . . your mother was everything in the world to you . . . everything in the world . . . you're missing her now . . . missing her . . . look through the window . . .

Erich von Stroheim during Foolish Wives *(1922). Ben Reynolds at camera. Maud George on right.*

Robert Vignola directing When Knighthood Was in Flower *(1922), a Cosmopolitan production with Marion Davies. Ira H. Morgan at camera.*

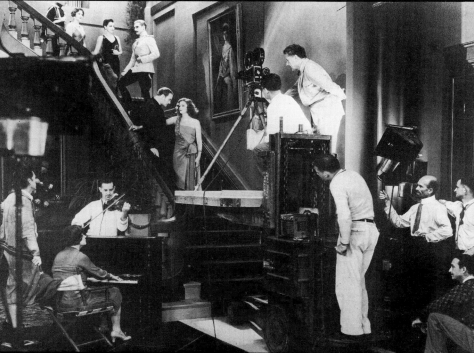

Fred Niblo directing Conrad Nagel and Greta Garbo in The Mysterious Lady *(1928). William Daniels at camera.*

the scent of the flowers reminds you of her . . . you feel the sting of tears . . . your throat's tight . . . now lean forward . . . gently . . . hold it . . . and *cut!*" The mood would snap with a sudden rush of noise and the actress would come to. "That's great, Mary, terrific. Print it, boys. On to the next setup—over here . . ."

Averse to intellectual or mystical terms, few of the old directors would admit to that strange, almost electric current that passes between actor and director. When I asked Allan Dwan about his methods of direction, he replied, "I have none. It all depends what I ate for breakfast."

King Vidor was more explicit. "In the silent days, the players were supposed to know the character they were portraying. Sometimes they didn't even read the script, but there was a thing that went on, almost telepathic, between the director and the actor. Things developed in scenes while the camera was going. And we had music on the set—that was very helpful to get the mood. In *The Big Parade,* when Gilbert encounters a German soldier in the shellhole, that was ad-libbed. I didn't have a big voice; I might say 'More,' 'Now,' 'That's wonderful,' 'That's great' . . . I wouldn't talk all the time and I'd get silent as quickly as possible. It was hypnotism.

"Gilbert never read the script of *The Big Parade,* and there were other actors of the period like that. They had faith and confidence in you. They knew you had a way of transferring emotion to them. I can't rationalize it. It's like a love affair; you just can't describe it. I actually remember moments when I didn't say a thing. I'd just have a quick thought and Gilbert would react to it."[7]

When the talkies came, the director could no longer direct during a shot. The musicians went, the megaphone went, the improvisation went. An icy, ghostly silence descended during shooting—a silence which was, ironically, to kill many talkies.

Accustomed to carpenters hammering on adjacent sets, accustomed to the music and the grinding cameras, and, above all, dependent on the voice instructing them through the megaphone, actors suddenly felt themselves adrift on another planet.

Once he had called "Camera!"—or "Interlock!" as it was now—even the director had to keep quiet and watch. All he had left was that vital element of hypnotism. It was working for him now as strongly as ever, and he was even more aware of it. More aware of it, but less likely to admit to it.

Silent-film directors have been dealt with by cinema books as impersonally as scientific specimens. Like the Latin names for butterflies, they appear in brackets after the titles of their films. Those considered outstanding are described in greater detail, their products discussed in a detached and clinical manner. Never do these specimens ever have the breath of life. Never do they seem human enough to have made mistakes, or to have done something accidentally. Every element of their work is described unremittingly as conscious artistic expression.

It is no part of a critic's job to investigate *how* effects were achieved. He has to confine himself to judging the final result as it affects him. He lays blame for a dull picture on the barrenness of the director's imagination; he cannot know

---

[7] *King Vidor to author, London, Aug. 1962.*

that the man was ill, that his mind was not on his job, or that he missed much of the shooting. A sudden, effective transition will be described as "inventive direction" even though the editor did it to cover up for some lost negative.

No critic can be expected to know such details. It would take a private investigator to uncover most of them, anyway. While the critic's appraisal may reveal artistic truths, descriptions by technicians of how the film was made reveal truths of another sort—about human strengths and weaknesses contributing to art, and about the accidents and mishaps that transform mediocrity into something fresh and unusual.

It is all too easy to become baffled and disappointed by the unexpected lapses of a favorite director. One can never fully appreciate the immense difficulties to be overcome. As an audience, one's attention is wholly with the film, and it is hard to realize that the mind of its creator may be elsewhere—affected by anxiety, temperament, thirst, or just plain fatigue. As Maurice Tourneur wrote, "You don't always do what you want, but most of the time what you can."[8]

To try to enumerate the great American directors of the silent era would be a difficult and largely valueless task. Such lists reflect personal opinion, based upon the number of films available; they cannot possibly be definitive. Griffith and von Stroheim would appear on all but the most radical lists. Rex Ingram and Raoul Walsh might be included by those with good memories. But other names would be forgotten because no examples of their work have survived.

No one could consider Hugo Ballin, for example, because all his films have vanished. Few could mention Maurice Tourneur, Frank Borzage, John Ford, or Rowland V. Lee unless they had access to archives or private collections. The regular group—Griffith, Chaplin, von Stroheim, Flaherty—would thus inevitably reappear, not only because of their undoubted greatness, but also because of the conservatism of film-appreciation societies.

The number of silent films in circulation is very limited, but more and more early productions are being unearthed, and names of hitherto unsuspected talents are achieving new reputations. Men regarded as competent at the time seem masterly today in comparison with some of the accepted paragons. Other forgotten directors, whose work is being rediscovered, may not prove masterly or great, but merely first-class film makers who have not deserved the obscurity of the past forty years.

A more interesting question than "Who were the greatest?" is simply "Who were they?" Who were the men who created the richest period in the cinema's history? What made them become motion-picture directors? What attitude did they have toward their work?

What sort of people were they?

---

[8] *Letter from Maurice Tourneur to E. Wagenknecht, quoted in* The Movies in the Age of Innocence *(Norman, Okla.: Univ. of Oklahoma Press; 1962).*

For students of the motion picture, Griffith's is the most familiar name in film history. Here, they are told, is the Great Master, the Great Innovator, the Man Who Did Everything First—apparently the only director in America creative enough to be called a genius.

The name appears with deadening regularity in film history books, inducing the sort of anathema some students of literature feel for the suffocating genius of Shakespeare. It is inconceivable that one man could be responsible for so many awe-inspiring innovations. Was he really alone? Was he never helped or influenced by anyone else? Were there no other great minds at this period?

The Birth of a Nation (1915), screened regularly by film societies, merely increases these misgivings. Expecting an earth-shattering masterpiece, students are shown a scarcely visible museum piece. They cannot know that it bears about as much relation to the original as a shriveled husk bears to a once fabulous butterfly. Technical considerations apart, *The Birth of a Nation* is an achievement which needs to be given a context. Astounding in its time, it triggered off so many advances in film-making technique that it was rendered obsolete within a few years.

"Just ten years ago," wrote a reader to *Photoplay* in 1926, "I sat enthralled before the wonder picture, *The Birth of a Nation*. Last night I saw it again. The wonder picture is mediocre enough now. The photography seems amateurish seen in the light of the marvelous effects produced now. The unnatural, jerky, rapid action is strangely reminiscent of the Keystone Cop era. De Maupassant tells us that he is wise who does not disturb the resting place of old letters; perhaps the same is true of pictures?"[1]

Griffith's genius is apparent enough in certain respects; in others, it can only be gauged by comparison. If *The Birth of a Nation* could be compared with other important films of the time—*A Fool There Was* or *The Spoilers*—its merits would become strikingly clear. Some of Griffith's films of 1911 and 1912, shown against the product of other companies, seem even more extraordinary than *The Birth of a Nation,* for they break completely new ground in their use of the medium. His techniques have been so thoroughly absorbed into the language of the cinema that many of his most dramatic innovations now seem little more than clichés. When these apparent clichés are projected at the wrong speed, with blurred, misty print quality, Griffith's reputation understandably suffers. Although renowned for his cinematic pyrotechnics, these were not a feature of every Griffith film, nor were they their most important quality. He made many quieter pictures—simple stories of humanity and warmth, the sort of film the silent era is noted for.

The story of D. W. Griffith is both inspiring and tragic. Writers have frequently used it to condemn the callousness of Hollywood. While the industry was far from blameless in its treatment of the man to whom it owed so much, generalizations are made at the expense of individuals. Many people within the industry tried to help Griffith. In most cases he refused their help.

Genius, being unpredictable, is a potential threat to the structure of an industry. It can only be properly considered and assessed in retrospect—and preferably after death. Had Chaplin conveniently expired after *City Lights,* Hollywood

---

[1] Photoplay, *April 1926, p. 10.*

D. W. Griffith on location for Way Down
East *(1920).*

would today be glittering with gold statues of him instead of bristling with
paranoia and ill will.

Griffith died on July 23, 1948, after sixteen years of virtual inactivity. Four
months before Griffith's death, the journalist Ezra Goodman went to see him:
"The father of the American film sat in an easy chair in a hotel room in the
heart of Hollywood guzzling gin out of a water glass and periodically grabbing
at the blonde sitting on the sofa opposite him . . . It was Griffith all right, his
lordly, arrogant, aquiline features surmounted by sparse white hair, attired in
pajamas and a patterned maroon dressing gown, and, at the age of seventy-two,
sitting alone, drunk and almost forgotten in a hotel room in the town he had
been instrumental in putting on the map."[2]

This makes a powerful opening for Goodman's tour of Hollywood, sightseeing through dung-colored spectacles. But how much truth is there in such
sensationalism?

Factually, there is truth. But truth also depends on your outlook, and on the
context of the facts. The real tragedy—for us—was the sixteen wasted years.
Goodman states: "They could not find a place for Griffith in the big, rich movie
business." In fact, many of his former associates tried to help him, but finding
a suitable place for D. W. Griffith in the much-changed industry was like trying
to fit Moses into the Salvation Army.

Besides this, Griffith was regarded in certain quarters as an anti-Semitic Jew.
The description is misleading; Griffith's Jewish origin had been absorbed into

[2] *Ezra Goodman:* The Fifty-Year Decline and Fall of Hollywood (*New York: Simon and Schuster;
1961*), *p. 1.*

his Southern ancestry. He saw himself as a Southern gentleman. As such, he expressed open scorn for certain immigrant members of the picture business. The recipients of this scorn felt themselves the victims of racial prejudice. As Griffith's power declined, he found his chances of recovery growing slimmer. One man who helped him, however, was the comedy producer Hal Roach. "D. W. Griffith was one of the great geniuses of this business," said Roach, "and there he was in Los Angeles doing nothing. He came to work for me on *One Million B.C.* [1940] just to have something to do. His name was never associated with the picture; there was no publicity that he was even working with us. But he was. He assisted on casting, and on the story, and on some of the phases of production. He did not go on location, but he was on the set when we were in the studio. I got on with him very well—he was an exceptionally nice person, and it was a shame what happened to him. I mean, I can't tell—when he was with me he was a brilliant man and could have been making brilliant pictures. Anything he said was intelligent. Why he fell by the wayside, I just don't know."[3]

Griffith's difficulties began in 1916 with the financial failure of *Intolerance.* The bankers expressed dismay at his reckless expenditure; in a fit of bravado, he relieved them of the picture, then found himself faced with enormous debts. After making *Broken Blossoms* in Hollywood, Griffith moved his company back to New York, an act which brought a further chill to the atmosphere. The Hollywood attitude, when Mamaroneck was selected as Griffith's permanent studio, was one of pique. Many hoped it would fail.

Way Down East, however, was a phenomenal success, and Griffith aimed for another with *Orphans of the Storm.* But it failed to reach the same financial heights and his fortunes began to change. James Quirk greeted the release of *The White Rose* in 1923 by asking: "Isn't it about time that Mr. Griffith made a picture that would go far toward maintaining his title of The Master? That reputation, which is not so secure as formerly, may slip further unless he comes back into the ring and upholds his championship." Quirk warned of four other directors who were endangering his prestige, and added that reputations cannot live long on past accomplishments. Referring to the fact that Griffith films were shown at two-dollar seat prices as a matter of course, Quirk ended on a stinging note: "White flowers at two dollars apiece are too high when other florists are selling them at fifty cents."[4]

Difficulties at Mamaroneck began to multiply. Film-colony gossip ignored management problems and blamed everything on an alleged romance with Carol Dempster.

In 1923, Griffith began work on *America,* starring Carol Dempster and Neil Hamilton. Tremendous enthusiasm was aroused; on location for this story of the Revolutionary War, local people brought out mementos and heirlooms. Historic buildings were placed at Griffith's disposal, and the Army offered full assistance. The industry, impressed by the advance publicity, smiled good-naturedly. Griffith seemed rejuvenated by enthusiasm. He waited impatiently for a snowstorm to shoot his Valley Forge sequence, achieving it only a few days before the première, February 21, 1924.

America was not a success. The film itself was made with painstaking care.

[3] *Hal Roach to author, London, July 1964.*
[4] Photoplay, *Sept. 1923, p. 27.*

The battle scenes were brilliantly staged. The fault lay with a great deal of unconvincing and uninteresting love interest, and insensitive editing. Every second shot seemed to be a title, with lengthy historical explanations. None of the sequences was cut with the care that had clearly been lavished on the shooting. The result suggested a historical epic made by learned men who knew nothing whatever about films.

Surprisingly, many critics liked the film. "I am a hard-boiled, hard-shelled critic and I say with equal frankness that tears coursed down my cheeks during several climactic moments. Test your patriotism—see *America!*" wrote one.[5] Exhibitors, too, acclaimed it as a masterpiece—"Audience appeal 100%."[6] But the picture's financial rewards were not so generous. It was many years before it earned back its cost.

Griffith had had a number of differences with United Artists, the company he helped to form. The Mamaroneck studios were in a crippling financial state. He concluded an undercover deal with Adolph Zukor of Paramount, who put up some of the money for his next film, *Isn't Life Wonderful?*, made on location in Germany. This beautiful film was a compassionate glimpse at ordinary people in a defeated country, suggesting that life can provide happiness under the worst of conditions.

On his return, Griffith made *Sally of the Sawdust* and surrendered his independence to Zukor. The Mamaroneck studios folded, and he faced debts of half a million.

"I'm not a bad businessman, honestly I'm not," said D. W. Griffith to Frederick James Smith. "I was never in difficulties until I turned my business over to others. In California, in the old days, when I both directed and managed, I got along all right. It was only when I came to Mamaroneck and turned over my business handling to others that I became involved. Of course, the collapse of everything at Mamaroneck nearly broke my heart. We missed success so narrowly. Bad management and bad releasing contracts caused the destruction."[7]

D. W. Griffith accepted a contract for three pictures at Paramount—so that once again he could take responsibility for his debts and pay back his stockholders every cent they had invested.

"Actually," he told Smith, "I'm working for nothing. Last year [1925] I went behind $15,000, but I will be out of servitude in another twelve months."

Paramount greeted his arrival with full-page ads—romantic paintings of the great man, surrounded by scenes from his famous films. "There is a point in the life of every great artist when, if he is free from cares, he can produce his greatest works," ran the copy. "Everything before, however distinguished, serves as preparation. Some critics feel they can pick out the place where Shakespeare's art reached its richest period. So it is with that master director David Wark Griffith, who is at work on a series of Paramount Pictures. In freedom from all worry and with the resources of the world's foremost film organisation at his disposal, D. W. Griffith is now in the golden age of his art."[8]

If this was a golden age, Griffith was not aware of the fact. When Cecil B. De Mille left Paramount, because the company objected to the expense of his

[5] *Charles Bahn, in the Syracuse* Telegram, *Nov. 1924.*
[6] *Rialto Theatre, Connecticut.*
[7] Photoplay, *Dec. 1926, p. 30.*
[8] Photoplay, *Nov. 1925, p. 4.*

unit and attempted to lower his percentage of the profits of his pictures, he left behind *Sorrows of Satan.*

"As soon as a director became powerful or famous," said Louise Brooks, "like Griffith or De Mille, the producers started thinking up ways to get rid of them. When they'd thrown out Cecil De Mille, they had this property. It was very silly and very old-fashioned, and they thought, 'Now who can we throw this at? Who do we want to get rid of?' And, of course, they thought of D. W. Griffith. With *Sorrows of Satan* they dug his grave."[9]

This Marie Corelli story was certainly unpromising and old-fashioned, but D. W. Griffith had wanted to film it since the days before *The Birth of a Nation.* With the help of a genius of a cameraman, Harry Fischbeck, he brought his techniques up to date and achieved a polished, sophisticated comedy. Some of it was strikingly well directed. Fischbeck's deep-focus photography and Griffith's use of low-ceilinged sets were not duplicated until Orson Welles and Gregg Toland made *Citizen Kane.* A melodramatic finish detracted from the fragile and imaginative delicacy of the rest of the film, and Quirk, in *Photoplay,* was able to call it old-fashioned. The picture created bad feeling between Griffith and his new employers, and it was eventually taken out of his hands to be recut by Julian Johnson.

James Quirk published the official verdict: "Well, all is over between D. W. Griffith and Famous Players–Lasky. Henceforth, Griffith will probably make pictures for Universal. There has been a lot of talk about this artistic divorce, but it all adds up to this; Famous Players–Lasky was dissatisfied with *Sorrows of Satan* and Griffith didn't like studio routine. It is hard to teach an old dog new tricks, and Griffith had been his own boss for so long that he couldn't adapt himself to new conditions."[1]

The news that Griffith would work for Universal confirmed his failure in the eyes of the industry. In those days, Universal compared to Paramount about as favorably as the YMCA compares to the Waldorf. However, he was offered *Showboat* and *Uncle Tom's Cabin*—both were favorite subjects. But both were eventually given to Harry Pollard.

Eventually, he returned to United Artists, the company he had helped to form in 1919, and through Schenck he made two silents and then a talkie version of *Abraham Lincoln.* It was not a great success, although *Photoplay* applauded it and welcomed the master back to the forefront of the industry. In 1931, he made *The Struggle;* this time *Photoplay* included it among the routine reviews in the back pages:

"Old Demon Prohibition Rum makes bum out of honest working man. Papa, full of red-eye, gets D.T.s and chases tiny tot round ruined garret, à la Lillian Gish, while audience snickers at phony thunderstorm. 'Father, Dear Father, Come Home with Me Now' and 'The Face on the Barroom Floor' done in the manner and with the technique of the early Biograph pictures. It's all too sad. Directed by D. W. Griffith, who, sixteen years ago, made *The Birth of a Nation.*"[2]

Douglas Fairbanks eased Griffith out of United Artists, and the years of inactivity began.

[9] *Louise Brooks to author, Rochester, N.Y., Jan. 1966.*
[1] Photoplay, *Jan. 1927, p. 45.*
[2] Photoplay, *Feb. 1932, p. 98.*

D. W. Griffith (left). William Fildew operating Pathé camera. G. W. Bitzer seated at right next to Mae Marsh.

German location for Isn't Life Wonderful? (1925); Carol Dempster and Frank Puglia.

During my interview with Adolph Zukor, I brought up Griffith's name, and it produced the inevitable response.

"He was a great man."

"Then what do you consider the reason for his failure?"

Zukor, ninety-two years of age, and very frail, lit a cigar and shook his head.

"He didn't fail. No, the procession passed him by. He couldn't keep up with the pace. It's age, you know. You can only do certain things up to a certain time."

"*You* say that?"

"Yes. I can't do today what I could do fifty or forty or thirty years ago by *any* means. Impossible. But Griffith was smart. He bought an annuity at a time when he did work, and he had an income of $30,000 a year. Nobody knew that. They told me—I'm not sure if it's true— that he began to drink before he died, which he never did before. Well, if that's true it wasn't because he was poor, or because of the way that he lived. He had that annuity and he couldn't change it. When he bought the annuity he made it so that under no condition could he ever do anything else but live up to it. So he never could lay his hands on any more than what he got annually. But he wasn't poor, he wasn't downtrodden. Some people say he had pants all rumpled and bad shoes—if he did, it was because he was a careless dresser, not because he couldn't afford to live any different."[3]

That was all Mr. Zukor intended to say on the subject. As I began another question, he turned away and said, "Well, I hope you got all you wanted." So the interview ended.

It is surprising that such a man could assuage his twinges of guilt—which all Griffith's contemporaries must feel—by bringing up the matter of the annuity. No pension can allay the corrosive misery of inactivity.

"Griffith knew he was a goner when they threw him *Sorrows of Satan*," said Louise Brooks. "I wish you could have seen him, walking round the Astoria studios . . . It's strange . . . they always make actors very pitiful. All the girls become drunken whores. All the men become broken-down drunkards, go insane and kill themselves. But with directors, they have a completely different story. They're all happy as heck living in retirement."

The life story of D. W. Griffith has proved to be the life's work of one man, Seymour Stern, who knew him well in his last days and who, while building up a biography, has written many illuminating articles on his work. He declared that Griffith's end was not the sordid tragedy it is assumed to be.

"Several attempts, as a matter of record, were made to bring D. W. Griffith back into the industry, but Griffith himself rebuffed them all. During the final years of his life, while living at Hollywood's Knickerbocker Hotel, he began to have, and had, something he was hungry for and hadn't had since the earlier days of his career; in popular vernacular he began having 'a helluva good time.' Actually, it was during the last eight months that Griffith began to take on what had every appearance of a new way of life."[4]

Griffith, said Stern, had announced plans for a new film, and, as soon as his decree was through, he intended to marry again.

"You think that man was having a happy time?" asked Louise Brooks. "A man who was drunk all the time . . . a man who was locked up in his room, or

[3] *Adolph Zukor to author, New York, Dec. 1964.*
[4] *Film Culture, Spring 1965, p. 88.*

out perusing cheap bars looking for cheap little girls . . . You think that man is happy? Everyone in Hollywood saw him walking around. Of course, no one wanted to have anything to do with him. They could hardly get anyone to go to his funeral."

D. W. Griffith died on July 23, 1948. At the funeral Screenwriter Charles Brackett, president of the Academy of Motion Picture Arts and Sciences, which had awarded Griffith an Oscar for his services to the industry, admitted in his eulogy that the award did not ease his heartache. "When you've had what he'd had, what you want is the chance to make more pictures, unlimited budgets to play with, complete confidence behind you. What does a man full of vitality care for the honors of the past? It's the present he wants and the future. There was no solution for Griffith but a kind of frenzied beating on the barred doors of one day after another. Fortunately such miseries do not endure indefinitely. When all the honors man can have are past honors, past honors take on their just proportion."[5]

D. W. Griffith has been called "the Shakespeare of the Screen" but has more in common with Charles Dickens. The use of melodrama amid settings of complete reality, the exaggerated, yet still truthful characters, the fascination with detail, the accuracy of dress and behavior, the sentimentality, the attitude toward religion, and the outrage over social injustice, are all points which their works have in common. Perhaps the most important element Griffith learned from Dickens was his method of switching from action to action—parallel cutting, a technique which gave the cinema the ultimate in dynamism.

For all his Dickensian melodrama, the memorable moments in Griffith's films are those which are handled with most subtlety and delicacy. Griffith had an uncanny ability of setting his camera on a close-up of an actress and wringing from her a performance of heartbreaking poignancy. He did this with a magical combination of hypnotism, ventriloquism, and sheer directorial ability. His one aid—for he used no music—was the actress herself.

"I am inclined to favor beginners," said Griffith, when asked what he looked for in an actress. "They come untrammeled by so-called technique, by theories, and by preconceived ideas. I prefer the young woman who has to support herself and possibly her mother. Of necessity she will work hard. Again I prefer the nervous type. I never engage a newcomer who applies for work without showing at least a sign or two of nervousness. If she is calm she has no imagination.

"To me the ideal type for feminine stardom has nothing of the flesh, nothing of the note of sensuousness. My pictures reveal the type I mean. Commenters have called it the spirituelle type. But there is a method in my madness, as it were. The voluptuous type, blooming into the full-blown rose, cannot endure. The years show their stamp too clearly. The other type—ah, that is different!"[6]

Lillian Gish, Mae Marsh, and Blanche Sweet were examples of the Griffith ideal, and their own natural brilliance as actresses fused with Griffith's genius to produce some electrifying moments.

Griffith's technique followed three stages. First he would rehearse the film as though it were a stage play. "These rehearsals are almost interminable," wrote

[5] *Charles Brackett, quoted in Goodman:* Decline and Fall, *p. 14.*
[6] Photoplay, *Aug. 1923, p. 35.*

). W. Griffith directing The Struggle (1931), his last picture. Joseph Ruttenberg at camera.

Harry Carr, a close associate. "For some actors they are very trying and embarrassing. He will tell them that two chairs are a trench in France over which they have to charge and die. They do this over and over again. If the actors do not satisfy him with their performance, he never storms and shouts. He changes actors. In *The Love Flower* he changed actors in one part eight times."[7]

These rehearsals, as Carr pointed out, were not meaningless repetitions. Griffith was constantly altering, modifying, polishing. And since he worked without a script, this was the way he familiarized his cast with the story.

Griffith enacted each part for his players. An ex-actor himself, he enjoyed this immensely. He was a ham, but his overacting was an inspiration; with such an example the most timid player would feel a surge of confidence.

Katherine Albert, who played in *The Greatest Question,* recalled Griffith's technique:

"I remember once he was doing the mother role and, his long, horselike face turned heavenwards, he called out 'My son, my son, can you hear me there in heaven? Say that you hear me—speak to me.'

"We were spellbound, but I realize now that it was pretty bad, pretty melodramatic acting. As he finished, quite pleased with himself, he happened to glance at my mother. She has a grand sense of humor and she was amused at Griffith's acting and showed it in her eyes.

"Sensitive, quick to see any play of emotion, Griffith realized that she knew it was phony. He shrugged his shoulders sheepishly.

" 'Well, something like that,' he said, and sat down."[8]

The people who worked with Griffith all acknowledge the hypnotic power of his voice. It was as effective as a musical instrument in its molding of the emotions. The tone, the resonance, the sudden harshness, the softening—all this had a profound effect on the performance.

Miss Albert recalled that during a rehearsal in the bare projection room, without costumes or props, she felt utterly wretched.

"I thought for a brief second that I should die right then, but I had read interviews about what being a trouper meant. Then, suddenly, a strange thing seemed to happen. Griffith's voice, a rich, deep, very beautiful voice, droned on telling us what we were to do. 'Now you stop by a tree. It's an apple tree. You pick up an apple, Bobby, and hand it to her. Don't forget you love her very much,' etc., etc. And the projection room and all those people seemed to fade away and I found myself actually on a Kentucky road, actually under an apple tree, not acting a part, not being spoken to by the great Griffith but living, really being, the girl I was playing. Bobby Harron stooped and handed me the imaginary apple. He took an imaginary knife from his pocket and peeled it. I took the peelings from him and threw them over my left shoulder. Griffith suddenly stopped me; 'What are you doing?'

" 'Why, you see,' I explained, 'you throw the apple peeling over your left shoulder and it falls in the shape of an initial. That's the initial of the man you're going to marry.'

"Griffith smiled. He turned to Lillian Gish, who sat on his right, and said, 'The kid's got it.' "

[7] Motion Picture Magazine, *May 1923, p. 116.*
[8] Photoplay, *Oct. 1931, p. 37.*

Orphans of the Storm (1921). D. W. Griffith directing from guillotine platform.

D. W. Griffith rehearsing Ivor Novello and Mae Marsh for The White Rose (1923).

On location for Way Down East *(1920).*

D. W. Griffith at the front, 1917, for Hearts of the World.

Such details pleased Griffith immensely. Dorothy Gish recalled that when in England for *Hearts of the World,* she and Griffith were walking in the Strand when they noticed a streetwalker sauntering along in front of them.

"Griffith suddenly said, 'Watch that!' I saw she had the darndest walk. And the way I walk in *Hearts of the World* is exactly the way that girl in the Strand was walking."[9]

Griffith constantly sought advice. He would ask for it from the actors, the assistants, the cutters, and even the property men and studio hands. Every member of his company felt they were contributing to the final result, and no one minded when they worked long hours or had to go without lunch.

When shooting started, Griffith's technique moved into its second stage. He blocked his scene in long-shot and mid-shot, much as a painter sketches an outline. The players, thoroughly rehearsed, generally found little difficulty in satisfying their director. The atmosphere was relaxed, and good-humored banter indicated the comparative lack of stress. If a scene went awry, Griffith would break the atmosphere. On one occasion, in the middle of a take, he began chatting to the actors about Lloyd George. He explained afterward that they were beginning to act—he wanted to confuse them, to jolt them out of the idea that they were doing something of importance.

"He knows just the instant an actor is spiritually reaching out for the lifeline," wrote Harry Carr. "At that instant he will speak the lines for them. Go to hell!' he will yell, as the hero defying the villain. It is wonderful to see the effect of this on the actors. It is just like an experienced jockey letting a horse feel the touch of his hand on the rein."[1]

Stage three began in the projection room. Running the dailies, Griffith would work out, simply by intuition, by the feel of the scene, where the close-ups should go—and where he should hit emotional climaxes. The blocking-in process was over; the master now added the rich details.

Emotional climaxes in Griffith's films, even more than spectacular crowd shots, were known as "big scenes."

"Griffith approaches a big scene carefully," said Frederick James Smith. "Mellowing preliminary—or 'working up'—scenes are shot for days preceding. Then the day comes. Someone has said that a cathedral hush settles upon the studio. Griffith goes to his room and rests for an hour. The player goes to his or her room and rests. Then the moment arrives. Stage carpenters' hammers are stilled. Griffith begins to talk to the player. He gives emotionally in direct ratio to the actor's response. Lillian Gish could reach an emotional climax easily. When the *Broken Blossoms* scene in the closet—still the screen's highest example of emotional hysteria—was shot in Los Angeles, the screams of Miss Gish, alternating with the cries of Griffith, could be heard in the streets outside. It required most of the studio staff to keep the curious from trying to invade the studio."[2]

Carol Dempster was not so pliable. A brilliant actress, she unconsciously put up a resistance to Griffith's hypnotic direction. It once took six solid hours' work for Griffith to induce Miss Dempster to cry. Refusing to resort to glycerine, Griffith had to work on her until she had achieved real tears.

[9] *Dorothy Gish to author, New York, March 1964.*
[1] Motion Picture Magazine, *May 1923. p. 116.*
[2] Photoplay, *May 1923, p. 34.*

Few people were allowed to witness the filming of these intense scenes. An actress being reduced to tears or hysteria does not enjoy being stared at by gaping bystanders, so Griffith would generally close the set. Harry Carr, however, was present when the scene with Lillian Gish and the dying baby was made for *Way Down East:*

"Griffith always gives me the feeling that it is his mind in the actor's body that is doing the work. I was the only one there behind the little fenced-in place, except the cameraman. I could feel the tenseness of a strange force. Something I had never felt before. It was impossible to endure it for long. I had to leave. I could feel myself literally slipping away."[3]

During the troubles at Mamaroneck, Griffith was understandably less enthusiastic about his work, and his preoccupied manner unsettled his actors. Alfred Lunt, appearing in *Sally of the Sawdust* (1925), said that he had very little contact with Griffith, and practically no direction:

"He'd set up the scene and that was it. It was all ad lib and I never saw a script. It was quite paralyzing, to tell the truth—I'd come from the theater, where I'd been brought up in a different way. Griffith was very pleasant, but he just didn't seem to bother. I remember in the grocery-store scene I said, 'What do I say to the grocer?'

"And he said, 'Oh, say anything—ashcans, tomato cans, ketchup. Just keep talking.' "[4]

But in *Sorrows of Satan* (Paramount, 1926), Griffith returned to his former methods to induce some shattering scenes from Carol Dempster. Again and again, throughout the film, a long-held close-up of Miss Dempster plays havoc with the audience's emotions. Seeing the film absolutely silent, with no music to help it, and just this lovely face in close-up on the screen, you can still feel something of the electricity that passed between director and actress and generated this extraordinary performance.

"I recall vividly making *The Sorrows of Satan,*" said Ricardo Cortez. "He took an awfully long time. I went to California for eight weeks and made *Eagle of the Sea* while he kept going with Lya de Putti, Adolphe Menjou, and Carol Dempster.

"Griffith was a strange sort of man—very quiet. There seemed to be an invisible barrier around him. You couldn't get near him. I was under the impression that he was a very lonely man—although I got to know him quite well. I felt terribly sorry for him and would visit him at his hotel—the Astor.

"He would go out for a walk, and end up at the Pennsylvania railroad station, where he'd sit on a bench and just watch people.

"During the making of the picture, I was playing in one of the attic scenes. We'd been working for six weeks, not getting very far, and for just thirty seconds I lost my temper.

"He had said, 'If you knew anything about acting you wouldn't do that.'

" 'I don't know a thing about acting,' I snapped, 'which was why I wanted to be directed by you!' "[5]

"I always think of him as *Mr.* Griffith," said Dorothy Gish. "I get so shocked

[3] Motion Picture Magazine, *May 1923, p. 116.*
[4] *Alfred Lunt to author, London, April 1965.*
[5] *Ricardo Cortez to author, London, Oct. 1965.*

when anyone calls him by his first name; I never did and never can. When I grew up, directors used to ask me if I disliked them. 'You never call me by my first name—it's always mister,' they used to say.

"But I cannot think of Mr. Griffith as anything but Mr. Griffith. We all had such respect for him. Oh, he'd get mad—and you'd just go quietly away and stay out of the storm until it had blown over. He was just marvelous."

Carmel Myers began her career at Triangle, with the Griffith apex. She was profoundly impressed by the care taken in setting up each production and felt that the rehearsals were one of Griffith's prime contributions. "At Universal I missed the spirit of D. W. Griffith. He was the umbrella that shaded us all. A fantastic man."[6]

Anita Loos regarded Griffith as a poet, one of the few able to extemporize with film. But in her view, there was only one person on the Triangle lot who was really dedicated to motion pictures—and that was not D. W. Griffith.

"He was always longing to go away and write plays," she said. "No, I think the only person who could really be called dedicated at that time was Lillian Gish."[7]

Lillian Gish agreed that writing plays was his real ambition. "His film career didn't give him the happiness that it ought to have done. I suppose I *was* dedicated—I knew the financial burden he was carrying. The others didn't. Griffith trusted me, I think, more than most. He wasn't a very trusting man with his business affairs.

"But it was a dedicated life then. You had no social life. You had to have lunch or dinner, but it was always spent talking over work if you were with anyone—talking over stories or cutting or subtitles or whatever.

"I don't see how any human being worked the way he did. Never less than eighteen hours a day, seven days a week. They say he saw other people's pictures, and took ideas from the Europeans. He never saw other pictures. He never had the time. If you insisted, he'd borrow a print of something outstanding, like *The Last Laugh,* and run it at the studio, but that was very rare. He didn't have time to see pictures; he was too busy making them."[8]

Nevertheless, one of the most profound influences on Griffith's determination to make big pictures was the Italian epic *Quo Vadis?* "Mr. Griffith and I went over to the theater in New York to see it," recalled Blanche Sweet—although Griffith always denied having seen it. "He was very impressed by the production and by its size. His attitude was, '*We* can make as big productions as *they* can!' I'm sure that picture influenced him because it wasn't long after that that he came up with the idea of *Judith of Bethulia.* We had never done as long or as large a picture, and at first the heads of the company turned him down cold. But he finally won."[9]

And Owen Moore, interviewed in 1919, remembered that Griffith had a deep admiration for French films. "Once he brought over a two-reel Coquelin film—a lovely little thing it was—an adaptation of *La Tosca.* He ran it off in the projection room for all of us as a model of pantomime. But when we began the next picture we were all trying to act like the French actors and the result was awful. Griffith never showed those films to us again."[1]

[6] *Carmel Myers to author, New York, March 1964.*
[7] *Anita Loos to author, New York, March 1964.*
[8] *Lillian Gish to author, New York, March 1964.*
[9] *Blanche Sweet to author, London, Sept. 1963.*
[1] Photoplay, *Dec. 1919, p. 58.*

Griffith was well aware of his own contributions to motion pictures. He once said he loved Orson Welles's *Citizen Kane,* "and particularly loved the ideas he took from me."[2]

While Griffith remained at the technical level he had evolved for himself by 1916, other directors took up his reins and swept onward. The 1920's were years of frustration and anxiety. He was no longer the industry's leader. Project after project was announced, then postponed or canceled. In 1922 he went to England, ostensibly for the première in London of *Orphans of the Storm,* but also to talk over with H. G. Wells a project for filming *The Outline of History.* The British government asked him to make a spectacular production in India, which they could use as an effective answer to Gandhi. Griffith announced plans for *Faust* with Lillian Gish, for *The White Slave* with Richard Barthelmess . . . When he went to Paramount, he was assigned *An American Tragedy,* a project that was later given to Eisenstein and several other directors before it was completed by Josef von Sternberg. He intended to do *Show Boat, Uncle Tom's Cabin, Romance of Old Spain,* and *Sunny* (with Constance Talmadge). He hoped to reissue *Intolerance* as a talkie with a new modern episode, and, in England, to remake *Broken Blossoms.*

Despite frustrations, Griffith continued to make pictures. But most of his films of the twenties were modest in both theme and execution and have led historians to complain of an artistic decline. Anything following *Intolerance*—still the biggest picture ever made—was liable to be anticlimactic. Griffith, saddled with debt, was forced to make smaller-scale, commercial productions. But he was still able to make pictures of the scale, and of the quality, of *Hearts of the World* and *Orphans of the Storm.* If *America* was a disaster, he fully compensated for it the same year when he took his company to Germany to make the exquisite and moving *Isn't Life Wonderful?* And if *Sally of the Sawdust* meanders somewhat aimlessly, the rich, vigorous *Sorrows of Satan* is almost entirely rewarding.

Griffith declined only in the sense that his opportunities decreased. In 1926, after his box-office disappointment with *Sorrows of Satan,* he retreated into writing his autobiography. (It was never completed.)

"Writers are the only ones who can express their ego," he said. "Directors can't, because they have to please the majority. We can't deal with opinions. All we can do is to weave a little romance as pleasantly as we know how."[3]

The irony of this understatement makes a bitter contrast with the heroic statements of the old Griffith advertisements. It recalls the phrase of Louis Gardy: "It would be impossible for the greatest master of language to picture the emotions as Griffith has perpetuated them."[4]

Our gratitude to D. W. Griffith will always be mingled with shame. For while his genius has gone, the spirit that destroyed him remains as strong as ever in our industry.

[2] *Goodman:* Decline and Fall *p. 10.*
[3] Photoplay, *Dec. 1926, p. 30.*
[4] *New York* Call, *quoted in* WID's Year Book, *1919, p. 151.*

9 / ALLAN DWAN

Allan Dwan —ex-engineer, ex-inventor—was a man whose mechanical skill brought him into the industry and kept him at the head of it, a man with a strong dramatic sense whose clear and logical brain and rich sense of humor ensured for his pictures the highest standards of entertainment and craftsmanship.

Capability Dwan—the man you turned to in a crisis. Astonishingly resourceful, Dwan's training as an engineer gave him a rare knowledge. Like the hero of *A Connecticut Yankee in King Arthur's Court,* his firm grasp of practicalities made him an object of wonder among those less fortunately endowed.

One of the Big Six directors in the twenties, Dwan has survived them all; he has the longest record of any director in the business.

"I once tried to draw up a list of the pictures I'd done," said Dwan when I met him in Hollywood in 1964, "Someone sent me a list with eight hundred titles on it, and I tried to help him by adding on the rest. I got to fourteen hundred and I had to give up. Just couldn't remember the others."

Unhappily, few of his pictures have survived, and a great career has been overlooked. But recently the young critics of *Cahiers du Cinema* rediscovered some of his talkies, and following their raves, *Film Culture* announced: "Dwan's career is still being mined for a possibly higher assay of gold to dross. Recent findings— *Silver Lode, Restless Breed, The River's Edge*—represent a virtual bonanza of hitherto unexplored classics. It may very well be that Dwan will turn out to be the last of the old masters."[1]

Allan Dwan was certainly one of the masters of the silent motion picture. He had to be; he made pictures so fast that anything less than mastery of the medium would have brought him early catastrophe.

When meeting such distinguished veterans as Dwan, preconceived ideas tend to make the actual encounter somewhat startling. Sparse facts, mixed with rumor and much supposition, had created for me a none-too-easy subject for an interview; I anticipated an elderly, rather fragile man, greatly embittered, impatient and short-tempered. For while the silent days were the peak years of his career, he has since kept himself in the background. "If you get your head above the mob," he has been quoted as saying, "they try to knock it off. If you stay down you last for ever."[2]

The stout man with the breezy grin who opened the door was, I assumed, a friend or a business associate; he was too youthful to fit my image. But when he swept me through to a study, decorated with stills from *Robin Hood,* my illusion was dispelled. Any question of age seemed ludicrous; the undiminished enthusiasm, the vitality, and the hilarious sense of humor proved that Dwan as a person hadn't changed much. From this encounter alone I fully understood why people like Douglas Fairbanks and Gloria Swanson selected him as a favorite director.

Recalling the past was no effort; the anecdotes flowed in brisk profusion, as though we were talking between takes on a silent picture. The thick glasses he wore as protection from the studio lights have now become permanent—otherwise those who knew him then would notice little change. Scripts for current projects were piled high on his desk; and on the wall was an appreciation from the U.S. Marine Corps for *Sands of Iwo Jima* and a graduation certificate made out to Joseph Aloysius Dwan.

[1] Film Culture, *Spring 1963, p. 23.*
[2] *Ralph Hancock and Letitia Fairbanks:* Douglas Fairbanks; The Fourth Musketeer (*New York:* Holt; *1953*), *p. 186.*

"That's a fine name to be known by." He grinned. "At school they used to say 'Aloysius to be a girl,' so I changed it to Allan.

"I went to work for the Peter Cooper-Hewitt company, and I developed the mercury-vapor arc for them—you know, the long tubes. In 1909 I fitted these mercury-vapor arcs in the post office in Chicago so that the men sorting the mail could work longer hours—it was a ghastly light, made you look mortified, but your eyes would last longer."

While he was fitting the mercury-vapor tubes, the attention of a passer-by was caught by the strange glare from the post-office basement. The man stopped, stared through the windows, and then walked down and asked for the person in charge. He introduced himself to Dwan as George K. Spoor and asked whether the lights would be suitable for photography.

"Yes,' said Dwan. "They ought to be very good."

Spoor, who was the *S* of the Essanay Company, Chicago,[3] placed an order for an experimental light. Dwan designed the first mercury-vapor arc bank, and the factory made up four, which he took to the studio.

"During this experimentation period, I watched what they were doing, and it kind of fascinated me—the silly pictures they were making under the lights. One day I asked them where they got their stories from.

" 'Well,' they said, 'we buy them from anybody.'

" 'What do you pay?'

" 'Oh—up to twenty-five dollars for good stories.'

"Well, I'd written a lot of stories for the magazine at university—*The Scholastic* at Notre Dame—so one day I brought over fifteen of them. They bought the lot."

They were so impressed, in fact, that they asked Dwan if he'd like to be their scenario editor—and they named a price far above anything a young engineer could earn. "I'll do both," said Dwan. "I'll supervise these lights *and* I'll be your scenario editor."

Two weeks later, most of the executives of Essanay left to form the American Film Manufacturing Company—and they persuaded Dwan to join them at twice his salary.

The new organization had a problem. Somewhere in California—no one knew quite where—was one of their companies. The supply of films had dried up and, despite frequent cables, so had the supply of information.

Dwan was asked to go and find out what had happened. He located them at San Juan Capistrano.

"They had no director because he was an alcoholic. He'd gone to Los Angeles on a binge and left the company flat. So I wired: 'Suggest you disband company—you have no director.' They wired back: 'You direct.' "

Faced with this sudden responsibility, Dwan called the actors together (among them was J. Warren Kerrigan) and announced: "Either I'm a director or you're out of work."

Replied the actors: "You're the best damn director we ever saw!"

Dwan asked what a director was supposed to do. The actors took him out and showed him.

"I found that was a very successful way to operate, and so I made that my policy. I just let the actors tell me what to do and I get along very well. I've

[3] *The A was G.M. ("Broncho Billy") Anderson.*

been doing it now for fifty-five years—and they haven't caught me yet."

Dwan made three pictures a week for American Film—*and* took the weekend off. Of course, the pictures were only one-reelers—later they graduated to two-reelers, and by 1913 they had reached feature-length.

"In those days we had full control of our companies, with no interference from the producers, subproducers, supervisors, and front offices that came later. We did what we liked and we hired whoever we liked. That's how I got Marshall Neilan, Victor Fleming, and fellows like that into the business. It's unheard of today, to walk out and see somebody you like the looks of, and say, 'Come on, come and work with me.' He has to do an apprenticeship, join a union, pass all kinds of muster, and do four thousand other things—even then he can't get in."

The start of Allan Dwan's career coincided with that of D. W. Griffith; from the very beginning, Dwan took careful note of the delicate feelers Griffith was putting into the primitive void of motion-picture technique. As Griffith gained confidence, as his experiments left the field of speculation and became bold innovations, Dwan admits he became his god.

"I watched everything he did, and then I'd do it, in some form or another. I'd try to do it in another way—I'd try to do it better. And I'd try to invent something that *he'd* see. He finally sent for me and said he was sick of competing, and would I join him at Triangle?

"What fascinated me about Griffith? Well, I think his lack of long gesture, his simplicity, and his use of facial expression. He developed a strange new panto-mime. I like pantomime anyway, but I don't like the extreme pantomime.

"Other actors exaggerated to make up for not having words. His players used short little gestures to get over their point—they were much more realistic. And I saw Griffith was expressing vividly a lot of things with very little effort.

"And then I liked the backlighting which his cameraman was using. I thought it was great. Nobody else would use it—they thought the sun should shine directly onto the person. I used to wonder how he had the faces beautifully lit when the sun was behind them, and then I went out to his studio one day and saw them using reflectors. So we learned to use reflectors.

"That wasn't new, of course; professional photographers often used reflectors in their portrait studios. But it was new to us. All we ever did was to go out on the street and photograph the shot just as it was. If there happened to be a shadow on the face, it stayed there. We never thought of easing it off with a reflector.

"And then, of course, he taught us the close-up. He had a terrible time with that. The theater managers almost canceled his pictures. They couldn't understand how people were walking around without legs. In the theater they were accustomed to seeing the whole body, and what it was standing on. But to see a head moving around, cut off at the neck, just wasn't acceptable. But I grabbed it immediately."

The question of who invented the close-up has long vexed film historians. Close-shots can be found as early as 1896, but close-ups were not in common use before Griffith's pictures. I asked Allan Dwan if anyone predated him.

"Oh no, nobody ever did. Nobody living ever did. He was the first person who ever dared put on a motion-picture screen anything but a full-length picture."

"But surely," I persisted, "you pioneering directors did *something* on your own?"

"We did. We did lots of things Griffith didn't do. But his achievements are the real, vivid things."

Dwan, right, on the set of Lawful Larceny *(1923), with (left to right) Conrad Nagel, Hope Hampton, Nita Naldi, and Lew Cody.*

Allan Dwan directing The Forbidden Thing *(1921). Tony Gaudio at camera.*

Dwan paused for a moment, and then said, "It's hard to remember and claim you were responsible for any one thing, but I was one of the first to make full use of the moving camera."

While running shots were becoming a familiar part of picture technique—the camera keeping pace with a moving vehicle—sustained traveling shots were a novelty. In *David Harum,* made in 1915 when Dwan was with Famous Players, the camera was mounted on a Ford, and it tracked right down the main street of a town, following William H. Crane as he chatted with another character, as people greeted him, as he paused, talked, and continued walking. *David Harum,* for most of its length, employs the simple, static technique prevalent in 1915— but occasional camera mobility gave it the look of a more mature silent film. And the opening is first-class cinema; iris-in to a masked close-up of a cup of coffee and a plate . . . the coffee is poured into a saucer, and the mask irises out to full frame. The camera then follows the saucer on its upward journey, to reveal a close-up of William H. Crane as David Harum. Then it pans across to reveal Kate Meeks as Aunt Polly. The smooth movement is interrupted by introductory titles, but the effect is still striking.

It would be a mistake, however, to give the impression that Dwan was obsessed by tricks of technique, and that his early experiments flowered into riotous camera movements and shattering montages. He just wasn't that kind of director. Warm and humorous, he had a great feeling for people—and his use of cinema was always subservient to the performances, to the story. He played around with every cinematic device, mastering each before discarding it in favor of absolute simplicity and a pure directness of style.

But his untypical flourishes are fascinating to consider while forming a picture of this important director's work. As Griffith's close-ups had met with bewilderment, so Dwan's traveling shots met with admonishment. "They made the people feel seasick," reported the theaters.

Another pet innovation was what would now be called a crane shot—the camera moving up and down like an elevator. No suitable equipment existed at that time, so Dwan secured a construction derrick, mounted the camera in a cradle, and raised it upward.

"That again was astonishing to people," said Dwan. "They visualized the cameraman having the camera on his back—you know, walking up a ladder. Nobody could figure out what we did with the camera to make it move around that way. We got so fascinated with the effect that we tried others, like starting low and pulling away until we were up in the air with the characters way down below. That startled people."

Dwan put his engineering experience to good use when he enabled D. W. Griffith to achieve what is still the most gasp-producing shot in film history—the crane shot over the huge Babylonian set in *Intolerance.*

"I was working on the Triangle lot as director with Fairbanks and the Gish girls, and, beyond this piece of advice, I had nothing at all to do with the making of *Intolerance.* Griffith, in fact, was across the street, on another section of ground, where he had his big set. Nobody knew what he was making until it was practically ready for release—we just knew he was making a big picture. In one of my pictures I had a poem—I always like poems to express things—and in it was a line: "The tolerance of opinion and of speech . . ." Now I had that ready, and since Griffith saw all scripts, he had read this one. He called me in and asked me if I'd mind dropping the poem.

" 'Not particularly,' I said. 'But why?'

" 'Well,' he said, 'I'll tell you, if you'll keep it confidential. I'm using that very thought in the picture I'm preparing—the big one. In fact, my title is *Intolerance*—and you've accidentally struck the key of what I want to do.'

"I agreed to drop the poem, and after a period of time, his cameraman, Billy Bitzer, came to me and said, 'The boss wants to know if you'd mind talking with me about a problem we've got—because he knows you're an engineer.' "

Bitzer told Dwan about the shot Griffith had in mind. The camera had to be able to rise up to the top of the colossal Babylonian set, and then descend to ground level again.

"Neither Griffith nor Bitzer could think how to do it. They first had an idea that I immediately pied—they planned to build a ramp, and slide the camera up that ramp. The problems attached to rolling a camera up that thing with any degree of steadiness were enormous. And you'd have to build it like a piece of pie in order to get it level. It would be difficult, it would be expensive, you'd have no control over the exact angle or height, and you'd have no flexibility.

"I finally induced him to construct a device on a railroad track with an elevator in it. The device was very simple, built of tubing so it could easily be dismantled and put together. I designed the idea of what to work for and suggested the use of railroad tracks, made utterly smooth so there would be no vibration, and railroad wheels.

"To do this shot today would require a boom—but we have no boom that would go that high. If we did have, it would need a very long arm and the vibration would be severe. This had to be rock-steady. And it was controllable—you could stop it where you liked, continue it from where you liked. It operated from donkey engines with a system of signals."

For all his mechanical skill, Allan Dwan is best remembered in the film industry for other sorts of innovations—devices to streamline production efficiency, engineering miracles in set design, and, most simple and least common, for his uncanny ability to think up ways of keeping cast and crew happy.

On *Zaza*, for instance, a Gloria Swanson picture, the company found the torrid New York summer heat quite intolerable while working under the sizzling Kliegs in Astoria Studios. To keep production going, Dwan had huge cakes of ice brought in and placed on either side of the set. A battery of electric fans was then placed behind them to keep a constant flow of cold air blowing over the actors.

Speed, too, was a celebrated Dwan trademark. James Quirk called him the Paavo Nurmi of directors: "He has just dashed off *Night Life in New York*. Rod la Rocque said it was completed before he knew it was under way."

"You will never hear Allan Dwan prate about 'My Art' " ran the caption when *Photoplay* devoted a full-page picture to him. "He has always been too busy making pictures. He believes in the photoplay as an art and as an industry, but he doesn't waste time telling everybody about it. Dwan is a sane director. His enthusiastic imagination is tempered with an amazing fidelity to the realities. If you remember the earlier Douglas Fairbanks films, notably *Manhattan Madness*; the vivid and adventurous *Soldiers of Fortune*; the whimsical *Luck of the Irish*; the thunderingly dramatic *The Scoffer*; that splendid celluloid hazard *A Splendid*

Hazard, you have acknowledged Dwan's versatility, energy and devotion to detail."[4]

One of Dwan's most acclaimed films was *Big Brother,* which introduced an astonishing child star called Mickey Bennett. "We made it in the toughest neighborhood in New York, at night," recalled Dwan. "I am still dodging the bricks the hoodlums threw from the roofs."

On the picture's release, Quirk paid unprecedented tribute: "Right on top of Pikes Peak, with the thermometer below zero, I would take off my hat and make a low obeisance to Allan Dwan for this production. He has made a truly great picture. It is a classic. It is an art work. *Big Brother* couldn't have been made more human, more appealing, more worthwhile with an added million of cost. More power to you, Allan. May your shadow never grow less."

I have not seen *Big Brother,* but the human qualities of *Manhandled,* made shortly afterward, are so strong that I do not doubt *Photoplay's* claims. In those films of his I *have* seen, Dwan has always drawn marvelous, lifelike performances —portrayals of real sincerity, never for a moment marred by overacting. I suppose one should except certain scenes in *Robin Hood,* especially those in which Sir Guy of Gisbourne (Paul Dickey), with burning eyes and grinding teeth, scorches the screen with the ultimate in villainy. But those scenes demanded that kind of playing. In realistic situations, Dwan never overstepped the mark; his players are so thoroughly and undeniably in character that I began to wonder about his directorial techniques. Did he employ some complex forerunner of the Method? Quite the reverse. The term "director" has never been so apt. His methods were utterly direct.

Madge Bellamy, a talented player who had innate skill but was often misled when directors exploited her aura of innocence, worked with Dwan on *Summer Bachelors* (1926). "He is a very wonderful man," she told Agnes Smith in *Photoplay.* "He always tells me the truth. We had an interesting conversation on the set this morning. I had been playing a sad scene and when I finished Mr. Dwan asked me what I had been thinking about, and I told him that I had been thinking about something sad. 'Well,' said Mr. Dwan. 'You should have been thinking about the muscles of your face.'

"Now I see what has been wrong with me. I have been trying to feel emotions and express them. I never have thought much about the technique. So I have been sitting here practicing with the muscles of my face. Look!" And Miss Bellamy drew her eyebrows. Instantly the tears slowly rose to her eyes. "See, I am crying and yet I am not thinking of anything sad. It's just a muscular reaction."[5]

"Artistic efficiency, that's Dwan!" declared Adela Rogers St. Johns—quoting him as saying, in 1920: "It's the most doggone fascinating game there is—directing motion pictures. It's a sense of power and a sense of creation in one. It's a gamble. Even if you know something about it, you're not so sure you know anything about it at all. The pictures that I have loved, that I thought were great, have been flivvers nine times out of ten. The ones that I sort of turned up my nose at went over with a bang.

"I am a businessman. I have a commercial mind. A man can make the most artistic picture ever filmed, but if it plays to empty houses it hasn't achieved a

4 Photoplay, *June 1921, p. 47.*
5 Photoplay, *Oct. 1926, p. 128.*

Mickey Bennett and Tom Moore in Big Brother *(1923).*

Gloria Swanson in Manhandled *(1924).*

thing for Art or for Humanity. The great problem of the pictures is the welding of art and business. Waste is not artistic. Inefficiency is not artistic.

"Pictures must be made fast. If you muddle around with them, you lose your clear vision. You cannot hurry art, of course, but you can hurry commercial production. Get your art in hand before you start to produce and you'll save yourself a lot of time and trouble."[6]

Artistic efficiency was an important contributor to Dwan's success, but the real secret was the fact that he never took the job too seriously. A practical realist at work in a Cloud-Cuckoo-Land, he loved making movies—but he never allowed crises or temperament to worry him. They made so little impression, in fact, that today he can look you in the eye and say that all his productions were trouble-free!

"The fellows that take the job too seriously, you know, start out half-licked. They don't know where they're going, and they have trouble all the way. But if you see your way clear, it shouldn't be too hard to make the picture. Always have something you can go to real quick—to keep things moving in case something blows. When we had control of our pictures, we had no trouble. Our trouble has happened when others have control."

Despite his straightforward simplicity, Dwan's pictures have a definite style. There is a penchant for high angles, which he uses intelligently, and an obvious dislike of bold, screen-filling close-ups.

"I felt the big close-up was embarrassing," he explained. "I still do—I think some of them are grossly overdone. You can almost see their tonsils on the giant screen. Of course it's very difficult to balance up this idiot screen they now have—this long thin thing. It's very hard to get art on *that*. The only thing that ever really fills it is spectacle. But you don't always want to see spectacle.

"Any story worth a damn must be intimate. It must be close to you. It must move you. Size will never move people. They may gasp—and that's it. It's over. You go to New York to see the tall buildings—and once you've seen them, you're satisfied. It's the same with the pyramids; you take a look and you've seen them. You don't want to go back every day for another look. For the average entertainment you need an intimate story—and an intimate story requires good scenes between two people. Occasionally more, but basically two people.

"I haven't really any stylistic objections. I get offended when I see a trick angle used purely for effect, without reason . . . but mostly it depends on the way these technical devices are used."

"After fifty-five years of directing," I asked him, "do you still get as much enjoyment out of it?"

"Yes, I do. It isn't a job, it's a disease. It's more than just work. It's fun to do it, it's fun to see the results, and it's even more fun to see how it affects people. I'm starting a big Marine Corps picture for Warner Brothers next. Directing movies—I'd do it free, I like it that well."

[6] Photoplay, *Aug. 1920, p. 56.*

10 / HENRY KING

Some film historians find it beyond belief that Hollywood—Griffith apart— produced any talent whatsoever. If one director's work shone above the others, then his brilliance is attributed to the master. "Henry King," wrote Paul Rotha, "learned from Griffith all that was good, combining the spoil with his own filmic knowledge."

Henry King never worked for Griffith, although he benefited, like everyone else, from Griffith's innovations. King's was an individual talent. In his films, each element was subjugated to the narrative. There were never any cinematic pyrotechnics. Filmically, his production of *Stella Dallas* (1926) is prosaic. It consists of medium long shots and close shots; there are few traveling shots, few dramatic angles. Yet warmth and humanity pervade every scene. *Tol'able David* (1921) is more striking cinematically, with a brilliantly edited fight scene, but overall it displays the same restraint—and the same deep affection for its subject. *Tol'able David,* which greatly impressed the Russian film makers, has been a film-society favorite for three decades. It was this film, more than any other, that established King's reputation.

Henry King, whom I interviewed in Beverly Hills in April 1967, is still a leading Hollywood director, and, although in his seventies, he still flies his private plane. On location, however, he wears the distinctive dress of the silent era—riding breeches and boots. His height, his powerful face, and his upswept blue eyes fit the romantic image of a Roman emperor. The voice, however, is pure Virginia. He is an excellent raconteur, with a strong sense of humor—and he transmits the warmth that so often distinguishes his films.

Born in Christiansburg, Virginia, King first appeared as an actor in school plays. Later, against his parents' wishes, he joined a local stock company. He rapidly gained so much experience that a repertory company in Chicago asked him to direct. The actors, accustomed to conventional melodramatics, were shaken by his fresh approach. He was fired. He went to California and into motion pictures, as an actor. He began directing at Pathé in 1916. Thomas Ince hired him, and he made *23½ Hours Leave* in 1919 with Douglas MacLean. Unfortunately, he spent considerably more than his budget allowed and the studio manager, in Ince's absence, decided to fire him. *23½ Hours Leave* was a great success, and when Ince returned he asked for King to be put under contract.

"I'm sorry," said the studio manager. "I let him go." Ince then fired the studio manager.

After a period with Robertson-Cole, a company that went bankrupt, King joined forces with Charles Duell and Richard Barthelmess to form the Inspiration Company. They made *Tol'able David* under the First National banner.

HENRY KING: *Tol'able David* was a Joseph Hergesheimer short story set in Virginia. With part of the picture I relived the days of my boyhood. I was born over the mountains, less than eight miles from where we photographed the picture. Mr. Duell didn't want to make it on location. "I had an idea we'd do it here in Pennsylvania," he said.

"There is a great difference," I said, "between Pennsylvania and Virginia. I can find all the locations I want in Virginia—up here I have no idea where to look."

I sent my assistant down to Staunton, Virginia, and I told him what to look for.

Henry King with Italian nuns, during the making of **The White Sister** *(1923).*

The most important thing was rail fences. Do you know what a rail fence is? Abraham Lincoln used to make split rails when he was a boy. He made the fences with split logs intermeshed. I told him a number of other things to look for. He called me from Virginia. "I stood on top of a hill," he said, "and I could see everything you told me about."

"Come right back," I said, "and let's get ready to go down there."

We went down two days ahead of the company. I found all my locations within one day—all within a six-mile radius.

We had a writer on the picture, Edmund Goulding, who became a director later. He was an Englishman, and he didn't know too much about Virginia. There were things in the story I disagreed with. It didn't develop. I talked to Eddie about this. I talked about the boy, the type of person he was, the family he came from. I talked about the family kneeling around the chairs each night, saying their prayers, which was done in my home for as long as I can remember. But Eddie didn't quite understand what I was talking about. I took my secretary down to Virginia, and I rewrote the middle of the story and some of the things pertaining to the end. I rearranged the conflict between the girl and the boy and the intercutting of the girl escaping and the boy fighting. When I got back to New York, Eddie Goulding was very much afraid I had ruined the story. But Hergesheimer thought I had enhanced it.

"You put into this," he said, "all the things that I left out." Had he written a full novel, he said, he would have incorporated my scenes, but this was not possible in a short story. Eddie was unhappy until the picture opened and then he found himself author of the screenplay of the best picture of the year.

None of the other five pictures that I did with Dick Barthelmess ever compared with *Tol'able David. The Bond Boy* was a story with a lot of feeling, however. It was about the conflict between a young boy and his stepmother—when the step-mother starts to make passes at him. Another Barthelmess picture was *Fury,* also written by Edmund Goulding. No one liked this story except me. I said, "Eddie, if you finish the screenplay, and it's as good as this all the way up, I will give you five thousand dollars for it." Well, five thousand dollars was a lot of money for a story at that time. It was Goulding's original story. While I was doing *Bond Boy,* Eddie came down to Virginia to discuss it. I talked about the story with such enthusiasm that Eddie became excited himself.

"You've fired my enthusiasm so much," he said, "that I'm going to turn this story into a book!" Putnam published it, and I did the picture. It was one of the most interesting experiences I ever had in my life.

I chartered a four-masted sailing ship with a German crew, owned by a Greek company and flying a Swiss flag. It had brought a cargo of bones from Santiago, Chile, to Philadelphia. We had to have it fumigated three times before we could put the people aboard. It didn't even have a radio. It took seven hours to raise the anchor, with the seamen turning winches and singing shanties. We set sail and went seven-hundred miles north of Bermuda, where we ran into a storm. We carried on photographing during the storm, with the waves crashing over the deck—and then we ran out of food. We had been sixteen days at sea. We restocked at Gloucester, then went back to sea again.

Tyrone Power (Senior) was playing Dick Barthelmess's father, and the old man didn't care very much for our sailing ship. It didn't have all the comforts of home. In the midst of a big scene, Mr. Power went up in his lines. He forgot what he was going to say. He also forgot, being a stage actor, that the line wasn't important. He twisted his head around and said, in a hoarse whisper, "Throw me the line! Throw me the line!" Well, I sat there in the chair and enjoyed it very much. When the scene was over I said, "Very good, very wonderful. That was a great, great, great performance."

Mr. Power said, "Well, thank you very much. But if you'd thrown me the line it would have been a great deal better."

"No, Mr. Power," I said. "You misunderstood me. The whole scene was awful. But I'll never forget as long as I live the deep sincerity with which you turned to me and said 'Throw me the line.' I believed that here was a man in distress, asking for something he desperately needed. That was the only thing in the entire scene I believed in."

Mr. Power, who had told me how much he hated motion pictures, and that he played in them only for the money, said, "Henry, I think I'm going to *like* motion pictures."

Having been an actor of some kind myself, I rehearse in a different way from most directors. I may have doubts that a scene can be done. So, without you know-ing it, I walk through the scene and try all the bits of business, just to see the difficulties. I don't want anyone to imitate me, but if I walk through it and it works out well, why, I know an actor can do it. I don't tell the actors to do what they want. We are telling a story, and everything must fit into the framework of this story. We don't want people two miles out of character. The entire thing must be as a whole. One angle may cover so much, another angle may cover so much, and I may make a close-up. But all these things are shot as one piece. When they're put together you must never be conscious of going to a closeup or of going to a long shot.

I generally shoot the other way around from most directors. For a scene in here, I would start on a great big closeup of you and let you take me into the room. Gradually, I would reveal the whole place.

Many times, art directors will build lavish sets. I've had them standing around chewing their fingernails, thinking, Are we *never* going to see this big set? Well, the set is nothing but a set. To me, it is completely wrong to photograph it just because it's lavish. We are telling a story. We should reveal the whole set only when it's necessary, when it will mean something.

I had an art director with me in Italy, a very fine American architect named Robert Haas.

Now, because I had a French governess in *The White Sister,* he immediately designed a room with French windows for her. The morning after the set was completed he found the French windows had been replaced by Roman windows. He pulled them out and put the French ones back. He came to me and said that he couldn't do anything with these Italians.

"It's ridiculous," he said. "Don't these people know about anything but Roman windows?"

"Now, Bob, wait a minute," I said. "This story takes place in modern Rome. Now get in the car . . . let's drive through the residential area and see how many French windows we can find. Don't let's damn these people too hastily. Maybe they're doing the right thing. Maybe they don't have French windows here."

"Oh," he said, "you can have French windows any place."

We drove through the residential area on two different sides. There were no French windows. Rome has windows all of its own—and they're Roman windows.

"I'll be good," said Bob Haas. "I'll never mention it again."

The Italians were not arguing with him, they were saving him from ridicule. Can you ask for anything better than that? The Italians are the hardest-working people I ever saw. They *want* to get the right effect. They *want* to please you. They don't want to do anything to disturb the atmosphere you're working in. I think that a great deal of the trouble the *Ben-Hur* people had in Italy was due to a lack of understanding for the people. I was there at the same time they were, and I had no trouble at all.

On the way over to do *The White Sister,* I met an archbishop, the papal delegate to Washington. He was very much concerned with the story of the film.

"You have a vivid imagination," he said, "and that is what worries me. The scene in *The White Sister*—where she becomes a nun—is sacred to the Catholic Church. I wish you'd eliminate it."

Now, I am a Catholic convert. I was not a Catholic then. "I'll make a deal with you," I said. "Would you prefer me to do this sequence with my imagination or with your help?"

"By all means, with my help," he said. "If you must do it, I will give you someone who will guide you so that you will not go wrong."

We arrived in Rome, and on the morning we were to shoot the sequence a short, fat little priest came on the set. He had his script with him, and it was very thick. He had the whole ceremony there. I spoke no Italian and he spoke no English; through the interpreter I told him to go ahead and stage the ceremony. It took him from eight in the morning until seven at night to get through it. I made no notes. I merely sat and watched, working out what we could cut and getting a complete picture in my mind.

When he had finished, we gave him dinner, and then I took Lillian Gish and J. Barney Sherry and the other players and worked through until the next morning. I shot the entire thing while it was fresh in my mind, without a scene of it being written down.

Now, I have worked with a lot of New York stage directors, but I never saw a man with such quiet authority. He handled people with great skill. He knew exactly what he was doing. When I saw the archbishop, I thanked him for sending the priest over.

"You know," I said, "he is the greatest stage director I ever saw. I have never seen a man with such an ability to impart information."

"Well," said the archbishop, "he's had a lot of experience. The last show he put on had sixteen thousand people in the cast."

The priest was the head ceremonial director from the Vatican!

For the volcano scenes in *The White Sister,* I went to Vesuvius. The only way you can get up to the top of the mountain is on horseback. So I took the cameraman, Roy Overbaugh, his assistant, a guide, and one other person. We rode up to the top, then we started down inside the volcano.

It was about a thousand feet straight down, but it didn't look deep at all, because it was so far away. Using ropes, we somehow got down to the bottom. There were little craters which would burst into life every few minutes, discharging gases. Then the wind would change and all you could do was lie on your stomach and put your handkerchief over your face. You'd be asphyxiated if you didn't. Fortunately, we were all young and full of enthusiasm. When the gas cleared, we set off again and came to a crack in the lava. It was about half the width of this room. We could see the lava cooking down there. We had to jump over to the other side, carrying the equipment. The camera assistant began to have fainting spells and had to go back. The craters kept bursting and firing little stones that looked about the size of pebbles. One of them fell near Roy Overbaugh and me, and it was at least a foot in diameter.

Well, we carried on up the side of the main crater, and I wanted to look inside it. The hole in the top was about sixty feet across and it was banked up with ashes. I had a Leica. I gave it to the cameraman and told him to photograph me when I reached the edge. Well, the heat was so intense I couldn't stand it. It singed my eyebrows and my hair. When I came back my face was blood red and the guide was lying on his stomach, praying. I asked him what the matter was. "Only one other man ever did that," he said. "The bank of ashes gave way and he went right on in." I never thought of that; I was just being stupid. That little expedition took twelve hours—but we got our film. It so happened that Vesuvius was in a kind of semi-eruption. When we intercut this with the scenes we had made in the studio, and with what we had shot on the side of Vesuvius, it looked rather convincing.

The burning of Savonarola from Romola *(1925). This amazing set, built on the grounds of the Vise Studio, Florence, covered seventeen acres. To achieve the texture of the stonework art director Robert Haas made plaster casts from the walls of the Davanzati Palace. "According to history," said Henry King, "as the flames enveloped Savonarola's body a small cloud, the size of a man's hand, grew into a thunderstorm. The gentlemen on the high ladders are there to produce the downpour."*

When doing *The White Sister,* I worked all over Italy. I worked in Sorrento and Capri and Rome and around Lago Montagna and Tivoli. We didn't go over there to make a picture of interiors. The hunt scene was staged by a local master of the hounds. Instead of hiring a lot of extra people, I just took the principals and used the social set of Rome as extras.

Romola was also made in Italy, but it was a much bigger and a much more difficult picture. It was a fifteenth-century costume thing. The ships were built at Livorno, by Tito Neri, the port captain. We named them after the members of the cast—the *Liliano* and the *Dorothea,* after the Gish sisters. We took a studio in Florence; our big set there covered seventeen acres, and the highest building was 274 feet. This was a reproduction of the Duomo and the Campanile. Robert Haas was again the art director, and I cannot praise too highly the Italian workmen. Nothing was too much trouble. They patiently worked over those sets to make them exact replicas of fifteenth-century architecture. I made some scenes in front of the real Duomo and the real Campanile; they matched so well you couldn't tell the difference.

After *Romola,* I left Italy and came back to California to make *Stella Dallas* for Samuel Goldwyn. *Stella Dallas* was a grand book and a tremendously emotional story. We had a problem about Stella Dallas's daughter. Sam Goldwyn suggested Lois Moran for the part. He had met her in Paris, and had had some close-up pictures made of her. Abe Lehr, his general manager, showed them to me.

"I think she's adorable," I said. "But Sam has seen her personally, what does he think?"

"If you like her, Henry, he likes her."

When Sam Goldwyn returned to New York, he called me. "If you like her pictures well enough," he said, "I'll try and make a contract with her now, because she's going to do a stage play with Marc Connelly."[1]

"Well, Sam," I said. "From the neck up she's marvelous. But she has to play a child as well as a woman. What kind of legs does she have?"

"You know, Henry," he said. "Much as I've been around in my life, this is the first time I forgot to look at a girl's legs."

"She's a dancer," I said. "If she has those big muscular legs, she'll be awful."

"She's opening in Baltimore. Why don't you come to New York as quickly as you can?"

The moment I arrived, Goldwyn suggested I take the midday train to Baltimore, see the show, and return that same night.

So I went down to Baltimore and met Mrs. Moran and her daughter at their hotel. We went into the dining room, and everything was very gay and chitter-chatter.

"Now, Lois," I said. "I have to tell you frankly why I am in Baltimore. I liked the test that Mr. Goldwyn made of you in Paris. I've seen you and I like you personally. But this girl has to appear as an eleven-year-old, and I must see what kind of legs you have."

So she pulled up her skirt. "There they are—how are they?" In the dining room!

"Well, that one's very pretty. How about the other?" I said, laughing. "Now, Lois, mission accomplished. You're fine."

---

[1] The Wisdom Tooth.

We finished dinner and saw the show. I went backstage to congratulate her and Marc Connelly, and I left in a cab, went to the railroad station, and returned to New York. All that way—from California to New York to Baltimore and back— just to see a girl's legs!

Frances Marion wrote the scenario for *Stella Dallas*. She had great talent for picking people. When I returned from New York she said, "I don't know if you have given any thought to the actress to play the mother, but if you haven't and before you settle on anyone, please think in terms of Belle Bennett." Well, I had known Belle Bennett when she was playing in *The Wandering Jew,* with Tyrone Power. She gave a tremendous performance, although she was in only one act. And I remembered when she was dabbling about in pictures, trying to get most anything she could.

"This woman has just what it takes," said Frances Marion. "She is a mother, she has two children, and she has had everything on earth happen to her. Both on stage and off, she *is* Stella Dallas." So we brought her in, and she was magnificent.

But the problem of her daughter remained. She had to play a child of eleven and grow to womanhood. Sam Goldwyn thought we should get an eleven-year-old girl out of school and let Lois play the older part. I agreed. We interviewed fifteen or twenty girls, trying to find one who was a tolerable double. Then Sophie Wachner, in charge of wardrobe, had an idea. She dressed Lois for eleven; she gave her ribbed stockings, to make the legs look straighter and thinner, and we took five girls of similar measurements. I photographed them first individually and then all together.

Sam Goldwyn ran the tests through. He ran them a second time and said, "Henry, are you pulling my leg? I don't know whether I'm making a fool out of myself or not. That girl next to the end—that *is* Lois Moran! Why do you want a double? She's the best one of the group!"

So Lois played all the stages, right on up till she married Doug Fairbanks, Jr. I gave Doug, Jr., a little mustache. I told him that a boy gets a little conscious of a mustache, and he should stroke it occasionally. He went back to see his father, and his father said, "What are you doing?"

Doug, Jr., said, "I'm trying to get into the habit, because I'm wearing a mustache in the picture."

So Doug, Sr., who was a little vain about his age, said, "Now, listen. What was that? You're wearing a mustache—?"

He called me on the phone. "Henry," he said. "Remember that I'm still in pictures. Don't make Junior look too old—"

"He won't," I said. "He'll look even younger." The mustache just made the difference to that scene of puppy love, when he climbed out of the boat and kissed Lois on the cheek. There was a lot of controversy about that scene. People asked why he didn't kiss her on the mouth. I said that little boys and little girls of that age don't kiss on the mouth. If they do, they're wrong. Anyway, that was another picture with a great deal of enthusiasm from everyone concerned with it. And the money that rolled in was quite fantastic.

The Winning of Barbara Worth was another great experience. I found the location up in the Black Rock Desert, Nevada, on the edge of Nevada and Idaho. This was an elevation of 6,000 feet and the most barren desert you have ever seen. But it was just right for our picture. We built a whole town up there. A railroad passed over by the mountain, and we had a railroad station put in. We had to haul our drinking water from two hundred miles away, although we drilled a well for showers and so on. Our camp could accommodate twelve hundred people, and we'd bring in another twelve hundred by train.

Now, you generally do your exteriors first, and then the interiors in a studio. We decided it was just as easy to reverse this. Carl Oscar Borg was my art director. The picture was about the reclamation of the Imperial Valley, the harnessing of the Colorado River into a huge irrigation project. Ronald Colman, whom I had discovered for *The White Sister* played the Eastern engineer, Willard Holmes. Vilma Banky had two parts—as a pioneer mother, who dies in a sand-storm, and as Barbara Worth, her daughter. The actor I'd cast to play Abe Lee was over at Warner Brothers, working for Lubitsch. I was ready to start his scenes, but Lubitsch was still shooting.

One morning, I arrived at the studio and noticed a man sitting outside the office of Bob McIntyre, the casting director. He had his knees up and his arms around them, and he looked at me as I went by. I asked Bob who he was.

"Oh, just a kid, a rider. He wants to get into the picture. He says he has a test."

"Send the test over to the projection room," I said. "I'll slip out the back door and have a look at it. Meanwhile, bring him in and introduce him."

So this fellow came in and said, after a long pause, "I'd like to play the part of Abe Lee."

"I'm sorry," I said, "that part's taken." I excused myself from him and went over to the projection room and looked at his test. He had paid to have it made on Poverty Row. All he did was ride up on a horse, make a gallant dismount, look at the camera, and walk into a saloon.

I came back and said to Bob McIntyre, "Well, anyway, he can ride a horse." I made a deal with the boy. "I'm taking about ten riders up to the location." I said, "I have nine of them, and I would like to take you. You get fifty dollars a week and we keep you in the camp."

"All right," he said. "I'll take it—on the understanding that if you have a little part you'll give it to me."

Well, we got ready to start the picture, and this other actor still hadn't shown up. So I took this boy and put him in Abe Lee's costume.

"All you have to do," I said, "is to keep your eyes on Vilma Banky."

Do you know, that man stood there from eight in the morning until twelve? No matter where Vilma Banky went, his eyes followed her—whether we were shooting or not. I think he had done some extra work but that was all. He had come down from Montana and was new to pictures. Well, he did some other scenes for me and while he didn't have much to do, he did it well. So I thought to myself, if he can do the scene at the hotel—where he rides across the desert for twenty-four hours to bring the news to Mr. Worth—then I'm not going to wait on the man from Warner Brothers. I didn't say anything to anyone. I didn't want any arguments—how do you know how good he is, or how good he isn't?—or anything.

I had this scene with Ronald Colman, Charles Lane, and Paul McAllister. Abe

Lee is supposed to knock on the door, completely exhausted after his ride across the desert. I went to the studio that morning and the first thing I did was talk to the boy. I wet his face and covered it with fuller's earth, and I walked and I talked. Tired—tired—tired. That was my subject. Tired—tired—tired. I walked around with him and I talked about how one feels when one is exhausted. Why *I* wasn't exhausted, I'll never know. I kept him walking between scenes, then I'd go back on the set. When I'd rehearsed those people, I'd go back to him. I worked with him for an hour before I asked him on the set.

"If I wanted you to come up to this door," I said, "and fall flat on your face —flat, even if it smashes you to pieces, could you do it?"

"Yes, sir."

"I don't mean you to break your fall with your hands. I mean you to fall flat. Like a corpse."

"Yes, sir."

"When you knock on that door, I want you to knock like a tired man. How tired would a man be if he'd ridden twenty-four hours on a horse?"

"Mighty tired."

"Well, I want you to *be* that tired. You've got to be tired in your mind as well as your body. When they open the door, I want you to look across the room. You see Mr. Worth, but you can't move your feet. You say 'M-m-mister . . .' and you collapse, and I want you to fall full length. Just as though you had died."

"Yes, sir," he whispered. "I'll do it."

I believed he would. I told Ronnie and Paul, "This boy has never done anything before. He's going to fall on the floor and he's going to smash his face.

Vilma Banky and Henry King during the making of **The Winning of Barbara Worth** *(1926).*

When he goes down, catch him under the arms and carry him over to the bed."
We rehearsed this without the boy. Irving Sindler, the property man, came up
and said that Mr. Goldwyn wanted to see me. Now, I had the set blocked off
with black cloth, so that no one could see what was going on. I laid back the
cloth and went outside.

"Henry," said Goldwyn, "I just want you to understand one thing. When you
spend a dollar of my money, you're spending a dollar of your own."

"Why, what's the matter, Sam?" I asked.

"You're going to put that damn cowboy in one of the biggest parts in the
picture."

"How did you know?"

"I just saw yesterday's rushes."

"How were they?"

"They were good—for that. But how are you going to do the big scene? That
is a big dramatic scene and no damn cowboy can play it."

"Well, now," I said, "to ease your mind, Sam, we have finished everything we
can. The actor we hired from Warner's is still working for Lubitsch and I don't
know if he'll get here by Christmas. It isn't costing us anything to continue with
this boy. We have to pay for everything anyway. We're just using up some film."

"I just wanted to tell you that when you spend a dollar of my money, you
spend a dollar of your own." And he turned on his heel and walked away.

So all right. I returned to the set and got the people back into the mood. Then
I went outside to the actor, wet his face again, and pasted more fuller's earth
till his eyes were just two cracks. It was the darnedest make-up you ever saw in
your life, because it had been on for about four hours. We kept wetting his face
and applying more fuller's earth until the dust caked his ears, his eyes, his clothes
—everything was white. When I was ready to shoot, I gave Sindler the sign
for this fellow to knock on the door.

And you know, he knocked on that door like he could hardly touch it. Ronnie
Colman stood up, opened the door, and revealed the most pathetic case I've ever
seen in my life. I don't think anything will remain in my memory as long as
the sight of Gary Cooper standing full length in that door, looking across the
room and saying, "Mr. W-W-Worth . . ."—and falling flat on his face. As he
went down, Ronnie Colman and Paul McAllister grabbed him, and Cooper's face
missed the floor by two inches. They carried him over to the bed and I said to
George Barnes, the cameraman, and Gregg Toland, the second, "Right, over
here, quick!" If I let this make-up deteriorate, we could never replace it. They
were lining up for a close-up when Irving Sindler came up.

"Mr. Goldwyn wants to see you."

"Oh—not *now!*" I went outside.

"Sam, what *is* it?"

"Henry," he said, "you're always trying to tease me. Why didn't you tell me
that man was a great actor?"

"Because he isn't," I said. "He's a cowboy from Montana—"

"Henry, he's the greatest actor I have ever seen in my life."

"How do you know?" I asked.

"Because I was peeping through a hole in the curtain. Let's sign him up."

"Sam, I've got a scene to shoot. I'll come back and talk to you about this later."

"Let Abe do it," he said. "We'll make a deal."

"Later," I said.

"Listen, we're partners, aren't we?"

"Of course we are, but unless we shoot this scene, we won't have a picture."

I ran back onto the set and I made the close-up of Gary. Then I said, "Gary, you have the part." He was just as bewildered by that as he was when he stood in the door. How do these things happen? The boy had his heart and soul set on playing Abe Lee. He knew the book backward. He came down to California, I gave him a part riding a horse as an extra man, and he ends up playing Abe Lee. Now if you can explain that, explain it. I'm not going to try to.

11 / MARY PICKFORD

To those who have never seen her—and two generations have grown up since she left the screen—Mary Pickford epitomizes the tear-jerking stories for which the silent era is celebrated. She is seen as a tragic little orphan, lost in the cruel world, at the constant mercy of Fate. Her name is as well-remembered as Chaplin's; while he is the undisputed representative of silent-film comedy, she has come to represent silent-film tragedy.

Nothing could be more ludicrously inaccurate. Mary Pickford was essentially a comedienne, although that description cannot do justice to her rich talents as a dramatic actress.

Her films were almost always comedies, the light episodes being laced with genuine pathos and much excitement. They were sentimental, but seldom mawkish. The character of Mary Pickford was an endearing little spitfire. She was delightful; she projected warmth and charm, but she had the uncontrollable fire of the Irish. Whenever a situation got out of hand, she would not submit to self-pity. She would storm off and do something about it, often with hilariously disastrous results.

Her playing was completely naturalistic; neither her acting nor her later silent films have dated in any way. She seems as fresh and vital now as when she was America's Sweetheart. She had legions of imitators, but no rivals. The ideal American girl is still the Mary Pickford character: extremely attractive, warm-hearted, generous, funny—but independent and fiery-tempered when the occasion demands.

The public adored Mary Pickford's little-girl character, and she felt obliged to play it until she was well into her thirties. As early as 1918, however, she made a stand against the "sweeter-than-light" approach—with a film called *Stella Maris*. Written by Frances Marion, from a novel by William J. Locke, and directed by Marshall Neilan, *Stella Maris* was an honest and brilliant production. Mary Pickford played two parts; Unity Blake, an uncannily realistic portrayal of a pathetic Cockney slavey, and Stella Maris, a rich girl, paralyzed from childhood, whose foster parents protect her from life's unpleasantness. When Stella Maris leaves her sickbed and confronts reality, she is profoundly shocked. She turns, in despair, on her foster parents: "By trying to shield me you have destroyed my happiness and my faith in human nature." The message was loud and clear, but the public preferred Mary in the one part they knew so well. Fortunately, she handled this role with intelligence and portrayed a young girl rather than a child, sometimes growing up within the story. Neilan's hilarious *Daddy Long Legs* (1919) begins with Mary as a baby, discovered in a garbage can, shows her days as a child in an orphanage, and ends with romance. She played adult roles in *The Love Light* (1921; Frances Marion), *Rosita* (1923; Lubitsch), *Dorothy Vernon of Haddon Hall* (1924; Neilan) and *My Best Girl* (1927; Sam Taylor).

While Mary Pickford's portrayals as an actress have been misrepresented, her importance in the history of the cinema has been grossly underestimated.

It would be no exaggeration to state that Mary Pickford and her husband, Douglas Fairbanks, exerted more influence on American productions than anyone else in the industry, apart from D. W. Griffith. And by 1920, even Griffith's importance was on the decline. His films had made their indelible impression on methods and technique. Now his contemporaries were overtaking him, with highly polished, highly imaginative productions. Mary Pickford and Douglas Fairbanks,

Jack Pickford discusses a setup with his sister, visiting the set of The Hillbilly (1924), *and director George Hill. The Hillbilly was based on the same John Fox story as* Heart o' the Hills, *which Mary Pickford made in 1919.*

Maurice Tourneur directing Mary Pickford in Poor Little Rich Girl (1917). *Lucien Andrio at camera.*

thanks to their phenomenal commercial successes, became the new pace-setters. The industry awaited a new film from their studios with the same eagerness that, some years earlier, they had awaited a new Griffith.

Pickford and Fairbanks were able to recognize talent, and they had business acumen enough to be able to employ it. Their choice was dictated as much by commercial considerations as by artistic merit, yet their films attained the highest possible standards in every department. Mary Pickford employed the finest cameraman, Charles Rosher. Douglas Fairbanks used brilliant men like Arthur Edeson and Henry Sharp. They both signed top directors—Sidney Franklin, Marshall Neilan, Raoul Walsh, Ernst Lubitsch, Maurice Tourneur—and they drew from lesser-known directors the best pictures of their careers.

Although Mary Pickford says she seldom exercised control over directors, her cameraman, Charles Rosher, declares that she did a lot of her own directing. "The director would often just direct the crowd. She knew everything there was to know about motion pictures."

With Chaplin, Griffith, and Fairbanks, she founded the aptly named United Artists in 1919, which gave her the independence she needed.

Her last film, *Secrets,* a talkie directed by Frank Borzage, was released in 1933. In it she played the wife of Leslie Howard, a pioneering homesteader, and proved once and for all that she was among the greatest actresses of motion pictures, both silent and sound. In this strong, dramatic role, she provided many fine moments, but one of them was particularly memorable—a familiar scene given new impact by her performance.

Gunmen are besieging the shack in which she and her husband are living. While Leslie Howard, firing from the window, holds them at bay, Mary goes into the back room to make sure that her baby is unharmed. She finds it dead. Cradling it in her arms, she sits, numbed by shock, in the middle of the room oblivious to the bullets whistling around her. There are no histrionics; she just sits there as the camera creeps forward. But in her face, in her eyes, is the most moving expression of despair. Mary Pickford lived her parts, and, as she said when I met her in London in September 1965, "That one really got me."

In her early seventies, Miss Pickford retained the humor, energy, and vitality that established her as the most important woman in the picture business. She was still among the richest people in the world. Married for nearly thirty years to Charles "Buddy" Rogers, her leading man in *My Best Girl* (1927), she still lived in Pickfair, the home that became the focal point of Hollywood society. Her attitudes strongly reflected the period to which she will always belong, and while she seemed progressive then, she now appeared conservative. She was defiant and proud of her views, however, and strong in her condemnation of moral liberalism. She had grown to detest politics, and she withdrew her support from the Hollywood Museum project when it became a political issue. "If a politician comes to my house," she said, "I have to go. I'm finished."

An attitude that had always been foreign to her was cynicism. She was baffled and annoyed by it, and she was equally bewildered by sly innuendo. Thus her relationship with the great Ernst Lubitsch, whom she brought to America, was doomed from the start. His cynical wit and his delight in sly innuendo and double-entendre collided with a determinedly straightforward and utterly uncomplicated approach. Her description of her skirmishes with Lubitsch indicates that she was still puzzled by the man. She concluded that he was incapable of directing women—which was very far from the truth. In actuality, he was as much of a dictator as Miss Pickford herself, and the humiliation of submitting to the control of a woman was almost more than he could bear.

Von Sternberg's monomania also upset her, as did Griffith's gentle taunting. She was a completely direct and straightforward person and she expected others to be the same. Fortunately most of her associates and employees worshiped her as much as the public. For she was one of the few great stars who was also a great producer—and a great person.

MARY PICKFORD: Everyone thinks that I took the name Mary Pickford out of the sky. My grandfather's name was John Pickford Hennessey, and my great-aunt, who was killed by a tram in London when she was seven, was called Mary Pickford.

I wasn't named after her, however. I was baptized Gladys Marie by a French priest—Gladys Marie Smith.

David Belasco settled on Pickford after I told him the various names in my family—Key, Kirby, Bolton, De Beaumont . . . Marie he changed to Mary.

It was my mother's name, anyhow. She was Charlotte Mary Catherine Pickford Hennessey. I had an aunt named Elizabeth, and a fan of mine in Boston, who traced my family tree, discovered that the names Mary Pickford and Elizabeth Pickford reappeared all the time—from the eleventh century. Originally the family were yeomen from Denmark.

I went into pictures in 1909. I refused to exaggerate in my performances, and my brother Jack wouldn't either. Nobody ever directed me, not even Mr. Griffith. I respected him, yes. I even had an affection for him, but when he told me to do things I didn't believe in, I wouldn't do them. I would *not* run around like a goose with its head off, crying "Oooooh . . . the little birds! Oooooh . . . look! A little bunny!" That's what he taught his ingenues, and they all did the same thing.

"I'm a grown girl. I'm sixteen years old. I won't do it!" I said.

"You'll do it," he said, "or you'll leave."

"All right, I'll leave. I'll go. I won't do it."

But he taught me a lot. For instance, in one picture I was a poor little girl, and I had this miserable little coat on, with a moth-eaten fur collar, and a funny little hat with a bird on it. I came into my room, threw the hat on the bed, and threw my coat on top of it. Griffith stopped the camera.

Now to stop the camera in those days, with film costing something like two cents a foot, was unheard of. He walked over to the set and said, "Pickford, you'll never do that again. You'll never come in and throw your hat on the bed and put your coat down without shaking it. You must take care of your clothes. No heroine is untidy."

I said, "Yes, sir."

"Now, Pickford, you go back and come in again. Camera, Bitzer."

I thought, "Mr. Griffith's right." So I went outside and came back in, took my coat off, shook it, brushed the fur, fixed the little bird on the hat, put it down on the chair, and put my coat carefully on the back.

Mr. Griffith said, "Very good."

That was the way he directed me. He once said that he could sit back of the camera, think something, and I'd do it. He also said that there were only two people who ever outworked him—Lillian Gish and Mary Pickford. I think in his way he loved me, and I loved him. Yet I never wanted to go back to pictures when I left him to return to Belasco; we had this great argument.

He was bringing people in from the outside who were without experience, and I didn't like that. There was a great controversy over who was going to do *The Sands of Dee* (1911). Blanche Sweet wanted it, I wanted it, and Dorothy Bernard and Mabel Normand wanted it. Griffith asked me to do *Man's Genesis*, and I refused because the part required bare legs. Well, not bare legs entirely— a sort of grass skirt that came down to the ankles. All the others said, "If Mary won't do it, we won't do it."

"All right," said Mr. Griffith. "Anybody who will not do *Man's Genesis* will not play *The Sands of Dee*." And he gave the part to Mae Marsh.

I thought, "It serves him right; she'll give a bad performance." When the film was made, we all trooped in to see her, and she was magnificent. I came out of the darkroom, and I went up to Mae Marsh.

"You did it better than I could," I said.

She had had no experience; she had previously worked in a department store. And I thought, "This does it. I've spent ten years in the theater,[1] and if she can do that without any experience, I don't belong in pictures. I'm finished."

On the train, going back to New York, Mr. Griffith and a group of us were having dinner together, and I was talking about Billie Burke. I was too young to realize what a splendid actress she was. I was completely wrong; I thought that she was insincere, and I said so.

"What!" said Mr. Griffith. "You—criticizing Billie Burke! You can't hold a candle to her!"

"Well," I said, "I can have my likes and dislikes—"

"No," he replied. "You're not privileged."

"And you're not privileged to criticize me," I said. "I'm going to tell you something now, Mr. Griffith. You can take these amateurs. I'm going back where I learned my *métier*, my profession. One year from tonight, I will be on Broadway."

"That's ridiculous," he said. "They won't even let you in the back door."

"Why not, sir?"

"Because you have disgraced yourself by being in motion pictures."

"Well, I'm going to tell you something. I'm going to be in a Belasco production!"

"Don't make me laugh," he said.

Having boasted, I now had to prove myself. When I got to New York, I called up the Belasco Theatre and asked to speak to Belasco's manager, William Dean.

"Mr. Dean," I said, launching straight into my prepared speech, "I've called you because I want you and Mr. Belasco to see a moving picture that I wrote and made. It is called *Lena and the Geese*—"

"Who is this?" he asked.

[1] *Miss Pickford's debut on the stage, as Baby Gladys Smith, was at the age of five.*

"This is Betty Warren."[2]

"Not little Betty—with the curls?"

"Yes, Mr. Dean."

"Where have you been? We've been looking all over the place for you."

"I've been in motion pictures."

"Shame on you," he said. "Do you still have your long curls?"

"Yes, sir."

"How long will it take you to come down to the theater?"

The theater was in the Forties, and I was on 72nd Street. "I'll get right dressed," I said.

I went down, and Mr. Dean was very excited. "I want to surprise Governor," he said. "I'm going to put you back of the scenery. Take the hairpins out of your hair, take your high heels off, and don't say a word."

Soon I heard Mr. Belasco.

"Dean, what is the surprise?"

"Oh, Governor, I'm not going to tell you. You'll have to find it yourself. It's right over there—back of that piece of scenery."

Belasco peeked round.

"Come out," he said. "Who are you?"

I had no shoes on, and my hair was down.

"Is this my little Betty?"

"Yes, sir." He was delighted and I was overjoyed.

"Dean, where has she been?"

"She has been a very naughty little girl. She has been in those flickers."

Belasco looked at me. "Is that true, Betty?"

"Yes, sir . . ."

"Oh, *Betty!*" he said, with mock horror.

"I'm sorry, Mr. Belasco," I said.

"Darling, you should be! Now, do you want to come back to the theater?"

"Yes, sir—with you."

"Are you under contract?"

"No . . ."

"Well, I've a wonderful part for you. It's Juliet, the blind girl in *A Good Little Devil*. Could you start rehearsals next Monday?"

"No, sir," I said. "Not until I talk to Mr. Griffith."

I left the theater, in the Forties, and went down to 14th Street in the subway. I couldn't afford a car in those days. When I reached the Biograph Studios, Mr. Griffith was rehearsing. He was the Czar; he sat in the middle of the stage, and he had his company all around him.

"Mr. Griffith," I began.

"Go away!" he snapped.

"I'm sorry, sir, I can't."

"I've told everybody in this studio never to interrupt me when I'm rehearsing."

"I wouldn't," I said, "but this is important. I have to leave."

"Leave?"

"Yes, sir."

[2] *Miss Pickford's previous Belasco success had been in* The Warrens of Virginia.

"Where are you going?"

"I'm going back to Mr. Belasco."

"No! When?"

"I'm due Monday morning, ten-o'clock rehearsal."

"Do you mean to say you're leaving Biograph?"

"I'm sorry, sir. I'm unhappy to leave Biograph, but more unhappy to leave your direction."

"Company dismissed," said Mr. Griffith. There were tears in his eyes. He took my hand. "Well, Pickford, bless you."

"Thank you," I said.

"What are you going to do?"

"I'm playing the lead in *A Good Little Devil*. Here's my script."

"Be good," he said. "Be a good actress."

"I'll try," I said.

I made one more film for him—*The New York Hat*.[3] When *A Good Little Devil* opened in Philadelphia, Mr. Griffith brought the whole company to see the opening night. Before the performance, he told me, "Don't you eat now, because I'm afraid you'll be sick with nerves. Just have a little piece of toast and a cup of tea."

But he was the one that became sick with nerves! He followed us to Baltimore. "Forget everything I told you," he said. "I did a wrong thing. I might have gone against Mr. Belasco. Go back to what he taught you."

We remained very good friends to the day of his death.

A Good Little Devil took me back into motion pictures. Adolph Zukor bought the rights for his Famous Players in Famous Plays. They thought I was just another actress, but when I made *Tess of the Storm Country,* that was really the beginning of my career. Tess was a character completely separate from what I'd been doing. The picture saved the company; Mr. Zukor told me later that he had taken his wife's necklace and his own insurance to pay salaries. Never once did he complain. Our salaries were there every Saturday. Edwin S. Porter, who made *Tess,* knew nothing about directing. Nothing. So the film's success was all the more surprising. We never saw any rushes. The negative was sent to New York for developing, which was very dangerous; so none of us knew what the picture was going to be like.

Edwin Porter had none of the ideas, like close-ups, that Griffith had developed. I developed one original idea myself. I was playing in *Poor Little Rich Girl,* directed by Maurice Tourneur, and one morning I was getting ready at about six thirty. My mirror was lying at an angle, and it caught the early-morning light and reflected it onto my face.

"That makes me look younger," I thought; I was supposed to be a girl of ten in the picture. I went to the studio and asked Maurice Tourneur if I could have a light placed low. Tourneur said no.

"Well, would you kindly take it? Take my close-up as you usually do, then would you get me a little spot, and put it on a soapbox or something, and direct it at my face? Then you can see it in the darkroom and choose."

[3] *From a story submitted by Anita Loos.*

Poor Little Rich Girl.

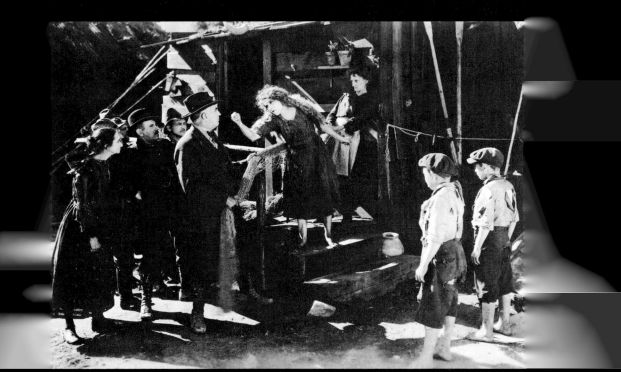

Mary Pickford, spitfire; Tess of the Storm Country *(second version, 1922), directed by John S Robertson.*

Mr. Tourneur saw my point when he saw the rushes, and from then on we used what was called a baby spot. That was the origin of it.

Griffith used to say of me, "She will do anything for the camera. I could tell her to get up on a burning building and jump—and she would." There is something sacred to me about that camera.

When we did *The Little American,* directed by Cecil B. De Mille, about the sinking of the *Lusitania,* I had to flounder in the ocean at San Pedro. In those days I couldn't swim more than two or three feet—but I did the scene. I tell you, that was some experience. It gets very cold at night in California, and I was wearing only an evening dress. I was frozen. A number of people were badly hurt when they slid down the side of the boat and got splinters. I avoided that, luckily, but I was plenty cold!

De Mille was a great producer, but I don't think he had any heart. He was a very commanding person, but he wasn't a great director. However, I loved him.

I lived my characters. That's the only way you can be. You have to live your parts. My mother walked into my bedroom one morning during the production of *Suds,* and was quite startled. "Oh, Mary!" she said. "You look like that ugly little girl!" I was *Suds.* I was Unity Blake in *Stella Maris.*

There was none of this nonsense of nine to five in those days, believe me. I worked from six in the morning until nine at night. When I finished on the set, I had to write all the checks and give the orders for the next day. We had no break. No coffee break—not even a glass of water. You see, I conducted three establishments: Pickfair, my bungalow at the studios, and the beachhouse. Instead of lying down and resting for twenty minutes, I entertained people like President and Mrs. Coolidge. Oh, I could name a dozen that came to the studio.

When luncheon time came, and we were in the middle of a scene, we'd go on for two hours. Then we'd work that night. I remember one night there were ninety-two people back of the camera, and I was the only one in front of it. It was pouring rain, and I was soaking wet.

You know how long it took to make up? Three hours. First they washed the hair. Then they set it. Then they put the make-up on. It took fifteen minutes to get to the set, and you were there at nine o'clock or else. That applied to everybody.

In addition to everything else, when my mother passed on I had to take over her duties, which was an eight-to-ten-hour-a-day business.

It's ridiculous what labor is doing today. Ridiculous. I wouldn't go back for anything in the world. What with their likes and dislikes, their coffee breaks and their overtime . . . how can people make pictures?

I never thought my films were important. I never did anything to save them. I just put them in storage and forgot them. I intended to destroy them because, frankly, I didn't want to be compared to the modern trend. If you look at the magazines of forty years ago, their writing is ridiculous. I mean, it's so sentimental. I was afraid my films would be the same. When the Hollywood Museum started, I tried to help, but I found the tins of film were just full of red dust. Then we had two fires, one in our office building, another in the stores, and films were lost in both. Private collectors won't give up the pictures of mine—and they know they're bootlegged. But it's just as well—otherwise they'd be gone.

I will not allow one picture to be shown: *Rosita*.[4] Oh, I detested that picture! I disliked the director, Ernst Lubitsch, as much as he disliked me. We didn't show it, of course, but it was a very unhappy and very costly experience.

Lubitsch was on his way over from Germany when the American Legion held a big meeting. I was on the platform. The supreme officer of the Legion got up and said, "I hear the son of the Kaiser is coming here. I would to God that the American Legion would go down to meet him—and throw him in the water. He doesn't belong here. He's still our enemy. And why are they bringing German singers over here? Do we not have enough good singers here, in the United States, without going to Germany?"

"Oh," I thought, "here it comes. I'll be next. 'What is she doing bringing Lubitsch over here? Do we not have good American directors?' " I wasn't going to take it sitting down. I decided that I would get up and speak. Perspiration began to break out on my forehead. This is what I planned to say:

"General, ladies and gentlemen. Since when has art borderlines? Art is universal, and for my pictures I will get the finest, no matter which country they come from. The war is over. And it is very ill-bred and stupid for the General to stand up and talk like that. A German voice is God-given if it's beautiful.

"Yes, I am bringing Mr. Lubitsch over here. Yes! I'm proud that I can. And General, you be grown up, you be a good boy and don't you say that to me, because I'm white, twenty-one, and an American citizen, and I contributed to the war as you did. But you're not contributing to anything with opinions like that."

I remember that speech to this day. I had it all set—and he never called on me. I was very disappointed.

Lubitsch was on the water, coming over, so I said, "We're in trouble. The American Legion may meet him." We arranged for a little pilot boat to take him off the ship. He was instructed not to mention Mary Pickford, where he was going, or what he was doing, and above all he was told not to mention Germany.

When he arrived in Hollywood I naturally sent Mrs. Lubitsch a large bunch of flowers. The newspaper people immediately wanted to know about it.

"What are you doing here, Mr. Lubitsch?"

Putting the card in his pocket, Lubitsch replied, "I'm not talking."

"Are you going to work?"

"*Nein.*"

I first met him on the studio lot, with Edward Knoblock and Douglas Fairbanks. Knoblock spoke perfect German, and he introduced us. Lubitsch took my hand, and suddenly threw it away from him.

"*Ach, mein Gott!*" he exclaimed. "She is cold!"

"Oh, he's just nervous," I thought.

"*Ja,* cold!" he repeated. "She cannot be an actress!"

"Our actresses are paid to act," said Knoblock. "They don't act when offstage, or away from the camera. You're judging her by German actresses."

Lubitsch was watching me all the time, to see if I would blow up. I kept my temper.

---

[4] Rosita *was shown in a Lubitsch retrospective at The Berlin Film Festival in July 1967. It was received with acclamation as "a masterpiece." The print came from the Moscow archives.*

Mary Pickford, Ernst Lubitsch, and cameraman Charles Rosher on Rosita *(1923).*

Charles Rosher on Sparrows *(1926).*

Our first production together was to be *Dorothy Vernon of Haddon Hall,* and he had read the script. I had spent a quarter of a million dollars in preparation. I remember seeing Knoblock and Lubitsch moving through the wheatfield at the back of the studio—the wheat was chest high, and they were swimming through it. "There goes trouble," I said to my mother.

Knoblock approached us and said, "I'm sorry. Lubitsch won't do *Dorothy Vernon.*"

"Edward!" I said. "Why not? He read the script in Germany, he came over here, he's been receiving salary, I paid his fare, and that of his wife . . ."

"Will you see him?" asked Knoblock.

"Of course," I said. "I'll have to."

I went over to my bungalow, which I had just had painted a dove gray. Lubitsch used to eat German-fried potatoes three times a day, and I was dismayed when the grease on his hands left little frescoes all around the room.

"All right, Mr. Lubitsch," I said. "What's wrong?"

He pounded my beautiful table with his fist and he shouted "I'm not making *Dorothy Vernon!*"

"Well," I said, "you read the script . . ."

"*Ja.* I don't like it."

"Why didn't you say that in Germany?"

"Vell, now I'm telling you."

"What's wrong with *Dorothy Vernon?*"

"Der iss too many qveens and not enough qveens."

Elizabeth and Mary; he objected to their story being more interesting than that of Dorothy Vernon. Queen Elizabeth and Mary Queen of Scots could have been a story on their own, but there wasn't enough in the script to make that possible.

"All right," I said. "I can't force you to do something you don't want to do."

"I go back to Germany."

I told him he could if he wished to. When he'd cooled down I said to Edward, "Let's find another story." We settled on *Rosita.* What an ordeal! I had to fight to get the story right. Lubitsch was a man's director, he had no sensitivity about women. He figured himself in every scene—as the man.

We had some amusing things, though. Lubitsch spoke very bad English; he would say the most censorable things on the set, and everybody would roar with laughter.

One morning I got onto the set early.

"Now look, boys and girls, if you went to Germany and tried to direct, you might say things that weren't proper yourselves. But you wouldn't like everybody to laugh at you. Now the first person that laughs on this stage will have to leave."

Lubitsch came in, and promptly said something and everybody disappeared. Charlie Rosher, my cameraman, hid his face under the black cloth of the stills camera, other people climbed up the walls of the set, and the only person who laughed was me. I can't remember this particular remark, but another occasion was equally amusing.

It was the big cathedral scene. I guess there were two or three hundred extras there. I was in my little dressing room, with my Alsatian maid, who spoke perfect German.

My Best Girl *(1927), directed by Sam Taylor.*

Charles Rosher, Henry Cronjager, Mary Pickford, and Marshall Neilan pose for a gag shot on Daddy Long Legs *(1919).*

Lubitsch was outside. He was very pompous and very important, like all little men. "Komm, pliss," he called, clapping his hands. "Dis is de scenes vere Miss Pickford goes mit der beckside to ze altar!"

There was an explosion of laughter. "Bordermayer," I said, "please go out and tell Mr. Lubitsch that he's not to say that." He came in and apologized.

"That's all right, Mr. Lubitsch. I understand. You're trying to learn the language."

"So," he said. "Correct, pliss, Miss Pickford, is it right to say 'Go mit der beck to ze altar?'"

"Perfectly good."

"So!" he said. He went outside, clapped his hands again, and announced: "Dis is de scenes vere Miss Pickford goes mit der . . . beck . . . to ze altar."

Lubitsch was a nice enough man, but he was stubborn. He walked off the set when Edward Knoblock questioned the accuracy of a scene. He let out a torrent of German, and then looked around at everyone. He evidently wanted to say "Oh, good *night!*" Instead of which, all he could remember was "Oh, how do you do!" And he stalked off the set. We waited till the door had shut, and then you never heard such a roar of laughter.

In the story, Don Diego [George Walsh] is shot by a firing squad with blank cartridges. He's lying on the ground, and I'm supposed to think he's dead. Lubitsch was a frustrated actor, and he had to act out everything: "You say, 'Don Diego, Don Diego, anschver me! Anschver me!'"

I tried not to imitate him. "Don Diego!" I cried. "Answer me!" But Lubitsch corrected me. He called from behind the camera, "Miss Pickford! Again, pliss— 'anschver me!'"

To keep him happy I imitated him, and George Walsh's stomach started going up and down in convulsions of suppressed laughter.

"George," I said, "I'll kill you!"

"I'm not making a sound," he giggled.

"Your stomach's moving all over the place! I can't act!"

Mr. Lubitsch cried, "Stop! Stop! Miss Pickford—vat iss to laugh?"

"Nothing, Mr. Lubitsch. I'm sorry."

"Don't make mit der laugh!"

I tried once more: "Don Diego! Anschver me!"

It was no good. George's stomach went up and down again, and I fell across him and we both laughed till we cried.

Poor Mr. Lubitsch.

The climax came toward the end of production.

"Look, Mr. Lubitsch," I said. "This is a love story. You've got to put in a sequence that makes the ending important."

"*Nein,*" he said. "I'm not making it!"

I thought it over, and I went to his office.

"Mr. Lubitsch. This is the first time you've met me as the financial backer and producer."

"Vatt iss dis?"

"I'm telling you that I am the Court of Last Appeal. I'm putting up the money, I am the star, and I am the one that's known. I won't embarrass you; I will never say anything before the company. If I have anything to say, I'll say it as

I'm saying it now. I didn't ask you to come to me, I came to your office. But you are not going to have the last word."

"Not for a million dollars!"

"I don't care if it's for ten million. You are not going to have that privilege."

With that he started tearing all the buttons off his clothes. Well, I wasn't losing *my* temper.

"That's final, Mr. Lubitsch."

He went to Edward Knoblock's desk and began tearing up valuable papers—papers that had been written in longhand. What a man. He shook his fist at me, and he really lost control.

We were going to do *Faust* with Lubitsch supervising. But Mother didn't know the story of *Faust,* so Lubitsch told her. *"Ja,"* he said. "She has a bebby, and she's not married, so she stringles the bebby."

Mother said, "What! What was that?"

"Well, Marguerite is not married, she has a bebby, so she stringles it."

"Not my daughter!" said my mother, outraged. "No sir!" So I didn't make *Faust. . . .*

I parted company with him as soon as I could. I thought he was a very uninspired director. He was a director of doors. Everybody came in and out of doors . . . He was a good man's director—good for Jannings and people like that. But for me he was terrible. To tell you the truth, I never saw his later pictures, because of my miserable experience on *Rosita.* He was very self-assertive, but then all little men are. . . .

I always tried to get laughter into my pictures. Make them laugh, make them cry, and back to laughter. What do people go to the theater for? An emotional exercise. And no preachment. I don't believe in taking advantage of someone who comes to the theater by teaching him a lesson. He can go to church, he can read the newspapers. But when people go to a motion picture they want to be entertained. It is not my prerogative as an actress to teach them anything. *They* will teach *me. They* will discipline *me.* And that's how it should be, because I am a servant of the public. I have never forgotten that.

My picture *Sparrows* wasn't too successful, comparatively speaking, because of an error of judgment. We tried to put too much drama into it. In the swamp scene, I had to carry some children along a narrow board—five or six inches wide—across an alligator-infested pool.

The alligators were alive, and very active. The old ones are rather sluggish—they live to quite an age—but the young ones of seventy-five are vicious. I carried this heavy baby on my shoulder, and she kept moving from one side to the other. It was very dangerous. I was worried most about the baby—although I admit I didn't exactly relish the idea of the alligators' teeth. . . .

I said to the director, "I'll have to rehearse this with a doll on my back. We can weight it to make it heavier." I made the trip across three times one way and three times the other. Then Douglas Fairbanks was told about it, and he raced over. He was furious.

William Beaudine, the director—who had been a property boy at Biograph—told him it was necessary. "It's nothing of the kind," said Douglas. "You can make a double exposure."

But by then I'd been across six times. . . . Quite frankly, I've never liked Mr. Beaudine since. I could understand it if he wanted to get rid of me, but not a little baby! That was malice aforethought, and I'll tell him so to his face. No director has a right to do that.

I had complete control over the direction if I wanted to use it, but, you see, I didn't use it. I would today. But now I'm older—and as we get older we get more positive.

Anyhow, it was so terrifying for many people seeing babies in such danger that *Sparrows* didn't do as well as it might have done.

They used to call me "Retake Mary Pickford." I was never pleased, and that's why I'm not today. I see one of my pictures, and I say to myself. "Well, Mary, you're pretty good in that scene, but in this one you're dreadful!"

For a long time, I saw none of my pictures. Then a strange thing happened to me quite recently. A picture called *Suds* came out of the nowhere into the now. And she's funny! She's pathetic, too, without wanting to be. I seemed to inject into the character—what shall I say?—individuality. I was not standardized. Maybe it's a form of gratitude, I don't know, but I will not put my films on television. I will not do anything to that young girl who made everything possible for me. I will not exploit her.

I left the screen because I didn't want what happened to Chaplin to happen to me. When he discarded the little tramp, the little tramp turned around and killed him. The little girl made me. I wasn't waiting for the little girl to kill me. I'd already been pigeonholed. I know I'm an artist, and that's not being arrogant, because talent comes from God. I could have done more dramatic performances that the ones I gave in *Coquette* and *Secrets,* but I was already typed.

My career was planned, there was never anything accidental about it. It was planned, it was painful, it was purposeful. I'm not exactly satisfied, but I'm grateful, and that's a very different thing. I might have done better; I don't know. There are unexpected circumstances that hinder us, and we just have to put up with them. We have to do the best we can under pressure.

I think Oscar Wilde wrote a poem about a robin who loved a white rose. He loved it so much that he pierced his breast, and let his heart's blood turn the white rose red. Maybe this sounds *very* sentimental, but for anybody who has loved a career as much as I've loved mine, there can be no short cuts.

ALWAYS REMOVE
ALL RECORDS FROM RECORD DRAWER
BEFORE STARTING THE INSTRUMENT
« CLOSE DOOR WHILE PLAYING »

Clarence Brown is one of the great names of American motion pictures —one of the few whose mastery was undiminished by the arrival of sound. Thanks to the widespread fame of his Garbo pictures—*Anna Christie, Conquest,* and *Anna Karenina*—Clarence Brown is unlikely to become a neglected master. His *Intruder in the Dust,* a study of racial conflict in the South, is the finest picture ever made on the subject. His *The Yearling* has become a classic.

Yet his films of the silent era have been completely forgotten. Although highly successful financially, they tended to be overlooked at the time when the volume of big specials crowded out fine productions of more modest budgets. Superb films like *Smouldering Fires* (1924) with Pauline Frederick and *The Goose Woman* (1925) with Louise Dresser were well reviewed and well received, but they were not to receive the unrestrained enthusiasm they deserved until rediscovered, forty years later, by a new generation. Their revival, at the National Film Theatre, London, the Theodore Huff Memorial Film Society, New York, and the Cinémathèque Française, Paris, caused some hurried reappraisal of Clarence Brown's early work. Audiences were struck by the freshness of the films, and many people commented on "the remarkably modern techniques."

Due to his success with Garbo, Brown has become celebrated in the narrow classification of "a woman's director." Yet he drew from Valentino what was probably his finest performance in *The Eagle* (1925). He handled action sequences with real vigor and with *The Trail of '98* (1928) proved his mastery of spectacle.

His style is one of deceptive simplicity, but the apparently effortless ease is the result of tremendous care. Clarence Brown as a director was concerned not only with performances, but with lighting, composition, editing, story construction —every stage in the process of film making.

Brown was a brilliant technician, but he also had a warm feeling for people. In his handling of players, and of situations, he achieved a naturalism that, even when stylized, was always convincing. *The Eagle,* for instance, was a highly romantic story, in settings of deliberate artificiality, but Brown's evocation of atmosphere, and his gentle humor, gave the slight story real stature.

Apart from their expert skill, the trademark of Clarence Brown pictures has always been their imaginative visual values. This, he says, he owes to Maurice Tourneur, the great director who gave him his first job in films.

"Maurice Tourneur was my god. I owe him everything I've got in the world. For me, he was the greatest man who ever lived. If it hadn't been for him, I'd still be fixing automobiles." I interviewed Clarence Brown in Paris in September 1965 and October 1966.

Born in Clinton, Massachusetts, in 1890, Clarence Brown was the son of a cotton manufacturer, Larkin H. Brown. The family moved to the South when Brown was eleven; after high school, he attended the University of Tennessee, and graduated at nineteen with two degrees in engineering. His father wanted him to enter the cotton business, but Brown's passionate interest in cars caused him to leave home and start work with the Moline Automobile Company, in Illinois, and later with the Stevens Duryea Company, of Massachusetts.

CLARENCE BROWN: I became the traveling expert mechanic for Stevens Duryea. One of my calls was to a dealer in Birmingham, Alabama, who took a

Clarence Brown directing Jack Pickford and Constance Bennett in The Goose Woman *(1925)*

Greta Garbo gazes at a portrait of her rival, Dorothy Sebastian: A Woman of Affairs *(1928*

liking to me. He had the agency for several big makes of automobile, and he set me up in a subsidiary company, called the Brown Motor Car Company. I had the agency for the Alco truck, the Stevens Duryea, and the Hudson.

It was around this time—1913, 1914—that I became interested in the picture business. Pictures were still in shooting galleries, but I used to watch for the product of the Peerless Studios. There were four directors there—Frank Crane, Albert Capellani, Emile Chautard, and Maurice Tourneur. Whenever I saw "Produced at the Peerless Studios, Fort Lee, N. J.," those were the pictures I went to see. I decided I could make motion pictures, and when I went to New York, it was primarily to see one of those men.

Going over to Fort Lee on the ferry, I overheard a couple of extra people talking about Maurice Tourneur. Apparently he was looking for an assistant director. When I reached the Peerless Studios I asked for him. "He's out on location," they said, but they wouldn't tell me where. I noticed some actors going back and forth for lunch, so I followed them out to the set. Tourneur was making *The Cub,* a moonshiner story, about a mile away from the studio. I went up to him and said I wanted to speak to him about his new assistant. He told me to wait.

He made me wait until six o'clock, when they'd finished shooting. Then he dismissed everybody and came over and said, "What do you want?"

"I understand," I said, "that you're looking for a new assistant."

"Yes, yes! I am!" He was very happy that someone was approaching him. I told him I'd come for the job.

"Who have you been working for?"

"Nobody," I said. "I'm in the automobile business."

He was taken aback. "Well, how do you expect to be an assistant to me?"

"What about the man you're trying to replace?" I asked. "Did he have experience when he came to you?"

"Oh, yes—"

"You don't like him," I said. "Why don't you take a fresh brain that knows nothing about the business and bring him up your way?"

He fell for that argument.

"You start next Monday at nine o'clock," he said. "I will pay you thirty dollars a week."

I was in.

Tourneur was an artist. He had been a painter, and although he did little painting while he was making pictures, he painted on the screen. Many of the tricks they use in the picture business today were originated by Tourneur, with his cameraman, John van der Broek. He was a great believer in dark foregrounds. No matter where he set his camera up, he would always have a foreground. On exteriors, we used to carry branches and twigs around with us. If it was an interior, he always had a piece of the set cutting into the corner of picture, in halftone, to give him depth. Whenever we saw a painting with an interesting lighting effect, we'd copy it. We had a library of pictures. "Rembrandt couldn't be wrong," we'd say, and we'd set the shot up and light it like Rembrandt. At least we stole from the best!

Tourneur was great on tinting and toning. We never made a picture unless every scene was colored. Night scenes were blue, day scenes amber, sunsets blue-tone pink or blue-tone green. The most beautiful shots I ever saw on the screen were in Tourneur's pictures. He was more on the ball photographically than any other director.

His cameraman, John van der Broek, a Dutchman, was a close friend of mine. I think he might have been the greatest cameraman today, if not the greatest director—but he was drowned while shooting one of the episodes of *Woman* (1918). I'll never forget the moment we parted. I was going into the Air Corps in 1917. He put his arms around me, in his European way, and said, "Clarence, I'll never see you again. Don't go." And in two months, *he* was dead.

I think I was Tourneur's first editor. In those days—1915—the only two people who knew anything about the film were the director and cameraman, so they had to edit it between them. I used to watch this process with interest. I once saw Tourneur with twenty pieces of film in his mouth. I got it into my head that I could do it. Within a month I was editing his pictures and writing his titles, relieving him of that end of the business entirely. I took to cutting like a duck to water; timing meant a great deal to me, having been an engineer and having dealt with inches, feet, rods, acres, and so forth. I think you'll find in all my pictures that I take trouble over tempo. Tempo is one of the most elusive things, but when you get it right there's nothing greater.

I would finish cutting a picture in two weeks. It took about four weeks to shoot a picture; and because Tourneur hated exteriors, I worked the rest of the time doing exteriors with my own cameraman. While he was shooting in the studio, we would exchange casts and work as two units. In that way we were able to make a number of pictures in one year.

I once had a hell of a fight with Tourneur. We were going to Florida to do two pictures with Olga Petrova, *Law of the Land* and *Exile* (1917). I had worked day and night to get the costumes ready. He wanted to see the actors wearing them, and I had to tell him I hadn't had time to get the actors. We were in Florida two months and he never spoke a word to me. If he wanted to tell me something, he addressed me through the other assistant.

In the meantime, a stage actress named June Elvidge, who had been in our pictures, told William A. Brady, whose World Film Corporation released Tourneur's pictures, that there was a young fellow with Tourneur who looked as if he had something on the ball. She wrote me a letter, and I had this at the back of my mind. I figured that if I could hold out until we returned to New York I could get another job with Brady.

When we got to New York we were still not speaking, and I was dying. I felt two inches high. I went to see Brady, and he signed me to a three-year contract at one hundred and fifty dollars a week—all I was getting from Tourneur was thirty-five. I didn't quite know how to approach Tourneur, so I said nothing.

I carried on, cutting the pictures we had shot in Florida. Finally, Tourneur called me into the projection room.

"Haven't you something you want to tell me?" he asked.

"Yes, Mr. Tourneur. I'm leaving you."

I've never seen anything so startling come over a man. He gasped, "Why?"

"Well," I said, "you haven't talked to me for two months. I know I'm fired, and I went out and got myself another job. I'm going to work for William A. Brady."

"You can't go," he said. "You can't go."

"But I signed a contract, Mr. Tourneur."

"You can't go," he repeated, and he cried. He *cried.*

He finally went to Brady and told him that he couldn't release me, and Brady gave in. Tourneur raised my salary and I was with him for seven years.

In 1919, I bought a story that I liked very much, but Tourneur was afraid it wouldn't make a good picture.[1] We compromised, and found another story in a San Bernardino newspaper article. This told of a cowboy artist who had been jailed and had made fine drawings on his cell wall. That was the gimmick of the picture. H. H. Van Loan wrote the story; a jail inmate painted the Crucifixion on his cell wall. During the night, the moon was uncovered by a cloud for a few moments, a ray of light fell on the picture, and it looked alive. A murderer, across the cell block, saw this apparition. He called a priest, spent the rest of the night confessing, and went to his death with a smile on his face. That was the story.

John Gilbert was an actor and an assistant with Tourneur at that time. He wrote the script with me in the old Garden Court Apartments in Hollywood. I directed the picture with a completely green crew; my cameraman was Charles van Enger—he had been an assistant; my assistant director, Charles Dorian, had been an extra; my art director, Floyd Mueller, had been an architect downtown. Jack Gilbert had never written a script. The only experienced man I had was the chief electrician, Freddie Carpenter, whom we brought out from New York.

When the picture was finished, I showed it one afternoon in the projection room at Universal. Jack was there, Tourneur, and myself. When the picture was finished, Jack was almost hysterical.

"My God!" he cried. "He's ruined my story!" He started damning the film. "This is the worst thing I've ever seen in my life!" And so on and so forth. Little Clarence went out and leaned over against a tree. I think I lost my cookies. Tears were in my eyes, and my career was ended.

Then Tourneur came out of the projection room. He came over to me, put his hand on my shoulder, and said, "Mr. Brown, that is a wonderful picture."

The Great Redeemer, as it was called, made a great hit. It was the first Metro picture to play on Broadway. I got the award from Sing Sing for the best picture of the year!

That was my first picture. Then Tourneur, with Allan Dwan, Tom Ince, J. Parker Read, Mack Sennett, and Marshall Neilan formed Associated Producers. Our first was *The Last of the Mohicans.* We hadn't been on that picture more than two weeks when Tourneur fell off a parallel and was in bed for three months.

I made the whole picture after that. We made it at Big Bear Lake and Yosemite Valley. I had learned by this time never to shoot an exterior between ten a.m. and three p.m. The lousiest photography you can get is around high noon when the sun's directly overhead. You only get depth on black-and-white exteriors with backlight, or three-quarter light, and a fill light to get photographic quality on the face.

We were up at four a.m. and we stopped at ten. We wouldn't go out again till three p.m.—but we shot till six and so we had a full day's shooting. I never

---

[1] *Brown eventually sold the story to M-G-M. It was* The Unholy Three.

The Great Redeemer *(1920), with House Peters. Clarence Brown, center.*

The Goose Woman: *Louise Dresser, Gustav von Seyffertitz, and George Nichols.*

shot an exterior in flat light in my life—until color came out. In color, it doesn't make too much difference. You get color depth. As you go to infinity, the color gets weaker and weaker until you get depth, even with flat light.

I had one cameraman who came to me, standing in for someone who was sick, and the back of his neck was wrinkled and sunburned, like a piece of old leather. "I can see you work with front light," I said. He thought I was mad.

But this lighting business is important. Today, I'm in real estate. If I want to build a house, my scenic values are important. So I am careful how I place the picture windows, with their view of the mountains. I wouldn't give you thirty cents for a north light. It makes the mountains look as if they were painted on a backdrop with gray paint. But with backlight, or three-quarter light, you get real depth.

In *The Last of the Mohicans* we made much use of lighting effects and weather atmosphere. We used smokepots to create the suggestion of sunrays striking through woodland mist. The rainstorm in the forest was simply a fire engine and a hose. We got clouds because we waited for them, and used filters. Clouds normally did not register on the old ortho film.

When the girls are escaping from the Indian ambush, I put the camera on a perambulator. We built it from a Ford axle, with Ford wheels, a platform, and a handle to pull it down the road. We follow the girls running away; suddenly, two Indians block their path. The camera stops—the perambulator stops—and this accentuates the girls' surprise.

Tourneur saw all the rushes. He could be very blunt. The first raspberry I ever heard came from Maurice Tourneur—and when I heard it, I knew it meant a retake.

Toward the end of production, we ran out of money. The directors of Associated Producers trooped out to Universal and I told them it would take another twenty-five thousand dollars to finish. I ran them all the material and then, and only then, did they vote me the money to complete the picture. It proved to be the only financial success Associated Producers ever had.

After Tourneur, I went to work with Brulatour. Jules Brulatour financed many of Tourneur's pictures. He had a controlling interest in the Eastman Kodak Company, and his star was Hope Hampton. Tourneur and Brulatour had a fight. Tourneur refused to direct Miss Hampton again, and he split with Brulatour, who virtually finished him in the picture business at that time. He had to get out and fend for himself. Brulatour took Jack Gilbert to New York to direct— and I went too. I made *The Light in the Dark,* with Hope Hampton, Lon Chaney, and E. K. Lincoln. It had an idea that intrigued me, but it was a dog. It was awful. Don't let's talk about it.

While I was with Brulatour, I did tests on Kodak's color system. This was around 1922. We built what I'll term a camera obscura, for want of something better. It was a room lined with glazed cardboard paper, white to reflect light. On one side was a bank of incandescent lights. With the light coming from one point, the reflected light gave us the halftones. Hope Hampton made a beautiful color subject.

My next assignment was a thing called *Don't Marry for Money,* with House Peters and Rubye de Remer, for Preferred. From there I signed a contract with

Universal and made five hits in a row: *The Acquittal, The Signal Tower, Butterfly, Smouldering Fires,* and *The Goose Woman.*

For *The Signal Tower,* we took over a railroad in northern California and worked among the big trees for six weeks. Ben Reynolds was my cameraman. We used to get up at five a.m. and shoot the locomotive climbing the gradient, with the sun coming up and the steam mingling with the trees . . . it was just beautiful. We made everything on location, even the interiors of the signal tower, which I had built at a switch track. When it got too bright outside we fitted amber glass in the windows to balance the exposure.

The whole railroad was ours. They had one train a day. Once we let that through, it was our set. I had a terrific wreck in the picture, when the train broke loose at the top of the mountain and came down wide open.

Pauline Frederick, who took the lead in *Smouldering Fires,* went through the worst attack of stagefright I ever witnessed. She had been a great Broadway star and had made a number of pictures. Her last real success had been *Madame X* (1920). The first two days on this one I thought she was going to give up. But she was a great artist and she pulled through bravely. When I made *This Modern Age* (1931) she came over to play Joan Crawford's mother.

It was *Smouldering Fires* that got me my contract with Norma Talmadge. John Considine was then working with Joe Schenck; one night he had nothing to do, so he dropped into the Forum Theater, Los Angeles. He didn't even know what picture was playing. He came in after the titles, and he thought Lubitsch had made it—until he saw the credits—"A Clarence Brown production directed by Clarence Brown."

He called me on the phone the next day and started talking about a contract. I was in the middle of *The Goose Woman.* I think I got twelve thousand five hundred dollars a picture for the five pictures I made at Universal. I jumped to three thousand dollars a week with Schenck.

The Goose Woman, with Louise Dresser, Jack Pickford, and Constance Bennett, was a Rex Beach story about a goose woman who was once a famous opera singer. She accidentally involves her son in a murder just to see her name hit the headlines again. Rex Beach got his inspiration from the Hall-Mills murder, one of the most famous trials in New Jersey—the woman implicated in that was a pig woman.

We had to search the whole of California and New Mexico to get enough geese for the picture. I even broadcast an appeal on the radio. We bought the Goose Woman's cottage off in the country somewhere; it had been lived in and it looked great. We moved the whole thing to the Universal backlot for our set.

Louise Dresser was great as the Goose Woman. I paid her three hundred and fifty dollars a week. I used her again as Queen Catherine in *The Eagle,* for Schenck, and this time I paid her three thousand a week!

A year after *The Goose Woman* was released, a murder was committed exactly like the one in the picture, when Marc MacDermott was shot dead at his front gate. The only difference was that the real victim was shot against his garage door.

The picture I did for Norma Talmadge, *Kiki,* in which she starred with Ronald Colman, was pretty good. Norma was the greatest pantomimist that ever drew breath. She was a natural-born comic; you could turn on a scene with her and she'd go on for five minutes without stopping or repeating herself. She was a tragedy of talking pictures. *Mme. Du Barry* with a Brooklyn accent wasn't too convincing and she never made another film.

With Schenck, I also made *The Eagle,* a Russian story with Valentino, Louise Dresser, and Vilma Banky. There was one elaborate effect shot I did in that; a long track down a banquet table. The camera started with a character (James Marcus) eating at one end. Then it traveled along the middle of the table, past all the other occupants, right the full length of the table—which must have been sixty feet long. To get the camera in that position was very difficult; no equipment existed to do it. So we made two perambulators. We put one on each side of the table and we constructed a bridge, with stressbeams so that it was rigid. Then we dropped a crosspiece and fastened the camera from the top, so that the bottom of the camera could travel along the top of the table. Of course, nothing could obstruct the movement of the camera, so we had prop boys putting candelabra in place just before the camera picked them up. I liked the effect so well I did it again in *Anna Karenina.*

I have had the opportunity and the pleasure and the good luck to direct the two people I consider were the greatest personalities of the screen—Rudolph Valentino and Greta Garbo. You'll be hearing about Valentino, who's been dead for forty years, and you'll be hearing about Garbo from now on as you have in the past. See how many of the other big stars are remembered in ten years. Garbo and Valentino are the two who are going down through posterity.

Flesh and the Devil was my first picture for Metro-Goldwyn-Mayer, and it really made Garbo. It also triggered off the Garbo-Gilbert romance.

Greta Garbo had something that nobody ever had on the screen. Nobody. I don't know whether she even knew she had it, but she did. And I can explain it in a few words.

I would take a scene with Garbo—pretty good. I would take it three or four times. It was pretty good, but I was never quite satisfied. When I saw that same scene on the screen, however, it had something that it just didn't have on the set.

Garbo had something behind the eyes that you couldn't see until you photographed it in close-up. You could see thought. If she had to look at one person with jealousy, and another with love, she didn't have to change her expression. You could see it in her eyes as she looked from one to the other. And nobody else has been able to do that on the screen. Garbo did it without the command of the English language.

For me, Garbo starts where they all leave off. She was a shy person; her lack of English gave her a slight inferiority complex. I used to direct her very quietly. I never gave her a direction above a whisper. Nobody on the set ever knew what I said to her; she liked that. She hated to rehearse. She would have preferred to stay away until everyone else was rehearsed, then come in and do the scene. But you can't do that—particularly in talking pictures.

We could never get her to look at the rushes, and I don't think she ever looked at any of her pictures until many years later. When sound arrived, we had a projector on the set. This projector ran backward and forward so that we could match scenes and check continuity.

When you run a talking picture in reverse, the sound is like nothing on earth.

That's what Garbo enjoyed. She would sit there shaking with laughter, watching the film running backward and the sound going *yakablom-yakablom*. But as soon as we ran it forward, she wouldn't watch it.

She took her work seriously, though. Her attitude was this; she came on the set at nine, made up and ready for work. She worked hard. At five thirty or six, when she was done, she was through. That was it. There was always a signal on the set—her maid would come in and hand her a glass of water. She would then say good night and go home. And when she was outside the studio, she wanted her life to remain her own. She didn't think her privacy belonged to the public. She used to say: "I give them everything I've got on the screen—why do they try to usurp my privacy?"

Greta Garbo did the greatest thing for a company that any star, living or dead, has ever done. She had a fanatical following in the United States, but unfortunately all those fans were not enough. Her pictures opened to bigger grosses than any other pictures we handled, but they didn't hold the extended run. Once the fanaticism was over, the box-office takings went way down.

On the other hand, in Europe, Garbo was queen. Over there, Garbo was first, second, third, and fourth. In 1942, M-G-M made a picture called *Two-Faced Woman,* but it wasn't rated very highly. Number one, that scared Garbo. Number two, the war started, the European market was virtually finished, and her American takings fell.

Under the terms of her contract, M-G-M were obliged to pay her whether they made another picture or not—win, lose, or draw. The company couldn't afford to make another Garbo film without the vital European market, and she understood the situation. She went to Mr. Mayer and released him from the contract for two hundred and fifty thousand dollars. She never took a nickel of the rest of the money she was entitled to under the contract. Is there a motion-picture star in the world who would do that? I wouldn't. But that's Garbo . . .

Flesh and the Devil was for a long time a favorite of mine—until I saw it recently at the Cinémathèque, Paris. They must have run it at the so-called silent speed of 16 f.p.s. or they must have stretch-printed it—printed every frame twice to make it run slower at sound speed. It was miserably slow. The tempo was completely destroyed, and I was sitting there, sweating. Originally the tempo was perfect.

I had a montage in that film of John Gilbert leaving South Africa to return to Germany. It started with a shot of Gilbert on horseback, and I synchronized the beat of the hoofs with Felicitas, which was the name of the girl Garbo was playing. Fe-li-ci-tas . . . Fe-li-ci-tas . . . I superimposed short cuts of the title over the picture, much as they do today for foreign-language films. From the hoofs hitting the sod, we went to a steamer, and the pistons seemed to be saying "Fe-li-ci-tas . . . Fe-li-ci-tas . . ." A double exposure also gave a close-up of Garbo's face. In the train, he's getting more excited at the thought of seeing her; *clucketty-cluck, clucketty-cluck*—Fe-licit-as . . . Fe-licit-as. Each cut was faster as the method of transportation became faster.

Flesh and the Devil had a horizontal love scene—one of the first. Toward the end of the scene, Gilbert, playing Garbo's lover, throws a cigarette out of the window. Marc MacDermott, playing Garbo's husband, is getting out of a cab when the cigarette falls at his feet. He looks up at the window, so the audience

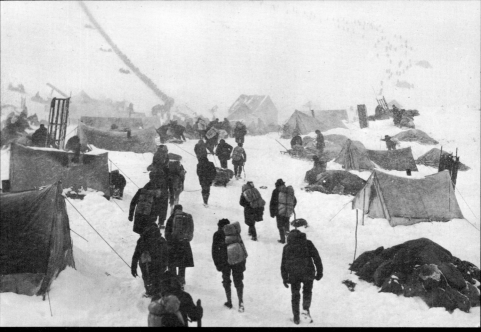

The Chilkoot Pass from The Trail of '98 *(1928).*

Greta Garbo and John Gilbert in Flesh and the Devil *(1926).*

knows he's prepared for something. When he bursts in on them and finds them in this compromising position on the couch, I put the camera down by Mac-Dermott's hand. I shot through his fingers at Garbo and Gilbert as he clenched his fist over them.

MacDermott challenges Gilbert to a duel. I shot this in silhouette. The two men start back to back, then they walk out of picture. There are two bursts of smoke from each side of screen. We dissolve out to a shot over Garbo's shoulder as she tries on a black hat in a millinery shop. In her hand is a handkerchief with a black border. She has a slight smile on her face. That's how we told who was shot—without a subtitle or any other sort of explanation.

They put a happy ending on *Flesh and the Devil*—I had to shoot it and it killed me. When we ran it in Paris, I told them to cut it off.

I look back on my second M-G-M film, *Trail of '98,* with mixed emotions. It wasn't too hot. Storywise, directionwise, and actingwise I was never too happy with it. It was just one of those conglomerates.

I was a year making it, and I lost twenty pounds. It was my toughest assignment. It was the story of the great Klondike Gold Rush, and to duplicate the Chilkoot Pass we used a location at the Great Divide, about sixty miles outside Denver, 11,600 feet with temperatures as low as sixty below zero. And I had to have two thousand extra people up there—from a town like Denver! But we got it. We duplicated the Chilkoot Pass. Old sourdoughs who saw the picture thought it was the real thing.

John Seitz was my cameraman—he was one of the greatest. Harry Carey was wonderful in it, but I had a lousy leading man. We went to Alaska to do the rapids scenes, and we lost three men up there. When I left Denver, part of the company stayed behind. A large section of snow fell and two or three more men were killed. It was a tough picture. Oh God, it was tough.

At night, you'd look at a mountain and the snow would be covering the peak. The next morning, that mountain would be dry and the snow would be on the next peak. Fifty- to sixty-mile-an-hour winds had moved the whole lot over during the night. That's the kind of weather we had.

We lived in a train. We had about a hundred and twenty-four altogether in the company, with six Pullman cars and two diners. At the Pass was the highest railroad in the country—on the old Denver—Rio Grande, which ran out of Denver and right over the top of the mountain. At the top they had snowsheds.

The first night we spent in the snowsheds, I nearly went out of my head. I woke up in the middle of the night, almost suffocated by the fumes from the engine and the smoke pouring in from other trains passing through. I tried to get some air, but I couldn't find a way out. I'll never forget that experience.

When we came to the scenes with the two thousand people climbing up the Chilkoot Pass, we built a track parallel to their route and built a sled for our cameras. We lashed three cameras to the sled, with three different lenses. At the top was a power windlass, which could be controlled by signals from the camera, so that we were able to follow people up, stop, go back, and take close-ups of the incidents that happened on the way up.

As luck would have it, the railroad ran from the lower slopes of the pass and went around it, emerging again on the level at the top of the pass. This was of great assistance logistically.

We went through the city of Denver and picked up derelicts off the streets—tramps, people who were broke, and people who were starving. We got them to the railroad station ready to leave at two in the morning. During the trip to the Great Divide, which took about four hours, the assistants clothed them. Now this is two thousand people—they put rubber boots on them, heavy underwear, heavy socks, mackinaws, and dressed them just as they would have been at the time of the Gold Rush. They were given their breakfast en route.

The train arrived at eight a.m. As they got off, we handed them their packs and steered them so that they had to climb the pass. Our cameras were all set and rehearsed, and I had telephones to each of the three or four camera locations. By the time they reached the top, and we had got what we wanted, it was two p.m. We picked them up in the train and fed them on the way to Denver.

But we had a problem. We needed them for a second day of shooting. We couldn't bring them back the following day—they didn't get back to Denver until eight p.m. So we had to skip a day—we gave them a call for the second day at two a.m. We probably lost twenty per cent, but it didn't matter so much because by then I had all my long shots.

We worked at eleven thousand six hundred feet for five weeks. I had to send a number of people down; they just couldn't take it. We couldn't walk fast, we couldn't run—we could hardly do anything at that altitude. We had little oil lamps on the cameras, with pipes fitted to the interior, to prevent the mechanism from freezing and to control static. [Static was a bugbear at that time; the intense cold caused electrostatic flashes to register on the film. Moving through the metal camera gate the film built up its own electricity.] Some of our scenes were just streaked with static.

Trail of '98 was the hardest picture I ever made. The next hardest was *The Yearling;* instead of fighting cold we were fighting heat—in the middle of Florida, in the summertime.

A Woman of Affairs, with Greta Garbo, John Gilbert, and Dorothy Sebastian, was my last silent picture. [Clarence Brown also remade most of *The Cossacks,* with John Gilbert and Renee Adoree, but did not seek a credit. Direction was attributed to George Hill, who had made the original.]

The talkies had already arrived, and John Gilbert went completely ham in the middle of shooting, demonstrating what he was going to do in his first sound film. He began speaking the titles with great flamboyance.

He wasn't alone in this. Many other actors—particularly those with stage experience—went back to that melodramatic, expansive-gesture stuff. Well, I was never on the stage. I knew nothing about that type of acting. I only knew what was human and what I saw in real life.

We taught the Broadway stage how to act. They used to come on the set, those stage actors, and throw their voices up to the gallery. Whenever I had to direct a New York stage actor, I did an imitation of him.

"This is how you're playing it," I would say. "Is this how a human being behaves? You're talking to me when you make a scene. It's intimate. The camera is there, and I'm here, right beside it. But you're projecting yourself way out to an audience."

I would never impose a performance on an actor, however. That was one of the troubles with Lubitsch's pictures. He was one of the greatest directors, but every player that ever worked for him played Ernst Lubitsch. He used to show them how to do everything, right down to the minutest detail. He would take a cape, and show the star how to put it on. He supplied all the little movements. He was magnificent, because he knew his art better than anybody. But his actors followed his performance. They had no chance to give one of their own.

If I hire a star at three thousand dollars a week, he's supposed to know something. In talking pictures, he'll know his lines better than the director does. He knows his scenes. So you're ready to start, with a loaded gun.

In silent pictures, nine times out of ten an actor didn't know what he was going to do when he came on the set. Everything was transmitted by the director. So you needed good actors.

I want everything an actor knows. If it's a woman, she'll know more about playing a woman than I know. I want to get her angle on the picture. So I always rehearse without giving a word of direction. I follow them around, and watch, and listen, and I get their interpretation first.

If their interpretation doesn't agree with the one I have in mind, then we begin to talk. A little shading here, a little shading there, a few quiet directions—"Come down . . . you're going overboard there . . . that's a little better . . . that's fine"— and by the time we're through we've got a pretty good scene. Sometimes it can be a composite scene, made up of ideas by everyone on the set. If an extra man

Brown, on the platform with William Daniels, directing Garbo and John Gilbert in A Woman of Affairs *(1928).*

comes up and says, "Mr. Brown, I just don't feel natural doing that," then I want to know why. When we've found the reason, we'll get it right.

If we couldn't get it right, we kept at it. I fought schedules all the time. I shot till I got it right. I can't make anything unless it's the best that I can do. Until I got that I kept going and I'd get holy hell from the front office. But they knew I'd come up with a good picture, so they put up with me.

I'm a perfectionist. I can only do it one way. That way may be terrible, but at the time I think it's great. A lot of the time it isn't good—but equally often, it is.

I couldn't make a quickie if my life depended on it. How Woody Van Dyke could shoot a picture in twenty days is beyond me. I marvel at it.

Occasionally I would go and see my own pictures at public theaters—and sometimes I would sneak out before they began. At M-G-M we previewed our pictures three, four, or five times. That allowed the producer to put his finger in the pie. The audience filled in their reactions on special cards, but I didn't need cards to tell me how they reacted. I can sit in on an audience and read them just from their actions. I'd hear a cough in one scene and my ears would prick up. My heart would start beating . . . "Here it comes—here it comes." Maybe that's the only cough, which would be fine. But maybe it would spread, and half a dozen people would start coughing. And that's when I put my mark against the scene; there's something wrong with it somewhere. I've lost the audience. Sometimes you'd get an audience that had grown accustomed to previews; they had become so professional that the preview was not worthwhile.

Now I see a picture of mine on television, cut from an hour and ten minutes down to forty-five minutes. At the point where you've got to see what happens next, up comes a commercial for underarm deodorant. Then they go back to the picture. Well, I don't. That's it. Commercials every five minutes stretch the length to two and a half hours, and kill every effect. Unless you can start a picture at the beginning and go through the end, there's no point in seeing it.

My favorite silent picture? I would have said *Flesh and the Devil,* but after that Paris show I'm not going to open my mouth about it again! Of talking pictures, I would pick *The Human Comedy, Intruder in the Dust, National Velvet, The Yearling,* and maybe *Song of Love,* which was the only thing I had to do with music in the picture business.

There were many directors I admired. If I like a picture, I shout about it, and if I don't like it, I shout too. I admired Griffith, Lubitsch, Murnau . . . Murnau! There was a great talent. When I saw that set he built at Arrowhead for *Sunrise.* I crawled over it for a day and a half. It was wonderful. We all felt he was great. Von Stroheim was a genius, and a very close friend of mine. He had only one fault; every sequence in one of his pictures was as important as every other sequence. He made a five-reel picture out of every scene. He didn't know how to space, how to get to the climaxes to keep the story going. Everything had to be meticulously accurate from start to finish. When they cut his picture from twenty-one reels down to eight or nine, it wasn't a picture any more. But in twenty-one reels, it was one of the greatest masterpieces ever made.

I admired Victor Seastrom greatly; he was a fine man. I visited him in Stockholm shortly before he died. I was going to do *The Wind,* which he finally did. I worked on the script, but then got cold feet. People just don't *like* wind!

Sidney Franklin was a good director—good producer, too. Too good; he overemphasized goodness. He was beyond perfection in his work. He was a wonderful talent, and the closest friend I have in the picture business.

Inevitably, however, I come back to Maurice Tourneur. Everything he did, I did. It wasn't inborn in me at all. Anything I have has rubbed off on me.

He had only one failing in his pictures—he was cold. He had no heart. Sometimes he would ask me to retake a scene.

"What is the matter with it?" I'd ask. "It looks all right to me."

"That's the way I wanted it," he'd say. "But it's no good. You do it."

So I'd get the actors in a corner of the set and we'd talk and kid around awhile. Then we'd take the scene again, the same way as he had taken it. But now it had a little something that it didn't have before—warmth.

I went over to France around 1948 and called on him while he was working at Joinville studios. In 1952, I returned. In the meantime he had had an automobile accident. A suitcase fell from the top of his car into the road while he was driving. He pulled off to the side, and ran out into the road to pick it up.

When I saw him again he had had his leg amputated, and he was fitted with a pegleg he could hardly walk on. Finally, he became bedridden.

In August 1961 I was in St. Moritz when he passed on. I came over to Paris and buried him and that was it.

I owe everything I've got in the world to Maurice Tourneur. Now I'm through with the business. I've finished my work. I lead an entirely different life. I haven't seen two pictures in ten years. Why? Well, I'm like an old fire horse that still races off when he hears the fire bell. If I see a picture and it's bad, I'm okay. But if it's good, the old instincts start working and I want to go racing off and get back to work.

13 / THE LOST WORK OF EDWARD SLOMAN

Archives are short of space and desperately short of money. They do their best to preserve films of accepted importance and films by well-known directors. But they cannot gamble. They cannot afford to waste space or risk funds on unknown films by unknown directors.

So the work of men like Edward Sloman has largely vanished. The National Film Archive, which has inherited many complete collections, and thus preserves many surprising items, has a copy of Sloman's *The Ghost of Rosie Taylor* (1918). The Museum of Modern Art has a few reels of *Shattered Idols*. Otherwise, his name has been forgotten; it appears in none of the history books, and Sloman himself has retired into obscurity.

I became interested in the work of Edward Sloman after acquiring a rare print of *Surrender* (1927), a Universal picture which marked the only American appearance of Ivan Mosjoukine. The story of *Surrender*, based on Alexander Brody's play *Lea Lyon*, is improbably melodramatic, but the direction is remarkable. It suggests the work of one of the more flamboyant continental imports—Paul Fejos, perhaps, or Dmitri Buchowetski—while preserving a very American smoothness of narrative.

Mosjoukine, a Russian star who achieved fame in his own country before the Revolution, and in France after it, plays an aristocratic Russian officer. He is first seen hunting in a forest. He catches sight of game, and raises his gun. Dissolve to close-up of his eyes as they squint down the barrel . . . dissolve to a closeshot of his dog, straining at the alert . . . dissolve to Mosjoukine's viewpoint, as he sights down the barrel of the gun. The camera gently tracks forward down the barrel, and settles on a close-up of a squirrel sitting in a tree. Cut back to Mosjoukine, who grins and lowers his gun. The squirrel darts away. The dog rushes off, but ignores the squirrel, and returns with a shoe. Intrigued, Mosjoukine discovers Mary Philbin paddling in a stream nearby.

Such inventive camerawork (the cameraman was Gilbert Warrenton) was time-consuming and expensive, so *Surrender* does not outdo this sequence. But there are other good scenes; the atmosphere of a village on the Austro-Hungarian border is beautifully evoked, the reality heightened by an intelligent use of the long-focus lens. The Russian invasion is extremely well done; two peasants are plowing a field on the outskirts of the village. One of them stops to mop his brow—and he catches sight of a column of infantry on the horizon. Feverishly, the peasants unshackle the horse and then both of them leap on its back. As they gallop into town, shouting the news, shots of advancing troops are intercut with shots of unsuspecting villagers. Again, Sloman makes effective use of Warrenton's camera dissolves as the glamorous Cossack cavalry advance force mixes through to the dust-covered, shambling infantry.

The Ghost of Rosie Taylor, made nine years earlier, suggests that many of the most attractive elements of *Surrender* were Sloman's stock-in-trade. Once again, the atmosphere of a European market town is beautifully evoked, and once again the approach is good-humored and full of charm. Mary Miles Minter, the star, plays a similar role to Mary Philbin's at the beginning of *Surrender,* and her relationship to her father, George Periolat, is shown in the same amusing light. But this time there are no melodramatics; despite its early date, 1918, *Rosie Taylor* needs no excuses. It is convincing, fast-moving, and expertly directed.

The film opens with a teaser scene, anticipating the modern television approach;

Mary Philbin in Surrender.

Edward Sloman with Ivan Mosjoukine, and authentic Russian extras, during the making of Surrender (1927).

some society ladies meet, and one thanks another for recommending Rosie Taylor, "a most excellent domestic."

"But," says the other, astonished, "Rosie Taylor is dead!"

"Impossible. Rosie Taylor, or her ghost, has been cleaning house for me."

They decide to investigate. The house certainly seems haunted; a mysterious white shape floats across the window . . . there is the sound of chains (suggested visually with skeletal hands rattling a chain) . . . and a song that Rosie Taylor always sang. Horror! The women flee in terror from the house.

The film flashes back to France, and introduces us to Mary Miles Minter, coping with her aged father, hopeful young men, and general chaos in the market. The film traces her voyage to America after the death of her father, her weeks of poverty, and the discovery of a letter—a letter of recommendation for one Rosie Taylor. For the French girl, it brings a new life.

Perhaps the most striking element of the treatment is its fast, parellel-action editing. When Mary Miles Minter sees the letter, which a garbage man accidentally drops in front of her, she leans forward to pick it up. Sloman cuts to her room; her landlady is knocking on the door for the rent. Cut back to the letter being opened; there is money in the envelope. Cut to the landlady clearing out the girl's baggage.

The cutting is rhythmic, swift, and informative. The existing archive print is damaged by deterioration, so it is sometimes hard to judge Ira H. Morgan's photography, but the exteriors are beautiful.

Mary Miles Minter, perhaps Mary Pickford's closest rival, was nowhere near such a fine actress; her performance rested with the skill of the director. It is to Sloman's credit that all the performances are consistently good, enlivened by frequent flashes of invention.

I wrote to Sloman, care of the Screen Directors Guild, Hollywood. I had heard he was still living in California, but had no idea where. Nor had the Screen Directors Guild. They returned the letter marked Unknown; scribbled alongside was the suggestion "Try Screen Actors Guild."

Sloman *had* been an actor, but not for fifty years. I tried some of his old colleagues, but they had also lost touch. Finally, Alfred Lunt, who had worked with him on *Backbone* (1923; Lunt's first screen appearance), remembered hearing of him recently. "He was a very good director," recalled Lunt, "and a dear man. *The Daily News* sent me a clipping, something he'd written about me after a television show we did. It was charming. He was such a good director."

Thanks to Alfred Lunt's information, I eventually made contact.

"So-o-o-o, here I am!" Sloman wrote back. "But I'm afraid there isn't much to tell. I've been out of the motion-picture business since 1939, when I entered radio as writer, producer, director—and *banker!*

"I got quite a glow out of your mentioning Alfred Lunt, James Morrison, Patsy Ruth Miller, Gilbert Warrenton, and others I worked with who remember me. All of them are part of so many happy memories. Do you realize that an actor and/or director, at my advanced years, practically lives on memories? It's so nice to know that someone remembers and appreciates the hard work and dreams that went into one's efforts in those struggling days of the motion-picture art. Or is it a business? Perhaps both."

Edward Sloman was born in 1885, in the Harrow Road, Bayswater, London. He spent his youth in the East End; his family was Jewish. He left England when he was nineteen, and began his theatrical career in 1909.

"For several years I earned a precarious living as an actor, and later as a director in stock and vaudeville. In a sketch entitled *Gringoire* (a name for François Villon) I played that funny, old, sly King Louis XI; years later, the leading lady, Hylda Hollis, became my wife.

"After a season in vaudeville, in a comedy sketch of our own, we fell out of favor with United Booking Offices. We listened to the persuasion of a character actress friend who was working in Hollywood, and we left for California. I was introduced to Universal's top director, Wilfred Lucas. Our actress friend had evidently given me a tremendous send-off [recommendation] and I was immediately engaged as leading man to the star, Cleo Madison, at the munificent sum of seven dollars and fifty cents per day. Lucas kept me working every day except Sunday, so the pay wasn't too bad for 1915, although we had earned ten times as much in vaudeville.

"An early picture was *The Severed Hand.* I remember it both for its title (ugh!) and for the fact that I had to carry my leading lady, who weighed a hundred and thirty pounds, up a specially built flight of twenty stairs, murmuring sweet nothings in her ear, yet!"

While acting in pictures, Sloman began writing scenarios and selling them for twenty-five dollars per reel. His wife appeared in one- and two-reelers by such directors as Allan Dwan and Joseph de Grasse, so their combined earnings reached an impressive sum. But Sloman was not satisfied. He demanded sixty dollars a week, was refused, and quit.

Fortunately, he was by now well known in Hollywood and he quickly landed other parts. He wrote a feature-length story, a war subject, and submitted it to his old director Burton King. King turned it down, and Thomas Ince bought it for four hundred and fifty dollars, one of the highest prices so far paid for an original. Ince, exercising characteristic prudence, managed to make four separate pictures from four incidents in the story.

Sloman was hired by Lubin's West Coast studios at Coronado as their one and only director—at a hundred dollars a week.

"My first picture was called *Saved From the Harem.* We sailed a real battleship, discharged a full complement of sailors in white battle dress, who charged up the beach with rifles at the ready. The U.S. Navy to the rescue!"

One of the two-reelers Sloman made at Lubin, in 1915, was a modern version of *Faust.* Besides directing, Sloman played Mephistopheles, in a dress suit.

"I was stuck over a scene in which Faust is changed from a ragged old man into a handsome youth, and is transported from a hovel to a glittering palace. Then I had an idea. I got the carpenter to make a platform, with four bicycle wheels. We mounted the camera and the cameraman on this traveling platform and started to photograph old man Faust, in a full-length shot. We moved toward him, refocusing all the time, until we came to a full head close-up. Then we started the dissolve. We marked the head close-up in the camera finder, and sent Mr. Faust to change his make-up to the handsome youth. Meanwhile, the hovel set was changed to the palace. The rejuvenated Faust returned to his former position, the other

George Sidney in We Americans *(1928).*

The Foreign Legion *(1928),* ***directed by Edward Sloman.***

half of the dissolve was started, and the camera pulled back to the full-length shot—disclosing Faust, impeccably dressed, standing before a huge fireplace. Presto!

"After some other one- and two-reelers, the studio head insisted that I star in all my films from then on. Three or fourth months of this were exhausting. I lost thirty pounds. Then he cut the lunch hours in half, and I quit.

"I went over to the Flying A studios in Santa Barbara, California, and directed five-reelers with Franklyn Ritchie, William Russell, and Mary Miles Minter.

"*The Ghost of Rosie Taylor,* with Mary Miles Minter, was not one of my mightiest efforts. I didn't like the story, and I didn't like the star. Mary Miles Minter was quite young then—sixteen—and very beautiful. Without doubt, she was the best-looking youngster I ever saw, and the lousiest actress.

"We rehearsed one scene all morning, but she didn't seem to get it. Finally, knowing she wasn't doing so well, she said, 'You do it—just as you think I ought to do it.'

"You can imagine a hulking, thirty-year-old six-footer playing the part of an ingenue—but I did it. And you know what she said after I finished?

" 'You're crazy! I can't do that!'

"I had to rewrite it so she could.

"I did several pictures with her, but was never happy with any of them. When Mary Pickford left Paramount, they immediately signed M.M.M. in her place at an unusually high salary. They got in touch with me to direct her—at a figure I never dreamed of. But the script was terrible—I never read a worse one. That was the end of my connection with M.M.M. Finally, they shot the impossible script, but the picture was never shown and the director was fired.

"The director of today yells to his staff, 'I need this—I want that.' The director of yesterday, if he wanted something special, often had to invent it.

"At that time, all night scenes were shot in daylight, and the positive tinted blue. No matter how blue, you always knew the scene was shot in daylight, and to me it was cheating. I tried something else. With the aid of a truck, half a dozen barrels of rainwater, a couple of pumps, some pierced pipes and flares, I made a series of medium close-ups of my leading man driving an auto through the streets of Santa Barbara at night, in a rainstorm."

Sloman made one of the first big feature westerns, *The Westerners,* in 1919 for Benjamin Hampton, a magazine publisher who was breaking into pictures. For J. L. Frothingham, he made a number of successful pictures, climaxed by *Shattered Idols.*

"This was highly rated, but it was the beginning of my undoing with one of the powerful producers. I had owned *Bride of the Gods,* the book from which *Shattered Idols* was made, and when this producer took over Frothingham's interests, I asked for payment for the story. He threatened that if I dared to sue he would blackball me out of the business. I dared and he blackballed. For two years, no one would hire me. So I made a picture on my own, with my own money, *The Last Hour,* with Milton Sills and Carmel Myers. C. C. Burr of Mastodon Pictures was to distribute it. I had a solid contract with him; it called for my receiving seventy-five per cent of all foreign sales. Among the many reprehensible things he did was to pawn the picture to a firm in England for a loan of ten thousand dollars. I never received a single cent from foreign sales.

"Eventually, I returned to Universal, and that love of a picture which brought me a five-year contract with Universal, *His People*. This is my favorite film, not because it was the best thing I'd done, but because it was such a sure-fire picture. I knew when I started that it was going to be a great hit. It was voted one of the ten best of that year; it cost ninety-three thousand dollars and netted three million."

This outstanding picture led to *Surrender*. Universal, anxious to repeat the success, considered that the one vital element was its ethnic background.

"The play *Lea Lyon* was a hardy annual of the German stage, being especially popular among the then considerable Jewish population of the principal cities. My boss, that forever old man Carl Laemmle, never gave up his native Germany; he used to spend several months there every year. He retained a warm spot in his heart for this creaky old play, since it showed how the Jews triumphed over their hated persecutors.

"Originally, I balked at doing the thing, but word came from Laemmle that Sloman *must* do the play. He himself adamantly cast Ivan Mosjoukine in the lead, over the objections of almost everyone at the studio. In spite of what the credit cards say, the script, good or bad, was all mine—every word. The name sharing the credit with me—Edward J. Montagne—was the head of the script department. He was put there for political reasons and to give me a free hand in the writing. We were troubled at that time by a bombastic, know-nothing studio manager, a former bookkeeper who only a few months before had never seen the inside— or the outside—of a movie studio.

"Mosjoukine was quite pleasant to work with, in a stand-offish sort of way. And he was rather a good actor, although he and his interpreter bothered hell out of me when it came to my giving him direction. He spoke not a word of English (or pretended not to) so I had to give the direction to the interpreter, which I did painstakingly. I would spend between five and eight minutes explaining what I wanted Mosjoukine to do. The interpreter would then relay my instructions in a few quick Russian syllables, which took him less than a minute.

"Time and again, I would ask, 'Did you tell him *everything* I told you?' And he would always reply, 'Oh, yes, Mr. Sloman, *everything!*' Evidently he did, because Mosjoukine would rehearse the scene just as I had visualized it.

"I really haven't a penchant for Jewish pictures. I've only done three, and these were forced on me by the powers that be because of the success of *His People*.

"*We Americans* was the other Jewish picture I did in the silent days. It had been a Broadway play, which starred an actor fresh from the Yiddish theater whom no one had heard of: Paul Muni.[1] He was very anxious to do the picture, but all we saw was a young man in the stage make-up of a middle-aged man, and we were afraid he wouldn't be convincing on the big screen. So we took George Sidney. Only a few years later, Muni became the biggest star on the Warner lot, celebrated for his make-ups."

Photoplay chose *We Americans* as one of the best pictures of the month, May 1928, and said that George Sidney and Albert Gran gave superb character dilineations.

"Much credit," *Photoplay* added, "must go to Edward Sloman, director, who is consistently making pictures above the average. This picture is of permanent value

[1] *Paul Muni was billed as Muni Wisenfrend; his real name was Muni Weisenfreund.*

(in the sense that *His People* and *His Country* are), and while highly entertaining to any audience, should make better citizens of us all."[2]

Sloman's method of direction was developed during his stage career.

"In those days, a stage director was also a teacher. There were very few schools where an aspirant could learn the rudiments of his art. So it was up to the director to tell him how to walk, to stand, to kneel, to enter and exit a door, and above all, to read—and the hundred and one other things he's supposed to do naturally and gracefully. I carried some of this over into pictures. I always believed in full and thorough rehearsals, and I augmented this by coaching the players while the camera was grinding.

"As a case in point, I once used a German actor who was an excellent type for an English country squire, but he was a very bad actor. I had to coach him in every little thing he did before the camera. On my next picture, *Butterflies in the Rain,* I needed a similar type. Everyone in the front office suggested the German actor. 'He played that part beautifully,' said they. I refused. 'He didn't play that part,' I said. '*I* played it!'

"On the other hand, directing Rudolph Schildkraut was a marvelous experience. I'd talk to him from behind the camera. If he was playing too broadly, I'd call to him, 'Tighter, Poppa, tighter,' and his control over his amazing technique was so perfect that, without losing the sense of the scene, he would diminish the overplaying and ease the action into perfect balance. Whatever you planned with Schildkraut always came off—sometimes even better than you'd dreamed it. Rudolph Schildkraut was one of the great actors of his era.

"I'm sure the early days in pictures were much more glamorous, much more romantic, much more soul-stirring, and much more edifying than anything today's directors can experience. We planned, and tried to create, something *new*. In many instances, we actually *did* create something new. And by so doing, we grew with the art."

[2] Photoplay, *May 1928, p. 53.*

14 / WILLIAM WELLMAN

The inadequacy of film preservation organizations is highlighted by the case of William Wellman. The early career of this director has, over the years, been practically obliterated. *Wings* was rescued by the Cinémathèque française, and *Beggars of Life* by the George Eastman Museum. But apart from these, no other examples of Wellman's silent work survive.

His career is associated almost exclusively with the sound era—and pictures of the quality of *Public Enemy, A Star Is Born,* and *The Ox-bow Incident*—yet Wellman started in the industry as long ago as 1918. He had been a flyer with the Lafayette Flying Corps. and an actor with Douglas Fairbanks.

But acting was an occupation contrary to his aggressively masculine nature. After two pictures he switched to the production side, and assisted such directors as T. Hayes Hunter, Clarence Badger, E. Mason Hopper, and Bernard Durning.

"Bernie Durning gave me my first chance to direct," he told me. "He was six feet six, and besides being a director he was an actor—and a bad one. He was the handsomest guy I've ever seen in my life. He took me on because he liked me. He said there were only two things he insisted upon; one was loyalty, which he knew he'd get from me, the other was no women—never to fool around with any of the dames on the picture. I made one mistake. Now he was a big man, but I was in pretty good shape, and I wasn't going to let a guy kick the hell out of me for not doing something. He took me into Buck Jones's dressing room; I broke chairs over his head and slugged him and everything else. But he still cooled me off in no uncertain way; he picked me up and dropped me in a chair, and he said: "Listen you son of a bitch, get some meat and put it on that eye of yours, and you'll be on that set tomorrow morning. Because, look, I need you . . . I *need* you." And then he told me why—he told me about this sickness that he had. Well, good Christ, I'd have committed murder for this guy. He gave me two of the greatest years I've ever had, and taught me more than anybody in the business. He made all those thrilling melodramas, *The Fast Mail* [1922], *The Eleventh Hour* [1923], and you learned everything from them—action, pacing, stunts. This was the greatest school a director ever had.

"When we were down at San Diego, doing some air stuff at North Island, he got one of his attacks. He called me up and told me he was in bed. 'It's all yours, Willie,' he said. I went out and shot that stuff, and saved a day on schedule. When it was all over, we went back to the Fox studio, and Winnie Sheehan and Sol Wurtzel, who were running the place, ran the stuff in the projection room. None of the cast or technicians had said anything about Bernie being off the picture— they loved him too much. But he was there in the theater, and when it was all over he unwound himself and stood up. And, goddam it, he stood high. 'How do you like that stuff?' he asked the two guys.

" 'Bernie,' they said, 'it's as good as—if not better than—anything you've got in your other pictures. Congratulations.'

" 'Congratulations hell,' he said. 'I was on a little trip I make every once in a while—and I was in bed all the time. Wellman did it; make him a director. And by the way, Dustin [Dustin Farnum the western star] is crazy about him and so am I.' Then he walked out of the room and they made me a director right then and there."

Shortly afterward, Durning died—from typhoid fever. Wellman directed a number of Dustin Farnum westerns, was promoted to Buck Jones pictures, and

Wings *in production: 1927.*

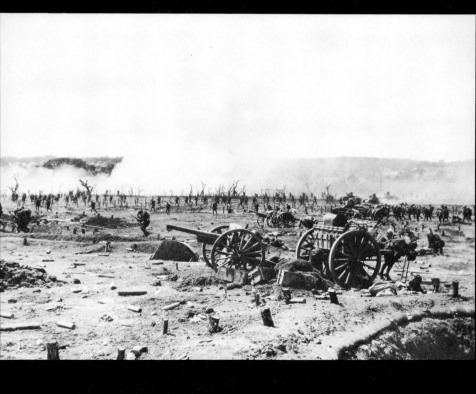

was fired by Fox when he asked for a raise. Eighteen months without work—and then he made a film in three and a half days for Harry Cohn. Cohn was then a poverty-row producer, and he offered Wellman a job at two hundred dollars a week. B. P. Schulberg, another independent producer, head of Preferred Pictures, saw Wellman's quickie, liked it, and offered two hundred and ten dollars a week. When Schulberg joined Paramount as the head of their West Coast studio, Wellman went with him. His first assignment was *The Cat's Pajamas*—"one of the most horrible pictures ever made," says Wellman—with which he was instructed to bring Betty Bronson, star of *Peter Pan,* from her youthful roles into maturity with an adult part in a sophisticated comedy.

"When they saw the picture, they decided I was no good and they were going to let me go. But Schulberg had to keep me, and the next one they gave me was *You Never Know Women.* I sort of bounced back on that one. Then I got *Wings.*"

Wings (1927) is one of the most excitingly directed war pictures of any period. Spectaculars have frequently attempted the same subject, but *Wings,* staged on an awesome scale, remains supreme. The story and the characterizations have not received the care and skill lavished on the action; the relationship between Charles "Buddy" Rogers and Richard Arlen is particularly hard to accept. But this is primarily an action picture, and death and destruction have seldom been more lyrically and sweepingly portrayed. The camera is in an aircraft for the most memorable scenes; the audience is given the vicarious thrill of shooting down balloons, engaging the enemy in a dogfight, bombing a village, machine-gunning columns of troops, and chasing and destroying a general's staff car. Normally such scenes are carefully staged within a confined area. The cameramen take care to avoid factories or roads which kill the illusion of a battlefront. But Wellman has half Texas and a whole army to play with. He can carelessly sweep across a five-mile radius and reveal nothing but battle-scarred countryside, columns of troops, and gun placements.

Wings and *You Never Know Women* both made flamboyant use of the moving camera, a style which Wellman adopted in the mid-twenties as it was becoming fashionable in Europe.

"Camera movement I loved—and then I got awfully sick of it. I did the first big boom shot in *Wings,* when the camera moved across the tables in the big French café set. Then everybody got on a boom, and both me and Jack Ford got right off. We both agreed we'd never use the thing again. There's too much movement. It makes some people dizzy—it really does, and they become more conscious of the camera movement than they are of what the hell you're photographing. I don't know what made me begin to move the camera around. I'd seen fights, and wanted to get closer to them, so I'd run forward. Then I thought I'd do that with a camera. But what I loved most was composition. I used to get some wonderful odd angles, but then everybody started odd angles—shooting through people's navels—so the idea was destroyed. Then I realized that the best thing was to make the picture the simplest way you could; if you wanted movement, or anything like that, use it where it really meant something, where it would help the picture. I used that theory completely in the last pictures I made."

Wellman's last picture was *Lafayette Escadrille* (1958). Since then his name has become shrouded in mystery, his reputation, particularly in England, resting on two infrequently revived pictures, *Public Enemy* and *The Ox-bow Incident*. But in 1965, new light was thrown on this neglected master when *Beggars of Life* was screened at the National Film Theatre. The original contained some sound effects and a song by Wallace Beery; this version, a sixteen-millimeter print loaned by the Danish Film Museum (originating from Eastman House) was silent throughout, and of a somewhat murky quality. Nevertheless, the rich, highly polished surface of technique gleamed through, revealing a style of astonishing elegance—an elegance which seemed out of place in such a picture.

Beggars of Life, with Louise Brooks and Richard Arlen, is a story of tramps, by the hobo writer Jim Tully. The customary freshness and unstudied casualness of most American silent films is replaced here by a dignified, carefully studied style, suggestive of the European cinema, and indicating a conscious striving toward artistry.

The American film makers produced their most satisfying results when they turned a picture out to the best of their ability, allowing for time and budget. When the European success began to disturb Hollywood, a penchant for artistry affected many of its directors. Their rough enthusiasm and vigorous pace were immobilized under treacly layers of respect. The sets and lighting became complex and studied, the pace slowed—and spontaneity began to give way to contemplation, and a meticulous care.

In Wellman's case, this did not destroy his natural flair for filmic storytelling. *Beggars of Life* is brilliantly thought out and superbly made. But this is the wrong subject to develop into a fine art; it is as though Jack London had borrowed the delicacy of Galsworthy to write *Call of the Wild*.

Wellman himself, whom I met in Brentwood, California, in 1964, is a true Jack London character. A colorful, vivid, and fascinating personality, he suggests an authentic figure of the Old West; tall and lean with a tough, weatherbeaten face and a voice exactly like John Wayne's, he is constantly on the move. Pacing about his Hollywood home, as restless as a caged lion, he described his career—emphatically declaring that he was sick of the "goddamned business." But from the way he talked about film, the way he described the problems of production, the excitement of direction and the triumph of success, it was obvious that he had a deep love for motion pictures—a love which soon eclipsed his contempt for the business itself.

WILLIAM WELLMAN: Most people think I was in the Lafayette Escadrille. I wasn't. I was in the Lafayette *Flying Corps,* which was a little different. The Escadrille was formed by a lot of crazy American guys who were either in the Ambulance Corps or in the French infantry—before America was in the war. This started something, and a lot of kids over here wanted to get into it. So the Lafayette Flying Corps was formed, an outgrowth of the Escadrille, and it was kind of hard to get into. You couldn't get into it out of prison, you know, you had to be a *fairly* decent kind of a kid, and have someone pay to get you abroad. I joined the Norton House Ambulance Corps, which was what you had to do, and that got me to Paris. There you had the choice of staying as an ambulance driver or joining the Foreign Legion attached to the French Air Corps, which in turn put you in the Lafayette Flying Corps.

The boom constructed for the remarkable Café de Paris sequence in **Wings**. *William Wellman lies on the platform. Harry Perry stands by the camera, which is mounted on an extension, below the boom, to enable it to glide over the tabletops. El Brendel and Richard Arlen are seated below.*

So that's what we all did. At one time there were two hundred and twenty-two of us in it, either training, or at the front, or dead. When you finished your training you were sent to Le Plessis-Belleville, just outside Paris, and there you had a few trips in a Spad, and you waited until some guy got bumped off in any of the sixty-odd escadrilles along the front. If your name was up, then you took his place. It was just a matter of luck.

I joined the Chat-Noir, the Black Cat Group, and was sent to Lunéville; I don't think they'd ever seen an American, much less hear one talk. I was nineteen. A guy named McGee joined us, and was killed in his first week, and then Tom Hitchcock, a great polo player, took his place, and Tom and I had a lot of luck together. When I got back to this country I joined the American Air Corps purely because I needed the dough. They made me an officer, and I was with them the last six months of the war. I was sent down to Rockwell Field, San Diego, and it was there that I got acquainted with some of the Hollywood people.

I'd known Doug Fairbanks from when he was playing at the Colonial Theatre, Boston; he used to watch me play ice hockey. He once sent me a wonderful cablegram, which I still have, saying that when the war was over, and if I needed a job, he had one for me. So I used to fly along the ocean and land in his backyard at Beverly Hills in a Spad, and spend weekends with him. I had a hell of a good time—met nearly everybody, Mary Pickford, Marion Davies. . . . I was a kid with some decorations, and a flyer, so I sort of fitted in. I had a limp that I used to exaggerate whenever I met a pretty girl. It depended entirely on how pretty she was as to how much I limped.

Doug made me an actor, and I played in two pictures. The first was *Knicker-bocker Buckaroo,* directed by Albert Parker, in which I was the juvenile, with Doug and Marjorie Daw. The other was a thing which Raoul Walsh did, *Evangeline,* with Miriam Cooper. She was the star, and in my great moment I was playing a British sublieutenant—is that what you call them, sublieutenant? Well, whatever the hell it is, with a powdered wig, I looked like a fairy.

I couldn't stand being an actor. I haven't liked many actors anyway, and I've directed most of them. One of my sons is an actor and it breaks my heart, but there's nothing I can do about it. I used so many of them, and had *so* many problems—you get a little sick of it, you know.

I saw *Knickerbocker Buckaroo,* and saw myself . . . well, I've got a long face, and the camera made it look like a fairground mirror. So I went to Doug and asked him if he could get me another job. "What do you want to do?" he asked. I pointed to Al Parker. "What does he make?" Doug told me, and I said, "I want to be a director. It's purely financial." He said I'd have to start way down at the bottom, and he got me a job at the old Goldwyn studios, as a messenger boy. That's the way I started.

I can say one thing about myself. I was probably the most hard-working director that ever lived. This was because I couldn't sleep. I've never slept well anyway, but while making a picture I would sleep only three hours a night. All the rest of the time I worked. If I wasn't on the set, I was working on the script, and trying to do the best I could with what I'd got.

Frankly, if you review my whole background, it's not very good. I can tell you that for every good picture, I made at least five or six stinkers. But I always tried to do it a little differently. I don't know whether I ever accomplished it, but I tried.

I didn't like many actors, and I didn't like many producers. But I loved David —David Selznick. He was not only a man with great imagination and great courage, but he had that wonderful thing—great taste. I'd known him long before he became a producer, and his brother Myron, too. David, Myron, and myself were all pals when we were broke. I loved his dad, Lewis, too—in fact I became the greatest Irish pinochle player in the world when his old man was alive. So I was literally one of the family.

If you went to David, he didn't have to go to anyone else for an opinion and an answer. You got it then and there—yes or no. He didn't say "Wait a minute" and then call some guy in New York. You worked directly with David, and kept the enthusiasm and drive. This is no longer with us. Now there's a guy who thinks he's running a studio, but there are two men in New York who are his bosses. Two men! Well, maybe one of those men's wives doesn't like it, or maybe he's living with some dame who doesn't like it. Or maybe he takes his opinion from some broker or lawyer. Either way, they're not in the motion-picture business. If they were they'd be out here *doing* something.

A great hit to me is a picture that has lived for years. It's unfair, I guess. Guys say to me, "Gee, you made *Wings!*" Well, they're too goddam young ever to have seen it, but they tell you that it must have been a great picture. Well, it was great, but it wasn't anywhere near as great as they think it was. So few people

Richard Arlen and Louise Brooks in Beggars of Life *(1928).*

William Wellman directing Wallace Beery and Edgar Blue Washington in Beggars of Life
Henry Gerrard at camera.

The Battle of Saint-Mihiel, re-created for Wings.

The camera crew on Wings included three of today's top cameramen: Russell Harlan (top row, far left), Ernest Laszlo (far right), and William Clothier (bottom row, second from right). Wellman and Lucien Hubbard, center.

today have seen it, but you still get great enthusiasm which has been handed on, sincerely and honestly, from the people that did see it. With luck, this will be a picture that will be remembered. Do you think anyone will ever hear of *Cat Ballou* years from now?

They gave me *Wings* because I was the only director who had been a flyer, in action. I was the only one who knew what the hell it was all about. That's literally the only reason—except that I had fortunately made a successful picture just before that, *You Never Know Women,* with Clive Brook, Lowell Sherman, and Florence Vidor, the story of the Chauve-Souris. It was very interesting, and it got an artistic award that year, so with that, and my being the only director with experience at the front, they gave *Wings* to me—and I really gave them a screwing on it. This was my big opportunity and I took advantage of it.

That was quite a picture to control. I had the army lined up to put on this battle at St. Mihiel. The guys were all right, it was their officers you had trouble with. The reason we had such trouble was because of their general. There were two things that he hated worse than anything. One was anyone or anything to do with motion pictures, and the other was flyers. And Christ Almighty, I was both of them. The minute he met me, he hated me.

The generals and their wives had a big dinner; there must have been a couple of hundred of them there. They'd met Lucien Hubbard, who was the supervisor, and John Monk Saunders, the writer, but they'd never seen me. They expected a De Mille to walk in, you know. The leading Mister General had got up and when he saw me, he didn't know who I was. (I was twenty-eight years old, with a lot of hair.) And he sat down again, and so did everyone else.

I'll tell you right now, that's a pretty tough spot. When I was asked to speak, I started off in a humorous way. I told them that I knew they expected someone a little more mature, but I said I was born on February 29, 1896, which was a leap year, so in reality I was only seven years old. I put it to them: "If Paramount Pictures are idiots enough to hire a seven-year-old kid to do this big job, then I have to have the help and assistance from all you older people!"

Turning it into a comedy thing sort of worked, and I talked to the big man's wife, who was wonderful, and I got onto the good side of her. I knew I was going to be helped that evening by pillow talk—and sure enough I got cooperation from then on from everyone but this goddam old general, who now hated me more than ever because I had gained a foothold.

Well, it was tough. When you're that age, which isn't very old for such responsibility, your inclination is to go off the eyeline a bit. But I don't know. . . . I think what kept me going was the selfish feeling that I was getting two hundred and fifty dollars a week, making a picture that was going to cost a couple of million bucks, and *I* was the guy that was doing it!

We did a fantastic amount of stuntwork. I did one of them myself. I got mad at the stunt guy and I went up and cracked up his plane for him—so if I was willing to do it, I didn't see why the hell I couldn't ask someone else to do it. Some of the men wouldn't lie on the ground during the retreat because they were scared of being trampled. So I lay on the ground. I was lying right there, with a German helmet on, and all these doughboys coming down. They knew I was there, but no one stepped on me. If they'd been sore at me they could

Gary Cooper and Charles "Buddy" Rogers in Wings.

Legion of the Condemned (1928).

have killed me. But there was none of that sort of feeling about; they didn't like the general any more than I did.

The only stunt man who got hurt on *Wings* was Dick Grace, who's the greatest of them all, and he got hurt doing the simplest thing in the world. Instead of turning his plane over, he *almost* went over—and snapped his neck. Well, that's his fault, not mine. If he'd gone over the way he cracked the Spads up he'd never have been hurt. They put a big thing on his neck and sent him to the hospital, and I went to see him every day. He was supposed to keep that cast on for a year at least. He had it on for six weeks. I happened to be dancing at the St. Anthony's Hotel, San Antonio, and I saw this guy Grace dancing with a dame. He'd gotten a hammer and broken the cast and escaped through a window. He never went back and he never put the thing on his neck again.

We staged the big battle with the help of army officers.[1] The underofficers were all great—the captains, the lieutenants, the majors. Up to a lieutenant colonel, you had no trouble. From there on up you were in hot water. So all that was necessary was to explain the scene to the guys that were going to do it; you had a blackboard to show them, and you rehearsed them.

We had dozens of cameras. On the big scene, we fanned out a series of camera parallels, and had about twenty-eight Eyemos, hand-held 35mm cameras, stuck about. I played the explosions from a detonator keyboard on the third level. I wouldn't allow anyone up there. I kept the barrage ahead of the advancing troops. A guy came up to ask me a question and I pushed the wrong button. I kicked the son of a bitch off there so fast it would make your hair stand on end. I never even saw him, because while I was kicking him off I was still playing with the keyboard. It turned out he was Otto Kahn, the big banker. When I found out, I was sure I was going to be fired, because I had taken a chance— it was all a question of sun.

We hadn't had a break for a hell of a time, and it was vital to have clouds *and* sun for the dogfight. B. P. Schulberg had gotten mad at me for the delay, and he sent Sam Jaffe, his brother-in-law, down to the location to straighten me out. Say you can't shoot a dogfight without clouds to a guy who doesn't know anything about flying, and he thinks you're nuts. He'll say, "Why can't you?"

I told him that it's just unattractive. Number two, you get no sense of speed, because there's nothing there that's parallel. The clouds give you that, but against a blue sky, it's like a lot of goddam flies! And photographically, it's terrible.

So I waited until I got clouds. I waited over thirty days. Then they sent Otto Kahn, Sir William Wiseman, and William Stralem, who owned Camel cigarettes. Three big money men. And they arrived right when we were doing the big scene.

I'd been looking at the sun for a long time, when I was flying, and I just had a hunch that I could do it. It was just as dark as hell, but I got everything ready. I got a hundred and sixty-five planes in the air, the thousands of troops we'd had sitting around, my cameramen, the whole thing. They all thought I was nuts, but I had seen that little light coming, and all of a sudden I could see the blackness disintegrating. Now I'm telling you the truth—I'm not exaggerating

[1] *The Production Manager on* Wings, *who secured unprecedented cooperation from the army, was Frank Blount.*

one second—I gave the camera crew the order to start because I just had a feeling I'd get away with it. The big scene started, and at the end of the three and a half minutes, when the scene was over, the clouds closed in solidly, and the sun never came out again for another three weeks. I got it that quickly. That night, the three big money men came up to my suite. I was alone, and I was loaded. I came out of the shower to open the door, and there were these three guys. I thought they were going to fire me.

"Have a drink," I said; I only had a towel around me.

Otto Kahn said, "No."

"I'm sorry," I said, "I'm drunk . . . What do you want?"

"Nothing," they said. "We just want to tell you that you can have anything you want. The whole thing is yours. You're one hell of a man." Then they shook my hand, and left. I waited till the door closed, then I fell down and cried.

As far as directors were concerned, Cecil B. De Mille mounted the greatest show on earth. Commanding absolute loyalty from his staff, he directed as though chosen by God for this one task. To suit his role, he wore breeches and high boots, and carried a revolver. The boots supported his legs, he explained, and protected him from the snakes so often found at his California ranch; the snakes inspired the revolver as well. Cynics wondered whether the serpents in the picture business caused him to wear such garb at the studio. Despite their laughter, De Mille made no secret of the fact that he adored dressing up.

For practically the whole of his career, De Mille was a powerful force in the film industry. But in his early days, he was also an exceptionally good director.

The Cheat (1915) was a masterpiece. The story suggests the favorite De Mille mixture of sex, sadism, and sacrifice, washed down with lurid melodrama. Yet so sensitive was De Mille's handling that a potentially foolish melodrama became a serious, bizarre, and disturbing fable.

A society lady (Fannie Ward) gambles with Red Cross funds, borrows from a wealthy Japanese, Hara Arakau (Sessue Hayakawa), and instead of paying him back in the style he considers customary, presents him with cash. Infuriated, he brands her as though she were an item in his collection. Her husband shoots Arakau, wounding him; to save her husband, the society lady sacrifices herself publicly, and reveals her brand in court.

Tautly constructed and excellently played, the film owes a great deal to Wilfred Buckland, art director, and to Alvin Wyckoff, cameraman, who created a remarkable visual style known as Lasky lighting. The branding sequence, and the subsequent shooting, are lit in a way that ignites the imagination; the scenes are as powerful as ever today.

The Cheat is one of those rarities—a film designed to shock which retains its artistic integrity.

Between *The Cheat* and a film of the banality of, say, *Manslaughter* (1922) lies a chasm of commercialism in which a great talent perished. The turning point was *The Whispering Chorus* (1918), in which De Mille sunk not only a large sum of money but also his heart.

The film was that bane of exhibitors, a picture with a message. *The Whispering Chorus* represented man's impulses for good and evil; they torment a young husband who absconds with his employer's money to bring his wife the things he cannot afford. On the run, he discovers a corpse washed up by the river. Feeling he has killed himself spiritually, he decides to be dead to the world. He dresses the corpse in his own clothes, destroys the face with lime, and is eventually arrested for his own murder. His wife meanwhile has married again, and is expecting a child. To save her from disgrace, he goes to his death.

There were protests against the "abnormal morbidity" of this picture. "It was poetic and very interesting," recalled Agnes de Mille, "but it lost a great deal of money. Cecil had to make money or he couldn't survive."[1]

De Mille changed his attitude toward his audiences. As he lowered his sights to meet the lowest common denominator, so the standard of his films plummeted. The decline was not immediately apparent. *Male and Female* (1919) was a delightful version of *The Admirable Crichton,* and the famous bathroom scene

[1] *Agnes de Mille to author, New York, March 1964.*

Cecil B. De Mille.

Cecil B. De Mille (with binoculars), Alvin Wyckoff, and Charles Schoenbaum shooting The Woman God Forgot *(1917).*

The Ten Commandments *(1923).*

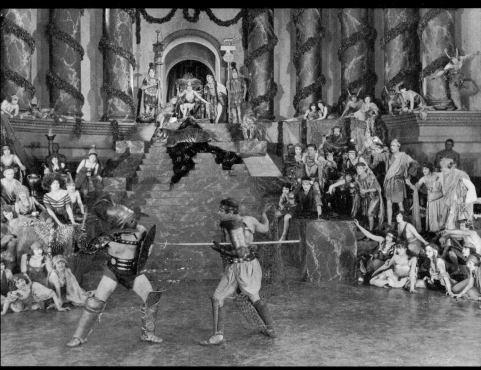

Gladiatorial combat from Manslaughter *(1922).*

was introduced with sly humor: "Humanity is assuredly growing cleaner, but is it growing more artistic? Women bathe more often, but not as beautifully as did their ancient sisters. Why shouldn't the Bath Room express as much beauty as the Drawing Room?" Gloria Swanson upbraids the maid (Lila Lee) for permitting the temperature to rise above 90°, and at breakfast declares that the toast is spoiled; "it is entirely too soft." "Are you certain, my lady, that the toast is the only thing that's spoiled?" asks the maid. The sense of fun, and the sense of cinema, gradually dispersed. During his sad metamorphosis, De Mille seemed to lose his grip on the medium. His films no longer cut together smoothly, and his showmanship, so splendidly displayed in *Male and Female* (when he flashed back to Babylon and, incidentally, to a provocative dance by Martha Graham), became tawdry. He preferred to work inside the studio, even for exteriors, thus sacrificing the freshness that made silent pictures so attractive. His box-office returns justified whatever he did in the eyes of his financiers. Even so, he took a considerable personal risk with the biblical prologue to *The Ten Commandments* (1923), expending enormous sums on a sequence which, although cinematically uninventive, is impressive in terms of sheer size.

"De Mille didn't make pictures for himself, or for critics," said Adolph Zukor, "he made them for the public. He chose stories if he thought the public might like them. He was a showman to his smallest finger. He never started shooting until he had completed every detail of the script, and he followed through as he had prepared. With other directors, the management had to sign the stars and make the decisions. But Cecil did it all himself."

The garish naïveté of the new De Mille inevitably alienated certain sections of the public. "For a long time," wrote an Ohio moviegoer in 1922, "I have wished to protest at the frightful superficiality of Cecil De Mille's productions. It seems to me that his photoplays are a real menace to the artistic growth of the silent drama. I became interested in De Mille when I saw his *Joan the Woman* and *The Whispering Chorus*. That is, until I saw his *Saturday Night*. Now I stay away and save my pennies for Chaplin, Griffith, and Ingram."[2]

Manslaughter is a fairly representative example of De Mille's view of the intelligence of his audience. "If the name of Paul Sloane or Christy Cabanne had been attached to it," wrote William K. Everson, "one wouldn't be too surprised." Everson presented it to the Theodore Huff Society in 1963, hoping that it might confound the critics of De Mille. It failed to do so. "It is hard to believe that such a crude and unsubtle film could come from a veteran like De Mille, harder still to believe that this came from the same year as *Orphans of the Storm, Down to the Sea in Ships,* and *Foolish Wives*. The amateurish and crudely faked auto chase scenes that start the film are of less technical slickness than Sennett had been getting ten years earlier. *Manslaughter* is exactly the kind of picture that the unknowing regard as typical of the silent film—overwrought, pantomimically acted, written in the manner of Victorian melodrama, the kind of film that invites laughter *at* it rather than with it."[3]

The celebrated orgy is drawn into the story in a surprisingly offhand manner. Thomas Meighan watches some flappers indulging in an energetic but perfectly

[2] Photoplay, *Dec. 1922, p. 8.*
[3] *Theodore Huff Memorial Society notes.*

innocent pogo race and declares: "This dance, with its booze and license, is no better than a Feast of Bacchus!"

Then follows a sustained flashback of a Roman orgy, an excruciating combination of cardboard costumes and half-naked extras. Gladiators enter the set, and De Mille dissolves back to girls boxing.

"You see," intones Meighan, "it's just the same—Gladiators and Prize-Fighters, Drink or Booze—it's the same in a modern roadhouse or in Ancient Rome."

The "heroine," Lydia Thorne, who has everything in the world she wants, except a mother and father, accidentally kills a speed cop. The cop (Jack Mower) had just received sergeant's chevrons for rescuing some children. As he dies, his wife (Julia Faye) kisses the chevrons, places them on her husband's sleeves, and salutes them, while Leatrice Joy emotes outside.

An encounter in jail between Lois Wilson and Leatrice Joy (who both give far better performances than the film deserves) provides this final example of *Manslaughter's* unconscious humor: "Doesn't this donut remind you of a life preserver? That is what prison has meant to most of us—a life preserver."

I saw *Manslaughter* with its star, Leatrice Joy. William K. Everson screened it for her daughter's birthday. Miss Joy thought it hilarious; she had not seen it for over forty years.

"Mr. De Mille was so kind to me that I'd do anything," she said. "Although I must admit I thought a lot of it was pretty corny. In those early scenes, where I'm chasing trains, they built a platform on the side of the car to accommodate two cameras and Mr. De Mille. I was horrified when I realized that they depended entirely on my driving for their safety. After that, I admitted to myself that I couldn't complain at the things De Mille asked me to do."[4]

During the show, Miss Joy handed out bags of popcorn to her friends and merrily recalled the day she saw De Mille sporting two pearl-handled revolvers.

" 'What,' I asked myself,' could a director be doing with *two* pearl-handled revolvers?' He told me to go and sit on the throne. Suddenly two unchained Bengal tigers came in. De Mille shot a number of scenes in which the tigers wandered all over the set. I was very frightened. Between takes, my maid ripped the stitches from where my nineteen-foot train joined my costume at the shoulders. And she put in tiny safety pins. I asked why she was doing this.

" 'Land sakes,' she said. 'If those tigers go wild, Mr. De Mille starts shooting, and all those people start running, I don't want to be bothered with no nineteen-foot train!' "

In the prison scene, Miss Joy said that the assistant director, Cullen "Hezi" Tate, forgot to tell her that the big soup tureens were hot, and she scalded her hands. De Mille seized on the opportunity and made her scrub the floor for the camera. "It'll show up those blisters," he said delightedly.

Hezi Tate passed into legend after a banker's convention at the studio, during which De Mille was staging his exhibitionistic routine. He yelled through his radio-loudspeaker system: "Where are my one thousand assistants?"

Hezi Tate strolled on to the set. "Here's nine hundred and ninety-nine of 'em," he said. "What do you want us to do?"

"De Mille had a basic reality," said Adela Rogers St. Johns. "He could always

---

4 *Leatrice Joy to author, Riverside, Conn., Dec. 1964.*

fool the public and he always knew it. He was one hundred per cent cynical. I had great fun with C.B., and I knew him as the biggest ham the motion pictures ever produced. There wasn't a moment when he wasn't acting. He was so good a ham that he could sell anything. This was the postwar period, remember, when flamboyance was at its peak. De Mille was as much a product of his age as he made the age a product of what he was."[5]

David O. Selznick acknowledged that much of what De Mille did was absurd but strongly defended him. "I don't know to what extent it was tongue-in-cheek or to what extent he was a combination Belasco and Barnum. But his early pictures, like *Old Wives for New,* dealing with marital relations and showing women with cold cream on their faces, provided a contrast to the Cinderella approach, and were revolutionary.

"You cannot judge De Mille by regular standards. You cannot compare one of the most successful of all film makers in terms of whether he's as good a film maker as somebody in Japan or Sweden. As a commercial film maker, he made a great contribution to our industry."

"Directorially," said William Wellman, "I think his pictures were the most horrible things I've ever seen in my life. But he put on pictures that made a fortune. In that respect he was better than any of us."

Most people who came into contact with De Mille found him kind and courteous. Bessie Love said that it was a pleasure to be turned down by him. But

[5] *Adela Rogers St. Johns to author, New York, Dec. 1964.*

H. B. Warner as Christ in Cecil B. De Mille's **The King of Kings** *(1927).*

De Mille was an unsuccessful actor, and he found directing actors very difficult. If an actor asked him how to interpret a scene, De Mille would tell him that he wasn't running a school. "I hired you as an actor. Get out there and act. I'll tell you when I don't like it." But for those who understood his requirements, he was considerate and appreciative.

"He was a man I respected tremendously," said Gloria Swanson. "He demanded discipline, and got it. He never said a cruel thing to me in the three years I worked for him. He had great gentleness and appreciated anybody who tried to do a good job.

"In the Babylonian sequence on *Male and Female* one of the lions got loose and came within ten feet of me. The next day, when I came on the set, I was rather shaken from this experience. I'm a Swede, you see, so there's a delayed reaction. Mr. De Mille decided to cut out the shot where the lion is on my back.

" 'Mr. De Mille,' I said, 'you can't do that. I want to do it. Please—you promised me I could.'

" 'Young fellow,' he said, 'why do you want to do this?'

" 'Well,' I said, 'when I was a little girl, I used to sit at my grandmother's piano. On the left-hand side there was a copy of a famous painting called *A Lion's Bride*. You told me you wanted to reproduce this painting, and I'd like to take part.'

" 'All right,' he said, 'I thought maybe it was a little too much for you.'

"In the arena, there was Mr. De Mille, the cameraman and his assistant—and my father, in army officer's uniform, standing on top of this arena, looking at his one and only with his eyes bulging out of his head. There were also two trainers, armed with whips. They folded up canvas and put this on my back, which was bare to the waist. They put the animal so that his front legs were resting on me, and little by little they eased the canvas out from under his paws. Then they cracked their whips till he roared. It felt like thousands of vibrators. Every hair on my body was standing straight up. I had to close my eyes. The last thing I saw was Mr. De Mille with a gun.

"There is a postscript to that incident. We had been on Catalina Island, doing a lot of sea scenes, which were dangerous for me because I don't swim. Then came the incident with the lion—and they wanted me to change into another gown for another sequence. I just couldn't do it. I went to see Mr. De Mille in his office and I started to cry.

"He put me on his knee and treated me like a young child. Well, what was I? Eighteen, nineteen years old.

" 'At last,' he said, 'you're a woman. Now I know it.' He'd always thought of me as a young boy, which was why, I suppose, he called me 'young fellow.'

" 'I was going to give you this after the picture,' he said, 'because of all the things that have happened to you—and because you never complained even when your blood was running to your knees.'

"And he brought out a tray of jewels from a jewelry store. 'I want you to choose one as a memento of this picture.'

"My eyes were popping out of my head. I saw a tiny gold-mesh change purse, not more than four inches square. In the center was a beautiful sapphire. He said, 'Is this what you really want? Be sure. Look again.' I did.

" 'Yes, Mr. De Mille, I would like this.'

" 'That,' he said, 'is your gift for being a brave boy.' "[6]

If public taste was the criterion of artistry, Cecil B. De Mille would be the finest exponent of the arts in the history of mankind. But his success was viewed with concern by some directors, who felt his tasteless extravaganzas negated everything they stood for.

"When I saw one of his pictures," said King Vidor, "I wanted to quit the business."

"I had great admiration for him," said Howard Hawks, who began as De Mille's property man, "but I never saw anything that I thought was good. If I tried to tell people to do some of the things he did, I would burst into laughter. Yet he made it work. I learned an awful lot from him by doing exactly the opposite. He was a great egotist and he could charm people into doing what he wanted. I once asked Gary Cooper how on earth he could read those goddam lines. 'Well,' he said, 'when De Mille finishes talking to you, they don't seem so bad. But when you see the picture, then you kind of hang your head.'

"On the set, he was a Nero. Off the set, he was charming, and he was terribly appreciative. He asked me to help him one time. He'd made a picture that was quite bad. I wrote the titles for the picture, and changed the whole tenor of the story so that it no longer took itself seriously. It became semi-humorous. He previewed it and was very pleased with the laughs he got. The picture was *The Road to Yesterday* (1925). I was called in very often to help him after that."[7]

Lost in the clamor is Cecil's elder brother, William, who spelled the de with a small d. Unhappily, most of the films of William C. de Mille have disappeared. Only *Miss Lulu Bett* (1921) survives, at the Museum of Modern Art, although other titles are rumored to be in the Moscow archive. *Miss Lulu Bett* shows de Mille to have been a man of great warmth and perceptiveness. He cared more for psychological reality than melodramatic action, and his style was as different from Cecil's as a miniaturist's from an epic painter. This brilliantly directed film tells the story of a young woman (Lois Wilson), a spinster, considered unattractive, who works as a household drudge for her sister's family. The opening title indicates the unusual approach: "The greatest tragedy in the world, because it is the most frequent, is that of a human soul caught in the toils of the commonplace." The sense of observation reaches a standard very seldom excelled, and de Mille's compassion and his realistic treatment give every scene a truthfulness still rare in the cinema. It retains its magic, and this fragile, delicate little story can still move its audience to tears.

Agnes de Mille explained the difference between her father and Cecil De Mille: "Cecil was operatic, whereas William was more interested in human values. He was concerned with humor, and with half-light, with the psychological states where emotions are mixed and graduate one into the other. He was absorbed by

---

[6] *Gloria Swanson to author, London, July 1964.*
[7] *Howard Hawks to author, London, June 1967.*

the characters of ordinary people. Cecil, however, was still throwing velvet cloaks over his shoulder and pacing the stage in high boots, although I think he had a finer eye for pictorial effects.

"On Father's set it was always quiet. They called him Pop. Cecil was The Boss. Pop wore a battered old hat which he would never give up. He wore it for thirty years. He always looked rumpled, and he slouched around and spoke very quietly. If he became angry, it was a quiet and powerful anger. Cecil indulged in a great deal of ironic tongue-lashing. Father was normally very patient and very intimate. I remember once he had a boy who had never acted before. He had photographed him all day, but the boy was inept and stupid. Father stayed up all night wondering if he had the heart to tell him to go. Most directors wouldn't have hesitated: *'Out!'* Cecil spent his life building up a legend. Father was interested only in the truth."

16 / JOSEF VON STERNBERG

The living legend, the once great artist, is a vulnerable creature. His life's work completed, appraised, classified, he alone remains at large, uncertain and unpredictable. Rediscovery seldom leads to regeneration; the most he can contribute now is disappointment.

Many artists, *enfants terribles* of their day, have emerged, mellowed by wealth and praise, as kindly, good-humored old men. However, no devotee of Josef von Sternberg need fear such a decline. With his autobiography, *Fun in a Chinese Laundry,* he launched himself from comparative obscurity to a notoriety greater even than that of his golden days. So inflammatory was this book that those who considered themselves friends became his enemies overnight. Others, realizing that the book told them more about von Sternberg than it did about themselves, forgave him because of his greatness as an artist.

From the beginning of his career, a sense of insecurity forced von Sternberg to adopt an armor-plating of contempt. Inspired by Erich von Stroheim—young Sternberg first assumed the same immaculate dress, white gloves, and cane. But he went one step further. He carried Stroheim's arrogant character of The Man You Love to Hate from the screen into real life.

"I first met Jo when he was an assistant director on a picture in England," recalled Clive Brook. "He was Jo Sternberg then. On location in Wales, we slept in the same bedroom and I remember seeing him one morning staring into the mirror.

" 'Which is more horrible,' he asked. 'With a mustache or without one?'

" 'What do you want to look horrible for?' I asked.

" 'The only way to succeed,' he said, 'is to make people hate you. That way they remember you.' "[1]

Whatever the value of this psychology, von Sternberg has yet to be forgotten; his is still a magic name to anyone interested in the cinema's past. Rediscovery programs have been held all over the world.

A London season was climaxed by the presentation of the BBC's *Epic That Never Was,* a documentary which investigated the mystery behind the fate of von Sternberg's *I, Claudius,* and which reconstructed the surviving fragments of the film. The producer of this enthralling piece of archaeology, Bill Duncalf, said that when he discovered forty-seven cans of *I, Claudius* in the laboratories at Denham, he enlisted the aid of the present London Films. He then tried to persuade von Sternberg to take part. Eventually he received a guarded letter agreeing to participation, and the project went forward.

"In California," said Duncalf, "I went to von Sternberg's office at the University. I knocked on the door. A voice inside said 'Come.'

"This was a great moment for me and I didn't try to hide my feelings. I strode forward, holding out my hand, and made some remark indicating my emotion. Von Sternberg, this little white-haired figure, just sat there. He ignored my hand and said coldly, 'Why have you come here?'

"I explained that I had written him three letters, one of which he had replied to. It was then that he noticed the package under my arm. He took it from me and opened it up. It was full of production stills from *I, Claudius.* He began

---

[1] *Clive Brook to author, London, March 1965.*

Josef von Sternberg directing Docks of New York *(1928).*

Olaf Hytten and Georgia Hale in The Salvation Hunters *(1923).*

sorting them out, muttering, 'This is mine . . . this is not mine . . . this is mine . . .'[2] until there were two piles.

" 'I want these,' he announced.

" 'You can't have them,' I said. 'They are unique. They are the only ones in existence. I will have to have them copied for you.'

"And that was the condition he made for his participation—copies of the stills *and* a print of the completed film."[3]

When von Sternberg arrived for the interview, on the University's stage, the scene had already been lit. As he lowered himself into the chair, he looked upward.

"Is that your key light?" he asked Robert Kaufmann, the American cameraman. Kaufmann said it was.

"Raise it," he ordered.

During the filming of the interview, he was extremely nervous. When he felt he was drying up he said, "Better stop that." When the shooting was over, the tension subsided and von Sternberg relaxed.

"He suddenly displayed a most unexpected charm," recalled Duncalf. "He went round to each of the crew, shook their hands and thanked them. Then he went out alone into a torrential downpour—just this little figure with a large umbrella. I couldn't help thinking of Chaplin."

Ironically, it was Chaplin who began von Sternberg's rise to fame when he publicly praised his first film, *The Salvation Hunters,* which had been made on almost an amateur basis. Chaplin arranged for it to be distributed by United Artists, and engaged him to direct Edna Purviance in *The Sea Gull.* (He later refused to release it, and it was hinted that his praise for *Salvation Hunters* was a joke, designed to see how far people would go in accepting predigested opinions.)

Mary Pickford also put the young director under contract, but she considered her eagerness a mistake.

"Mon Dieu! He proved to be a complete boiled egg. Not even a *boiled* egg. This business of *von* Sternberg, and carrying a cane, and that little mustache! I'm so glad I didn't do the film. It was to have been called *Backwash,* set in Pittsburgh. It was a very sad story, and everything was covered in dust. I liked *Salvation Hunters,* but you never know who was really the guiding hand . . ."

One person who was quickly convinced of von Sternberg's talents was Mrs. Ad Schulberg, now a prominent agent, then the wife of B. P. Schulberg, head of Paramount West Coast studios.

"I don't know how I happened to be at the Mary Pickford studios when I saw *Salvation Hunters,"* she said, "but I was very impressed, and came back and told Ben about it. I was always an agent at heart! Ben didn't get around to it, and Harry Rapf signed him at M-G-M. But there was a stormy session there and eventually Ben got him for Paramount."[4]

After reshooting part of Frank Lloyd's *Children of Divorce,* von Sternberg was given his first big chance with *Underworld.* The stars of this gangster story were Evelyn Brent, George Bancroft, and Clive Brook.

[2] *He was referring not to ownership but to the original photographer.*
[3] *Bill Duncalf to author, London, Dec. 1965.*
[4] *Mrs. Ad Schulberg to author, New York, Dec. 1964.*

"He acted like a Prussian," said Brook. "He was a very dictatorial director. But I always got on pretty well with him, except for one memorable occasion. He kept me working twenty-four hours at a stretch. I was walking off the set when he called me back.

" 'Where are you going?' he asked.

" 'To my dressing room,' I replied.

" 'Why?'

" 'To perform one of two functions, neither of which I will attempt to explain.'

" 'You do not leave this set without my permission!'

" 'Look,' I said, getting really furious. 'You are a thoroughgoing———.'

"Von Sternberg stopped work, called off all the extras—this was the big fire scene—and sent them home. By this time I didn't give a damn. But I was a trifle uneasy when I was summoned into the office of Hector Turnbull, the producer.

" 'Mr. von Sternberg has told me that you used obscene language to him and walked off his set.'

" 'Yes,' I confessed. 'I called him a ———.'

" 'Splendid,' said Turnbull. 'He's had that coming for a long time.' "

If Sternberg set out to inspire general dislike he succeeded impressively. And angry feelings were in no way placated when his pictures turned out to be breathtakingly good. Far from becoming easier to work with, von Sternberg's irascibility increased.

"I tried to learn my parts like a human being," said Olga Baclanova, star of *Docks of New York*. "And I tried to play them that way. He wanted me to play a scene a certain way—I felt this was not right. 'Why do you tell me to do that?' I asked him.

" 'Do what I told you,' he said. 'Just because you were at the Moscow Art Theatre, don't think that you understand everything. Follow me.'

"So I started to do what he wanted.

" 'It's terrible! It's awful!' he shouted. We argued, and he yelled at me, and I was so scared I cried like a baby. And that, of course, was what he wanted. The scene in the picture was very good.

"When *The Docks of New York* came out, he said, 'You see what I did for you?'

"Now I see him in Europe, at Cannes, at the festival—at Venice, at the festival. He looks wonderful. We kiss each other and he says, 'You have forgotten me.'

" 'Do you think I could forget *you?*' I ask. 'I only began to make pictures and you started to yell at me!' "[5]

"He was very positive with actors," said Clive Brook. "But he didn't use any sort of Method approach. He would go on indefinitely taking shots. He was a great man to wear an actor down. Poor Lawrence Grant, on *Shanghai Express,* was kept hard at it from nine until six one day until the poor man burst into tears. 'I don't think I can go on, Mr. von Sternberg.'

" 'You have done it,' he said. 'The last take is good.'

"On the same picture, he asked me what I thought of some rushes. 'But Jo,' I protested, 'everyone is talking in the same dreary monotone.'

[5] *Olga Baclanova to author, New York, March 1964.*

" 'Exactly,' he replied. 'I want that. This is *The Shanghai Express*. Everyone must talk like a train.'

"I have a novel by him. He didn't just write it, he designed it as well—format, cover, everything. That was typical of him."

Today, von Sternberg claims to have done virtually everything on his pictures—including the photography. The late Georges Perinal (cameraman on *I, Claudius*) told Bill Duncalf that he learned more from von Sternberg than from anyone he ever worked with. David O. Selznick, while producing at Paramount, admitted that he was instructed to give von Sternberg carte blanche, even though he thought many of his ideas "ludicrous."

Considered by some the greatest cameraman in the world, von Sternberg's grasp of narrative was seldom more than tenuous.[6] The majority of his sound films were carried by the visuals alone, for von Sternberg had a richer sense of visuals than any director since Maurice Tourneur. He not only understood the subtle art of lighting—he knew that art direction and set dressing could have an emotional effect as well as fulfilling practical requirements. Von Sternberg could film the telephone directory and make it exciting, mysterious, and sensuous.

Von Sternberg's silent films are superior to his talkies. Ideally suited to the medium, artistically and emotionally, he kept a firmer grip on the drama.

Salvation Hunters was von Sternberg's first film, although he had taken over *Children of Divorce* from Frank Lloyd. It is a pretentious and unpromising start and a flat and largely unimaginative exercise in filmcraft. The artistic arrogance of its opening title is not, unhappily, transmitted to the film. "There are important fragments of life that have been ignored by the motion picture because Body is more important than Thought. Our aim has been to photograph a Thought."

Salvation Hunters tells the story of a man's fight for victory over himself and his surroundings. "It isn't conditions," says Sternberg in a final title, "nor is it environment—it is faith that controls our lives!"

The film lacked subtlety yet it displayed a certain austere dignity. The surroundings chosen were mudflats, on which a dredger ceaselessly worked. "For every load of mud the claw dislodged, the earth laughed and shoved in another."

The young man (George K. Arthur) meets a girl, "her soul encrusted with a bitter contempt for life," played by Georgia Hale. Seeing a small boy being beaten, the girl pushes the young man forward. He hesitates; she calls him a coward. He knows it. Eventually the three derelicts—"Flotsam, Jetsam, and company"—link up and decide to get away from the mud, to seek their fortune in the city. The salvation hunters fall foul of exploiters. The young man's struggle with himself is depicted as an actual fight scene, in the style of *Tol'able David*. The fight is more picturesque than exciting. Sternberg stages part of it behind a real-estate sign: "HERE Your Dreams Come True."

Sternberg's first commercial production is so superior in style as to be unrecognizable. *Underworld* had been intended by Paramount for Frank Lloyd. They finally assigned it to Art Rosson.

---

[6] *Asked at his London press conference how much the story meant to him, von Sternberg replied, "Nothing."*

"So here's what happened," recalled Monte Brice, a comedy writer who was at the studio during production. "They're working on the script. Von Sternberg is hanging around; he's going to be on the picture, but nothing has been decided. He's sitting around reading a book *that* thick. It's got nothing to do with a picture—it's just a big book. Every once in a while someone would come up and he'd lift his head and give them an answer. And it was usually a pretty good answer, to a problem that was going on over the other side of the room. All of a sudden this big switch. Art Rosson is out entirely, and von Sternberg is the director. Hush-hush; closed sets and all that stuff. I noticed that von Sternberg was the first one to shoot with one camera. We had to use two on account of the foreign negative; he just insisted and that was it. Guess he was cutting in the camera. Anyway, rumor gets out that *Underworld* is going to be a hell of a picture."[7]

Underworld was all of that. It was the film that began the gangster cycle, and it remains the masterpiece of the genre, containing all the elements which became clichés in later pictures. The characterizations are very rich; George Bancroft, the gangster, constantly roaring with laughter, is offset by his dignified and eloquent accomplice, Clive Brook, and the disturbingly attractive Evelyn Brent.

In von Stroheim style, von Sternberg sketches the atmosphere with staccato titles: "A great city in the dead of night . . . streets lonely . . . moon clouded . . . buildings as empty as the cave dwellings of a forgotten age."

Fade in to a clock; the camera pulls back and tracks down a skyscraper to the street. Dissolve to the front entrance of a bank; there is a shattering explosion. Clive Brook, as Rolls-Royce, unshaven and down-at-heel, stands on the sidewalk as George Bancroft emerges from the bank.

"The great Bull Weed closes another bank account," he says, sardonically. Bancroft grins, grabs him, and they make their getaway as the cops race up, firing.

Von Sternberg handles the film with a controlled narrative style, enlivening sequences with sudden flashes of imagination; it is the work of a mature artist.

In a bar scene a rival of Bull Weed tries to bait Rolls-Royce. "How'd you like to pick up ten bucks?" he asks him. He produces a bill, screws it up and throws it in the cuspidor. The camera whip pans from Rolls-Royce's tense face to the cuspidor and back again. The suspense builds. Finally, the gangster hits Rolls-Royce on the jaw—and as he does so, the camera jerks upward as though the audience, too, has felt the blow.

One magnificent sequence is the gangster's ball, "the underworld's armistice when, until dawn, rival gangs bury the hatchet and park the machine gun." Larry Semon, playing "Slippy" Lewis, looks at himself in a distorting mirror; von Sternberg rapidly cuts close-ups of other criminal faces, equally distorted, but not by any mirror . . .

When Bull Weed has broken jail, and is in Rolls-Royce's apartment, he suddenly freezes at the sound of policeman's feet echoing down the corridor. Von Sternberg evokes the sound by cutting from Bancroft's alarmed face to a

[7] *Monte Brice to author, London, Sept. 1962. The man who suggested that von Sternberg should take over was Howard Hawks, at that time a Paramount producer. His first position on the picture was as director of photographic effects.*

tracking shot of a pair of shoes. Cut back to Bancroft; he listens intently. Then he whips open the door. There is just a kitten and a milk bottle; the shoes belonged to the milkman. In his book, Sternberg recalls that he had the kitten fed by the gangster—pointing to this as one of his many concessions to commercialism.

The climax is as spectacular and exciting as any gangster film produced since; Bancroft is cornered in the apartment by a whole motorized column of police, who take up the offensive from outside. They even produce an armored motorcycle equipped with mounted machine gun. During this battle, the story is resolved; Bull Weed discovers that his trusted friends have not, after all, betrayed him. When he gives himself up, the prison officer says, "And all this got you was another hour."

"There was something I had to find out," says Bancroft. "And that hour was worth more to me than my whole life."

The Last Command is more subdued in style. *Underworld,* although replete with what were to prove characteristically rich visuals, was suggestive of German studio work. Bert Glennon, who photographed it with von Sternberg, brought the knowledge gained from working on *Hotel Imperial* with Mauritz Stiller. Glennon again worked on *The Last Command,* but the studio work has a different quality. The film represents a transitory stage, a compromise between stylized realism and the self-contained world of von Sternberg's later films.

The Last Command is extremely clever, but the ending is unsatisfactory because of an obvious story flaw. The story is supposed to be based on an idea casually mentioned by Ernst Lubitsch, but most people in Hollywood accepted it as an imaginative elaboration of the case of General Lodijenski, of the Imperial Russian Army, who was for a while a penniless film extra.

The story was von Sternberg's, although credited to Lajos Biro. Herman Mankiewicz wrote the titles.

Emil Jannings plays an old Hollywood extra, whose photograph is recognized by a director. The director, a Russian, remembers when this man was the general in command of the Russian Armies. "Have him report tomorrow," he says, "and put him into a general's uniform."

The general's story is told in a flashback to the days when he was Grand Duke Sergius Alexander, cousin of the Czar. Revolution is smoldering; two actors are brought before him, who have been entertaining the troops but who are suspected of being revolutionists. One is Leo Andreyev (William Powell), director of the Kiev Imperial Theatre. The other is Natacha (Evelyn Brent). The Grand Duke disposes of Andreyev, but takes Natacha for his personal attention. Natacha goes along with him, intent on killing him. But when the opportunity at last arrives, she is unable to fulfill her mission. "Why did you not shoot me?" asks the Grand Duke. "I suppose," she replies, "it was because I could not kill anyone who loves Russia as much as you do."

Bolsheviks ambush the Grand Duke's train, and Sergius Alexander comes face to face with the new Russia. He tries to reason with them. "People of Russia, you are being led by traitors!" The mob replies by trying to tear him to pieces. Even Natacha joins their cause. "Make him sweat as *we* have sweated. Make him stoke the train to Petrograd!" she cries.

The Grand Duke is stunned by Natacha's treachery. But in the locomotive she comes to him. "Don't you understand? It was the only way I could save your life. I love you." She gives him her pearls, so that he can pay his way out of Russia. He manages to drop from the train—just before it crashes through a bridge and into an ice-packed river.

So great is the shock of losing both the country and the woman he loves, that Sergius Alexander develops a nervous affliction; his head now shakes from side to side in stunned disbelief.

In the film studio, the Grand Duke undergoes all the indignities of movie extras. Eventually, he is brought before the director—Leo Andreyev. "I have waited ten years for this moment, your Highness." He looks him up and down. "The same coat, the same uniform, the same man—only the times have changed."

He gives him command of a troop of extras in a battle scene. As the cameras grind, an extra cries, "What's the difference who wins this war? You've given your last command. A new day is here!" The general does not notice the camera; he is oblivious of the pretense. He sees only the mob at the railway station—and he delivers an impassioned speech to them. At the end, he collapses. "Have we won?" he whispers to Andreyev. "Yes, your Imperial Highness, you have won."

Grand Duke Sergius Alexander dies. "Tough luck," says the assistant director. "That guy was a great actor."

"He was more than a great actor," says Andreyev. "He was a great man."

The story is extremely well told, but the basic flaw remains; Andreyev encountered the Grand Duke once, when he was arrested, when the Grand Duke struck him. He could not have known about the general's true personality since he never saw him or Natacha again.

Aside from this lapse, *The Last Command* is a most unusual and effective production. At no stage does it try to present an accurate picture of the revolution —von Sternberg had no interest in realism—but as a rich character study it is unforgettable.

The Hollywood scenes gave von Sternberg ample opportunity for some home truths. When the director is shown examining the still pictures of extras, he produces a cigarette. Instantly a dozen lighters cluster obsequiously around it.

A title "The Bread Line of Hollywood" introduces a bitingly observed sequence; mournful faces jammed against the studio gates . . . the desperate rush forward as the gates open . . . the panic to get to the right section. The costume department is split into sections, each provided with its own pigeonhole window. "One corporal!" yells the man at the window. A bundle of uniform clothing is thrown from the back of the costume department. The man who throws it takes wicked delight in throwing it as hard as he can. "One general!" Track along shoes to next window, track along hats to the next window, track along swords. . . .

Eventually, the old general is fitted up, and he makes his way to the make-up room. He is frail and slow, and his nervous affliction irritates the extra beside him. "Quit shakin' your head! How do you expect me to make up?"

"Excuse me please," says the old man sadly. "I can't help it. I had a great shock once."

He brings from his wallet his star of the Order of Alexander Nevsky and adds it to his uniform. "Where'd you get that gadget from? Steal it from a hock shop?" The other extra man grabs it. "I'm your pal. I want to show it to every-body!" The extras taunt the old man; they stick the decoration on the tip of a bayonet so that he has to struggle to the table to reach it.

The assistant director is treated by von Sternberg with caustic humor. The extras regard him with, great deference, standing up whenever he appears. The assistant is a conceited little man with a mustache and a permanent cigar. He tells the general: "The director has an important part for you, Pop. You've got to look nice." He pins on a decoration in a patently absurd position.

The general moves it to its correct place. "In Russia that was worn on the left side," he says. "I know because I was a general."

"I've made twenty Russian pictures," retorts the assistant. "I should know about Russia!" He puts the medal back where it was.

The flashback opened with a tour of inspection by the Grand Duke. Now von Sternberg lines up his uniformed extras and stages a tour of inspection by the director. The camera tracks with him from behind the bayonets; he stops before the Grand Duke with an air of triumph and blows cigar smoke in his face. Then he walks around him, examining him with immense satisfaction. Andreyev may have been a theater director and not a soldier, but he is Russian; and the Order of Alexander Nevsky on the wrong side offends him. He places it on the correct side.

The echoes of von Stroheim are evident at other points in *The Last Command;* in the flashback, the Grand Duke's batman is caught wearing his fur-collared overcoat.

"If he does it again," orders Sergius Alexander, "remove the coat and shoot the contents."

In order to humor the Czar, the Grand Duke is forced to withdraw a division from the front for a parade. During the royal inspection, von Sternberg intercuts heavy guns firing.

Jannings characterization is very fine. Perhaps the most moving moment occurs when the mob sets upon him at the railway station, and Natacha joins them. Natacha is a very potent element of the picture. Von Sternberg was a master of cinematic eroticism; a few delicately suggestive touches in *Underworld* carried more impact than the previous decade of vamp pictures. Few directors have displayed such intelligence with such scenes; a moment in the locomotive in the flashback of *The Last Command* when Evelyn Brent distracts a sentry from Jannings' escape by making love to him is an example of von Sternberg's mastery. As Jannings kills the engineer with a shovel, Evelyn Brent, embracing the sentry, clenches her teeth and gasps—a brilliant piece of visual double-entendre.

Von Sternberg's talent at conveying the physical attractiveness of women was to reach its height with the sound films of Marlene Dietrich. *Docks of New York,* however, was a remarkably sensuous picture. Two well-contrasted players, Betty Compson and Olga Baclanova, gave electric performances in a highly charged atmosphere, an atmosphere created almost entirely by light.

Docks of New York (1928) is the greatest film von Sternberg ever made. He achieves a feeling of warmth and humanity—he seems to care about his characters, instead of using them as in some of his sound films merely to form patterns of light and shade. *Docks of New York* looks like a massed collaboration of the finest European and American directors, art directors, and lighting cameramen.

(It was photographed in collaboration with Hal Rosson; the art director was Hans Dreier.)

Because he is again dealing with life on the waterfront, von Sternberg can repeat elements that appealed to him in *The Salvation Hunters*. He has rejected the documentary starkness of his first film, however, and any similarity is purely coincidental. This is an artistic achievement out of all proportion to the pretentious little quickie that began his career.

George Bancroft plays a tough stoker, in the days before oil-fired boilers "made stoking a lady's job." With only one night ashore he determines to make it memorable. The evening starts ominously; he rescues a girl from drowning. The girl (Betty Compson) is not grateful; she was trying to commit suicide. "After a month in the stokehold," Bancroft tells her, "I've got no sympathy for anyone that wants to quit a wonderful world like this." They spend the evening together in the dockside bar, and half-drunk, Bancroft marries her.

Next morning, Bancroft starts out to return to his ship when the girl is arrested for shooting the third engineer, who had tried to rape her. But the engineer's wife (Olga Baclanova) marches in and announces, "I shot him an' nobody else is goin' to get the credit for it."

The girl tries to hold Bancroft, but he leaves once more. "Sorry, baby, sailing in an hour. Never missed a ship in my life." When she tries to draw attention to his responsibility, he protests: "Now don't get sore. I never did a decent thing in my life. I've always been like this. No power on earth could keep me ashore."

Betty Compson is heartbroken, but she tries to retain her dignity. "It would have been kinda funny if this had been on the level, even for a couple of months."

"If I stayed ashore for a couple of months, I might get to like it," says Bancroft with a grin. Just as the girl sees hope dawning, Bancroft's mate (Clyde Cook) arrives. "Time's up."

The girl has tears in her eyes. "Well—good-bye, Bill." Bill hesitates, and his mate tugs hard on his shirt pocket. The pocket rips, and the contents spill on the floor. Bill, finding just the excuse he needed, starts a row over this trivial incident. The girl smiles through her tears.

"I'll fix it for you, Bill. You can't go to sea like this." She sits him on the bed, and she tries to thread a needle. But she can't see through her tears. Von Sternberg uses a blurred subjective shot of the needle; never has the subjective camera been used so poignantly.

Bancroft sees that she cannot thread the needle, and he impatiently takes it from her. At that moment, she knows she has lost him. This moving scene ends with Bill leaving; the girl goes into a corner, averts her face and weeps. Bill tries to console her, and she turns on him savagely, pushing him through the door and slamming it.

"The nerve of that dame," he mutters to his mate. "Bawling me out after all I done for her."

His ship leaves, with Bill at work in the stokehold. "Lucky for you I happened along," his mate tells him. "If I hadn't prised you loose, she'd have stuck you like a barnacle."

The replacement third engineer appears. "I want steam, not talk."

Bill has suddenly had enough. He hands over his shovel, leaps overboard, and swims ashore. He finds his wife in jail; in the night court he discovers that she is charged with possessing stolen clothing. He confesses. "Break in any-where—take what you want," remonstrates the judge. "Sixty days. Release the woman."

The girl is overwhelmed at seeing him. "Sixty days ain't a long cruise, baby," he tells her. "An' it'll be my last if you'll wait for me."

"I guess I'd wait forever, Bill."

Docks of New York was one of the finest achievements of a period when fine achievements were commonplace. Its impact has gained strength with the passage of time. It is one of the enduring masterpieces of the American cinema, a triumphant vindication for a man whose behavior suggested to so many that of an artistic charlatan.

My own experience with this extraordinary man confirmed all I had heard. He allowed me to interview him, qualifying the invitation with a daunting order not to outstay my welcome.

"I am a polite man, and I do not wish to injure our future relationship. I will ask you to stay for half an hour. Then you will go. Do you understand?"

He received me at his Hollywood home. His study, in the depths of the house, was an attractive room crammed with books and Oriental statuary and decorated with diplomas—mostly commemorating recent awards from European countries. The room was cluttered in the way a Sternberg set is cluttered; every-where was something to intrigue and excite the eye.

I began the interview somewhat nervously; von Sternberg, seated behind a huge desk, was quick to notice this.

"What I would like to ask you first of all—" I began.

"Half an hour is a long time, Mr. Brownlee," he said. "Compose yourself. Relax. I will tell you when the half hour is over."

"You're very considerate . . . The technical aspect of your photographing your pictures . . ."

"What is the nature of your project in general?"

"Well, I'm trying to get to the secret of the silent-film era—which I regard as the richest era in film history, an era which you brought—"

"But Mr. Brownlee, why do you couch your question in parentheses? Why don't you tell me your inquiry, without what you regard as the richest era in film history?"

"You asked me what the nature of my project was—"

"Yes, yes."

"Well, I'm telling you."

"You asked me how some things were. I can't agree with you about those things. So just tell me what you want to know. What your inquiry is. Do you follow me?"

"Yes I do."

"Well, you're making parenthetical observations."

"You don't agree?"

"They're debatable. They cause a great deal of confusion in my mind about the nature of your inquiry. I want to find out what it is you're investigating."

"Well, I'm investigating the silent film—"

"You said the secret."

"Did I?" I said resignedly.

"There's no secret about it, so I don't know—"

"I'm trying to get to the root of it; perhaps that's a term you may not understand quite—an English term for—"

"Are you suggesting, Mr. Brownlee, that I do not understand? Look around you at my books. You assume that I do not know anything about the English language. I know what the word 'root' means."

"I'll get to my question any moment now! I'm getting over barbed-wire obstacles at the moment."

"No, I just don't want you to . . . I'm useless in any primitive approach to any cinematic problem."

"Well, I'm not trying to give a primitive approach, but I'm certainly being battered down to it. Look, I'm writing a book. About silent pictures. I'm writing a book about silent-film directors, cameramen . . . the men that made this period to *me* the richest of all. I'm trying to find out how it was that *you* managed under Hollywood conditions to control the photography of your films. And I would like to know the technical details of how you achieved it—right down to the stock you used . . ."

"You have the most amazing parenthetical approach with everything you say that I have ever heard in my life."

Although infuriated that I could make no headway, I have to admit, in retrospect, that von Sternberg was right. I can see just what he was objecting to. I was approaching him with a set of preconceived ideas; his replies had to fit those ideas. Accustomed to being misrepresented, he wanted me to understand what he was saying from *his* viewpoint.

Gradually, his replies, while remaining guarded, became fuller and more enlightening. I asked him how such great cameramen as Lee Garmes were able to work with him when he controlled the photography.

"Lee Garmes did exactly as I told him to. Exactly. To the extent that I would always be beside the camera. No picture of mine has ever been independently photographed. I always liked the best man I could find—Lee Garmes was excellent. One of the best men I had was Bert Glennon. Every time I had a different cameraman. They were learning. They were pleased to be instructed."

"Where did you learn photography?" I asked.

"Photography is not an independent art."

"Lighting?"

"Is not an independent art. One of the interesting things about the acquisition of knowledge is that one does not necessarily acquire this knowledge in a direct line from someone who was expert in it before. Otherwise there would never be anything new. There are always new approaches—and I began to photograph with a still camera long before I did anything else.

"James Wong Howe, a very good photographer, came to me the other day. 'I'll never forget what you taught me.' I said, 'What did I teach you?' He said, 'You said to me, "The sun only throws one shadow." You questioned why I had six or seven shadows in everything I was doing. From that moment on I never had more than one shadow.' This is a very simple observation; it would take a very nondiscerning person to so illuminate something that it throws creeping shadows. It's still being done . . ."

Von Sternberg has no interest in accurate detail on the screen—unlike von Stroheim, who fanatically checked everything down to the last tunic button to ensure authenticity.

"When I made *Underworld* I was not a gangster, nor did I know anything about gangsters. I knew nothing about China when I made *Shanghai Express*. These are not authentic. I do not value the fetish for authenticity. I have no regard for it. On the contrary, the illusion of reality is what I look for, not reality itself. There is nothing authentic about my pictures. Nothing at all. There isn't a single authentic thing. When I made *The Blue Angel* in Berlin I had never been in Germany before. That is, I'd passed through Germany—was there a couple of days. They wanted me to visit the school system and find out something about what the pressures are. It was very humorous. I didn't want to see. It would only confuse me.

"There are other values that I'm after. For instance, for some strange reason there are certain films which have been made by very capable directors and which have retained the power that was not quite evident at the time. The power has lasted long enough—visually long enough—for people to wish to see the films again or to look at them as something that had an impact other than they thought at first.

"For instance, I made a film called *Scarlet Empress*. This film was seen and was generally derided. The reviews were very bad. But today when it is seen, thirty years later, there seems to be another quality there, that makes it more valuable than it was at the time.

"The German government gave me a ribbon—a gold ribbon of special distinction—for making *The Blue Angel*. It is in fact dated 1963. Thirty-four years after I made the film! They didn't do these things while I was there.

"There are some qualities which seem to last, and it is these lasting qualities which should talk. It is something that is not evident to analysis at the time. You see, for instance, Bunuel makes *Los Olvidados*. At the time you say, "Well, that's a fine picture,' but somehow or other you want to see that again and again . . . students want to look at it as they will want to look at *Viridiana* perhaps thirty years from now.

"There are other qualities there than those achieved by discernible technical effects. For instance, Mr. Eisenstein wrote a book about the theory of montage. He never used that in his own work. This is what he composed for some people who needed to read such a thing."

No glib, psychological summing-up can rationalize this extraordinary personality. His tolerance may be poised on a bayonet tip, but once that obstacle has been overcome, he displays a genuine warmth, wisdom, and charm. These qualities were revealed when von Sternberg came to England to launch his book. He snapped at one or two importunate journalists, but otherwise he was uncharacteristically benevolent. At the crowded press reception, von Sternberg answered questions courteously, in a very soft, quiet voice so that his interrogators had to strain to hear him above the general noise. He wore a houndstooth jacket, with a colorful tie.

"My goodness!" said a woman critic, "what a wonderful von Sternberg tie you're wearing."

Without a flicker of amusement, he replied, "I have a good tailor."

Evening Standard critic Alexander Walker interviewed him persuasively, and von Sternberg responded with more information than he usually imparts:

"I regard actors as marionettes, as pieces of color in my canvas. When I direct, I am ice cold. I can't be emotionally involved. I watch a motion picture as a surgeon watches an operation. If the patient dies, that does not diminish the interest of the operation. How can a man who starts work at six a.m. and finishes at eight p.m. have any feelings? If he did he would die at the end of the first day. I have no affection for anything which comes as I expect it to come. I have affection only when the film or the sequence is better than I planned it."

Walker asked him why the character of Lionel Atwill in *The Devil Is a Woman* was made up to look so much like von Sternberg.

"Everyone in my films is like me," he replied enigmatically.

"Physically? Morally?" asked Walker.

"Spiritually," said von Sternberg, smiling slightly.

Some autograph hunters descended. As von Sternberg signed each one with his name, the recipient's name, and "Affectionately," a woman came to say good-bye. Von Sternberg turned to her as she spoke, and gave her all his attention. Then he gently took her right hand and held it, speaking to her very softly. The woman practically melted under his charm. "Good-bye," she said, backing away starry-eyed. "It really was wonderful to have met you. I think you're . . . you're *wonderful!*"

Later, Von Sternberg explained his theory of photography.

"A landscape must be photographed in the same way as a human face. You have the hills, the trees, a lake if possible. I always gauze the sky at the top— I burn holes in the gauze with a cigarette to give me an irregular edge. The landscape, you see, is the same as a face, which has as its main features the eyes, the nose, and the mouth and hair. I always have a light in the frame, which is very bright. It can be any part of the frame. I place a light directly above a face so that the nose shadow is very short. I do not use fill light. Cameramen always want fill light. Why? I use very simple lighting. Cameramen cannot reproduce it because they cannot continue with this simplicity. Also, they have not my talent."

Von Sternberg offered an explanation for the apparent inconsistency of the story line in *The Last Command:*

"William Powell, as the director, is commenting on the difference between a great actor and a great man. It is necessary to point the difference. What was actually said was, 'He was more than a great actor. He was a great man.' He said that based on his observation of Jannings' performance in the trenches in the studio."

I asked if von Sternberg allowed his actors any interpretation of their own.

"What interpretation could they give?"

"Well, they could deliver the dialogue—"

"What dialogue could they have learned?"

"From the script."

"What script? There was no script. If I gave my actors a script they would spend all night rehearsing before a mirror, and it would be very hard for me to undo all that. When they come on my set they have no idea what to do.

The Last Command (1927). Emil Jannings as a former Russian general, now a Hollywood bit player. The assistant director appraises his uniform; a property man stands by with a boxful of medals.

George Bancroft and Evelyn Brent in Underworld (1927).

The Docks of New York (1928). *Betty Compson tries to repair George Bancroft's torn pocket. At right, Clyde Cook.*

You must realize that first I set up my camera, then my lights, and then I am ready for my actors to come on."

"Did you improvise?"

"On *Anatahan,* which was carefully planned, we improvised only two or three scenes. On other films, the actors did not know what they were going to do. Since my scenes are short I can do this. The dialogue is short, there are no extended passages. Unless there is singing or dancing, the scenes are short, therefore I can improvise."

Asked about his contributions to *Children of Divorce,* to *It,* and to *Duel in the Sun,* von Sternberg replied that they could not be recognized.

"I can imitate the style of any other director. When I did *Children of Divorce,* I did it in the style of Frank Lloyd. I had nothing to do with *It.* Clarence Badger directed. Wait a minute—I know how they mix us up. Badger got the silver medal for *It* and I got the gold medal for *Underworld."*

I asked him to elaborate his remark about his lack of emotion.

"I am ice cold. You cannot direct unless you have contempt for your camera, contempt for your lights, contempt for your actors."

"Is contempt the right word?"

"Well, if not contempt—indifference."

"You talk of all this coldness, but you yourself are not a cold person."

"Ice cold."

"When talking with you, one doesn't feel you're cold."

"That depends what you mean by a cold person. I love human beings. I am a warm friend. I am a loving husband and a loving father." He paused. "Imagine me saying I am a loving father! You got that out of me by insistence. But I have been in Europe a month. When I return I shall embrace my family. But where films are concerned, you must lose your emotional involvement, otherwise you will not be in full control of your scenes. People will see things that you did not know were there. You cannot be sure you have the effect, because of the emotion you had at the time."

In answer to my questions about his photographic technique, von Sternberg offered to demonstrate. "Give me a camera and some lights, and I will show you," he said. With BBC producer Barrie Gavin, who was planning a program on von Sternberg, I arranged for a studio to be available the following Sunday.

Isleworth Studios, in a suburb of London, are generally shut on Sundays. This Sunday, however, especially for von Sternberg, they had been opened by the owner of the studios, Ralph Solomons.

Von Sternberg climbed out of the taxi and walked into the studio. "This will take five minutes," he said, "if everything is ready."

Everything was not ready. A full staff was not available, and several people were doubling up. A two-man television camera crew shadowed von Sternberg's every move.

"Where is the floor light?" Von Sternberg's customarily soft voice now had a commanding ring about it.

The electrician brought up a heavy lamp, known as a 5k. Without removing his coat or scarf, von Sternberg set to work. He pushed the lamp forward, until it stood a few feet from the girl who was acting as model. He asked the electrician to raise the lamp to its fullest extent. Then he produced a chair for the girl to lean against; it also marked her position.

He ordered the camera to be set up with a two-inch lens. The assistant did so, and von Sternberg saw him peering through the finder. "You don't mind me looking through it, do you?" von Sternberg asked. The assistant grinned sheepishly.

Von Sternberg removed his glasses and looked at the shot. He straightened up from the camera and appraised it with the naked eye.

"Would you take this bench away and move your light closer? Now get up there and put the back light on." The electrician clambered up the ladder to the lighting gantry.

"Not so fast, it is dangerous," said von Sternberg, with concern.

The light clicked, but did not come on. The second electrician fiddled with the junction box. No result.

"When I work I use a light bridge over my camera, so that I don't have to reorganize my lighting each time," said von Sternberg, ignoring the delay.

"Does this apply to traveling shots as well?" I asked.

Von Sternberg was silent for some time. Then he said, "Well, you ask extraordinary questions. How could it apply to traveling shots?"

"If the light bridge moved, the light would remain constant with the camera."

"The trick is not to make the light constant." At last the lamp came on. "Now get me one of those little baby spots." A second backlight came on. "Take that off, will you? Just this one. Throw it down on the girl's hair, and make it hot— as hot as you can."

He altered the position of the girl's head and aimed the spotlight behind her at the wall, then gazed at the result for a few moments.

"I want a black gauze," he announced.

"What does he want the black gauze for?" asked the electrician from among the lights.

"Who said that?" demanded von Sternberg. There was a momentary silence. "Er—me—up here."

"You want to know what I want it for?"

"Which lamp—"

"Huh?"

"Which lamp?"

"Get a gauze down here. You don't want to know what I want it for."

Von Sternberg returned to the camera and looked through the viewfinder.

"You have moved," he said to the girl. He went up to alter her position and decided she should remove her jacket. He was not pleased with her black sweater.

The gauze was put over the 5k, and a wooden board, known as a flag, placed in front.

"That's it. Now raise it up. See if you can cut across her forehead. Move that clock on the mantelpiece, will you? More. Hold it. Take this light and turn it, easy—easy—whoa!"

He looked up at the flag. "This thing is wrong. Have you got such a thing as what we call a cookalourus?"

The English technicians knew it as an "ulcer," and one was soon produced.

"That's better. Take the flag off and put that on. That light is not on her head. That light is on her shoulders. Put it up on her head. Put it on *her!*"

Suddenly, a transformation took place. The backlight moved, and an authentic von Sternberg close-up began to appear.

"My God," whispered the electrician, "look at that! He's making a Dietrich out of her. She looks really *beautiful!*"

Von Sternberg looked at his shot through the viewfinder, then straightened up. "This damn thing isn't right," he muttered. The television camera, constantly aimed at his face, began to irritate him. "I wish you'd stop. I mean you've taken enough, haven't you?" The cameraman hurriedly switched off and backed away. Von Sternberg went up to the model and put his hand gently on her chin. He brought the face down fractionally.

"Now, if you want you can shoot this, but this is not the right unit here," he said, indicating the cookalourus. "You need one that hasn't got such straight lines, one that is made of cellulose. A regulation broken line. You haven't got one here." He turned back to the girl. "Now move from right to left. Your face should be reasonably pleasant—reasonably. Just relax and move. All right, it's not perfect but take it."

The assistant switched on the camera. The 5k, directly above the girl, produced a very short nose shadow and a soft modeling to the cheekbones. The cookalourus protected the forehead; the backlight lit up the hair.

Josef von Sternberg demonstrating his lighting technique, Isleworth Studios, London, Nov 1966.

The final lighting; the cookalourus produces shadows of varying shapes.

"As you see," explained von Sternberg, "the forehead must be slightly shaded. The hot light should be on the chin. The background should be broken; you see what the spotlight did for the background. She should not wear a black dress. I would take a spray gun and spray that with aluminum. It is not photographic. She should wear a light dress. But in general, there's your scene. Now let's go home, huh?"

Von Sternberg signed a few more copies of his book, said good-bye to everyone, and was driven back to his hotel. The studio staff began to relax. They came to the conclusion that this use of two heavy lamps and one small spotlight was "the simplicity of genius." The electrician was particularly interested. For the record, I asked his name.

"Ralph Solomons," he said—the man who owned the studio. . . .

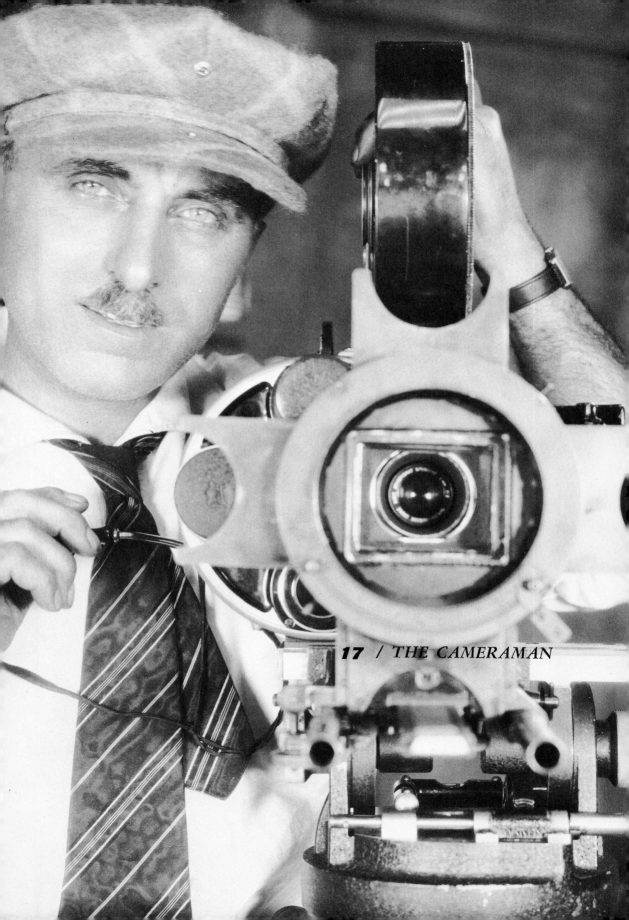

17 / THE CAMERAMAN

The value of the cameraman's contribution to a motion picture cannot be overestimated. Not that there is much danger. Reviewers still talk in terms of a director's "fine, atmospheric lighting" or his "brilliant handling of the camera." Hardly ever does the cameraman rate a mention.

This misconception has led to the assumption that lighting and composition are elements controlled by the director, with the cameraman merely carrying out instructions.

Only a handful of directors—Maurice Tourneur, Josef von Sternberg, Clarence Brown, Rex Ingram—have ever influenced the photography of their pictures. In each case they worked with a cameraman who was little short of a genius. These cameramen—John van der Broek, Lee Garmes, Bert Glennon, Hal Rosson, Jackson Rose, Arthur Miller, Milton Moore, William Daniels, John Seitz—respected their directors, understood what they were aiming for, and achieved the finest possible results.

On a regular commercial production, there is no time for a director to do more than select the basic setup, or camera position, and leave the cameraman to light it. A director often appreciates composition, but he seldom knows anything about lighting; few can tell what effect the lighting is producing until they see the rushes. Even then, most directors are satisfied if their scene is adequately illuminated.

The cameraman captures the visuals. The director sets them up, controls them, judges them . . . but it is the cameraman who records them on film. Consequently, his responsibility is enormous. Everything rests on his skill; the creation of the atmosphere, the translation of the director's ideas, the whole look of the film—and the work of dozens of people, whose combined efforts could be wiped out with one mistake.

Today, this responsibility is shared by several technicians, who make up the camera crew; the director of photography, who has overall control; the operator, who actually handles the camera; the first assistant, who follows focus to keep the picture sharp and acts as general assistant to the operator; and the second assistant, who loads the magazines and is general handyman to the crew.

In the silent days, the photography was the responsibility of one man—and that man did practically everything. He sometimes even supervised the developing of the negative.

The close association between cameraman and laboratory was of the highest importance. A marginal error in developing or printing could ruin valuable work. Frequently, the cameraman would be in there with the lab men, hours after his work was officially over, checking his negative on the developing drum with a red light.

"Motion-picture photography of the silent era," said John Seitz, the great cameraman of *The Four Horsemen of the Apocalypse* and *Scaramouche,* "was an optical and chemical business. The addition of sound changed it to more of an electrical enterprise. The talking picture made it necessary to standardize film developing, thereby taking away much of the individuality of the cinematographer."[1]

---

[1] *John Seitz in a letter to author, Jan. 1963.*

Cameraman John Boyle on Lambert Hillyer's
Her Second Chance *(1926).*

Until the introduction of panchromatic film, which gradually came into use in the early twenties, silent pictures were photographed on orthochromatic film. Although ortho film was crisper than present-day film stock, it was much slower. Its ASA rating would have been 24, compared to today's average of 200. Consequently, accuracy with focus and exposure was imperative.

Astonishingly, few Hollywood cameramen used exposure meters. The photo-electric cell had not been invented, of course, but a number of actinometers, or visual-extinction meters, were available—including the Watkins, designed especially for motion-picture work. This meter was fitted with a pendulum for counting half seconds and crank turns; it was the size of a small watch. Yet few cameramen even tried one. Said a veteran cameraman, when asked how he managed without meters: "You gauged exposure from past experience." He added that when faced with unusual conditions, such as snow, he would expose a short test, and develop it on the spot with a portable developing unit he always carried with him.

But back in the early days at Universal, there was a sign outside the camera department which read: "If in doubt, shoot at 5.6."

Cameras in the silent days were cranked by hand from choice, not because motors were unavailable. The old Biograph studios used motor-driven cameras for a time, and when Bell and Howell brought out their metal camera, in 1912, they made a motor for it. But it was not considered an essential part of the camera, and few used it. Bell and Howell also introduced the use of ball bearings for their camera, which made cranking easier. After a good turn, you could release the handle and it would revolve a turn or so on its own. The same Bell and Howell is still in use in optical departments, where a high degree of precision is required.

One of the most important advances was the arrival of the Bell and Howell perforator, in 1912. The perforator was a precision instrument that standardized the shape and number of sprocket holes and, together with the Bell and Howell printer, ensured a far better negative and release print.

Studio shooting, 1928. Monta Bell directing Leatrice Joy in The Bellamy Trial. *Arthur Miller at camera. In the foreground, Betty Bronson; Charles Middleton at extreme right.*

Director Sidney Franklin, wearing roller skates, works out a traveling shot for Quality Street *(1927). The camera is the newly introduced Bell and Howell Eyemo, especially designed for hand-held shooting. The actress is Marion Davies.*

Cameraman William Daniels lines up a top shot for The Kiss (1929), *while Jacques Feyder directs Greta Garbo and Conrad Nagel.*

Many veterans aver that if talking pictures had not banished the crank, in order to standardize shooting speed, films would still be ground by hand. For cranking, besides being reliable, had an added advantage; it allowed the cameraman to slow down or speed up the action during shooting.

If an actor took a long time to mount a horse, the cameraman could slow down. The actor would then appear to leap nimbly into his saddle. As the horse galloped away, the cameraman would return to normal, adjusting the exposure so that the density of the shot would remain even. Comedian Larry Semon had a trick of skidding to a halt during a chase, and then whisking around the corner. On the screen, this effect was always greeted by roars of laughter. To achieve it, cameraman Hans Koenekamp would reduce his cranking speed to a slow turn just as Semon threw his feet out, braked, and then vanished around the corner.

When ground slowly, the action would be speeded up. Slow motion was produced by grinding very fast; usually the speed required for miniatures was so fast that a motor had to be used.

The official rate of cranking was sixteen frames per second. Everything was calculated to this figure; the amount of stock required, the amount remaining in the magazine, the length of the film in projection. Camera motors, when used, were governed to turn at precisely this speed.

But sixteen frames per second proved to be a myth when the Western Electric sound engineers investigated the average speed of projection. Checking with the first-run Warner Theatre, they were told "between eighty and a hundred feet per minute." In other words, between twenty and twenty-six frames per second. The Western Electric men settled upon an average speed of twenty-four frames per second for their sound films; ninety feet per minute.

This wide divergence came about because projection motors were rheostatically controlled. There was no fixed standard rate; it was up to the operator to control the speed. Some unscrupulous theater managers, trying to squeeze in an extra house, would speed up the films until the action appeared ludicrously fast. Cameramen became wise to this practice, and they would increase their rate of cranking. By the mid-twenties, films would be photographed between eighteen and twenty-two frames per second, and projected between twenty and twenty-six. The slight increase was imperceptible on the screen but gave the action an added zest.

On most feature films, two cameras ground side by side. The first cameraman, in charge of photography, operated one camera, a second cameraman operated the other. The first camera supplied the domestic negative from which American prints were made; the other supplied the foreign negative.

The cameras themselves, which look so primitive, so apparently crude today, were actually very well made.

"All cameras use the same principle, then as now," said Arthur Miller. "The image is transmitted through the lens to an aperture, behind which the film is exposed while the shutter is open. When it is closed, the film is moved down for the next exposure. It's just as simple as that, no matter how it is dressed up."[2]

Said George J. Mitchell, writer and historian on motion-picture photography:

[2] *Arthur Miller to author, Hollywood, Dec. 1964.*

"It is a fact that you can load these cameras with modern film and place them beside a new Mitchell or Arriflex. You will not be able to tell the difference on the screen."[3]

Don Malkames, a silent-era assistant cameraman, who is now a director of photography and a collector of movie equipment, claims that he can shoot equally good pictures on the Pathé which Billy Bitzer used for *The Birth of a Nation* as on his newest machine.

"Of course," he says, "the new camera is handier to use, with many labor-saving gadgets, but the final result looks the same."[4]

From the earliest days, interiors were made on open stages, with sunlight providing the illumination. The stages were built so that the sun stayed at the back of the sets for most of the day. But inevitably, a few shadows would fall in the wrong places. Some studios overcame this bugbear by mounting their stages on a turntable and moving around with the sun.

The majority of Eastern companies, at the mercy of the weather, worked in glass-roofed buildings. Some of them used basic, theatrical-style artificial lighting. On the West Coast, where the sun was guaranteed three hundred days in the year, open stages remained in use much longer. These open stages were equipped with canvas and muslin diffusers.

At rough-and-ready Universal, the problem of whether or not to shoot in the face of an approaching cloud was solved by Lee Bartholomew, head of the camera department. If a cloud shadowed the main office building, or the light appeared yellow, he hoisted a "Don't Shoot" flag, which could be seen from all corners of the ranch.

Daylight lighting on interiors was adequate for comedies, since it was customary to photograph them in flat light. But for dramatic or atmospheric pictures it was too insipid. To relieve this pallid monotony, some lighting effects were essential. Griffith's cameraman, Billy Bitzer, said that he discovered backlighting by accident one day when he cranked a few feet of Mary Pickford and Owen Moore for fun, during the lunch break. The sun, coming from the rear and illuminating Miss Pickford's curls, created a striking effect, which Griffith was quick to notice when he saw the scene in the projection room. He was delighted, and Bitzer evolved a more efficient method of backlighting with mirrors. One mirror would reflect the sun into another, and this would be aimed at the back of the player's head. The men holding the mirrors could move around with the sun, enabling shooting to continue as long as the sun shone.[5]

Special effects are today the province of laboratory technicians. Fades, dissolves, superimpositions are produced by optical printers. But since such machines did not become available until the late twenties, special effects in silent pictures were the responsibility of the cameraman. He had to achieve them in the camera.

Fades were comparatively simple. To fade out at the end of a scene, the cameraman closed his aperture, or, in some cases, his shutter, while he cranked. The light was gradually cut off from the film, and a smooth fade was produced. Most cameramen fitted an iris to the front of the camera, used for those circular fades so

[3] George J. Mitchell to author, Hollywood, Dec. 1964.
[4] Don Malkames to author, New York, March 1964.
[5] Quoted by George J. Mitchell, in American Cinematographer, Dec. 1964, p. 710.

Paramount's Astoria studios, Long Island, N.Y., being converted into a Spanish village for Joseph Henabery's A Sainted Devil *(1924).*

A frame enlargement from A Sainted Devil *showing the result as it appeared on film, a fine example of a glass shot. The cameraman is Harry Fischbeck.*

A skillful double exposure from Rex Ingram's The Conquering Power *(1921) with Ralph Lewis. Cameraman, John Seitz.*

Cameras were used side by side to supply an original negative for foreign versions.

beloved of the early silents. If further fades were required after the picture was edited, laboratories offered a chemical fade process. This was not always successful; the chemicals tended to streak and the final effect was seldom comparable with camera fades.

Dissolves were more complicated. They involved fading out one scene, winding back, and fading in again over the same shot. If the incoming shot was unusable, the previous shot had to be retaken.

Allan Dwan made an early film from Gray's "Elegy" which he called *Paths of Glory*. A section of the poem required twenty-seven scenes to illustrate it. All of them were big scenes—one of them contained a parade through a triumphal arch by famous historical characters—and Dwan decided to link them with dissolves. Twenty-five dissolves . . .

"The cameraman would start on the first scene," said Dwan, "and at a certain point I'd say 'Fade,' and he'd start to count, 'One, two, three, four, five, six, seven, eight,' and he'd be out. It was faded. And he'd mark that number down. Now when we're ready for the second scene, he'd have to black his camera out, wind back eight, and we'd be ready to start. He'd fade in, and the scene would go on until I said 'Ready—fade,' and he'd count again and fade out.

"He had to do that twenty-five times on one piece of film. Any mistake on any one of them would wreck the whole works. Now the thing was sensational. When it went into the theater, people stood up and cheered. Everyone wondered how we did it. And I got a letter from Griffith about it. But the cameraman was so nervous that by the time he had fifteen of them on there, he'd take that roll of film and sleep with it! And he'd get up with his notes in the middle of the night and work it out to see if his numbers were right. When he put it in the camera his hands would shake so much that his assistant would have to take it away from him to be sure it was reloaded at exactly the right spot. I guess I was showing off a little. Twenty-five dissolves! It was a task to give a cameraman—I thought afterward it was a mean thing to do."

More complicated special effects, such as double exposures, split-screen, and glass shots also had to be executed in the camera. What the veteran cameraman achieved in the twenties would now be considered impossible without optical printers or traveling matte processes.

There is hardly a camera technique in existence that did not have its origin in the silent era. Wide screens, three-dimensional pictures, Technicolor, hand-held cameras, traveling shots, crane shots, rear-projection, traveling matte, Cinerama— all had made their appearance before the end of the twenties. Even the zoom lens had been developed by 1929.

Motion-picture lighting reached its peak during this period. From 1922 until the coming of sound, and intermittently thereafter until about 1935, cameramen achieved miracles with lights.

Photoplay pointed out in 1923: "It is a far cry from the glaring sunlight and monotonous floodlight of only a few years ago to the beautiful and effective lighting of today. Gone are the old-time diffusers which were like window shades, the mirrors covered with cheesecloth with which light was directed onto desired spots; the crude silver canvas reflectors. In recent years, the art of lighting for pictures has made marvelous strides. Hardly a week passes that some new discovery is not announced, and experimentation is going on all the time by directors and lighting experts. The day is coming—and coming soon—when the light expert will be as a skillful painter, using light rays as the artist does pigments."[6]

Picture after picture came out, each excelling the other in gauzed soft-focus effects, exteriors with a tangy sharpness that was practically three-dimensional, highlights glistening with an almost liquid intensity, tints and tones which subtly underlined atmosphere, brilliantly simulated effects such as candlelight, lantern light, moonlight . . . the lighting of the best silent-film cameramen infused the screens of the twenties with a luminescence that was magical.

How they did it is a saga of ingenuity and enthusiasm, energy, skill, and courage—and the love that these men felt for their work.

[6] Photoplay, *Nov. 1923, p. 44.*

18 / CHARLES ROSHER

Pancho Villa tried hard to be a director. He told me to film the funeral of a general. Villa's enemies, the Federal forces, had executed him by lashing him to the tracks and driving a train over him. The funeral spread over three days. I didn't have enough film for half a day. So I cranked the camera without any film in it. It was all I could do. I didn't want to be shot myself."

Mexico, 1913; Pancho Villa, bandit leader and rebel patriot, signed a contract with the Mutual Film Corporation, and triggered off one of the most bizarre episodes in screen history.[1]

"I accepted the assignment and went to Chihuahua, Villa's headquarters, accompanied by Mr. Dean, one of Hollywood's early cameramen, and father of Faxon Dean, who also became a cameraman," recalled Rosher. Part of the time, we lived in a boxcar, but during field operations we just slept on the ground. Our food consisted mainly of dried goat meat and tortillas. Our cameras, Williamson and Gillon, were packed on donkeys. It was a real treat to get back to Chihuahua and be able to bathe, change clothes, and get a good meal.

"I had to film everything; men digging their own graves . . . executions . . . battles. This was before World War I had started. I was right in there, in the trenches, listening to the *ping-ping-ping* of the bullets hitting the air above me.

" 'You don't have to worry,' they told me, 'so long as you can hear 'em!' I remember a man next to me stopping a bullet. It hit him right in the lung. He fell, and the blood poured out of his mouth—whoosh.

"I made many shots showing the primitive conditions. There was no Red Cross. They had one man with a shrapnel hole in his leg. They'd put a rag through the hole and moved it backward and forward to clean it. I made several still pictures of this sort of thing and gave them later to the American Red Cross. I had one of a man with his jaw blown off, lying on his chest like red meat . . . others of wounded men dying of gangrene. Hell of a mess.

"In Chihuahua, I met the British consul. He asked me to bring my still camera (a 3A Special postcard-size folding Kodak, the first of its kind) and come with him to the palace of Don Luis Terrazas, who was under house arrest, guarded by Villa's troops. Don Luis was one of Mexico's richest men. He owned huge herds of cattle, which Villa was now distributing to the poor peons. The British consul was one of the most respected men in Chihuahua, so we had no trouble in passing the guards. I made several pictures in the palace of Don Luis and his family, then the consul took one of me with the Don. Finally, Don Luis asked if I would take a letter to his son in El Paso.

"Every week I took the exposed film to El Paso to be shipped to Chicago for development and printing. It was about two hundred miles to Juarez aboard a military train, and everything was carefully checked. I had the Terrazas letter in my pocket, and I began to wonder what would happen if they searched me before crossing the border.

"As soon as we arrived at Juarez, I went to a photographer's studio and asked if I could use the darkroom. I placed the letter in one of the film cans. I knew

[1] *Gunther Lessing, a young lawyer, arranged the deal with Villa, depositing a substantial sum in an El Paso bank. Mutual made a separate agreement for a feature picture, a life of Villa to be directed by D. W. Griffith. Raoul Walsh went to Mexico to shoot background footage and action scenes. Eventually, D. W. Griffith, preoccupied with* The Birth of a Nation, *assigned the picture to Christy Cabanne, who made* The Life of Villa. *Walsh's footage was incorporated, and Walsh himself, with Villa's approval, played Villa as a young man.*

Charles Rosher, 1912, with Billiken camera. Made by Horsley of Nestor, this camera consisted of parts from the Gaumont and other models used by the Motion Picture Patents Company and was an infringement.

General Villa (extreme left) south of Chihuahua, 1913. Charles Rosher at right with William on camera.

they wouldn't dare open a can of film. When we reached the American side of the Rio Grande, I reported the facts to the U.S. officials. The can was opened in a darkroom, and they okayed the delivery of the letter.

"After many exciting experiences with Villa, I was captured by the Federal forces and placed incommunicado. There were five thousand Federal troops in this town, Ojinaga, surrounded by the Villaistas. I was taken before General Mercado, and he noticed the tiny Masonic pin I wore in my buttonhole. He gave me the Masonic greeting; he was a Mason too! Turned out that the current President Huerta of Mexico was this general's brother-in-law. Well, I was entertained royally in Ojinaga. Then General Pershing made some kind of a deal and the Federal troops were allowed to cross the Rio Grande—a shallow section which they could ford.

"The U.S. forces swooped in on them at El Paso and put them in a concentration camp. I took that general a big box of cigars while he was in the camp. Boy, was he glad! They freed him later.

"The film with Wally Beery, *Viva Villa!*, made in the thirties, was full of things imaginative rather than accurate. They didn't use any of our stuff. I don't even know what they did with it."

Seldom has a newsreel assignment had the benefit of such a distinguished cameraman. Rosher was already one of the industry's pioneers; although comparatively little known, he was soon to prove himself a master in his field. His work on the Mary Pickford pictures, over a twelve-year period, immeasurably improved the photography of American pictures and transformed motion-picture photography from a skilled craft into a fine art.

Rosher was born in London, on November 17, 1885. He studied photography at the Polytechnic, and covered several important assignments—the launching of the *Mauretania* and H. M. S. *Nelson,* and Harry Lauder's first pantomime at the Theatre Royal, Newcastle—before he joined the Bond Street firm of Speaight, Court photographers.

Visiting America in 1908, at the Photographers' Association of America Convention in Rochester, New York, he met George Eastman and George Harris, of Harris and Ewing, Washington, D.C. Rosher worked for this celebrated firm until 1909. Acquiring a motion-picture camera, he covered several events, and his work brought him to the attention of David and William Horsley, two Englishmen who owned the Centaur Film Company.

"The Horsleys had a studio in New Jersey. Well, I won't call it a studio. It was really nothing but a shop, with a lot of bathtubs for developing the film. They used to go out and make pictures with an improvised camera—an infringement of the Motion Picture Patents Company. This brought the Horsleys into the patents war, and they became the first independent producers."

In 1911, the Horsleys opened a West Coast branch, called Nestor Films—the first studio in Hollywood. Rosher became one of Hollywood's first cameramen.

"I was not always the cameraman. Wallace Reid, then playing small parts, could also crank the handle, and sometimes we changed places. While he shot the film, I was made up with side whiskers and a beard and I acted with the rest of the players."

During Hollywood's formative years, Rosher worked with Universal and Lasky, with Mae Murray, Sessue Hayakawa, with Cecil B. De Mille and William C. de

Mille. He was one of the cameramen on Cecil B. De Mille's *Carmen* with Geraldine Farrar.

"Alvin Wyckoff, an excellent photographer and a very easygoing man, was the head cameraman. De Mille used to shout at him, but he took it lying down. Wyckoff finally wrecked himself with De Mille when he founded the cameraman's union.

"De Mille was tough on lunch breaks. One day, about three p.m., he asked, 'Anyone hungry?'

" 'We're not, if you're not, chief,' Anne Bauchens, his cutter and script girl, replied.

"I yelled, 'Speak for yourself, Anne!' De Mille called lunch.

"But just in case, I'd carry sandwiches in a little bag hanging under the tripod head."

Rosher made the tests of Florence Vidor which brought her into pictures as a star. In 1915, on loan from Lasky, he shot a Lonesome Luke comedy, featuring the youthful Harold Lloyd. His wide experience, his background of still photography, and his mastery of lighting recommended him to Mary Pickford, the most important star in the business.

In 1917, he succeeded Walter Stradling, another Englishman and the uncle of Harry Stradling, as Mary Pickford's chief cameraman. Miss Pickford was already in a position of command; she was able to insist upon the finest artistic and technical values for her productions.

Rosher provided her with visuals of such astonishing quality than other photographic experts were awestruck.

Richard Speaight, the managing director of the Court photographers, who had employed Rosher in his early days, wrote a letter of congratulations:

"It is a long time since anything has made such an impression on me as the wonderful pictures you showed me of Mary Pickford." (Rosher was also responsible for Miss Pickford's stills.) "I have thought much about these and would first like to congratulate you on the wonderful results. In my thirty years' experience of studio work, and recently of cinema work, never have I seen such exquisitely portrayed portraits."

Speaight went on to ask how such results were achieved, and to wonder whether he had facilities adequate for such work. The technical advances achieved by Rosher while working for Mary Pickford are hard to exaggerate. Being a highly skilled portrait photographer, he undoubtedly felt a certain disdain for many of his fellow cameramen, some of whom had no training whatsoever. His scorn for this widespread ignorance spurred him to prove his worth. In this respect, he had something in common with D. W. Griffith; his temperament compelled him to treat motion-picture photography as though it were an art. The result was that he made it one.

And in doing so, he became the highest-paid cameraman in the world.[2]

When *Little Lord Fauntleroy* was released, in 1921, reviewers acclaimed Rosher's brilliant special effects.

"The double exposures are the finest that have ever been made in the history of the business. When Mary Pickford [playing a dual role], kisses herself as 'Dear-

---

[2] *D. W. Griffith offered him a job, but he was contracted to Mary Pickford.*

Sparrows (1926). *This scene was originally taken on location, but the sheep kept wandering away. Charles Rosher tried again on the back lot, and this time the sheep stayed put.*

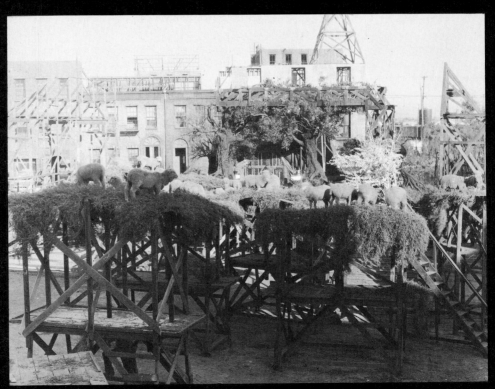

This reverse angle shows why.

est' and hugs herself, and when both characters walk off together, one ahead of the other—well, it's almost uncanny. Hats off to Rosher."[3]

These intricate trick shots were made in the camera. Rosher built a camera stand weighing two thousand pounds.

"Steel girders formed the framework; the base was lined with sandbags, and a huge, hollow block of steel supported the pan and tilt head. The contraption could be moved around on casters, but when I'd lined the shot up, packs secured it to the floor. Jacks held the pan head rigid, too, once it had been positioned. In front of the camera was the matte frame, and I moved the matte as Mary moved. The whole setup was so solid that you could jump around the floor without shifting it a thousandth of an inch."

As the *Motion Picture Herald* pointed out, not even an expert could spot the dividing line. "The embraces, the walks together, the various conversations indulged in by the figures—these not only bring forth the star's ability to differentiate them, but the double-exposure work is so fine that her performance is accentuated."[4]

Rosher went to extraordinary lengths to ensure perfection; in *Sparrows,* a dream sequence depicted Mary Pickford asleep in a barn. One wall of the barn dissolved away to show a flock of sheep being tended by a Christ figure. The dissolve itself was difficult enough, but the problem was increased by the flock of sheep. Whenever the scene was about to be shot, the sheep wandered away. Rosher had the

[3] WID's Daily, *Sept. 18, 1921.*
[4] Motion Picture Herald, *Oct. 1, 1921.*

Sunrise (1927) *directed by F. W. Murnau, photographed by Charles Rosher, with Janet Gaynor.*

carpenters build high platforms which were camouflaged with grass and foliage, and the sheep placed on top. Unwilling to break their necks by jumping off the edge, the sheep stayed put.

For *Rosita*, Mary Pickford's version of "Don Cesar de Bazan," directed by Ernst Lubitsch, Rosher created a new method of lighting.

Wrote a reviewer: "The really exceptional photography seen in *Rosita* . . . is likely to establish a new school of photographic art for the screen. The result Mr. Rosher has attained with his new method is an almost perfect perspective of the third dimension, or stereoscopic effect, showing the figures in bold relief in the foreground, at the same time keeping the background sharply in focus yet obtaining the long-sought-for effect of showing distance on a flat surface. 'Perspectography' is the new name applicable to this newest effect in the development of motion-picture production."[5]

The Los Angeles *Express* acknowledged Rosher as the industry's best-known cameraman. "He is one of our most competent, artistic, and thoroughly versed in lighting and camera values. He has invented more camera tricks than any other individual. Not even Bitzer, the veteran cameraman for D. W. Griffith, has anything on Rosher in this respect."[6]

Quite properly, Rosher has never underestimated his achievements. He is not naturally modest. Even so, he refuses to accept any superiority over Bitzer, whom he acknowledges as the greatest cameraman of all.

Rosher said that he found working under pressure quite intolerable. "If they made me mad, I used to walk off the set and disappear. No one could find me. I'd get the film in on schedule, often ahead of schedule, but I couldn't work with people breathing down my neck. Some shots take more time; others go very fast."

He admired Mary Pickford greatly. "I'll say definitely she was one of the finest characters I ever knew, and a clever businesswoman too. She did a lot of her own directing. The director would often just direct the crowd. At the end of a scene, whoever was directing, she would always ask me for my opinion. I often chose the setups; I'd get her to play a scene where I could light her favorably.

"On orthochromatic film, hair always looked dark unless you specially lit it. With Mary's curls, lighting was especially important. I often arranged her curls myself; I kept the hairpins by the camera. I also selected her make-up, which she applied herself. [Leichner German make-up.] There were very few make-up men in those days. I had a special powder mixed by Max Factor under my supervision in his hole-in-the-wall shop down in Los Angeles. The make-up was named 7R; it's still being made by the Max Factor organization.

"After Doug and Mary got married, I was with them in Europe and Doug went with me to the UFA studios in Berlin. I did special tests of their stars to demonstrate glamour lighting. They always lit them with heavy, dramatic lighting and deep shadows. Erich Pommer was there then, and he put me under contract for a year, with Mary's consent. I acted as consultant on F. W. Murnau's *Faust*. I didn't do anything on the picture, but Murnau expected to go to America, and he kept asking, 'How would they do this in Hollywood?'

"Carl Hoffman photographed *Faust* and I learned a great deal from him. I took

[5] *Unidentified review in Charles Rosher's press-cutting collection.*
[6] *Los Angeles* Express, *Aug. 13, 1921.*

Tempest (1927), directed by Sam Taylor, photographed by Charles Rosher, with Camilla Horn and John Barrymore.

The huge set built for Sunrise, designed by Röhrig and Herlth. The scale was intentionally exaggerated; this is the city seen by a young country couple, who are overwhelmed by its size. Motive sketches for this production were by Rochus Gliese.

several ideas back, including the dolly suspended from railway tracks in the ceiling, which I adapted for *Sunrise*, Murnau's first American picture.

'That was a very difficult film, *Sunrise.* We had many problems. My assistant was excellent, and very helpful—Stewart Thompson, later cameraman for Bing Crosby. For some scenes, such as the swamp sequence, the camera went in a complete circle. This created enormous lighting problems. We built a railway line in the roof, suspended a little platform from it, which could be raised or lowered by motors. My friend and associate, Karl Struss, operated the camera on this scene. It was a big undertaking; practically every shot was on the move. The German designers built an enormous set on the Fox lot, with false-perspective buildings. Real streetcars were brought in, and streetcar rails laid.

"For the forest scene, a mile-long track was built out at Lake Arrowhead; the end of the track came right in to the city. All of it was specially built, including the streetcar, which was mounted on an automobile chassis. On those big scenes, such as the fairground and the café, I think I used more lights than had ever been used before."

Sunrise is a great film; slow and classical. Photographically, it is a work of genius. Its European flavor is very strong, even though it was made in California. But however brilliant the European cameramen may have been, no one could have infused the visuals with such a combination of delicacy and richness as the great Charles Rosher.

Murnau clearly trusted his cameraman implicitly. "I found it difficult to get Murnau to look through the camera. 'I'll tell you if I like it in the projection room,' he used to say. I would have continued to work with Murnau on *Four Devils*, but I had to go back to Mary Pickford. I very much wanted to continue with Murnau; I was with him a few hours before he died in a car accident. We were very close friends."

Rosher's favorite director, however, was Sidney Franklin, for whom he shot two Mary Pickfords—*Heart o' the Hills* and *The Hoodlum.*

"Franklin did not know me, and wanted someone else as cameraman. Mary said, 'If you don't like him or his photography after you've worked with him, I'll talk to you again.' We got along fine, and after that he borrowed me whenever I was between pictures."

He photographed Sidney Franklin's *Smilin' Thru* with Norma Talmadge and *Tiger Rose* with Lenore Ulric.

"I got a bonus on that picture—the only time Harry Warner has ever been known to give a bonus. Ulric *had* to be back in the theater by a certain date. If we hadn't finished the picture by them, we'd have to go to New York and carry on while she was rehearsing. That would have been pretty expensive. Well, Harry Warner began to sweat.

" 'Charlie,' he said, 'I'd be very grateful if you'd help me over this. Try and put the pressure on before she returns.' He said that to me, see, because Sid couldn't put pressure on anybody; he was only concerned with the actors. Well, I did my best, and we managed to complete the picture before she went to her rehearsals. We were now back from location at the Sunset Boulevard studios of Warner Brothers. And Harry called me into his office.

" 'I want to thank you, Charlie, for putting on the pressure and getting us through. If we'd gone to New York it would have cost us twenty-five to thirty thousand dollars more to finish the picture.' And he proffered me a check. I took it, but he kept hold of his end. I said I was very grateful but that I was only doing my duty, and I shouldn't really accept. You see, I was getting a salary from Mary Pickford, who had loaned me, as well as a salary from Warners. But if I'd let go of that check, he'd have put it on the table, and I could hardly pick it up after all I'd said.

"So I just kept hold of it. He kept on talking and I kept on holding—and at last he let go. I looked at it, and found that it was for a thousand dollars. That was epoch-making—the Warners handing out a bonus."

David Belasco, the great impresario, who had produced the stage version of *Tiger Rose,* was so delighted with Rosher's work that he sent him a telegram:

YOUR CAMERA WORK IN THE TIGER ROSE PICTURE IS SO SUPERB THAT I HASTEN TO CONGRATULATE YOU   YOUR LIGHTING EFFECTS ARE GOD GIVEN IN THEIR NATURALNESS AND BEAUTY   YOU HAVE MORE THAN CONFIRMED ALL THAT I HAVE HEARD OF YOUR ARTISTRY
                                                    DAVID BELASCO

Belasco, the pioneer of elaborate stage effects, knew what he was talking about. Rosher claims, however, that it was only because he had made Lenore Ulric look good in the close-ups.

"Belasco was sweet on Ulric—she was his pet, and that was why I got that cable."

Rosher preferred to work with men who understood the problems of photography and who would allow him the time needed to achieve the effects they wanted. This was not always possible.

"Sam Wood was selfish; he wasn't interested in my job, and he never gave me enough time. He didn't want to devote time to photography—unlike Sidney Franklin, who was so tasteful, so highly sensitive.

"I liked working with Robert Z. Leonard, husband of Mae Murray. He used to call me Lord Plushbottom, and put a chair on the set with that painted on the back. I made *The Primrose Ring* for him in 1917, and I did some trick work that I was very proud of. It sounds simple enough today—fairies walking over Tom Moore's hand—but it had to be done with the old Pathé camera, and it was not easy at all. The fairies were children; one of them was Loretta Young.

"Another fine director who appreciated photography was Maurice Tourneur, for whom I photographed *The White Circle."*

In 1927, Rosher began work for United Artists' *Tempest,* originally planned as a von Stroheim picture, but now a Barrymore vehicle, directed by the Russian émigré director Viatcheslav Tourjansky. In France, Tourjansky had worked with Abel Gance on *Napoleon* and had directed the brilliant *Michel Strogoff* with Ivan Mosjoukine.

"Tourjansky was a perfect delight to work with. He had a camera eye, great taste, and a fine imagination. But he wasn't fast enough. I don't know the details of the dispute, but Schenck took him off the picture. Lewis Milestone was brought in, but Sam Taylor finished the picture. The leading woman, Dorothy Sebastian, was taken off as well as Tourjansky, and replaced with Schenck's girl friend, Camilla Horn, who had been in Murnau's *Faust.*

"By this time I had developed my Rosher Kino Portrait Lens. In Germany, in 1926, I had the opportunity with a big optical company there to develop this lens. It gave a rather marvelous quality, and roundness, almost a stereoscopic quality. The lens was tried out in Germany; the first time it was used was by Gunther Rittau on von Sternberg's *Blue Angel* for the close-ups of Marlene Dietrich. The first time I used it was on *My Best Girl* with Mary Pickford. And it is still in use in Russia, with my name on it.

"Barrymore was especially pleased with it because its softness smoothed away his dewlaps. For the first time he could be photographed properly full-face; before, they had to favor the famous profile. I was the only one who could get him on the set. He was half-stiff from drink most of the time. He used to get me in his dressing room to drink Napoleon brandy with him; I used to pour it surreptitiously into a flower vase."

Sam Taylor was a comedy director, hardly an ideal choice for a Russian melo-drama. He was a very imaginative director, however, with a full command of motion-picture technique; thanks to his direction, and to Rosher's beautiful camera work, *Tempest* emerged as a richly impressive production, the epitome of the romantic Hollywood spectacle of the late twenties.

After *Tempest,* Rosher did location work in the Canadian Rockies for another Barrymore film, *Eternal Love,*[7] directed by Lubitsch. Sam Taylor sent word that as soon as he returned from location, Mary Pickford wanted him to start on her first talking picture, *Coquette.*

Rosher went to the studio, and attended a meeting with Sam Taylor and the sound engineers. They produced a plan, showing the positions of the cameras. Each camera would be contained in an insulated booth; the plan was carefully worked out to enable entire scenes to be shot at one time.

"Taylor and the sound men must have spent a lot of time laying out these plans. No consideration had been given as to how the cameraman was to achieve satisfactory lighting."

At this time, 1929, the sound engineers had not found a way of recording close-ups and long shots and maintaining the levels, so scenes had to be shot in a sort of television style.

"Sound dominated everything in Hollywood, and photography took a great setback for over a year. Anyway, I expressed myself freely, and as a result my career with Mary Pickford came to an end—fortunately without any unpleasant-ness. I took no part in the production."

A new career began for Charles Rosher. While in Germany, he had received an offer from British International Pictures, in Elstree, which he had been forced to turn down. Now he told them he was available, and he was immediately engaged.

While E. A. Dupont set up *Atlantic,* the story of the sinking of the *Titanic,* Rosher photographed *The Vagabond Queen* (Geze von Bolvary) with Betty Balfour, known as the Mary Pickford of England.

After working in France, on *La Route est Belle* (Robert Florey), he returned to Hollywood in 1930, and started work at M-G-M. Having won the first Academy Award ever given to a cameraman—for *Sunrise*—Rosher received another Acad-

---

[7] *The working title was* King of the Mountains.

emy Award for *The Yearling* (directed by Clarence Brown, produced by Sidney Franklin, 1946). Numerous Academy nominations for his photographic achievements were still to come (he received eight) together with two Eastman Medals of Honor and *Photoplay's* Gold Medal. He also became a Life Fellow of the Royal Photographic Society, a fellow of the Photographic Society of America, and he received the first and only fellowship award to a cinematographer from the Society of Motion Picture Engineers, in 1950. He received his highest award when the Professional Photographers of America made him an Honorary Master of Photography.

But Charles Rosher's greatest accomplishment took place during the silent era when he, and a small group of top-flight cameramen, changed the look of American films. As Mary Pickford said, at the opening of the Eastman House Photographic Museum in 1950, "Charles Rosher is the dean of cameramen."

Charles Rosher was also one of the great masters of the motion picture.

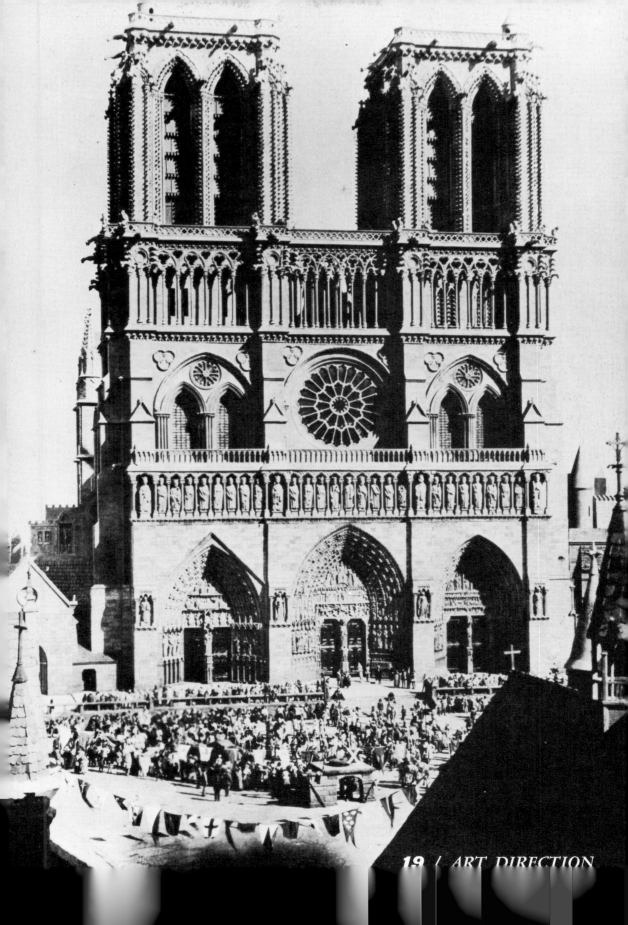

The more successful the art direction, the less likely it is to be noticed. Only when it fails, only when a set *looks* like a set, does the work of this much over-looked department become apparent.

Set design, set construction, and set dressing are items taken for granted by audiences. Unhappily, they are often taken for granted within the industry itself. All too frequently, a director sees his set first when he walks onto it to start shooting.

Art direction, or production design, determines the look of a picture almost as forcefully as the lighting. For it dictates the atmosphere—and atmosphere, particularly in films of period reconstruction, is tremendously important.

In the silent days, art direction was a late developer. The earliest pictures were shot against flats decorated by the property man. If a scene painter was needed, he was hired from a local theater. Audiences, accustomed to the inadequacy of theatrical sets, were not disturbed by the White House looking like a small-town grocery store. The miracle was that it was there at all.

The improvement in art direction paralleled the improvement in lighting. In 1914, one of the greatest theatrical designers in America, Wilfred Buckland, joined Famous-Players-Lasky. The ephemeral miracles he had achieved for Belasco he now created, more permanently, for films like *Carmen, The Cheat,* and *Joan the Woman.*

"Because Buckland had worked with the master realist of the stage," wrote Kenneth MacGowan in *Photoplay,* "he brought something besides the Belasco plays to Lasky. He brought tasteful richness of setting. Under the flat lighting of most movies [which were then lit by daylight] it would have bored and distracted with quite the force that it does on the stage. But made over by "Lasky Lighting"—as it is today in most of the Famous-Players-Lasky productions—it has a splendid and satisfying richness."[1]

Probably the greatest impetus to art direction at this period were the gigantic sets in *Intolerance,* built without any art director. They took three months to erect, and Frank "Huck" Wortman, the master craftsman who built them, aroused much anger in Hollywood when he refused to obey the instructions for instant demolition issued by the Los Angeles fire department. They stood, both a reproach and an encouragement, for almost a year, towering above the site where the Allied Artists studios now stand.

William Randolph Hearst, anxious that Marion Davies should appear in the richest possible settings, brought in Joseph Urban, designer for the Ziegfeld *Follies* and the Metropolitan Opera House.

"The motion picture offers incomparably the greatest field to any creative artist of brush or blueprint today," said Urban, in 1920. "It is the art of the twentieth century and perhaps the greatest art of modern times. It is all so young, so fresh, so untried. It is like an unknown ocean stretching out before a modern Columbus."[2]

A Viennese architect, Urban left Austria in 1913 and became as celebrated in America as Reinhardt in Germany. Said Julian Johnson in *Photoplay,* "The thing that has spread Mr. Urban's name about the United States has been the Ziegfeld *Follies,* in five gorgeous annual issues. However much Mr. Ziegfeld has done for

[1] Photoplay, *Jan. 1921, p. 73.*
[2] Photoplay, *Oct. 1920, p. 32.*

Mr. Urban, in either finance or notoriety, Mr. Urban has done incalculably more for Mr. Ziegfeld, for, in supervising every item of color and material form, from the lights to the gowns of the girls, he—no other—has created the most beautiful vision of its kind that the stage has ever seen. 'Urban lighting,' 'Urban gowns,' 'Urban scenery,' 'Urban curtains,' and, above all, a deep, tropic, furnace-like, fascinating, and almost intolerable shade known as 'Urban blue,' have become household words in every show-shop."[3]

Art directors, like Urban, ran into strong resentment from the carpenters and prop men who had had the field to themselves for so long. On the Hearst production *The World and His Wife* (Robert Vignola), the studio carpenter, evidently distrusting Urban's motion-picture ability, brought him a set of postcards as a guide, and some photographs of a Spanish house which he thought should be copied. Urban, with the crushing knowledge of the erudite European, gently explained that he had brought, as an example of the city architecture of New Castile, pictures of a new French château built in Andalusia by a war profiteer.

Not only carpenters were irritated by these design experts. The directors, too, grew impatient. They had to follow carefully laid plans, their movements were restricted, and they could no longer switch haphazardly from setup to setup without elaborate alterations to flats and overheads.

One director explained to Urban that he wanted a model of a Buddhist temple constructed for a dream sequence: "You build her right up there, about three feet high, and I wheel it up or push it back—she gets big or she gets small, just as I place the platform; you know what I mean?"

"Yes," murmured Urban, "I know. You want a rubber temple."[4]

The art directors were responsible for much of the improvement in the appearance of pictures around 1920; before that, the interiors of many of the straightforward, routine productions had a thin and empty look, like a rehearsal runthrough. Unfortunately, the change was so phenomenal that film makers fell in love with the unaccustomed beauty. For a while, some films became slow. "You don't run past a beautiful picture in an art gallery," was the current argument. "You stop and gaze at it."

Robert Brunton, an important early Hollywood figure, was among the first to contribute that most vital stage of creativity: elimination.

"He built his settings with taste and restraint," said Kenneth MacGowan, "but he made assurance doubly sure by blotting them out with shadows. Realism and minutiae he borrowed, and light from a single major source; but with one he killed the other. The actors held the stage, illumined and dramatized by light. Behind them were mere suggestions of place—surfaces that were at once atmosphere and a frame."[5]

A similar approach was that of Hugo Ballin, actually one of the few art directors to direct his own pictures—starring his wife, Mabel Ballin. Favoring simplicity, Ballin's method was one of mathematical precision. He made copious sketches for every scene, and worked out the camera position for each shot.

Ballin, Brunton, Buckland, and Urban were the advance guard of a wave of

[3] *Ibid.*
[4] Photoplay, *Oct. 1920, p. 132.*
[5] Photoplay, *Jan. 1921, p. 73.*

Treasure Island (1920), *directed by Maurice Tourneur. Art director, Floyd Mueller. Charles Hill Mailes, Bull Montana, Lon Chaney, Shirley Mason, Charles Ogle.*

The Four Horsemen of the Apocalypse (1921), *directed by Rex Ingram. Uhlans enter the village on the Marne. Art director, Joseph Calder.*

Joseph Urban set for **Buried Treasure.**

The essential combination: brilliant lighting (by John Seitz) and brilliant art direction (Leo Kuter) from Rex Ingram's Trifling Women *(1922) with Barbara la Marr, Lewis Stone, and Gareth Hughes.*

designers and craftsmen who descended upon motion pictures to embellish, to decorate, and to ornament. Later, their position was usurped by such great names as Cedric Gibbons and William Cameron Menzies. Eventually, this aspect of motion-picture production was so completely mastered that, in 1927, critic L'Estrange Fawcett was campaigning for a return to the days of the painted backcloth and the mere suggestion of sets. He conceded, however, that realistic detail could be amazingly significant in a film. "I believe the great mass of the public are captivated by it. A carelessly constructed set may often wreck the general effect of a film; the public simply loathes sloppiness or skimping. In time we may educate ourselves to look further and we may evolve scenic modes which are less expensive and provoke a greater esthetic reaction. Instead of mere soothing pleasure, we may secure dramatic effects by suggesting scenery in a tragic sequence—a few lines or shadows to represent door, window, and wall— or a humorous design behind comic action. But I fear it will take time to make the public appreciate the idea."[6]

Yet this very idea was used in Maurice Tourneur's *The Blue Bird* (1918), on which the art director was the brilliant Ben Carré. "A number of scenes," said Kenneth MacGowan, "showed the players against backdrops painted in fantastic flat designs—with perhaps a mountain or a castle in silhouette. There was no attempt to light these drops so as to imitate reality or to create an abstraction of vague dreaminess. It was a "stunt," an attempt at abstraction. The effect of individual scenes was pretty enough, but the contrast between these and succeeding scenes of three-dimensional realism was disconcerting."

The Blue Bird, though highly imaginative, failed financially, and Tourneur and Carré returned from their experimental meandering to ground on which they were more familiar and more expert. Their early films brought to the screen a degree of beauty seldom attained since, and both names were vitally important in the development of motion-picture design.

The real bugbear which haunted the art department was that conscience-pricking irritant, accuracy. For all the ability of designers of this period, many sets were pure Hollywood. Such structures could exist nowhere else. Beulah Marie Dix, a noted historian as well as scenarist, came to this conclusion: "I think Hollywood film makers were of one mind with that eighteenth-century English writer who was taken to task for introducing Negro slaves in a story laid in England in the Middle Ages.

"He replied that the blackness of the slaves contrasted dramatically with the whiteness of the princess, and if blue slaves would have contrasted even more dramatically, he'd have made the slaves blue."[7]

Nevertheless, the majority of silent-film designers, set decorators, property men, and technical directors aimed at accuracy. Their attitude was summed up in this highly commendable manner by the head of a property department in 1919:

"Maybe not nine hundred and ninety-nine people out of a thousand know or care what kind of candles an old Kentucky moonshiner would be likely to use in his cabin. But as there is always the possibility that the thousandth person does, we are taking no chances. We'll dig up an old candle mold from somewhere and get the real article manufactured on the premises."

[6] L'Estrange Fawcett: Film Facts and Forecasts *(London: Geoffrey Bles; 1927), p. 181.*
[7] Beulah Marie Dix in letter to author, Aug. 1964.

The set as it was originally used in The Spanish Dancer (1923), *directed by Herbert Brenon. A glass shot made it appear part of old Madrid.*

The set, redressed for Hotel Imperial (1927), *directed by Mauritz Stiller (in white at right).*

Cameraman Hal Mohr was married before this cathedral altar, built by Richard Day from Erich von Stroheim's design. **The Wedding March (1928).**

The alibi "The audience will never notice" was given the lie very early in *Photoplay's* "Why Do They Do It?" column—which was entirely devoted to blunders made in movies:

"As Nan in *The White Moll,* Pearl White, in order to ward off suspicion of the blood spots on the floor, has rare presence of mind to cut her hand on a broken lamp chimney. In a few minutes, when she becomes the 'White Moll' again, the wound is entirely healed, and she even allows the adventurer to squeeze her hand!" (—Marion Shallenberger, Johnstown, Pa.)[8]

Audiences spotted every conceivable error, and specialists in various subjects had a field day when films appeared dealing with their favorite topic. Sometimes these complaints were unjustified; many fans complained that Valentino, in Rex Ingram's version of *Eugénie Grandet—The Conquering Power*—was seen using a fountain pen. This caused a protest from Valentino himself: "Why did people object?" he asked. "The story was modernized . . . didn't they realize?"

What was extraordinary about the silent days was that so many film makers sincerely tried to attain authenticity. Griffith had a fine sense of period, and a historian's approach to his subject, which he managed to transmit to his players.

"We used to do our own research," said Dorothy Gish. "We went down to the public library and looked up what we wanted. But when you start researching, you have to be terribly careful you don't get sidetracked. I remember once working through *Leslie's Magazine,* and in the period I was looking up, Oscar Wilde was in the United States . . . and you know what a furore he caused! I was trying to find out what I was supposed to wear, and what I was supposed to do in this period—and I kept being tempted over the page by Oscar Wilde!"

[8] Photoplay, *Jan. 1921, p. 78.*

However authentic the detail, however correct the costumes, however accurate the characterizations, one element of Hollywood period films was always wrong: the women. Whether it was ancient Babylon or pre-war Vienna, the women's cosmetics, hair styles, and apparel were a compromise between the era of the story and the year of production. The same still holds true today—and the reason for it has yet to change.

Hollywood films are the fashion plates of the world. Not only do the latest releases reflect the newest styles in clothes, but also in hair styles, cosmetics, and interior decoration. The men behind these industries are also the men behind motion pictures; producers do not allow themselves to forget that.

If a period picture suddenly appeared depicting women correctly attired for that period, the shock for the uninitiated would be great. Fans would be appalled at the appearance of their favorite star. And their favorite star would be equally outraged.

"This habit of 'improving' the hair styles, make-up, and costumes of an earlier age to conform more nearly with contemporary taste was not a Hollywood exclusive," said Beulah Marie Dix. "The English artists of the Victorian era were doing just that. Millais's *The Huguenot* is an outstanding example. The female stars had much of the responsibility for the hybrid hairdos and costumes. When it was a question between the wishes of a star and the reputation of an art department, the management seldom hesitated."

The primary requirement of a Hollywood period picture was to break away from twentieth-century inhibitions. A situation which was unconvincing or scandalous in a modern setting somehow gained acceptability when transferred to a bygone era. For the ultimate in vicarious effect, therefore, the women's appearance could not be removed too far from the present.

The art direction, however, had to reflect both the period and the story's approach to that period.

When Valentino made his first picture for United Artists, art director William Cameron Menzies anticipated the usual torrid romance. He therefore designed highly stylized sets. The story took place in Russia during the reign of Catherine the Great, but neither Menzies' sets nor Adrian's costumes bore the slightest hint of the eighteenth century. They were anxious not to alienate Valentino's fans with a welter of period detail. The picture was originally titled *The Untamed*. By the time it was complete, it had become *The Eagle;* directed by Clarence Brown from a sly and witty script by Hans Kraly, Lubitsch's scenarist, it proved to be a romantic comedy along the lines of *Forbidden Paradise*. Naturalistically played, with tongue in cheek, it was a good-humored take-off of Valentino by Valentino. The art direction was now obtrusive and out of character, and the costumes mere fancy dress. *The Eagle's* charm was thus marred by the design, which was as perplexing as a Harold Lloyd comedy with Elinor Glyn decor.

The antidote for inauthentic art direction was supplied by the great Erich von Stroheim, who produced not only a full scenario, but scripts containing careful drawings of every set, every prop, every uniform. Scrupulously correct, and authentic in every detail, von Stroheim's cathedral set in *The Wedding March* (art director: Richard Day) was given the ultimate in approval when cameraman Hal Mohr elected to be married before its high altar.

20 / DOUGLAS FAIRBANKS IN ROBIN HOOD

Robin Hood (1922), if not the most flamboyant of Fairbanks's swashbuckling costume epics, is certainly the most awe-inspiring. Its centerpiece is an enormous castle, said to be the largest set ever constructed in Hollywood.

Purely on the level of art direction, *Robin Hood* is an unsurpassed and unsurpassable achievement.[1] All Fairbanks's costume films were impeccably researched and beautifully mounted, but *Robin Hood,* set in the reign of Richard Coeur-de-Lion, deals with a period more specific, and therefore more difficult to recapture, than *The Black Pirate, The Thief of Bagdad,* or *The Gaucho.* It proves that where authenticity is concerned, once given the impetus, Hollywood could outmatch anybody.

Fairbanks, of course, provided the impetus. Once he took on a project, his energy was prodigious, his enthusiasm obsessive. Although fascinated by the legend of Robin Hood since childhood, he was not convinced that it would make an ideal motion picture. When the idea was first suggested, he turned it down. Following the resounding success of *The Three Musketeers,* he wanted to make either *The Virginian* or a sequel to *The Mark of Zorro* or *Monsieur Beaucaire.* During his 1921 European tour, scenarists Kenneth Davenport and Mrs. Lotta Woods developed these stories.

Fairbanks returned to Hollywood just before Christmas. On the morning of January 1, 1922, with his collaborators assembled for New Year's Day, Douglas Fairbanks made a memorable pronouncement:

"I've just decided that I'm going to make the story of Robin Hood. We'll build the sets right here in Hollywood. I'm going to call it *The Spirit of Chivalry."*

Robert Florey, then in charge of the Pickford-Fairbanks "Foreign Department," was among the gathering:

"I will never forget the forcefulness with which Douglas made this pronouncement. He pounded his fist on a small table. Nobody said a word.

" 'Mary and I are going to have to buy a new studio, where we can all work together. I'm thinking of the old Jesse Hampton Studio on Santa Monica. There's nothing but fields around there, and we can put up some really big sets—Nottingham in the twelfth century, Richard the Lion Heart's castle, a town in Palestine, Sherwood Forest and the outlaw's lair. There's a big field to the south where we can set up the Crusader's camp in France. We'll have several thousand costumes designed from contemporary documents, we'll order shields, lances, and swords by the thousand, we'll stage a tournament, we'll—'

" 'And how much is all that going to cost?' asked John Fairbanks, Douglas's brother, who was company treasurer.

" 'That's not the point,' replied Douglas. 'These things have to be done properly, or not at all.'

"By midday on January 1, 1922, everyone was convinced that Douglas was absolutely right. *Robin Hood* must be made."[2]

A research team, led by Dr. Arthur Woods, moved into action. Books, documents, engravings, and photographs poured into the studio. A huge library, the Robin Hood Library, was established. Fairbanks, now completely absorbed by the

---

[1] *The art direction was based on the combined principles of Gordon Craig, Max Reinhardt, and Robert Jones.*
[2] *Robert Florey,* Le Film, *Montreal, Oct. 1922, pp. 6–11.*

Robin Hood (1922). *Wallace Beery as King Richard I.*

Wallace Beery, Robert Florey, Arthur Edeson, Douglas Fairbanks, and Allan Dwan pose for a publicity picture during the shooting of the tournament scene. In the background, wind machines, mounted on trucks, stand by to set guidons and pennants fluttering.

subject, steeped himself in the period, studying pictures and accounts and chronicles . . . of tournaments, costumes, weapons, castle life, furnishings and accouterments. Wilfred Buckland was made supervising art director; under him worked Irvin J. Martin and Edward M. Langley. Mitchell Leisen, costume designer for Cecil B. De Mille, was given the monumental task of producing everything from chain mail to kingly robes. Arthur Edeson, who had photographed *The Three Musketeers,* was signed as cameraman, with Charles Richardson as second; Allan Dwan was director, assisted by Dick Rosson.

Fairbanks intended to spend a million on the production, but a slump had hit the industry, and no one would put up the money. Fairbanks himself financed the picture, and became its sole owner.

With Mary Pickford, Fairbanks reluctantly left for New York to settle a lawsuit. The day after his departure, John Fairbanks hired more than five hundred workmen to build the sets, the plans for which had been finally approved.

Robert Fairbanks, another brother, and the company secretary, shared Allan Dwan's background as an engineer.

"We worked out a couple of interesting engineering stunts for the big sets," recalled Dwan. "On the interiors, the walls meshed together with a matrix, which we designed and built, so they could be put together rapidly in sections. The interior of the castle was very vast—too big to light with ordinary arcs. We didn't have enough. It was an open set, and certain sections were blacked out to give the right atmosphere. So to light them we constructed huge tin reflectors, about twenty feet across, which picked up the sun and shot the light back onto the arches inside. Then we could make effects.

"Another problem was the chain mail. If you made real mail, it would be impossible to wear, it would break your back. That stuff was very heavy—people were much tougher in the Middle Ages. We devised a method using heavy canvas, sprayed with silver paint. It looked exactly like chain mail, but it was flexible, and you could walk in it and work in it. We had small sections of real chain mail when we came in for close-ups—enough to stop a sword. The rest of it was just heavy burlap."

Fairbanks was due to return from New York on March 9, and the construction crews redoubled their efforts to finish the castle.

"After painting the castle walls to give them ancestral respectability," wrote Robert Florey, "the scene-painters then planted moss, ivy and other creepers in the crevices of the plaster. Work continued even at night—when we cursed the huge mosquitoes attracted by the searchlights.

"On March 8, the drawbridge, made from an enormous steel frame, was completed, and this meant that the whole facade was finished. The silhouette of the huge castle could be seen from miles away.

"At midday on March 9, the train arrived at the little station of Pasadena. As Douglas leaped out, his first word was 'Well?'

"He demonstrated some new tricks for the photographers, and shook hands with everyone. From their faces, he realized there was a surprise in store for him.

" 'Let's go and see what you've been doing at the studio,' he said. I climbed into Douglas's car, so that I could see his look of astonishment when he saw the splendid set. The chauffeur drove across Pasadena in a whirlwind of photographers and newsreel men, who were mounted on vehicles, trying to get to the studio before us.

"At the corner of Santa Monica and La Brea, about two hundred yards from the studio, Douglas caught sight of the castle for the first time. He opened his eyes very wide and exclaimed, 'My gosh! It's astounding . . . it's fantastic!'

The epoch-making structure towered ninety feet above the Boulevard. For hours, Fairbanks toured the sets, followed by his associates. He was amazed, but he grew more and more uneasy. Finally, he announced that the picture would be shelved.

"I can't compete with that," Fairbanks told Dwan. "My work is intimate. People know me as an intimate actor. I can't work in a great vast thing like that. What could I do in there?"

Fairbanks saw the film would have the mighty sweep that he first envisaged when he read about the Crusades. But where would he fit in? The competition from the lavish décor was too great. He would be lost.

"I induced him to come back to the studio one morning," said Dwan, "and I took him onto the set. About forty feet up, there was a balcony. I'd hung a big drape from the ceiling, sweeping down across that balcony to the ground.

" 'Now,' I said, 'you get into a sword fight with the knights, and they chase you up the stairs, battling all the way. You fight like mad, and you succeed in getting away, but as you run out onto the balcony, some more knights rush out of the door at the end and you're caught between them. You haven't a chance. So you jump on the balustrade, and you're fighting them—'

"And then I stopped talking. He said, 'Yeah, *then* what do I do?' I showed him. I climbed onto the balustrade and jumped into this drape. I had a slide, a kid's slide, hidden inside it and I slid right down that curtain to the ground, with a gesture like he used to make, and I ran out through the arch to freedom.

"He bought it like that. 'I'll do it!' he shouted. He immediately sent out for some people, ran up to the balcony, explained it to them, jumped in the drape and slid down. He did it a thousand times—like a kid.

"Then I had him appearing suddenly at the windows, which were so high up no one could ever reach them. 'How do I ever get up there?' he said. 'It's ridiculous.'

" 'You go up the vines outside,' I said. We had a wide moat around the castle, with water in it, about thirty feet across. Naturally, no one could jump it. But there was a little wall at one end, running toward the moat. 'Now you run along the top of this little wall,' I told him, 'and you jump over onto those vines and climb up to the window.'

" 'Who am I?,' he said. 'The world's champion jumper? You expect me to jump across *that?*'

" 'Sure,' I said. I had a Trampoline at the end of the wall. He ran and hit that and it threw him over to the vines, where we had hand holds on a net. He caught them, and climbed up to the window. Well, of course he started to play with that as well. These were the things that finally made him buy *Robin Hood,* but it wasn't easy to get him to do it."

There was no detailed script during the whole making of the picture; Fairbanks, under his pseudonym Elton Thomas, has credit for the story, but in fact he and

The castle, designed by Wilfred Buckland, was said to be the biggest structure built for a silent picture—including the Babylon set for Intolerance. Its size was further increased with a glass shot, which added towering height to the castle.

Paul Dickey as Sir Guy of Gisbourne.

This banquet scene indicates the care lavished on Robin Hood. (These stills were taken by A. F. Kales, printed to resemble engravings, and mounted in a presentation volume for Douglas Fairbanks. They are reproduced by courtesy of Douglas Fairbanks, Jr. The reproductions, unhappily, cannot do justice to the beauty of the originals.)

The departure for the Crusades.

Dwan and Lotta Woods molded it into shape during actual production. Fairbanks complained after the film was released that he had received many communications from intelligent people deploring the fact that the film wandered so far from the book.

"If these critics know what book they are talking about," he said, "they have a distinct advantage over me."

The shooting of *Robin Hood* was Hollywood's big tourist attraction. As it happened, few other studios were working; among the knights and ladies thronging the crowd scenes were writers, technicians, and actors, all out of work because of the slump and grateful for the activity.

"In the big crowd scenes, we organized carefully," said Dwan. "I divided them into groups of fifteen or twenty, selected a man as their boss, put him in uniform, and he was my assistant. As a matter of fact, the war made *Robin Hood* easy. There wasn't a single man among the extras or the technical staff without military training. I had a phone on my platform, and any changes I wanted, I just had to press a button. To get extras we took buses and went down to Main Street and piled people in. We brought them up to the studio, put them in costume, gave them a box lunch, and paid them at the end of the day. Half of them didn't know what they were doing."

"Nothing was too good for the production," said Enid Bennett. "I had a most wonderful time playing Maid Marian. Of course the part was not too demanding, I just walked through it in a queenly manner. But everything was so lavish. Douglas Fairbanks was wonderful, inspiring. He was very timid about love scenes, although we finally did a beautiful scene where my profile was drawn on the castle wall. Elinor Glyn got me the part. She spotted me at a reception and declared: '*That's* the girl to play Maid Marian.' "[3]

One of the most difficult scenes had no human participants at all; just two

[3] *Enid Bennett to author, Palm Desert, California, April 1967.*

birds. During the march to the Crusades, Fairbanks, as the Earl of Huntingdon, receives word from Lady Marian that Prince John is imposing cruel repressions in Richard's absence. He dispatches, by pigeon, a message saying he will return at once. The villain, Sir Guy of Gisbourne, sends up a falcon to bring down the pigeon. It is an astonishing scene; with a long-focus lens, the camera smoothly follows the birds, keeping them both in frame as the falcon executes his deadly maneuver. Grappling with the pigeon, the falcon brings it to earth, still alive. The message is removed and the pigeon released. The falcon was imported from England; it cost sixty pounds. Insured by Lloyd's for its journey to Hollywood, it had to be kept in the dark and fed only on raw meat. The actual scene ran to more than a hundred takes.

Wary of imitations, Fairbanks copyrighted his film as *Douglas Fairbanks in Robin Hood;* the advance publicity was the most intensive ever, and so was the welcome from the public. The picture broke box-office records almost everywhere. At Grauman's Egyptian Theatre it ran for so long that streetcar conductors, instead of announcing the carstop, yelled "All out for *Robin Hood!*"

Said Robert E. Sherwood in the New York *Herald:* "It represents the high-water mark of film production—the farthest step that the silent drama has ever taken along the high road to art. Back of all the vast display is an intelligence which is indeed rare. *Robin Hood* did not grow from the bank roll; it grew from the mind—and this is the chief reason for its superiority."

"More than anything else," said *Photoplay, "Robin Hood* is a show. It seems to be stretching the word photoplay to classify it under that name. In fact it's the last thing in spectacles. We doubt if the silversheet will go much further along this expensive road. Director Allan Dwan must be given great credit for his masterly handling of the massive and seemingly insurmountable difficulties. The spectacle is his triumph."[4]

One or two setbacks came to light as the exact costs were being totaled. The picture lost $90,000 on its Chicago run. The negative cost was $986,000, which did not include Fairbanks' own salary. Once the exploitation and release prints were taken into account, *Robin Hood* cost about $1,400,000—exceeding both *Intolerance* ($700,000) and the celebrated "million-dollar movie" *Foolish Wives.* But it earned $2,500,000.

The picture received the *Photoplay* 1922 Medal of Honor—there were no Academy Awards in those days. The award was presented not to the director, as was customary, but to Douglas Fairbanks: "In spite of the fact that a dozen or more men and women played important parts in the production of this picture, the credit for the conception and the execution of the idea goes to Mr. Fairbanks."[5]

Robin Hood, lost for many years, was discovered in America by a collector, and a number of prints are now in circulation. Few, unfortunately, retain any of the fine photographic quality of the original. Historian Rudy Behlmer, describing the Robin Hoods of the screen for *Films in Review* said that the picture was "much too long and not representative of the vintage Fairbanks."[6]

The picture is a study in atmosphere and adventure; it is sometimes stately,

[4] Photoplay, *Jan. 1923, p. 64.*
[5] Photoplay, *Dec. 1923, p. 91.*
[6] Films in Review, *Feb. 1965, p. 91.*

but never slow. The mood of the film is suggested by a typical Allan Dwan touch—the use of a poem at the beginning:

So fleet the works of men,
Back to their earth again;
Ancient and holy things
Fade like a dream.

The poem (Charles Kingsley's "Old and New") is followed by shots of ruined castles; a slow dissolve, and the ruins are restored to their former grandeur.

History—in its ideal state—is a compound of legend and chronicle and from out of both we offer you an impression of the Middle Ages.

The huge drawbridge is slowly lowered right into camera. Across it march first the squires, then the knights, in two columns, banners and pennants fluttering. Between them skips the King's jester (Roy Coulson). A powerful tracking shot introduces Richard the Lion-Hearted (a brilliant performance by Wallace Beery), striding out to where a tournament is about to begin. Beneath the castle walls is assembled the flower of English knighthood, hundreds of men preparing soon to march with Richard on the Crusades. The Earl of Huntingdon (Douglas Fairbanks) is pitted in duel with lance against Sir Guy of Gisbourne (Paul Dickey). To gain unfair advantage, Sir Guy straps himself into his saddle. But no such precaution can withstand the tremendous force of Huntingdon's lance. Sir Guy crashes to the ground, and King Richard cries:

"Huntingdon hath proved his knightly mettle! We hereby decree that on the Holy Crusade he shall be our second-in-command."

The excitement takes grip with this stirring opening, with the sight of thousands of chain-mailed warriors, cloaks and guidons flying in the wind, heavily built horses rearing and charging, lances splintering and armor crashing . . . the excitement sparked off by this sequence seldom leaves the picture.

Arthur Edeson's photography makes such magnificent use of Buckland's incredible sets that each new shot has an almost physical impact.

Fairbanks breezily throws away superlative shot after superlative shot, carefree in the knowledge that something even more stupendous is coming up.

Complaints of slowness are inexplicable. One logical explanation might be that film societies religiously run this silent film at silent speed, sixteen frames per second. The picture was originally intended to be shown at about twenty-two frames per second, much nearer sound speed. Projection rates at this period varied greatly, and the confusion is understandable. But the slower speed adds another forty minutes to the running time.

Further complaints border on the pedantic. Perhaps Fairbanks is not a convincing medieval character, but his presence is even more important to the film than historical accuracy. The people in *Robin Hood* are of less consequence than the settings. Enid Bennett, a very subdued Maid Marian, gives little life to the part. Paul Dickey (Sir Guy of Gisbourne), on the other hand, gives too much, and is too melodramatically villainous to carry real menace. Sam De Grasse, however, gives a fine portrayal as the sinister Prince John. The atmosphere of *Robin Hood* fully compensates for any lack of characterization.

"We knew that atmosphere was something beyond authenticity and the absence of anachronisms," said Dwan. "It was the atmosphere that we strived for far above anything else."[7]

In this respect, success has seldom been more triumphant. Equally successful are many of the cinematic ideas. When Robin Hood exacts revenge on the followers of Prince John, an arrow thuds beside them to give them warning. And each time this happens, a sudden gust of wind springs up, stirring the dust. This idea is perfectly in tune with the dramatic hyperbole of the early chronicles.

When Fairbanks takes on the role of Robin Hood, after being weighed down in chain mail and armor as Huntingdon, he and his men leap through the woods with the vitality of gazelles. Thanks to Fairbanks' grace and good humor, this evocation of the joy of freedom succeeds; had Robin Hood been played by anyone else, the response would be one of embarrassment.

After the climactic fight, a beautifully choreographed action sequence in which the castle is captured, King Richard cries "Huntingdon!" No response. Again he cries, at the top of his voice, *"Huntingdon!"* The Merry Men, sitting in a line high on the castle wall, tumble from their perch as though blown by the wind. A hilariously irresponsible element of comedy pervades the entire picture.

One great comedy moment, however, was never recorded. Charlie Chaplin asked Douglas Fairbanks if he could borrow the castle for a sequence in his next picture.

"I don't get it, Charlie," said Fairbanks. "What do you want to do?"

Chaplin demonstrated: the huge drawbridge was lowered and Chaplin appeared from inside, clutching a kitten. He put out the cat, picked up a bottle of milk, a newspaper and some letters, and sauntered back inside again. The drawbridge slowly closed.[8]

Fairbanks loved the gag, but he was too astute a businessman to allow his castle to appear in another picture.

Robin Hood was unique in every respect. Nobody connected with it ever achieved anything quite like it again. And the picture itself, one of the rarest of collector's items, has become as legendary as the story which inspired it.

[7] Motion Picture Magazine, *Feb. 1923, p. 25.*
[8] *Florey:* La Lanterne Magique, *p. 82.*

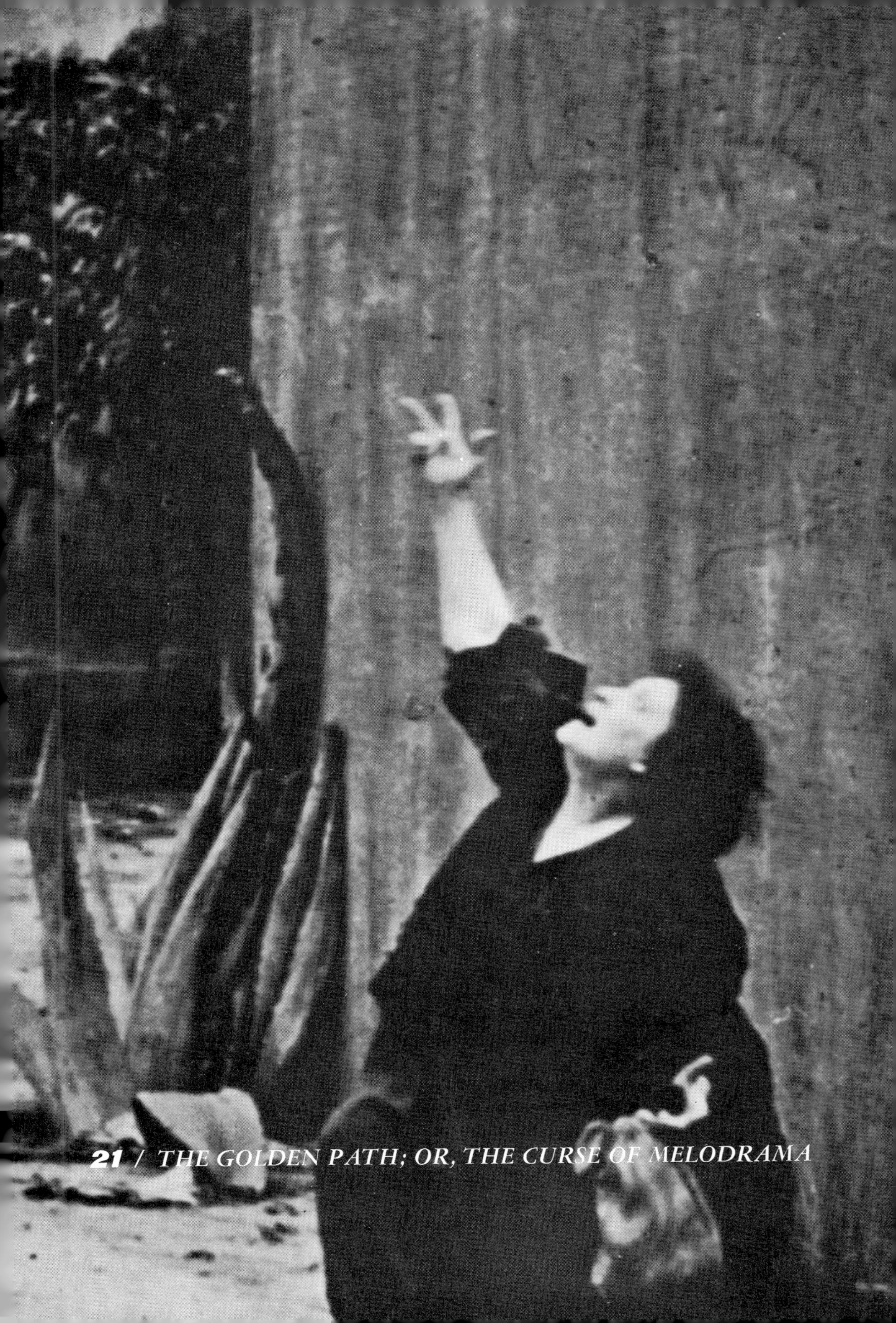

21 / THE GOLDEN PATH; OR, THE CURSE OF MELODRAMA

Complaining of the trend toward realism in motion pictures, a fan wrote to *Photoplay* in 1927:

"We can get morbid enough reading everyday life, but we want a rest at the movies. Life is so. But why choose the ugliest specimen to portray your heroes and heroines? Why be so realistic? Let us go back to the golden path. We don't want life, but something to make us happy. Let us live."[1]

The golden path—golden for quite another reason than its sweetness and light—was religiously followed by every producer of dramatic feature films in Hollywood. They are still swarming down it today, but both sweetness and light have long since been trampled into the dirt.

Reassured by the belief that their prime duty was to entertain, film makers bought material of great potential and intelligence, stripped it of motivations and complex overtones, and reduced the action to basic, easy-to-follow melodrama.

Even the dictionary defines melodrama with a certain distaste: "Drama marked by crude appeals to emotion."

The purveyors of entertainment find melodrama an invaluable asset. It requires not the slightest effort on the part of the audience. They are not required to think; they merely watch. They will not miss any subtlety because there will not *be* any subtlety. The values are simple, the threat is clear and the resolution action-filled and straightforward. There is seldom any characterization in pure melodrama, never any complex motivation. Life is reduced to the infantile level of an adventure strip.

This oversimplification was the most regrettable aspect of silent-film melodrama. In a fast-moving serial or action picture, it didn't matter that motivations were reduced to a minimum. The story had to move; no one cared why the hero did it so long as he did it effectively. Action was all that counted; one sequence to establish the hero as a regular fellow, another to show the sweet and innocent heroine, one more to reveal the villain's dark intent, and you could sit back and enjoy what the American silent-film makers made best—moving pictures that *moved*.

The action melodramas of this period are in a class of their own. The only comparable film of recent years has been *The Last Voyage*, made by silent-picture director Andrew L. Stone and photographed by silent-era cameraman Hal Mohr.

But melodrama in other contexts is less forgivable. In films about politics, for instance, its use is dangerous enough to border on the immoral. Political issues are far too important, far too intricate, and far too little understood to be presented as black-and-white hokum.

In the silent days, more people went to the movies than read books, consequently motion pictures carried greater influence than the ideas of current writers.

After the Russian Revolution, Americans based their ideas of Bolshevism on the sensational half-truths of newspaper reports and on the portrayals of Communist activity in films like *Dangerous Hours* (1920: Fred Niblo).

In this picture, Russian infiltration of American industry was foiled by Lloyd Hughes. The political complexities were ludicrously simplified. Audiences were shown the most heinous crime of all time: the nationalization of women. This abominable act involved a number of extras on horseback rounding up women, throwing them into dungeons, and beating them.

[1] Photoplay, *May 1927, p. 11.*

Patria (1917). L. Dick Stewart and Milton Sills menaced in episode seven: Red Dawn.

Laura la Plante in The Cat and the Canary (1927), *directed by Paul Leni; one of the best* *he spoof melodramas.*

Dangerous Hours *(1919). The meeting of the Bolsheviki.*

Dangerous Hours. *The meeting of the workers.*

It is easy to denigrate silent melodramas, and most film historians are only too adept at it. This picture can be faulted for its political irresponsibility, but not for the way it was made. That films were able to say *anything* as early as this is miraculous enough, let alone display the flashes of imagination with which director Niblo and cameraman George Barnes enliven the story.

Politically, the picture is childish, yet Fred Niblo had been to Russia and had photographed inside the Kremlin. *Dangerous Hours* has none of the atmosphere he must have felt on that trip.

The picture opens promisingly with a documentary-style exterior scene. Strikers —"with an honest grievance," as C. Gardner Sullivan's title tells us—gather during the second week of a silk-mill strike. We are introduced to some obvious Bolsheviki—"the dangerous element following in the wake of labor as riffraff and ghouls follow an army."

Lloyd Hughes plays John King, "graduate of an American university—but a disciple of the 'Greater Freedom' as painted by Russian liberal writers."

King demands to know why the police are driving the Bolsheviks away from the strikers.

"They don't work in the mills. They are only trouble-makers looking for a little cheap notoriety."

"They are fighting for the cause of humanity," replies King hotly.

"Well," says the cop, "they'll have to do it a block further down."

This dead-pan wit soon gives way to the most arrant melodrama. A Red Army officer with the lurid name of Boris Blotchi (Jack Richardson) tries to inveigle King into joining his espionage group in wrecking industry. Blotchi, says a title, "is carried away with a wild dream of planting the scarlet seed of Terrorism in American soil."

King agrees, and is misled through several reels. But he finally comes to with such patriotic fervor that the art titles break out in stars and stripes.

"At last I know you!" he cries. "You are not interested in humanity but murder. We in America do not fight this way, and what you say shall not be! THIS IS AMERICA!"

Sophia, the femme fatale (Claire Dubrey), advances and spits, "Damn America!"

King swings around and starts shouting at the assembled Bolsheviks. And, in a curious foretaste of the later Soviet method of titling, one phrase at a time appears on the screen, becoming progressively larger:

"And I say damn you!"

"You cowards!"

"You liars!"

"YOU SWINE!"

Some members of the public may have thought this was searing stuff, but fortunately few critics took it seriously.

"As propaganda," said *Photoplay*, "*Dangerous Hours* is negative. The story concerns the redemption of a parlor Bolshevist. A girl, who is two hundred per cent American (Barbara Castleton), persuades him that it is all wrong, Trotsky, all wrong. However, it is easier to start a mob than to stop one. Hence we have a swirling climax produced with a great deal of dash. Who remembers, by the way, when all villains were German?"[2]

So many distortions of the Red Revolution appeared that the magazines were moved to protest. "Please, oh please," *Picture Play* begged producers in 1920, "look up the meaning of the words 'bolshevik' and 'Soviet.' Neither of them mean 'anarchist,' 'scoundrel' or 'murderer'—really they don't!"[3]

Melodramatic treatment was dangerous enough for political subjects; when it appeared with racial connotations it became downright offensive.

After *The Birth of a Nation* outcries, the Negro did not appear again as a villain. He was relegated to atmosphere, or comedy bit parts. As it happened there were very few Negroes in California, and white actors often had to don blackface to play such Negro roles as railroad employees. In Los Angeles, the first real encounter with Negroes took place during the armaments drive in World War II.

The emphasis switched to the Yellow Peril. *Patria,* a serial financed by William Randolph Hearst, whipped up hatred against both Japanese and Mexicans to such a degree that President Wilson was forced to intervene. It was 1916; America was still neutral, but war clouds were gathering. The Hearst newspapers, which had recently covered the Pancho Villa campaign, were now running hostile articles about the Japanese "yellow peril" and about the Mexicans. The serial depicted America being attacked by an unholy, and somewhat unlikely, alliance between Mexico and Japan. Cashing in on the wide publicity given to the suffrage movement, the serial had the imaginary army foiled by Irene Castle.

Mexico could scarcely protest, since America had severed diplomatic relations. But Japan could—and did. Hearst's International Film Service received a letter about their serial:

Several times in attending Keith's theatre here I have seen portions of a film entitled Patria, *which has been exhibited here and I think in a great many other theatres in the country. May I not say to you that the character of the story disturbed me very much. It is extremely unfair to the Japanese, and I fear that it is calculated to stir up a great deal of hostility which will be far from beneficial to the country, indeed will, particularly in the present circumstances, be extremely hurtful. I take the liberty, therefore, of asking whether the Company would not be willing to withdraw it if it is still being exhibited.*

> With much respect
> Sincerely yours,
> WOODROW WILSON[4]

Patria was not withdrawn; it was modified. "The Japanese and Mexican flags were cut out of the picture," records Terry Ramsaye, "and it managed to squeeze by the censorship and back into the market, considerably crippled at the box office."

But the yellow peril, epitomized by Warner Oland and Sojin, continued to lure high box-office grosses.

Chinatown in silent movies seldom appeared as anything but a seething nest

---

[2] Photoplay, *May 1920, p. 111.*
[3] *Harry J. Smalley in* Picture Play, *April 1920, p. 58.*
[4] *Terry Ramsaye:* A Million and One Nights *(New York: Simon and Schuster; 1926), p. 779.*

---

of intrigue, vice, and dope-trafficking. The residents of Chinese quarters in American cities protested vigorously against these preposterous portrayals.

On one occasion, a unit arriving in New York's Chinatown to shoot Thomas Meighan's *Pied Piper Malone* (Alfred E. Green) was met with a hail of stones, fruit, vegetables, and old shoes. The riot, intended as a demonstration against the bad name the movies were giving the area, merely confirmed everyone's worst suspicions.

After a while, easily identifiable minority groups were avoided, but *Old San Francisco,* a Warner Brothers melodrama of 1927, was a full-blooded return to the worst days of spooky Chinatown. The astonishing aspect of the picture is that, as late as 1927, producers should consider the expense of such offensive silliness worthwhile.

The story centers around a noble family, last of the Spanish settlers, whose lives are threatened by the evil Chris Buckwell (Warner Oland). Buckwell has a Hideous Secret, revealed when he is discovered creeping around his victim's ranch. The mission bells ring out.

"Stop—stop those accursed Christian bells!" cries Buckwell. As Dolores Costello advances on his cringing form, carrying a sword like an avenging angel, Buckwell's terrible secret bursts forth; he has Oriental blood!

The film's premiere, at the Warner Theatre, was bathed in purple light, which seems appropriate enough. But the critics were not encouraged to use purple prose. The New York *Post* called it "violently melodramatic and preposterous in

T. Hayes Hunter directing stage actress Blanche Bates in **The Seats of the Mighty** *(1914).*

the extreme—and one of the silliest pictures ever made." The New York *Sun* gave credit to director Alan Crosland for the way he had fashioned this piece of lurid melodrama. "It cleverly provokes illusion despite the cheaply obvious and 'sinister' story."[5]

Crosland's treatment is in fact so skillful that *Old San Francisco* provides esthetic pleasure, despite Darryl F. Zanuck's distasteful story. The big climax of the San Francisco earthquake is indifferently staged with double exposures and models, but the handling of the melodrama is picturesque and compelling. The art direction, particularly on the underworld interiors, is fine, and Hal Mohr's lighting is exquisite. It seems sacrilegious to squander such talent on such material. But this was one of the strengths of silent-film makers; presented with the most unpromising assignment, the visual sense of director, cameraman, and art director frequently combined to produce a picture of real value.

The pure melodramas, the lashed-to-the-railroad tracks, saved-by-the-dog pieces of unabashed nonsense were still being made in the twenties, but they were the domain of poverty-row companies such as Gotham, or the serial manufacturers.

Most melodramas were skillfully embellished with rich characterizations, beautiful settings, and disarming light relief. Thus Hollywood stumbled upon its celebrated formula. Not all such melodramas, however, were surefire box office.

Wid Gunning's trade paper *Wid's Daily* urged a return to the primitive days. With the thick-skinned insensitivity of the exhibitor he urged, in 1921: "Put in the hokum. The red-blooded stuff. That gets them on the edge of their twenty-cent seat. Let's get some of the beauty out and the action in. Let's find a thrill or two or maybe more. Let's get back to basics—primal emotions—that is what the fans want."[6]

Exhibitors' reports, undiluted opinions of the theater men themselves, supported such philistinism.

Bits of Life, Marshall Neilan's experimental film which incorporated four short stories, one of which was a delicately handled Chinese episode, received this terse comment: "I tell you that Chink stuff of that kind won't do if we expect to stay in the game,"[7] said the owner of the Electric Theatre, Centralia, Kansas.

The Wedding March (1928; Erich von Stroheim): "Well, the agony is over. I am a glutton for punishment, but this picture sure made me run up the white flag as the people came out. I thought perhaps I might be mistaken, so I asked numerous ones what they thought of the picture and two of them guessed it was all right (notice they just guessed) and what some of the others said you would not print so I won't tell you." (Perkins Theatre, Holton, Kansas.)

The Wind, Victor Seastrom's masterpiece, received equally scorching words. But Lubitsch's *The Patriot* was treated with understanding: "Played this three days to an empty house, but it was no fault of the picture . . ." "Wonderful picture as far as acting is concerned, but a big flop at the box office. We lost money, and although the flu and bad weather had something to do with it, can't lay all of it to that alone . . ."[8]

But not even theater men were fooled by inept hokum. "*Speed*—a joke from

[5] *Quoted in "When Critics Disagree,"* Photoplay, *Sept. 1927, p. 84.*
[6] *Quoted in* Photoplay, *Nov. 1921, p. 64.*
[7] *Quoted in* Photoplay, *Dec. 1923, p. 114.*
[8] Motion Picture Almanac, *1929, pp. 208-9.*

end to end. Lucy was not cleared of the murder; in fact it seemed that the director forgot that a woman had been killed in the excitement of finishing the serial. It is 'punk.' " (Wigwam Theatre, Oberlin, Ohio.)[9]

Dramatic critic B. T. Clayton reluctantly agreed with the commercial view:

"Despite all their luted cacophonies in the public prints over 'Better Pictures,' 'New Faces,' and Art with a large A, the producers were long ago convinced by the extraordinary success of such yap-dazzlers as De Mille's *Anatol* that what the people want—today, yesterday and tomorrow—is the good old hokum. Probably in about 1955 some bold revolt will venture a Little Theater and be absolutely dumbfounded by the result—as was the New York Theater Guild, which started in a cellar somewhere near the Battery and awoke one bright day to find the art-starved populace flocking to its dugouts in hordes, fairly sobbing with gratitude.

"One theater for the intelligentsia, one for the patron of *A Telephone Girl's Temptation.* One theater for the story of lingerie and lily-love, and another for the throbbing, passionate symphonies of Lubitsch and La Negri, the swashbuckling fanfaronade of Fairbanks, the pastorals of Charlie Ray, and the intellectual operas of William C. de Mille. And gradually the patrons of the one would become more regular attendants at the other. The kindergarten pupil would, in time, become the high school student.

"But even hokum grows more delicate with each passing year. Consider the revolver dramas of twenty summers past when the crux of the evening's entertainment lay in the big scene in the lumber mill in which Curses-on-you-Jack-Dalton villain had the hero bound hard and fast to a Long-Bell log that was slowly slipping down the chute to a whirring buzz-saw.

"Compare the worst picture of 1921 to the old familiar dramaturgy of *Nellie, the Beautiful Cloak Model.* Is *Anatol* not superior to any play in which someone tied someone else to the railroad tracks just as the Limited whistled in the distance?"[1]

The improvement was immense. But not until the light touch of Chaplin's *Woman of Paris,* and of Lubitsch, Frank Tuttle, Mal St. Clair, and a host of sparkling sophisticates, did heavily spread melodrama begin to melt.

Although ridiculed by comparison, it never left the movies. Today it remains an integral part of the dramatic feature film. Compare the letter written to *Photoplay* in 1927 with this one, written to the specialized magazine *Films in Review* in 1964:

"I have never been able to understand the intellectuals' denigration of melodrama. Because good always triumphs over evil in melodrama, beautiful little lamps are temporarily lit in the lousiest of us. I think melodrama has been a more powerful and inspiring force than any other literary or cinematic form."[2]

A great many melodramas have enriched cinema history. But without this element, the cinema might now be incalculably richer.

[9] *Quoted in* Photoplay, *Dec. 1923, p. 114.*
[1] Picture Play, *June 1922, p. 33.*
[2] Films in Review, *Jan. 1964, p. 58.*

22 / SCENARIO

The first place in which a film is seen is in the scenario writer's imagination. And that is where it looks its best. The imagination short-circuits practical issues and reveals the film in all its glory, untarnished by effort and undiminished by compromise. It will never look so good again.

For the imagination can never compete with reality. It can only provide a springboard for the artist to transfer his dream—an incentive to help him realize it.

The scenario writer, poring over his typewriter, may visualize the most awe-inspiring scenes, but he has to shackle his imagination. If the picture has a budget of sufficient size, he can describe the Flood and leave the special-effects department to simulate the catastrophe. But however impressive the final result, it will never match that first wonderful glimpse. For no words can accurately describe the vision of the mind.

More than any other narrative art, motion pictures have had to endure a series of creative blood-lettings. These occur from the moment the original conception is drafted to the moment the final print reaches the screen.

When the cinema began, no such danger existed—because no scenarios existed. Those primitive one- and two-reelers were shot in a couple of days by directors who had a rough idea of the story and who improvised as they went along. Off-the-cuff directors carried on well into the twenties, having grown highly proficient and capable of rapid invention. D. W. Griffith was the dazzling example. A man who could shoot *Intolerance* without a script has methods that defy analysis. None of the great comedians—Chaplin, Lloyd, or Keaton—ever worked from a script until talkies came. But then few silent comedies were ever shot from a conventional scenario; that was their secret.

"Thousands, perhaps hundreds of thousands of writers," wrote Alfred Cohn in 1917, "have wondered why they haven't been able to sell a comedy scenario to one of the big film companies. The chief reason is that there is no such thing as a scenario or 'script of a slapstick comedy. No continuity is written and the writers do not write. In one of the biggest comedy plants, a staff of about twenty is employed. Yet perhaps not more than a few of these writers have ever written anything, or could if their lives depended upon it. The finished product is the result of conference work."[1]

Gags, hammered out and argued over the scenario department conference table, are likely to be stronger and funnier than those sweated out over a typewriter by a single writer, lacking the stimulus of competition. While shooting, the gags were further developed by improvisation.

Scenarios for dramatic feature films had to be written; as the standard of production improved, better stories were sought and top writers from the field of novels and magazines were signed.

The last of the shoot-from-the-cuff directors was supposed to have been Marshall Neilan. Late on the set one day, a member of the cast suggested that he might have lost his script. "Sure," said one of the crew, "and now he's hunting through the Hollywood Laundry to find it."

The word "scenario"—replaced today by the term "screenplay"—did not mean shooting script. It was the sequence of scenes, the story told in visual terms,

[1] Photoplay, *Sept. 1917, p. 119.*

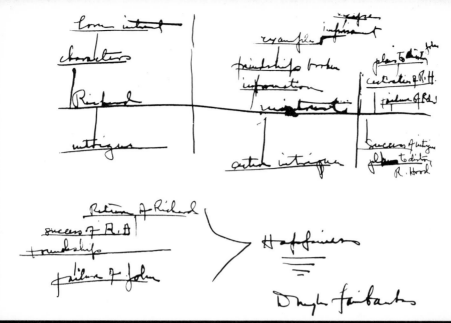

Douglas Fairbanks wrote his scenarios under the pseudonym of Elton Thomas. Robin Hood was made from an outline no more elaborate than this.

Douglas Fairbanks and Edward Knoblock working on The Three Musketeers (1921) *at Pickfair.*

originally devised to explain as clearly as possible what its author had in mind. From this scenario was written the continuity, or "shooting script," as it is known today.

Scripting for dramatic feature films was always an intricate process, but it should not be overestimated. Frequently, writers were employed merely to set down the story of the film on paper so that it could be budgeted, cast and put into production.

The process of writing a motion picture in the silent days began in much the way it does today. A picture, then as now, generally had its basis in another form —a book, a play, or even a poem. When this original was acquired by the motion-picture company it became what was called a property, and it underwent a series of radical changes.

So that a producer could be acquainted with the story without having to read the book, it was reduced to synopsis form. A special story-reading department coped with this, and members of this department were often expected to read the synopsis to the producer. They may have misunderstood the plot, they may have misconstrued the theme—more likely than not, they had no interest in it. But it was on this synopsis, this report, that the fate of the property depended. Blood-letting number one.

The producer then assigned the property to a scenario writer, usually a woman, Her adaptation of the author's work was liable to be specialized, cold and professional. She read the book knowing that she had to make visual sense of the narrative, so she was hardly likely to become as emotionally involved as the author intended. Many episodes relevant to the general reader were valueless to her. Atmosphere setting, character building, suspense heightening—while a novel can legitimately take pages to describe a simple scene, a motion picture's prime requirement is pace and speed.

The scenario writer's blue pencil slashed through line upon line, however delicately written. This treatment did not necessarily hurt the film. A story, bought for motion-picture use, becomes an independent work and should not be judged by the standards of another medium.

Yet much anger was aroused when a popular novel was altered, when characters were dropped, or when the ending was changed. Many silent films were panned by the critics when they departed from the original. In many cases, the films have lived far longer in the memories of those who saw them than the novels or plays from which they were made.

Fannie Hurst's short story "Humoresque," published in *Cosmopolitan Magazine,* was made into a successful film in 1920 (adapted by Frances Marion and directed by Frank Borzage). She went to see it at a special screening at the Ritz-Carlton.

"A cousin of mine, a writer herself, accompanied me and was very shocked. 'Why, it's a travesty of the story,' she exclaimed. 'The liberties they've taken!' I made a sound signifying agreement, but I thought they'd done rather well. I enjoyed it.

"The author's ego is something very difficult to overcome or to overlook. I felt that if you sold something you made it over to those who had bought it. They should be able to do what they liked with it without interference. Very occasionally, I felt that they had improved on my concept, but only occasionally. An author's concept is very precious and belongs to him only. If anyone else does it, however well, you feel 'it isn't me . . . it just isn't mine . . .' "[2]

To the scenario writer, the adaptation was an assignment. However dedicated she may have been, her interest understandably fluctuated from job to job. She was anxious only that her retelling of the story should be clearly understood by those who had the task of translating her words into pictures.

As silent pictures grew more complex, as supervisors came into being, and as more and more people became connected with production, the adaptation was tampered with by many hands, not all of whom could claim competence.

The final continuity itself usually went through several rewrites before it met with approval from the head of the scenario department, the head of the studio, the supervisor, the director, the star, the star's agent or manager, and, somewhat infrequently, the author himself. Many versions, many conceptions—all of them a compromise between literary convention and cinematic compression, all of them involving further creative blood-lettings.

In the great days of M-G-M as many as ten writers would work on the script before the cream of their work was skimmed off for the final version.

No wonder scenario writers shared the highest mortality rate with racing drivers.

Most celebrated of the early scenario writers was Anita Loos. Her best-known achievement was the book *Gentlemen Prefer Blondes,* but her accomplishments in other fields were even more astonishing.

"She is a brilliant woman," said Louise Brooks. "Do you know what she was doing when she was fifteen? She was writing three scripts a week for Griffith, she had two vaudeville acts playing in top vaudeville, and she was writing a Broadway column for a New York paper, and she had never been out of California!"

Miss Loos diffidently corrected Miss Brooks. "I did not write the Broadway column," she said, "but contributed to one, when I was twelve. And I only had *one* vaudeville act playing in top vaudeville." She affirmed that she also wrote the titles for *Intolerance.*[3]

In her father's theater, Miss Loos watched the films which were screened between acts. The stage manager would raise the curtain so she could watch the reverse side of the screen.

"I saw them all, and it occurred to me that they must need stories. So I wrote one. It was inspired by Mary Pickford. I mailed it in and it was accepted immediately. The title was *The New York Hat;* Mary Pickford played the lead and D. W. Griffith directed. I got twenty-five dollars. I was twelve years old."

Miss Loos wrote stories for Biograph, Lubin, Kinemacolor, and Kosmik.

Griffith's Biograph Company was her chief customer, however, and the company eventually decided to put her on the payroll. When Anita Loos visited the studio with her mother, she watched first the company secretary, and then Mr. Griffith, mistake her mother for herself.

When Griffith had recovered from his surprise at finding his author four foot nine, with pigtails, he asked her to work at the studio. The company had been buying so many Anita Loos stories he felt she might just as well be on the lot.

[2] *Fannie Hurst to author, New York, Nov. 1964.*
[3] *Anita Loos in a letter to author, Jan. 1966.*

William de Mille, Jeanie Macpherson, Elinor Glyn, Cecil B. De Mille.

Dolores del Rio and Count Ilya Tolstoy, eldest son of Count Leo Tolstoy, pose for a publicity shot during the production of Edwin Carewe's Resurrection *(1927).*

"I worked in the scenario department. I *was* the scenario department. There was nobody else on the lot who was writing. Fine-Arts used to buy scenarios, and I think there were two or three writers who sent things in rather regularly, but I don't remember anyone being right there on the lot but me."

Her early scenarios, for two-reelers, consisted of a page and a half. By 1916, her feature scripts ran to forty pages. She wrote them in longhand, and a stenographer typed them. She has never learned to used a typewriter.

"I would sit on set during rehearsals and if one particular actor showed special talent, I could put something in for him—much as you do in stage rehearsals if someone pops up and is funnier than you thought. I'd be there during shooting and I'd be around at the cutting stage, putting in the titles. Quite often, you'd find mistakes in the shooting which you'd have to conceal with titles.

"It was all very easy in those days. We had so much fun that I don't really remember when the work got done."[4]

Miss Loos's pictures were gay, but they were far from inconsequential. Their characteristic element of satire raised already entertaining stories into subjects of importance. She and her director husband John Emerson kidded all the popular idiosyncrasies with the Douglas Fairbanks–Triangle comedies—vegetarianism, the craze for publicity, spiritualism, Coué-ism, ruthless big business, snobbery—and the films' freshness after fifty years proves that the satire still works. This satire sprang not from a suppressed social conscience, but from a bubblingly creative sense of fun. "It was the way my mind ran," said Miss Loos. "I couldn't have written any other way."

At this same period—1916—William de Mille was initiating Famous Players-Lasky into the idea of scripting their pictures. "Coming from the tradition of a literate theater," said Agnes de Mille, "my father suggested that it might be useful to write out in detail beforehand what they planned doing. He wrote complete little synopses for Cecil. Then he asked a writer friend, Margaret Turnbull, to come west to help him. The two of them wrote synopses sitting at desks in a small wooden house with screen doors on the lot. Pop got the studio painter to make him a sign which he hung on the doorknob, SCENARIO DEPARTMENT. And this was the first time these words appeared in Hollywood."[5]

These two pioneers were joined by Hector Turnbull, later head of the Lasky scenario department, Marion Fairfax, and Beulah Marie Dix.

"In those early days of silent pictures," said Miss Dix, "a writer often sold an original to the company and then worked on it, frequently in collaboration with the director. One learned quite quickly what could and couldn't be done with a camera. For instance, one did not write in the script: Scene 40—the supply train is blown up.

"C.B. vowed that was the description of one episode that was handed to him. He developed it into fifteen scenes and took two days to shoot them.

"It was all very informal in those early days. Anybody on the set did anything he or she was called upon to do. I've walked on as an extra, I've tended lights—and anybody not doing anything else wrote down the director's notes on the

[4] *Anita Loos to author, New York, March 1964.*
[5] *Agnes de Mille:* Dance to the Piper (*Boston: Little, Brown & Co.; 1952*), *p. 12.*

script. Script girls were only slowly coming into being. I also spent a good deal of time in the cutting room."

Such apparently casual conditions, embracing all departments of production, were ideal training for scenario writers, whose ability rested on their appreciation of practical production problems.

A solid core of first-class writers, nearly all of them women, grew up as the importance of the work began to be recognized: Frances Marion, Eve Unsell, Clara Beranger, Edith Kennedy, Bess Meredyth, Ouida Bergere, Beulah Marie Dix, Marion Fairfax, Jeanie MacPherson, Lenore Coffee, Hector and Margaret Turnbull, and June Mathis were to remain top scenarists throughout the silent era.

Sam Goldwyn, who has always regarded the writer as the most significant single contributor to a film's artistic success, attracted to his company a number of celebrated authors, both American and European. He called this group "Eminent Authors, Inc."; it included Cosmo Hamilton, Channing Pollock, Avery Hopwood, Mary Roberts Rinehart, Gertrude Atherton, Edward Knoblock, Henry Arthur Jones, Somerset Maugham, Sir Gilbert Parker, and, most valuable, Rupert Hughes, who later became a director. These illustrious names were brought in at enormous cost to raise the reputation of the industry; it was a valiant but foolhardy move. These authors had spent their working lives expressing themselves in words, and they were completely unprepared to develop plots and delineate character in terms of pictures. Enormous effort was expended by Goldwyn to teach them the various crafts of the motion picture, but the scheme was doomed from the start. Goldwyn lost little, fortunately; his financial deficit was offset by a tremendous gain in prestige. The Eminent Authors was a sort of talkie revolution in reverse—the finest exponents of literary narrative suddenly found themselves in a medium which seemed to require their talents but which proved as baffling as a new language.

Regular continuity writers, despised as hacks, were called in to rescue many an Eminent Author from many an elementary muddle, just as stage men were later called in to bail out directors foundering amidst the flood of talkies.

Some of the scenarios written by the Eminent Authors have remained in Hollywood legend as Awful Examples.

"Edward Knoblock wrote a scenario for my father," said Agnes de Mille, "but, like most of the other famous novelists and playwrights, he couldn't think visually. One line in the scenario came up as: 'Words fail to describe the scene that follows.'

"Father said that was wonderfully helpful to a director! Then there was another phrase, which cropped up in *Midsummer Madness,* written by Cosmo Hamilton: 'Not by accident, they found themselves alone in a cabin in the mountains that summer night . . .'

" 'Not by accident,' father said, took him five sets and two weeks to shoot!"

Most of these writers were frank in pointing out their real interest in motion pictures—money. They were openly contemptuous of the medium. In some cases, this contempt sprang from a feeling of inferiority, hard to face after years of success, when the absurdity of their position dawned on them. A few grew difficult to handle, became temperamental, and expressed their derision with what they considered grand gestures against the small-mindedness of film producers. One playwright presented a three-page scenario for a seventy-minute feature. Soon, most of the original group had left; other companies continued to import big names, such as Elinor Glyn, Michael Arlen, and even Goldwyn refused to admit defeat. He persuaded Belgian writer Maurice Maeterlinck to come to California.

Writers *were* important, and, in retrospect, the Eminent Authors scheme was a stage it was vital at some point to pass through, if only to prove its impracticability.

By 1920, it was open season for scenarios. Everyone was writing for the movies; studios were overwhelmed by scripts and stories from amateurs all over the world. This was the only side of picture production in which the public could participate. It needed no training, no technical knowledge, and no equipment more complex than a typewriter. Advertisements for photoplay writing schools ousted those for acting.

"Millions of People Can Write Stories and Photoplays and Don't Know It!" stated an ad for the Irving System. "Don't you believe the Creator gave you a story-writing faculty, just as He did the greatest writer?"

People did—only red-eyed scenario editors were liable to dispute the point.

Elinor Glyn published a series of books entitled *The Elinor Glyn System of Writing*. The third volume was devoted to the photoplay, and Miss Glyn advised her readers to cultivate visualization: "Find a quiet spot where you will not be disturbed by anyone or anything. Close your eyes and concentrate on your play. Don't dream. Visualize!"[6]

It would have been ideal, said the studio story departments, to have left it at that—but Miss Glyn was just beginning. Explaining the development of character, she exhorted: "Keep Your Hero Smiling! A laughing, active man full of the spirit of modern life. Understand, he should not be a grinning idiot. He should not smile merely for the sake of smiling. There should be a reason for his smiles. They should radiate cheer and optimism and determination to forge ahead!" Miss Glyn advised her students to make him a normal, red-blooded young man "But Keep Your Hero Clean. He may err—but his mistake should be the result of carelessness, thoughtlessness, mischievousness or recklessness, but never the result of direct intent."[7]

Another popular course was supplied by successful scenario writer H. H. Van Loan, who wrote *Virgin of Stamboul* and whose name was the first among photo-dramatists to appear on a theater marquee—the Strand, San Francisco, in November 1920. In Van Loan's endearingly bombastic book *How I Did It* he describes the adventures that led to his successful scenarios, and offers advice for the amateur:

"First, establish a reason for your story, then introduce your characters, and after you've done that, make a dash for the climax. That's all there is to it. Establish a premise and then rush for the final scene. Don't waste any time en route. Be sure that it contains action, action, and then some more action. Mix a few thrills with it. Bring a tear to the eyes of your audience. Then, the next instant, chase away the tear with a smile. If you do that, then you've got a story."[8]

The Palmer Institute of Authorship enjoyed success for a time when a story written by Ethel Styles Middleton, the wife of a Pittsburgh factory foreman, was

[6] *Elinor Glyn:* The Elinor Glyn System of Writing, *Book 3 (The Author's Press; 1922), p. 264.*
[7] *Ibid., p. 284.*
[8] *H. H. Van Loan:* How I Did It *(Los Angeles: Whittingham Press; 1922), p. 24.*

produced—by the Palmer Photoplay Company. It was distributed (by FBO) and it received a great deal of publicity. Lloyd Hughes starred, and former cutter Del Andrews directed.

"This picture is the advance guard of screen drama which is genuinely of the people, by the people, and for the people," said Palmer's advertisement, adding that Mrs. Middleton's story was based on "an astounding dramatic episode in the lives of people of her acquaintance."[9]

The Advisory Council of Palmer Photoplays contained some significant names: Thos. H. Ince; Rex Ingram; Allen Holubar, then an important director; C. Gardner Sullivan, and for good measure, James R. Quirk. One of the 1923 advertisements was for a lady named Frances White Elijah: "HER FIRST STORY WAS BOUGHT BY D. W. GRIFFITH!"[1]

Palmer also went into print, and *Representative Photoplays Analyzed* is a historically fascinating series of stories of current pictures, given in full and intelligently examined.

Soon, a number of phony writing schools were exposed. One of them, offering valuable advice by Mr. Lawrence McCloskey "of the Lubin Company" neglected to add that the Lubin Company had been nonexistent for years.

Wrote Agnes Smith, *Photoplay* staff writer: "The allurements of a writer's life are touchingly set forth as follows: 'No physical exertion required—invalids can succeed. Learn in five days' time. Start to write immediately. Each story accepted should mean from twenty-five to a hundred and fifty dollars for you.'" But, added Miss Smith, this doubtful organization understated the situation. "Any writer, these days, receiving only a hundred and fifty dollars for a story would go out and hang himself in Joseph Hergesheimer's barn."[2]

Cecil De Mille, speaking for the Lasky Corporation, said that as the drama was the most democratic form of amusement, so scenario writing was the most democratic and popular form of indoor sport. "Inexperienced writers dash off scenarios as they would a letter home. It takes one of our trained writers from four to eight weeks to prepare a story for the screen. Amateurs think they can turn them out at a rate of three to four in an afternoon."[3]

This was 1920, and the Lasky Corporation was still encouraging amateur scenarists in the hope that talent would raise its periscope above the sea of words. Out of every two hundred manuscripts submitted, said De Mille, one might contain an idea that would form the basis of a photodrama.

By the mid-twenties, the work of the amateur photoplay writer was no longer destined for the screen but for the wastepaper basket. The motion-picture business was now the exclusive domain of professionals. The days of experiment were over.

[9] Photoplay, *Jan. 1924, p. 99; the film was* Judgment of the Storm.
[1] Picture Play, *April 1923, p. 15.*
[2] Photoplay, *May 1927, p. 29.*
[3] *Quoted in Frances Taylor Patterson:* Cinema Craftsmanship (*New York: Harcourt, Brace; 1920*), p. 169.

23 / EDITING: THE HIDDEN POWER

An editor's job is no more limited to the joining up of scenes than a poet's to the rhyming of words. Both are essential functions, but both are merely mechanical stages in a creative process.

Editing is directing the film for the second time. To gauge the psychological moment—to know exactly where to cut—requires the same intuitive skill as that needed by a director.

The director controls the action and judges the point at which it should occur. So does the editor. The editor's field of operation is narrower, because he has to work with what he has been given. If a director is dissatisfied with the contents of a scene, he can augment it, or subtract from it, and then reshoot. The editor has to put up with what he has, or discard it. But by careful placing and selection, he can transform an inferior scene into a perfectly acceptable one. With the director and cameraman, the editor is one of the three major contributors to the quality of a motion picture; he is capable of destroying a well-directed film and of rescuing poorly directed material. But his efforts are never fully appreciated, except by the director. The producer, and the members of the unit, seldom realize the effort that goes into the various editing stages. It is small wonder that those outside the industry have the idea that an editor merely joins up the scenes as they come from the studio.

This, however, is the way he operated in the most primitive days. At that time, the scenes were lengthy and generally required a title to separate them from the next scene. The material was screened in the projection room; the director would tell the cutter how he wanted the scenes to go. The cutter would make notes, and would take the material to the cutting room, where he would join up the shots in the order described.

As filmic storytelling became more imaginative, so the cutter's job became more complex, more responsible. The role of editor was created. Editing gave the cinema an identity of its own. The pioneer's strict adherence to stage tradition and practice was undermined by several elements. One was the work of D. W. Griffith. But his experiments were counterbalanced by a large number of routine and frequently dull films, made much as any other director might have made them. Experiment took time; Griffith was paid by men who were satisfied that the industry had made all the progress it needed and it was not often that he could spare that time.

The real impetus to break away from the confines of the stage was provided by the comedy producers. They were not obliged to imbue their films with an aura of dignity, as were the dramatic producers. The less dignity the better. They realized that to keep the audience laughing continuously, the action had to move and more *fast*. All dead footage was therefore ruthlessly slashed. Instead of a character-leaving shot . . . *hold it . . . hold it . . . cut to next . . . hold it . . . hold it . . . character enters. . . .* Instead of this deadly routine, the editors of comedy pictures adopted a different rhythm—and cut on action, before the screen was empty. The transition was as fast as it was smooth, and this technique made some of the musty, stagebound dramas look so ponderous that around 1914 they began to follow suit.

Fast cutting was not a conscious invention, but a logical development. In many ways, film making was a game, and with youthful enthusiasm the comedy

Tom Miranda, Goldwyn editor.

producers sought ways to make the game more enjoyable, more elaborate. Soon, the work of the leading comedy producer, Mack Sennett, was hailed as art—a term which shook him into self-consciousness. Like Chaplin, he was made acutely aware of his talent, and he depended upon outside influence for judgment, rather than relying on his own intuition. But until that time, the Keystone rough-and-tumble, guided by such fine directors as F. Richard Jones and Del Lord, produced a constant stream of real cinema, the influence of which cannot be overestimated.

The ability to cut quickly does not necessarily imply an ability to cut well. The complexities of editing are not solved simply by speeding up the pace. But at least this fast cutting, in its influence on the dramatic film, brought about a refreshing metamorphosis.

Scenes were no longer photographed from one fixed position in one long take. They were broken up into a form which was to become the basic grammar of motion pictures—long shot, medium shot, and close shot. For a while, around 1914-15, the cinema carried on with a solidly based grammar, but with no syntax. The long shot was followed by the mid-shot, which was followed by the close shot; there was little attempt at rearrangement to heighten the effect.

The work of Griffith certainly changed all that. *The Birth of a Nation,* released in 1915, was the first feature film to exploit fully the extraordinary power of editing. In the truest sense of the word, this was a masterpiece; it served as an example for the rest of the industry.

The editing of this film, although often frenetic and uncontrolled, is still powerful. But it lacks the polish that Hollywood was later to become famous for; it lacks *smoothness*. This is a quality common to most other American film makers which Griffith, strangely enough, seldom displayed.

For Griffith, the master of editing, could conceive the most complex and amazing cutting. But when it came to its execution, he seemed to lose interest. It is one of the incomprehensible features of this great man that he was capable of the most meticulous staging, ensuring the correctness of every detail, yet he could be blind to glaringly mismatched editing.

A long shot would be taken in bright sunlight; the following shot would be dull and overcast. A warrior would sheathe his sword in the long shot; in the close shot he would sheathe it again.

Andrew Stone worked with Griffith's editor, Jimmy Smith. "Jimmy Smith said, as I recall, that Griffith had a great habit of shooting everything in long shot. He'd then sit in the projection room and decide where he wanted close-ups. Jimmy often bemoaned the fact that Griffith just never gave a damn about matching. He'd pick out where he wanted his close-ups and then he'd go on to any stage with any background and get these beautiful art close-ups and cut them in. Now, number one: it's very difficult to look at the action in a projection room and then come back and try to repeat it for the close-up. If you do it at the same time, fine—you repeat the same action at the same speed. But if you do it a month or two later, well, the other action may have been faster, it may have been slower. You're just relying on memory. When you put the two shots together, you'll see how wrong you are! If you're going to make a retake of a close-up today you first study the film in the projection room, then you take the Moviola out on the set and you have the cutter study the master shot while you shoot the cut-in—just so the section matches exactly. If an actor sits down in the master and he's taking off his jacket, you can't have him sitting down in the close-up taking off his tie! And this is why Jimmy Smith was so sore about Griffith never giving a damn about matching."[1]

A theory has been put forward[2] that this was a deliberate style, that Griffith, in common with several other directors, quite intentionally created these obvious double actions. This could be true—and it is interesting that Griffith's early Biograph films and his 1919 *The Greatest Question* had none of these overlapping cuts. *Intolerance* (1916) and *Orphans of the Storm* (1922) were riddled with them.

So while Griffith forced an awareness of the power of editing on the industry, and while he laid its foundations, the refinements and polish were supplied by others.

Editing, in common with other aspects of techniques, settled down to a solid professionalism around 1918. Astonishingly, most editors worked without the animated viewers considered essential today. They cut in the hand. Modern film editors are baffled by this; how could they possibly judge the pace, or the rhythm? William Hornbeck, one of the great film editors, insisted that it was perfectly

[1] *Andrew Stone to author, London, April 1962.*
[2] *Notably by Ray Angus, editor of the* Silents Please *TV series* (*conversation with author, New York, March 1964*).

simple once you grew accustomed to it and that he still uses that method occasionally.

Animated viewers, particularly the celebrated Moviola silent head,[3] which operated by foot pedal and was motor driven, appeared in the twenties. There were also some hand-cranked models, and other experimental bits of machinery. But most editors preferred to use the ordinary ground-glass screen on their bench, which had a light beneath it, enabling them to examine the frame; some of them fitted a magnifying glass on a rotating stand, which they could swing across for close examination.

Experience in the cutting room, ideal training for directors, was also sought after by people from other departments.

When Bebe Daniels was making comedies for Paramount in the mid-twenties, she used to work with the writers.

"One day, the editor, Dorothy Arzner, came to me and said, 'Bebe, you could have heightened this scene a great deal. . . .' She started to explain, but I didn't get it. 'Come up to the cutting room some night and I'll show you what I mean.' So I went up with her, and I became fascinated. I went up every night, if I wasn't working at night myself. It taught me more about writing for motion pictures than anything in the world could have taught me.

"Dorothy used to hold the film up to the light and cut it in the hand. I remember my first lesson; she held the film up and said, 'Well, now, look—this is dead from here to here—we're going to put this close-up in here—so we'll go to here. We don't need this—wait a minute, we can come in here. . . .'

"Gradually I began to understand, and learned to cut film myself. We used to mark the frame with a wax pencil, scrape the emulsion off with a razor blade, apply the glue, then put the other piece of film on top and press it down hard. Then we'd check our sprocket holes, and examine the cut under the magnifying glass. Dorothy used to cut as we went on those comedies, and it was very helpful to see the cut rushes in the morning. We could keep the pace right. We might have slowed down as we went along, but seeing the cut rushes kept us to the right speed.

"Every night I'd trudge up there and work with Dorothy until seven or eight, then I'd go home with my· nails full of glue. I remember saying to Dorothy that I didn't want to bore her by coming up all the time.

" 'Bebe,' she said. 'I love this.' "[4]

Cutting in the hand died out when sound brought synchronization problems—but it continued long after the introduction of Moviolas.

"The old cutters would not use them," said Bebe Daniels. "They were like old cooks who refused to use pressure cookers."

That cutting in the hand produced satisfactory results with surprising speed cannot be denied; the best editors maintained the rhythm of sequences to perfection. And rhythm is the basis of film editing, just as it is in music. A change of shot, or movement within a shot, sets up the beat, and once this is established it has to be preserved. Some editors cut without bothering about the beat of the scene; few people are aware of the mistake, just as few people notice when a

[3] *The first Moviola appeared in 1904.*
[4] *Bebe Daniels to author, London, July 1963.*

uper-Hooper-Dyne Lizzies, *a Sennett comedy of 1925, directed by Del Lord, edited by*
William Hornbeck. Billy Bevan disturbs some parked cars as he pushes his old jalopy up

…he street. This sequence appeared in Robert Youngson's When Comedy Was King, *released* …by Twentieth-Century Fox, *from which these frame enlargements were taken.*

shot is slightly soft. But while an audience may not remark on it, or even be aware of it, such errors are subliminally disturbing. One feels slightly uneasy without knowing why. In silent pictures, the rhythm of the picture was especially important—and a bad cut could be as offensive esthetically as a missed beat in a symphony.

Editors are passed over by film historians because their work, when successful, is virtually unnoticeable. No historian, without knowing the problems, without knowing the director's working methods, or without being an editor himself, could possibly evaluate the editor's contribution. As Anthony Wollner, A.C.E., pointed out: "An editor need not be a writer, but he must know story structure; he need not be a cameraman, but he must understand pictorial composition and the compatibility of angles; he need not be a director, but he must feel the actors' performances and the dramatic or comedy pacing as surely as the director."[5]

Editing is an art, completely satisfying in itself. At the same time, editing experience is ideal training for direction. Dorothy Arzner, following her years as an editor, became Hollywood's most successful woman director.[6] She began at Famous Players in 1919, typing scripts. These scripts gradually aroused her interest, and she discussed them with the cutter. At that time, the cutter also acted as script clerk on the set; this was known as "keeping script."

"One cutter, Nan Heron, was particularly helpful," said Dorothy Arzner.[7] "She was cutting a Donald Crisp picture, *Too Much Johnson;* I watched her work on one reel and she let me do the second, while she watched and guided every cut. On Sunday I went into the studio and assembled the next reel. On Monday I told her about it and she looked at it and approved. I finished the picture under her guidance. She then recommended me to keep script and cut the next Donald Crisp picture, *The Six Best Cellars,* with Bryant Washburn.

"I was a very fast cutter. I cut something like thirty-two pictures in one year at Realart, a subsidiary of Paramount. (Their main star was Bebe Daniels . . . whose courage and talent I greatly admired.) I also supervised the negative cutting and trained the girls who cut negative and spliced film by hand. I set up the film filing system and supervised the art work on the titles. I worked most of the day and night and loved it."

After about a year with Realart, Miss Arzner was recalled to Paramount to cut and edit *Blood and Sand* starring Rudolph Valentino, and also to keep script. Paramount planned to spend $50,000 on a double-exposure process to matte Valentino into the Madrid Bull Arena. As a temporary solution, Miss Arzner cut the three bullfights from existing stock footage. She then asked to shoot some close-ups of Valentino to match the long shots. The result was so effective that the picture was released with Miss Arzner's bullfights intact.

"I was running *Blood and Sand* in the projection room when Jim Cruze passed through to reach the adjoining theater. He paused to watch. Suddenly I heard

---

[5] *Quoted in* The Cinemeditor, *Spring, 1965, p. 17.*
[6] *Dorothy Arzner's first directorial assignment was* Fashions for Women (1926) *with Esther Ralston. Brooks Atkinson commented: "If fashion pictures must be made, let Dorothy Arzner make them." It is often claimed that Miss Arzner was Hollywood's first and only woman director. She was undoubtedly the most successful, but other women directors included Alice Guy-Blache, Lois Weber, Lillian Gish, Mabel Normand, Ida May Parks, Ruth Jennings Bryan, Grace Haskins, and Jane Murfin.*
[7] *Dorothy Arzner in letter to author, April 1967.*

an exclamation. 'My God, who cut that picture?' I wasn't sure if this meant approval or disapproval, but I quietly admitted I did. When the lights went up, he asked me if I would cut his next picture, *The Covered Wagon*."

It was her association with *The Covered Wagon* that brought Miss Arzner's name into the film history books—the only editor from the entire silent period to be officially remembered.

Editing became more complicated mechanically with the introduction of sound, but it was never more challenging esthetically than at the height of the silent era, when, with bravura action sequences like the chariot race from *Ben-Hur*, the land rush from *Tumbleweeds*, and the battle scene from *The Big Parade*, it exploded in a pyrotechnic display of cinematic ferocity. Such sequences still stand as supreme examples of the editor's art.

The Cov

a Ja

24 / *TWO UNIQUE PROCESSES: TINTING AND TITLING*

Sepia-toned photographs have gone out of fashion; so, for different reasons, has tinting for motion pictures. Sepia-toning for still photographs was a hang-over from the Victorian habit of dressing everything up; naked black-and-white was felt to be harsh and, in portrait work, occasionally unkind. Tinting for motion pictures was introduced for similar reasons, but it quickly began to serve a much more useful purpose.

Night scenes were difficult and costly to photograph. Film stock was very slow, and a great deal of light was needed to illumine long shots satisfactorily. The mob scenes in *Hunchback of Notre Dame* (1923; Wallace Worsley) required every arc in Hollywood before they were properly lit for the camera.

But with an all-over blue tint, close-ups taken at night could be intercut with long shots taken by day—and the tinting would provide the uniform night effect. (Some of these day-for-night sequences have been duped onto ordinary black-and-white stock, and the apparent carelessness has puzzled audiences, who place the blame, inevitably, on the "primitiveness" of the silent days.)

Regular daylight scenes were tinted amber, fire scenes were red, early-morning scenes were gold, and there was a wide range of subtler tints, such as peach-glow, for firelight or sunsets. These tints were not just a substitute for color—they were also remarkably effective in creating, and changing, the atmosphere of scenes and heightening the dramatic effect.

Smouldering Fires (1924; Clarence Brown), a brilliant drama about the un-happiness of a woman of forty who falls for a man of twenty-five, employs tinting most creatively. For a party scene in which the woman (Pauline Frederick) becomes painfully aware of the youth of her husband and his friends, the screen goes a deep red—a color which returns for the final, tension-filled denouement, when she realizes her own defeat. Elsewhere, the atmosphere is carefully sustained with the yellow candlelight, the gold dawn, the pink firelight, the deep blue of the night. . . .

Tinting in motion pictures first appeared when enterprising projectionists held colored gelatin before the lens.[1] Soon, the film itself was not merely tinted but toned as well. Toning was a process which converted the blacks to color but left the highlights untouched. When a tint was added to toned stock, a two-color effect was obtained. In *Back to God's Country* (1920; David Hartford), the forest scenes were given an added dimension: the trees were green; the back-ground and highlights were a light yellow. The effect was superb. In *Napoleon* (1927; Abel Gance), as Bonaparte watches the burning of the English fleet in Toulon harbor, his face is bathed in the reflection, while the night sky behind him is a deep blue. This process was called blue-tone pink.

Tinting was generally the responsibility of the editor. He decided upon the colors in consultation with the director; he spliced together all the scenes for amber tint, all those for blue, sent them to the laboratory, and then re-sorted them into their original order in the work print. Laboratories kept tinting baths working full time. Every print had to be tinted separately, and the stock treated *after* printing.

Tinting has often been equated with the hand-coloring of postcards, which is a totally false comparison. There was nothing crude about this process. An

[1] *The films shown at Koster and Bial's, New York, in 1896 were tinted by hand.*

original tinted print of a well-photographed silent picture was esthetically both stimulating and satisfying. The only reason the process died out was that tinting interfered with the sound track of talkies. Occasionally, sound films appeared on amber-toned stock, but the changes of tint from scene to scene did not appear again until color stock enabled the makers of compilation pictures to evoke a faint suggestion of nostalgia.

Years before regular tinting became commonplace, when nine colors were introduced in 1921, and long before experiments with Technicolor began, films were available which were hand-tinted in full color. Again, the idea suggests tinted postcards. Some of the films were almost as offensive, but others were remarkably successful.

Pathécolor, as the best process was called, was introduced in the early nineteen hundreds and was used on special sequences of dramatic films, in trick films, and for Pathé's regular fashion reports. It was a costly and elaborate process; other companies tried to emulate Pathécolor, but they could never match it for accuracy. Their attempts at hand-tinting produced blobs of color which wobbled on the screen like sections of colored jelly. Pathécolor, being a stencil process, was almost always in register and seldom suffered from that disconcerting short-coming—when a character walked off screen, leaving his color behind.

Arthur Kingston, a veteran cameraman, who worked in France and England and who became a prominent inventor, was with the Pathé Company before World War I.

"At Vincennes," he said, "Pathé employed about three hundred women. Each worker sat at a bench. On her right was a ground-glass projection screen and a handle. Each turn of the handle moved one frame of the film to be tinted. The frame was enlarged to 6½ by 9½ inches.

"On her left was another copy of the same film, which was to be the stencil. In front of her was a pantograph with a ten-to-one reduction, to which an electro-magnetic vibrating needle was attached. This was fed by a fifty-cycle supply, and it cut the stencil for each section. There were never more than three sections. One woman would work on the blue, another on the red, another on the yellow.

"To add more color, the release print would be specially toned. Then the three stencils would be lined up in synchronization on a special machine, and rollers would spread the dye. The biggest difficulty was the rapid shrinkage of nitrate film. If any of the prints involved shrunk to any extent, the colors would overlap. So we designed special shrinkage charts which worked in conjunction with an accurate projector. Then we could repunch one sprocket hole per frame. We could depend on our color prints being almost perfect."[2]

Hand-tinting was never widely used in America, but it continued to be used for certain scenes in continental pictures—the fireworks display in *Casanova,* the exotic sequences of *Mille et Une Nuits.* The Americans had access to Technicolor two-strip by the mid-twenties, and they employed this much as the French em-ployed their hand-tinted color, using it for the scenes with Christ in *Ben-Hur* the fashion parade in *Fig Leaves,* the final love scene in *King on Main Street.*

Full color made hand-coloring unnecessary, but nothing has ever replaced the tinting process. Many pictures shot in black-and-white today would benefit from

[2] *Arthur Kingston to author, Denham, Bucks, July 1965.*

Developing bath; the same apparatus served for tinting.

RICHARD A. ROWLAND
PRESENTS

The Barker

WITH

MILTON SILLS AND DOROTHY MACKAILL

SCREEN PLAY BY BENJAMIN GLAZER

A GEORGE FITZMAURICE
PRODUCTION

A First National Picture

To avoid lengthy credits, the main title carried as much information as possible.

John Emerson and Anita Loos examine a set of art titles.

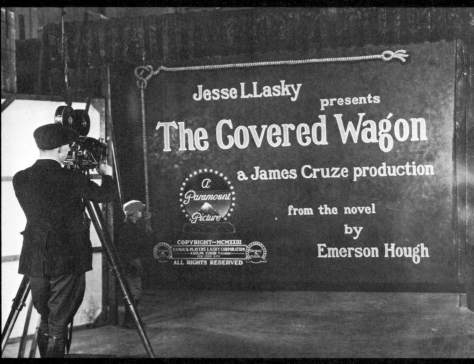

Karl Brown photographing the opening title for The Covered Wagon *(1923). The title card was enlarged to this enormous size so that a curtain could be raised to reveal it. This particular take was scrapped. The title was remade to read: "Adolph Zukor and Jesse L. Lasky present."*

some imaginative uses of color washes, particularly period pictures. Most laboratories have forgotten how to do it; the method popular in the silent days was to replace the silver by a colored metallic compound. This was usually a ferrocyanide; sulphide a warm brown, vanadium a greenish yellow, and uranium ferrocyanide a reddish brown. The film was dipped into vats which contained the necessary chemicals.

"The use of delicate tints," said *Motion Picture Photography,* "both removes the contrasting black-and-white effect and adds a touch of warmth to the black deposit of silver."[3]

And it added magic to the movies.

Title writing, a process unique to silent pictures, was an art in itself. In those days, a fiction writer received from one to ten cents a word. A motion-picture title writer got about two dollars and twenty cents a word—not for the number of words he wrote so much as for the number he avoided writing—while still managing to tell the story.

Titles are regarded as the blight of silent pictures, an insurmountable obstacle to full enjoyment by a modern audience. Obviously, if you are not used to them, the sudden appearance of printed captions can be unsettling. It is really a matter of growing accustomed to the convention. Writers, directors, and editors did all they could to keep titles to a minimum—and to ensure their effectiveness when they *were* used.

Despite the attempts to make title-free pictures, film makers realized that the most enlightened audience would be unable to follow a plot without the aid of titles. Eliminating titles from a silent film was about as simple, and desirable, as eliminating dialogue from a sound film. It could be done . . . it *was* done; but the results were invariably grossly overlength. Tortuously explanatory visual passages were needed to dispense with one simple title, and the effect, far from being a satisfying artistic achievement, was frequently irritating and gimmicky.

"Not long ago," wrote Gerald Duffy, Mary Pickford's title writer "a mighty producer made the maniacal assertion that the perfect picture would be one in which there would be no titles whatever. Others of his insane colleagues accepted this delusion as a fact.

"I was frantic. It would mean the destruction of my business and the picture business—but particularly *my* business. The nonsense spread to the point where the adventurous Charlie Ray made a picture without any titles, hoping, I suppose, that it would turn out to be the perfect picture: *The Old Swimming Hole*—that was it. And the innovation well-nigh ruined it.

"That picture without titles was the strongest argument possible for the picture *with* titles. And as thunderous proof of the truth, the biggest laugh was provoked by a substitute for a title. Charlie wrote on a slate: 'I'm through with wimmin,' and then, immediately becoming the victim of a romance, he erased the resolution with ardor in view of the audience. Without the words, where would the laugh have been?"[4]

The Old Swimming Hole, directed by Joseph de Grasse, was a charming picture,

[3] *Carl Louis Gregory, ed.:* Motion Picture Photography (*New York: New York Institute of Photography; 1920*), *p. 197.*
[4] Picture Play, *Aug. 1922, p. 22.*

and practically plotless. As Burns Mantle pointed out, "No one in it could possibly have anything worth titling to say."[5] But a few delicately placed titles might well have removed the occasional *longueurs,* without damaging the flow.

Titles, like any other creative process, depended on skill and judgment for their success. Sometimes they overweighted a picture and caused squirms of agony rather than the squeals of delight which greeted the bon mots of top title writers like Ralph Spence, Gerald Duffy, Joe Farnham, and George Marion, Jr. These men possessed a unique facility for turning out snappy, witty, epigrammatic, or atmospheric titles which would not have seemed out of place in the works of Wilde or Conrad.

Writing these titles was a strange business. Economy and conciseness would appear to be the primary requirements. Yet some of the most effective titles were lengthy and rambling. The explanatory titles for *The Covered Wagon* impart simple facts, but with the use of place names and atmospheric description they gain an almost epic poetry, exactly fitting the mood of the film. It would have been simple to have written:

"Banion's train arrives first at Fort Bridger."

But explanatory titles in dramatic films communicated feeling as well as information. The actual title reads:

Across Wyoming and over the first range of the Rockies—chilled by early October frosts—the Banion train pulled in at old Fort Bridger a few miles ahead of Wingate.

The epic simplicity is again apparent when the character of Tully Marshall is introduced:

The next day came a trader—that lone nomad of the prairie with his small caravan—traveling between the new frontier and civilization—unmolested because he carried no plow and sought no land.

To add an extra dimension to the following scene was a primary duty of the explanatory title. Here another example from *The Covered Wagon* has a three-pronged emotional appeal:

The whispered secret of Gold flashed like magic through the Liberty camp—California became the promised land. But Banion thought only of Molly's wedding as he gave the order that separated the two trains forever.

Since Molly (Lois Wilson) was about to marry the villain (Alan Hale), any glimpse of Banion (J. Warren Kerrigan) after that title was of immense interest to the sympathetically aroused audience. And again the utter simplicity of the title has real beauty:

Month after month, over the Western Rockies, Northwest across the thirsty land of the Shoshones and the mighty Snake, the Men of the Plow held to their purpose.

Titles were indicated in the script—sometimes they were written in full, sometimes sketched in:

---

[5] Photoplay, *May 1921, p. 51.*

S.T. INDICATING THAT WHILE PETE SHOULD BE AT WORK HE IS COURTING SHIRLEY [*His Picture in the Papers*—1916]

It is fascinating to see how a perfectly adequate title in the scenario can be transformed by the title writer into a jewel. In the Sam Taylor–Tim Whelan script for *Exit Smiling* (1926; Taylor), comedienne Beatrice Lillie was introduced with this title:

Violet, the Patsy of the show. Born and raised on the stage, she knew life only as the stage reflected it.

Title writer Joe Farnham rewrote this, altering the sense, but emphasizing the characterization and ensuring a laugh:

Violet, the drudge of the troupe . . . who also played parts like *Nothing* in *Much Ado About Nothing*.

Comedy titling was a more hazardous occupation than titling for dramas. Dialogue titles had to be funny, but not funnier than the scene. If the scene was a bit flat, however, the titler had to brighten it up. Ralph Spence was the master at this; in a Marie Dressler–Polly Moran comedy, when the two were swilling synthetic gin, he had one say to the other:

"This stuff makes me see double and feel single."

Ralph Spence was a film doctor. By switching sequences and rewriting titles, he could alter a complete story—change drama to high comedy. He had a daunting advertisement in the *Film Daily Year Book:* a full-page picture of himself with the legend: "All bad little films when they die go to Ralph Spence."[6]

Changing all the titles in a picture was not as easy as it seems. Many members of silent-film audiences became adept at lip-reading. They could tell whether the title bore any relation to what the character had just said. Editors usually cut as the character began to speak, and returned to the scene as he finished. But sometimes this was not practical.

"In an effort to be funny," wrote Louise Brooks, "old actors and directors have spread the false belief that any clownish thing coming to mind could be said in front of the camera in silent films. They forget the title writer had to match his work to the actors' speech. I remember late one night wandering into Ralph Spence's suite in the Beverly Wilshire, where he sat gloomily amidst cans of film, cartons of stale Chinese food, and empty whisky bottles. He was trying to fix up a Beery and Hatton comedy, *Now We're in the Air,* and no comic line he invented would fit the lip action. Silent-film fans were excellent lip readers and often complained at the box office about the cowboy cussing furiously trying to mount his horse."[7]

Lip-reading became obligatory for full enjoyment of *What Price Glory?, Beau Geste, Old Ironsides,* and *Sadie Thompson.* The language of the players, especially McLaglen and Beery, was too hot for any titles. Gloria Swanson was able to ride all her censorship problems and still give a down-to-earth realistic portrayal of Sadie Thompson by sandwiching discreet titles between honest-to-goodness

[6] Film Daily Year Book, *1926, p. 180.*
[7] Sight & Sound, *Summer 1965, p. 123.*

Anglo-Saxon, delivered silently—but scorchingly for lip-readers. The new sport became known as the "cuss word puzzle."

Eddie Sutherland was very anxious to use Spence on his first big success, *Behind the Front.*

"Spence was a great man—but quite irresponsible. I could never find him. His hobby was railroad trains, and he had a whole room full of them. He was a good drinking man, liked girls, liked fun, and he had a room at the Hollywood Plaza. I found out what room he was in, and engaged the one next to it. Next morning, as his breakfast was taken in, I went in too, with the film in my arms.

" 'Oh, you rat. You found me.'

"So we stayed in the room while he wrote the titles. He'd run the film on a little Moviola thing, and he'd say, 'What do you want on this thing? What do you visualize, Eddie?'

"Beery and Hatton were in the front-line trenches for the first time, so I said, 'Something to show the danger that they're going into, and that they don't like it much, I guess.'

"So he wrote a title:

" 'Listening post—where men are men, but wish they weren't.' "[8]

By the late twenties, Ralph Spence was earning ten thousand dollars a picture, and *Photoplay* noted another significant fact:

"A Hollywood theater announces, in electric lights, 'Titles by Ralph Spence,' being the first time on record a title writer rated billing."[9]

The development of the silent film title (or subtitle, to differentiate between the caption and the main and end titles) took in as much ground as the development of the motion picture itself.

"Do you know," said D. W. Griffith, "that the first pictures we made were without titles? We decided that titles—provided they are the right sort—help a picture. Many important feet of film are saved by the simple expedient of using a few printed words. Every foot of film is precious."[1]

The earliest titles were bold statements: "That night" or "Next day"—with the occasional adornment of "Came the dawn." As technique became more elaborate, so did the titles.

Wrote Peter Milne in *Photoplay,* "Title writers have now swung around to the other extreme. A situation calling for a simple fact such as the passing of a night is liable to blossom forth in such a literary hemorrhage as:

" 'Came the sweet-voiced harbingers of a new day, putting to rout the somber blackness of the night.'

"The excuse for employing such a wasteful combination of words is that it provides an alleged poetic touch. We have made an exhaustive study of the elaboration of simple statements into wordy subtitles that are calculated to induce an emotional state of mind:

" 'That night' becomes 'Inky black darkness, dotted with a myriad twinkling lights . . .'

" 'The next day' becomes 'Comes another rising sun and the troubles of yesterday are forgotten in the brilliant new avenue of opportunities it unfolds.'

[8] *From tapes transcribed by Oral History Research Office, Columbia University, New York, Feb. 1959.*
[9] Photoplay, *Jan. 1929, p. 101.*
[1] *Article by Griffith in* Motion Picture Magazine, *July 1926, p. 25.*

"Shifting the action of a picture from a large city to the western plains offers a fine opportunity for literary fireworks:

" 'Alone . . . under the dome of God's vast cathedral of nature.'

"If titles continue to progress from brevity to superverbosity we expect to see 'Passed by the National Board of Review' appear as 'Pronounced worthy of the gods and of the great American public by the venerable men and women who make up that great and august body . . . guardian of the public morals . . . the National Board of Review.' "[2]

Early title writing went through two other unfortunate stages. In the first, the title would dispense with the possibility of any suspense or excitement by announcing the contents of the incoming scene and giving away the outcome. It was rather like prefacing a murder thriller with the words, "The butler did it." D. W. Griffith was as much of an offender as anyone; in *Goddess of Sagebrush Gulch,* he kept pulse rates low during a potentially exciting scene with this giveaway title:

> *Help, when Help is Needed!* Tom, a courageous young man, saves Gertrude from the serpent's fangs.

Such a lack of confidence in the audience's ability to follow the action was more forgivable at this early period, when a large percentage of American audiences were immigrants, often without any knowledge of American customs and lore, who might have mistaken the meaning of certain scenes without this careful guidance.

In some theaters in the Jewish community of New York, spielers enacted the male and female voices, reading out not only the titles but carrying on an ad lib accompaniment all the way through the picture. These spielers were relics of the days before titles were in common use. A spieler had to have great presence of mind; often working without rehearsal, he could be caught off guard by a sudden twist in the story:

As the heroine embraces the young man, the female spieler purrs: "Oh, Lionel, I do love you—I do—" At the appearance of the real love, the spieler, realizing that she has mistaken the brother for the lover, continues unabashed, "—but as a sister. You see, here comes my fiancé now."

The second unfortunate stage through which the title passed—a stage which could have aided only the spieler—appeared in *The Spoilers* (1914), when dialogue titles were reinforced with the name of the character who was speaking. Since *The Spoilers* also employed the giveaway title, the picture was somewhat handicapped.

Early titles consisted of plain lettering, usually in upper- and lower-case typeface, sometimes equipped with the title of the film and the name or symbol of the production company. As film makers became aware of the importance of the title, they began to provide backgrounds, counterpointing or complementing the title itself.

These art backgrounds were normally reserved for explanatory titles at the beginning of sequences; titles were embellished with silhouettes or allegorical *motifs*. These designs and backgrounds were subdued, to preserve the clarity of

---

[2] Photoplay, *Oct. 1925, p. 132.*

the title, but they were more than mere embellishment. The principal purpose was to maintain the continuity of thought; but they were useful, too, to prevent a violent change from picture to the pure black-and-white of the caption. A light shot suddenly cutting to a black title may be good exercise for the eyes, but it tires them rapidly; art backgrounds smoothed the transition.

The idea of superimposing titles over the scene, as is now customary for foreign-dialogue movies, had occurred to silent-film people, and was used to retain the flow of movement, as in the *Ben-Hur* chariot race, or the chase through the streets in the gangster film *Walking Back* (Rupert Julian). But for general use, the problems of duping and overlays were too costly and complex, particularly when foreign versions were needed.

As it was, foreign negatives could be shipped with flash titles—titles of two or three frames, which cut down the overall footage, reducing shipping costs and import duty. (Since England, in an attempt to profit from the invasion of American films, had raised its import duty to fourpence a foot, these flash titles represented quite a saving.) The distributor could then make up full-length titles by stopping the flash frames in the printer gate, and running off as much positive as he needed. Producers adapted this method by photographing titles direct onto small glass plates, which were then placed in the printing machines and used as flash frames; this ingenious method saved thousands of feet of negative stock.

Further footage was saved by the use of simplified spelling: "programme" became "program," "employee" became "employe."

But, always, the major problem of the title writer was how to squeeze what may be a complex thought into a few words.

"In Mary Pickford's *Through the Back Door*," wrote Gerald Duffy, "one particular title had a burden to bear. It had deftly to insinuate that Mary was eloping—but it couldn't say it because she wasn't. We simply wanted to deceive the audience into thinking she was. Also, it had to suggest that her mother was contemplating divorce. Moreover, the last time we had seen the characters they had been on Long Island. Now we were to show them in a New York hotel— and it was necessary that we tell the audience that it was a New York hotel.

"Another vital point was that the title had to be funny. Writing that title was a staggering undertaking. But the furniture in the picture saved me. My title read, 'If it were not for New York hotels where would elopers, divorcees, and red-plush furniture go?' Seventeen words told everything."[3]

---

[3] Picture Play, *Aug. 1922, p. 22.*

25 / MARGARET BOOTH

Margaret Booth is one of the great motion-picture editors. Today, one of the top executives at M-G-M, she holds the all-embracing title of editor-in-chief. One of the few to survive every regime since the days of Thalberg, Miss Booth now holds immense control. Her uncanny perceptiveness, which has something of Thalberg about it, is the result of a long career and a complete devotion to this most demanding craft.

Perhaps her most celebrated achievement was the first version of *Mutiny on the Bounty* (Frank Lloyd). She also cut scores of other M-G-M films: *Mysterious Lady* (Fred Niblo) with Garbo, *The Enemy* (Niblo) with Lillian Gish, *Lady of Chance* (Robert Z. Leonard), *Telling the World* (Sam Wood), and *A Yank at Oxford* (Jack Conway).

Miss Booth is reticent about her work and modest about her achievements. She is well known for the fact that she entrusts nothing to writing. It was hard to persuade her to describe her career. Finally, just before she left London for California, after a visit in 1965, surrounded by suitcases and unpacked clothes in her hotel suite, she relented and recalled enough about her work to hint at the sort of problems she overcame and the sort of person she is.

MARGARET BOOTH: I had just come out of school, and I started as a patcher [film joiner] with the D. W. Griffith Company. While I was there, I learned to cut negative; in the old days we had to cut negative by eye. We matched the print to the negative without any edge numbers. We had to match the action. Sometimes there'd be a tiny pinpoint on the negative, and then you knew you were right. But it was very tedious work. Close-ups of Lillian Gish in *Orphans of the Storm* would go on for miles, and they'd be very similar, so we all had to help one another.

This lasted a few months, then I went to work in the laboratory at Paramount, assembling the tinted sections for release prints. That lasted two or three weeks. Finally, I went to work for Mr. Mayer at the old Mission Road studios.

Louis B. Mayer was then an independent producer, releasing through First National. At Mission Road was a remarkable director, John M. Stahl. I became his assistant. I used to stand by him while he cut, and he used to ask me to come in with him to see his dailies in the projection room. This way he taught me the dramatic values of cutting, he taught me about tempo—in fact he taught me how to edit.

In those days, one did everything, and sometimes I went on location with him as script girl. When the Mayer company merged with Metro and Goldwyn, I went to work at the Culver City studio. I was still an assistant, but I used to go back at night and cut the out-takes—the takes Stahl had discarded. After a while, he started to look at these efforts of mine, and sometimes he'd take a whole sequence that I had cut and put it in the picture. Then gradually I got around to making his first cut—and that's how I got to be an editor.

Learning how to cut was hard going because Stahl was a very hard taskmaster. He was a perfectionist; he kept doing things over and over again. He shot every sequence so it could be cut in many different ways.

Irving Thalberg was that way too. In *Romeo and Juliet* [Cukor], I had five versions of the balcony scene. One with tears, one without tears, one played with

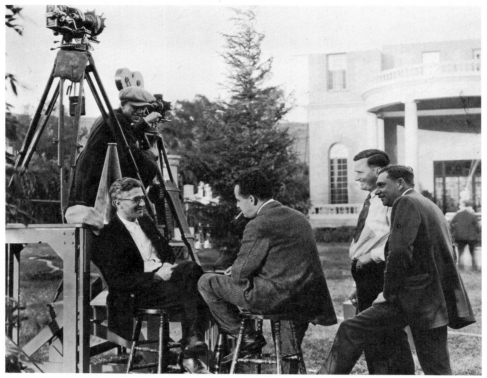

John M. Stahl during the making of The Wanters *(1923) with Paul Bern, Amos Meyers, and Sidney Algiers at the Mayer Studios.*

close-ups only, another played with long shots only, and then one with long shots and close-ups cut in.

When Stahl left M-G-M, he asked me if I'd come with him. But I didn't want to work for just one man; I enjoyed working for everyone. . . . I feel people get tired of you, and you get tired of them by the time a picture's finished. I went on working at M-G-M, mostly with Thalberg—the greatest man who was ever in pictures. M-G-M was like home to me. I started there so young; I knew everybody there, and never wanted to work any other place.

I think we took longer to cut pictures in those days. There was more time to play with them. We were making many, many pictures—unlike today, when you have to make them fast and get them out fast. You could say, "We won't release this until we get it perfect." And you could go and reshoot things. If you needed a close-up to help the scene, you went down and shot it. You—or anyone else—could do it, and it cost nothing. Today that same close-up would cost you five thousand dollars.

When I cut silent films, I used to count to get the rhythm. If I was cutting a march of soldiers, or anything with a beat to it, and I wanted to change the angle, I would count one-two-three-four-five-six. I made a beat for myself. That's how I did it when I was cutting the film in the hand. When Moviolas came in, you could count that way too. You watched the rhythm through the glass.

We used the big screen more in those days. As we cut the picture, we would continually screen it. We would make the necessary adjustments, and then screen it again. Cut it and run it, cut it and run it. And gradually we would make our rhythm, our pattern, for the picture.

We didn't always have titles when we started editing. We would assemble the material, and run it for the title writer. He would give us a set of temporary titles to keep us going until we got the picture finalized, when we could insert the regular titles. The temporary titles were set up on a typewriter and shot down at the laboratory; sometimes the letters were quite large. Title-typing, we called it. Titles had to follow their own pace—a foot and half to a word, so that people could read them.

I think the director contributes a great deal toward editing. It's a combination. Some editors are given credit when the director has more to say than you realize. It isn't like writing a book, and writing it all yourself. You make a cut, and the director comes in and says, "I don't like that" or "Why didn't you punctuate this?" It's a combination of minds. There are very few editors who cut a picture on their own, without anyone saying anything.

Directors don't necessarily play the part of the editor down—but they *do* like to play the part of the editor. They like to edit. They like to get into the cutting room and play around with their own pictures. This is bad, I think. Everyone should be allowed to do their own work. Directors want to contribute to the editing part of it, but most of them are bad editors. They realize, however, that it teaches them about their cutting, and shows them where they've made their mistakes.

Clarence Brown was a wonderful technician; I cut a number of his pictures, and I never saw him in the cutting room. He worked in the projection theater; he used to run the picture again and again and make comments. He understood cutting. He was wonderful to work with.

Charles Brabin was a good director; he left cutting up to us. John Stahl cut his own pictures, of course, and Reginald Barker, a great outdoor director, whose films had a wonderful vitality, also worked in the cutting room. Fred Niblo, on the other hand, told you what he thought and what he wanted, but he would stay away.

Sound was very nerve-racking when it first came in. It was hard to get it synchronized. We were all new at it, and I thought it was terrifying. The first sound I had to cope with came along when I was cutting a silent picture, *The Bridge of San Luis Rey* [Charles Brabin]. It was decided to add a talking sequence at the beginning and end.

But silent films could be quite frightening too. When we went on a preview for *Trail of '98* [Clarence Brown], I was still putting the titles in on the train. I was handing them to an assistant so he could hand-patch them. The train was swaying and shaking, and I could hardly read them. I was very worried in case I handed them to him upside down. When we got to the theater, I could barely bring myself to watch the picture in case a title came on the wrong way round. . . . Thalberg was worried about the picture anyway, and I thought, "If I get into trouble over this. . .!" The film ran smoothly enough, but the preview went very badly. People just didn't care for the picture. We were all very disappointed.

We previewed at the Fox-Wilshire a Selznick picture I had cut, *Our Dancing Daughters* [Harry Beaumont], with Joan Crawford. When we went in, there were five hundred people outside the theater. So we put on a second preview. It was a tense time for me, because we were running working copies—and they used to break. That same night, I had to race back to the studio to fix a reel while they started on Reel 1.

Some cutters keep a record of their pictures, and they can remember everything they've worked on. This doesn't interest me. Remember, I have never been in a cutting room since 1937. I work in the projection room. Directors and editors work on a picture, and then I come in and finish it.

There has been no advance in technique since the silent days—except for one thing. They're doing away with fades and dissolves. I like this much better than the old technique of lap dissolves, which slowed down the pace. There was a time when we made eight- to ten-foot dissolves. We taught the audience for many years to recognize a time lapse through a lap dissolve. Now they're educating them to direct cuts—a new technique brought about by a new generation of directors who can't afford dissolves or fades. And I think it's very good.

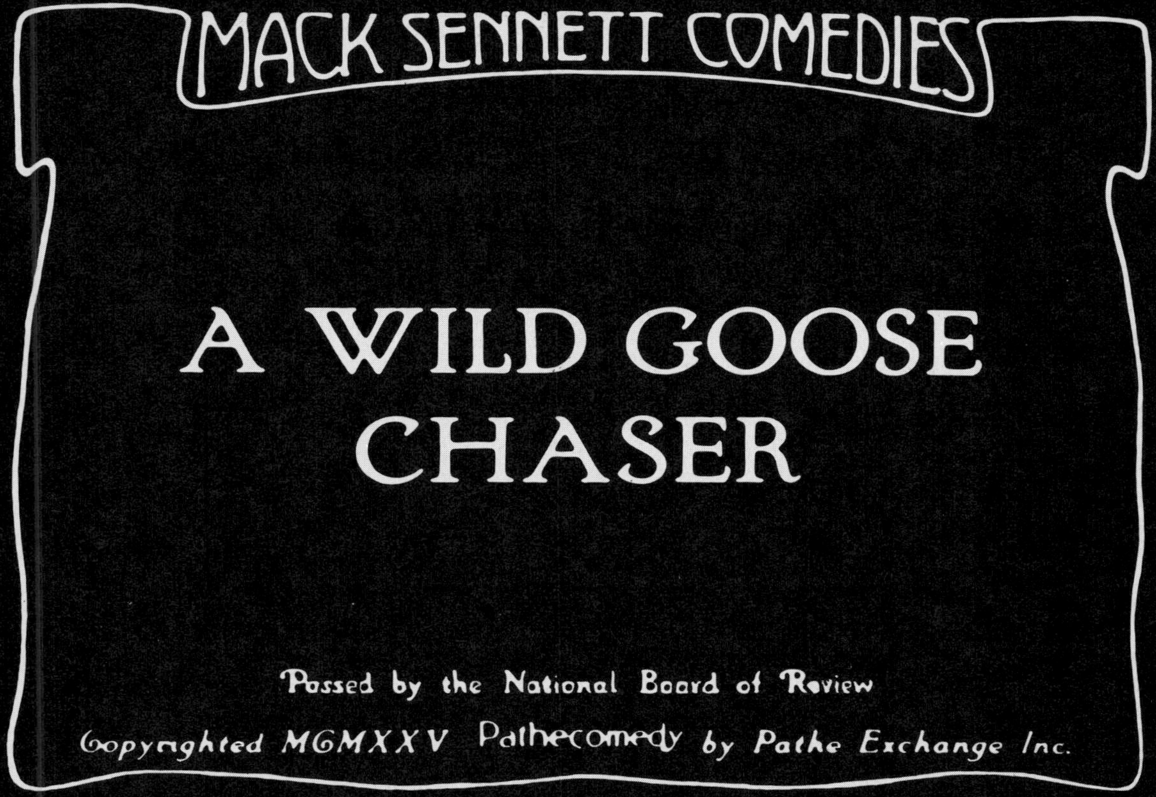

MACK SENNETT COMEDIES

A WILD GOOSE CHASER

Passed by the National Board of Review

Copyrighted MCMXXV Pathecomedy by Pathe Exchange Inc.

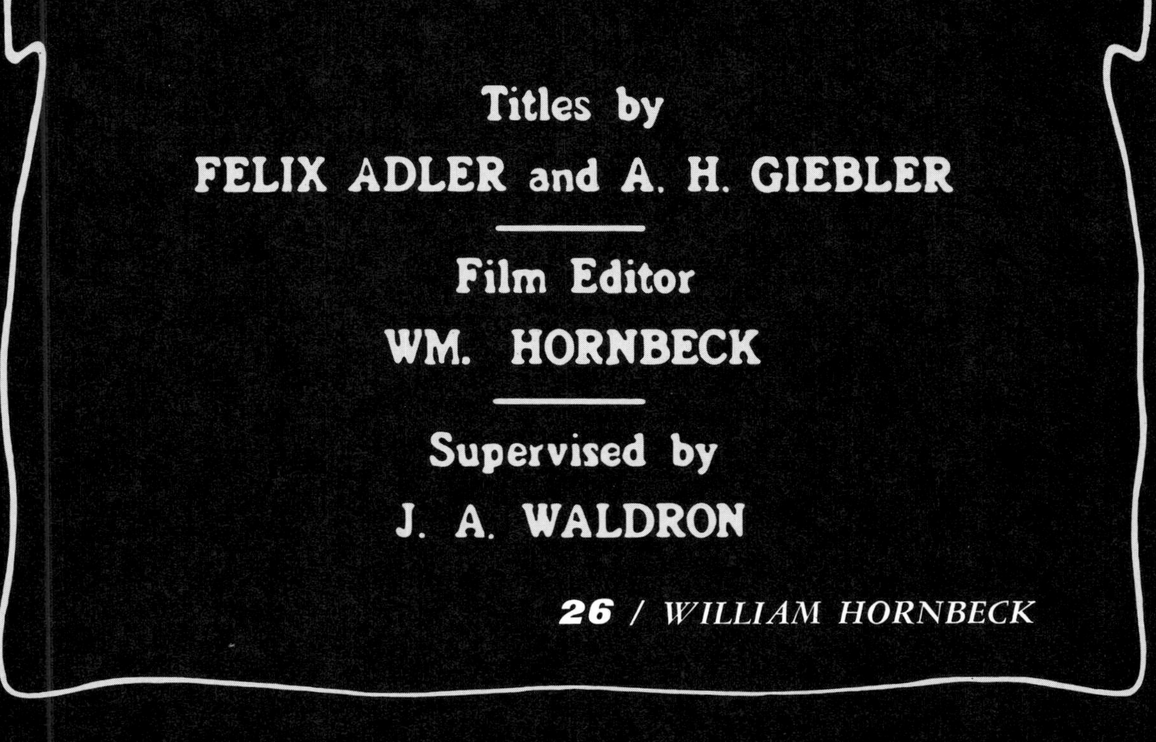

MACK SENNETT COMEDIES

Titles by

FELIX ADLER and A. H. GIEBLER

Film Editor

WM. HORNBECK

Supervised by

J. A. WALDRON

A legendary name in the industry for his masterly editing of *Shane, A Place in the Sun,* and *Giant,* William Hornbeck is equally celebrated for his work in England during the thirties, as supervising editor for Alexander Korda. Now he is vice-president in charge of editorial at Universal Pictures.

Perhaps because his well-known achievements are enough for anybody's life-time, his unknown early career comes as a surprise. For during the 1920s, William Hornbeck was supervising editor at the Mack Sennett studios. There he had complete charge of the editing of those two-reel comedies, so many of which are classic examples of motion-picture cutting.

WILLIAM HORNBECK: My mother was running a hotel in Los Angeles, around 1909, and some movie people came there to take rooms. They told her they were looking for a place to build a studio.

"Well," she said, "the nicest place in Los Angeles, where the sun always shines, is out where we live—a place called Edendale. We own some land there."

Unconsciously, she directed them right to where we lived. They bought some land from us, and eventually built studios there at Allesandro Street, which later became Glendale Boulevard. Later, Mack Sennett took them over, and they became the studios of the Keystone Company.

I was a kid of about ten, very excited about films, and I always watched them at work over the fence. Eventually, I got a job delivering newspapers at the studio. I knew everyone, and they let me go into any department I wanted. I especially liked the miniature department with the little trains. I tried to secure a regular job, but I was too young.

"You get long pants," they said, "and we'll give you a job."

Meanwhile, my mother started a restaurant, called Katie's. I was the dishwasher. I can remember one noontime, the dishes were piled high. Suddenly the phone rang. It was the watchman at the Sennett studio: "There's a job, if Willie wants it."

I threw off my apron, leaped on my bicycle, and raced to the studio.

I was now fourteen, and working in the laboratory—winding film. Later, I became a printer, at six dollars a week. I wanted to go into the editing rooms, but I was still too young. I became a projectionist, and then, in 1917, the war started and all the eligible males left. That gave me my break into the cutting rooms, and by the time the war was over I was editing. If it hadn't been for the war, it could have taken me years. By the time I was twenty, I was head of the department.

The man who taught me most about editing was F. Richard Jones, an extremely fine editor who later became an important director and producer and made feature pictures for Sennett like *Mickey* and *The Extra Girl,* both with Mabel Normand.

Of course, you can't teach anyone how to edit. You can only pass on advice and tips they should follow. These tips are not rules; if you had rules for editing, why, you could put it in a book and anyone could become an editor. But you can pass on advice; after that, you've got to use judgment.

A two-reel picture would take much longer in those days than you'd think—often up to three or four weeks to shoot. We had eight or ten companies to keep up a schedule of one picture a week. We had to get that one picture out, or else we didn't get paid.

The person who really had to know his business was the cameraman. He had to be very skillful with his grinding speeds. Cars had to race through at the right pace, while in fact they might be moving very slowly. Dick Jones was very interested in camera speeds, and how they can help a scene. He would try an action at varying speeds; fourteen frames a second, twelve, ten, six. . . .

The crew at Sennett was very small. The cameraman had no assistant; he did everything. He had to load his film in the morning, he had to carry his camera, he had to crank it, he had to put the slate up in front. Then he had to break his own negative film down in the morning after it had been developed. They never kept camera reports, so he'd go through and look for NGs (NG stands for No Good).

At the end of a scene, the director might say, "Well, I think that was a good one." So the cameraman would grind a few more frames, making the OK sign with finger and thumb. If the director said "NG," he would make the NG sign—the hand held out like a traffic cop.

Later, the director might decide to use an NG take; that was why the cameraman had to go into the laboratory and break his material down into the print takes.

We had our own laboratory. They would screen the rushes first for the director, then Sennett would get a special running, either at the studio or at his home, in the evening, where he had projection equipment. The editor would then take it and go to work.

At first, we cut the film by hand, running it over a ground glass. We constructed a sort of Moviola in 1921, but it was very crude and terribly noisy. For a long time we would never trust it, and we cut both ways.

On the Friday night, or the Saturday, when we had finally cut the work print, all the cutters would go over to negative cutting. The same editor who cut the positive cut the negative. We had light boxes all round the room. You broke the negative down into individual takes, and hung them in front of the light boxes so you could see the action at the start. There were often hundreds of cuts in a two-reeler, so we would each take a small section, say two hundred feet. There were no key numbers, so you found the first scene in your section, then you went around looking for the negative of that scene. Sometimes there were eight or ten takes. You had to try one, then another, until you found the one that matched.

We would try to finish before midnight on Saturday night, when he had to ship the negative to New York. We got close to missing once or twice. Sometimes it would be early Sunday morning, but we always got it on the train.

Of course it was more than a job to us. We worked very long hours. There were no unions, so you could do any job. Many times I shot a scene, an insert, or titles; consequently I learned many other aspects of the business. If you needed an insert, you went down to the camera department, picked up a camera and a short end of film, and shot it. We learned about exposures and lighting. . . . Today you would have to hire a whole crew.

Many of those cliff-hanging stunts in the Sennett comedies were done with piano wire. The wire was very strong, unless it had a kink in it. They rented my car for one picture—a Dodge. It was a nice car. They put it up about thirty feet on wires, and the wires broke. Luckily there was no one in it, but it damaged the car very badly. They fixed it, but it was never a good car again. The only serious accident I can recall was when cameraman Al Jenkins was photographing the Santa Monica Road Race. One of the cars broke off and hit his camera and killed him.

In 1926, Larry Semon signed with Mack Sennett to direct. This gag picture shows Semon and Sennett, and, behind, Del Lord and Eddie Cline, acting peeved at losing their jobs (left).

William Hornbeck, in charge of the Mack Sennett cutting rooms, 1921 (right).

Mack Sennett supervised his pictures all along the way. But he couldn't afford to reject any; good or bad, the pictures had to go. A lot of them weren't quite up to standard, but they went.

We had one we considered too bad to ship, so we held it back. The company wasn't doing too well; we were at the end of our contract with Pathé, and the contract hadn't been renewed. Pathé didn't think we were making good enough pictures. Eddie Cline got the idea of making fun of the picture. We overdid the titles, and made the name of the picture *The Gosh-Darned Mortgage*. We still felt it was horrible. We finally shipped it to New York. When the review committee saw it, they gave it the highest rating of all our films and gave us the new contract for the coming year. "Now this," they said, "is the type of film we want."

Sennett really knew comedy, but of course he made mistakes. He fired Frank Capra. Capra was a writer, a gag man, with an ambition to be a director. He kept trying to persuade Sennett to give him a picture, and Sennett finally did so. After a few rushes, he said, "This fellow will never make a director," and fired him.

But Sennett knew comedy. He wasn't a very educated man, having been a boiler-maker by trade, and there were several jokes about this. One of them concerned Hampton del Ruth. A title on Sennett comedies said "supervised by Mack Sennett in collaboration with Hampton del Ruth." The story goes that when Sennett found out what collaboration meant, he fired Hampton del Ruth.

In 1928, a feature about the war came up, with Johnny Burke—*The Good-bye Kiss*. I heard that Sennett was looking around for feature editors like Lloyd Nosler or Donn Hayes. A few of them worked on the picture for a while. Arthur Tavaris stayed the longest; he worked four or five weeks.

I wanted to do the film very much, but Mack said, "Stay on the two-reelers. You know you have a job, you always have that, and you do your two-reelers well. We want a prestige editor."

This made me pretty sore, because they were getting considerably more money than I. Well, Arthur Tavaris came in some time later and said he thought the boss was an awful hard man to work for. I'd almost forgotten about the picture, but I quickly realized what he meant.

Sennett never said much, during the screening of a picture. But I knew what certain movements would indicate. If he squirmed in his chair to the right, I knew what that meant. I knew he wasn't happy if he squirmed to the left. He had a terrible habit of spitting. He'd chew tobacco or cigars, and if he spat that meant he was *really* unhappy. Poor Tavaris didn't know this set of signals.

One day, Sennett called me. "Come and have dinner tonight and take a look at the picture."

I protested that I had a lot of work, but Mack insisted, so I went. And I saw all the signals that poor old Tavaris had missed. Finally, Sennett turned around and said, "Do you want the picture?"

I said I sure did.

"Can you get someone else to handle your two-reelers?"

"Sure," I said. "There isn't too much to be done to this, anyhow, because it's already assembled."

"What about your notes?" asked Sennett.

"I don't take notes," I replied.

"Tavaris and the other guys took notes."

"I don't need them."

"Just like I told them!" said Sennett. "You don't need them. *They* take notes, and they bring the picture back next evening and I say, Jesus Christ! It's exactly the same!"

So it was arranged. I would cut *The Good-bye Kiss*.

"Another thing bothers me about Tavaris," added Sennett. "He comes to dinner and he always has a pile of potatoes and nothing else, or a lot of meat and nothing else. A man with taste like that *can't* make a good film editor."

Stunting in the silent days meant walking on tigers' tails. It was an occupation with few veterans. Whatever your qualifications—whether you were a circus acrobat, a stunt aviator, an animal trainer, or a racing driver—you faced fresh challenges and unknown hazards at every call.

Film making had none of the modern conveniences of back-projection or traveling matte (although both were to appear before the silent era ended); with such devices, a man could appear clinging by his fingernails to a twelfth-floor window sill, while actually standing on the ground.

In those days, whatever you saw on the screen had actually been achieved—either by the actor himself, or by a stunt man doubling for him. As serials and thrillers caught the public imagination and drew increasingly large crowds, so the actors had to be placed in increasingly intricate situations. A stunt man, accustomed to falling off horses, would soon be asked to fall off motorcycles; then to leap out of airplanes. The first take would generally be his first attempt; there was no training.

Precautions were taken where possible, but many stunts depended on freedom of movement; you can do little to help a man leaping out of a train, or clambering from aircraft to aircraft in mid-air. It is up to the stunt man himself; all you can do is to keep the crank handle turning.

When "Suicide" Buddy Mason was asked if there was any standard by which stunt men were judged—by other stunt men—he replied, "Nope. It's just—well, when you get so they call you by your first name when you come into the hospital, then you belong."[1]

Some of the greatest stunt men were the stars themselves. Buster Keaton, former vaudeville acrobat, did almost all his own stunts—and he stunted for his actors as well.

"I developed more stunt men than any studio in Los Angeles. I've taken the goddamdest people and made stunt men out of them.

"You know the scene in *Sherlock Jr.* when I call a motorcycle cop, jump on his handlebars and we hit a bump in the street, and I lose the cop? Well, the cop that fell off was me. I took Ernie Orsatti, an assistant prop man, who was my size —put my clothes on him and I put on the cop's clothes.

"Then I had to do the scene where I ride on the handlebars. That was a hell of a job. Number one, I've got no brakes—there are only foot brakes, see. Well, I got some beautiful spills, some real beauties. I parked right on top of an automobile once. I hit it head-on. I ended up with my fanny up against the windshield, my feet straight in the air!"

In the same picture, Buster escapes to the roof of a train standing at a siding. He clambers up a rope, but the rope operates the water tower.

"The volume of water hit me so hard it tore my hands loose from the rope and I fell. And when I fell I lit on the track and my head fell right across the rail. Right here"—he pointed to the back of his neck. "I had a headache for a few hours, I remember. Mildred Harris's house was nearby, and she gave me a couple of stiff drinks—this was during Prohibition, when you couldn't just stop any place for a drink.

"I woke up the next morning, my head was clear, and I never stopped work-

---

[1] Photoplay, *Nov. 1927, p. 30.*

ing. But years later, I'm down at the Soldiers' Home in Sawtelle. They won't release you out of that until they've X-rayed everything you've got. If you've got
dandruff, they'll keep you there. The doctor calls me in and says, 'When did you
break your neck?'

"I said I never broke my neck. He says, 'Look at this X-ray. The callus has
grown over the crack, next to the top vertebra.' I asked him how long ago he
thought it happened. 'It could be somewhere between ten and fifteen years ago.'
I start thinking back—it's that damn fall on that track. Well, I never knew it.
Never stopped working. That's luck. No nerve pinched or anything. That's a
fluke. That could have ruined you . . . there are so many things in the vertebrae
that could cause you trouble!"[2]

Harold Lloyd's thrill pictures were shot just as high above the streets as you
see them. Sometimes a false section was constructed on the roof of a tall building,
at other times Lloyd worked above a wooden platform. All the same, he frequently
faced a drop of fifteen feet. Once, the unit decided to see what would have happened had Lloyd slipped. They dropped a dummy onto the wooden platform,
and it bounced into the street below. Lloyd's stunts are all the more remarkable
since he achieved them with only one good hand—the thumb and forefinger of
his right hand were blown off during a still-picture session in 1919, when a
property bomb, being used for a comedy pose, proved to be live.

The films of Richard Talmadge all centered on his athletic prowess; Talmadge,
whose real name is Metzetti, and who is not related to the Talmadge family, has
put his vast experience as a stunt man to profitable use, and is now directing the
second units on big feature films. At the front of a film he made in 1923, *Let's Go*
(William K. Howard) appeared the title: "The amazing athletic 'stunts' performed by Mr. Talmadge in this picture are *actual,* and are not achieved by means
of 'doubles,' 'dummies,' or tricks of the camera."

Richard Talmadge worked with Douglas Fairbanks, not so much as a double,
for Doug was famed as a star who performed his own stunts, but more as a
model. Fairbanks would watch him go through the full action to look for flaws,
hazards, and the most effective movements, then he would do the stunt himself
for the camera.

"Doug's stunts were not actually great athletic feats," said Allan Dwan; "they
were good stunts done with great grace. That was the whole key. If Doug had to
fight a duel and leap to a table top, I would time his leap—and I would cut the
table to exactly the right height to accommodate his ability to leap. And the same
with the climbs. Every set that we built I measured for handholds. They were
always there, and he would automatically feel for them. A longer-armed man would
have been awkward on them, or a shorter man, but with Doug it was perfect.
He was athletic and strong enough to do a hand climb, but we fitted handholds.
He would go up a wall, and the wall was all prepared. If he jumped, it was just
exactly the distance he could gracefully jump. Never a strain.

"Now we only used stunt men when there was danger, when there was a chance
the man might get hurt. In one of his pictures, that I wasn't on, Doug insisted on
doing a stunt that I would never let him do—and he got hurt. He jumped over a
balcony railing to a horse waiting below. Horses, you know, instinctively move

[2] *Buster Keaton to author, Hollywood, Dec. 1964.*

when they feel anything coming. That's what this one did, and Doug fell and was hurt. Now I'd have used a stunt man for that shot. That wasn't graceful. It was just foolish."

The average career of a motion-picture stunt man was under five years. He either got injured or he got money enough to leave this most dangerous game and take up another occupation.

How did a stunt man become a stunt man? Usually by accident. An extra or bit player would be paid more for stunt work and this proved a great incentive.

"Round about 1915," recalled Eddie Sutherland, "when I was working as an actor on a Helen Holmes serial called *The Hazards of Helen,* I was getting fifteen dollars a week. If I did stunts, like jumping off a moving train, I got an extra five dollars, and when you get fifteen dollars a week, five is very important.

"In one scene, the hero [Leo Maloney] and the heroine are on top of a train loaded with dynamite, and they have to get off. A character had lassoed a telegraph pole and had tied the rope to a tree across the track. Jean Perkins, a fine stunt man, doubled for Helen, and a fellow named Harold Lloyd—not the comedian—doubled for Maloney. They jumped up and grabbed the rope—and they missed. Perkins wasn't hurt—just shaken and bruised a bit. But the other fellow broke his leg, and took all the flesh off it, so they had to stop shooting for the day. Being anxious to get this job, I went to Perkins and said, 'Look, I know what you did wrong in that.'

"He said, 'Well, tell Mac [J. P. McGowan, the director].' I told McGowan that Jean and I could do it without getting hurt. He said, 'Oh, Eddie . . . if you get hurt, your family will kill me. I know them!'

" 'Look, it's a cinch. I know how to do it.'

" 'How?'

" 'I'm not going to tell you. If I do, you won't let me do it.'

"I prevailed on him to let me do it. The other two had jumped straight up at the rope, and I figured you had to dive at it to counteract the speed of the train. Now, the train wasn't going very fast, because they were undercranking the scene. We got all set to do it. Jean and I dove at the rope and we both made it. The train went down the track a few yards and blew up. It blew us right off the rope—and I went to hospital."

Cliff Bergere took to stunting out of desperation—to break into movies, and to acquire a full-length leather coat like the one he saw on stunt pilot Omer Locklear. Bergere, then very young, had a job at San Francisco, assisting a day-flip aviator.

"From that moment on," recalled Bergere "I watched Locklear like a hawk. I saw his exhibition over 'Frisco and I said to myself if that is what it takes to get that coat, then I'm going to be a stunt man."

Encountering Isadore Bernstein, general manager of Universal, Bergere remarked that he was actually a stunt man—although he was now selling stock. Bernstein offered him a job doubling for Robert McKim in a seventy-five-foot jump from the mast of a schooner; Bergere accepted. Then he realized what he had taken on and went into rapid training. For half an hour he stood on the diving board of his local swimming pool, unable to move—giddy and feverish. To his great relief the script was changed—and McKim merely fell overboard.

"Seventy-five feet! Good Lord, I'd have been split wide open!"

But the meeting with Bernstein had paid off. Bernstein's card, marked "Introducing Cliff Bergere," brought him an offer to double for Fred Thomson in a serial called *The Eagle's Talons* (Duke Worne). Bergere was to climb out of an aircraft, onto the roof of a moving train. His pilot was Al Wilson, himself an experienced stunt flier.

"At twenty-five hundred feet, Al motioned to me to get out of the seat and down the ladder. I looked around and couldn't see the train so I motioned, 'What for?'

"Al cut his engine and yelled, 'You ——, *Get out!*' I thought, 'Gee, if he's gonna get mad about it, maybe I'd better get out.' I climbed gingerly down the ladder until my feet were on the last rung. I had both arms wrapped around the ladder and a charge of dynamite wouldn't have gotten me away from that ladder. We gradually descended until we were directly over the train, which was going about twenty-five miles per hour. Al climbed the plane, and motioned to me to climb back up."

Bergere became enmeshed on the guy wires, but remembering Wilson's language, he loosened his grip, by a sheer effort of will, and freed himself. Anticlimactically, the plane landed; Wilson conferred with the engineer, and they decided that the train should go at fifty-five miles an hour. Then they took off once more.

"This time, I got down on the ladder and no sooner found my feet on the bottom rung than I landed in a sitting position right on top of the train.

"When I got back, I realized everyone from the director on down had seemed nervous, and when I remarked about it, I found out that just four days before, Jean Perkins had been killed trying this very stunt."[3]

Jean Edward Perkins was twenty-four when he died—one of the greatest of stunt men.

"When I first saw him," said Clarence Brown, "I thought he was the coolest-looking person I'd ever seen. His self-control was astounding. His eyes were like ice, yet they were always smiling. He had a hankering to play around with airplanes; I told him to stay on the ground. His sense of timing and distance was so perfect and his body control was so fine that he had a pretty good chance to pull through most of his stunts. But he didn't listen. They never do."[4]

Dick Grace, the most celebrated of the silent-era stunt men, considered Perkins the greatest double in pictures.

In an article in *Photoplay* he described how Perkins was to make a change from an airplane to the top of a passenger train, while Paul Malvern, doubling for the villain, was to catch him and start a fight on the train roof.

"Handicapped by a pilot unused to making changes, and a stiff side wind, the transfer was unusually dangerous. Twice they failed, and the train was signaled to make more speed. On the third trial, Jean on the rope ladder struck the side of the Pullman car. It did not seem to bother him, however, and he hung as before from the last rung as the plane made a wide sweep before trying it again.

"As the airplane approached the train on the fourth trial, Jean could be seen trying to climb the ladder. He made several attempts, but each time his strength seemed to fail. Finally, his struggles became feebler, and with a hopeless shake of

[3] Speed Age, *Nov. 1951, p. 13.*
[4] *Quoted in* Photoplay, *Nov. 1927, p. 32.*

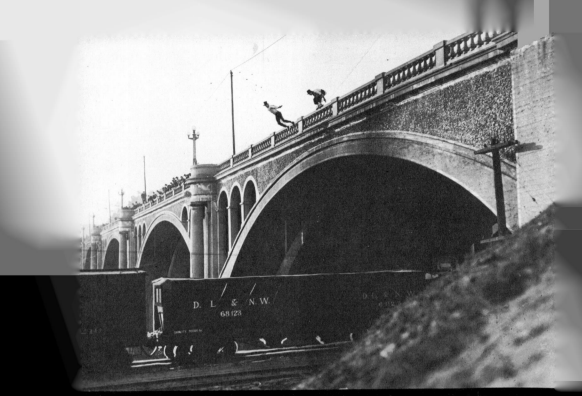

Some of the most hazardous stunts were for comedies: a scene from Loafers and Lovers (1920) a two-reeler directed by Melville Brown.

Hidden Dangers, *a 1920 serial directed by William Bertram.*

Charles "Lightning Hutch" Hutchinson making an 18-foot leap for The Whirlwind, a 1919 serial, directed by Joseph Golden (publicity matte shot).

the head his hands slid from the ladder. He fell probably fifty feet, but the speed of the airplane increased many times the force with which he hit."[5]

Reginald Denny, the comedian, was an eyewitness to the tragedy. He said that Perkins was doubling for William Desmond; that a friend of Perkins, who had recently bought a Standard airplane, was given the job instead of an experienced stunt flier like Al Wilson or Frank Clarke.

"The pilot should have leveled off and allowed for the drift of the wind when the train got into the straightaway. But this bird leveled off right over the train, and of course the cross-wind took him away from it. Then he came back again— but there wasn't enough straightaway there. Any of the real good fliers could have pancaked and dropped him off—there were plenty of good landing places. But this guy just flew around, and he got panicky around seventy feet high and in the end Jean had to let go and that was his finish. He might have been all right, but he didn't have the safety strap attached to the ladder, which you twisted around your wrist so you could rest."[6]

Reginald Denny, an athletic man, began his screen career in the boxing series *The Leather Pushers*. His big break came when he was cast in the thriller *The Abysmal Brute* (Hobart Henley, 1923), into which he injected the light comedy which was to make him famous. The picture, however, was an action melodrama —and Denny found that he had to do his own stunts.

"A sea-rescue scene was shot in February, and the breakers were anything between fifteen and twenty feet high. They brought some liquor down there—they thought I'd need it, which was true. But the whole crew got drunk on it instead.

"The man they sent for me to rescue, I really had to rescue. When they asked if I could get through those breakers, I said I'd try it first. 'Put a boat out there and watch me.' I knew enough about it; as one wave breaks, you go right out with it and get the next one, riding the green water. But if you get into one while it's boiling, you're through.

"We had five cameras. 'As soon as the white handkerchief is waved,' they said, 'anytime after that, start.' I told the man to be sure that he didn't go out while a breaker was coming in. 'Wait till it breaks, and go out with it.' But he was so scared that as the handkerchief waved, he ran out. He threw himself in as a breaker boiled and I really had to rescue him. When I got out to him he was in an awful state; he was full of water, and down quite a bit. It wasn't a rough sea, but the swells were very big.

"I managed to get it across to him that I was going to turn over—I was holding him up on my back—and he was to grab my ankles and straighten out, because we were going down. I saw this big one coming, and I yelled, 'All right!' and I turned over. He got my ankles all right, and I started down. But then he drew his legs up in panic and that did it. The breaker caught us both and boiled us. They got the shot—but they couldn't use it. We weren't *both* supposed to be rescued!"

The injuries suffered by motion-picture personnel—stunt men included—were no more numerous, nor more serious, than the general run of industrial accidents. In 1925, for instance, only three deaths occurred during actual shooting; stunt man R. D. Jones drowned while trying to shoot the rapids in a canoe for *The Ancient Highway* (Irvin Willat). Max Marx was killed at Universal City when a rope

[5] Photoplay, *Aug. 1925, p. 128.*
[6] *Reginald Denny to author, San Marino, California, Dec. 1964.*

Barnstorming aviator Omer Locklear, with Milton Moore, working on Cassidy of the Air Lanes (1919), directed by Jacques Jaccard.

The stunt that killed Jean Perkins.

snapped during the shooting of *Strings of Steel* (Henry MacRae). Electrician Carl Barlow died after falling from a platform during the filming of *The Big Parade* (Vidor). The records for that year show that seven actresses received severe burns, nine people were overcome by heat or suffered nervous prostration, four were hurt by automobiles, six were injured by horses, and four stunt men were injured while doubling for stars.

Nevertheless, newspapers always told of stunts going wrong, of highly experienced men getting killed. Lieutenant Omer Locklear, the brilliant barnstorming aviator, was killed when he lost control of his aircraft during a power dive for *The Skywayman* (James P. Hogan). With him died his assistant, Lieutenant Milton Elliott. The accident happened at night, and it was thought that Locklear had confused skyrockets, sent as signals, with the searchlights on the ground. Locklear left a wife and two children; Fox arranged for ten per cent of the profits of the film to be given to the aviators' families.

In 1922, a crowd gathered at Seventy-second Street and Columbus Avenue, New York, to watch a scene being shot for *Plunder* (George B. Seitz); Pearl White was the star, and Miss White was known as a star who did her own stunting. On this occasion, however, stunt man John Stevenson doubled for her, in a blond wig. From the top of a double-decker bus, he leaped to an elevated girder—missed his swing, and was thrown twenty-five feet before he fell to the ground. He died the same day from a fractured skull and cerebral concussion.

A stunt man's routine was the narrow escape. Dick Grace, doubling for a woman star he did not name—"it would be a breach of confidence"—was dressed in a flimsy ballet dress which was to catch fire. The property man soaked him in gasoline and threw a match at him.

"In a moment, I was a flaming human torch," Grace wrote. "It was too much, to feel those flames searing the flesh of the back, neck, arms, and face pierced my self-control. With an agonized scream of a person burning to death, I cleared the balcony in a bound, then down to the main floor.

" 'Help! I'm burning!' Everyone seemed paralyzed into inaction. Then everything began to fog before my eyes. I still had the presence of mind, however, to keep my arms locked above by head, thus preventing my face from burning seriously. I kept running, and so for the most part the flames and fumes swept behind me, although they reached ten feet higher than my head."

Grace was rescued by the assistant director, who tripped him, wrapped him in an overcoat, and fought to smother the flames. With help he succeeded; then Grace's physician examined the damage. There was no skin from the neck to the waist. The doctor promptly washed him in gasoline.

"The pain was unbearable and twice I fainted. I had seven hundred and eighty square inches of skin burned from my body, the greater part being third degree, extreme."[7]

A few months later, thanks to the doctor's ruthless speed, Grace was practically scarless.

Two years earlier, in 1923, Martha Mansfield, a star, was burned to death. Someone threw a lighted match on the ground. Miss Mansfield, dressed in a hoop-skirted costume for the Civil War film *The Warrens of Virginia* (Elmer Clifton),

[7] Photoplay, *Aug. 1925, p. 128.*

touched the match with her dress—and in seconds was a living torch. She died a day later from the burns and from shock. Shortly afterward, both Dot Farley and Bebe Daniels narrowly missed the same fate.

A great name in the stunt game was Leo Noomis, one of the few veterans of the business. In 1922, Noomis doubled for Jack Mower as the luckless speed cop, the victim of Leatrice Joy's craze for fast cars in *Manslaughter*. The action called for the speed cop to come tearing after Leatrice, for her car to slew around on the highway, and for the cop's motorcycle to hit it dead center. The natural result of such a collision prevented Jack Mower from doing it himself, although as a western actor he was perfectly capable. De Mille called Noomis in and turned the stunt into a circus turn.

"There were ambulances there, and hundreds of people came to watch. It was horrible . . . you wouldn't think they'd want to . . . ," recalled Leatrice Joy.

Miss Joy's place in the car was taken by Richard Arlen. Leo Noomis calculated that if he drove the motorcycle straight at the car at forty-five miles an hour he would have speed enough to be thrown clear.

" 'It's going to be an easy one,' said Noomis, 'unless I get tangled. I won't, of course. But if—Mr. De Mille, would you sort of keep an eye on the wife and kids?' " Adela Rogers St. Johns reported the event somewhat overdramatically:

"The impressive man in puttees said briefly, 'I'll take care of them as long as they live. So don't worry about that.'

"The giant motorcycle hummed. The quiet of the countryside was shattered by the horrible shock of tearing metal and crashing steel. A body vaulted into the air, flung as a child flings a rag doll, and lay very still on the other side of the car. Leo Noomis had finished his day's work."[8]

Reports differ over what happened to Noomis. Mrs. St. Johns reported that he suffered only a broken collar bone, and was stunting again within two weeks.

Leatrice Joy remembered it differently. "The man hit the car, and although they'd put mats on the other side, he broke six ribs and his pelvis and was rushed to hospital. He stripped the motorcycle. Now they shouldn't have risked a man's life for that shot. When you see it on the screen, it looks exactly like a dummy."

The justification for risking men's lives was that gasp of amazement from the audience; the stunt men were agreed on that. What appalled them was to hear their daring, carefully calculated exploits dismissed airily as "trick photography."

Trick photography had been an integral part of films for as long as they'd existed, but the thrillers and serials, ground out fast, seldom resorted to such deception. Audiences, reassured by the fan magazines that their favorite serial star did all his, or her, own stunts, protested when process and overobvious glass shots began to appear. Thrillers had acquired a reputation which studio work and Dunning process photography was undermining.

In 1924, *The Lone Wolf* (S. E. V. Taylor) was criticized in *Photoplay:* "It is made slightly ridiculous at the finish by a double airplane transfer in the clouds, a lot of which was too obviously done in the studio. The realism of some of the airplane stunts that have preceded it has not been achieved in this picture and the audience is inclined to chuckle."[9]

The freshness, vitality, and rugged honesty of the early silent melodramas, with

[8] Photoplay, *Dec. 1922, p. 30.*
[9] Photoplay, *July 1924, p. 45.*

their real locations and real backgrounds, gradually gave way to a more sophisticated, highly polished production, in which every technique was used to extract the maximum of excitement and production value. Sometimes studio work was resorted to—but most directors knew the value of a real thrill, and the last years of silents saw the most awe-inspiring stunts of all—the *Ben-Hur* chariot race, the *Tumbleweeds* land rush, *The Fire Brigade* (William Nigh) blaze, the crashes and stunt flying in *Wings,* the deluge in *Noah's Ark,* in which several extras were drowned, and the astonishing aerial dogfights in *Hell's Angels,* the only sequences retained from the silent version.

The old-time daredevils, their prestige depending purely on physical prowess, had values belonging to a past age; they were the skilled gladiators of the Hollywood amphitheater, performing feats of horrifying danger in order to amuse the crowds. Their reward was the roar of applause, just as it had always been . . . but now the emperors had gone, it was fate which gave the thumbs-down signal for the end.

What these men left behind, however, was not just the barroom anecdote. Without them, an essential realism would be missing from motion pictures. We have not matured enough to find action pictures displeasing—and for action to be attractive, the physical element is what counts. The same is true of the cinema as a whole. It is no fun to watch a man thinking. But to see him span a yawning chasm in a furious auto leap. . . . to swing from plane to plane. . . . to see him fulfill the wildest flights of fancy on our behalf is an exhilarating and gratifying experience. An experience without risk.

They have had no mention in the histories of the motion picture, yet without them there would be no history.

The grips, carpenters, property men, electricians, and assistants often had to work as hard as any director or actor, but without the reward of credit or the satisfaction of creative involvement. These men were the backbone of the industry —the rank and file of an Army of the Republic, winning battles for a whole echelon of Napoleons.

The Motion Picture Herald said, at the end of the silent era:

"People engaged in motion-picture production work as hard as those in any industry in America. In about seven out of ten cases they work longer hours than do those employed in any other profession or business. More careful or scientific regulation of habits of sleeping, eating, exercise, and recreation is required than in almost any field imaginable."[1]

Some of these technicians belonged to unions connected with their trades, but there were then no unions to protect them as film workers. Not that unions were unnecessary—men were frequently exploited, and they often worked long hours under almost intolerable conditions. But there was little demand for unions in those days because the general enthusiasm for pictures spread to every member of the company.

As one veteran director said: "I don't recall any gripes at any time from any of the crew on any production I was on about working too long or too hard."[2]

These men, like the movie star's proverbial mother, were the industry's best pal and severest critic. A really fine performance was rewarded with a burst of applause from the shadowy figures behind the lights. This most spontaneous and genuine of praise often meant more to the recipient than a handful of good reviews. Ann Harding, newly arrived in Hollywood from the New York stage, said that she got more kick out of appreciation from a studio crew than she ever did from a Broadway audience.

"These birds are hard-boiled, for a fact. When you do a scene as they like it, you're good."

These men knew what it took to give a top-class performance; they had seen almost all there was to see. They were not easily impressed.

The men with the most colorful jobs were those who worked in the property department. Some of them were phenomenal; equipped with almost psychic powers, they invariably managed to produce the right thing at the right time. Comedy companies used to go out on location with no script but a lot of ideas— the success of which often depended on the property man. Could he produce some obscure prop on the spot, or would he have to send back to the studio for it?

Bebe Daniels' unit at Realart included a prop man named Charlie.

"He always thought *ahead*," recalled Miss Daniels with admiration. "He could produce a rowboat out of his pocket. If you pulled something on Charlie, and asked him for something absurd, he had it—or he could make it. A donkey we were using had an incomplete ear, which looked slightly odd. We asked Charlie if he had anything that could improve it. He produced something so perfect that we asked him how he came to bring it with him. 'Well,' he admitted, 'I heard someone mention something about making a purse out of a sow's ear.' He had the purse, too."

[1] *Quoted in* Photoplay, *March 1932, p. 70.*
[2] *Andrew L. Stone to author, London, April 1962.*

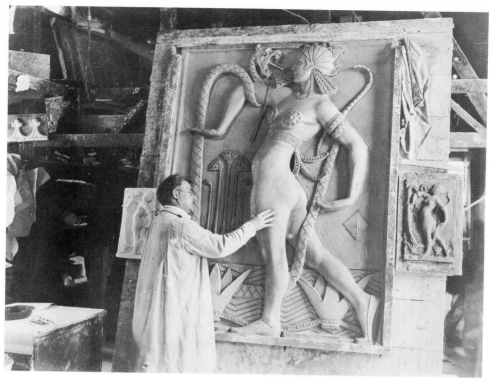

Plasterwork for **The Queen of Sheba** *(1921).*

Enterprise and personal initiative were never the sole prerogative of the higher-salaried technicians. Reve Houck, chief electrician at the Ince studios, became so exasperated at the inadequacy of studio lighting for certain effects that he invented his own. He developed a tiny arc, to simulate match light or the beam of a torch. The smallest automatic light up to that time, it was capable of a thousand candle power. An actor could conceal it in the palm of his hand, the wires running up his sleeve and down his trouser leg. When he lit the match, he pressed the button of his baby arc, and the flame appeared to be lighting up his face. The arc could be fitted in lanterns, mounted in car headlights; it was available in five different sizes, and so long as the trailing cable was concealed, the illusion was perfect.

A large proportion of all the technicians in Hollywood studios today are in their sixties; they have been in the industry since the silent era, and whatever the artistic failings of the films they have worked on, their own reputation remains unimpaired. All over the world, the man-behind-the-scenes in the Hollywood studio is acknowledged to be the best at his job.

"When I returned to Hollywood after thirty years," said Clive Brook, "I'd forgotten about these phenomenal men. But there they were—the same ones that had worked with me in silents. During an exterior, one of the horsemen we were using mistimed a jump and broke a five-barred gate. Anywhere else, this would have held production up for the whole day. Not in Hollywood. The property man had made up five spare gates."

29 / *IT WAS A TOUGH LIFE*

Work is the only dignity!" This Calvinistic observation, made, surprisingly, by F. Scott Fitzgerald, sums up the religion of the Victorian age.

In England, where Victorian puritanism found its most fertile soil, work was only dignified if the work itself had dignity. This was a period when leisure for many was spent in eating, sleeping, and traveling to work. A period when the thought of making money from entertainment—from ill-spent leisure—was considered immoral. The entertainment world was regarded with a lofty indifference; visits to the theater or music hall were accompanied by feelings of guilty indulgence. Hampered by such moral opposition, the silent-film industry in England never flourished.

The American social structure being less clearly defined, the attitude to work was more enlightened. The basic Victorian principles applied, too—often very strongly, but the emphasis was more on activity. You may not have achieved membership of the New York Four Hundred if your wealth came from toilet partitions, but elsewhere your work carried no social stigma, so long as you were *active*. The entertainment industries were regarded as essential, and the men who worked in them were accepted, if not respected, members of their society.

Nevertheless, many people in the motion-picture business had come from the emotional claustrophobia of nineteenth-century Europe, the camphorous aftertaste of which lasted well into the twentieth century. Practically everyone in films had worked in other jobs—some of them in the theater, but many in more mundane work, requiring strict hours and drab routine. The sudden break into the glamour and excitement of film production, combined with the equally sudden rise in salary, made many feel guilty. This guilt was seldom consciously expressed; it was sublimated into the almost fanatical amount of hard work of film technicians and players during this period.

For many of them, the fact of working at something enjoyable was a new sensation. Some had known great poverty. While they earned thousands a week in California, their families still struggled, refusing assistance.

It is no wonder that Hollywood cut itself off from the rest of the world, becoming a sort of Graustark, a dream factory, which was a bit dreamlike itself. The defenses it erected were not so much to repel outsiders as to conceal its true feelings. Hollywood was out of balance with the rest of the world and was acutely aware of the fact.

To allay the guilt which furtively gnawed at certain souls, technicians and players often endured the most incredibly rigorous conditions "for the sake of the picture."

For some, such an experience was an adventure, a challenge. To others, it was a purge.

Back to God's Country (David Hartford) was made in 1919 by a company based in Calgary called Canadian Photoplays Ltd.; the aim of Ernest Shipman, the company's organizer, was to produce James Oliver Curwood stories in their natural locations. This meant working in temperatures often twenty below zero. *Back to God's Country* was immensely successful—*Photoplay* thought it had "some of the most remarkable 'animal stuff' ever photographed."[1] and it set the style for future pictures starring Nell Shipman. Around 1923, she was making a series of

[1] Photoplay, *Jan. 1920, p. 115.*

two-reelers in freezingly realistic conditions, co-starring with Flash, the wonder dog, and Johnny Fox.

While on location in northern Idaho for one of these pictures, Nell Shipman and her director husband, Bert Van Tuyle, became separated from the others who were with them. Van Tuyle had injured his foot and it had become infected. Frequently delirious, he insisted on climbing out of the sledge and walking—and Nell Shipman had to handle it herself. Dragging the sledge across the ice on Priest Lake, she fell into the water several times through airholes. But she kept on —holding her husband's arm, or dragging him in the sledge when he was exhausted, even though her feet were frost-bitten. After twenty miles of this grueling endurance test, they reached a ranch, and Van Tuyle was rushed to hospital, where his foot was amputated.

Such accidents were not rare. Despite the appalling experiences of von Stroheim's company in Death Valley, Paramount sent the unit for *The Water Hole* (F. Richard Jones) to that same murderous part of the desert—in June, when the temperature was a hundred and thirty.

"We got up in the morning before dawn," said Nancy Carroll, the star of the picture. "We put on our make-up by the light of automobile headlights. Then we trooped in single file out to the location. We were careful to tread in each other's footprints, because if an extra set appeared in the sand, it would take some explaining. The men lugged the cameras out, and we started shooting as soon as there was enough light. About eleven thirty, the heat became unbearable, and we would fling ourselves on the ground, anywhere where there was a roof—a hut or tent—and rest. Luckily, I was very young and very strong, but the cameraman, C. Edgar Schoenbaum, went out of his mind with the heat. He made the fatal mistake of not wearing a hat, and after a time he began to see pink haystacks. The first sign of sunstroke is pink. The Chinese cook went mad one day and chased people with a knife. The film couldn't be left there because it would melt, so an auto would come and collect it. But frequently its tires would blow on the way back. It was terrifying. People would just sit down and cry."[2]

The silent era in Hollywood was a period of astonishing contrasts. Studios would go to immense trouble to mollycoddle their stars on the set, yet they would send them into the wilds as unprepared as Napoleon's army for the Russian winter.

Colleen Moore, filming *The Huntress* (John Francis Dillon), described for *Picture Play* what it was like to be on location in the High Sierras in mid-winter. She lived in a cabin in a summer camp which was utterly unfit for below-zero temperatures; it was built of rough pine slabs with inch-wide cracks between them. The cold was almost unendurable. "These hardy mountain folk," wrote Miss Moore, "don't feel all's right with the world unless it's about twenty below zero."

Her cabin was provided with smoky oil lamps and an inefficient stove. There was no running water; just a tin jug with cracked ice in it. To take a bath she had to travel three miles to a hot spring.

"When not registering joy and sorrow for the camera," she wrote, "I make a fire, carry water, heat it on the stove, keep the cabin clean, make the bed, whittle pokers for stove lids—in general, qualify for a covered-wagon wife. I am burned, blistered, frozen, dirty; my hands and face are rough and chapped. Oh, the great

[2] *Nancy Carroll to author, New York, March 1964.*

One of the best of the outdoor directors, Reginald Barker, with cameraman Percy Hilburn on Snow Blind (1921).

The lake on the Baker Ranch in the Snake Valley of Nevada was banked to form a river for the crossing of the Platte sequence in The Covered Wagon (1923).

Camera crew in trouble during the shooting of the rapids scene for The Hillbilly (1924) *directed by George Hill.*

Lunch break on The Covered Wagon: *Ernest Torrence, Charles Ogle, Ethel Wales, director James Cruze, J. Warren Kerrigan, Alan Hale, and Lois Wilson.*

West and the great Western hills . . . I do wish they'd leave 'em in fiction where they sound so much more romantic!"[3]

When Miss Moore came to England in 1962, she recalled this experience. "It was so awful!" she laughed. "And to think of the thousands they were paying me! Every morning the prop man would come in and build a fire in our little stove, and he'd put the water on it. We couldn't get out of bed, it was so cold. We had to put the make-up on the stove, too, so it would unfreeze.

"This was the only *really* rugged location that I had. *The Sky Pilot* [King Vidor] was pretty bad, except for one thing—we had good living conditions. While shooting in the snow was pretty difficult, we lived in a small hotel, which was over the railroad station and it was warm, and we had plenty of hot water, and it was nice coming home at night—and we had delicious food, so it didn't matter that we'd had a pretty tough day.

"On *The Huntress,* the food was so dreadful, you wouldn't believe it. For a while I actually lived on raw eggs and crackers because the cooked food was so horrible. But I must say that when you're young, and it's all so exciting, it's fun— so you crack the ice . . ."[4]

Film makers re-creating the old West on location sometimes went through the same rigorous conditions as the pioneers. The filming of the epic western *The Covered Wagon* (James Cruze) was an epic in itself.

"Conditions were rough," recalled Lois Wilson, co-star of the film with J. Warren Kerrigan, "but no worse than some of the other westerns I was on. I got slight frostbite, we ran out of supplies and had to live on apples and baked beans for a while, but I loved every minute of *The Covered Wagon*. It was an adventure. Oh, we were cold, but I don't think the film would have been as good if we hadn't been uncomfortable and if we hadn't run into unexpected circumstances. For instance, snow. Nobody expected snow in the desert at that time of year. The tents were so laden with snow they were practically falling on our beds. So Walter Woods, who was out there with us, wrote in a snow sequence.

"Do you realize that the covered wagons in that picture were practically *all* original Conestogas? Famous Players advertised, and people came from all over the Middle West with their wagons and horses. Some of them brought their families. They were paid two dollars a day each, and two dollars a day for stock, and they were fed. That was it.

"We had a great many Indians, too. The Arapaho Indians made James Cruze a chief; they called him Standing Bear. James was kind of like a bear. We had one old Indian who had been through the Indian wars, and, I think, the Civil War. Anyway, all he wanted out of life was a Union uniform, which the government had supplied him. He couldn't speak English, but Tim McCoy served as interpreter. The Indians had all been told the story of the film, and they entered into it with great spirit. This Indian was an expert with a bow and arrow, and when he heard that I was to be shot in the film, he volunteered to do it. 'Very good shot,' he said to Cruze, through Tim McCoy. 'Very good. Shoot arrow through lady's shoulder. Not hurt much. Not break bone. Go right through!'

"I grew deeply interested in the Indians. Their life and their customs fascinated me. I feel we have not treated them fairly and I contribute all I can afford to the

[3] Picture Play, *Oct. 1923, p. 54.*
[4] *Colleen Moore to author, London, Sept. 1962.*

schools—one in particular, the Holy Rosary Mission, Pine Ridge, Dakota, which takes care of five hundred Sioux children."[5]

On location for *The Love Flower,* the D. W. Griffith company left Miami, Florida, for Nassau, Bahamas, in the yacht *Grey Duck*—and they were not seen or heard from for five days. The Navy ordered all available craft to search for the missing vessel. Drifting without food or water for three days in a heavy sea, their troubles were climaxed when two members of the company were swept overboard.

"At the time the story gained circulation," said *Photoplay,* "many rumors were rife that it was only 'press stuff.' But it was a sure-enough adventure."[6]

About two weeks later came cables from Sicily telling of the disappearance of Herbert Brenon on Mount Etna. Making a picture for an Italian company, he had wandered away from the company at lunch and had been set upon by bandits.

"He was held for ransom," said *Photoplay,* "until the beastly fellows discovered he was an American citizen with his Government backing the search for him. He turned up safe and sound. Oh dear!"[7]

Marshall Neilan was snowed in in the San Bernardino Mountains around the same time, and Matt Moore walked fifteen hours through the snow to summon help, returning with guides and food; but the press agents, having made as much as they could of the Griffith-Brenon incidents, couldn't use the story.

More tragic was the fate of Lynn Reynolds, who was shooting snow scenes in 1927 when the unit was caught in a blizzard. Renee Adoree was one of the victims. Lost for several days, the company was found half-starved and half-frozen. Unnerved by the experience, Lynn Reynolds later shot himself.

Irving Sindler, property man on the Valentino picture *Son of the Sheik,* kept a diary in which he recorded the unit's life in the desert. He described how Vilma Banky put her spoon in a bowl of something that looked like blackberry jam but proved to be a sugar bowl crawling with flies; how the brackish water caused Montagu Love to fall ill, and how he carried on working; how the heat never moderated, even at night.

"At midnight, it is still too hot to sleep. Sheets are like fire."

How, after two hours' sleep in bed, the unit had to get up at four a.m. to work all day, toiling up a sand dune, sometimes on hands and knees, with flies penetrating the eyes and mouth. . . .

But Irving Sindler was stoically philosophic: "Well, we'll get Mr. Valentino's lovely, beautiful desert scenes. This can't last forever."

Son of the Sheik was Valentino's last film. His health was affected by the rigors of this production and he died from the effects of a double operation for appendicitis and peritonitis, in August 1926.

These extreme examples were counterbalanced by many well-organized location trips in which the company was billeted at good hotels, supplied with transport and portable kitchens, and treated with every consideration.

But those aren't the experiences anyone remembers!

[5] *Lois Wilson to author, New York, April 1967.*
[6] Photoplay, *March 1920, p. 105.*
[7] Photoplay, *April 1920, p. 88.*

30 / THE SILENTS WERE NEVER SILENT

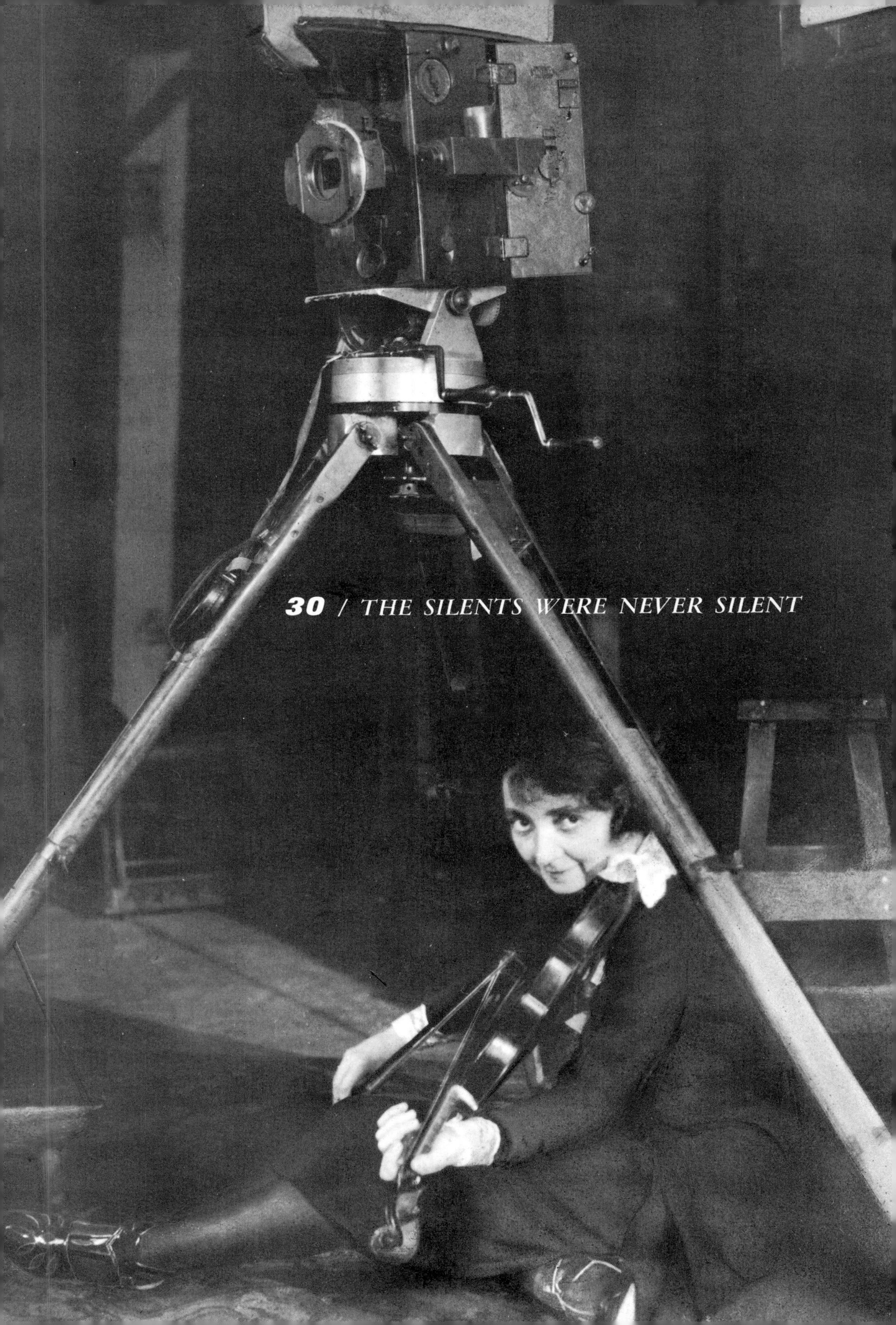

It was the aim of the exhibitor to eradicate the silence from silent pictures. A piano was at first sufficient to drown the whirr of the projector. Soon, even the cheapest theater could afford both a pianist and a violinist. With the improvement in production came an improvement in presentation. During the Golden Era, the reputation of a theater often depended on its orchestra. People sometimes claimed that they went to the movies "just for the music."

A first-class orchestra could make the dullest picture bearable, and careful scoring, combined with good playing, could provide an extra dimension to the magic of the movies.

The critics, however, generally saw a picture cold, with no accompaniment at all except the projector noise, coughs and comments. A film that survived the ordeal of a projection-room press screening and also received good reviews certainly deserved the praise it received.

Theater musicians worked from a standard repertoire, unless the picture was a big special; *Broken Blossoms* was released with a largely original score by Louis F. Gottschalk. A regular picture would be issued with a cue sheet, sent out by the exchange as part of the promotional material. Cue sheets read like this:

No.	Title or description	Tempo	Selection
1.	This is the tale	Light intermezzo	Melodie Caprice (Squire)
2.	But Paris	Light intermezzo	Demoiselle Chic (Fletcher)
3.	Jean Jacques	Love Melody	Melodie d'Amour (Engleman)
4.	The Ananias of Cadiz	Flowing romance	Serenade Italienne (Czibulka)

Also favored were the works of Grieg, Schubert, and Weber. Motion-picture theater orchestras brought classical music to the ears of many who had never previously heard it.

During the twenties, some theaters were equipped with gigantic organs, capable of accompanying the film with more volume and less manpower than an orchestra. They were capable of an added attraction; they could supply a wide range of sound effects—thunder, gunfire, or the whistle of a locomotive.

These organs were completely different in tone from their ecclesiastical counterparts. The Wurlitzer catalogue quoted a St. Louis theater owner: "The Wurlitzer is the only organ I know that gets away from the cathedral tone—or drone—that has no place in a theater's musical program."

In other enterprising establishments, sound-effects specialists would sit in the orchestra pit, or behind the screen, and attempt to synchronize the firing of a revolver or the thunder of hoofs with a reproduction of the sound. Complete outfits were marketed for this purpose, and special .22 caliber revolvers were manufactured for use in westerns. The barrel was blocked, in case the gun fell into unauthorized hands; since six shots were considered inadequate for a good western fight, the revolvers were equipped with eight, sometimes twelve chambers.

These attempts to drown the silence reached a high-water mark of absurdity in 1922 when an energetic laboratory tycoon, Watterson Rothacker, tried to prove that talking pictures were possible. He employed radio for his experiment; Frank Bacon enacted a spoken sketch at the Rothacker studios in Chicago, while a silent camera recorded his actions and a stenographer noted his departures from the script. Later, Bacon radiophoned his lines to a projection room where the film was being screened. Synchronization, to say the least, was sporadic.

While the French film *L'Assassinat du Duc de Guise* (1908) is accepted as the first to be provided with a specially composed score (written, at the request of the Lafitte brothers, by Camille Saint-Saens, and performed by the Orchestre de Salle Charras), *Judith of Bethulia* (1913) is acknowledged as the first to employ an orchestra on the set. D. W. Griffith, the historians allege, used it to help Blanche Sweet through some emotional scenes. But Blanche Sweet could not remember musicians being present at any stage of the production. As she pointed out, Griffith used music less than practically any director. He once said he would never employ a player "who could not feel the role enough to weep at rehearsals."

Griffith did use a brass band, however, to whip up the enthusiasm of the extras during the battle scenes for *Intolerance*. And the Denishawn dancers at Belshazzar's Feast required music.

The same year, 1915, Cecil B. De Mille arranged for Bizet music to be played during the production of *Carmen,* at the request of the star, the celebrated opera singer Geraldine Farrar. Miss Farrar called upon Charles Gardner's *The Lilac* for her love scenes.

Other directors also realized the value of music on the set. The grinding of the cameras could have a paralyzing effect on nervous actors—besides which, the noise of nearby sets being put up and pulled down was unsettling for everybody. Music helped to drown noise, it supplied added atmosphere, and it generally improved morale. Soon, almost every company had a small orchestra—a violin and a portable organ were the most popular instruments—and they played for exteriors as well as interiors.

Maurice Tourneur once declared that a unit he saw filming a chase from the back of a truck were accompanied by another vehicle racing alongside—full of frantically playing musicians.

For silent-film productions, sets were built alongside each other without sound-proofing. In some studios, four films might be working at once, on adjoining sets.

A story that circulated during the alleged Gloria Swanson–Pola Negri feud told of Miss Negri's insistence on soft, heart-rending music for an important emotional scene. Musicians on the other sets were requested to keep quiet while she went through this difficult scene. According to popular legend, Miss Swanson hired a brass band for the day, and it struck up a rousing military march just at the crucial moment. Actually, the band was brought in as a playful gesture by Allan Dwan, but Miss Negri always imagined it was Miss Swanson's work.

Mary Pickford, despite her Griffith training, frequently used music to stir her emotions. The Cadman Indian lyric *From the Land of the Sky Blue Water* was a favorite, together with Massenet's *Élégie,* which was played for the poignant scene in *Stella Maris* when Unity looks in the mirror and realizes her own ugliness. In *Tess of the Storm Country* (the 1922 remake), however, there was no music for the tender moment when she stands before the judge. As with Griffith, it was the moving voice of Forrest Robinson, as the judge, which brought the tears.

William de Mille with Efrem Zimbalist, Sr.

Pauline Starke and Conrad Nagel in Sun-Up (1925), directed by Edmund Goulding.

John Robertson, who directed *Tess,* did not care for music on the set. Nor did his star, Richard Barthelmess. Rupert Hughes, although an accomplished musician, refused to have music anywhere near him when he was directing.

Chaplin never had music on the set, but he often slipped away to a deserted part of the studio to play the violin while working out the details of a scene. The violin appeared in *The Vagabond.*

"I loved music," said William Wellman. "It's just too damn bad we can't use it now. I had the greatest combo in the world. I had a gal that played the organ, a gal that played the fiddle, and a funny old guy that played the cello. And boy, I tell you; they could play. They'd play between scenes and they'd keep the company going all the time. It was just wonderful."

King Vidor also acknowledged the value of music on the set: "It was very helpful to get the mood. John Gilbert liked "Moonlight and Roses" on *The Big Parade.* Other actors would ask for something from opera. All through *The Crowd* I had Tchaikovsky's *Pathétique* played. There'd be a theme that meant the picture."

"Every set would have musicians," said Conrad Nagel. "Mickey Neilan had an orchestra of four, so there was always fun on his set. On *Tess of the d'Urbervilles* he and his wife, Blanche Sweet, would have some rows. The minute a row started, this orchestra would start to play 'Poppa Loves Momma . . . Momma Loves Poppa' and laugh them out of it. These musicians would know a hundred to a hundred and fifty pieces of music, and they'd have a piece to go with whatever happened on the set. For hundreds of years, when you went to war, the regiment would take a band along. The music would give a great lift to the soldiers. And it was the same on a silent-picture set; the music kept you buoyed up."

Director Edward Sloman, however, did not agree. "The fallacy of music on the set was proved, of course, by the untalented or inexperienced actors. To my mind they were just kidding themselves. I tolerated it only because I didn't like to see the musicians lose their happy jobs. Mary Philbin always craved it, but believe me, hard-riding direction did her more good than all the music she ever listened to."

"In silent pictures," recalled Ben Lyon, "you'd hear the grinding of the camera quite loud through the music. For the final rehearsal we sometimes asked the cameraman: 'Will you give us the camera?' No film—but it was an inspiration to hear that grinding. And the music was a great help. If I had a scene that required me to be emotional, I always had them play 'My Buddy'—ye gods, it was effective!

"Then suddenly talkies came in and everything was soundproofed—everything was silent. The camera was sealed in a soundproofed booth and everybody kept absolutely quiet until the end of a take. In this complete silence we were at a complete loss. It took us a long time to get used to it."

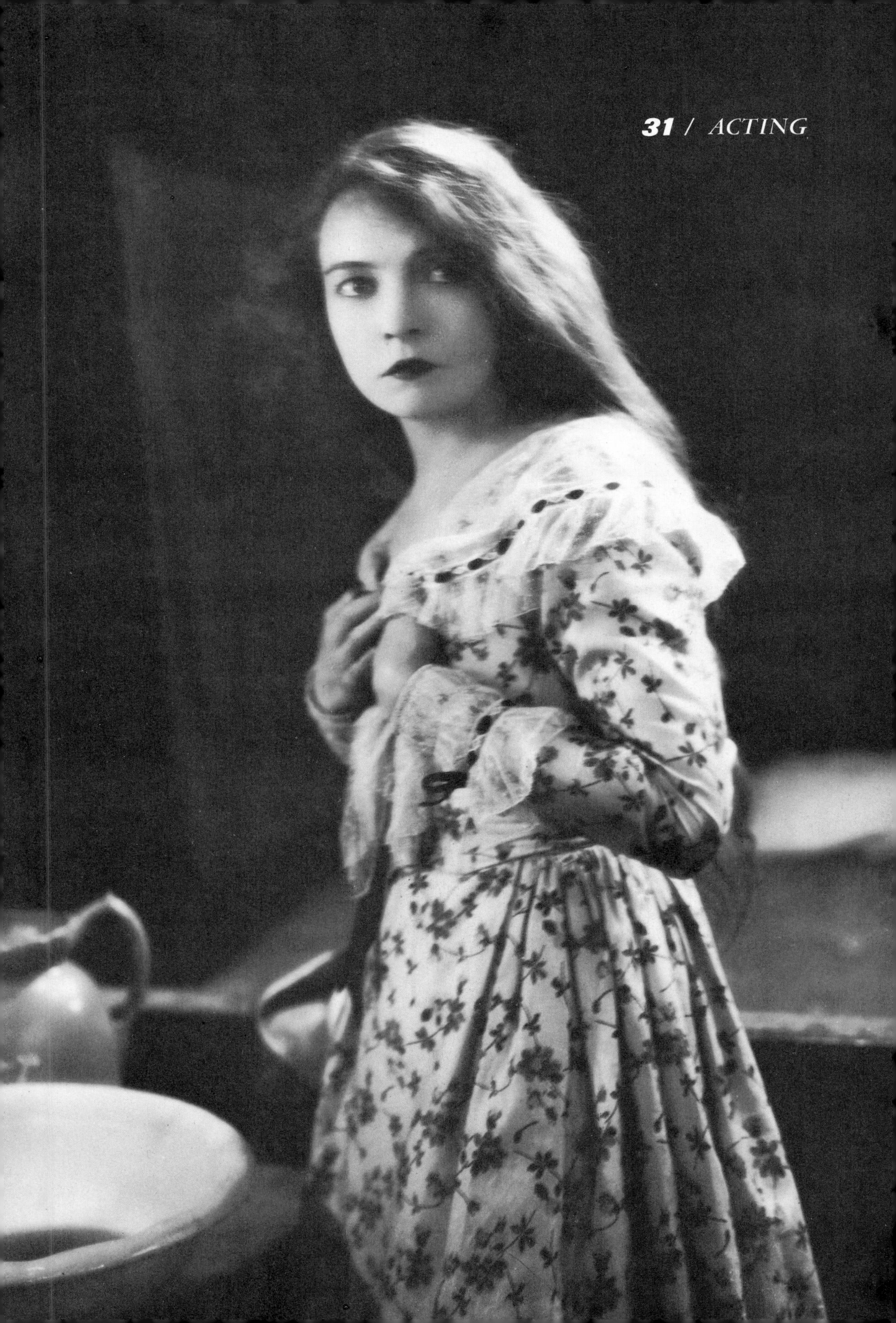

The very thought of a silent-film actor sends some people into hysterics. They imagine the acting of those days having as much subtlety as a cavalry charge.

Popular illusion often contains a germ of truth. No one would deny that silent-picture acting started out like this; the early productions were merely photographed versions of stock-company melodramas, and players saw no reason to alter their lavish style of acting for the camera. Many melodramas carried this tradition well into talkies.

But since its inception, the style of the theater has been that of emphasized representation. The Greek players, their faces concealed by masks, were heavily dependent on gesture. Playing in huge arenas, their movements had to be clearly visible from hundreds of feet away; gesture was expansive and elaborate.

Even now, when realism has changed the whole concept of acting, players in the theater still depend on a degree of exaggeration to project their life-size actions into something larger than life.

The cinema, however, is already larger than life. For an actor to give the same performance on a thirty-foot screen that he gives as a tiny figure on a stage betrays what appears to be a bewildering lack of common sense. But in the early silent days, it merely betrayed a forgivable ignorance of the medium.

Sarah Bernhardt, old and fixed in her ways, played for the motion picture as though for an audience in the theater—she thought the camera would record her performance in the same way a daguerreotype recorded her likeness. It did. It recorded it and transformed it. "I rely upon these films to make me immortal," she said. Memory and legend would have served her better. After half a century, the idol appears disillusioning, baffling, and ludicrous. "Did people really take her seriously?" ask modern audiences.

It is somewhat comforting to know that Mme. Bernhardt herself was as shocked by her screen performance as audiences are today. She is said to have fainted when shown *Camille*. By the time she came to make *Queen Elizabeth*, she found the whole process of picture-making quite ludicrous.

"Sarah Bernhardt gives you no idea of what she was like on the stage," said Alfred Lunt. "She was so extraordinary . . . she had an amazing voice. There was never a voice like that in the whole world, ever. She carried on a bit, if that is the expression to use, with gestures and so forth, but she was very effective. I don't think she treated motion pictures very seriously."

The old style of emphasized representation was rapidly dying in the theater by the early years of the century.

"There was very little left by the time I went on the stage," said Lunt. "Some of the old men who tottered around the stage, clinging to the proscenium—they kept up the old style. But elsewhere it had practically vanished.

"I remember when I was a little boy, I saw Richard Mansfield in *The Scarlet Letter*. I don't think I could have been more than eleven, so this would be 1904. Oh, I thought he was awful—he overacted so. Even at that age I knew he was carrying on far beyond the limits of truth."

Alfred Lunt, together with Lynn Fontanne, his wife, and Helen Hayes and Katharine Cornell, were part of a strong naturalistic trend which in the twenties had a great effect on the American theater.

But other theatrical personalities who appeared in motion pictures leave the impression that emphasized representation was in vogue well into the twenties.

Priscilla Dean's performances are as vivid today as ever—and remarkably naturalistic. A scene from The Dice Woman *(1926).*

The versatility of Norma Talmadge: scenes from some of her earliest features.

Ernst Lubitsch's concentration is as intense as Pola Negri's in this rehearsal shot from **For-bidden Paradise (1924).**

Apart from the Famous Players who enhanced Adolph Zukor's Famous Plays, and such stars as Beerbohm Tree and Constance Collier, who carried the dignity of the theater to Triangle's productions, names of the magnitude of Otis Skinner and Wilton Lackaye brought to their screen appearances a startling flamboyance which suggests that they, at any rate, had not embraced any particularly naturalistic tenets.

Dramatic styles date rapidly; acting acceptable a mere ten years ago can look absurd today. We have completely lost contact with the style of emphasized representation—so much so that we find it comic whenever we see it, and to judge those who used it with skill against those who were merely inept is impossible, because the whole method looks ludicrous.

But some outstanding performers, creating their own standards and not following convention, retain their original power; their style is timeless, and, luckily, some of their work has been captured on celluloid.

Eleanora Duse, in the Italian film *Cenere* (1916), is a model of restraint, employing delicate movements of the hands rather than the exaggerated sweeps of the arms customary to her period. It would not be true to say that she adapted her style for the screen; those who saw her on the stage during her 1924 American tour say that her performance then was somewhat similar. Although old and ill, and somewhat inaudible, she had enormous charm and a very expressive body.

"Very different," said Alfred Lunt, "from another Italian—a man called Rosso —whom I once saw. He really let go. When he reached a big, emotional scene there'd be a burst of applause. He'd stop, bow gracefully, then carry on with the play."

While the early silent pictures were forced to use players from the theater, a number of authentic film players were being established, who intuitively developed a naturalistic style ideal for the camera. It looked right then—and it looks right now.

Mary Pickford, from her very earliest films, had the characterization of a real person, which in no small way helped her win the title of America's Sweetheart. Other Griffith-trained actresses display the same freshness, inventiveness, and immediacy that made the slightest artificiality on the part of another player in the film seem shatteringly clumsy by comparison. Norma Talmadge, who started with Vitagraph, then went to Triangle, was one of the motion picture's great dramatic actresses and she was completely natural in the most contrived circumstances.

Her sister, Constance, was a brilliant comedienne, and in comedy no actor would dare overact unless to aim at burlesque.

Restraint and naturalism are in vogue today. Realism was not so popular then, and many actors and directors were totally opposed to it. They wanted to give their audiences something more enjoyable than life. They argued that people had enough realism during the day; they came to the theater or to the movies to forget, to be taken out of themselves, to be given a thrill, and to see people behaving as they *don't* in real life. And so stylized performances persisted, especially in melodrama. And it was felt that if you start with a true character, the portrayal will remain truthful—once you've found the truth, it can be emphasized or exaggerated and yet it will still be true.

It is hard to believe that the actors gesturing, flapping, and generally eating the scenery in a full-blooded melodrama were quite capable of a restrained, realistic performance—but it was so. They are surprised at the suggestion that they should have played their melodrama straight.

"But it's hokum," they protest. "You couldn't play hokum realistically—you have to go along with the spirit of the thing."

Today, veterans of the silent era tend to be self-conscious about the performances they think they gave, and they laugh off any references to their acting styles. Few of them have anything to be ashamed of. One or two were unable to act at all, admittedly, but the majority could not only act—they could act in at least two distinct styles.

Florence Vidor, as the dignified patrician of the Lubitsch and Mal St. Clair sophisticated comedies, merely had to incline her beautiful head to make her meaning starkly clear. In *Eagle of the Sea* (Frank Lloyd), however, she flaps around in true melodramatic style, having no more in common with her other roles than a serial heroine with Duse.

Elinor Fair's playing as the heroine of *Yankee Clipper* (Rupert Julian) raises hoots of raucous laughter from audiences today. But in the same year, 1927, she filled a lead role in the light comedy, *Let 'Er Go, Gallegher* (Elmer Clifton), charmingly and completely naturalistically.

The person who decided upon the style of performance was usually the director. To some, overacting was anathema.

"We had many traveling theatrical companies coming to Los Angeles," said Joseph Henabery, "and I got to see them all, because I'd do the job of an usher in the gallery and see the show free. It got to the point where I considered myself to be a good judge of acting, and when motion pictures came along it seemed to me that they were confused.

"There were two schools of acting on the stage—the first was the beginning of a naturalistic, realistic school. Then there was the flamboyant school. If you were interested in pictures, you were kind of divided as to which to choose.

John Griffith Wray demonstrating a scene for Anna Christie *(1923).* William Russell at left.

Edwin Carewe directing Alla Nazimova in My Son *(1925).*

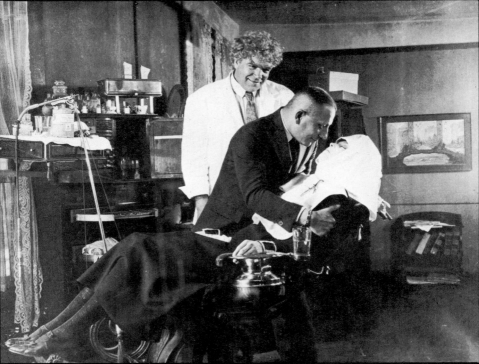

Erich von Stroheim shows Gibson Gowland how to ravish Zasu Pitts for the dentist-chair scene in Greed *(1925).*

Norma Shearer and James Kirkwood in Broken Barriers *(1924), directed by Reginald Barker.*

"But when you saw this Delsarte type of acting, silent, on the screen, you said, 'That's terrible!' As a matter of fact, I've had many actors from the stage see themselves on the screen for the first time and cry out in holy horror, 'Is that me?' They'd never seen themselves. They'd *never* seen themselves, so they could never realize how horrible they were. They were readier to appreciate that what had been considered fine acting was really ham acting, as we call it. I think motion pictures did more to change and improve the style of acting than anything else.

"They began to see that it was possible even in the theater to do things in a subtle way and convey ideas by suggestion rather than to blurt out some wild statement."

But other directors would not dream of permitting anything less than the grand style.

"There were a lot of people who wanted realism and not melodrama," said Blanche Sweet, "and we thought it was wonderful when Tom Ince decided to do *Anna Christie* (1923), which was a realistic play by every standard. But he didn't go far enough—he didn't try to play it that way. He even inserted some extra barge scenes to bring in some melodrama. We said, 'No, please don't. It isn't that kind of picture.' The director was John Griffith Wray. I liked him; he was so sincere, so interested in his work, but we just disagreed. Our style of working conflicted.

"He was a very violent man himself, and I liked to work quietly. It so happens that the other main characters—William Russell and George Marion, who'd worked his part out for the play—felt as I did. But Wray had a more melodramatic idea of the thing; we tried to hold it down and hold it down and we were constantly in conflict. Wray was a driving, noisy type of director—he used to use a megaphone for a close-up. He was a dear fellow and I was very fond of him, but he would insist on overstating and exaggerating everything.

"One doesn't like to have to go over the head of the director to the producer and ask for something to be changed, but I had to. I went to Tom Ince and told him that we were going to have to do over a number of scenes. And he said he'd do them himself. He hadn't directed for a long while, and I'd never worked for him when he was a director, so I didn't know what to expect. When he came along and redid the scenes, he was twice as violent as Wray!"

While naturalism did not sweep unopposed across the American film industry, it strengthened its hold year by year. When, in 1914, *Motion Picture Magazine* held a competition for the best answer to the question: "What Improvement in Motion Pictures Is Needed Most?" an honorable mention was given to reader Walter Scott Howard for his "eloquent conviction of the culprit 'Unnaturalness.' "

"To grimace, smirk, contort the physiognomy into a thousand twists may pass muster before a painted act-drop; but a scene depicting nature in all its reality revolts at the antics of a puppet and must be peopled by *genuine human beings*. Give us less nourishment, more naturally served. Human existence—genuine, throbbing life of the people! Bury your crude monstrosities before a second Don Quixote comes to ridicule from off the screen your morbid heroines, your sordid villains, your pack of painted manikins . . ."[1]

By 1916, a number of influential directors were endeavoring seriously to dispel the pervading, musty odor of theatrical acting.

[1] *Motion Picture Magazine, Dec. 1914, p. 126.*

Albert Capellani's career was comparatively short in America; he was one of the many French importations and he directed some of Nazimova's pictures.

"Capellani's excellence," wrote Allen Corliss in 1916, "lies more in his exquisite valuation of detail and finesse than in breadth and power such as Griffith's or Brenon's. He is as subtle as his mother tongue; he gets his effects by a stealthy artistry that sneaks up behind one, as it were, and stabs the heart in the back ribs. 'Be natural' is Cap's slogan, displayed in big letters on sign boards all around his studio at Fort Lee, New Jersey.[2] He doesn't want his actors to act, which sounds like a paradox but isn't. To be natural on stage is one of the most difficult things an actor has to do, because of the fact that he is addressing an audience and has to fight down self-consciousness. But, according to Capellani, there is no excuse for a motion-picture actor to feel self-conscious and become stagey in his work. Capellani will not tolerate the exaggeration of facial expression and gesture that was thought essential to motion-picture acting in earlier days and still is one of the great faults of so many screen players.

" 'Screen acting should be nature herself. My artistes—they must be natural. That is why I am what you say—so gentle with them. Oh! So hard they try to act—an' when they try it is worse. I speak soft, always soft. I try to coax them to be natural, to walk and talk like real people.' "[3]

Maurice Tourneur also brought a new, naturalistic style to dramatic acting. But whereas Capellani's underplaying was born of many years' experience with film, Tourneur's came from the theater.

"Before going to America," said Jacques Tourneur, "my father was at the Theatre Antoine. The director of that theater, Antoine, was a man of iron who forced his actors to underplay. He was fifty years ahead of his time, and his adaptations of Ibsen and Chekhov were played exactly as we'd play them today. I believe my father brought to America everything he'd learned from Antoine."[4]

Marshall Neilan, a potent, if somewhat wild, force as one of America's top six directors, summed up the motion-picture people's attitude to the theatrical smothering of their art:

"The sooner the stage people who have come into pictures get out, the better for the pictures," he said in 1917.

By the twenties, motion-picture acting in American films was an example to the world.

Other film-producing countries, slower at losing the links with the theater, were never able to match the Hollywood star system by producing personalities of their own. In Italy and Germany, emphasized representation held its own with surprising vigor. When Fritz Lang's *Metropolis* was released in America, *Photoplay* said that the film was almost ruined by its terrible acting. "The settings are unbelievably beautiful; the mugging of the players is unbelievably bad."[5]

And one writer described the acting in Italian pictures so graphically that he made further explanation unnecessary.

"The acting in these pictures," he said, "is like the moment after someone's shouted 'Fire!' "

[2] *This celebrated sign has also been attributed to Alice Guy-Blache, in whose studio—Solax—Capellani was working.*
[3] Photoplay, *Jan. 1917, p. 88.*
[4] *Jacques Tourneur to author, London, Oct. 1964. Antoine later directed films himself.*
[5] Photoplay, *May 1927, p. 52.*

Ziegfeld was crying outside my door with a string of pearls. But I simply couldn't go on with him . . . I simply couldn't go *on* with him! I decided to go to Hollywood because Jesse Lasky was offering me four thousand dollars a week. And when I got there, darling, oh—it was unbelievable. They picked up my car, my little car, and they carried me in it—all those wonderful boys carried me in it to my hotel! Oh, it was too divine, darling, too divine! And then the Prince of Wales . . ."

Louise Brooks shook her head, fatalistically. "It's the same over and over again," she said. "The stars will give you the same unmitigated rubbish; they just tell it different ways, that's all. Absolutely nothing bad ever happens to them. That's the kind of stuff you'll find in all these books they're bringing out; autobiographies, biographies. . . . Truth is foreign to them."

Louise Brooks was not one of the important stars of the silent era. She made comparatively few pictures in America; her two best-known films were *Diary of a Lost Girl* and *Pandora's Box,* both made by G. W. Pabst in Germany. But of all the personalities of that era, Louise Brooks has emerged most triumphantly. She has become the object of idolatry for thousands who are too young to remember her in silents, and who base their admiration on revivals at archives and film societies. Louise Brooks fan clubs have started up all over the world. Her youthful admirers see in her an actress of brilliance, a luminescent personality, and a beauty unparalleled in film history.

Lotte Eisner, in a first edition of *L'Écran Démoniaque,* asked: "Was Louise Brooks a great artist or only a dazzling creature whose beauty leads the spectator to endow her with complexities of which she herself was unaware?"

After Miss Brooks had visited Paris, the paragraph was altered. Now it reads: "Today we know that Louise Brooks is an astonishing actress endowed with an intelligence beyond compare and not only a dazzling creature."

"Damn Lotte," said Louise Brooks. "If I'd kept my big black mouth shut, hadn't teased her about thinking I was a dunce in 1928, she might not have changed, in that penetrating paragraph on me, its final intuitive question."

Louise Brooks is one of the most remarkable personalities to be associated with films. Superficially, the facts suggest a character from *Sunset Boulevard.* Miss Brooks describes herself as a recluse. She lives alone in Rochester, New York; she seldom goes out, she seldom receives visitors; and she spends most of her time in bed. In fact, she is a woman of immense creative energy. She is a brilliant writer; several of her articles have appeared in *Sight and Sound.* She has been divorced from motion pictures long enough to be able to look at them with objectivity. Her memory is excellent, and while she can recall all her experiences in the twenties, she does not belong to the period herself. She is not afflicted with morbid nostalgia; she loves silent films for their beauty and their quality. But she has matured since those days, and can discuss them in rational terms.

To talk to her is a creative experience. Relentless in her search for truth, she can detect hyperbole or elaboration instantly. The inventions of some producer or star will cause her to fly into a fury. "How can you *believe* such crap? They're just telling you how marvelous they are. Think for a moment; how could that have happened?"

She is completely honest—about herself and with herself. Her language is

The Iron Mule *(1925). The director, William Goodrich (center), was better known as Roscoe Arbuckle. Al St. John is the character lying down. Buster Keaton gave this accurate reproduction of the De Witt Clinton locomotive and train to his former partners; he had used it on* Our Hospitality *(1923).*

Louise Brooks.

colorful; unprintable adjectives fly without warning. Her voice is musical, and she sometimes has to harshen it to give the swear words any impact.

The exquisite Louise Brooks face is still there, with the additional contours of middle age. The hair is gray, swept straight back. The youthful vitality and humor, balanced by the eloquence of maturity, suggest that Louise Brooks has forgotten about the alleged disadvantages of being sixty.

"Another thing these stars do," she continued. "They've told these lies so often that they believe them. When I started writing my autobiography, I had to strip a thousand humiliating, protective lies off myself, one by one."

Miss Brooks threw her memoirs, *Naked on My Goat,* down the incinerator. Her carefully researched, beautifully written pieces about other stars and directors of the period have, fortunately, been preserved. She has thrown valuable new light on the motion picture and, equally important, upon our attitudes to the motion picture. One of her characteristic profundities was quoted by James Card in his article for *Sight and Sound:*

"The great art of films does not consist of descriptive movement of face and body, but in the movements of thought and soul transmitted in a kind of intense isolation."[1]

What follows are transcripts of conversations with Miss Brooks—observations on other stars, descriptions of directors, and anecdotes about her own career. She did not object to the use of a tape recorder—in fact she encouraged it.

"These other people," she said, "are writing books out of books. I had a journalist spend a whole day with me and he taped everything I said. What did he get out of it? Nothing. He didn't even play it back. These people have to have something written down, so they can sit at their typewriter and copy out what everybody else has written."

LOUISE BROOKS: I learned to act while watching Martha Graham dance, and I learned to move in film from watching Chaplin. He was doing imitations and clowning around one summer in 1925 when he was in New York for the opening of *The Gold Rush.* When he wasn't out with a lot of other people, we'd all gather in A. C. Blumenthal's suite at the Ambassador. There, Charlie was himself, and perfectly happy, doing imitations *all* the time. He'd been doing Isadora Duncan, then he said, "Look, Louise, guess whom I'm imitating." He walked away from me, wiggling his ass, oh, a disgustingly silly walk. Of course, I knew. He turned around and saw my face; it was grim and white. I was only eighteen. He rushed over and said, "Oh, I didn't mean it! I wasn't doing you!"

But of course he was, and it took me years to get rid of that ridiculous walk that I'd cultivated so carefully at the Follies. I thought it was terrific until he imitated it.

I discovered in that instant that everything is built on movement. No matter how well Ronald Colman played a scene, if you saw him lumbering across a room in that hideously heavy way of his, it took all the meaning out of it.

Speaking of Chaplin, he said in his book that we must get rid of walks . . . in and out of scenes. What the hell? He built his whole character on a walk. Garbo

---

[1] Sight & Sound, *Summer 1958, p. 240.*

is all movement. First she gets the emotion, and out of the emotion comes the movement and out of the movement comes the dialogue. She's so perfect that people say she can't act. People would much rather see someone like Peter Sellers performing than see real acting, which is intangible. People are pretty good judges of dancing, because they've all tried to dance a little. They can recognize a technique. They're judges of singing, because they've tried to sing, and they recognize a technique. So they must have some visible technique in order to judge acting, and there isn't any. Acting is a completely personal reaction.

That is why I get so inflamed when people tell me Garbo can't act. She is *so* great. Sarah Bernhardt was always a thousand times more popular than Duse because she gave a "performance."

Proust made a brilliant remark: "The degree of mediocrity produced by contact with mystery is incredible." Isn't that a wonderful line for Garbo?

The best actor I ever worked with was Osgood Perkins. Usually, when I played comedy with directors like Mal St. Clair or Eddie Sutherland we would laugh about a scene before we shot it. Not with Frank Tuttle. I didn't even know I was playing comedy until I saw that picture (*Love 'em and Leave 'em*) with an audience. I played it perfectly straight, and that's the way he wanted it.

You know what makes an actor great to work with? Timing. You don't have to feel anything. It's like dancing with a perfect dancing partner. Osgood Perkins would give you a line so that you would react perfectly. It was timing—because emotion means nothing.

Look at Adolphe Menjou. He never felt anything. He used to say, "Now I do Lubitsch number one," "Now I do Lubitsch number two." And that's exactly what he did. You felt nothing, working with him, and yet see him on the screen —and he was a great actor.

I adored Jack Pickford and I adored Mickey Neilan. Mickey was a far better director than anyone knew. And did you know Jack was an excellent director, too? But they didn't make anything out of it. A director nowadays spends a lot of time being interviewed. He uses esoteric words, and his films have seven thousand meanings, none of which you see on the screen. It's all something very special that exists in their words and in their imagination. But directors in the twenties went about their business in the most ordinary way.

There is one divine story: there were three great pals, Jack Pickford, Mickey Neilan, and Norman Kerry. They all drank a great deal. On this occasion, Mary Pickford was making *Dorothy Vernon of Haddon Hall* and Mickey was the director. They went up to San Francisco to shoot an exterior, which was the grand procession to the castle, in Golden Gate Park. It was nine o'clock in the morning; they had the great procession of horses, and hundreds of extras, and Mary was on her milk-white steed. They were all ready to shoot. It was a very expensive sequence, but there was no Mickey Neilan. So Mary said, "Who's in town?" "Well," somebody said, "we hear Norman and Jack are in town." They scouted around all the speakeasies where Mickey and Norman and Jack might be, and all the hotels, and they couldn't find them anywhere. So Mary directed the sequence. There was no trouble. She knew how to do it. Nobody thought a thing about it. Today, everyone would fall apart and nobody would do anything.

Shooting the procession, Charles Rosher was lining up a shot when he happened to look behind the ropes where the bystanders were watching. There stood Neilan, who said, "Say, you're doing pretty well!" and then disappeared again on his drunk.

As soon as a director became powerful or established, the producers started thinking up ways to get rid of him. With block booking, film companies were bound to make a great deal of money, no matter who directed the pictures. After a director got so big that he could defy the producers, and demand a certain cast and a certain budget, he was given a bum picture and thrown out of the studio. With all the pictures sold in advance, it didn't matter if some were bad.

I made three pictures with directors who suffered such fear and agony, being forced to direct, that I dreaded going on the set to watch their struggles.

Luther Reed didn't want to direct. He had been a writer. And in those days, a writer was not much more than a means of getting a film down on paper so that it could be budgeted, cast, and got into production. Frank Strayer had also been a writer. Most of the time, they stood silent behind the camera, letting the cameraman, Menjou, or Beery handle the direction.

I made *Rolled Stockings* with Dick Rosson; he'd been Allan Dwan's assistant, and it was an assistant that he wanted to be. During *Rolled Stockings* he sat sweating, with a trembling script. There wasn't enough Bromo-Seltzer to float him out of his chair.[2]

One director they tossed out was James Cruze—he was fascinating. The strangest man I ever knew. He directed *The Covered Wagon.* I made a picture with him and Tommy Meighan called *The City Gone Wild.* He almost never talked and he drank from morning till night. He was the man who invented the drink called The Well-digger's Ass. It was a pick-me-up. You asked, "Why is it called The Well-digger's Ass?" "Well, you know how cold the well-digger's ass gets!"

Jimmie hardly talked at all during the making of a film, and I never read a script. We were on location in Griffith Park. He said, "Okay, Louise, get in the car."

I got in the car.

"Well, get in the driver's seat!"

I got in the driver's seat.

"Now," he said, "drive off, fast—as fast as you can go."

"I can't drive," I said.

"You can't drive!" He glared at me. He absolutely glared at me. "You can't *drive??*"

It was as if I'd said that I couldn't talk. He was infuriated. It had never occurred to him to ask me if I could drive, or to tell me what the scene was about. So that day's shooting was all loused up, because they had to get a double, and get some clothes that would look like mine.

But Cruze was a wonderful man. I don't know what ruined him. I don't think it was booze, because it never changed him at all.

He was a very fast director, but that doesn't mean he didn't take his pictures seriously. Like Pabst, he would work over his script completely before shooting. When Pabst started a film, I never saw him pick up a script. Other directors never let the script out of their hands.

---

[2] *Dick Rosson later became an exceptionally good second-unit director.*

I don't say that's bad. A director works fast who knows everything ahead of time. He sees the picture finished, whole, cut, titled. Pabst would take one shot, bang—that was it. I remember I was going to do my famous Follies-girl walk across the stage in the theater scene of *Pandora's Box*. I'd planned it all out. I took four steps on stage and Pabst said "Cut." That was the end of it. I had given him all he wanted.

Those young comedy directors—Eddie Sutherland, Mal St. Clair—they thought they were geniuses, like Chaplin and Sennett. What they didn't know was that when they were out drinking and playing around and dancing all night, Chaplin and Sennett were thinking about tomorrow. Chaplin would think about a picture for years. I went down with him once in 1925 to a Hungarian restaurant in the Jewish ghetto in New York. He went there every night. God knows why; nobody knew why. He would get the violinist to play, and give him five-dollar bills. And how many years later did he do *Limelight?* And there was the scene. He was the violinist.

But Mal St. Clair, who worked at Sennett, and Eddie Sutherland, who worked with Chaplin, imagined that Sennett and Chaplin really did think up their scenes right there on the set. And Mal and Eddie would try to make pictures that way . . . with large hangovers to boot.

When I was married to Eddie Sutherland, he was having a great deal of trouble on *Fireman Save My Child*. He'd done no preparation. If he wasn't inspired on the set, he would think of a reason why he couldn't shoot. He would say, "That building is too close to the camera. Now move that building back

Eddie Sutherland and Louise Brooks during the making of It's the Old Army Game (1926).

and we'll shoot tomorrow." And he would come waltzing home at two in the afternoon. Then he and Monte Brice, the writer, would get together with Tom Geraghty, another writer. They'd come into the living room and Eddie would say, "Now, shall we have a few cocktails?" He had a cocktail shaker to hold about a gallon. He'd shake up the martinis and they'd start their story conference. In about an hour, they'd be telling stories about the time they did this or Jack Pickford did that and Tommy Meighan did the other. By that time, I'd be off upstairs, reading a book. But I would hear the conversation getting farther and farther away from what they were going to do the next day. We would wind up all going to a supper club.

The next morning, Eddie would get up and put on a red tie. He used to say, "When I put on a red tie, people don't notice that my eyes look like two Venetian sunsets." Then the building would have to be moved again. . . .

I sat in the projection room many, many times with producers, looking at new films. They didn't have the slightest idea of what they were looking at. Gangsters, chorus girls—if it was their favorite subject, they liked it. Gambling, prize fights, horse races—those are the things they loved themselves.

That little guy in the tight coat sitting behind the big desk with a couple of hoodlums standing on either side, with guns to defend him—that was the life!

When I worked a little bit for Harry Cohn, at Columbia studios, there was an office set, a street where they ran cars up and down, a penthouse, and a night club. You could make all of Cohn's pictures in those days on those four sets. Just get some guys in tight black coats, the cars, the guns, the babes—and start shooting.

When I worked in night clubs, and in the theater, I knew all the real gangsters. Men like Capone. They were the most disgusting, idiotic boors. But, oddly enough, they had one great talent. During Prohibition, they owned a lot of night clubs and they would hire people for these clubs that nobody else would have. A girl like Helen Morgan, for instance; nobody wanted her. She had a delicate little voice, she had very long legs, she had a large bosom, which wasn't fashionable then; she wasn't very animated, and she sat on the piano and wouldn't use a microphone. The gangsters loved her. They put her in a night club called The Backstage, and all of a sudden Ziegfeld "discovered" her.

Nobody could compete with the amount of money made by the producers and executives, because one of the chief sources of their income was absolutely impossible to trace. When Otto Kahn was elected to the board of directors of Paramount, he tried to find out what "overhead" meant. After a production was budgeted, the producers would simply add a figure for overhead. At that time [1928] an Eddie Sutherland production would cost three hundred and fifty thousand dollars. The producers would add to that anywhere from thirty to fifty thousand dollars overhead. The cleverest accountants working for a brilliant financier, Otto Kahn, could not find out where the money went.

Do you know my favorite actress? The person I would be if I could be anyone? You'll never guess. She worked at Universal. She came in with talkies. She was very special in her appearance, her voice was exquisite and far away, almost like an echo. She was an excellent actress, completely unique. She killed herself. She had an Irish name and she was married to a very famous agent and producer, Leland Hayward. Margaret Sullavan. This wonderful voice of hers —strange, fey, mysterious—like a voice singing in the snow.

Another element that is very important to me: clothes. A woman's clothes are not only the key to her personality and her pretensions and aims, they give you an instant image of a period, its morals and manners. History at a glance. I had to go to Berlin and Paris to find directors who understood that costumes and sets were as important as actors and cameras.

Maybe that's why people like von Sternberg's old films. They are wonderfully exciting to the eye after looking at westerns, and spies in offices, spies in beer joints, spies rolling broads over beds. Or those goddamned ugly war pictures. This is surely the age of ugliness.

Dietrich's clothes in *I Kiss Your Hand, Madame* were fantastic. What she couldn't wear she carried. She was big, strong, and she naturally had the energy of a bull. Sternberg tried turning her into a Garbo. He stopped her dead and posed her. Every time I see her pictures, I ask myself, 'What in hell is she thinking about?'' And I remember von Sternberg's story about one scene. He said to her: "Count to six, then look at that lamp as if you could no longer live without it."

And you can see that she would do these things. In true acting you never think of what you're really doing—it's just like life. Right now, I'm thinking of seven different things and so are you.

Did you know I made a picture with Roscoe Arbuckle when he was directing a series of shorts called *Windy Riley*? This one was *Windy Riley Goes to Hollywood*. He was working under the name William Goodrich. He made no attempt to direct this picture. He sat in his chair like a man dead. He had been very nice and sweetly dead ever since the scandal that ruined his career. But it was and to find my director was the great Roscoe Arbuckle. Oh, I thought he was and to find m ydirector was the great Roscoe Arbuckle. Oh, I thought he was magnificent in films. He was a wonderful dancer—a wonderful ballroom dancer, in his heyday. It was like floating in the arms of a huge doughnut—really delightful.

The moment I heard I had to work with a certain director, no matter what I thought of him, I was sold. And as long as that picture was being made, he was wonderful. I think actors who fight with directors during a picture have everything to lose. It's *their* faces they're going to see on the screen, not the directors'.

Wallace Beery used to scheme all day to figure out ways to get my back to camera in two-shots. Billy Wellman said to me, "Don't let him do that to you." I said, "I don't give a damn what he does. You're the director. If you don't want him to back me up, you tell him." The result was that he'd have to take close-ups of me to get my face in the picture. So I'd be in a close-up while Wally would be in a two-shot!

I think the auteur theory of *Cahiers du Cinema* is crap; I read the first English issue. It took me two hours and three dictionaries to get through the Bazin auteur article to find out what everybody has known since the beginning of films: that some writers and some directors are jealous of the stars' glory and the auteur theory is just another attempt to wipe the stars off the screen with words. And the silliest yet devised. After a film is finished, words can't help the poor director; and a great director doesn't need them.

"I was standing with one of the exponents of this sort of stuff in the lobby of the Dryden Theatre at Eastman House, watching a film in the theater through the glass doors. I said, "Who directed it?" He said "I don't know." To me, that was incredible. He himself had selected the film to be shown to a group of people up from New York. The first thing I want to know about a film is who directed it.

Looking through an old dictionary with the flyleaves pasted with quotes from Goethe, I came upon this one: "The novel [film] is a subjective epic composition in which the author begs leave to treat the world according to his point of view. It is only a question, therefore, whether he has a point of view. The rest will take care of itself."

33 / GERALDINE FARRAR

To call the legendary Farrar a motion-picture star is like referring to Winston Churchill as a painter. She was first and foremost a great opera singer. Her performances were invariably greeted with wild enthusiasm; she was pursued by adoring young student fans, known as Gerry-flappers.

She was born in Massachusetts in 1882;[1] her father, Sid Farrar, was a celebrated National League baseball player. Geraldine made her debut in Berlin in 1910, and became a leading member of the Berlin Opera and the Metropolitan Opera Company, New York. In 1915, Morris Gest and Jesse Lasky persuaded her to enter films. In his autobiography, *I Blow My Own Horn,* Lasky suggested that Miss Farrar's acceptance was due to the fact that she had seriously overstrained her voice. "Be that as it may," he wrote, "she proved the most charming, gracious actress I ever brought to Hollywood, and was completely devoid of temperament, contrary to the tradition of prima donnas. If the script called for her to be in mud up to her waist, or with clothing, skin, and hair fireproofed for burning-at-the-stake scenes, she didn't demur for an instant."[2]

Miss Farrar, at eighty-two, confirmed Lasky's description. She had no hauteur, none of the mannerisms attributed to once great stars. She was warm and talkative, and her sense of humor left little doubt of her Irish parentage. The meeting was arranged by Agnes de Mille, a close friend since Miss Farrar's first days in Hollywood; we drove out to Miss Farrar's home in Connecticut, and spent an afternoon in March 1964 recalling what she called "those wonderful days."

GERALDINE FARRAR: It was vacation time for me. I was in silent pictures and I could save my voice. The pantomime fascinated me particularly; we used our faces, our eyes, and projected *ourselves.* We put on our own make-up and our own costumes. You have to be very careful with hair styles, because everything was shot out of sequence, so you had to know where you were; shot twenty-two had to match with shot three forty. I'll never forget *Joan the Woman* [1916]. Mr. De Mille was very worried about my safety in the battle scenes, and particularly about the effect of all the smoke on my throat. At one point I was up to my waist in mud, wearing heavy armor and carrying a sword. Mr. De Mille had two men holding something over me to prevent things falling on my head. However, they weren't always in the right place at the right time. . . . I remember slipping off a ladder in my armor, which was made of aluminum silver and weighed eighty pounds.

I was always frightened of horses, and couldn't ride at all. They gave me a superb white horse; the animal immediately knew that I was an amateur and was less than gallant. In Griffith Park, it ran away with me and I was rescued, petrified, by Jack Holt. I saw myself falling on my spiked helmet, being pinned down by my heavy armor, and being stuck there with my feet in the air. They supplied a double, Pansy Perry, for the long shots. But how I hated riding! "Prepare to mount!" they'd shout, and I'd groan, "Not *again* . . ."

I remember overhearing two cowboys discussing me. One of them said, "I've never seen her on the screen, but they say she sings. I know damn well she can't ride a horse."

There was an aura of mysticism attached to *Joan the Woman.* It was before

[1] *Miss Farrar died March 11, 1967.*
[2] *Jesse Lasky (with Don Weldon):* I Blow My Own Horn (*London: Victor Gollancz; 1957*).

Reginald Barker directing Geralding Farrar in The Turn of the Wheel *(1918). Percy Hilbur, center.*

Geraldine Farrar in Carmen *(1915), directed by Cecil B. De Mille.*

the war; later my esquires actually went to France. The cowboy who played St. Michael captured six enemy soldiers and saved his gun position. He never came back. Another went to Rheims; he wrote to say that he had just been through something exactly like the assault we'd made at Orleans. He said that a *curé* he'd been talking to couldn't understand his interest in the historical aspect of it all. Another man was actually killed at Compiègne, the battle he'd fought in for the film. The thrill of having taken part in the event, having used the weapons and worn the costumes, made a deep impression on them.

I went into motion pictures because the European war had closed the opera houses there. Morris Gest had seen me as Carmen, and since Famous Players was taking theatrical people at the time, he suggested I make a motion picture of it. It was wonderful—arduous, but wonderful. The worst part of it was the dreadful white make-up. It was terribly hot, and the Klieg lights made it worse. In no time at all the make-up was streaming down your face, and back you had to go to make it all up again. You kept getting Klieg eyes—an inflammation caused by arc-light dust[3]—and you spent most of your time trooping down to the infirmary. The Kliegs were a great nuisance. You'd make the most inspired gesture, the arc would sputter, the light on your face would flicker, and the shot would be ruined.

I thought De Mille was a genius, and I was very fond of him. He would never shoot you in close-up against white, and he would never allow a moving background behind a close-up. He wanted all the attention focused on the expressive moment.

My blue eyes photographed blank.[4] I was horrified at the first day's rushes, but he solved the problem. A man held up a black velvet strip. When I stared at it, my pupils dilated. He was a genius at solving that sort of problem.

William de Mille wrote the scripts—*Maria Rosa,* magnificent; *Carmen; Joan the Woman; The Woman God Forgot; Temptation; The World and the Woman* . . . Cecil De Mille directed them, all but the last—that was directed by Frank Lloyd. He was always good on sea pictures; he later did *The Sea Hawk* and *Mutiny on the Bounty.* I liked him as a director, but he had better luck with ships than with people.

Cecil De Mille loved Wagner and always wanted to do *The Ring.* He was so considerate. In *Joan the Woman,* I was confined to the cell. He said he'd like to make a suggestion. If I didn't like it, he wouldn't go ahead, but he'd like to put it forward. He wanted to take some white mice, paint them brown, and have them run over me. Well, he was so nice about it, I couldn't refuse. And I told myself, if I live through this, let's hope he won't want a retake.

De Mille seldom did more than one take. He explained the scene, but never demonstrated it. Everybody improvised. The trouble with *Joan the Woman* was that the sword alone was almost impossible to handle. The standard, flapping in the wind, was three and a half yards long and had a terrific pull. I don't want to be dogmatic, but a girl with a Hollywood diet couldn't do it. You have to be sturdy to play that part.

These pictures were spontaneous. All the elements combined with enthusiasm; that was the secret of their success. When pictures eventually moved inside studios

[3] *Klieg eyes, it has since been found, were caused by ultraviolet rays.*
[4] *Orthochromatic film was not sensitive to blue.*

they lost the large horizon, they lost the ability to capture the best moment of our largely improvised performances. There was too much machinery. On our pictures, there was a great feeling of life.

California, you see, was a dream. The people were kind and generous—but we worked hard. Not that Sam Goldwyn thought so. He always arrived by the same train, and always found us having lunch. "Don't you ever work around here?" he asked.

I told him to take another train and he'd find out. Goldwyn was a man with a great responsibility. The Famous Players studio on Vine Street was no bigger than a pie plate, yet he and Lasky and De Mille managed to make these big pictures. Extras got five dollars a day; they'd come panting in from the streets: "Any work today?" All they had to do to get extras was go on the roof and whistle.

After the films for De Mille, there was a split between Lasky and Goldwyn. I went to Goldwyn at Fort Lee, where Mary Garden was doing *Thaïs*.

Willard Mack was married to Pauline Frederick. Mack could charm the birds off a branch. Somehow, he bedazzled Goldwyn with a script for me. I was to be Panka O'Brien in a film called *Hellcat,* the daughter of an Irish lady and a sort of Pancho Villa character. He had very strange ideas in the script; I would steal into a tent, cut up the American flag, and drop the pieces in a dung heap. What about the censors? Oh, we'll worry about that later, he said. Another idea was to have me cutting the ropes that bound a man's wrists, and slashing his veins at the same time. As I say, charming—but a lousy writer.

Instead of a gay Mexican costume, I wore long calico which dragged on the ground—between sheep and cattle! It was ghastly; I had to try and shoot a gun. All I could do was to wave it from side to side trying to pull the trigger. I could shoot a gun about as well as I could ride.

Nobody was ever ready. Reginald Barker was the director; he was all right, except that he was never ready either. He was always thinking. I had a piano there, and I learned my programs, so there was no time lost.

Caruso made films, too, but he wasn't careful enough. When I told Caruso's manager that I was going back into pictures, he said, "But won't it hurt your opera?" I told him it hadn't so far. Caruso was a beautiful singer, but he was no actor. He couldn't do love interest. We used to tell him. "You sing, and we'll drape ourselves around you." In his films, they had to provide the romantic couple to support his performance.

Why did I leave motion pictures? It happened like this: I was having a dinner party for Fritz and Harriet Kreisler. It was all rather formal. The butler came up; he was old, and he creaked at the joints.

"Mr. Goldwyn wants to see you," he said. "He has a very urgent message."

Sam was looking very embarrassed.

"Have you brought the script?" I asked him, expecting to go out on a picture, and wondering why he had called at this hour. "If I'd known you were available, I would have invited you to dinner."

No, he hadn't brought the script. He kept fingering his collar nervously. It seemed he'd had a serious conversation with his bankers. He kept hedging, and seemed unable to say what he had come for.

"What's the matter?" I asked.

Finally he said that my contract had two years to go, and he wondered if we could come to some arrangement. My films were apparently not bringing in what he'd hoped. He wondered if we could alter the terms to a percentage basis. I went to a drawer and brought out a paper.

"Is this the contract?" He said it was. "Well, why don't we just tear it up?"

He was astounded. "Would you really do that?"

"Of course," I replied, "if you're going to worry about whether my pictures make money or not. I can't spend my time watching figures. Let's just tear it up."

He was amazed; he had never known anyone who would do that. The next time I saw Sam was years later, at Noel Coward's *Bittersweet,* in Boston. When we'd greeted each other, he said, quite seriously, "Why don't we make a *Carmen* with words?" I was white-haired even then, so I took it as the nicest compliment. But I said I'd save him the embarrassment.

Of all my films, I liked *Joan the Woman* the best. I have a list of abhorrences, which include microphones and records, but I don't include motion pictures. I think I liked them because they were silent. They also saved my voice. You could give yourself entirely to expression. Of course, we spoke our lines aloud. Full out. So on second thought, I suppose they didn't really save my voice much after all.

The ageless Gloria Swanson, magnificently attired in a flowing diaphanous evening gown, lay back on a couch in the Carlton Tower Hotel, London.

The television executive, transfixed by her clear blue eyes, expressed astonishment that this heroine of his youth should retain all her magic.

"The story of *Sunset Boulevard*—how much of it was your story?" he asked.

"All of it, dear," said Miss Swanson, adopting a Norma Desmond drawl. "I really *am* the greatest star of them all. But I hide away from people. I live in the past. And if you take a quick look in the bathroom, you'll find a body floating face downward right now."

The most unexpected quality about this great star is her talent for self-deprecation.

"Oh, it's been wonderful having you here," said the maid, as Miss Swanson prepared to leave the hotel.

"Thank you—how kind you are," she replied graciously.

"I've always wanted to meet you—and at last I have," said the maid.

"And I bet you were surprised at the little runt you found," murmured Miss Swanson.

Sensitive about her five feet two, she nevertheless draws attention to it. No one else ever notices. You leave Gloria Swanson convinced she is six feet two. A woman of tremendous energy and lively humor, she is a constant surprise. She is a food faddist, she supported Goldwater, and has other characteristics regarded by many as almost antisocial. But she disarms angry critics with completely frank and charming explanations for her beliefs. She has no talent for subterfuge or falsity. Despite being the most popular star of her generation, she has survived as a real person. Expecting Gloria Swanson to talk about the past betrays ignorance of one of the basic facts of the motion-picture business. For Gloria Swanson is *not* Norma Desmond—which is why she so thoroughly enjoyed playing the part. Miss Swanson does not live in the past, and it takes a great deal of persuasion to get her to talk about her career.

In fact, her career is so unique, so extraordinary, that trying to condense it would be like trying to write *War and Peace* on the head of a pin. But one episode she described throws a great deal of light on her attitude to her work and on her personal courage:

GLORIA SWANSON: Most people, even in the profession, believe that I was a Mack Sennett Bathing Girl. This is not the truth. It doesn't make any difference one way or the other—except that I still cannot swim. When they put me with Mack Swain and Chester Conklin in *The Pullman Bride,* this was the first time I ever had a bathing suit on. We went down to the beach where some publicity stills were taken. Phyllis Haver and I stood on a rock; I wore a silly bathing suit with a big bow in my hair. I hated all this. I was only seventeen, and I had no sense of humor. In those days, I was rather a prissy young lady.

I did my comedies like Duse might have done them. I guess I was one of the first deadpan comedians. I was funny because I didn't try to be funny. The more serious I got, the funnier the scene became. And I hated it all; I loathed *Pullman Bride* because it was the first time Mr. Sennett had put me in low comedy. Up to then I had been with Bobby Vernon in Clarence Badger comedies—but Vernon had been sold to Triangle. Mr. Sennett retained me—he wanted to

Gloria Swanson, Tom Kennedy, and Bobby Vernon in Nick of Time Baby, *a 1917 Keystone comedy directed by Clarence Badger.*

Thomas Meighan and Gloria Swanson in Male and Female (1919), *Cecil B. De Mille's version of Barrie's* The Admirable Crichton.

make me a second Mabel Normand. I told him I didn't want to be a second anybody, so he tore my contract up. When they tried to make me do a pratfall for *Pullman Bride* that was the end; I left.

Well, I saw a green suit in a shop window. It attracted me, but I couldn't afford it, so I felt it was about time I went back to work. Now I could have worked for any comedy company—Sunshine . . . Christie . . . Universal . . . anywhere. But I wanted to go into dramatic pictures. So I went to Triangle, where my old buddy Bobby Vernon was.

They were just starting a picture; the first shots were on location. There was some idea in this comedy about two women wearing identical hats. I played one of the women, but I couldn't keep my hat on because of the strong breeze, so I returned to the studio to get a hatpin. Why I went, and why they didn't send someone else, I don't know; maybe they weren't ready for me at that moment. Anyway, I returned to the car from the wardrobe department, clutching my hatpin, when the chauffeur said he couldn't take me off the lot. I thought I must have been fired.

I sat there, wondering what was going on, when I saw this man wearing a camel-hair coat over his shoulders. At first, I thought it must be D. W. Griffith, who always wore a camel-hair coat in this way, but presently someone came up and said that Mr. Jack Conway wanted me to go to his office.

He wasn't there, but a secretary gave me a script to read. It was a *Saturday Evening Post* story called "Smoke."[1] As I read it, I became alarmed. The main character, Patricia, was the athletic type. She rode horseback—that was all right because I had a horse of my own—and she drove a car, which I could also do. But when it came to diving off a pier, I was petrified. Part of the story required her to save the life of a man who loves her.

Suddenly I heard footsteps: Mr. Conway. I didn't know what to say or do. Here was opportunity knocking at my door: I can't say I can't swim, because they'll get another girl. I'll have to learn to swim.

Mr. Conway looked into my face and said, "Well, what do you think about it?" I stammered, "I think it's wonderful—which part do I play?"

"Why, Patricia," he replied. "The leading girl."

I said, "Why, yes, of course, I'd love to do it." And he told me to report for work tomorrow morning.

The moment I left the studio, I went straight to the YWCA, got into a bathing suit and got into the pool—at the shallow end, of course. When I looked down the deep end, I saw that the instructor was having somebody floating on her back. This was all I needed. If he wants me to do this, I thought, I'll sink; I'll go backward. My head'll go down, my feet'll go up. So as he approached me, I scrambled out of that place fast and ran. I never went back.

Well, we started the picture, and I omitted to tell them I couldn't swim. Naturally, the first scenes were interior. But the frightening moment approached—and Mr. Conway finally announced that tonight was to be the night that we'd all go down to Wilmington Docks, where the big ships came in. And I was going to have to rescue this man.

Fortunately, Mr. Conway flirted a bit with me on the way out and I thought,

[1] *Release title:* You Can't Believe Everything.

Gloria Swanson as Sadie Thompson *(1928). The marine is Raoul Walsh, who also directed the picture.*

"Isn't this nice? He likes me, so he'll be very understanding." In the front seat of the car was a young lady I'd never seen before. I thought maybe she was one of the script girls. When Mr. Conway left to set up, I said to her, "May I ask who you are?"

"Why," she said, "I'm a professional diver." Well . . . that was music to my ears. But why did they get me out here? I wondered. With that, Mr. Conway arrived and said, "We're ready for you. Now this is the scene where you see from your car this man who's in love with you. He's on his crutches, walking out on this dock, and he jumps over, trying to commit suicide. You jump out of the car, run over, pull your evening dress off and dive in and save him."

You can imagine me saving anybody. "Mr. Conway," I said. "I may swim a little, but I don't dive."

He looked at me as if he couldn't believe his ears. "But you're a Sennett Bathing Girl!"

I pointed to the girl in the front seat of the car. "She does!" I cried. "She does, she does!"

"I know," said Mr. Conway. "But you've not only this to do, you've to dive off a yacht in the other episode, and you have to do one off a cliff. . . . You'd better start now—there's so much to be done."

"Look, give me five minutes alone," I told him. I went to the end of the dock, looked into the black nothingness. There was no moon, no stars, just black, black, black. I thought, "This is the end." Then I said to myself, "If I become unconscious, at least I'll come up and float. So I'll tell the leading man that if he sees something floating around out there, it'll be me—and he's to come and rescue me." And I didn't think I was going to die anyway, so I said to Mr. Conway, "All right, I'll do it. I'm not going to die tonight."

Now I was like a prancing horse at the starting gate. I wanted to get on with it. And this man took such an interminable time to get out on the dock. He was being overdramatic, I thought. Some shipbuilders nearby muttered about "these crazy motion-picture people." We only had flares that lasted a minute and a half. After that, nothing. So I might strike my head and never come up. I might be lost underneath the piling because there was no light. But when my name was called, I went out as if I'd been shot from a cannon. I ripped off the evening dress, posed like I'd seen them posing in ads, and dived overboard. Just as I was leaving, I heard someone say, "There must be sixty feet of water there."

The last thing I wanted to do was to dive into sixty feet. Three inches and I'd have been happy—but sixty feet! While I was under water, all I could think of was sixty feet. The man had been warned to look for me—he didn't have to. I looked for him. And I swam to him. I certainly did; I swam. And all through the picture. When it was over, I was invited to a swimming party, and I was so proud of myself that I bought a bathing suit and went to the pool. It was just as if I'd been nailed to the springboard. It was only two feet off the surface, but I couldn't jump. I had to walk back feeling like an idiot. And I've never swum since.

35 / BETTY BLYTHE

The reactions of the old stars to requests for interviews was frequently startling. "I'm sorry," said Dorothy Phillips, once known as the "Sarah Bernhardt of the screen," "but I have neither the time nor the inclination to discuss the past."

Betty Blythe, legendary star of *The Queen of Sheba* (1921), was disarmingly friendly.

"How funny you should mention *Sheba* and J. Gordon Edwards," she said. "Why, I was just thinking about him over breakfast this morning. What a wonderful director! Do come round—I should love to tell you about him."

Miss Blythe was still living in Hollywood in 1964, at a house with the whimsical number 314¾ and she was still active in motion pictures. She had appeared, as queenly and elegant as ever, in the ballroom scene of *My Fair Lady,* in which she was photographed by her former cameraman, Harry Stradling. Although temporarily immobilized after a foot operation, Miss Blythe was hospitable and charming.

On the wall was a painting of her late husband, the director Paul Scardon. The Spanish-style windows looked down on to a fine panorama of Hollywood; the evening light shrouded the service stations and the motels and threw the tall palm trees into silhouette. The scene looked like something out of *The Queen of Sheba.*

Miss Blythe remembered the picture vividly; because it was her most important role, *The Queen of Sheba* still meant a great deal to her. She was selected by J. Gordon Edwards to succeed Theda Bara. The vamp cycle had ended, and he was anxious for a new style.

BETTY BLYTHE: Strangely enough, my husband and I bought a home when I returned from Europe, after *Chu Chin Chow* and *She,* and it was right across the street from Theda Bara.

Anyone she loathed in this world, I'm quite sure was me. Because I succeeded her. Well, she could succeed me now—I'm almost as fat as she was. I've been lying in a hospital bed for three months, so what are you going to do about it? These are the only shoes I can get on, but oh—you don't know how nice it is to have a shoe on again. Oh, brother!

I rated Mr. Edwards one of the finest gentlemen I have ever known. You see, my husband was an Englishman; he was just the same type. Mr. Edwards wasn't English, but he was the same gentlemanly sort of person. He was such a scholarly man, just as fine as silk.

And he had an awful lot of power. If he wanted something done, it was done—right, boom. But he had this love of the theater, love of the entertainment world. It was just part of his vibrations that he put into these wonderful pictures.

We worked side by side for six or seven months on *Sheba* and until the last day it was still "Mr. Edwards" and "Miss Blythe." We never sat around and talked or laughed. He was always thinking, thinking of the next scene: Was this right? Was that right? So one was very quiet on the set. I never went over and sat with Mr. and Mrs. Edwards, as I had with other directors.

There was something quite powerful about him. He was always watching and thinking, so I never wanted to intrude. We became friends only when the pic-

The Queen of Sheba *(1921)*.

ture was finished; I used to go to their house in New York for dinner, and they came to my house in Paris later.

He had been a very fine stage director. He had conceived the idea of *The Queen of Sheba* years before. He started writing it in hotels, traveling with a theater company from city to city. He had spent something like twenty years on it.

After finishing all the Theda Bara pictures, he conceived a completely new approach. He wanted a younger woman. Fox was on his uppers, on the verge of bankruptcy. He was a man mad for money—it was all he knew, all he could think of. It was just then that Mr. Edwards produced this idea. I don't know how Fox managed to finance it, but I do know Mr. Edwards had an interest in it.

Now Theda Bara was pretty well sold by then. She had a world public. She filled a marvelous niche in our business, in her style. The world took it—and demanded her.

I had been in California about a year; I was born out here, but I'd spent my acting days in New York. I started in the theater, and when I got great notices in Arthur Guy Empey's *Over the Top,* Vitagraph contracted me for two years. Then I decided on Hollywood.

One day my press agent, Herbert Howe, a brilliant man, called me on the phone and said, "They're casting for a queen over at Fox. I'd like to take you over this afternoon."

I remember I wore a little white summer dress and a purple thing around my hair that hung way, way down. You know, drama stuff. Probably looked pretty funny and tacky, but Hollywood's casual and I was young.

Mr. Edwards made an immediate impression on me. He looked at me so keenly, so alertly. The walls of his office were bare except for one painting—a magnificent picture of Solomon's Temple. Afterward, it was duplicated for our set.

"Miss Blythe," said Mr. Edwards, "would you kindly remark on that painting for me?"

I had been put through the works in Paris for my education in art. The curriculum had called for two days a week at the Louvre; I had had to write down exactly what I had seen and what I had felt. So I was well trained in art appreciation and understanding. I stood for a few minutes looking at the painting. I don't remember exactly what I said, but something about how its greatness and expansiveness were quite overwhelming, emotionally and historically. "They must then have been great lovers of the arts to have lived in that style."

Well, nothing else happened, and I didn't hear from him or from anyone else. Mr. Edwards went to New York—he and his wife told me what happened later, when we became good friends.

Fox said to him, "Well, we've got to find Sheba now, haven't we?"

"No," said Mr. Edwards. "I've found her—in California."

I don't suppose I was in his office for half an hour—but the discernment of that man! A feeling, I suppose, that I had been a student of the arts . . . I don't know what it could have been.

"Well," said Fox. "Get some movies she's been in."

They got my first movies over from Vitagraph. "Oh, she's terrible," said Fox. "Look at this . . . look at that . . . *that* could never play a *queen!* What are you talking about, Jack?"

"Never mind," replied Mr. Edwards. "That's my Sheba. But I'll play ball with you, Mr. Fox. I'll do anything you want to do."

So they started to photograph every woman, even the great Geraldine Farrar. I don't know if Mr. Edwards thought she was too old by then, that she didn't

J. Gordon Edwards and John Boyle during the making of The Queen of Sheba *(1921).*

have the warmth of youth, but he held his ground. Fox saw more films, brought over thousands of stills of me from Vitagraph. He was still completely opposed to having me.

Of course, I spent these five months on my knees, praying for this part. I was working nearly all the time, too. It was always in my mind, but no communication came whatsoever.

Then one morning, at my apartment in the Hollywood Hotel, the phone rang; a voice said that Mr. J. Gordon Edwards would like me to have a screen test tomorrow afternoon, made up at three o'clock. But first I had to be in wardrobe to select my gown.

A test! Even that far gave me hope. My glory be, I was palpitating like a wild deer. At the wardrobe department, I was introduced to Margaret Whistler.

"Here are your thirty-six gowns for the part," she said. "You may choose. I'll leave you completely on your own."

I chose one with a great peacock. I'm mad for peacocks; later we had twenty-two of them on our ranch in the country. When you walked in this costume, which had pearls to the knees, the legs would come out. When you stood still, there was that glorious peacock right across the body. "Oh," I said, "the peacock—that's my deal." Maybe it was luck; I don't know anything about luck.

With the costume went a long train—miles of it. It went all over the wardrobe room.

"Walk," said Margaret Whistler. "Walk, and watch yourself." So I went way back, and walked toward a long mirror. And I saw my body. I saw my legs, my torso, my long, long arms. I said, "Is that I?"

Well, I'd washed and bathed it and walked and fed it and put it to bed at night all my life. But I had never looked at my body as a piece of statuary. So much for those two years at the Louvre!

I had this marvelous feeling; it was most extraordinary. I can still feel the chills all over my body.

"Talk about the ugly duckling!" I said. And I thought: "Why have I got a medium like this? Where has it been?"

That afternoon I was made up and on set at two o'clock. The actor who played Solomon was there—Fritz Leiber. The wonder of J. Gordon Edwards, that he chose Fritz Leiber. With his great height, and the classic modeling of his face, he could have stepped right out of biblical times.

Fritz Leiber escorted me to the throne. "Ad lib this," said Mr. Edwards. Since Leiber was a marvelous Shakespearean actor, he read a Shakespearean phrase to me. I received it in silence, and then replied in some sort of poetry which sufficed for expression, and for the contact that was so important between players.

The scene ended; while we were waiting for the lights to be changed, Sol Wurtzel, who ran the Fox Western studios, came over and said, "Miss Blythe, we will let you know in about three days. It's very nice of you to come over and go through this."

I said, "I'm very grateful, Mr. Wurtzel."

We worked on for a couple of hours. Mr. Edwards by now could see how well we wove together. We were both tall, Leiber and I, both artistic people, and it was just sort of right.

At the end of the test, Mr. Edwards asked me to sit down for a few minutes.

I was there about half an hour. Mr. Edwards had tea brought to me, but we didn't talk. He was around, doing things.

Then Sol Wurtzel came over with the contract in his hand. He handed me a pen.

If you could imagine what I felt. This was the most coveted role in the country. There wasn't an actress in New York they hadn't tested. Even the great ones, like Jane Cowl. Everyone in Hollywood was grinding their teeth for the part.

I should imagine that J. Gordon Edwards was about sixty at this time. Of course, I was young; maybe he just looked older to me than other men I knew. He used to take two hours for luncheon, during which time he would go to his lovely home in the hills and lie down and rest. So I imagine he was around sixty then.

He directed more by feeling than by what he said. Chairs would be brought up for his wife and himself, and we'd start our rehearsal.

"Now we're going to play the love scene. This is your position . . . your thrones are here. . . ."

He'd watch carefully as we read our lines—lines taken direct from the Bible.

"No, no—not that way, Miss Blythe. Come back—let's try it again."

Gradually, he would weld us with rehearsals. I'll never forget the love scene. My! We were just *wrung* when it was over. We were both of us trembling. Edwards had that effect upon one. Under his direction, depth and sincerity came to the fore—and all of your knowledge of screen etiquette.

He never talked during a shot; he left us to it. But he always had a five-piece orchestra on the set. For the beginning of the picture, we had to go down to Laguna, up on the topmost peak of the highest rock. The water would hit the rock below, and spray would fly over us. And right behind me, there was the five-piece orchestra! Mr. Edwards would never suggest what music to play; he would say to an assistant, "Ask Miss Blythe if she wants a change." I was very fond of Brahms. I was a singer, and had had music training, so I knew what I wanted. I was fond of *Thaïs* and arias from operas.

The wonderful thing about Mr. Edwards was this: no matter how dramatic it was, it was never hammed.

Sheba sent word to Solomon that she was sending him a gift. She would like to accompany the entourage and see him again, but for the moment she wishes him to accept the gift. It was their child.

They shot that from so far back, the cameras were practically on Vine Street. They crept slowly forward, trucked slowly toward the little boy. He's only five years old, and about this high, but as he sees Solomon he makes a tiny movement with his arm. Then Mr. Edwards cut to the close-ups of Solomon as he says, "Our child!" It was great drama.

The picture had great spectacles. The chariot race was really thrilling. Vashti, the heavy, was played by Nell Craig, and she was insanely jealous—not of me, of the part. Oh, brother! She loathed me as no woman has ever loathed another. I couldn't win her over, I just couldn't. But she was a very good actress.

I had four white horses, and she had four black horses. I had great strength in my legs and my feet. Of course, they had a man down on the floor of the chariot in case anything went wrong. And did those horses tear! It seemed like

The arena set from The Queen of Sheba. *Tom Mix supervised the chariot race.*

Solomon and Sheba see their dead child brought back to life. Fritz Leiber and Betty Blythe in The Queen of Sheba.

we were going through the air—flying. The horses get a feeling of competition.

Then Nell Craig was pulled forward by their power. She had beautiful hands, but there was no strength in them. She broke three ribs. So they had to put in a double; one of the men dressed up in her costume, and we carried on with a marvelous chariot race. It really was a race. The audiences in New York stood up with excitement. Tom Mix organized the horses . . . they wouldn't speak of it to me, but several were hurt.

There were some terrific night scenes, with hundreds of soldiers. I wasn't permitted to be there that night, because I wasn't in it, but there were at least a hundred trained swimmers and stunt men jumping from great ridges into water. Bodies were flying through the air like popcorn. Mike Miggins was Mr. Edwards's assistant director. He was a character of the world, and as clever as anything. He had been with Mr. Edwards through the Theda Bara films, so that if a mass formation was needed, he could do it very well.

Our farewell scene was tragic drama done in the stillest form of suffering. We were standing way, way down one of the great rooms of the court. As the cameras started to grind, Mr. Edwards called "Action," and we just looked into each other's eyes. Then I walked slowly with the little boy right to the very edge of the great doors and then hesitated. I turned around and with my back full upon the audience I just raised an arm and stood there. And he did the same. No blubbering, no weeping, none of that stuff. We just knew the timing because we were both emotional people. And finally, I brought the hand down and turned, just looking into the years ahead without him. I put my arm around the child. I didn't look at him. I just looked into the ages I would have to spend without this great love.

Mr. Edwards had his handkerchief out. Miss Whistler heard him say, as he wiped his eyes, "That can never again be made like that. Cut. Everybody go home."

Everybody went home. It was three in the afternoon. . . .

We were to go over to Italy to make *Pelleas and Melisande* and *Pygmalion.* Mr. Edwards had five all laid out to follow *Sheba.* He went over and had all these great sets made and then that man Fox did him in about me. He ruined his career and he ruined mine. I was to have gone right on as Theda Bara had gone, with one great production after the other. Mr. Edwards returned to this country and his whole flash of genius as a director just went to ashes. I don't know the details, except that the blame lay with Fox. Now I just carry in my heart the love of this beautiful thing—*The Queen of Sheba.*

J. Gordon Edwards's obituary, in *Photoplay* 1926, states that he died on Christmas Day, 1925. "He was about to check out from the Plaza Hotel, Manhattan, to start for Hollywood, and make another stab at re-entering pictures. Edwards had been a big director. Yet the last time he visited Hollywood hunting for work he couldn't get a chance. He was about to start out again on Christmas Day. He was 58 and jobless. A broken heart. They called it pneumonia."[1]

Edwards is a lost name of film history. None of his films survive. Only some fascinating stills suggest the quality of the productions. His grandson, Blake Edwards, is an important Hollywood director. But the name of J. Gordon Edwards is scarcely even a memory.

[1] Photoplay, *March 1926, p. 34.*

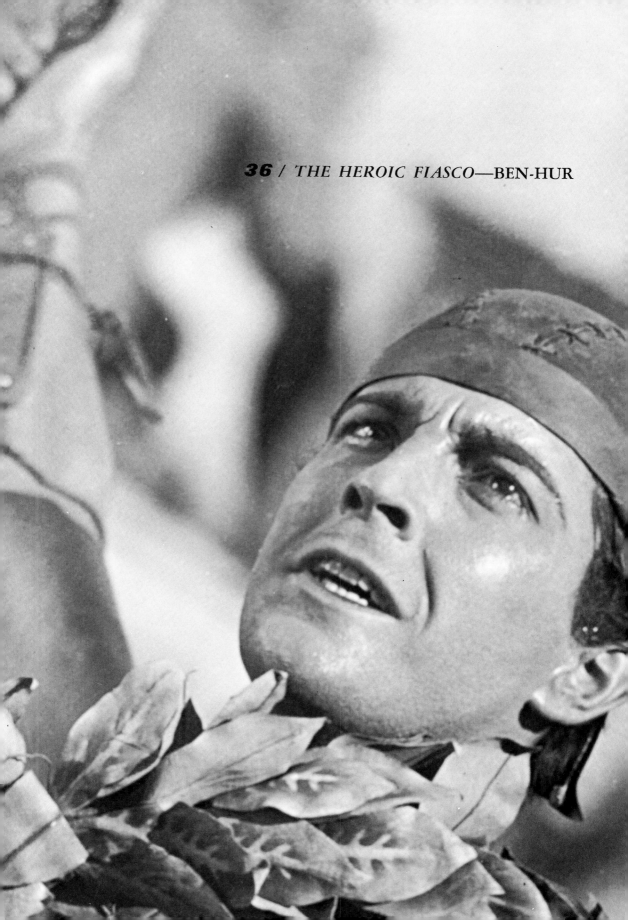

Courage displayed under controlled conditions, is impressive enough. Under conditions of chaos it becomes heroic. The technicians and players who worked on *Ben-Hur*—enduring seemingly endless hazards, and supporting men who were bewildered and confused—displayed courage on a level almost unparalleled in film history. They established the production as a sort of Dunkirk of the cinema: a humiliating defeat transformed, after heavy losses, into a brilliant victory.

Ben-Hur was a project of impressive proportions from the beginning. General Lew Wallace spent five years writing the book and, although he expressed doubts about its financial success, he lived to see it break all publishing records and achieve the largest single sale of any book, apart from the Bible.

Ben-Hur was the first work of fiction to be blessed by the Pope; while this honor assisted sales of the book, it presented an insuperable obstacle to the ambitions of theatrical producers. General Wallace announced that for religious reasons he would permit no dramatization of the story. Mark Klaw and Abraham Erlanger, America's most celebrated impresarios, persisted doggedly for nine years. When the General finally relented, he confronted them with a number of unusual clauses, among them a stipulation that if the play was not performed every season the rights were to lapse.

The original production opened in November 1899 and cost $71,000 before the curtain went up. Dramatized by William Young and staged by Ben Teal, it ran for a year on Broadway. The scale was immense, with elaborate crowd scenes and vast choruses, intricate lighting effects, a sea rescue, with stagehands positioned in the wings, shaking lengths of cloth to simulate waves—and a chariot race, with two horses pounding a treadmill while a painted panorama of the Circus Maximus revolved behind them. Ben-Hur was played by Ernest Morgan, Messala by the future star of westerns, William S. Hart. Later William Farnum, another future motion-picture star, replaced Morgan in the title role.

The spectacular elements were subject to constant improvement; the two horses became five, then eight . . . for a long time, *Ben-Hur* could only be performed in eight cities, which had theaters large enough for the mammoth production.

In 1905, General Wallace died; *Ben-Hur,* now on tour, was regarded as the most profitable production in theatrical history.

The motion-picture business, however, had advanced little further than the Kinetoscope. No film could challenge the stage play in either story or production value. But *Ben-Hur* was a magical title, and when a chariot race was staged, as an added attraction to a fireworks display at Sheepshead Bay, director Sidney Olcott of the Kalem company seized the opportunity of producing a version for practically nothing.

"I took a cameraman and a couple of actors down to the track and shot the race," said Olcott "A reel of interiors added to this and presto, *Ben-Hur* was screened!" [1]

The little film was released in 1907: "Sixteen magnificent scenes with illustrated titles, positively the most superb motion-picture spectacle ever made." Harper and Brothers, the publishers of the book, and Klaw and Erlanger, producers of the play, promptly sued Kalem for breach of copyright. Kalem, filled

---

[1] Motion Picture Magazine, *Feb. 1925, p. 100.*

Charles Brabin directing on board the pirate galley at Anzio, 1924. The young man with his back to camera is Basil Wrangell.

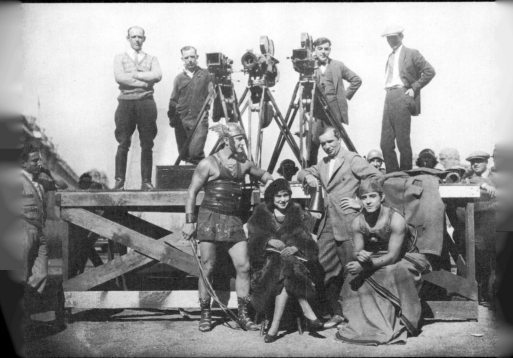

Reaves Eason with megaphone, Francis X. Bushman with whip, Ramon Novarro, seated. On parallel, Percy Hilburn, first cameraman on chariot race. Third man is Jay Rescher.

with righteous indignation, stoutly defended their film as being a good advertisement for the book and the stage play. Motion-picture rights had never been discussed before, and the test case dragged on until 1911, when Kalem, conceding defeat, settled for twenty-five thousand dollars.

Not long afterward, in 1913, the first motion picture to seriously rival *Ben-Hur* opened at the Astor Theater, New York: the Italian *Quo Vadis?,* which shared with *Ben-Hur* both the religious and the mystical elements—*and* the chariot race.

In 1915, Griffith's masterwork, *The Birth of a Nation,* was released and the heart-stopping excitement of its Ride of the Klan somewhat tempered the thrill of *Ben-Hur's* treadmill-pounding horses.

Now the motion-picture industry began to pursue the property. Henry Wallace, however, proved as much of a stumbling block as his father, whose distaste for the stage was reflected in Henry's attitude to the screen. The same religious scruples were presented as an excuse, and it was not until 1919 that Wallace's stubbornness was overcome by the winning enthusiasm of Douglas Fairbanks.

Through the show-business grapevine came the hint that Wallace would dispose of the entire property for four hundred thousand dollars. Abraham Erlanger was galvanized into action. Anxious to maintain the validity of the stage rights, Erlanger had carefully kept to the letter of his contract; revivals of *Ben-Hur* had taken place, as stipulated, each season. While he owned the theatrical rights, he considered himself first in line for the film rights, which he then intended to sell for a heavy profit. But now that Wallace seemed willing to sell, other producers expressed interest: Adolph Zukor, D. W. Griffith, Marcus Loew. . . . Soon every major company had made some kind of an approach to the property.

Erlanger instigated some swift moves. Linking his resources with those of Florenz Ziegfeld, of the famous *Follies,* and Charles Dillingham, he formed a company—the Classical Cinematograph Corporation—whose sole object was to purchase the rights to *Ben-Hur* and sell them again for as high a price as possible. In 1921, the Classical Cinematograph Corporation bought the rights for six hundred thousand dollars—and Erlanger offered them for sale for a million dollars.

This huge figure flabbergasted the industry. The property was now out of reach of everyone. *Intolerance,* the biggest picture ever made, had not cost that much—and to pay a million before a foot of film was shot seemed an absurd proposition. But the unfulfilled potential of a film of *Ben-Hur* nagged like toothache at the business instincts of major executives.

William Fox, with a cavalier sense of showmanship, produced the lavishly mounted *Queen of Sheba.*

The following year, 1922, Frank Godsol, the financier behind the Goldwyn company, found a solution to the problem. He needed a prestige subject, but clearly could not hope to raise the required million. Instead, he shrewdly suggested to Erlanger that the Goldwyn company be entrusted with the property. They would produce it to a guaranteed standard—"a caliber equal to *Birth of a Nation, Orphans of the Storm,* or *Way Down East*"—and they would divide the profits equally.

Erlanger was amenable to this unprecedented arrangement, but he laid down strict conditions. Following General Wallace's practice, he insisted on full control over everything—director, cast and scenario writer—and he demanded approval of the final show print. He repeated the stipulation that the figure of Christ should not be shown—that it should be suggested by a shaft of white light. The Goldwyn scenario department replied that a shaft of white light could hardly be expected to play a dramatic part for three whole reels. . . .

While the two parties wrangled over negotiations, the Goldwyn company's all-powerful head scenarist, June Mathis, took the next positive step forward by winning the confidence of Mr. Erlanger. Miss Mathis, responsible for the scenario of *The Four Horsemen of the Apocalypse*, and for the casting of Rudolph Valentino, was one of the most important figures in the industry. Breaking with Metro, who had produced *The Four Horsemen*, she and Valentino had signed with Lasky. Following a dispute, she had been tempted over to Goldwyn by Frank Godsol's offer of an enormous salary and autonomous control. A woman of indomitable strength and energy, Miss Mathis threw herself into this new task with an enthusiasm that ground to dust all obstacles and objections. Her word was law, and her first decree was that the picture should be made in Italy. A number of Americans had produced pictures in Italy, notably J. Gordon Edwards, whose *Nero* company encountered many of the obstacles that were to cripple *Ben-Hur*.

A committee of two men was sent to Rome to reconnoiter the possibilities; Major Edward Bowes, vice-president of Metro and later of radio fame, was accompanied by J. J. Cohn, a studio account executive.

With business-like objectivity, Cohn ignored the scenery and concentrated on facilities. He concluded from what he saw and from what he was told that Italy, from a film-making point of view, was an uncharted wilderness.

Major Bowes, however, was of a different mind. According to a witness, he was easy prey for the rapacious Italians. They were determined to lure this huge production, with all its accompanying benefits, to help bolster their unhappy economy. They took one look at Major Bowes, and they knew they had their man. J. J. Cohn was all set to recommend that the picture be made in Hollywood. Major Bowes, however, had been out to dinner with some Italian film representatives. He returned to the hotel room three sheets in the wind, and threw on the bed the contract to make *Ben-Hur* in Rome.

Miss Mathis had won the first round. Over her choice for director and star, however, the Metro executives were still indecisive.

Anxious to supply proof to Mr. Erlanger of their high artistic intentions, they postponed a decision while they sifted through the work of every major director, and made tests of every possible actor.

Miss Mathis continued her work on the project, supremely confident in both the power of her position and the wisdom of her choice. She allowed one or two close friends to know the names she wanted; George Walsh to play Ben-Hur opposite Francis X. Bushman's Messala, and she intended that Charles Brabin should direct.

Rumors about the latest contenders enlivened Hollywood gatherings for months; Valentino seemed the obvious choice for Ben-Hur, but after his angry dispute with Famous Players–Lasky, he had walked out of the studio. His contract with Lasky prevented him from working for anyone else.

The Goldwyn company tested John Bowers, Robert Frazer, Antonio Moreno, Edmund Lowe, Ramon Novarro, William Desmond, Allan Forrest, and dozens of others, including Ben Lyon.

"June Mathis sent over to First National and said they wanted to test me," said Ben Lyon. "When the powers-that-be told me, I said, 'This is ridiculous. I can't do Ben-Hur. My ribs are showing—I'm skinny. I haven't been eating very regularly . . .' But they insisted that I go over, so one night I went to the Goldwyn studios, and into their make-up room. When I took off my clothes, the make-up man almost laughed. I looked like a greyhound coming out of Trap Four. The make-up people said, 'Well, we'll have to do something about it. We'll *paint* muscles on you.' They began to shade the body and arms to give slight light and shadow to make me appear more muscular. Then the make-up man's assistant got a brilliant idea: 'I know how we can make him look tougher; spray oil on him, like you do on the beach!'

"So they did—and I went on to the set to make my test. They had tremendous lights there, and it took them fifteen minutes to light me. By the time they were ready to shoot, all my muscles had run, so I didn't get the part. I ended up Ben Lyon instead of Ben-Hur."

For a short time, cowboy star Charles "Buck" Jones was being seriously considered; his histrionic ability was in doubt, but Hollywood admitted gleefully that if he couldn't act, at least he could drive a wicked chariot. Virginia Pearson, an early-day vamp, was expected to play Iras.

Herbert Howe quipped: "It looks like *Ben-Hur* might win the *Photoplay* Medal for being the best picture of 1940, if there isn't a world war in the meantime. We have a tip on the actor who will finally get it. It's Jackie Coogan. Our sleuths in Hollywood report that Jackie spends several hours every day driving his scooter in training for the big chariot scenes."[2]

One of the few important roles to be assigned without argument went to Francis X. Bushman, the great lover of the early days of pictures. Paradoxically, Bushman was not overjoyed.

"They didn't ask any questions, they just offered me the part. But I'd always played a hero, and I was afraid of it. I went to Bill Hart, who'd played Messala on the stage for years, and I said, 'Bill, do you think I ought to do this filthy Roman?'

" 'Frank,' he said, 'that's the best goddamned part in the picture.' He told me how they once got him to play Ben-Hur, and he got sick, longing to be back playing Messala. So he sold me on it, and I accepted."

Bushman tried hard to persuade Valentino, his next-door neighbor, to take the title role. "What if I do that?" answered Valentino. "Where can I go after Ben-Hur? I have no place to go but down." He himself strongly favored Antonio Moreno for the part.

Over at the Metro studios, a young actress named Carmel Myers found herself being scrutinized by a business-like woman from behind the cameras; the woman introduced herself as June Mathis, and arranged for her to have pictures taken in various Egyptian costumes. From these stills—no motion-picture tests were made—Carmel Myers was given the role of Iras.

[2] Photoplay, *May 1923, p. 57.*

The man who originally expected to direct *Ben-Hur* was Rex Ingram, director of *The Four Horsemen,* and a close friend of June Mathis. So keen was he on the subject that he had a clause inserted in his Metro contract. He was to direct *Ben-Hur;* if the property was bought by another company, Metro would still give him permission to make it.

"While we were making *Where the Pavement Ends,*" recalled Ingram's cameraman, John Seitz, "Rex received word that *Ben-Hur* was going to be made without him. This made for a sudden change in his personality. Everything had been going so well and he was having his way in almost everything. This came as a great shock."

Ingram's star, Ramon Novarro, confirmed the fact that Ingram was very upset. "Marcus Loew himself had promised him the picture. His reaction, when he lost it, was a hundred per cent Irish—and you know what I mean."

"The latest report," announced James Quirk in *Photoplay,* "is that von Stroheim is to make *Ben-Hur.* If so, we wouldn't be surprised if he went to Europe and rebuilt Palestine and the Roman Empire with all their ancient glory."[3]

In the fall of 1923, the winners in the *Ben-Hur* contest were announced to the waiting crowds—but there was no applause. June Mathis was the real victor, for George Walsh was to play Ben-Hur and Charles Brabin was to direct. A widespread reaction was one of dismay; George Walsh, brother of director Raoul, was physically well matched to Bushman, but as an actor he was rated little higher than the routine. Gertrude Olmsted was to play Esther.

"The cast would discourage me completely if it weren't for the fact that Charles Brabin is to direct, and he is a good director, and June Mathis is a good scenario writer—so there you are," said *Photoplay.*[4]

The choice of Charles Brabin came as a surprise, for he was not in the front rank of American directors. Born in Liverpool, he had worked in the American motion-picture industry since 1908, and had married Theda Bara. June Mathis, who had worked with him when she was an unknown actress, admired him greatly and considered his directional technique "perfect." She once said that she had selected Rex Ingram for *The Four Horsemen* only because he had worked under Brabin. For many years, Brabin had made modest program pictures, but when, in 1923, his independent production *Driven* was released and acclaimed a masterpiece, her faith in him was justified. Hollywood Cassandras, however, considered him "a wallpaper director" and predicted his failure.

Gradually, the company assembled in Rome. When Francis X. Bushman landed, Charles Brabin greeted him with the news that hardly anything was ready. "François," he said, "I won't get around to your scenes till next August." Bushman took advantage of the situation and arranged to go on a tour with his sister. Progress on the picture was so slow that he was able to visit twenty-five countries, from Norway to Africa, before being summoned to the location.

Carmel Myers was not required immediately, either; she had time enough to make a picture in Germany with Julanne Johnston and Edward Burns.

George Walsh was not so fortunate. Delighted with the prospect of raising himself in one move to the pinnacle of stardom, he agreed to a salary cut when offered the role.

[3] Photoplay, *Sept. 1923, p. 27.*
[4] Photoplay, *March 1924, p. 76.*

The original Circus Maximus set, showing the miniature out of register. In the foreground editor Lloyd Nosler.

The original Circus Maximus set with miniature in register; the upper galleries are crammed with miniature people. The same system, with improvements, was employed on the Culver City set. In the foreground the Ben-Hur editing team—the two Italian assistants, Basil Wrangell, and Lloyd Nosler.

He received neither the salary nor the treatment generally accorded a star. On the boat to Italy, he discovered he had been allocated second-class accommodation. On arrival in Rome, he was kept in the background and almost totally ignored.

June Mathis, too, received a severe shock when she arrived in Rome. She was informed that under no circumstances would she be permitted to interfere with Mr. Brabin on the set. As it happened, there was hardly any set for Mr. Brabin, anyway. Art director Horace Jackson and technical director Colonel Braden were endeavoring to build the enormous Circus Maximus and the Joppa Gate sets outside the Porta San Giovanni, close to the Appian Way, but labor disputes were making progress impossible.

Italian labor was not costly, nor was it fast. The country was in an unsettled state; since Mussolini had seized power, Socialist workers had been doing their utmost to harry the economic system by staging strikes and slowing down operations.

Mussolini was much admired in Hollywood, where he was considered the political equivalent of Douglas Fairbanks. He had issued orders for the Americans to be given every assistance. But as soon as he realized the discrepancy between the salaries earned by studio hands in Hollywood and the rate his Italian carpenters were paid, he contrived some behind-the-scenes harrying himself.

With the big sets far from complete, Brabin, with his cameramen John W. Boyle and Sylvano Balboni, arranged to shoot the sea battle. Hoping for seventy ships, he was finally given permission to build thirty. The labor troubles had affected the shipyards too, and Brabin realized there was nothing he could do. The constant holdups gradually blurred the keen enthusiasm of the *Ben-Hur* company. Weeks of inactivity had an insidious effect on their sense of responsibility.

Francis X. Bushman visited Brabin at Anzio and was appalled to find the entire company immobilized, lying around in the sun.

"Charlie Brabin was a lovely fellow, and we were very dear friends," recalled Bushman. "He was the storyteller superb—he could describe the most marvelous picture in the most beautiful language, but he'd never do it. I was with him at Anzio for several days, and all the time he was telling stories and drinking wine. I didn't realize that out on the beach he had hundreds of extras roasting and doing nothing."

After many delays, about twelve vessels were made ready. Only two were complete in every detail; the pirate flagship and the Roman flagship. The remainder were profiles, mounted on rafts, or on existing hulls, and used as backgrounds for the scenes shot on the decks of the principal ships.

The Anzio port authorities decided that these vessels were not seaworthy and ordered them back to harbor. More work was carried out to make the ships safer, but the authorities still objected. They refused to allow the battle scene to be shot unless the ships were anchored. The cameramen were faced with creating the illusion of a full-scale sea fight while the vessels involved remained stubbornly static.

A further problem was supplied by innumerable fishing boats, which continually sailed into shot. A group of speedboats was given the job of racing out across the bay and changing the course of these little ships. In charge of the patrol was Basil Wrangell, a young Russian whose mother was Italian, and who was hired as an interpreter. He was to see longer service on the production than anyone.

Back in Hollywood, the Goldwyn company was merging with the Metro and the Louis B. Mayer companies. *Ben-Hur* was the headache transferred by Frank Godsol, who had sold out to Marcus Loew, to Louis B. Mayer, Irving Thalberg, and Harry Rapf. The new triumvirate discussed the picture at length, and they screened Brabin's rushes. Louis B. Mayer's daughter Irene remembered the screenings:

"The whole company had lost their frame of reference. There was no efficiency. The script wasn't completed and the picture had not been set up professionally. Brabin's footage was terrible. They'd got huge sets over there, but you never saw them on the film. What did appear looked cheesy. The make-up was awful, the wigs terrible. They'd lost contact with their own taste. The atmosphere was fraught, people were getting hurt, and a great deal of money was being wasted."[5]

Mayer, Thalberg, and Rapf agreed that there could be no retreat. Although they considered the existing material inadequate for the amount of money expended, they realized that the project could not be abandoned. Instead, they decided upon drastic surgery. Everything shot to date would be thrown away. George Walsh had not yet appeared, so they replaced him with Ramon Novarro, a promising Metro star who was being built up, at considerable expense, as a box-office attraction.

Charles Brabin was to be withdrawn; Fred Niblo would take his place. Of the original cast, Francis X. Bushman and Carmel Myers were retained. Harry Edington took over as production manager. June Mathis was replaced by scenarists Bess Meredyth and Carey Wilson.

Such strong measures were undoubtedly called for. What hurt the people who had worked so long on the project was not the replacements so much as how they were replaced.

Under a cloak of secrecy, rescue operations swung into action. Ramon Novarro was spirited out of Hollywood to join a train at Pasadena. He was instructed by Marcus Loew to meet press inquiries with the explanation that he was taking a short vacation.

Fred Niblo boarded the *Leviathan,* explaining to reporters that exteriors for his latest production, *The Red Lily,* had to be shot in France; from there he intended to travel to Monte Carlo for a Norma Talmadge picture.

Hollywood was convinced that he was the replacement director, but conjecture took a new turn when Marshall Neilan was seen to board the *Olympic.* For a day or two, he became the current favorite. Would he and Niblo perhaps share the job? Then someone discovered that he was journeying to France to make *Sporting Venus* with his wife, Blanche Sweet.

The party from Metro-Goldwyn, sailing aboard the *Leviathan,* included Marcus Loew, titular head of the new combine; Fred Niblo and his wife, Enid Bennett; Bess Meredyth and Carey Wilson; Ramon Novarro; J. Robert Rubin; and Joe Dannenberg (Danny of the *Film Daily*). Louis B. Mayer, who had accompanied the party to the dock, bade them farewell with a remark of optimistic jocularity: "Be sure to have a lot of camels in the picture!"

[5] *Irene Mayer Selznick to author, New York, March 1964.*

Reported *Photoplay:* "The excitement surrounding the making of *Ben-Hur* in Italy goes on, and is about as interesting to the film colony as the picture itself is likely to be."[6]

In Italy, morale had foundered. Attempting to reorganize the company at the last minute, June Mathis had offered several people the job of direction. None of them envied Brabin his immense responsibility, and all had refused. Miss Mathis herself was without authority, and her last-ditch efforts to save the film were fruitless.

Perhaps the hardest blow fell on George Walsh. "George and I used to take a run together every morning," said Francis X. Bushman. "We'd fence and box and wrestle together, and I knew him intimately. One day I read about the new plans for the picture in the *Telegraph* in the American Express office in Rome. We used to get the *Telegraph* in bundles every four or five days, and I saw this article about Novarro being signed for the lead. I went out and showed it to George.

" 'Do you know anything about this?'

" 'You know, Frank, he said. 'I felt this was going to happen. But to leave me over here for so long, to let me die in pictures—and *then* to change me!' "

In New York, Metro-Goldwyn made an interim announcement; Charles Brabin was being replaced because of illness. No mention was made of either Walsh or June Mathis.

"The great injury I incurred," said George Walsh, "was in their not announcing publicly the full facts. Unfortunately for me, the public figured that I had failed to fill the bill."[7]

Brabin quickly made the true position clearer by filing suit against Metro-Goldwyn for breach of contract; he demanded $583,000 damages. He alleged that when he arrived in Italy to start production the necessary equipment had not been provided, and that a general condition of chaos and futility existed.

June Mathis, although relieved of her post, stayed on in Rome with her fiancé, Sylvano Balboni, who had lost his job. In statements to the press she placed the blame for the disaster squarely on the shoulders of Charles Brabin. She disassociated herself from the material he had shot, and declared that while she had anticipated supervising the production herself, she had found Brabin in full authority. She added that despite her own disappointment, her chief regret had been the treatment of George Walsh.

"I had complete faith in his ability to play Ben-Hur. I realize many other people did not believe in him, but the same thing occurred when I selected Rudolph Valentino for the role of Julio in *The Four Horsemen.* Valentino justified himself, and I am confident that Mr. Walsh would have done the same thing. Actually, he was given no opportunity to succeed or fail. He was withdrawn without a chance. Indeed, Mr. Novarro was in Rome for three days before Mr. Walsh was notified that he had been succeeded in the leading role."[8]

As soon as he returned to America, Charles Brabin was signed by Colleen Moore to direct *So Big.* This success restored his prestige, and, some time later,

[6] Photoplay, *Oct. 1924, p. 36.*
[7] *George Walsh in letter to author, March 1966.*
[8] Photoplay, *Oct. 1924, p. 84.*

he was actually re-signed by M-G-M. Ironically, his association with that company ended, once again, with his replacement.[9]

"Miss Mathis reacted bravely about the take-over," said Ramon Novarro. "In fact, she told me of a dream she had had in which she had gotten hold of some object that was on fire and then threw it away. But, as we say in Spanish, 'we see faces, but we do not know what goes on in the heart.' "[1]

June Mathis was also put under contract by Colleen Moore; she died suddenly in 1927.

Late in 1924, an official explanation for the general reshuffle was issued from Culver City. "Now, so late that the act is done with poor grace and savors of an agreement in a legal settlement," said *Photoplay,* "the company explains that the merger of the Metro and the Goldwyn interests made the change of players necessary, as they had Mr. Novarro under contract, and it was good business to play him in the important role to build up his value as an attraction. Mr. Loew explains why they felt constrained to annihilate Walsh, and then wishes him good luck. But what we wonder is—will Mr. Walsh deposit the good wishes in his bank? A strange business this."[2]

July and August 1924; no shooting. Fred Niblo and Harry Edington were faced with countless pre-production problems caused by the decision to scrap Brabin's footage and start from scratch. Technicians arrived and departed with the regularity of tourists. In early September, Louis B. Mayer set out for Italy with his wife and two daughters.

Back in Hollywood, *Ben-Hur* jokes abounded; a director meets a friend on Broadway. "I'm between productions," he explains. "Which productions?" "Er— *Cabiria* and *Ben-Hur.*" Says a flapper, *"Ben-Hur* has taken so long to make— won't the costumes look a little old-fashioned?"

Rex Ingram, who had originally expected to be signed for the picture, and who had been deeply hurt when Brabin was chosen, now had his hopes crushed again. Bitterly discouraged, he announced his retirement from the screen. His retirement fortunately proved to be little more than an extended vacation; both Erich von Stroheim and Dmitri Buchowetski campaigned for his return, publicly declaring him "the world's greatest director."

When Louis B. Mayer arrived in Italy, Fred Niblo was reshooting the sequence which had brought about the downfall of the previous regime: the galley battle. The ships built for Brabin looked too small to be really impressive. They had been discarded, and the sturdy vessels which appeared in the final picture were newly built, from designs by Italian art director Camillo Mastrocinque, and were completely seaworthy.

But a worse catastrophe than any that had befallen Brabin at Anzio was to beset Niblo at Livorno. "I really dreaded leaving the shore each morning," he wrote later, "fearing that our luck could not last, that there might be an accident this day. . . .[3] He went on to point out that none had occurred, thus drawing a discreet veil over one of the most dramatic disasters in motion-picture history.

As a curtain-raiser, Niblo discovered a pile of sharpened swords concealed under some canvas on the deck of the pirate flagship. Investigating further, he

[9] *The Picture was* Rasputin and the Empress, *with the Barrymores. It was taken over by Richard Boleslavsky.*
[1] *Ramon Novarro in letter to author, March 1966.*
[2] Photoplay, *Jan. 1925, p. 92.*
[3] Motion Picture Magazine, *April 1926, p. 98.*

learned that the man casting the extras had separated the crews into fascists and anti-fascists. The sea fight would have resulted in a classic naval engagement if this had gone unnoticed.

As it was, disaster was in the air. The script called for the Roman triremes to be rammed by pirate raiders. After fierce fighting, the Roman flagship would be set alight, and extras would leap into the water. For the establishing long shot, the ship was soaked in oil so that it could easily be set afire by torches.

Both ships were crammed with Italian extras, men from the poverty-stricken areas around the location who, just for the money, had said they could swim. Few of them could.

The ramming was impressively staged. The pirate vessel was attached by cable to a high-speed motorboat which dragged it through the water and sent it splintering against the side of the Roman trireme.

It was not necessary for the ram to penetrate the hull; the effect would be achieved later by cutting inside as the galley slaves were engulfed. Nevertheless, as the pirate ship thudded against the Roman trireme, the extras were seized by panic. Many of them, appalled by their plight, dropped to their knees and implored the saints for aid.

Thoroughly demoralized, they were unprepared for real emergency. When the shots of the burning trireme were lined up, a sudden wind fanned the flames more quickly than had been anticipated. The fire spread through the whole ship, and the extras forgot their safety instructions.

Al Raboch, who was handling the crowds, tried to muster them, but few paid any attention. They poured over the side. Raboch himself was saved from injury when someone deflected a flaming timber by holding a shield over his head.

Some of the extras were supposed to leap into the water, and dinghies were standing by to pick them up. But others were wearing armor.

"I heard their cries for help," said Francis X. Bushman. "I said to Niblo, 'My God, Fred, they're drowning, I tell you!'

" 'I can't help it,' he yelled back. 'Those ships cost me forty thousand dollars apiece.' "

That evening several extras were missing. Fred Niblo and Enid Bennett, with Claire McDowell and several members of the company, stayed up all night checking the names. Eventually, there were three sets of unclaimed clothing left. An assistant director, a Frenchman with a professed loathing for Italians, took out a boat loaded with chains and weights. He intended not only to sink the clothes but any bodies he might encounter.

Bosley Crowther, in his book *The Lion's Share*,[4] describes how three men, still dressed as Roman soldiers, turned up two days later, angrily demanding their clothes. A fishing boat had picked them up and landed them farther down the coast.[5]

Opinions differ as to the casualty rate. Francis X. Bushman said that he had asked the Italian wardrobe man how many had drowned. "Ah, Mr. Bushman," was the enigmatic reply, "many costumes missing. . . ."

Basil Wrangell considered that some extras must have drowned. "Many could not swim, but had lied in order to get the job. Also, after seeing the film, I can't

---

[4] *The book contains a chapter on the making of* Ben-Hur.
[5] *Bosley Crowther:* The Lion's Share (*New York: G. P. Dutton; 1957*), p. 97.

The Jerusalem miniature. In the foreground, Lloyd Nosler.

The pirate galley rams the Roman trireme, the start of one of the most alarming episodes in motion-picture history.

Rescue boats pick up the extras.

The end of the trireme.

The Jerusalem miniature as it appeared in the film. Kathleen Key (Tirzah) and Ramon Novarro (Ben-Hur) at the moment the tile falls.

M-G-M's publicity department matted together all the elements to produce this composite picture. The border between miniature and actual set is all too obvious. However, in the film, it is undetectable. The publicity department has added spurts of dust under the chariot wheels.

see how it's possible that some weren't. In any case, this is something the studio would have kept quiet, and only those on the scene could really tell you."[6]

Among those on the scene, Ramon Novarro was certain that no one was drowned. "I was next to Mr. Niblo when this happened, and I feel I am right about my statement."

"There would have been a hell of a stink if there had been any casualties," recalled Claire McDowell's son, Gene Mailes. "It would have led to an international incident. I'm certain no one was killed.[7]

"I was on the shore, watching, as the galley caught fire," said Enid Bennett, wife of Fred Niblo. "I was helpless. All I could do was pray. I remember that one man was missing. They said Fred would be arrested if that one man didn't turn up. So M-G-M said that the Niblos must return to Rome at once, which we did. It was a scary journey. Every time a carabiniere appeared on the train we thought it was the end. I've heard it said that three were missing, but I remember one. And I remember the wardrobe man, to protect Fred, did away with his clothes and effects. When he turned up, he had to make them up to him."[8]

The galley sequence was still incomplete; for further shooting at sea, strong safety precautions were taken, and a diver was assigned to the company. "Just to rescue the costumes," was the cynical view.

The abrupt curtailment of the battle scene, however, forced M-G-M to resort to model shots for the missing angles. This miniature work was handled by Kenneth Gordon Maclean.

For the galley interiors, a pool was built, thirty feet deep. The depth—and the water—was necessary to show the galley slaves' view of the ramming; the hull was to be gashed open, and tons of water were to pour over the helpless slaves, while the camera swung violently from side to side.

While digging, the construction crew breached some ancient catacombs. "Oh, my God!" cried the frantic production manager. "If Mussolini ever hears about this . . . if the museum people ever hear about this . . . we're done for."

The catacombs had to be waterproofed. This meant delay, and further unbudgeted expense. But the company discovered to their delight that the whole area was rich in Roman remains. They were soon energetically digging up archaeological rarities, some of which proved to be two thousand years old.

Meanwhile, the main unit was filming the raft scene, out in the Mediterranean, exposing the elderly actor Frank Currier, as Quintus Arrius, to the bitter winds and the icy water for almost four hours at a stretch. Novarro, who shared this endurance test, saved him from pneumonia only by slapping him constantly, between takes, and pouring into him generous doses of the brandy sent over from the camera boat.

"The shooting of the raft scene took three full days," said Novarro. "They could have used doubles since the raft started a good mile from the camera."

In the film, Currier looks deathly pale, and is shivering plainly. (The 1958 version of *Ben-Hur* avoided such rigorous demands on its players by staging the scene inside the studio, with a painted sky backdrop.)

Fred Niblo was working under immense pressure; and dealing with crowds of Italian extras, few of whom could speak a word of English, was sometimes

[6] *Basil Wrangell in letter to author, Feb. 1966.*
[7] *Gene Mailes in tape to author, Sept. 1966.*
[8] *Mrs. Sidney Franklin to author, Palm Desert, April 1967.*

more than he could stand. Normally an urbane and charming man, he lost control at one point. Francis X. Bushman walked off the set.

"I was through. I wouldn't have him doing that. Why, Italians are born actors. You don't have to tell them what to do. They could have told *him*. But he wanted it done differently, and he began to throw things at these men, women, and children. That made me mad."

Fred Niblo's wife, Enid Bennett, was the epitome of tact and diplomacy. Niblo's dogged single-mindedness was offset by her disarming charm and genuine concern for the welfare of the company. She persuaded him to apologize, and shooting was resumed. Those who worked on the second stage of *Ben-Hur* acknowledge their gratitude to Miss Bennett and the stimulating effect she had on morale.

Despite the praise which other American units had expressed for Italian technicians, the *Ben-Hur* company found it impossible to locate a competent Italian electrician. Eventually, a group of electricians were imported from Vienna, and the lighting unit was built on the spot.

Horses were also a problem. Some superb white steeds, ideal for the chariot race, were found in Bulgaria, but their owner had another offer. Each bid made by Metro-Goldwyn's representative was countered by the unknown competitor. The price kept rising. Finally, inquiries were made; and the other bidder proved to be an agent of the Pope. The Pope got the horses.

Carmel Myers, who had been one of the few to enjoy the inactivity of the Brabin regime, discovered that now Niblo was in charge, things were beginning to hum. "It had all been divine. My mother and I lived in the Excelsior Hotel, and we used to go sightseeing. The Italians adored us—we'd brought a lot of money with us— and we adored them. We made a great many friends. When Mr. Niblo took over, we talked about the costumes for my role as Iras. He told me he wanted me to have the most exciting headdress ever seen on the screen. I was a bit bewildered; hairdressers usually do this for you. 'Where do I—what do I. . .'

"He dismissed me. 'Go find it,' he said.

"My mother and I had a little conference, and she decided to go back to Vienna, the city of her birth, where the most exotic and stylish women used to come from. We toured the hairdressing parlors there, and in one of them I discovered this white silk wig. That headdress was considered very startling. It sort of made history."

The constant warring between fascist and anti-fascist was turning *Ben-Hur* from a motion-picture enterprise into a political bloodbath, as savage as anything in Roman history.

Said Fred Niblo: "It's as though a crowd of Republicans and a crowd of Democrats were to start hurling hammers, rivets, boards, or any other weapon at the other faction."

The Colosseum set was still not complete. Apart from the political riots, work had been delayed by the attitude of the Italian laborers.

"One day I came on the Colosseum set and saw about five hundred workmen sitting on the ground," said Bushman. "I got mad, and I tackled the foreman. 'You promised to have this arena ready in seven weeks and here it is seven months and you haven't finished yet.'

" 'Well, Signor Bushman,' grinned the foreman. 'We have no work when this is finished. Why should we work ourselves out of a job?'

"I knew it was Mussolini who was causing all the trouble," added Bushman. "He'd get this crowd to strike one week, that crowd to strike the next."

By the time the Colosseum set was finished, the days had shortened and the autumn sun stayed low. It was now impossible to obtain even lighting conditions.

Shooting the chariot race against daunting odds was second-unit director, B. Reaves Eason. Chosen for his proficiency with horses, Eason was a director of low-budget westerns. Although Fred Niblo had nominal control over the material Eason shot, he had nothing to do with the actual direction. Eason was able to spend a considerable time covering the chariot race while Niblo was completing other sequences. *Ben-Hur* had been planned like this from the beginning; Brabin was to have handled only the intimate material with the main stars; Italian and German second-unit directors were to have been simultaneously shooting the mob scenes.

Eason was a remarkable man. While his westerns were adequately shot, they revealed none of the genius for action which he was to display with this scene— and with the land rush in *Cimarron* and the charge in *The Charge of the Light Brigade*. An expert horseman, he was ruthless in obtaining the effect he wanted. The death toll of horses in Rome was alarming. As Francis X. Bushman said, "They never had a vet attend any horse. The moment it limped, they shot it. There was a guy named Cameron who rented them. I asked him how many we were losing. 'Oh,' he said, 'about a hundred.' "

In America, surveillance by the SPCA was keen, and the casualty rate fell dramatically. (But in Eason's sequence of *The Charge of the Light Brigade*, 1936, the carnage was so appalling that special legislation was passed to protect animals in future productions.)

Interviewed toward the end of his life, Eason explained his attitude toward the direction of action scenes: "You can have a small army of people charging across the screen and it won't matter much to the audience. But if you show details of the action, like guns going off, individual men fighting or a fist hitting someone in the eye, then you will have more feeling of action than if all the extras in Hollywood are running about. That is why real catastrophes look tame in news-reels. You need detail work and close shots in a movie. Only then does it come alive."[9]

Securing this detail work took four months. Eason tried to shoot the scene in Rome, but he had to admit defeat. The lengthy shadows restricted the field of vision, and the surface of the racetrack itself was far from satisfactory.

"During one take," said Bushman, "we went round the curve and the wheel broke on the other fellow's chariot. The hub hit the ground and the guy shot up in the air about thirty feet. I turned and saw him up there—it was like a slow-motion film. He fell on a pile of lumber and died of internal injuries. We found the ruts around the curve of the Spina were too dangerous."

This was not the only accident. On another occasion, Bushman's chariot was racing behind Novarro's when Novarro made an uncertain move and turned

[9] *Ezra Goodman:* The Fifty-Year Decline and Fall of Hollywood (*New York: Simon and Schuster; 1961), p. 300.*

the wrong way. At once, Bushman's chariot crashed into it and rode over the wreckage. Everyone was convinced that Novarro had been killed, but although one of the horses had died, Novarro was uninjured. The superstitious stunt men put his miraculous escape down to the power of the scapulas he wore on his costume.

"Ramon didn't really have the right technique," said Bushman. "He held the reins like he was on a carriage. You've got to *wrap* that stuff around your wrist, jam your feet up against the front, and lean straight back. That's the only way you can turn the horses, because they're running away. All the noise is exciting them—forty-eight horses, twelve chariots—and no springs in them, either."

The Circus Maximus set saw the entire cast and crew only once—when the King and Queen of Italy made a tour of the *quadrero*.

"It was the coldest day I ever lived through," recalled Carmel Myers. "We all lined up out there and stood for an hour or more waiting for the King, the Queen, the Prince, and Princesses to come by. None of us knew what we were supposed to do when they *did* arrive."

No one had told Francis X. Bushman about the visit, and he drove up in an open car, in the full regalia of Messala, ready for work. Seeing the crowd, he told his driver to continue. Acknowledging the multitude with an imperious gesture, Bushman made a grand sweep around the arena and disappeared.

The rest of the arrangements went hopelessly awry, in true *Ben-Hur* tradition. The royal family met neither the cast nor any of the distinguished visitors, such as Norma Talmadge, Julanne Johnston, and Loro Bara, sister of Theda, who had made a special point of attending that day. The royal cortege swept straight past. Novarro swore he would put in for an extra day's pay—until another royal vehicle passed with the Princess, who recognized him, bowed, and smiled.

"That saved you five dollars," Novarro told the business manager.

The retreat was sounded in January 1925, hastened by a fire which swept through the property warehouse.

Irving Thalberg had regarded the entire Italian expedition as an act of economic madness from the outset, but Loew, Mayer, and the other executives held on to the hope that the Italian investments would be recouped. Mayer had run into a severe altercation with Fred Niblo, and had left for a tour of Europe.

Before leaving, however, he had arranged for Basil Wrangell, who was now Mr. Mayer's personal interpreter, to run him all the best European pictures. Wrangell translated the titles to enable Mr. Mayer to follow the story. One of these pictures was Mauritz Stiller's *The Atonement of Gosta Berling*. During his tour, Mr. Mayer signed up Stiller and his protégée, Greta Garbo.

Wrangell, on Mayer's departure, was transferred to the cutting room, to assist Lloyd Nosler. Nosler, who had worked with Niblo on several pictures, had replaced Brabin's editor, Aubrey Scotto, and was confronted with two girl assistants (Irene Coletta and Renata Bernabei), neither of whom could speak English. Wrangell's knowledge of Italian had won him yet another job.

Most of the sets were struck, but the Circus Maximus was left standing, in the hope of returning to complete the chariot race in the spring. Eventually, Thalberg managed to scotch even that idea.

"When archaeologists unearth Rome in years to come," said Fred Niblo, "and chance upon the ruins of this great set, they will say, 'Ah, how great was the civilization of those days.' "[1]

M-G-M officially announced that the *Ben-Hur* company had sailed on January 17, 1925—and by declaring that all work possible abroad had been completed, they turned a retreat into a tactical withdrawal. They admitted, however, that weather conditions had not been favorable, but added that the film was practically complete; it would be finished in Hollywood by the first of March.

Remaining behind until early February were the cutting staff. Basil Wrangell was the only foreigner retained by M-G-M and invited to America. "This was because we had catalogued and canned about a million feet of exposed film and, outside of Nosler, I was the only one who knew where to find it. This cataloguing was quite a job, but believe me, it saved a lot of time after we got to the final editing. During my first year in America, I worked on this picture; I never got home before midnight and had only two Sundays off. It was a hard way to meet and see a new country."

Encouraging news brightened the horizon for the homeward-bound veterans; Sid Grauman, the famous exhibitor, had contracted to show *Ben-Hur* for a solid year at his Egyption Theatre, at a minimum profit to M-G-M of three hundred thousand dollars. The Knickerbocker, in New York, had been leased for a two-year showing.

James Quirk said in *Photoplay* that there was little doubt that when the picture was finally released it would be exploited with a full use of superlatives: "The Greatest Story of All Times," "The Sweetest Love Story Ever Told," "Masterpiece Supreme," and, perhaps, "The Picture Every Christian Ought to See."

"Not only every Christian," he added. "Every Mohammedan, every Hebrew, every Buddhist, and every Sun Worshiper in America will have to buy a ticket for it, if the picture is to make money. At least seven and a half million dollars will have to come through the box office before M-G-M will receive a cent of profit. We have to excuse them, then, if they use up every adjective in the dictionary, the *Encyclopaedia Britannica* and a full library of crossword-puzzle books. It's just got to be a good picture."[2]

Conscious of the attention of the world, Metro-Goldwyn-Mayer were acting in the grand manner. Despite the expenditure of more than three million dollars, they continued to lay out extravagant sums on an impressive scale.

Now that the Circus Maximus set in Rome was to be written off, a new one had to be built in Culver City. Cedric Gibbons, M-G-M's chief art director, and A. Arnold Gillespie designed it, following the example of the Italian set, and combined carefully-matched miniatures with the full-size construction.

With the company working on home ground, assisted by skilled Hollywood technicians, it was fervently hoped that the *Ben-Hur* jinx might be lifted. Such hopes were rapidly dashed.

No sooner had building started on a large vacant lot behind the M-G-M studio than the City of Los Angeles decided to start digging a huge storm drain on that very site. M-G-M construction crews arrived to find a steam shovel demolishing their set. Frantic telephone calls revealed that more wrecking equipment was on the way.

---

[1] Motion Picture Magazine, *April 1926, p. 98.*
[2] Photoplay, *April 1925, p. 27.*

An alternative site was eventually found at the intersection of La Cienega and Venice Boulevards. Eight hundred men worked in shifts; after four months, Breezy Eason was able to resume the chariot race sequence.

Saturday was a Roman holiday for the film colony. Among the thousands who crammed the Circus Maximus were stars of the magnitude of Douglas Fairbanks and Mary Pickford, Harold Lloyd, Lillian Gish, Colleen Moore, Marion Davies, and John Gilbert. Sid Grauman was there to speculate on the last stages of his investment. Directors, too, turned up en masse; Reginald Barker, a fine action director himself, George Fitzmaurice and Henry King, both of whom had recently worked in Italy, Sidney Franklin, Rupert Julian, and Clarence Brown.

Since this was to be the most spectacular moment in an epoch-making picture, Fred Niblo arrived to superintend operations from a high platform. B. Reaves Eason and his assistant Silas Clegg, continued directing from ground level.

Forty-two cameramen were hired for the event. Their cameras were concealed in every position that might yield an effective angle. They were hidden behind soldiers' shields, concealed in the huge statues on the Spina, buried in pits, mounted on overhead parallels . . .

The crowd was split into sections, and each section was under the control of an assistant director. Urgent calls had gone out for extra assistants, and among those who had offered their services was a young man from Universal, William Wyler.

"I was given a toga and a set of signals," recalled Wyler. "The signals were a sort of semaphore, and I got my section of the crowd to stand up and cheer and to sit down again, or whatever was called for. There must have been thirty other assistants doing the same job. People have said that I was the assistant director on the entire sequence, but that's all I had to do."[3]

Thirty-four years later, Wyler was to direct M-G-M's second version of *Ben-Hur*.

There were twelve chariots and forty-eight horses. Stunt men drove ten of them, and Bushman and Novarro rode their own for this special day. The stunt drivers were range riders, polo-pony breakers, and circus men, as well as being movie doubles. To ensure a real, hell-for-leather, no-punches-pulled epic race, a special bonus was offered to the winner. The fact that the race was fixed for Ben-Hur didn't matter; the day was being devoted to establishing shots with massed crowds. Ben-Hur could win another time.

The incentive given the stunt men stimulated the crowd as well. Once the bets were placed, the assistants no longer worried about whipping up general excitement.

This Saturday was more in the spirit of a carnival rodeo than a filming session. The stunt men put on an astonishing display. During the opening race, a horse-shoe flew off one of the chariot teams, hurtled past a camera stand and narrowly missed some spectators. Anxious assistants tried to persuade the crowd to sit down, but the excitement was too intense. By the next race, which was enlivened by a spectacular pile-up, the crowds were responding like the audience at the original Circus Maximus, in Antioch.

[3] *William Wyler to author, London, July 1963.*

At the end of the day, Douglas Fairbanks and Harold Lloyd fought a mock duel with spears, and then the crowds of extras trooped out of the arena, as exhausted as the charioteers themselves.

This one big day had been so impressive that many assumed the sequence was finished. But Eason and his crew spent weeks working in an empty arena on the complicated details of the race—close-ups of racing wheels, thundering hoofs, flaring manes, flexing muscles, and lashing whips. Despite precautions, the inevitable mishaps occurred. When a rescue team of four black horses set out to drag a wreck clear of the arena, Eason arranged for other chariots to flash past them, to increase the excitement. Alarmed by these oncoming chariots, the rescue team panicked and crashed into a camera platform. Eason, who was standing underneath, saved himself by diving between the horses.

In the film, Messala's wheel is wrenched from its axle by Ben-Hur's chariot. Messala crashes, and the other chariots, tearing at breakneck speed around the Spina, cannot avoid him. One ofter the other, they pile into the wreck, beneath which lies the battered Messala. Ben-Hur races on to victory.

"M-G-M convinced everyone that not a horse had been killed," said Francis X. Bushman. "In that big crash, those stunt men drove straight for the wreck. They knew what to do, and although there were some scratches, and a little blood here and there, none of the men were hurt. Everybody saw the men were okay, so M-G-M say, 'Think of it—not a horse touched!' But there were five horses killed outright in that one crash."

The crash had been planned for a certain turn where ten cameras were positioned. The axle had been sawn through with such careful precision that it broke at exactly the right point.

"The last day we raced," said Bushman, "I was anxious to get home for Christmas. The horses were all wet, and we were pretty exhausted. All of a sudden, smoke bombs went off, pistols were fired, and all hell broke loose. It was our farewell. We shook hands all around, and do you know?—there were tears in our eyes. We had been through so much for so long. . ."

The forty-two cameramen had shot fifty-three thousand feet of film on the big day, but editor Lloyd Nosler had to cope with two hundred thousand feet altogether for this one sequence. On the final show print, the chariot race ran to seven hundred and fifty feet.

But those seven hundred and fifty feet are among the most valuable in motion-picture history. For this was the first time that an action director, realizing the potential of the cinema, had possessed courage and skill enough to fulfill it.

Ben-Hur opened at the George M. Cohan Theater, New York, on December 30, 1925.

"The reception was all the director, stars, and producers could have wished," reported *Photoplay*. "Ramon Novarro, Francis X. Bushman, May McAvoy, and Fred Niblo and Enid Bennett all came from Hollywood to attend the premiere. But Ramon had bad luck. He had contracted a slight cold on the train, and arriving in New York was ordered to bed at once where he was obliged to stay throughout his entire visit East.

"The others attended the opening and were greeted with tremendous applause.

Ramon Novarro with victor's laurels.

For the first time in picture history, the blasé Broadway audience forgot itself so far as to cheer madly during the chariot race.

"Fred Niblo was rushed at the finish of the picture, and it looked as if he'd never get out of the theater. A hundred friends wanted to congratulate him. He apologized for the dampness of his palm, which was plainly caused by the nervousness he felt waiting for the picture's reception."[4]

The reviews were equally encouraging. *Photoplay* thought the picture justified the four million dollars and the years of work. "*Ben-Hur* is not a flat picture upon a screen. It is a thing of beauty and a joy for ten years at least. This is a truly great picture. No one, no matter what his age or religion, should miss it."[5]

Motion Picture Magazine agreed that it was a masterpiece, but felt that it had faults—the faults of motion pictures as a whole. "Under the spectacle," wrote critic Agnes Smith, "it has little brain and not much heart. It pleases your eye without touching your soul. Except for Miss Bronson's scenes and Mr. Novarro, it astonishes you rather than moves you."[6] Miss Smith singled out the fine titles of Katherine Hilliker and H. H. Caldwell for especial praise.

Reactions outside America were, on the whole, rapturous. But Mussolini was infuriated by it. He had imagined that Bushman, the superb Roman, was to have been the hero. When he saw the Roman defeated, he banned it from Italy. The picture was banned in China as well. "*Ben-Hur* is Christian propaganda decoying the people to superstition, which must not be tolerated in the present age of revolutionary enlightenment," ran the edict.

[4] Photoplay, *March 1926, p. 49.*
[5] Photoplay, *March 1926, p. 54.*
[6] Motion Picture Magazine, *March 1926, p. 49.*

The total negative cost was just under four million dollars. The picture grossed more than nine million, but the distribution costs, and the fifty per cent royalties to Erlanger's Classical Cinema Corporation, left M-G-M with just over three million —a million less than the film cost to make. The prestige value, however, was inestimable.

When it was all over, an M-G-M executive remarked with justifiable cycnism: "Nothing like it ever has been. Nothing like it ever will be. And nothing like it ever should have been."

Ben-Hur was reissued with music and sound effects in an abridged version in 1931. The abridgment did not help it, and it was cold-shouldered by talkie-struck audiences who thought it old-fashioned. The picture disappeared and the title passed into legend. *Ben-Hur* as a film had proved as ephemeral as the stage play, and it survived only in the memories of those fortunate enough to have seen it.

In the late fifties, however, a print was rediscovered in America. At the same time, M-G-M's second version was nearing completion, under the direction of William Wyler, and the company had taken stringent precautions to ensure that no copy of the original was in existence. To their indignation, just as the Wyler version was premiered, they discovered the celebrated film collector William K. Everson holding a rival premiere of the Niblo original. M-G-M alerted the FBI, and Everson learned that a jail term was a threatening possibility. Being a distinguished motion-picture historian, he was saved by the last-minute intervention of Lillian Gish, who testified on his behalf. The case was dropped.

M-G-M's anxiety to suppress the original was not due to any fear of comparison. Few of the company's employees had seen the 1926 version. They merely wanted to remove obsolete merchandise to clear the way for the new product. They wanted, too, to prevent any unauthorized exploitation which might harm the new release.

But Everson's point had been made with the maximum effect, even though he was projecting a battered 16mm mute copy of the sound reissue—that *Ben-Hur* (1926) was superior to *Ben-Hur* (1959). Undoubtedly one of the best epics ever made, the original has retained its impressiveness. The performances are remote and theatrical, but their dignity ideally fits the sagaesque quality of the story. The picture, being the achievement of an organization rather than the work of one man, is not consistent. But it is like a great art gallery, in which one or two halls have been emptied for redecoration. You walk through them without complaint, certain of other treasures to come. Passages in *Ben-Hur,* particularly some of the interior dialogue scenes, are unexciting and exist merely to propel the narrative. But such scenes do not impair the effect of the film as a whole; *Ben-Hur* carries almost as powerful an impact today as it did on its release.

The chariot race stands out as the finest scene in the picture, followed closely by the galley battle. The worst elements are the vamp scenes, which are dated and ridiculous and would have seemed foolish in 1926. The Technicolor nativity scene, with Betty Bronson as the Madonna, is a garish example of the commercial art of the twenties, and is as esthetically offensive as a neon advertisement in a church. Fred Niblo refused to be associated with this scene, which was directed by Ferdinand Pinney Earle, but his objections were directed more against the idea of Miss Bronson as the Virgin Mary than against the design. Miss Bronson's exquisite serenity is the sequence's saving grace—but nothing could compete with her shimmering Technicolor halo.[7]

The film has a stronger period feeling than the 1959 version, although the women remain true to Hollywood tradition and mirror the period of production rather than the era of the story.

The make-up required by orthochromatic film leaves the players strangely pale; there are no olive skins or tanned complexions. Since the story takes place in the countries of the Mediterranean. where the climate is hotter than California's, the white faces are a real drawback to conviction.

The opening sequence splendidly evokes time and place with a light-hearted touch which, unhappily, never reappears. Ben-Hur is introduced with his back to the camera, watching a column of Roman troops. As he turns toward us, we track back with him through the crowd. Esther (May McAvoy), sitting on a donkey, is playing with a dove which suddenly flies from her hand. It flutters down near Ben-Hur, who leaps forward to rescue it from the trampling feet of the crowd. But his sharp movements frighten the bird, and it flies off again. Ben-Hur, aware of the beauty of its owner, gives chase. The dove alights in the most dangerous spots. Horses' hoofs brush past it, cartwheels nearly crush it. Eventually, Ben-Hur removes his skull cap, creeps up behind the bird and pounces. . . . He returns the dove to Esther, and, as he takes his leave, she strokes the bird tenderly with her cheek. This interplay of drama, comedy, suspense, and romance is very well directed.

The Joppa Gate sequence, one of the few Italian exterior sequences to survive, is also impressive. The columns of troops pass; a man spits as the mounted centurions canter by. The governor is very fat, and is crowned with a laurel wreath. Standards flutter in the wind. From the roof of his palace, Ben-Hur and his sister Tirzah lean forward to get a better view. A tile is dislodged from the wall. It falls. Hold his reaction. Then cut to a high angle from the other side of the road; there is a commotion, but we cannot see exactly what is happening. A close shot reveals that the Roman governor has been struck on the head by the tile. Soldiers charge up to Ben-Hur's palace; we cut inside, the door bursts open in close-up, and soldiers pour in. Behind them, Messala rides arrogantly in on horseback.

The galley sequence opens with shots of the seven Roman triremes under full sail. Then a title: "Stately and beautiful, but under the beauty, deep-locked in the heart of each ship, a hell of human woe." The camera tracks slowly toward the hortator, who is keeping time with hammer blows; behind him is a naked slave, pinioned to a whipping block, his back scarred with lash marks. In time to the rhythmic hammer blows we cut to shots of the galley slaves heaving on their oars—first in close-up, working back to extreme long shot, while the camera tracks closer and closer to the relentless hammers.

Suddenly, one of the slaves goes berserk and tries to bite through his chains. He is beaten with whips, while one of the slaves calls out, "He is dead, but still they lash—and lash—and lash."

A fleet of pirate vessels is sighed on the horizon. Battle stations are called. The

---

[7] *Christy Cabanne, in charge of tests, favored Myrna Loy for the Virgin Mary, but Thalberg insisted on Betty Bronson. Miss Loy was compensated with a single-shot appearance in the chariot race. Raboch's build-up to the nativity, slow tracking shots of Mary, Joseph, and the donkey, is excellent; it precedes another sequence by Ferdinand Pinney Earle of the star of Bethlehem. This looks considerably better on tinted original prints; copies tend to make it seem as artificial as the halo.*

pirate chief orders a Roman prisoner to be lashed to the prow—"I will return you to Rome, in my way"—then his ship rams the trireme. The battle is exceptionally well staged and extremely savage; the audience is not spared the sight of pirates brandishing decapitated heads, or of broadswords being plunged to the hilt. One terrifying shot shows a wounded Roman lying helpless on deck, surrounded by the snakes the pirates have been throwing. The vigorous, rhythmically cut onslaught reaches a climax with a shot of shackled galley slaves screaming as the flames engulf them. Perhaps the most remarkable shot shows a pirate ship sailing alongside a trireme, and snapping the oars like matchsticks.

The chariot race is breathtakingly exciting, and as creative a piece of cinema as the Odessa Steps sequence from *Battleship Potemkin*. The 1959 *Ben-Hur* recreated the opening of this sequence shot for shot; they managed to include many more spectacular crashes, but dispensed with some of the more striking angles of the race, such as the dramatic pit shot.

The sequence fades in on a line of mounted trumpeters, signaling the start of the event; the camera then tracks slowly behind a squadron of cavalry as it leaves the building and enters the arena. The line of horsemen advances through the huge pillars into the amphitheatre; the camera emerges with them and draws to a halt. There is a momentary pause. The horsemen continue trotting forward. Then, very slowly, the camera tilts up and reveals what appears to be the biggest set in film history, filled with the largest crowd ever seen on the screen.

For once, actuality exceeds legend. Every film enthusiast has heard about that huge set, but no one ever expects it to be *that* enormous. . . .

This is the miracle conceived by Cedric Gibbons and A. Arnold Gillespie and built under the direction of Andrew MacDonald. Having designed miniatures which would combine with the full-size set in much the same way as a glass shot, they added a triumphant master stroke; a set of galleries with ten thousand tiny people, all of whom could stand up and wave. The camera photographed miniature and full-size stand together. Since the motion picture is not three-dimensional, the perspective is destroyed, and the model appears to be an integral part of the main set. But most extraordinary of all, Gibbons & Gillespie designed the miniatures so that the camera could pan over them, and not lose register. On a glass shot, the camera has to be in a rigid position; a fraction of an inch out of place, and the painted top of a building will appear on the screen several yards away from the full-size lower half. This design gave the cameraman complete freedom, and saved M-G-M hundreds of thousands of dollars.

Other special effects are almost as impressive; the collapse of the huge Senate building, an effect for which Gillespie cooperated with Frank Williams, is a masterly example of Williams's new traveling-matte process.

The Christ motif throughout the picture is subtle and effective—far more so than the shaft of white light which Erlanger had insisted upon. The finest example is contained in Raboch's sequence of the scene at the well, when Christ's hand gives water to the thirst-crazed Ben-Hur; the motif is first seen as a hand sawing wood. Niblo uses a hand, an arm, or a footprint in later scenes. The majority of these are in Technicolor. The photography, despite the number of cameramen—Rene Guissart, Percy Hilburn, Karl Struss, Clyde de Vinna, George Meehan, E. Burton Steene—is beautiful, and the lighting is quite consistent.

Judging the performances by modern standards is difficult, because the players act in the grand manner. But the use of emphasized representation is dramatically and choreographically justified, although it prevents one becoming involved with the characters.

Novarro is remarkable. At first his style seems hopelessly dated; gradually, the electric power of his brilliance takes over.

Francis X. Bushman has the physique of a magnificent Messala, but he conveys menace in a roaring, melodramatic style which is now hard to accept.

May McAvoy, an intelligent and beautiful actress, is wasted in a role which requires little more than some innocent gazes.

Frank Currier, as Quintus Arrius, gives a careful, restrained performance which remains in the memory.

Claire McDowell, as Ben-Hur's mother, typifies the acting style. Everything she does is in the grand manner, and it *is* grand. She gives the film its most poignant moment; the scene in which she and her daughter, released from prison suffering from leprosy, return to the old Hur palace and find Ben-Hur asleep outside. She dare not touch him; instead she tenderly kisses the stone upon which he sleeps. Miss McDowell was a great actress.

Director Fred Niblo's style was usually lifeless (*Blood and Sand, Mark of Zorro*), but with the impetus of a large budget and the expectations of the world, he produced a *film,* rather than his usual series of cardboard pictures. The fact that the narrative slackens during the last third is no more his fault than the scenarists'; the chariot race, the ultimate in excitement, appears in the first half of the picture. The mood changes from bloodthirsty action to religious mysticism; this may work in a novel, but in a film it seems anticlimactic.

The editing is impeccable throughout; whenever Nosler is offered a challenge, as with the chariot race and galley battle, he surmounts it with genius. Other editors, who cut some of the smaller sequences, were Bill Holmes, Harry Reynolds, and Ben Lewis.

Ben-Hur epitomizes the skill of motion-picture technicians at this stage of film history. It proves what they could accomplish under the most arduous of conditions. Of the many production disasters since—the most notable parallel is *Cleopatra*—none have ended so victoriously as the original version of *Ben-Hur*.

Nothing like it had ever been. Nothing like it has ever been. But the film industry should be grateful that it *was* made. For while *Ben-Hur* may not have enriched its makers, it certainly enriched the technique of the motion picture.

37 / PRODUCERS

Producers are the eternal thorn in the flesh of creative film makers. Their role is as difficult to define as their contributions are hard to distinguish. They are the men who reduce motion pictures to the level of merchandise.

Some producers are responsible for the choice of material, the choice of stars, and the choice of directors. Some, like Sam Goldwyn and David O. Selznick, carried their responsibility further and, by a deep personal interest, enabled great things to happen. But the majority have little constructive part in the creative process.

They are essentially businessmen, promoters concerned only with administration and finance. This is not to denigrate their value. No industry can survive without such men, and those producers who realize their true function, and who carry it out efficiently, are indispensable. They can greatly reduce the burden or responsibility for a director.

All too frequently, however, producers use their financial knowledge to wield a dictatorial power. Feeling that they deserve a say in the artistic treatment of their productions, they try to impose their own tastes; while this may be beneficial in the case of a Goldwyn or a Selznick, it usually proves disastrous. At best, the result will be a forced compromise.

Producers are safeguarded by anonymity. Whereas the work of a director can usually be judged from the screen, the work of a producer remains a mystery. Yet his name on the screen is given the same prominence as that of the director. What right has he to accept credit for someone else's artistic achievement?

He has the right in most cases because either he or his studio has found the finance for it. Without his participation, the film might never be made. The only requirement to achieve recognition as a producer is money—for money brings its own contacts. Today, a shrewd investment can lead to a producer's being credited without his ever having worked on the picture.

In the silent days, corruption was somewhat less rampant, but the same problems existed. Carl Laemmle, head of Universal, became the joke of the industry because of the number of relatives he employed. By 1927, he had fourteen.

"He had all his relatives from Laupheim," recalled Erich von Stroheim. "Most of them were unable to do anything—you took them whether you liked them or not. Some were nice, others were arrogant bastards. The first script girl I had was a niece, and a spy for the front office. If I had caught her spying, I would have thrashed her; but oddly enough—I don't know whether it was my looks or my uniform—she didn't squeal."[1]

James Quirk indignantly published the case of a conscientious studio manager who had gently remarked on the inefficiency of the family crew. Apparently he was told to mind his own business and was fired three months later.

"It is a notorious fact," added Quirk, "that these relatives have demoralized the whole studio with their family politics, and cost the company at least a million dollars a year. The minority stockholders bear it—but they don't grin."[2]

In retrospect, Laemmle appears to have been prompted more by traditional Jewish family ties than by brazen nepotism. He was a kind-hearted man, who enjoyed his power and used it to give opportunities to the young and inexperi-

---

[1] *Erich von Stroheim on tape recorded by John Huntley for the British Film Institute, London, 1953.*
[2] *Photoplay, Nov. 1927, p. 28.*

enced, and to assist charities and those friends who were in financial straits. When business associates told him his sympathies were frequently misplaced, Laemmle would shrug and say, "Well, it can do no harm, and I won't miss the money."

It was Laemmle who first recognized the talent of Irving Thalberg, and who had perception enough to overlook his extreme youth and to accept his unusual maturity. Thalberg was twenty-one when Laemmle went abroad and left him in charge of the studio.

Universal at that time concentrated on quantity, and the studio was a seething mass of activity. To offset its factory reputation, the company sank its resources into "specials"; *Blind Husbands,* directed by Erich von Stroheim, brought Universal wide prestige and von Stroheim was given carte blanche for his next production, *Foolish Wives.*

Appalled by his extravagance, Thalberg stepped in to try to curb von Stroheim's enthusiasm. At first, he was not successful. Shooting had continued for a year, and the budget had reached unparalleled proportions when Thalberg made his most courageous—and unpopular—move: one night, in Westlake Park, von Stroheim's cameras were physically removed and shooting ceased.

Thalberg and von Stroheim were to do battle over several pictures, and many observers felt that their disputes epitomized the eternal struggle of art versus commerce. The true situation was not so clear-cut: von Stroheim was a brilliant director, and Thalberg recognized his brilliance. He was also wildly extravagant, and it was Thalberg's job to curb his excesses. It is doubtful whether von Stroheim would have received such freedom, and such costly concessions, with another organization. A story told at M-G-M describes Thalberg's reaction as he watched some rushes on *The Merry Widow*—long, long scenes in which von Stroheim had shot the contents of a baron's wardrobe—boots, shoes, slippers, shoe trees. . . .

"What the hell is all this about?" asked Thalberg.

"I wanted to establish that this man is a foot fetishist," explained von Stroheim.

Thalberg was nearly apoplectic. "You," he said, "are a footage fetishist!"

Von Stroheim was not the first to suffer from producer interference. Thomas H. Ince instituted the system, and stole credit for the direction of any film he fancied. Terry Ramsaye, in *Million and One Nights,* tells how Herbert Brenon's name was removed from the credits of his 1916 spectacular, *Daughter of the Gods,* by producer William Fox, and how the entire picture was recut. Fox, offended because Brenon was receiving all the publicity, went as far as to give orders to exclude him from the premiere. Brenon gained admittance, claimed Ramsaye, by wearing a false beard.[3]

Fox's interference, significantly, occurred *after* shooting, because at that time directors worked entirely on their own. Important directors were their own producers, handling the financial as well as the creative aspects of their pictures. Few were troubled by front-office interference, because the front office knew little about production methods.

The arrival of supervisors was a blatant insult.

"Supervisors," said Terry Ramsaye in *Photoplay,* "are supposed to guide, inspire, and encourage writers, directors, and actors. But with few exceptions, they grope about in the darkness of limited mentalities, have not a creative cell in their

[3] *Terry Ramsaye:* A Million and One Nights (*New York: Simon and Schuster; 1926*), *p. 706.*

brains, and do not know the difference between encouragement and the bully-rag."[4]

Maurice Tourneur left Hollywood rather than submit to the supervisor system. The trouble began during the making of *The Mysterious Island*.

"After four days' shooting," recalled Jacques Tourneur, the son of Maurice, who was cutting the picture, "I was present on the set when a man appeared. He wasn't a technician, and he wasn't connected with the production. He was just watching.

" 'Would you get that man off the set?' asked my father.

"The assistant director told him to leave, and he did so. Five minutes later, an irate call came from Louis B. Mayer.

" 'Did you throw —— off the set?'

" 'Of course. I can't tolerate anyone on the set,' replied my father.

" 'But he's your producer!'

" 'My what?' said my father. 'What does a producer do?'

" 'The producer supervises the entire production, and sees the dailies and makes comments and everything.'

" 'There's no such thing as a producer. I don't want one. If he steps on the set, I'll throw him out.'

"Well, next day, the producer comes on the set again. It wasn't his fault; this

[4] Photoplay, *Sept. 1927. p. 78.*

Adolph Zukor and Jesse Lasky plan the Paramount studios.

The changing face of the picture business: United Artists, 1919; D. W. Griffith, Mary Pick-
ord, Charles Chaplin, and Douglas Fairbanks (top). United Artists, 1956; the signing of th
agreement under which the United Artists management group acquired Mary Pickford'
stock interests (bottom).

was his job. My father said, 'I won't work until this man leaves the set.' And he sat down and waited. Finally, the producer left. He was very nice about it. The next day, Mayer called again.

" 'Mr. Tourneur, you must have a producer. Every director must have a producer from now on. It's the studio's new policy.' "

Tourneur walked off the set; within three days he was on the train to New York, from where he sailed for France.

Rex Ingram too, refusing to knuckle under, and remaining a sworn enemy of Louis B. Mayer, persuaded Marcus Loew to provide him with a studio at Nice.

But in Hollywood, the autonomy of the director was seriously endangered by the growing number of "snoopervisors."

"They're like goldfish," quipped humorist Irvin S. Cobb. "They can swim around with their eyes open and still be asleep."

The intellectual qualities of this unpopular species were also open to attack. "What's a supervisor?" asked M-G-M's Douglas Furber. "A man who knows what he wants, but can't spell it."

One of Wilson Mizner's sardonic remarks was even more enlightening. "An after-dinner coffee cup," he said of one producer, "would make that man a sun bonnet."

The term "supervisor" reverted to "producer," and at the end of the silent era they were firmly entrenched as part of the industry. Among them were some excellent men—David O. Selznick, who became the industry's finest independent producer and who, with Thalberg, gave the term a new dignity. Al and Ray Rockett, two enthusiasts who had produced the astonishingly successful *Abraham Lincoln;* Julian Johnson, former editor of *Photoplay;* Benjamin Glazer, writer and colleague of Erich von Stroheim; Bertram Millhauser, a veteran of serials, one of the rare supervisors who allowed the director to operate on his own. . . . But most of them were as unnecessary as they were uncreative. Hollywood summed up their value by calling them "glacier watchers"—"they stand around making sure the studio isn't engulfed by a glacier." The bitterness aroused at this time spelled ruin for many.

38 / *LOUIS B. MAYER AND IRVING THALBERG*

The producer who used his powers to the fullest was perhaps Louis B. Mayer. He is said to have finished the careers of practically all his enemies. A slight, real or imagined, would never be forgotten; Marshall Neilan's remark, "An empty taxicab drove up and Louis B. Mayer got out," ensured that his days as a top director were numbered. Mayer was sufficiently powerful to ensure that other companies, besides M-G-M, would cold-shoulder those on his blacklist.

Mayer comes out of the period very badly; history has shown him to be a childish, melodramatic paranoiac.

"But," says Clarence Brown, "everything that has been said about him has been the case for the prosecution. Louis B. Mayer was my closest friend. He was one of the greatest brains in the picture business. He made more stars than all the rest of the producers in Hollywood put together. He wasn't a producer who had anything to do with the artistic side of the business at all, but he was a great human being. He knew how to handle talent; he knew that to be successful, he had to have the most successful people in the business working for him.

"He was like Hearst in the newspaper business. Hearst reached out and took the cream of all the newspapermen in the United States and put them in his organization at a much higher salary. He made an empire out of the thing.

"Mayer went into the horse-race business as a sideline. He didn't know the front end of a horse from its hind end, so he treated it exactly like he treated the picture business. He went out and got the finest breed that money could buy. He went to South America, he went to Ireland, he went everywhere, until he worked up a stable producing horses that were finishing first, second, and third."

Objective observers have relayed spine-chilling stories of Louis B. Mayer's behavior—suddenly sinking on his knees and crying out during a discussion with a producer, bursting into tears and staging a petulant scene during a talk with another.

To expect Louis Mayer to behave with Anglo-Saxon stoicism reveals ignorance of his make-up as a person, or his background. Mayer was the best actor on the lot.

"He could play the part of any star in the studio, and play it better," said Adela Rogers St. Johns. "That's how he used to make them do it. Greer Garson didn't want to play Mrs. Miniver, so Mayer called her into his office and played the role himself. He was the best Mrs. Miniver there ever was. He was hypnotic. And Miss Garson took the part.

"Don't let anyone ever undersell Mayer. He had absolutely infallible judgment. And that's the only thing that is required of a producer. He was a fantastic man; he headed the greatest studio that ever existed, and he was the only immovable figure in it.

"Thalberg was a great creative artist, but without Mayer he could not have operated. If you think of the British War Office and the commander in the field, you have a correct parallel. Whatever the commander may achieve, he does so because the War Office supplied him with the troops and ammunition to do it with."

After Thalberg died, at thirty-six, his reputation unsullied by domestic scandal or financial failure, he was virtually canonized by Hollywood. For his was a success story previously seen only on the screen.

Mary Pickford, Calvin Coolidge, Louis B. Mayer, Cecil B. De Mille, and Will Hays; visiting day at M-G-M.

Henrik Sartov, King Vidor, and Irving Thalberg pose with Lillian Gish for a publicity picture during **La Boheme** *(1926). Sartov's matte box, the longest in the business, accommodated gauze in six positions.*

Irving Thalberg was born in Brooklyn in 1899. He inherited many of his remarkable qualities from his mother, whose redoubtable spirit brought him through a long illness. Just before graduation, he had been struck down by rheumatic fever, and forced to leave school. During that period, he read avidly, and this concentrated study proved invaluable during his motion-picture career.

As soon as he was fit enough, he did light, occasional work in a drygoods store. In the evenings, he studied typing and shorthand, and these qualifications secured him a thirty-five-dollar-a-week job as secretary to a cotton broker. He rose to the position of assistant manager of his department, but felt that the job held no future.

During a vacation on Long Island, he met Carl Laemmle, of Universal. Laemmle, impressed, offered him a job. Thalberg turned down the offer, but when he failed to find other work that interested him, he talked himself into a job at Universal's distribution office. There he was again discovered by Laemmle, who, remembering his enthusiasm and intelligence, transferred him to a secretarial post with D. B. Lederman. Thalberg, efficient, conscientious, and extremely interested in his work, was soon promoted; he became secretary to Laemmle himself. He was observant, and, fascinated by the business, he began to learn the intricacies of running a huge motion-picture concern. During conversations with his employer, he told Laemmle of his reactions to the company's products. Laemmle realized his value and when he made one of his regular visits to California, in 1919, he asked his secretary to accompany him.

Thalberg, seeing production methods of California at first hand, quickly realized the inefficiency of local management. Laemmle took charge whenever he was there, but the general manager, Isadore Bernstein, had an immense problem to face. Universal, unlike Famous Players or Metro, was not a series of studio buildings but a ranch that sprawled over four hundred acres, ideal for scenery, but difficult to manage. Trying to control Universal was like trying to control a game reserve; the studios had been operating for only four years, and jack rabbits and mountain lions still treated it as their rightful domain. Tracking down a company and rounding up lost extras was like going on safari.

Thalberg made clear to Laemmle that things could not continue as they were; when Laemmle went to Europe, he left his twenty-one-year-old secretary in charge.

Thalberg's baptism of fire was the *Foolish Wives* debacle. No sooner had that picture been completed than he and von Stroheim grappled again, over *Merry-Go-Round*. Thalberg dismissed von Stroheim from the picture, and replaced him with Rupert Julian—an act which aroused much controversy.

"This was the first time a director had ever been fired, I believe," said David Selznick. "It took great guts and courage. Thalberg was only twenty-two. Remember that a matter of hundreds of thousands of dollars in those days could wreck a company, particularly a company which was not that strong. I certainly could not defend from a creative standpoint the substitution of Rupert Julian for von Stroheim, but von Stroheim was utterly indifferent over money, and could have gone on and spent millions, with nobody to stop him.

"I can well imagine that Thalberg reasoned with him, but finding von Stroheim adamant, he had the courage to do what had to be done. I know that when he fired a director in the middle of a film, he was faced with the problem of who was available, who will step in on something they haven't prepared, to pick up shooting overnight. It wasn't easy to find a replacement, because in those days there was great resentment, and since Julian was under contract to Universal, they threw him into the breach."

Von Stroheim apart, Universal did not offer further challenge. Thalberg grew restless; a romance with Rosabelle Laemmle was not progressing and he was disappointed with his four-hundred-and-fifty-dollar-a-week salary. Following his principle, "Never remain in a job when you have everything from it you can get," he began to investigate offers from other studios. He decided to accept a post with Hal Roach, but Louis B. Mayer, who then ran his own studio on Mission Road, offered him six hundred dollars a week, and Thalberg accepted.

When Mayer merged with the Metro and Goldwyn companies, Thalberg was rewarded with a vice-presidency and a greatly increased salary. He rapidly established himself as a brilliant and perceptive mind; his opinion was sought by practically everybody on the lot. By the time he was twenty-six, he was in control of the company, producing an almost unbroken series of box-office successes.

Clarence Brown explained Thalberg's genius:

"You would be working with your writer, and you would come to this scene in the script. It didn't click. It just didn't jell. The scene was no goddam good. You would make a date with Irving, talk to him for thirty minutes, and you'd come away from his office with the best scene in the picture. That's how good he was."

Said Margaret Booth, chief editor at M-G-M, "I think he was the greatest man who was ever in pictures. No one has equaled him. No one *will* ever equal this man. He had a mind like an electric buzz-saw."

Few of those who worked for him expressed anything but the deepest respect. One of the dissenters was Eddie Sutherland, who worked at M-G-M in both the silent and sound days.

"In my opinion, the whole producer system was started by Thalberg. He would inspire us to spend all night kicking around his stories—for free. He would tell the director all the thoughts he had. Then he'd look at the result on film and decide he could do it better, and do a lot of retakes. This had never been heard of. We used to say, in the days before Irving, 'Take one shot at it. If you're no good, you'll be fired.' But the Metro system was: 'Let the producers make it till they're happy,' which is expensive, incompetent, and makes for mass regimentation of pictures. M-G-M's studios at Culver City became known as Retake Valley.

"I think that when the producer came in as, theoretically, the artistic head of production, pictures started to deteriorate."

Clarence Brown felt that Thalberg understood motion pictures, and that the retake idea was extremely valuable. He said that Thalberg never looked at rushes; he waited until the film was finished and then began his analysis.

"We always made a picture with the idea that we were going to retake at least twenty-five per cent of it. We went through and made the picture, then took it out to an audience, previewed it, and found the weak spots. We then rewrote and redid them.

"They didn't figure when a picture was complete that it was finished. That was the first cut—the first draft. It paid off in the long run. I think they made a series of the best pictures that were made in that era. And nobody has ever touched Thalberg."

When the name of Irving Thalberg first gained prominence, the movie magazines sent writers to find out his secret.

Dorothy Herzog wrote a piece in *Photoplay* which reflected the general astonishment at this luminescent new personality:

"Mr. Thalberg comes to town haloed by glamorous publicity. No man can be twenty-six years old and merit such awesome titles. A girl interviewer lolled in the anteroom.

" 'Have you seen him?'

" 'Have I seen him!' Her optics rolled upward. 'My dear, he is so wonderful. So boyish, so modest, so natural.'

"Bosh, likewise piffle, we murmured, and followed the guardian of the Miracle Man's room into 'the presence.' We failed to discover 'the presence.' Instead, a human being of medium height, slight physique, passable good looks, and extraordinarily alive eyes of brown greeted us with direct scrutiny and boyish smile.

"We introduced ourself as the girl interviewer who meets all the incoming trains. Whereupon the youth before us actually blushed. He protested mildly on being interviewed when New York was full of movie stars. The more Mr. Thalberg talked, the more intrigued we became. To us, he seemed a combined Horatio Alger hero, Peter Pan, Napoleon, Falstaff, and J. Pierpont Morgan, and we aren't being prodigal with these names simply to demonstrate how well versed we are in the classics."[1]

Agnes Christine Johnson, scenarist, exclaimed, "If he were a politician, he'd be a Mussolini; if he were a poet, he'd be a Shelley; if he were an actor, he'd be a Barrymore! He's so marvelous that no one who doesn't know him can believe it. Seeing him sitting in with all the important people, looking such a boy, and deferred to by everybody, you'd think that either they were crazy or you were. But if you stayed and listened, you'd understand. He has a mind like a whip. Snap! He has an idea—the right idea—the only idea!"[2]

Thalberg summed up his own success by saying that if you believe in a thing hard enough, and you have enthusiasm to make others believe in it, you can't fail.

"It's not so much what one man does, but what he can get from the other fellow that counts. Nine out of ten things that any man does, anybody else could do. It's the tenth thing that makes the man."

Thalberg's day lasted nineteen hours—he found he needed only five hours sleep.

"Most people sleep too much. They think they must have eight or nine or ten hours sleep, and if they don't get it, they think they ought to be tired. 'I didn't get to bed till midnight last night, and it's almost two now. I'll be worn out tomorrow,' they say, and instead of going to sleep, they worry—and drag themselves out of bed completely exhausted."[3]

Thalberg retained the habit of reading in spare moments; his favorite works were those of Epictetus, Kant, and Bacon. "They stimulate me," he said. "I'd drop out of sight in no time if I didn't read and keep up with current thought—and the philosophers are brain sharpeners."

Thalberg's skill lay in his uncanny ability to judge the pacing of a picture, and

[1] Photoplay, *April 1926, p. 66.*
[2] *Quoted in* Motion Picture Magazine, *May 1926, p. 56.*
[3] *Ibid., p. 97.*

in his infallible, intuitive skill in the placing of emotion. He drew attention to strengths and weaknesses, not by momentous announcements at company meetings but during screenings.

"He made his points by mumbling," recalled Margaret Booth. "He'd mumble all the way through, 'I don't like that bit' . . . 'I wish you'd done so-and-so'. . . . 'See what you can do with that.' I never took any notes, I just listened. No assistant ever took any notes either—no assistant ever came in when I ran with Thalberg, and I ran every day. I remembered what he said, because I knew what he was talking about."

Director Hobart Henley pointed out that Thalberg did not want pictures containing his ideas alone.

"He wants pictures with the ideas of the people who are paid for them. He wants me, for instance, to give him the best stuff I have—mine, not a rehash of his. But if something that read well turned out not so good on the screen, I go to him and, like that"—Mr. Henley snapped his fingers—"he has a remedy. He's brilliant. But he wasn't only born that way. He's on the job every second of every hour."[4]

Donald Ogden Stewart, who won an Academy Award with his *Philadelphia Story* for M-G-M and who wrote *Brown of Harvard* for them in the silent days, acknowledged Thalberg as the one real genius he met in Hollywood, Chaplin apart.

"There was a father-and-children feeling at M-G-M when Thalberg was around. You wanted to please Daddy. The best you ever got was 'that's not bad,' but coming from Irving that was as good as an Academy Award. He was Poppa to everyone. Even though he was so young, he advised people about their investments, about their wives; he felt it was part of his duty as a producer.

"He was so dedicated to his job that when he accompanied visiting executives from the East to Lee Frances' [a Hollywood bordello], he would sit in the hallway, in a rocking chair, reading *Variety*."[5]

Metro-Goldwyn-Mayer achieved, within a few months of its inception, a prestige envied by every other company. Their challenge was taken up by Paramount, which itself staged a spectacular comeback. The last years of the silent era saw the American film industry, led by these two companies, reach its peak of artistic and commercial achievement.

"Next to D. W. Griffith," said Anita Loos, "Thalberg was the greatest man in pictures. We used to have a preview every week at M-G-M. Fifty-two previews a year. And every one of them was a smash hit. We never had a dud. If a picture proved a failure in the studio, he knew how to fix it. By the time it hit the screen outside, it was great. He had a completely fresh viewpoint on everything. He never did anything that was banal or trite. I was with him for eight years and when he died, I said 'Hollywood is finished. I'm going to get out.' And I did."

[4] *Ibid., p. 56.*
[5] *Donald Ogden Stewart to author, London, Oct. 1963.*

39 / DAVID O. SELZNICK

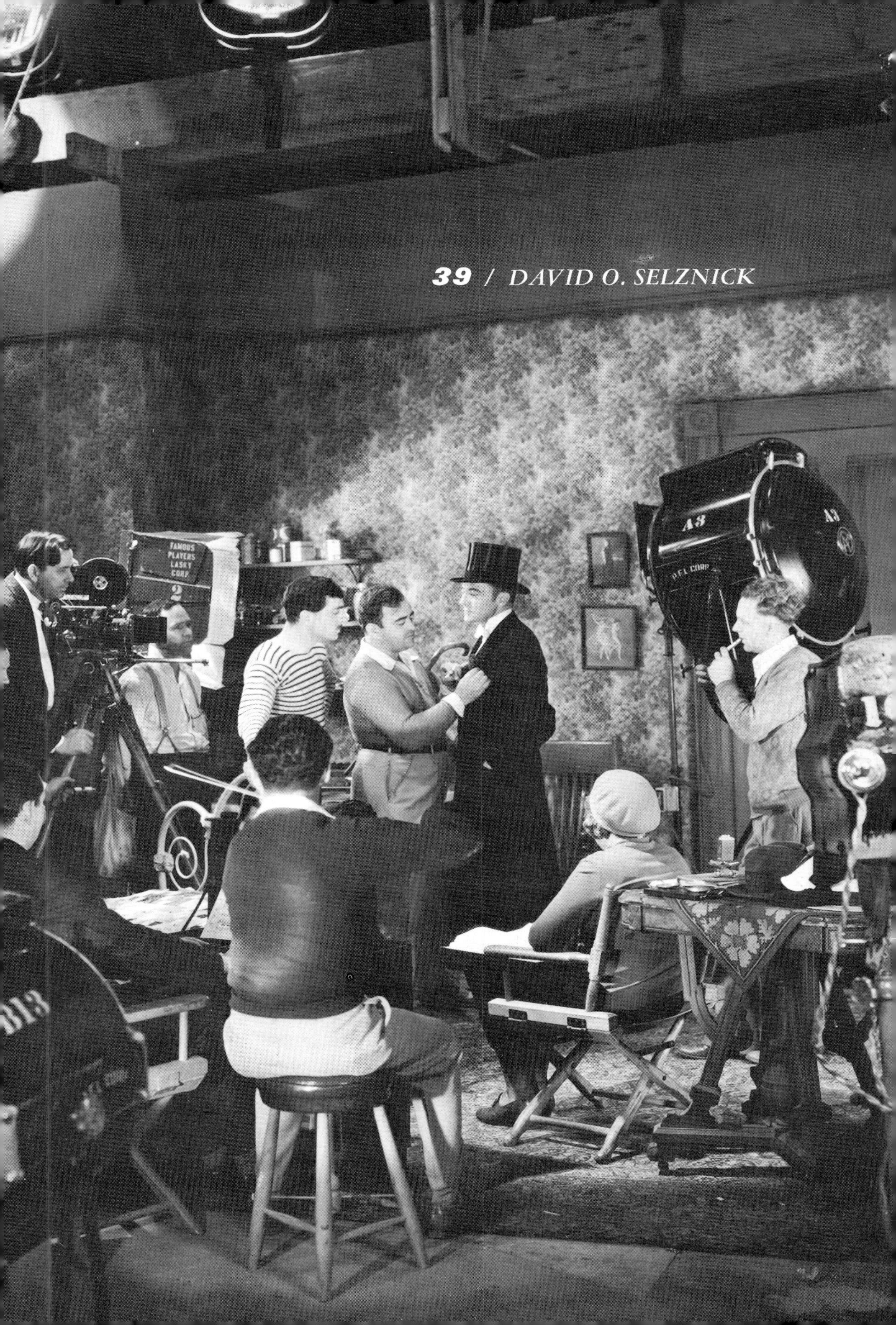

A protégé of B. P. Schulberg, David O. Selznick became the industry's most respected independent producer. He died on June 22, 1965, and the obituaries concentrated on his most celebrated achievement, *Gone with the Wind.*

His early career was overlooked because it was practically unknown. David Selznick was the son of the pioneer producer Lewis J. Selznick, and to understand his unique character, it is important to know something about his father.

Lewis Selznick was an immigrant from the Ukraine. He went to America via England, settled in Pittsburgh, and opened a bank and three jewelry stores before he was twenty-four. Selznick had vigorous ideas; he could promote ventures, but could not always sustain them. In New York, in 1912, his "world's largest jewelry store" collapsed. An old friend, Mark Dintenfass, owner of one of the small independents which made up Universal, brought Selznick into the battle-front of the Pat Powers–Carl Laemmle conflict. While this conflict raged, Dintenfass was caught between two fires. His stock in Universal was up for sale, but neither side expressed the slightest interest. Selznick tried to help; he interviewed both Powers and Laemmle, at the same time surveying the workings of the motion-picture business. His promotional instincts were thoroughly aroused.

"This was duck soup for me," he later recalled. "I knew what I was after, so I appointed myself to a job, picked out a nice office, went in and took it. This got by with bells on. People came in and talked to me about everything that was going on, and pretty soon I knew all about it."[1]

Selznick discovered that Universal lacked a general manager, and he assumed the post himself. Since the company was in chaos, no one questioned the validity of this appointment.

Selznick's activities blossomed until Laemmle asked for his resignation, by which time he was an expert in the Machiavellian maneuvers of motion pictures. He became vice-president and general manager of the World Film Corporation. As Terry Ramsaye points out, "He also appointed himself the general disturbance of the motion-picture industry." When Laemmle, in his series of trade-paper advertisements, asked exhibitors "to use the brains that God gave you," Selznick replied that the motion-picture business "takes less brains than anything else in the world."

Eased out of the World Film Corporation, he formed his own company to produce pictures with Clara Kimball Young, who had been World's most important star. The Clara Kimball Young Film Corporation set a fashion, which was at once adopted by Mary Pickford with the Mary Pickford Film Corporation. Selznick published an open letter in the trade press, congratulating Miss Pickford on her shrewdness in following an idea which he had originated.

"Will you please express to my friend, Mr. Adolph Zukor, my deep sense of obligation? It is indeed delightful to encounter among one's co-workers a man so broad-gauged that neither false pride nor shortsightedness can deter him from the adoption of an excellent plan, even though conceived by another."[2]

Lewis J. Selznick Enterprises produced pictures starring Miss Young, Norma and Constance Talmadge, Olive Thomas, Elaine Hammerstein. . . . Meanwhile, he trained his sons, Myron in production—he later became a top agent, and David in promotion.

[1] *Lloyd Morris:* Not So Long Ago (*New York: Random House; 1949*), *p. 124.*
[2] *Terry Ramsaye:* A Million and One Nights (*New York: Simon and Schuster; 1926*), *p. 764.*

The Selznick Company, later Select Pictures, was annihilated by its competitors. At the same time, David Ó. Selznick (the "O," officially Oliver, actually stood for nothing; it was adopted to distinguish him from a relative he disliked) began his first venture into motion-picture production.

DAVID O. SELZNICK: In the early days, I think my father cared as much as I do about pictures. With films like *War Brides,* with Nazimova, directed by Herbert Brenon, I think then he cared greatly. But everything became swamped with the details of building a huge company with branches all over the world. I don't think then he had time for it. He was too concerned with empire building.

I think silent pictures were marvelous entertainment—extraordinarily creative, and a wonderful medium that we've lost. There have been instances of its use and influence in sound pictures, and of course that influence continues. In retrospect, I think Hollywood did an absolutely fantastic job, under the greatest of difficulties, when everything was new and everyone was starting from scratch.

In those days, one of the marks of whether we were doing well with a scene was the number of titles. If we had to use too many of them in discussing a scene, we'd automatically throw the scene out. So that we learned to tell stories with film. We would describe a scene in terms of cuts. We'd say, "They do so-and-so, and then you cut to a close-up, and then you cut to such-and-such" . . . and we would tell the scene to each other in editing terms, rather than in dialogue terms. If the scene didn't stand up cinematically, we'd say, "Oh, that's no good," and start over again. That's what made it such a marvelous medium. Today, a scene is judged by how it reads on paper in terms of dialogue. We constructed each scene, too, so that it had a beginning, a middle, and an end. Each scene told its own story, and followed into the next scene. All this is an art that has been lost.

David O. Selznick.

I think it's a pity that so much of the knowledge of cinematic craftsmanship in this country passed with the death or retirement of so many of the old hands. A contrast with directors abroad, who, whatever their shortcomings as makers of entertainment for American audiences, know more about the telling of a story on film than a regrettably large percentage of American directors of today. I think that, for instance, the greatest cinematic talent to come along in many years is Fellini. You must remember that the silent era was a very young man's business. Everybody was learning. There were no such things as experienced experts—unless they had gained their expert knowledge in a relatively short time. The cutters had started sweeping up the cutting-room floor; they'd learned how to patch film and how to cut. The actual mechanics of cutting are not all that difficult to learn, but creative cutting is something different. A man's ability to contribute became discernible from projection-room conferences, discussions at rushes and first assemblies, so that as far as the directors were concerned, they came largely out of the technical ranks.

That was a tremendous advantage that they had over a large percentage of today's directors. They understood that good cinema, so to use that term, is, or should be, a cutting medium. They learned these things on the way up, and understood them as directors. They understood the technical side of telling a story with film, whereas many of today's directors do not know the cinematic crafts; they've come from the ranks of stage directors, or writers, and therefore are dependent upon their crew or, in rare instances, upon their producer. Kazan told me, after he had directed several pictures, that he was only then learning how to tell a story with film. I think he did learn.

This isn't to say that a good picture from an entertainment standpoint cannot be made by someone who does not know these things. If the scenes are effective enough, as to writing, construction, dialogue, and performances, they can be very good entertainment, and very successful films. But without the benefit of expert cinematic craftsmanship, I would remake them.

I worked with a substantial number of the good directors of that period. I was particularly smitten with the talents of Bill Wellman, whose contributions to film have never been properly appreciated by students of film. Wellman was, to the best of my knowledge, the first director in America to use the moving camera.

I don't mean a camera car, such as Griffith used for the Ride of the Klansmen in *Birth of a Nation*, but I mean actually trolleying with the camera, actually bringing fluidity to camera movement. This was brought to this country by Wellman, simultaneously with its use by some of the German directors.

I was also present on the stage when a microphone was moved for the first time by Wellman, believe it or not. Sound was relatively new [this was *Beggars of Life*, 1928] and at that time the sound engineer insisted that the microphone be steady. Wellman, who had quite a temper in those days, got very angry, took the microphone himself, hung it on a boom, gave orders to record—and moved it. That was the end of what had been a complete loss of cinema; if you look at the first sound pictures, you'll see that the people were stationed in one spot and were not permitted to move by the sound engineers.

Those were among the contributions made by Wellman, which I have always felt were due to the fact that he had been an aviator in World War I; he had the eye of an aviator who was used to constant movement. The opening sequence of his *Legion of the Condemned* (1928) I've many times quoted as one of the most brilliant uses of film to tell a story that I've ever seen. He told the whole story of four individual men in, I think, less than one minute each. He was really a remarkable talent. Wellman was a close personal friend of mine, and, of course, in our youth we would talk nothing but pictures. Morning, noon, and night, seven days a week. Indeed, we worked six days a week on the stages.

My first feature was *Roulette* (1924), which was made for seventeen thousand dollars. I managed to persuade Henry Hull to do his part for a new dinner jacket. Before that, I directed and edited a newsreel, for Ford, and my cameraman was Ernest Schoedsack; he carried all the gear up in the woods in a different part of the country every couple of days, and he was a remarkable semi-documentary fast cameraman. I also did a film of Firpo, who had come to fight Jack Dempsey, called *Will He Conquer Dempsey?,* and a newsreel of Valentino judging a beauty contest.

When I went over to Paramount, after an abortive association with *White Shadows of the South Seas,* a story called *Heliotrope,* which became *Forgotten Faces,* was my first real production, other than some westerns and the previous enterprises of my adolescence in New York. I was out to make some good pictures; *Forgotten Faces* turned out very well. It went very smoothly, and I got on very well with the director, Victor Schertzinger. Ah, things were easier in those days.

I was answerable to B. P. Schulberg, who was head of Paramount (West Coast) Studio. But he actually had nothing to do with the picture beyond setting it up in the first instance. In those days, as a supervisor, you were never *entirely* responsible for anything so long as you were working under the studio head. I would say that I was as responsible for *Forgotten Faces* as any producer today could possibly be responsible for a film. But I never achieved absolute autonomy until RKO in 1931.

A supervisor had, if anything, more authority than any studio-employed producer has today. He was more intimately connected with the details because it was not so departmentalized—as it is now within the big studio format, or whatever's left of it. You had complete autonomy on sets, costumes, and all the other details of production, so long as you were within budget.

I became very speedily executive assistant to Schulberg, which made me second in charge of the studio and, therefore, always connected with the whole program. Then Schulberg went away for six months and at the age of twenty-seven I took over the whole studio. I'd only been in Hollywood a few years. I varied the extent of my controls—although with Josef von Sternberg, I abided by Schulberg's instructions that I was to let him do as he pleased. Von Sternberg's great talent was photography; he was one of the greatest cameramen that ever lived. He had an extraordinary eye for composition, he knew how to photograph a woman glamorously and how to teach her movements that in today's terms seem a little absurd but which in those days had tremendous appeal. He had a great sense of specious glamour, and while there were many things about his way of working, about his scripts, and about the way he staged his scenes that were little short of ludicrous, they nevertheless made for big box office. He created Marlene Dietrich as a star; he made her up out of a lot of old cloth—I should say old cloth trimmed with a lot of sequins—so he was also a great showman in his day. In Schulberg's absence, I would debate with Sternberg and would invariably surrender to a lot of ideas that I thought were absolute nonsense. On other directors I exercised great control and I got along extremely well with them.

But there were few pictures in the silent era which actually I was sole producer of. And my connection with them varied from picture to picture, according to who was the producer and who was the director. Getting a picture into work every Monday morning and shipping one every Saturday didn't allow too much time for the fine details.

Schulberg was a remarkable factory foreman. I learned a good deal from him about studio management. His tastes were very set; he had all sorts of silly taboos, all sorts of rules about what you could and couldn't do in pictures. But he was a remarkably efficient man and he ran his factory well—a factory that turned out a series of pictures with Nancy Carroll, Wallace Beery and Raymond Hatton, Richard Arlen, James Hall, Ruth Taylor, Esther Ralston. . . . We made three to six pictures a year, with each of these stars, or combination of stars; their cost was predetermined, their gross was predetermined. You knew that you could make X dollars of profit on each picture you made for X dollars. And then there would be the occasional fling: films on somewhat higher limits for the Emil Jannings pictures, the Lubitsch pictures—or higher budgets for the Dietrich-von Sternberg pictures. And once in a while they would take a chance on something like *An American Tragedy*.

There was *one* picture which I practically produced—*The Four Feathers*. Cooper and Schoedsack did the location material; the breaking of the British square and the charge of the rhinoceroses, and they did a brilliant job of it. Schoedsack had been my cameraman—and Merian Cooper had been a soldier of fortune. He'd a brilliant war record, and had fought in Poland against the Bolsheviks. Actually, there was a statue of him in Poland! And I really co-produced it with them, although I produced all the studio work, with Lothar Mendes directing. It started as a silent, and we added sound and dialogue.

So I had this extraordinary, beneficial training—under Schulberg—running a big plant. It proved invaluable in later years.

40 / *WE'RE NOT LAUGHING LIKE WE USED TO*

The silent era was the golden age of comedy. That much, at least, has been generally admitted, thanks to the reissues and the compilation films, which have given silent comedies a second run of popularity. Several attempts have been made to emulate the unique silent-comedy style in current releases. The most elaborate example has been Stanley Kramer's *It's a Mad, Mad, Mad, Mad World,* a Cinerama colossus with a huge cast of old-time stars in guest roles.

But a new Golden Age of Comedy cannot be created simply by *re*-creating the style of the original one. Kramer's picture merely drew attention to the fact that even without color, Cinerama, and stereophonic sound, comedies had been a lot funnier forty years before.

Although the picture was not a financial failure, reviewers brought up the old question: why don't they make pictures like they used to?

They don't because they can't. Film makers today do not necessarily lack the skill; they lack the resources. It is no longer economically possible to take comedy units away on location and make the picture up as you go along. Everything must be planned, scripted, and scheduled. And as the great comedians realized from the beginning, comedy can seldom be planned. It has to happen.

Silent comedies had that wonderful spontaneity because they usually *were* spontaneous. The majority of silent comics never worked from scripts, but that does not mean they were slapdash film makers. Chaplin, Lloyd, and Keaton had genius, but they did not depend on that abstract quality alone to see them through. Apart from Chaplin, all the top comedians surrounded themselves with gag men— men who were paid not so much to write gags as to think them up, pass them around, improve them, polish them, and then to work out a way of shooting them.

Buster Keaton employed four of these gag men, Lloyd as many as ten. They were paid as highly as directors, which many of them became. Often, they would accompany the unit out on location, and when the shooting got bogged down they would throw in new ideas and elaborate old ones. Silent comedies would sometimes cost more, and take longer to make, than regular feature pictures. But it was this method of inspired improvisation that led to the era becoming known as the Golden Age of Comedy.

The most impressive quality of the comedy men was their astonishing capacity for hard work. They would keep going day and night if they thought it would help their picture. They would never give up. If a gag failed the first time, they would try again and again until they had achieved the effect they wanted. And their tenacity did not finish at the end of production.

If the audience reaction was wrong, if the gags fell flat, they would take the film back and reshoot the weaker sections. Not all producers could afford to do this; run-of-the-mill two-reelers were seldom previewed. But the feature comedies generally were, and the products of the Roach and Sennett studios were frequently slipped into a normal program. Harold Lloyd laid the most store by previews, and Irving Thalberg credited him with their innovation.

Perhaps the most endearing aspect of this period was its lack of self-consciousness. No one knew they were creating a Golden Age. No one, apart from Chaplin and Sennett, had so far been hailed as a genius. Film making was still fun. On the Keaton lot, the favorite sport was baseball. When he needed camera crews or gag men, Buster would hire men for their proven ability not so much in the picture business as on the baseball field. When they also proved to be expert technicians, this was sheer coincidence.

But then the whole period was an amazing succession of happy accidents and splendid coincidences—from the moment Chaplin stumbled upon his immortal tramp make-up, to the accidental casting of Oliver Hardy opposite Stan Laurel.

Chaplin, Lloyd, and Keaton have been recognized as the three great figures of comedy pictures. But the silent era presented many other fine comedians, whose work has almost entirely vanished.

Harry Langdon made comparatively few features, and the best of these, *Long Pants* (1927) and *The Strong Man* (1926), both directed by Frank Capra, are fortunately still in circulation. They reveal Langdon as the fourth genius of screen comedy. Chaplin introduced pathos at certain important moments; Langdon used it, in varying forms, almost consistently. His was a simple, childlike, and immensely vulnerable character, whose innocent charm made the audience feel warm and protective. Langdon's character stared at the world like a startled white mouse. He was a completely individual comedian and a brilliant pantomimist.

Born in Council Bluffs, Iowa, Langdon was a newsboy, with a fascination for the stage. He managed to get a job as property boy, and then ran away from home to join a stock company. He spent some time with the Kickapoo Indian Medicine Show, for which he did a turn on the bill, then sold medicine to the crowd. Later he joined the Gus Sun Minstrel Company, for which he did a song-and-dance number, a chair-balancing specialty, assisted in a juggling act, took care of the wardrobe—until one night their special Pullman car burned down at Council Bluffs, Iowa, and Langdon went home to bed.

He broadened his experience by working as a circus tumbler and clown, a newspaper-strip cartoonist, and a vaudeville player.

"Each is hard in its own way," said Langdon, in a *Photoplay* interview. "Newspaper comics are hard because you have four or five frames in which to tell your comedy. You don't have the elbow room of the circus, the stage, or the screen.

"Vaudeville is sometimes harder and sometimes easier than the newspaper or screen ways of cracking jokes. If you get a cold house, it's harder than anything else on earth. The oddest thing about this whole funny business is that the public really wants to laugh, but it's the hardest thing to make them do it. They don't want to cry, yet they will cry at the slightest provocation. Maybe that's why so many comedians want to play tragedy—they want a sort of vacation."[1]

While Langdon was playing in Los Angeles, Mack Sennett signed him. His screen character retained the costume of his vaudeville days—a little cloth hat, a large overcoat, and a pair of broad, flat shoes.

Most of Langdon's comedies for Sennett were routine for the period, but some matched the highest standards of silent comedy. His films were nearly all the work of the same team—Harry Edwards, director; Arthur Ripley and Frank Capra, gag men; William Williams, cameraman; William Hornbeck, supervising editor; and Al Giebler, title writer.

In 1925, *Photoplay* reported that Harry Langdon was the favorite comedian

[1] Photoplay, *June 1925, p. 86.*

of the movie colony: "Ask Harold Lloyd who gives him his biggest celluloid laugh. Ask any star. They will all say Langdon. In a year, he has taken up his comedy post right behind Keaton and Lloyd."[2]

The enormous success of Langdon's first independent feature, *Tramp, Tramp, Tramp* (1926) fully justified this claim. With the increase in footage, Langdon hired more gag men. Credited were Frank Capra, Tim Whelan, Hal Conklin, J. Frank Holliday, Gerald Duffy, and Murray Roth. Joan Crawford played the girl.

"This picture takes Langdon's doleful face and pathetic figure out of the two-reel class and into the Chaplin and Lloyd screen dimensions," said *Photoplay*. "Not that he equals their standing yet, but he is a worthy addition to a group of comedy makers of which we have entirely too few."[3]

In *Tramp, Tramp, Tramp* Harry plays the son of a bootmaker (Alec B. Francis) whose livelihood is threatened. Harry promises to find some money— "I'll get it in three months if it takes a year." He enters a marathon cross-country walk, an advertising stunt for Burton Shoes, determined to win both the $25,000 prize and the girl on the Burton billboards. This framework supplies the basis for some wonderfully inventive gags. Occasionally, an episode tends to be funny for the sake of being funny and conflicts with the Langdon character; there is a lengthy thrill scene (repeated in *The Chaser*) which is expertly done but belongs more properly in a Harold Lloyd film. But the majority of *Tramp, Tramp, Tramp* is delightful.

The scene with Harry in a chain gang is a masterpiece of careful timing. Marched out to break rocks, Harry is ordered to pick up a sledgehammer. It is too heavy. He puts it back on the pile and selects a tiny hammer. The guard forces him to pick a full-size one. This time the head falls off. Now the guard angrily sorts out another one, and from the blur of hands and hammers, Harry emerges with the guard's rifle. Being Harry, he doesn't know what to do with it, so he throws it away. It goes off, and another guard dashes up. Startled, Harry drops a heavy hammer on the guard's foot—and the man goes off, hopping and cursing. Harry quickly turns back to the pile, rummages through, and when the other guard turns away, he departs with the tiny one after all. He sits down before a huge rock and taps it gently, like a child with an egg. Nothing happens, so he takes a pebble and breaks that instead. Langdon conveys the charm of infancy without being infantile; his comedy, however violent, is always delicate.

At the end of the film, Harry and Joan marry and we are introduced to baby Harry. Langdon plays this part, too. A tiny Harry in a cot, he sneezes, throws a ball out of his cot—and it bounces off the wall and hits him. The startled reaction, the wide-opened eyes, and the delayed double take are all typical Langdon gestures and they fit his baby to perfection. The Langdon crew obviously fell in love with this scene—which was a retake when a real baby failed to cooperate— and it goes on and on, becoming more and more enchanting.

With this feature, Edwards should have established himself as a top comedy director, but according to the evidence that survives, he took too long, ran over budget, and Langdon assigned his next production to Frank Capra. (However, Harry Edwards remained a close friend and worked with Langdon in later years.[4])

[2] Photoplay, *March 1926, p. 110.*
[3] Photoplay, *August 1926, p. 88.*
[4] *Mrs. Mabel Langdon to author, London, Sept. 1967.*

Edwards may have been first-rate, but Capra was brilliant. He understood Langdon's character better than anyone, including Langdon. *The Strong Man* proved to be a masterpiece.

"It's a grand and glorious laugh from the start to the finish," said *Photoplay*. "It begins with one laugh overlapping the other. Chuckles are swept into howls. Howls creep into tears—and by that time you're ready to be carried out."[5]

The Strong Man is frequently shown by archives and film societies all over the world. Its tremendous climax matches that of the best action pictures. It takes place in a sin-ridden, bootlegging town; the strong man gets drunk, and to soothe the infuriated audience, the manager of the saloon steers his assistant (Harry Langdon) on to the stage. Harry is lost. Faced with the scowling disbelief, he does a little olé gesture. He looks around at the heavy weights and the huge cannon, and does another olé. He tries to lift a weight, fails, so he goes into a tap-dance routine. Outside the saloon marches the local congregation, determined to drive the evildoers from among them. Inside, the restive audience finally goes berserk, and Harry opens fire with the cannon in a fantastic action scene which culminates in the total collapse of the Walls of Jericho, to the awe of the preacher and the congregation. On the most basic technical level, *The Strong Man* is a great achievement, superbly photographed by Elgin Lessley, who had worked with Roscoe Arbuckle and Buster Keaton, and very well edited by Harold Young. The picture stands today as one of the most perfect comedies ever made.

Long Pants, made by the same team, has inexplicably lost the polished veneer of *The Strong Man*. It remains an important comedy, and often a highly successful one. But the final result indicates that something was wrong somewhere.

Explanations conflict with each other, and the parties concerned are unwilling to talk of the incident. What seems to have happened is basically this: After the success of *The Strong Man,* Langdon was at last able to relax, confident that with Capra and Ripley he had found a perfect team. He went on a four-week golfing trip. When he returned he found that writer and director had quarreled; Ripley insisted that Langdon's entrance into the picture came too late. Capra refused to be interfered with. Langdon supported Ripley, and the picture, *Long Pants,* was made under intolerable conditions. Langdon fired Capra.

Infuriated, Capra wrote a letter to the movie columnists. He said that Langdon was impossible to work with, that he wanted a finger in every pie, that he was conceited, egotistical, and considered himself the biggest shot in pictures. The substance of the letter was printed and the story was picked up and exaggerated by newspapers everywhere. Frankly, I find this episode hard to believe, for Capra is revered as a kind and considerate colleague as well as a great director. But it is told by the usually reliable Katherine Albert[6] and the evidence of Langdon's collapse is irrefutable. Capra is sure to provide the full explanation when he publishes his autobiography.

Langdon was knocked out by the blow, but he had a First National contract to live up to, even though he had lost his will to work. He directed his next picture, *Three's a Crowd,* himself, from an Arthur Ripley story. It was heavily influenced by *The Gold Rush*. To his little shack in the slums, reached by an incredibly long and probably symbolic stairway, Harry rescues a girl he finds in

[5] Photoplay, *Nov. 1926, p. 52.*
[6] Photoplay, *Feb. 1932, p. 40.*

The Harold Beaudine company on the Christie lot.

Benjamin Stoloff directing Roaring Lions at Home *(1924). Sid Wagner at camera.*

Raymond Griffith, during the making of Hands Up *(1926), with gag writer Monte Brice.*

Douglas MacLean and Doris May in The Jailbird *(1920), directed by Lloyd Ingraham.*

the snow (Gladys McConnell). She has a baby and he looks after it as his own. There are very few laughs in the picture. It is a surprisingly mournful comedy and, although full of gentle, poignant charm, it is flatly directed. In a sad ending, the girl's husband arrives to take her away. Harry lights their departure with a little oil lamp. As their car drives off, he walks down his long, long stairway into the snow-covered street, stunned by what has happened to him. At the corner, he blows out his lamp and all the street lights go out.

Photoplay was unnecessarily harsh: "A few more like this, and he'll be sent to that limbo of lost movie souls—vaudeville. Langdon reaches for the moon—and grasps a feeble glowworm."[7]

If *Three's a Crowd* conveyed Langdon's depression, *The Chaser* indicated a good recovery. Langdon directed this one, too, and it establishes him, in retrospect at least, as an excellent comedy director—not in the Capra class, but certainly as good as Edwards. Its style is so similar, in fact, that Edwards might have returned and helped out his old friend. The long-held single setups of *Three's a Crowd* have been abandoned and the pace of the old two-reelers restored. The idea of Harry as a girl chaser is hard to conceive, and the single scene he devotes to his amorous conquests can be quickly passed over; it is uproarious, a spoof Valentino, but wildly out of character. Far more effective are the scenes in which, by court order, he has to take his wife's role as housekeeper. Dressed in a voluminous skirt, he shuffles out to the chicken house with a frying pan and tries to induce a hen to lay an egg. He holds the hen over the pan, hoping for the egg to drop straight in. When nothing happens, he looks curiously at the sleepy chicken, puts it to his ear, and shakes it like a defective alarm clock. Meanwhile, another hen has crawled under his skirt, deposited an egg, and crawled out again. When Harry lets the first chicken go, he steps back and is startled to discover an egg that he has apparently produced himself. *The Chaser* is full of such unexpected delights.

Heart Trouble was Langdon's last independent production. It has not been seen since its original release, but I doubt whether it justifies *Photoplay*'s merciless review; "If this is shown in an open-all-night theater near some mission where you pay fifteen cents for the privilege of slumber—buy a ticket. It won't keep you awake a moment. But if you wish to enjoy a movie, stay away. Just a lot of silly gags, no story, and enough inane situations to spell the exit of Harry Langdon."[8]

Langdon's exit was headlined all over America. "Funny Man Goes Bankrupt." Besides his financial crises, his marriage was broken. Technicians and producers alike cold-shouldered him. When, in 1929, he signed for a series of two-reelers with Hal Roach, he learned that the Capra letter had not been forgotten. "Now see here," said Roach. "None of that high-handed stuff you pulled at First National."

"Harry Langdon was a wonderful comedian," said Eddie Sutherland, who later directed him. "I think he destroyed himself. By the time I had him in this sound comedy, the poor man was a beaten, defeated fellow. Sound hurt Langdon, too. He was not so funny articulate."

Another tragedy of the sound film was Raymond Griffith. A silk-hatted comedian, Griffith was a cross between Adolphe Menjou and Max Linder. His

---

[7] Photoplay, *Oct. 1927, p. 125.*
[8] Photoplay, *Sept. 1928, p. 111.*

character was that of a man of polish and assurance thrown completely off balance, usually by women.

First and foremost, Griffith was a brilliant actor. A former dancer, he moved with astonishing grace. After a number of supporting roles, in which he effortlessly stole every picture, Griffith was awarded his own comedy series at Paramount.

"I first happened to see him in *The Eternal Three* [Marshall Neilan]," wrote a fan from Philadelphia in 1924, "which was just an ordinary picture with ordinary acting—but for one exception, Raymond Griffith. His acting is superb, as it is in every one of his pictures, and I don't believe that I have missed any with his name in the cast.

"But even a profound admirer of his must admit that he has been in some very bad pictures. *Poisoned Paradise* [1924, Louis Gasnier] was AWFUL. Someone behind me said, 'For heaven's sake, what's this Barrymore doing in this den of wax dummies?'

"I hope, as do a great many others, that some sensible producer will offer him a starring contract as soon as possible."[9]

Success for Raymond Griffith brought the inevitable resentment; columnist Adela Rogers St. Johns claimed that he had taken success so seriously "that it is quite the funniest thing he has ever done." His conversation, she alleged, consisted chiefly of possible subtitles for his future pictures.

"He doesn't even play the game to the extent of differing with his director in privacy, but openly asserts his authority, as I have seen myself."[1]

Raymond Griffith was undoubtedly a vain man, but he was immensely talented. When he won his star contract, he won the right to dispute with his director. Keaton and Lloyd had achieved this right; Griffith felt that he, too, had progressed far enough to understand what was best for his pictures. His trouble lay in the way he asserted his control.

"I've met a few stubborn people in my life, but he was about the tops," said Monte Brice, writer on *Hands Up* (1926, Clarence Badger), one of Griffith's finest comedies. "Right off the bat we had a big row about Mack Swain. We were out on location and Mack's supposed to come rushing out of this store. Someone's stolen his horse. I remember the title—'Nobody ever steals my horse and lives to warm the saddle!' All the townspeople standing around gave Mack a big laugh. Griff was standing against a fence, watching the thing, and chewing his fingers.

" 'Hey,' he said to me. 'Get rid of him.'

" 'Get rid of Mack Swain?'

" 'Get rid of him.'

" 'Jesus, I don't hire and fire people. You can do it. What's the matter with him, anyway?'

" 'Too goddam funny!'

"So now we call it off. Mack doesn't know what the hell's happened. We all go back to the hotel.

" 'You can't tell from one little scene,' I said. 'The guy comes out, he's a funny man—they recognize him from the Chaplin pictures and that's why he gets the laugh.'

[9] Picture Play, *Jan. 1925, p. 13.*
[1] *Cal York column,* Photoplay, *Dec. 1925, p. 110.*

" 'Don't want him.'

"Clarence Badger, the director, gets sick—too much heat or something, and he retires to his room. And I'm the sucker for the whole thing.

"Finally I pin Ray down to the fact that what made Mack so funny was his big floppy hat. We have to send to the studio for another hat, so he can play it straighter. Well, that's a whole day gone . . .

"Griff was a great gag man, but boy, he was stubborn. We had a lot of fun, though. *Hands Up* was a hell of a funny picture."

An accomplished pantomimist, Griffith saw to it that an opportunity for mime was included in every one of his pictures. In the stagecoach-ride scene in *Hands Up,* he recounted a ghost story to two young girls. Every event was described in mime, hilariously and brilliantly. In *Miss Bluebeard* (Frank Tuttle), he mimicked a cat. His natural talents for mime were especially important to Griffith; he lost his voice at an early age and his husky whisper was far from adequate for stage delivery. When a company of French pantomimists toured the vaudeville theaters in America, he joined them, and toured Europe for a season.

He used to say that he lost his voice as a boy, playing in the famous old melodrama, *The Witching Hour.* Every night he had to scream when threatened with a beating. One night he managed a shriek and nothing more. He was unable to speak any of his lines. But a story emanating from Griffith was automatically suspect. It is more likely he lost his voice through bronchial pneumonia.

"Griffith was a congenital liar," said Eddie Sutherland, who directed one of his most successful pictures, *He's a Prince.* "And I don't mean that maliciously. But if he'd done all the things he said he'd done, he'd have been a hundred and eighteen years of age.

"Ray and I were dear, close chums off stage. He was a very determined, very ruthless, very shrewd fellow. His big failing as a comedian, which I pointed out to him, was that he didn't know the difference between comedy, travesty, farce, or light comedy. He'd mix it all up. And he would never be the butt of any joke. Now the success of almost all great comedians comes from being the butt of jokes. Griff was too vain for this. He would get himself into a problem, and then he'd want to think himself out of it. This worked well for a few pictures, but it wasn't a solid basis."

Griffith had a more thorough groundwork of comedy training than any other comedian. Besides the years he spent as a dancer, as an actor, on the vaudeville circuits, with the mime company, he also went through the various grades of the Mack Sennett company. He not only acted for Keystone, he worked as a gag writer, and became Sennett's right-hand man.

"When he left Sennett a few years later," said Herbert Howe, "he was a master mechanic of comedy. He could gag. He could time his business to a second. He knew to an inch how much footage a scene should have to get the biggest laugh. In addition to being an actor, he was qualified as a director and a scenario writer. His attitude toward the art of screen comedy is that of the mathematician. There is no emotion about it, he will tell you; it is pure mathematics."[2]

Raymond Griffith vanished from the screen toward the end of the silent era, written off as just another talkie tragedy. His voice, they realized, could never record.

[2] Photoplay, *May 1925, p. 39.*

But in 1929, *Photoplay* announced that Griffith's husky whisper recorded "far better than many a bell-like baritone![3] He was on his way back. Howard Hughes, the twenty-five-year-old millionaire, put him under contract for $75,000. Hughes finally had to write the deal off. Ray Griffith's comeback was a myth.

But he had one more brilliant role to essay. With grim irony, he was asked by Lewis Milestone to play the part of a dead French soldier in the shell-hole scene with Lew Ayres in *All Quiet on the Western Front* (1930).

Griffith had disappeared from the silent screen because of contract troubles. After *All Quiet,* he turned to writing scripts at Warners. By 1934 he was one of Darryl F. Zanuck's writers. He ended his career as a producer.

"Griffith is one of the brainiest men in pictures today," wrote columnist Selma Robinson in 1926. "A man with a brilliant mind, scintillating humor, an instinctive feeling for proportion, a genius for writing and directing motion pictures and an infallible rhythm that makes his characterizations so perfectly timed."[4]

In 1923, Raymond Griffith was hired as a gag man by Douglas MacLean, another forgotten master of screen comedy. MacLean was trained as a civil engineer, but he had become a bond salesman, reporter, auto salesman, actor on the legitimate stage, film salesman, studio assistant, and bit player. He enjoyed a certain success as leading man to Mary Pickford in *Captain Kidd, Jr.* and *Johanna Enlists.* Henry King's *23½ Hours Leave* brought him stardom, in the company of Doris May. He decided he had a future as an independent comedian; when no one would back him, he financed his own picture, *Going Up,* and prudently hired Raymond Griffith to write it.

"*Going Up* is one of the most amusing comedies that has recently come to the screen—the best chance that Douglas MacLean has had, since he became a star,"[5] commented *Photoplay*. The picture was a great financial success, and established MacLean as a top comedian.

"Make your audience feel superior to you," was MacLean's advice, "but don't let them get derisive. Make them feel a bit superior to the characters in the story, but don't let them feel superior to the picture. Don't let them know it is a picture. Make it a bit of human drama—or humor—that is going on before their eyes. I don't try to make my pictures comic. I try to make them entertaining."[6]

MacLean, like Griffith, ended his career as a producer.

In Hollywood, I made several attempts to contact him. Eventually, a man answered the telephone. He seemed genuinely bewildered when I asked to speak to Mr. MacLean.

"Did you not know he was ill?" he said. "I'm his male nurse."

"I'm extremely sorry," I said. "Would it be possible to write to him?"

The male nurse was patient. "I don't think you quite understand. Mr. MacLean has lost all powers of communication."

That remark was very poignant. For not only had Douglas MacLean been forgotten. Not only had the work of a lifetime been lost. The memories had gone, too.

[3] Photoplay, *April 1929, p. 78.*
[4] Motion Picture Magazine, *May 1926, p. 35.*
[5] Photoplay, *Dec. 1923, p. 74.*
[6] *Quoted in* Photoplay, *Nov. 1926, p. 139.*

Reginald Leigh Dugmore Denny was born in Richmond, Surrey,[1] and was educated at St. Francis Xavier College in Mayfield, Sussex. These biographical details, unexceptional though they may seem, explain why the career of one of the finest comedians of the silent screen was wrecked by the arrival of sound.

Denny's characterization was that of a typical young American entangled in the problems of suburban life. When talking pictures revealed an impeccable English accent, his characterization and his career came to a sudden halt.

With *Madame Satan* (C. B. De Mille, 1931) he began his second career: as a featured player. One of Hollywood's best, he played everything from Benvolio in M-G-M's *Romeo and Juliet* (Cukor) to a less demanding role in *Abbott and Costello Meet Dr. Jekyll and Mr. Hyde*. With Sir C. Aubrey Smith, Basil Rathbone, and Alan Mowbray, he became one of America's favorite Englishmen. His career in silent pictures was forgotten, not only by movie audiences but by Denny himself.

When I met him, in Hollywood, he admitted he had not seen one of his silents for over twenty years. He clearly had little idea of how good he was, and it took some persuasion before he agreed to see *Skinner's Dress Suit*. He and his family gathered in the Hollywood home of collector David Bradley, awaiting the film with a trace of nervousness. First in the program was an episode of *The Leather Pushers*, the boxing series which brought Denny to Hollywood. This two-reeler showed Denny as a likable but rather flat character; what humor there was came from other members of the cast.

Skinner's Dress Suit, however, was a revelation. Smoothly and expertly directed by William A. Seiter, it showed Denny at his best—as a comedian whose polish and technical brilliance matched, but never outshone, his genuine warmth.

As the Denny family watched this 1926 comedy, the atmosphere noticeably changed. The picture's gags at first received restrained, relieved chuckles. But as the story took hold, the audience, which included Sennett comedienne Minta Durfee, roared with laughter, giving the film their wholehearted approval.

Mrs. Denny spotted herself as an extra, and identified Janet Gaynor as another. At the end, Denny was assailed with congratulations. Grinning shyly, he confessed that he had expected the picture to creak. "It certainly stands up a lot better than I thought it would."

The Denny style of comedy has been part of Hollywood's staple diet since Mr. and Mrs. Sidney Drew and Mr. and Mrs. Carter de Haven, several of whose films were directed by William A. Seiter, popularized light comedy on the screen. Universal featured Doris Day and Rock Hudson recently in a series of situation comedies remarkably similar to those in which they once starred Reginald Denny and Laura la Plante.

Denny's attributes as a comedian seem much higher in retrospect than they appeared at the time. The twenties, of course, were a golden age: with Chaplin, Keaton, Lloyd, and later, Langdon, occupying the highest echelons, other comedians suffered by comparison. Denny's style, however, was individual enough to withstand such searing competition. He did not direct or conceive his pictures in the way that Chaplin, Lloyd, or Keaton did, nor did he exercise such close supervision. But his talents are impressive enough for him to be placed, with Raymond Griffith, on a level only slightly below that of the masters.

[1] *Reginald Denny died in June 1967—in Richmond, Surrey.*

One of the secrets of Denny's success was William A. Seiter, his director for five years. A good-natured man, who loved golf almost as much as he loved pictures, Seiter ambled through his comedies with contented ease. "He didn't want to be a big picture director," said one of his players. "He enjoyed making nice, medium pictures. Simply, easily, quietly."

Seiter is a vital part of Denny's career, because he appreciated his talents and brought them out to their fullest advantage. Denny's best pictures invariably have Seiter's name on them, even though his most financially rewarding productions were directed by Harry Pollard.

"Pollard didn't have the real comedy touch," said Denny. "He didn't have Bill Seiter's ability. Pollard was all for the broad comedy and I was for the lighter. We just couldn't agree.

"But we started out together with *The Leather Pushers*. We made these independently, in New York. We had to make them independently because no one would touch them. 'Prize fighting? Who would go and look at it?'

"We made two, didn't have enough backing, and folded up. Then Pat Powers became interested, and anything that Powers wanted, old man Laemmle of Universal would grab away from him. They'd had a battle once. So Laemmle gave us a deal—eleven thousand five hundred dollars for the negative and one working print.

"They never thought they had anything, but when they released them—boy, they went over! We made four more. Of course, we owed money all over the place, but Universal said they would advance us the money so we could pay off our bills. Trouble was, we didn't get it in the contract. As we went to make number six, Universal shut down on our credit, notified all our creditors, and forced us into bankruptcy. Then they bought the whole thing out.

"While the legal angle was being attended to in New York, they shipped me out to California. In Hollywood, they always seem to resent anybody who comes from New York. I was sitting around doing nothing, and they didn't like that, so they started a series of Northwest Mounted Police stories, with one of old man Laemmle's relatives, Nat Ross, directing. *Jaws of Steel* was one of them. I'll never forget it. I'd hardly ridden a horse in my life, and they had me trying to bulldog a guy. I got thrown, and I broke my ankle. We made two pictures, that was all, then Universal stopped the series; they said, 'God, look at that!' They wanted me in condition to go on with *The Leather Pushers*.

"Harry Pollard came out and made all but the last six. Then they assigned me to *The Kentucky Derby* [King Baggott], which was an adventure story with no comedy at all. They had no idea of using me as a comedian. But when we did *The Abysmal Brute,* the Jack London story, that was the first time I suggested putting in some comedy ideas. It was when the character went into the big house for dinner. This boy, whose father was a fighter, had never been anywhere except lunch counters. He'd never been in a big home; he wouldn't know what to do. So I started to play it for comedy, and the director, Hobart Henley, thought I was kidding.

" 'Why not, for God's sake?' I asked. 'Let's put some comedy in here. It's true to nature, and it'll get some laughs.'

"Henley agreed, and we got some light comedy into the hokum. The picture was a great success."

Denny's career as a comedian was launched with his next film, Harry Pollard's *Sporting Youth* (1923), a picture designed along lines similar to the Wallace Reid auto-racing comedies. *Photoplay* thought it was almost as good, and added that Denny came nearer to filling the place left vacant by Reid's death than any other leading man.

Pollard and Denny had a disagreement over the leading woman in this film; Pollard wanted his wife, Margarita Fischer, whom Denny did not consider suitable. Eventually, Denny secured a young girl he had noticed in a western, Laura la Plante.

From the Del Monte location of *Sporting Youth,* Miss la Plante wrote a graphic description of the company's happy-go-lucky atmosphere to *Picture Play Magazine:*

"Reggie is such a fine actor that he can burlesque a scene, saying funny words, without losing any of the dramatic effect. I mean, he can act the fool and still make his face behave dramatic, which I can't. In the scene where he was supposed to walk the plank to eternal oblivion, he assumed a tense pose, raised his hands to heaven, and as he dived, called back, 'I have but one life to give for Universal Picture Company—'

" 'Corporation,' corrected Eddie Stein, who is very careful about such matters, being our business boss, and it almost broke up my scene."[2]

When Denny was assigned William A. Seiter, working conditions became even sunnier. With cameraman Arthur Todd, and some supporting players who appeared often enough to warrant the term stock company, the Reginald Denny company grew very close; it included editor John Rawlins, assistant director Nate Watt, casting director Fred Datig. Universal's suspicions that it was developing into a family affair were confirmed when Miss la Plante married William Seiter.

"We never had an argument," said Denny, "never a cross word, and we always brought the picture in within budget. The front office never had to worry, yet they finally separated us. We were getting on too well, Bill Seiter and I.

"We used to sit down and talk the story over before shooting. There was a great interchange of ideas; we'd listen to anybody. If someone thought we could do something better, why not? We'd try it. But basically, the great secret was that Bill Seiter and myself would get the script, and we'd make suggestions, and argue like hell. Finally, we'd get it right. You can't be a comedian unless you think what you're doing is funny.

"If you get too tired, you quit. That was the wonderful thing with Bill Seiter. If we worked Saturday and wanted to go golfing, I'd get a dizzy feeling around lunchtime. We'd get all our stuff in the box, then Bill would say, 'You can't work any more if you've got that dizzy spell again.'

"They'd take me in and check me, and I'd be fine. But you can't prove you're not dizzy. If I wanted to go to a football match, it would be the same thing. 'All right,' Bill would say, 'you get dizzy around twelve o'clock.' "

The sense of enjoyment spread to the screen in the Denny comedies, and was reflected in the playing of the cast. However good a comedian may be, his timing can be ruined by one clumsy move on the part of a supporting player. In these Seiter-directed films, the cast was impeccable: Otis Harlan, the little fat man with the anxious expression; Ben Hendricks, Jr., the smooth brother-in-law with the

[2] Picture Play, *Jan. 1924, p. 70.*

mustache; Emily Fitzroy, the mother-in-law with the soul-chilling glare; William Austin, tall, effete, and infuriating . . . As *Motion Picture Magazine* said: "We have yet to see Denny try to hog a picture—his aim being to surround himself with competent performers."[3] But these players were a great deal more than competent.

Reginald Denny's background was the theater. His father, W. H. Denny, was an actor; his grandmother, Mrs. Henry Leigh, was an actress. Denny himself made his first appearance as a small boy at the Royal Court Theatre, London, in 1899. He ran away from school at sixteen, considering that his theatrical career had been interrupted long enough. In 1911, he was brought over to America as one of the eight chorus men of *Quaker Girl in New York;* he ended up playing the more substantial role of Prince Carlo when the original actor fell ill.

Returning to England in 1912, Denny toured the music halls in a dramatic sketch; the following year, he left for India and the Orient with the Bandsmann Opera Company. In 1914, he returned to America, where he toured until 1917.

"As America had entered the war, I thought it time for me to enlist, which I did at the British Recruiting Mission in New York. My wife, whom I had married during the Indian tour, thought this was a terrible thing to do as we now had a daughter, Barbara, born in 1916."

Accepted by the Royal Flying Corps, Denny started his pilot's training course at Hastings, where he won the brigade heavyweight boxing championship. Before his course was complete, the Armistice was signed and he was discharged. But if drama was lacking during his wartime service, it was awaiting him on his return.

"As an officer, I was entitled to a first-class passage, but at the R.C.A.F. repatriation camp at Folkstone, we were told that if we had urgent reasons for returning, we could sail the next day, although no first-class accommodation would be available. The voyage, aboard a small United Fruit boat, the *Taloa,* was ghastly. The boat was badly overcrowded, with troops packed in the hold. A mutiny broke out when the officer in charge tried to organize fatigue parties to clean up the ship. I was one of the three remaining commissioned officers on board. It was impossible to try to regain any form of discipline, so we hopped overboard to the pilot boat at Halifax, and were given rail transportation to New York."

Denny had not told his wife of his arrival, since he would not normally have received his return passage for several weeks.

"When I arrived in New York, I discovered that my wife was in a play called *Nellie of N'Orleans.* She was in her dressing room, making up, when I reached the theater. I entered the room and went to embrace her, but she pushed me away, saying she was through with me.

"I went up to her apartment and saw my daughter Barbara. When my wife returned that night, I tried to reason with her, but to no avail. She was in a highly nervous state, and I found out she was also rehearsing in a new play in which she was being starred. She allowed me to stay in the apartment only until I got a job, which was a couple of days later."

At the Blackstone Theatre, Chicago, Denny was told that his wife had had a

[3] Motion Picture Magazine, *May 1926, p. 84.*

Reginald Denny in His Lucky Day *(1929) (left).*

What Happened to Jones? *with Otis Harlan (right).*

What Happened to Jones? *(1925); Zasu Pitts. Otis Harlan, Reginald Denny.*

Skinner's Dress Suit *(1925); Reginald Denny and Laura la Plante.*

Fast and Furious *(1927).*

complete nervous breakdown; he raced back to New York and placed her in a sanitorium. Barbara was taken to a farm by her nurse, and Denny went back to Chicago. His play lasted three weeks. Broke and stranded, he borrowed enough to get back to New York, where he signed a contract for *The Passing Show* of 1919.

The title was ironic; before rehearsals were over, the Actors' Equity strike was called and Denny was again out of work. But this catastrophe led him to the World Film Corporation at Fort Lee, New Jersey, where he made two pictures with director Oscar Apfel: *Bringing Up Betty* and *The Oakdale Affair.*

Back to the theater; Denny played in *The Passing Show* until he was loaned out to play with John Barrymore in *Richard III.* He and Barrymore became close friends, and Denny still considers *Richard III* the finest thing this great actor ever did. Offers from motion-picture producers were now plentiful, and Denny worked for directors John Robertson—*39 East* and *Footlights*—and George Fitzmaurice—*Experience.*

"Then I had an idea for a series of stories around famous paintings. I made one called *The Beggar Maid,* for which I chose Mary Astor. She was about fifteen then. A man named Isaac Wolpe put up the money, and we made it for peanuts. We had a cameraman by the name of Lejaran A. Hiller, who was way ahead of his time; he was terrific. He was a commercial photographer who specialized in magazine illustrations. I wrote most of the first story, and Herbert Blache directed. I wrote a second story, *The Angelus,* by Millais. They released the first one, and oh, it was sensational! Ninety per cent of its success was its marvelous photography. It was beautiful.

"Famous-Players released it, and they offered Wolpe this contract to make some more out at Astoria. I told him not to accept the offer. 'You can't have Hiller,' I told him. 'They'll use their own cameraman, and Hiller's your best bet. Stay independent, and use the Famous-Players release.' But no, he went for it. So I quit. The next picture stunk; they made a small print order and that was the end of the contract. Isaac Wolpe committed suicide; he jumped off the Knickerbocker Building."

After *The Leather Pushers* had initiated his Hollywood career, Reginald Denny became Universal's most important star and, next to Chaplin, the highest-paid Englishman in pictures. Nevertheless, Universal stubbornly refused to give him his own unit. With Bill Seiter he virtually had one, but when Seiter was taken off the Denny comedies and assigned to directing la Plante pictures, the need returned.

"They gave me Freddie Newmeyer, who had been Harold Lloyd's director. He was supposed to direct *That's My Daddy.* But we didn't have the same ideas of comedy. So I directed it. I came out and told him that I didn't approve of the way he wanted to do the sequences, and he said, 'Well, Reggie, go ahead.' I had already written the story myself; I refused to make the awful story they gave me. From my story, they wrote their own scenario [written by Earle Snell], which I promptly threw out the window. We shot from my original.

"I rehearsed the actors, and everything else, and wrote the titles. Universal took it and had a sneak preview which they tried to keep from me. I managed to go out and see it; they had gagged it up with silly titles and ruined it. It was vile.

" 'I refuse to do another picture for you,' I told them, 'unless I get that picture back for recutting.'

" 'Impossible,' they said. 'The negative's all been sent away.'

" 'I don't give a damn,' I said.

"I made them send the negative back. I had an awful time, but I managed to restore the cuts and the original titles.

"*That's My Daddy* was the story of a guy who's engaged to be married to a wealthy gal, and also the story of a little orphan. The orphan has always dreamed that she had a real daddy somewhere, a daddy with a silk hat and everything else. She runs away from home, and gets hit by a car, and is taken to hospital. Meanwhile, this guy is on his way to his wedding. He's in a silk hat and cutaway, and because he's in a hurry, he's driving his own limousine. He's in too much of a hurry, and a speed cop stops him.

"I alibi to the cop: I tell him my little child has been in an accident and I have to get to the hospital. It's an Irish cop. 'Sure,' he says. 'I know. Follow me, I'll take you there.'

"At the hospital, they take me to the little kid, and tell her 'Your daddy's here!' It's just what she's dreamed of. And I'm landed with the kid . . . on my wedding day.

"The girl I had was a sweet little thing, Jane la Verne. Harry Pollard later used her in *Uncle Tom's Cabin,* and Universal put her under contract. She was only six years old; I treated her very carefully, and made her really believe in what she was doing. She was terrific. Then Universal took the picture and made her a wisecracking kid with gag titles. It was terrible.

"After I had recut the film and it was released, the general manager called me into his office and showed me a letter from the New York office. They thought it was the worst picture they had ever seen.

"Old man Laemmle wasn't there; he was at some hot springs. I got in my airplane and flew over and crash-landed at the sanatorium and went to see the old man.

" 'Look,' I said. 'I know a report has been sent from the Universal office about this picture, but I tell you what I'll do, Mr. Laemmle. If that picture doesn't make more money than the last four pictures we've made—and it cost only half as much—then I'll work for you for nothing until the difference is made up. And I'll sign that. But if it makes more money than the last four, then you give me my own unit.'

"The old man said, 'Do you mean that?' I told him I did, and he almost made a final agreement. But then they got to him and said, 'He's trying to dictate to you,' and he wouldn't go for it. Of course, the picture just cleaned up. Even with bad write-ups. They got to the press, too. 'Denny's Swansong' it was called. Afterward, the old man came to me and said, 'I'm sorry. I realize I listened to the wrong people.' "

The stories of the Denny comedies, presented in print, suggest pure farce, or the most contrived situation comedies. But Denny enjoyed taking the most extravagant, absurd, and impossible situation and playing it realistically. He disliked playing broad comedy, as his clashes with Pollard and Newmeyer indicate, although he appreciated it when well used.

"Good hokum, I love—low comedy, pies in the face, pratfalls, and so on. But it's got to *belong*. The timing and everything else has got to be right. Just to take a pratfall, or jump into a bucket of paint, for no reason—this offends me. It's got to be real. You've got to believe it.

"To do farce properly, you take an almost impossible situation but you play it legitimately. Eddie Horton [Edward Everett Horton] was a great farceur. He was sincere and legitimate. To quote an example: in one scene, he's in love with a young girl, his secretary, but he doesn't know she's married. All of a sudden, she starts talking about her baby.

" 'You had a baby?' he says. 'How did you have a baby, may I ask?'

" 'By the natural means—.'

" 'You are married?'

" 'Yes.'

" 'Well, where's your husband?'

" 'I shot him.'

"His reaction to that was sublime. He turns to the audience with this expression of stunned surprise. Then he says, quietly, 'Rubbish.'

"To me, this was legitimate, and superb.

"Today, they take an impossible situation and burlesque and hoke it up. Maybe I'm getting old, but I often see what is supposed to be a comedy, and I just don't see where the humor is. I did a comedy show recently on TV; I was ashamed of doing it. But they pay you for it; you do it. It was absurd—nothing funny, idiotic burlesque. Everything abstract and absurd is today supposed to be comedy. That's the way I feel about it."

The astonishing career of Harold Lloyd represents Hollywood's ideal. Yet it is unprecedented in Hollywood history. A likable young man makes good, marries his leading lady, crowns success with success, becomes the world's tenth richest entertainer, buys a sixteen-acre estate, and withdraws from motion pictures. At this point, catastrophe is usually imminent. But not in the case of Harold Lloyd. He remained extremely wealthy, he remained married to his original wife, he retained his estate, and, even more surprisingly, he stayed the same likable man he was before, his personality unchanged by the ultimate in success.

This success was richly deserved. Harold Lloyd, with Chaplin and Keaton, was one of the three supreme masters of the comedy film. And like Chaplin and Keaton, he was not merely an actor but a creator. He closely supervised every stage of his productions and was responsible for much of the direction.

Chaplin, Keaton, and Langdon presented unique characterizations. Lloyd began his career by virtually imitating Chaplin. In 1917, he switched to a characterization that was individual but certainly not unique. His bespectacled eager-beaver epitomized the young American of the era—the sort of character popularized in fiction by Harry Leon Wilson, Homer Croy, and the Horatio Alger stories.

"I was one of the first comics that you could believe in," Lloyd claimed. Lloyd's character was the only one the audience felt they knew in real life. Chaplin and Keaton portrayed the underdog, and there were many occasions when the audience could identify with them. Lloyd, however, was closest to the American middle classes. He was the guy across the street, the guy in the next office—a regular fellow.

Harold Clayton Lloyd was born in Burchard, Nebraska, on April 20, 1893. "It is impossible to cast any glamour over my youth," he wrote, in his autobiography.[1] "It was exciting enough and filled with incidents and what, to me, was adventure, but there was nothing romantic about it. I was just a plain, freckled, ornery American kid."

Lloyd organized his own shows; his first appearance on the stage was a fleeting role in *Macbeth*. Later, his stage appearances became more frequent. He recalled that one stage director, Lloyd Ingraham, who became a director of silent pictures, told him he would make his mark in the business.

Lloyd's parents separated when he was sixteen, and he decided to try another profession—boxing.

"But I didn't like to fight, and while I got a little thrill out of the crowds, my career as a pugilist was brief and not particularly brilliant. I only fought a few times and then I decided that I had been right in the first place and returned to my first desire, the stage."

Lloyd's father won heavy compensation for an accident, in 1911, and was anxious to use the money to help his son. "But I didn't know whether to go to New York, the mecca of show business, or to California, where I would be accepted in the stock company. We actually tossed a coin and California won. But it was through the kindness of my father that I was able to go."

The Edison Company had established a studio at Long Beach; on one occasion they came to San Diego for location shots. Lloyd was an assistant teacher at a dramatic school there, and he did a day's work as an extra, playing a Yaqui Indian.

---

[1] *"The Autobiography of Harold Lloyd," Chapter 1*, Photoplay, *May 1924, p. 32.*

"It was during those days in San Diego that I hit the bottom. It was the hardest of any time in my career. I was literally down to one nickel. I bought six doughnuts with it and they were the finest doughnuts I ever ate in my life. I went twenty-four hours on them, and then I bobbed up again with some salary that somebody owed me."

Eventually, he became a bit player with the Morosco stock company. When it was rumored that the company was closing, Lloyd went to Hollywood for the first time to look for work in motion pictures.

To his dismay, the gate men barred him from the studios. He paced outside the Universal gate for hours; the gate man was kind but firm.

"The next day it dawned on me that I could get through that gate. I had my make-up box with me, the one I had used in the theater. I sneaked out behind the building, put on a make-up, turned my hat into a new shape, and when the gang of extras swept back through the gates after lunch, I was with them."

He was in the studio, but he was not yet *working* in the studio. He soon discovered that the man to watch was the assistant director, who hired the extras. After a couple of days of sneaking through the gates in make-up and besieging assistant directors, Lloyd was given some extra parts. Working with him was a young man who was to play a decisive role in his career, Hal Roach.

"We became very fast friends. Hal was given a part in a J. Warren Kerrigan picture. He really wasn't an actor. He didn't have the stage background that I'd had, and he couldn't do the part to the satisfaction of the director, J. Farrell MacDonald. So I got the opportunity, and did it perfectly all right.

"Hal thought 'Damn . . . ,' but funnily enough, that was what really started our partnership. He had kind of a respect for my histrionic art, if you'd call it that!"[2]

Lloyd and Roach were paid five dollars a day as extras. When Universal decided that no extra was worth more than three dollars, they decided they were getting nowhere. Shortly afterward, they left the studio.

Roach was anxious to produce comedies, and wanted Lloyd to join him. When Roach inherited a few hundred dollars from a relative, he realized his opportunity had arrived. He made a few inexpensive pictures, the last being *Just Nuts* with Jane Novak and cowboy star Roy Stewart. When Lloyd, who played the comedian opposite these two names, discovered that Stewart was being paid ten dollars a day, while he only got five, he was disturbed.

"I thought about it a few days, and I felt pretty bad. Then my spunk began to get up. So I went to Hal, and Hal said he couldn't get Stewart unless he paid that price, but he couldn't possibly afford to give me that.

" 'Well,' I said, 'I would have stuck for five if that's all you paid anybody. But if you can't get him for less than ten, you can't get me for less either.' And I quit."

Lloyd went to Keystone. Roach tried to replace him with Richard Rosson, but soon had to abandon the idea. He went to work as a director at Essanay.

"Then Hal got things worked out, and Pathé offered him a contract if he got the three of us—Stewart, Jane Novak, and me—back again. Well, Roy Stewart had been signed on another western series, and Jane Novak had involved herself

[2] *Unless otherwise credited, the remaining quotations are from conversations between Harold Lloyd and the author in London and Hollywood between June 1963 and Dec. 1964.*

in other commitments, and I was just about ready to sign a contract with Sennett. But Hal offered me fifty dollars a week, so I left Keystone. And that was when we really started off in full measure."

Roach began directing Lloyd in a series of one-reelers for Pathé, based on a character called "Lonesome Luke."

"I didn't like Luke," said Lloyd. "Luke was a semi-imitation character. I tried my best to stay away from anything Chaplin did, and my clothes were really the reverse of Charlie's, being too small instead of too big. All the same, Charlie had the corner on comedy clothes. Lonesome Luke was a broad comedy character, and Charlie had the corner on that, too. He was king in that department.

"I was looking at some Lonesome Lukes recently. He was a rough, hard-driving character. The gags were rough and cruel and certainly violent. But Luke was pretty fair commercially and they were making money on it. When I said I wanted something completely individual, no one wanted to let me do it. Luke was making too much money for them."

Pathé pointed out, with indisputable logic, that they had spent a great deal of money exploiting Lonesome Luke—but nobody had heard of Harold Lloyd. His name had never even been on the screen.

By now, Bebe Daniels had become Lloyd's leading lady, and one night they were in a theater, waiting for one of their comedies. As the Lonesome Luke character appeared on the screen, Lloyd heard a small boy saying, "Oh, here's that fellow who tries to do like Chaplin."

"If I knew where that boy was," Lloyd wrote afterward, "I'd send him a medal, because that settled it for me. I went back and told Roach I was going to quit. I wasn't going on forever being a third-rate imitator of anybody, even a genius like Chaplin."

Roach wired Pathé again, and this time they agreed to allow Lloyd to try his new character. To replace the Luke two-reelers, Roach signed a celebrated clown, Toto, and asked Lloyd to continue making two-reelers himself.

"I said, 'No, I want to go back to one-reelers.' They thought I was out of my mind. 'Why?' they said. 'You were making two-reel Lukes. What do you want to go back to one-reel pictures for?'

" 'Because,' I said, 'the character has to be established. We do a one-reeler every week. Two-reelers we do one every month. If I had a bad one, the public's got to wait four weeks—with the stench of a poor one still around. But with a one-reeler, we cover it up the next week."

The character sprang from Lloyd's desire to get as far away from Lonesome Luke as possible, and to play a more natural character. "I wanted to make comedies where people would see themselves and their neighbors. It was then that I hit on the straight make-up with the glasses."

Lloyd, a dedicated moviegoer, had been inspired by a picture about a bespectacled and apparently inoffensive clergyman who became a tough he-man when the need arose. Lloyd found his glasses in an optical shop on Spring Street, Los Angeles. They cost seventy-five cents.

"I had to direct the first few glass-character pictures myself. I didn't intend to. I didn't even intend to do the first one. I hired a director for it—J. Farrell MacDonald, who had directed pictures Roach and I were extras on. He had never directed comedy. He would say, 'Harold, how do you want this scene?' I

The Lonesome Luke period: Bud Jamieson, Bebe Daniels, Harold Lloyd, Gus Leonard; 1917

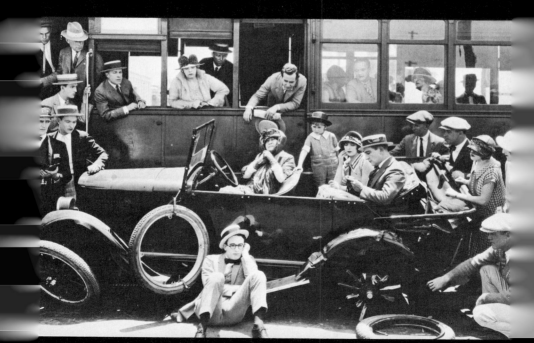

Hot Water *(1924).*

had to tell him exactly how the scene should go, and he would go in and tell the people. This happened on every scene. About a third of the way through the picture, he came up to me. He was most honest. 'Harold,' he said, 'I'm lost in this. I don't know where I'm going. You're telling me everything to do. I have to consult you on every little thing, and I feel foolish. I think you'd make much faster progress if you'd take it over yourself.' "

Lloyd directed this first comedy with the glasses character—*Over the Fence* (1917). For the next one he hired Gil Pratt. Gilbert Walker Pratt had begun his screen career with Kalem, and with the New York Motion Picture Company; with Roach's company he co-directed with Lloyd, and played heavies. Alf Goulding, an Australian with a great deal of stage experience, who was working at Fox, was the next director to make his appearance on the Roach lot. Pratt and Goulding alternated on the first five. When Roach's venture with Toto failed, Roach took over one of the units. Pratt went on to Vitagraph, and Roach and Goulding alternated.

In 1919, Roach signed with Pathé for nine two-reelers. *Bumping into Broadway* was the first, *Captain Kidd's Kids* was the second. It was also the last film with Bebe Daniels. She and Lloyd had been at a dancing contest two years earlier at Sunset Inn in Santa Monica. Cecil B. De Mille had also been there: "I'd like to have you in my company," he said. Miss Daniels pointed out that she was under contract. "Well, when you aren't, let me know," said De Mille. Miss Daniels was anxious to become a dramatic actress, and at her first opportunity she left Roach. To her surprise, De Mille was still interested.

The problem of replacing Bebe Daniels was solved by Roach. He had seen a girl called Mildred Davis in a Bryant Washburn comedy, *Marriage à la Carte* (1916; James Young). He screened it for Lloyd, who thought her ideal. (He later married her.)

Pathé was enthusiastic about the two-reelers, but held them up until all the remaining one-reelers had been released. Meanwhile, they asked Lloyd for some publicity shots. A photographer from the Witzel studio, Los Angeles, arrived at the studio and began to take pictures. One of them was to show Lloyd holding a mock bomb and looking up to heaven.

"And I damn near went to heaven!" said Lloyd.

The bomb was live. Three bombs with full charges had been put in a box with fake bombs, and the property boy had produced a live one.

"I had that bomb right in my face, where it would have blown my head off, but some providence made me lower it to say something to the cameraman. That one little gesture saved my life."

The explosion shattered the window, cracked the ceiling, and laid him up for nine months. His hand was injured and it seemed certain that he would be blind for life. His face was torn and covered with powder burns.

"The months that followed were so tough that I can't speak about them without turning cold," wrote Lloyd in his autobiography. "Up to that time, I'd led a normal, carefree, happy life. I'd known discouragement, poverty, worry, hard work. But nothing mattered because the future was rosy, I was young and strong, and everything was fun. With that explosion I knew real suffering for the first time."

Certain that he would be disfigured, he made up his mind that if he could see at all, he would become a comedy director. If not, he would become a comedy writer. But his acting days were over.

Miraculously, his recovery was complete. A special glove was fitted to his right hand, and Lloyd began work on *Haunted Spooks,* his fifth two-reeler, soon after leaving hospital.

"As a rule, when I put on the glasses, I never did anything you couldn't believe in. It may be a little improbable, but you could figure it could happen. In *Get Out and Get Under,* I did something I very seldom did, but it was quite funny.

"I was fixing my Ford, and I had the hood up. I had my head inside, then my shoulders went in, then half of me was in the car, and pretty soon my feet disappeared inside the engine. We were treating the picture as a satire. In those days, you felt the Model T could run without anything, so I ran it for a while, and I discovered I didn't have an engine. The Ford people were after me to use that film only about eight months ago. They were *delighted* with it. But I didn't let them have it; not unless I knew how they were going to use it."

Lloyd has always been very careful about the fate of his old pictures. Collectors may have acquired prints of *Safety Last* or *Grandma's Boy,* but most Lloyd features are held by Lloyd himself. He keeps a close watch on the activities of archives, film societies, and re-issue theaters. Gradually, he is releasing his best pictures in compilation form: *Harold Lloyd's World of Comedy, Harold Lloyd's Funny Side of Life. . . .* As in the silent days, he is dependent on audience reaction and previews.

"A movie audience is your best and worst critic. If you ask them outright to tell you what's wrong, they'll be hopeless. But if you sneak in and listen to them, they'll tell you everything.

"In the old days, it used to be a delight to sit in the audience and hear the reaction. They completely let go. They screamed. Today, they don't want to do that. They're restrained. Inwardly they may enjoy it as much, but in the old days they really got into the spirit. Everybody else was doing it, so they just let go.

"The real challenge to me on reissuing these pictures is to see if I can intrigue or capture a lost generation. How many teenagers know Lloyd? They couldn't be less interested in Lloyd. They're not familiar with the comedy of that era, and they couldn't care less. We ran *The Freshman (Harold Lloyd's Funny Side of Life)* in the Encino Theatre, San Fernando Valley. The house was full of teenagers, and predominantly girls. And the reaction—I don't think we'll ever hear it go better than it did. They wrote cards afterward and we got almost one hundred per cent favorable reaction.

"Irving Thalberg gave me credit for starting previews. I don't think he was right there, but I was certainly one of the early ones. When we took a one-reeler to have it previewed, an old theater manager over in Glendale took it as an occasion. He put on his white tie and tails to come out and explain to the audience what was going to happen.

"When we shot a picture, we did it as well as we could, but without going overboard. We knew we were going to preview—to let the audience be the final judge. Then we would come back and work two weeks, three weeks, six weeks—as long as it took to remake certain scenes. Then we would go and preview again.

"When *I Do* was a three-reeler, the first reel simply didn't click. It started with an elopement: the girl's parents are delighted, because they like the young man, and they are secretly helping them to elope. It was funny, but it laid an egg at the first preview. So we junked the whole reel, started from reel two, and it became one of my most successful two-reelers.

"*Grandma's Boy* was another example. I had had the idea for some time. We tried two or three times to get off the ground with it, but we kept going for something else. It was a lovely idea, but it was different from our usual comedies. So finally, we started it as a two-reeler. Like *Sailor-Made Man* just before it, it kept growing. 'Never mind the footage,' we said. 'Let's just go as long as we want to . . . we'll develop it the way we think it should be developed.' It ended up not a two-reeler but a five-reeler. Our first preview was a great disappointment. It was good, but not good enough. I remember Roach and I had brought our families, so we left the girls in one car and Hal and I went and sat in the other one to fight this out. We were there almost an hour in his car, with the girls not being happy at all.

"Hal said, 'Look, Harold, we are making comedies. We are doing things to make people laugh. Let's get back to the kind of picture we *should* make.'

"I said, 'Hal, this has got heart. It's different from what we've ever done. It's much finer. It's really got feeling.'

" 'But it hasn't got any laughs,' he said.

" 'Hal, you're absolutely right. Maybe we'd better go back and build a lot more laughs into this picture.'

" 'I'll say we'd better,' he said.

"We put in about twenty gags—sorted them all through the picture. Then we spent a lot of money on a little cartoon character called Icky, representing the boy's good and bad spirit. We previewed again. We found little Icky didn't help us at all. But oh, my, how the gags helped! We went back and shot still more gags, but we never lost any of our theme. I wouldn't let go of one inch of it.

"And if I had to choose my favorite of all of my films, I would choose *Grandma's Boy*. It could have been a drama just as easily as a comedy. It was about a boy who was a coward; his grandmother gives him a talisman, telling him that it belonged to his grandfather who, in the Civil War, was an even worse coward. She tells him how it enabled him to triumph over all odds. The boy takes the talisman and, knowing he will win, strides into his toughest opponent— a tramp. He is beaten again and again, but he never gives up because he knows he will win in the end. Then he finds out that his talisman is nothing more than the handle of his grandmother's old umbrella. But she tells him it worked; it gave him faith enough to persevere. He goes ahead and finally wins simply because he believed in himself. If you wanted a tragic picture of a coward, you could do it just as well with this theme."

In the comedy studios, the director did not share the same glamour, or the same responsibility, as his counterpart in dramatic work. Comedies were invariably the creation of a number of people. Harold Lloyd was most dependent on his gag men.

"When Hal and I started, we had to think up our own gags. When Hal went off to direct Toto, and I started my first picture with glasses, I had to think up all the gags myself. As the pictures began to make money, I hired as many idea men as I could get that I thought were good.

"One of them was a man named Frank Terry. He was one of the best, but he was also one of the worst. He'd give you ten ideas, and only one of them would have a germ in it. The others were horrible. He had an original mind, but no judgment at all. When I wasn't working for a while, I sent him over to Fox so he could earn some money.

" 'He'll give you lots of bad ideas,' I said, 'but he's a good man.' They kept him two weeks. 'Harold,' they said, 'were you kidding us?' They let him go. They couldn't pick that little wheat out of the chaff. Poor Frank. . . . He was Australian. He'd come in and tell me six gags, and I'd say, 'No, Frank—no, no, no!' He'd go out and say, 'Lloyd's in a terrible mood—a *terrible* mood.'

"I would come into the gag room in the morning, or whenever I had the time, and they'd all start throwing their ideas at me. I had some very good boys: Fred Newmeyer, who had been our property man, Ted Wilde, Tim Whelan, Sam Taylor, Clyde Bruckman, Jean Havez, Johnnie Grey, Tommy Gray. . . .

"Sometimes I felt fit to send them out alone, to work by themselves, or in pairs. Or divide them up, and let them work that way. You have a scene—say it's the magician's coat in *Movie Crazy* (1932). We're starting to build that, and we've arrived at the point where I am to dance with the wife of an important personage. It is vital that I make a good impression. Of course, I don't know that I have a magician's coat on, full of white mice and doves, nor does she. So how are we going to fill that out? I send the boys out to work on ideas. Maybe they'll come back with one idea we can use, but very seldom did it happen that way. Generally, they produced an idea, and we sat in there and worked it out. All of it was left entirely to my judgment; I had to routine everything.

"We had no script, but we made minute notes of the particular sequence that we were going to shoot. We would even suspend work for three or four days to work out exactly what we wanted. But when we finished shooting, the result might be completely different from our original idea. We allowed ourselves to remain open. If something came up that was better than what we'd conceived on paper, well, we did it. If you were working to a set script, you could get yourself completely fouled up. After you've changed it a few times, you might have to throw the script away, because you'd lost yourself. This way we built as we went along, like building a house. Building was of great importance.

"We'd have a certain number of pieces of business, gags, that we knew we were going to do. They were called 'islands.' We knew we had to go there. But whatever we did between those was up to us. We would ad lib, and make it up as we went along.

"Sometimes I'd take five, six, seven, or eight takes. They'd say, 'Oh, Harold, you've got it!' I'd say, 'Well, think of something else.' Some other little thing would come, and you would ad lib it. Of course, there were times when we did ten takes, and we went back and used the first, because it had a certain spontaneity, a simplicity, maybe, that the other ones didn't have. But generally, the takes we kept building turned out to be the best. You may start with only one or two little ideas. By the time you finished, you had ten ideas in the scene, none of which you had even conceived in the gag room.

Harold Lloyd and Mildred Davis in Grandma's Boy (1922).

Grandma's Boy; *Dick Sutherland, Harold Lloyd, Anna Townsend.*

For Heaven's Sake *(1926)*.

Welcome Danger *(1929); Mal St. Clair, director (the film was eventually credited to Clyde Bruckman); Wally Howe; Walter Lundin at camera; Gaylord Lloyd (Harold's brother) just visible; Jimmy Anderson; "Bard" Bardwell, head electrician; Jake Jacobs (Lloyd's double), holding board; Barbara Kent.*

"That's one of the things that working without a script did for you. It allowed you complete freedom. When I worked with Preston Sturges on a picture called *Mad Wednesday,* he would want a scene played as he wrote it in the script. We were tied down and we lost our freedom. I think it ruined the picture.

"I never took credit for direction, although I practically directed all my own pictures. The directors were entirely dependent on me. I had these boys there because I felt they knew comedy, they knew what I wanted, they knew me—and they could handle the details. When you're acting in front of the camera, you can't see yourself, and these boys were able to say, 'Harold, don't you think it would be funnier if you didn't do so-and-so?'

"If anything went wrong and I didn't like it, I had nobody to blame but myself. I had complete control over all my pictures.

"Now a picture like *Mad Wednesday,* that is a hundred per cent the other way. I only had control over the first third. Up to the barbershop. And Howard Hughes, who was producing it, left that alone, I'm glad to say. But he cut the barroom terribly, he cut some of the best stuff out of it, and then he just cut straight on through. But by that time, in my estimation, Sturges had already ruined it. The first third, however, I liked.

"Of all the directors, Sam Taylor was the most valuable man I ever had. He was a tremendous help to me. He had a brilliant mind. He parted from me, amicably, because I had stopped producing for a while, and he went off and directed Pickford, Fairbanks, Bea Lillie, John Barrymore. He was an academic type, and was one of the biggest helps I ever had.

"I'm not counting Hal, because Hal wouldn't drop into that category. Hal and I were in a different period. He wasn't actually a very good director. He had fortitude, he had drive, and he had worlds of confidence. But in the early days, on the Lonesome Luke pictures, he would work until he got up to the last five or ten minutes, then he would say, 'All right, this creaks.' And he'd quit. He'd just wind it up.

"But there was a sort of affinity between Hal and myself. He used to say, 'No matter what the scene is that I think up, Lloyd has the knack of putting it on the screen the way I visualized it.' Roach was very creative, he was a very good gagman, and he had great courage."

Lloyd paid the best salaries in the business for his gag men. They got between five hundred and eight hundred dollars a week, which was exceptionally high. He managed to tempt gag men from every studio.

"We had a very funny situation once over a playwright named Frank Craven. He had written many fine Broadway hits, such as *The First Year,* in which he starred. He was an excellent actor and an excellent comedian. He was doing things in pictures and doing exceptionally well, and one day I met him at a party. We got talking about the number of men I hired to deliver pieces of business.

" 'Harold,' he said, 'why do you go to all that expense? You pay these fellows a lot of money. Why don't you get one man who can do all this for you? It would save you all that expense.'

" 'I've never found such a man,' I said.

" 'I think I could do it, Harold,' he said.

" 'Frank,' I said, 'I've got all the respect in the world for you. You're a great talent. But I don't think you could do it.'

" 'Would you like to take a chance on it?' he said. 'I'll cost you more money by far than any one of those men, but it won't come to anywhere near what you're paying the group.'

" 'Frank,' I said, 'would you like to try an experiment? Would you like to come over and just sit in with this group for a while? Then I'll give you some things to work on and if you can do it, maybe we can make a deal.'

"He came over, and sat in with my gag group for three days. I left him alone. I went in and talked to them and they threw ideas at me. Finally, after the third day, Frank said, 'Good-by, Harold!' Then he said, 'What irritates me is this medium. In my own medium, I can think of ideas galore. But I sat in there for three days and these fellows were throwing ideas all over the place, and I couldn't think of one damn thing. It really hurt my pride. I would have liked to help you, but Harold, it's your medium!' "

The technicians at the Lloyd studio were a closely knit group, nearly all of whom had been with the company for years. Walter Lundin, first cameraman; Homer Scott, second cameraman; Fred Jackman in the earlier days; Freddie Guiol, property man; Bill MacDonald, property man; Jack Murphy, production manager; H. M. Walker, title writer; Joe Reddy, press agent; Red Golden, assistant director; Tom Crizer, cutter.

"These men I kept all the year round. We may lay off for four months, but it made no difference. Their salaries went right on, and they just went ahead and did whatever they wanted. They weren't happy when unions came in, I can tell you that right now! They were better off without the unions. That wasn't the case, of course, at other studios where they didn't treat their personnel the way I did.

"We kept up the comedy spirit at the studio—comedy on as well as off. I stopped work for a whole day once because the boys had led someone to believe that Lloyd was half rooky. So I did everything to make him think that, and we had a wonderful day of it. Of course, we could do that sort of thing in those days.

"Property men—talk about property men being important! Oh! They were your lifeblood, believe me. They were instrumental in saving your life. They were the ones who worked out the safety factors. Of course, they missed occasionally, but not very often, and we had great confidence in them. If someone said, 'Freddie's okayed it,' I went ahead and did it. I felt that Fred [Guiol] wouldn't let anything go by that he hadn't tried out thoroughly and was satisfied was safe. Same thing with Bill MacDonald. They were both with me for years. Freddie Guiol finally became a director, and he worked as an associate with George Stevens, who had been a Roach cameraman. George Stevens swore by him—he didn't want to do a picture without Guiol.

"The safety factor was always important, but never more so than on *Safety Last*. I got the idea for that picture when I was walking down Seventh Street, Los Angeles, and I saw a tremendous crowd outside the Brockman Building. I asked what all the excitement was about. 'A man's going to climb this building in a little while,' they said. So I stood around, and sure enough, a steeplejack named Bill Strothers came out and was introduced to the crowd. The usual ritual, I guess, that goes with that. Then he started climbing. I watched him for about three floors, and it had such an emotional effect on me that I started walking up the street. I was afraid that at any moment he'd fall and kill himself. I walked about a block up the street, but my curiosity held me back. I didn't go away, but I went around the corner, so I could peek around every so often and see where he was. There were other people there, too, and I'd inquire, 'How's he doing?'

" 'Oh, he's on the sixth floor.'

"He went up via the windows, from one window to another. I still don't know how he could possibly have done it, but he did. When he'd finished climbing the building, he rode a bicycle around the edge—and went up a flagpole and stood on his head. When it was all over, I went up and introduced myself. I told him I was in motion pictures, and I asked him to come in on our next one. I figured that if *I* was affected that way, an audience would be, too. We could incorporate his climb into our story.

"Roach and I signed him up, but we spent the next two or three weeks working on our story, and Bill got bored doing nothing. He was offered another job climbing a building, and he asked if we'd let him do it.

" 'No, no,' we said. 'You might break a leg!'

"Time dragged on. Eventually we let him do it. It was only a three-story building, but he fell from the first floor and broke a leg. *I* had to do the climb in the picture, while Bill Strothers was being chased by the cop. If you look carefully you'll see that he has a limp. We called him Limpy Bill.

"We did the climb first in *Safety Last*. We weren't sure how the picture was going to start. But we had our climb, and we were very happy with it. It gave us great enthusiasm.

"There was no back projection in those days, of course, so when you see me climbing, I'm *really* climbing. We had platforms built below the skyscraper windows—they were about ten to fifteen feet below, covered with mattresses. After the picture, we dropped a dummy onto one of the platforms, and it bounced off into the street. I must have been crazy to do it."

Besides the real building, specially constructed sections were put up on the roof of other buildings.

"You're taking a hell of a chance on all of them, believe me. It was not at all soft. We took at least a month and a half to make the climb. We could only shoot a few scenes a day, because of the shadows blotting out the middle of the street down below. We could only work from eleven to one thirty. We'd get there early to get everything lined up, and we would rehearse some of the scenes so that the moment the shadows were right, we could move fast."

For the extreme long shots, in which the familiar straw-hatted figure is dwarfed by the building, Lloyd used Bill Strothers. A circus acrobat did the stunt in which Lloyd's foot catches in a rope; he swings off the building, describing an arc, and comes to rest on a ledge. But practically all the other scenes were performed by Lloyd himself.

At the end of production, he visited a fortune teller at the beach. Feeling the calluses on his hands, she informed him that he earned his living through manual labor.

"I'll say I did. At first, I was just scared to death. But after I'd worked up there a few days, I got just as goofy as anybody."

Look Out Below was Lloyd's first thrill picture, a one-reeler, followed by *High and Dizzy* (two reels). *Never Weaken,* a three-reeler, staged its climax among the girders of a half-built skyscraper. *Safety Last* was the first feature thrill picture.

"We made it because after *High and Dizzy* everything seemed to be an anti-climax. We just *had* to do another thrill picture."

Lloyd is perturbed, however, when he is constantly reminded of his skyscraper exploits. "Doesn't anyone remember my other pictures?" he asked. "I made close to three hundred, and only five were thrill pictures."

Lloyd refers only to his skyscraper comedies when he talks of "thrill pictures." But there were thrilling sequences in many of his comedies. In *Girl Shy* (1924), Lloyd finds himself with only a few minutes to stop his girl from marrying another man. He commandeers every means of transportation—from a streetcar to a horse and cart—to make it to the church on time. This sequence is as excitingly shot as the chariot race from *Ben-Hur,* even though it was made a year earlier.

Another thrill sequence, equally well shot, is featured in *For Heaven's Sake.* Harold has charge of a crowd of drunks, who take over a double-decker, open-top Los Angeles bus and hurtle through the streets at breakneck speed. Again, Lloyd uses no process shots. The bus screeches around corners, apparently on two wheels, lurching as drunkenly as its occupants. One of them does a tightrope walk along the rail on the top deck. . . .

"That whole bus was on a truck, but on rockers. It was terrifying up there because it felt like the bus really was going over. As it tipped, we all went over the edge; it gave the perfect illusion of the bus cornering on two wheels.

"The tightrope walker was done by a brace, an iron brace that came up one leg and fitted to his body. It was up to him to bend his body, and his loose leg, so that you couldn't tell that one leg was completely stiff. Oh, we did things quite elaborately, believe me!

"A scene like that might take two weeks. We would get a whole cordon of police and rope off probably three blocks. We used all our own traffic and all our own pedestrians. All those people that we run through there are our own people, being paid."

Film historians and critics, while praising Harold Lloyd's comedies, have said that he was funny only because of his material. They allege that Lloyd himself was not a comedian.

"I could give them so many answers to that. It is completely erroneous. I mean, you couldn't capture the comedy if you weren't a comedian. Comedy comes from inside. It comes from your face. It comes from your body."

Lloyd now tends to give the impression that he was always confident about his work, that he never suffered from the agony of doubt. An interview with him in 1924 revealed another side to this great comedian:

"There is one thing about Harold that is always amusing. If you ask him how his picture is going, his face falls, he looks utterly downcast and miserable. 'I'm afraid of it,' he says."

Lloyd withdrew from motion pictures, dissatisfied with his 1938 production, *Professor Beware.* He says he was rushed into it, and it was below his usual standard. He determined not to make another picture until he found the right subject.

"Then I got to doing other things. I made one last picture, *Mad Wednesday,* and I didn't like it. So I withdrew altogether."

Lloyd became immersed in a vast number of activities and hobbies, all of which he approached with his characteristic dedication.

His aim is the attainment of excellence. He has become a stereo photographer of brilliance, and has won national awards. A passionate music lover, he has constructed a stereophonic sound system rivaling the finest in the world. His record library receives every new release in the way the British Museum receives every new book. He has carefully catalogued it, and page after page is filled with the work of his favorite composer, Beethoven.

A long corridor in his huge, thirty-two-room house is lined with framed photographs with signed tributes from Frank Capra—"To Harold, who started all of us gag men"—from Chaplin, from Cecil B. De Mille: "To Harold Lloyd, hoping that my spectacles never get as many laughs as yours."

He keeps his films in fireproof vaults, and there is a cutting room attached. His impressive estate, "Greenacres," will be handed over to the Beverly Hills community on his death; he is a director of the Beverly Hills Chamber of Commerce, and very active in civic organizations. He is a leading figure in the major project of the Shriners—the maintenance of seventeen hospitals for crippled children in the United States, Mexico, and Canada.

He never lost touch with motion pictures, however, and occasionally considered directing other comedians. He says he would like to direct Dick van Dyke. He has produced comedies, and one of them was a Lucille Ball film.

"There was a scene when Edmond O'Brien comes across a girl who tries to make him by dropping her handkerchief. I suggested that he should walk past, pick up the handkerchief with his toe, and drop it in her lap. They tried it again and again. Not being on the set, I didn't know how things were going until they told me it wasn't working.

" 'It just isn't funny,' they said. 'Shall we throw it away?'

" 'No,' I said. 'It *is* funny. I did it in a picture myself, *Welcome Danger*. Let me see how you're doing it.'

"It was so clumsy.

" 'No—you have to do it on the beat. You walk forward and you mustn't pause.' I showed Ed, and everyone roared, and he was raring to go. He did it as I'd showed him and he was perfect.

"I have seen many of the modern comedies, particularly the slapstick spectacles. The trouble with most of them is that there's not enough conditioning for the gags. I'll explain what I mean; they don't build up the comedy, they don't condition the audience to expect a certain gag, and when the gags happen they don't work on it enough. They don't cap it with another one to bring an even louder laugh. Sure they get laughs—they often have some big gags. But then the audience doesn't see it through my eyes. They could be *so* much better!"

Harold Lloyd is undeniably pleased by the warm affection with which his films have been received.

"We really didn't think about posterity, in those days," he says. "But we're happy to accept the credit they're giving us for these old pictures being classics. Generally you have to die before something of yours becomes a classic. You don't enjoy it in your own lifetime!"

43 / BUSTER KEATON

NAVIGATOR.

At least he died in a blaze of glory. Few stars have staged such spectacular returns. Even fewer have been welcomed with such warm affection.

Buster Keaton died on February 1, 1966, just as the publicity surrounding his comeback was reaching its peak. A retrospective had brought him to the Venice Film Festival, where critics, journalists and film makers gave him a standing ovation. Further offers were pouring in, from motion-picture producers and from television. Tributes were being paid him in newspapers and magazines the world over. A long-awaited biography was about to appear.[1]

Keaton was delighted, but he knew that the value of such applause was academic.

"Sure it's great," he told film historian Lotte Eisner after the Venice triumph, "but it's all thirty years too late."

When he really needed encouragement and support, in the early days of talkies, he received it from no one. Joseph M. Schenck, his producer and his brother-in-law, and probably the most powerful figure in the business, persuaded him to cease independent production and to join M-G-M. Keaton admitted it was the biggest mistake of his life. He lost the unit that had worked with him from the start. He lost his gag men, and was forced to shoot from written scenarios. Worse still, arguments with producers, and the closely supervised studio routine, caused him to lose his enthusiasm. He became an alcoholic. His wife, Natalie Talmadge, sister of Norma Talmadge, who was married to Schenck, sued for divorce.

"What a raw deal they gave poor Buster," said Louise Brooks. "When his wife divorced him, Joe Schenck made sure that he didn't own his films, so he could never resell them. They weren't his own property, like Lloyd's or Chaplin's. He didn't have a cent. He lived in a magnificent house, on the same scale as a millionaire. But a millionaire's income comes in every year for ever. Poor Buster lived in a mansion with eight or nine servants on three thousand dollars a week. Schenck was making money out of actors, out of films, out of stories. What did it matter to him or Sam Goldwyn if they lost two thousand to four thousand dollars a week in the big bridge games? Or went to the Clover Club and lost twenty thousand? They forced the actors, like Buster, to take part because the moment you haven't any dough you're through. You aren't brave any more. No actor could compete financially with a producer. Poor little Buster with his three thousand dollars a week, trying to live like a millionaire. It was impossible. So they broke him."

The majority of Keaton's sound films were lamentably unsuccessful and both they and he were quickly forgotten. In 1945, an article by James Agee in *Life* revived his fame in America. Film appreciation societies began to circulate *The General* and *The Navigator*. As audiences for these comedies increased, Keaton's mangled reputation was restored. In the mid-fifties, further Keaton pictures were reissued. A few years later, the Cinémathèque Française held a Keaton retrospective; almost every Keaton picture, two-reeler and feature, had been tracked down. Keaton announced plans for a series of reissues, to be released through a Munich film company. The plans were sabotaged when Schenck executors claimed ownership. At the time of his death, the work of Buster Keaton's entire motion-picture career was locked in a vault in Germany.

---

1 Rudi Blesh: Keaton (*New York: The Macmillan Company; 1966*).

Coney Island *(1917); Alice Mann, Roscoe Arbuckle, Buster Keaton.*

Donald Crisp directing Keaton's underwater descent for The Navigator *(1924). The underwater sequence was shot later in Lake Tahoe.*

Keaton's house, in the San Fernando Valley, was called "The Keatons." It was a bungalow, pleasant enough, but scarcely comparable with his former residence (only recently occupied by James Mason). Buster spent his spare time looking after his chickens and watching television. His spare time became less and less toward the end, however, as producers and agents tried to sign him. "I won't do a weekly TV series," he said. "It's too much like hard work. Guess I turn down eighteen offers a season."

His last projects had included a Samuel Beckett film, simply called *Film*—"that was a wild daydream he had"—several commercials, including one for Ford recreating the style of *Cops*. A color film called *The Railrodder*, which showed Buster traversing Canada on a mechanized handcart, some of the *Pajama Party* series and Richard Lester's *A Funny Thing Happened on the Way to the Forum*.

Keaton talked about his career with detachment. When he described the mechanics of a gag, or the difficulties of staging an intricate scene, only then did he become really engrossed. In between bouts of coughing (he died of lung cancer), he demonstrated some hilarious moments, and paced the room with that unique Keaton walk.

The room was decorated with photographs, certificates, and awards. A billiard table occupied one side of it; on the other was what Keaton called his saloon. It was about the size of a telephone kiosk, but fitted with authentic swing doors, and a sign: "Stage Door."

"Everybody has a cocktail bar, I go for one of these. It has a spittoon, a brass rail, and draught beer. If you like beer, this is the best in town. This is a seven-and-a-quarter-gallon tank; instead of the old system of running it out of a wooden keg through coils, this is an icebox. I use an aluminum barrel, so it's the temperature of the icebox. No coils. No ice."

In the far corner hung two cowboy hats, from Texas and Oklahoma cattlemen's associations, and next to them a fireman's hat, signifying honorary membership of the Buffalo, New York, fire department. There was also a replica of a Confederate kepi. An Oscar stood on a table—"To Buster Keaton for his unique talents which brought immortal comedies to the screen"—next to an Eastman Award. It was the Eastman Award which Keaton seemed most proud of and most anxious to display.

"There are only twenty of those in existence," he said. "They gave one to the five male stars of motion-picture history—and it's one of those I've got."

A photograph of Roscoe Arbuckle smiled down from one wall; an original colored lithograph of the old General locomotive dominated another. Beneath was a hilarious shot of three Busters sitting beside each other on a bench, their hands covering eyes, ears, and mouth like the three monkeys. There was a still of Buster's father, Joe Keaton, with the train he drove in *Our Hospitality*. A more recent photograph showed Buster with Harold Lloyd and Jacques Tati.

"Here's a picture for you," said Keaton. "This is the best still picture I've got. It shows a dinner held at the Roosevelt Hotel to welcome Rudolph Valentino into United Artists. Here are eight of the ten top stars of motion pictures—William S. Hart, Norma Talmadge, Douglas Fairbanks, Mary Pickford, Charlie Chaplin, Rudolph Valentino, Constance Talmadge, me—the two missing are Harold Lloyd and Gloria Swanson. It's a great photograph. Today you couldn't duplicate it, because if you managed to assemble eight of the top stars, by the time you could get them together a couple of them wouldn't be in the top ten. They come and go too fast."

After pausing in front of pictures of his children and grandchildren, Keaton pointed out the oddest item of all—a stunt check for seven dollars and fifty cents, carefully placed in a frame.

"That was a stunt I did for Lew Cody. The gag was that he comes down to the cellar to turn on the boiler or something, dressed in full-dress clothes, and he steps on this cake of soap. Well, Cody can't fall off a chair without putting himself in hospital, so he's got these two stunt men. They each do good falls, but they aren't funny. Eddie Sutherland, the director, didn't want a straight dramatic fall—it had to look funny or he can't use the scene. Well, I was doing *The Cameraman* with Ed Sedgwick and I figured Sedgwick wouldn't need me for a while, so I said, 'Give me Cody's clothes.'

"I put on his full-dress suit, came down the steps, and instead of hitting the piece of soap with both legs going from under me, I did it the other way. I took my foot out so it threw me on my head, and as I came down I threw a neck roll and lit with the tails of my coat over my head. It was an ideal cut. It hid me completely when I lit, so all I had to do was to move Cody in there in the exact same spot, move the camera up a few feet, and he just took the coattails back off his head, shook himself, and went on with it.

"Now they moved the camera up without putting a number board between the shots, so it looked like it was a continuous scene. In the projection room, poor Eddie Sutherland is there watching his dailies with Irving Thalberg. And Thalberg says, 'You must never let Cody do a thing like that! Do you realize the chance you took? Cody could be laid up for weeks!'

"They gave me a stunt check for seven-fifty. I never cashed it. They owe me an awful lot of interest, because that was shot in 1928!"

Keaton's obvious enjoyment of this recollection was significant. He was fascinated by the mechanics of film making, by the careful and intricate preparations that go into the ultimate goal of the comedian: a laugh from an audience.

He took immense care over such details. His gags were never hit-and-miss; they were calculated with the precision of an engineer's bluprint. And he was a past master when it came to stunts involving physical prowess for comic effect.

He had ideal training. He was born in the middle of a cyclone, on October 4, 1895, in Piqua, Kansas.

His father, Joseph Keaton, in a rare interview, recalled that at the time he was playing *Kathleen Mavourneen* with his medicine-show troupe of four.

"Between the acts we sold patent medicines, guaranteed to cure everything and stop anything—including cyclones. But after the cyclone passed, all we had left was the repertoire. The tent and the medicines were gone. That evening, when I got back to our little roominghouse in Piqua, after chasing our tent all over the country, the landlady told me our troupe had been increased to five.

"My wife had given birth to a son—our first baby. I was awfully glad. I could see the time coming when the little feller got some older, when I wouldn't have to play the bloodhound in *Uncle Tom's Cabin*."[2]

The baby was named Joseph, after his father and his grandfather, and he was

[2] Photoplay, *May 1927, p. 98.*

renamed by his father's partner, Harry Houdini. When he was six months old, young Keaton fell downstairs. He was completely unhurt, but he burst into tears, and Houdini picked him up to comfort him. "That's some buster your baby took!" he said. From that moment, Joseph was Buster Keaton.

Buster had an exciting childhood. Said his father: "Billed as 'The Three Keatons,' Buster, his mother, and I had a burlesque acrobat act in which my wife and I threw Buster about the stage like a human medicine ball." As "The Human Mop," Buster was not so much a performer as an indestructible prop. Official investigations were made into the act after complaints of cruelty. But Buster remained unscathed by his experiences.

His formal education amounted to one day—a day he said he played strictly for laughs, using the rest of the class as an audience. The school felt it advisable for general discipline that he should not return.

William Randolph Hearst tried to sign "The Three Keatons" for a two-reeler. Later, he suggested a series, based on a comic strip in his newspapers called "Bringing Up Father." Joe Keaton, however, had no time for the movies.

Buster left "The Three Keatons" when his father got drunk once too often. He went to New York to try for work as a single act. He struck success right away when Max Hart, New York's most influential agent, secured him a part in *The Passing Show of 1917.*

Just before rehearsals started, at the Winter Garden, he met an old friend from vaudeville days, Lou Anger.

"You've never been in the movies, have you?" asked Anger.

"No," replied Keaton. "Joe got mad at them."

"Well, come on down to the Norma Talmadge studio."

Anger and Keaton went to the Colony Studio where Norma Talmadge and her sister Constance were working, and where Roscoe Arbuckle was due to start a comedy called *The Butcher Boy.*[3]

"The making of a motion picture started to fascinate me immediately," said Keaton. "So I stuck with them, and went in and out of that picture. First thing I did was ask a thousand questions about the camera, then I went into the projection room to see things cut. It just fascinated me."

Keaton was so enamored of motion pictures that he asked Max Hart if he could break his two-hundred-and-fifty-dollars-a-week contract to work in pictures at forty a week. Surprisingly, Hart approved and told Keaton that he was making a very wise move.

At the Colony Studio, Keaton met his future wife, Natalie Talmadge, sister of Norma. After an unsuccessful attempt to establish herself as an actress, she was working with the Arbuckle unit as script girl and secretary.

"Arbuckle at that time was considered, next to Chaplin, to be the best comedy director in pictures. He directed all his own films. He was a good man to watch. I was only with him about three pictures when I became his assistant director. I don't mean that in the sense of an assistant director like we have today who sees

[3] *Keaton told me a slightly different story from the version in Rudi Blesh's book. He said that he met both Anger and Arbuckle on the street, and that Arbuckle invited him over to the studio. I checked with Rudi Blesh, who pointed out that most of his interviews were secured during 1952—1953. "If I were choosing," he said, "I'd take the earlier story, which he told me when he was still in his fifties and his memory was very clear." In deference to the authenticity of the Keaton book, I have altered this story to correspond with that of Blesh. All other material remains as Keaton described it.*

people are on the set. I mean when he was doing a scene and I wasn't in it, I was alongside the camera to watch it. I directed when he was in the scene. So by the time I'd spent a year with him, it was no problem at all to direct when I set out on my own."

Keaton's career was interrupted by the draft board. "I went into the infantry. I spent eleven months in the army, seven months in France. I was close enough to hear it, but by the time I hit the front, the Germans were in retreat, which was a great thing. I was tickled to death at that."

On his return, in 1919, he received offers from Fox and Warner Brothers; Warners was then an unimportant little company, but Fox suggested a salary of a thousand dollars a week. Keaton preferred to return to Schenck at his former salary of two hundred and fifty. He admired Schenck, and was deeply indebted when he discovered that Schenck had sent regular weekly checks of twenty-five dollars to the Keaton family while he was in the army.

"I'm back out of uniform, and I do two pictures with Arbuckle—*The Hayseed* and *The Garage*. Then Schenck in New York tells Marcus Loew that he's going to sell Arbuckle to Paramount for feature pictures, and he's going to make two-reelers with me. Now, Loew knew me from the stage—he knew 'The Three Keatons.' And he probably had seen me in a couple of Arbuckle pictures. He's a theater owner; he's just bought Metro studios and the Metro studios were next to the new Keaton studios. He's also bought the Metro exchange, which operates throughout the world, and he's taken over the contracts of all the Metro stars. And he says, 'I'll take the Keaton pictures'—before we even started to make them!

"He goes to New York's leading theater producer, John Golden, who did *Seventh Heaven, Turn to the Right* and *Lightnin'*, and says, 'I want one of your famous shows. I want to make a special immediately to try and improve the quality of pictures at Metro.'

"Golden and Belasco were the two leading producers of dramatic shows, although Golden didn't hesitate to do light comedies, such as *Officer 666*. Golden suggests *The New Henrietta*. The original show starred William H. Crane and Douglas Fairbanks. This is one of Fairbanks' big hit shows on Broadway—before he ever sees a studio.[4]

"Loew says, 'Get me William Crane to play his own part, and give me the stage director. Has he had any experience in a studio?'

" 'No,' says Golden.

" 'Well, we'll put a motion-picture director in with him.' So they get Herbert Blache.

"But they can't get Fairbanks. He's now a big star with United Artists. They ask him who should take his role, and he says 'Keaton.' "

The picture was renamed *The Saphead* (1921), and was rewritten to make Keaton's role, Bertie, the main character.

The Saphead was an elegantly staged light comedy, very well made, with scenes of great charm. Keaton's presence gave the film more than just a top-flight performance, since many of the gags were his and the final riot in the stock exchange was a typical Keaton sequence. *Photoplay,* however, gave it mild praise; they considered the picture intelligently directed (Herbert Blache shared a credit

4 *Fairbanks' first motion-picture role was Bertie, the Lamb of Wall Street, from* The New Henrietta. *The picture was called* The Lamb (1915; *Christy Cabanne*).

with the stage director, Winchell Smith), edited, and titled, and thought it furnished good light entertainment.

"Buster Keaton is a natural and agreeable comedian,"[5] was their only comment on Keaton's first feature appearance.

At this same time, Roscoe Arbuckle was also making his first feature appearance. George Melford was directing him in *The Round Up,* a western romance in which his namesake Maclyn Arbuckle had starred on the stage. Much of it was played straight. As *Photoplay*'s reviewer put it: "I don't suppose anyone could possibly take 'Fatty' seriously as a sheriff with notches on his gun, but it is something of a triumph for him that he keeps the faces of his audience straight while he is suggesting the possibility."[6]

An uncredited bit was played by Buster Keaton—the last time the two men played together.

"Right after *The Saphead,* I was up hunting at Long Pine, on the edge of the Mojave Desert. It's good quail country, and I went up there to shoot. And there's Arbuckle, on location. Now I had no connection with the picture—it was Paramount—but they had a scene to make and Arbuckle said, 'Put make-up on Keaton and let me shoot him.'

"George Melford, the director, says, 'All right,' so they get me in Indian make-up and they put the camera shooting over Arbuckle's head. You could see him take aim at me and shoot . . . and when he shot, I died. But I was going at top speed, and when he hit me I sailed through the air and then plowed the dirt—right over a fifty-foot cliff. Ever see a rabbit hit in the back of the head—what it does to him? Well, that's what it looked like it did to me.

"The silly part of it was that my mother, living in Muskegon, Michigan, went to see it because she liked Arbuckle, and remembered the show from Broadway. When that Indian died on the screen, she said, 'That's Buster.' How in God's name she could pick me, I don't know. No one told her I was in the picture. and I never thought of writing. It was just a long shot of an Indian. But she knew it was me. 'Nobody else could do that,' she said."

When Joseph Schenck sold Arbuckle's contract, Keaton inherited the Arbuckle company.

"Then he got me the studio. The studio was the old Chaplin studio before Charlie built the place on La Brea. So I had a city lot there, a good-size block, for my studio. We had all the room in the world for one company. Of course, we used location an awful lot.

"On location, your big problem is people. People standing watching, getting in the way. But we didn't have so much trouble. If we were going to be in a congested section, we'd always tell the police department. They'd send down two or three motorcycle cops to control traffic, or do whatever we needed.

"We never actually paid them for this, but we used to give them an extra's check or a stunt check. That was probably ten dollars, or something like that. If we wanted the fire department, they'd say, 'Which one do you want?' We went down, told them what we wanted, and they sent them out on a call. It cost us nothing. Never did. None of our railroad things ever cost us anything. The Santa Fe people were tickled to death to see SANTA FE on the screen. It was on their

[5] Photoplay, *May 1921, p. 53.*
[6] Photoplay, *July 1924, p. 107.*

boxcars, on their engines, on everything. They were perfectly satisfied. You can't get cheaper advertising than that!"

The Keaton company comprised director Eddie Cline, who co-directed with Buster Keaton, and a nucleus of three gag men. Jean Havez and Clyde Bruckman were Keaton's favorites. Havez, a genial, fat man who looked like Roscoe Arbuckle, used to write shows for Kolb and Dill. He composed the song, "Everybody Works but Father."

Clyde Bruckman was one of the best gag men in the business. When Keaton credited him for the co-direction of one of his pictures, he was signed up by Harold Lloyd. In fact, he had had no directorial experience at all, and the responsibility of his new job unnerved him. On top of this, marital troubles led him to drink.

In 1953, Bruckman borrowed a gun from Keaton. After a meal in a Hollywood restaurant, which he was unable to pay for, he went to the rest room and shot himself.

Other gag men on the Keaton company included Joseph A. Mitchell, who came from a background of vaudeville and the legitimate stage, and Thomas Gray, who had written for *The Greenwich Village Follies* and *Music Box Revues*.

Later, Keaton tried Robert E. Sherwood, Al Boasberg, Carl Harbaugh, and other important writers. He found them all unsuitable for silent comedy work.

The chief technical man was Fred Gabourie, responsible for set building and for special effects. His achievements with the Keaton comedies were to make him one of the most sought-after technicians in the business.

The studio head was Lou Anger, officially the production manager. But most of the time Gabourie filled this role. Bert Jackson was the property man, Denver Harmon the chief electrician. Elgin Lessley was first cameraman, Byron Houck, former baseball player with the Philadelphia Athletics, was second cameraman. Bert Haines was camera assistant. Later, Devereaux Jennings joined as a first cameraman.

"By the time we were ready to start a picture, everyone on the lot knew what we've been talking about, so we never had anything on paper. Neither Chaplin, Lloyd, nor myself, even when we got into feature-length pictures, ever had a script.

"After we stopped making wild two-reelers and got into feature-length pictures, our scenario boys had to be story-conscious. We couldn't tell any far-fetched stories. We couldn't do farce comedy, for instance. It would have been poison to us. An audience wanted to believe every story we told them. Well, that eliminates farce comedy and burlesque. The only time we could do something out of the ordinary had to be in a dream sequence, or in a vision. So story construction became very important to us.

"Somebody would come up with an idea. 'Here's a good start,' we'd say. We skip the middle. We never paid any attention to the middle. We immediately went to the finish. We worked on the finish and if we get a finish that we're all satisfied with, then we'll go back and work on the middle. For some reason, the middle always took care of itself."

Keaton's first independent comedy was a two-reeler called *One Week*.

Sybil Seely was the leading lady. She was an unknown.

"If my studio manager coud get a leading lady cheap, he did it. He just didn't consider it important."

College (1927); James Horne, foreground.
Keaton on parallel.

Buster Keaton in The General (1926).

The General.

But then Keaton was not overparticular himself. She had to be attractive, and have some acting ability. But he never insisted on a sense of humor in case she broke up during a scene. Only occasionally did he use an established name, such as Phyllis Haver (in *Balloonatics*).

One Week set the style for all the future Keatons; the opening gag sequence . . . the slow build-up . . . the frenetic climax . . . and then that climax outmatched by the final sequence. Buster and his new wife have bought themselves a build-it-yourself home. The jealous rival changes all the numbers on the sections. Result: chaos. The house is a nightmare jumble, with doors where the windows should be and the kitchen stove halfway up the outside wall. Making the best of their predicament, the newlyweds hold a house-warming party. A storm springs up, the rain leaks through the roof, and the guests are drenched. After the rain—wind. The fragile little house is unable to withstand the gale, and it starts spinning on its axis, hurling the guests through the windows. One elderly gentleman braces himself against the furious wind, examines his watch, and thanks Buster for his hospitality. The guests depart. After the storm, more problems. The house has been erected on the wrong lot. Ordered to move, Buster attaches his house to his Ford and drives across town. Mounted on barrels, the house proceeds smoothly until the barrels jam between the tracks of a railroad crossing. A train is hurtling toward them. Desperately, they try to move the house. It is no use. Buster drags his wife to safety, and they cover their eyes, waiting for the crash. The train steams harmlessly past—on an adjoining track. Relieved, they turn back to the problem of shifting their house. But before they can move, another train from the opposite direction crashes straight through it. Buster places a FOR SALE notice on the rubble and resignedly saunters away. Then he remembers something and returns; he pins to the notice a leaflet entitled "Instructions."

One Week not only established the gag formula which the subsequent Keatons were to follow, it also established their technique. The simple setups, the flat comedy lighting, the spare use of titles—and the overall excellence of the direction. Buster Keaton gave credit to co-director Eddie Cline, but there can be no doubt where the responsibility lay for the final result. Cline was a successful comedy director in later years, but few of his films have the panache of these early Keatons. In retrospect, Buster Keaton was probably the best comedy director in the business. Chaplin's use of film was pedestrian by comparison.

Keaton was also an intuitively brilliant editor. He said he learned how to cut from experience. But in 1920, he could have had very little experience. Keaton thought about this. "Yeah . . . well, I don't know—" Mrs. Keaton suggested that perhaps the timing of actors gave him skill enough to be able to pace comedy.

Keaton agreed. "I was a veteran before I went into pictures. I was twenty-one years old by then. I made my first picture when I was twenty-five. Pacing—for fast action, you cut things closer than normal. For a dramatic scene, you lengthen them out a little bit more. Once we've seen the scene on the screen, we know what to do. We get in the cutting room and run down to where the action it. There—as he goes out that door, rip it. That's it. Give him the next shot. Get it down to where he's just coming through the door. Get the two spliced together. We didn't have regular Moviolas. We had machines with little cranks, but they were a nuisance.

"J. Sherman Kell was my cutter. Father Sherman, we called him. He looked like a priest. He broke the film down and put it in the racks. I'd say, 'Give me that long shot of the ballroom.' He'd get that out. 'Give me the close-up now of the butler announcing the arrival of his lordship.' As I cut them, he's there splicing them together. Running them onto a reel as fast as I hand them to him. There was quite a fire risk in those days, with nitrate film, but we never paid any attention to it. If a match got near one of those films, brother, it went up fast . . .

"There was one big advantage in those days, when you owned your own studio, and you were the only company in there. The skeleton of your outfit— that's your technical man, your head cameraman and his assistant, your prop man, your head electrician—these people are all on salary with you for fifty-two weeks of the year. So if I'm sitting in the cutting room, and the picture's been finished, and I want an extra shot, I can do it. If I want to take a sequence out—'If I turned to the left in that alley there I could drop this whole sequence and pick it up right here'—we can get the cameras out that afternoon and go back to the alley and shoot it. Now to do that would cost me the gasoline of the car we owned, and the amount of film we bought from Eastman to put in the camera to take it. Which, when it's all added up, means about two dollars and thirty-nine cents.

"You try that at any major studio today, and I'll tell you the least you could get that scene for would be around twelve thousand dollars. Just to go out and grab that scene and get back. Because everything is rented. Everything. And of course you don't move a company today, but the union forces you to take so many prop men, so many make-up men . . . this has to go, that has to go . . . the dressing-room truck goes . . . the commissary truck goes."

The most striking aspect of the Keaton pictures was the enormous amount of trouble lavished over every gag. Production value on such a scale requires more than a simple desire to make people laugh. It is not surprising that Keaton's childhood aim was to be a civil engineer. On many of his pictures, he actually exceeded his ambition, for no civil engineer was ever faced with such bizarre problems.

"The gag was that I should launch this boat I've built," said Keaton, referring to the 1921 two-reeler *The Boat,* "and it should slide down the launching ramp into the water—and straight to the bottom.

"It took us three days. We kept running into problems. We put something like sixteen hundred pounds of pig iron and T-rails in it, to give it weight. We cut it loose and watch it slide down the ramp. But then it slows up—so slow we can't use the shot. You don't like to undercrank when you're around water, because you can spot it immediately. The water's jumpy.

"Well, first thing we do is to build a breakaway stern to the boat, so that when it hits the water it'll just collapse and act as a scoop—to scoop water. That works fine except the nose stays in the air. We've got an air pocket in the nose.

"We get the boat back up and bore holes all through the nose and everywhere else that might form an air pocket. Try her again.

"Well, there's a certain buoyancy to wood, no matter how you weigh it down, and this time the boat hesitates before slowly sinking. Our gag's not worth a tinker's dam if she doesn't go smoothly straight to the bottom.

"So we go out in the Bay of Balboa and drop a sea anchor with a cable to a pulley on the stern, and out to a tug. We get all the air holes out of the boat, we made sure that the rear end would scoop water, and with the tug right out of shot we *pulled* that boat under the water.

"When they made *The Buster Keaton Story,* with Donald O'Connor, they ran into the same problem trying to re-create the gag. So I told the construction department all about the bugs, how to eliminate them and how to prepare it in the first place. They improved on me one way. Although they went out with a sea anchor, they built an extension to the launching ramp so that they could control the boat more easily. And then they brought the cable right back under the launching ramp to a powerful truck."

For sheer technical genius, *Sherlock, Jr.* is an eye-opener. It is undoubtedly Keaton's cleverest film. But its success as a comedy is debatable. The gags, brilliantly conceived and executed though they are, amaze the audience rather than amuse them. They are greeted not so much by laughter as by gasps of astonishment.

"That happened often," said Keaton. "Another one of those was in *The General,* when I dislodge one railroad tie by hitting it with another. They laugh later a little bit."

Sherlock, Jr. was started by Roscoe Arbuckle. Keaton always acknowledged his debt to Arbuckle—"I learned it all from him"—and after his trials, when Will Hays refused to let him return to the screen as an actor, Keaton hired him as director.

"He daren't use his real name, so I give him the name William Goodrich. First I wrote it out Will B. Good. Well, that's all right for a laugh, but William Goodrich is the one we decided upon. All right, that's it. At the end of about three days' shooting we notice a mistake. He's now so irritable and impatient that he loses his temper easily. He screams at people, gets flushed and mad—and of course, things don't go well. He hadn't recovered from those trials, of being accused of murder and nearly convicted. It just changed his disposition. In other words, it made a nervous wreck out of him."

Lou Anger suggested a solution. William Randolph Hearst, he said, was having difficulty finding a director for *The Red Mill,* Marion Davies' new picture. Why not put forward Arbuckle's name?

Keaton approached the matter subtly; he talked to Marion Davies, pointing out that Arbuckle was in a terrible state after the trials, and that one directing job might make all the difference.

"Roscoe and I are such close pals that getting the job from me wouldn't mean anything," explained Keaton. "He'd think it was charity."

Ironically, the Hearst newspapers had been instrumental in blowing the Arbuckle affair from a court case into a nationwide scandal. The Hearst–Marion Davies relationship was receiving open criticism and Miss Davies' pictures were suffering financially as a result. According to rumor, Hearst gave the go-ahead for scandal in Hollywood to be uncovered—scandal lurid enough to swamp any of his own. He struck it rich almost at once, and Arbuckle became the scapegoat for the whole of Hollywood.

Keaton said that he once heard Hearst declare that he had sold more newspapers during the Arbuckle trials than when the *Lusitania* went down.

Arbuckle was placed in a dilemma when Marion Davies persuaded Hearst to hire him; he was anxious not to let Keaton down, but he dared not miss the chance of an expensive picture. Keaton said he understood: "This is too great an opportunity, Roscoe. We hate to lose you, but—"

Arbuckle needed no further persuading. He took the job. Keaton scrapped the first three days' work, started again from scratch, and completed *Sherlock, Jr.* as sole director.

Sherlock, Jr. is a young motion-picture projectionist whose ambition is to be a great detective. In the most startling sequence, Buster falls asleep in his projection box . . . and a dream sequence shows him walking down the aisle and clambering into the screen. The characters in the film become characters from his own life, and they promptly throw him out. He picks himself up and climbs back into the screen again. As he does so, the scene changes—and instead of being inside a room, he finds himself outside the house. As he turns to walk down the steps, the scene cuts again, and he falls off a garden bench. He is about to sit on the bench when the shot changes to a city street, and he sits down violently on the sidewalk.

Buster picks himself up and walks along the street, finding himself suddenly on the edge of a cliff. He slips, scrambles to a safer position. Then he peers over the edge. Cut—and he is in the same position, but in a jungle, flanked by lions. He starts walking nonchalantly away, and the lions follow. Cut again—and he is in an empty desert. Suddenly a railroad train roars through the shot. . . .

This is too intricate to be funny. It provokes admiration, astonishment, but not always laughter. It holds up the main narrative, it even holds up the film-within-a-film, for the scenes have no connection either with the story or with themselves. It is exhibitionistic and self-indulgent. It also happens to be one of the most brilliantly contrived special-effects sequences in film history. Buster Keaton was still very pleased with it.

"Every cameraman in the business went to see that picture more than once, trying to figure out how the hell we did some of that. Oh, there were some great shots in that baby! We built a stage with a big, black cut-out screen. Then we built the front-row seats and orchestra pit and everything else. It was our lighting that did it. We lit the stage so it looked like a motion picture being projected on to a screen.

"For the location shots, all we needed was the exact distance from the camera to where I was standing. Then the cameraman could judge the height. As we did one shot, we'd throw it in the darkroom and develop it right there and then —and bring it back to the cameraman. He cut out a few frames and put them in the camera gate. When I come to change scenes, he could put me right square where I was. As long as that distance was correct.

"On *Seven Chances,* I had to use surveyor's instruments. I had an automobile, a Stutz Bearcat roadster. I'm in front of a country club. Now it's a full-figure shot of that automobile and me. I come down into the car, release the emergency brake, and sit back to drive—and I don't move. The scene dissolves and I'm in front of a little cottage. I reach forward, pull on the emergency brake, shut the motor off, and go on into the cottage. Later, I come out of the cottage, get into the automobile, and the scene changes back to the club. I and the automobile never moved. Now the automobile has got to be the same distance, the same height and everything to make the scene work. For that baby, we used surveying instruments so that the front part of the car would be the same distance from the camera—the whole shooting match."

Sherlock, Jr., despite the immense care lavished over its production, did not

The General *again.*

receive the acclaim one might expect. *Photoplay*'s reviewer was not even awed by the special effects: "This is by no means Keaton's most hilarious offering, but it is short, snappy and amusing. Comedies are like oases in a celluloid world, rare and refreshing, and you don't want to miss Buster with his immobile face and unique composure in his new setting."[8]

"It was all right," said Keaton; "it was a money-maker, but it wasn't one of the big ones. *Hospitality* outgrossed it, *Battling Butler* outgrossed it, *College* outgrossed it, *Steamboat Bill* outgrossed it. And then at M-G-M, both *The Cameraman* and *Spite Marriage* outgrossed it. Maybe it was because at the time it was released the audience didn't pay so much attention to the trick stunts that were in the picture."

Buster took no chances with his next production, which was to outgross them all and become his biggest money-maker. Reversing the basic idea of the desert island, Buster and his girl find themselves stranded aboard an ocean liner. The desert island, when it heaves to, is far from deserted, but is swarming with cannibals. Having taken the idea this far, Keaton and his scenario staff foresaw dramatic scenes. Always a stickler for authenticity, Keaton wanted his cannibals realistically portrayed—"legitimate, not burlesque"—and he wanted the spy scenes at the beginning of the picture handled dramatically. So he hired Donald Crisp, because Keaton thought he had directed the successful *Goose Woman,* actually made by Clarence Brown. A veteran from the earliest Griffith days, Crisp worked on *Birth of a Nation* and directed films for Reliance-Majestic and Mutual;

⁸ Photoplay, *July 1924. p. 46.*

during the twenties he made programmers for Lasky and, later, for De Mille's PDC. He is best remembered for his acting appearances.

Crisp proved a bit of a problem. Hired for his flair for drama, he became enthusiastic over the comedy.

"We told him not to worry about the gag department. We'd take care of that. Well, we started, and he directed the dramatic stuff all right, but he wasn't fussy about it. He was only interested in the scenes I was in. He turned gag man overnight on me! He came to work in the morning with the goddamnedest gags you ever heard of in your life. Wild! We didn't want him as a gag man, for God's sake! We let him go before we did the underwater scene. That was a tedious job, and a lot of trouble to us. A director can't do anything with a scene like that; it's strictly between me and the cameraman and the technical man.

"Actually, after I let him go, I went back and shot a couple of dramatic scenes again. One of them was when they'd dragged the girl onto the cannibal island and all those black feet were around her and we went to her close-up, surrounded by feet. He shot it in such a way that it looked like all she was doing was smelling feet. Which would be perfectly natural if we were looking for laughs—but we weren't. Not at this point. So I shot that again so she wasn't half-unconscious and their feet weren't bringing her to, or something. I just had her looking more scared.

"Then there was another scene in the first part when Crisp let the spies who cut the boat loose do a little overacting. I was always a little fussy over that. I don't like overacting."

The Navigator cost $220,000. Keaton's comedies always ran about a third more than a regular dramatic feature, such as a Norma Talmadge, which would cost around $180,000. They took longer to make because of the complicated tricks; Harold Lloyd's comedies were even more expensive, and Chaplin's were the costliest of all.

"We paid no attention to footage. First of all, we were making five-reelers; then, in 1925, we went to seven-reelers because everyone else did. As for the amount of raw stock we used, we never paid the slightest attention to it. We could generally tell when we were over footage, but we didn't mind. It's much better to be able to cut and throw away than go short. We shot our two-reelers in the same way. Say we shot a scene eight times. Well, we didn't print all those takes. The second and fourth were pretty good—just print those two, that's all. The others were thrown away."

This was normal procedure, and remains so today. Another regular procedure for silent pictures was the second camera for the foreign negative. But there were certain occasions when a second camera was impractical, and sometimes it was not even possible to shoot the scene twice.

"I'm in the cage out at Universal, where they had all the animals at that time. It's a big round cage, about sixty to eighty feet in diameter, full of tropical foliage. With a whip and a chair and a gun, the trainer gets the two lions in position, and I go to mine. My cameraman is outside the cage, shooting through one hole. The trainer says, 'Don't run, don't make a fast move, and don't go in a corner!'

"Well, there *is* no corner in a round cage!"

Buster laughed, pushed the table out of the way, and began to demonstrate. He re-created the scene from the film-within-a-film in *Sherlock, Jr.,* when he found himself flanked by lions. He did his unique Keaton walk across the room, whistling nonchalantly.

"I start to walk away from one lion—and lookit, there's another one, there! I got about this far and glanced back and both of them were *that* far behind me, walking with me!" Buster was almost helpless with delighted laughter. "And I don't know these lions personally, see. They're both strangers to me! Then the cameraman says, 'We've got to do the shot again for the foreign negative.'

"I said, 'Europe ain't gonna see this scene!'" More laughter, and then Buster returned to his seat, chuckling. "Years later, Will Rogers used that gag—'Europe ain't gonna see this scene' . . . we made a dupe negative out of *that* baby! I've worked with lions since, and some nice ones."

The most famous Keaton comedy is *The General,* because it has been revived so frequently; it has even been shown on television. Far too often, a revival is among the least representative of a star's work. But *The General,* although not typical, is a fine example of Keaton's work. Reissues have dampened the original impact by removing titles and apparently inessential scenes and thereby wrecking the whole pace and shape of the picture. Fortunately, the original silent version is still available, and still fresh and vigorous enough to make *Motion Picture Classic*'s 1927 review totally incomprehensible: "A mild Civil War comedy, not up to Keaton's best standard."[9]

"*The General* was my pet. It was a page out of history, although I couldn't use the original finish. Walt Disney tried to do it later [as *The Great Locomotive Chase*], but he couldn't use the real finish either. Because the Southerners took all eight of those guys and hanged them. They felled a pine tree into a crutch, and pulled all the eight horses out at the same time. They hanged all eight men at once. That was the real finish to that. Then, of course, Disney makes the mistake of putting Fess Parker in the lead as a Northerner. He's trying to make villains out of the Confederate Army.

"Well, you can't do that with a motion-picture audience—they resent it. And the same goes if I was in Michigan, Maine, Massachusetts. They lost the war anyhow, so the audience resents it. We knew better; when the story ended, the South was winning. This was correct. All this took place in 1862, and the South lost in 1864. But I wrote my own finish to get my engine back. From the time I deserted with my engine it becomes the real story.

"Now this was my own story, my own continuity, I directed it, I cut it and titled it. So actually it was a pet. Not my biggest money-maker though—that was *The Navigator.*

"I went to the original location, from Atlanta, Georgia, up to Chattanooga, and the scenery didn't look very good. In fact, it looked terrible. The railroad tracks I couldn't use at all, because the Civil War trains were narrow-gauge. And the railroad beds of that time were pretty crude; they didn't have so much gravel to put between the ties, and you always saw grass growing there.

"I had to have narrow-gauge railroads, so I went to Oregon. And in Oregon, the whole state is honeycombed with narrow-gauge railroads for all the lumber mills. So I found trains going through valleys, mountains, by little lakes and mountain streams—anything I wanted. So we got the rolling equipment, wheels

9 Motion Picture Classic, *April 1927, p. 80.*

and trucks, and we built our freight train and our passenger train, and we re-modeled three locomotives. Luckily, the engines working on these lumber camps were all so doggone old that it was an easy job. They even had burners. At that period they didn't pay much attention to numbers of engines—they named them all. That's why the main engine was called 'The General' and the one I chased it with was 'Texas.' It was the 'Texas' I threw through the burning bridge.

"We built that bridge and dammed up water underneath so the stream would look better. I planned the scene with Gabourie and a couple of his right-hand men, one of them a blacksmith. We had a forge and a blacksmith's shop right on the lot.

"Extras came from miles around to be in the picture. None of them were experienced—we had to train them. And when we did the battle scenes, I got the State Guard of Oregon. That location was around twelve hundred miles from Hollywood.

"Railroads," added Keaton, "are a great prop. You can do some awful wild things with railroads."

A great deal of the chase was shot, not from the engine, but from a vehicle, tracking alongside from the road. The tracking shots are perfectly timed so that the engine is held center of frame, and there is no vibration. Keaton fitted Westinghouse shock absorbers on the automobile and used a road scraper to smooth the surface down before shooting. "We were pretty fussy about that," he says.

Keaton's next was *College*. James W. Horne, a young director who had made a success of *The Cruise of the Jasper B,* and who was to direct many of the Laurel and Hardy comedies, took the credit for directing this one.

But once again, Keaton said that he did most of the directing. "James Horne was absolutely useless to me," he said uncharitably. "Harry Brand, my business manager, got me to use him. He hadn't done many pictures, and no important ones. Incidentals, quickies. I don't know why we had him, because I practically did *College*."

Keaton viewed credits with indifference. Carl Harbaugh was given screen credit for writing *College* and *Steamboat Bill, Jr.,* but Keaton said he was one of the most useless men he ever had on the scenario department. "He wasn't a good gag man, he wasn't a good title writer, he wasn't a good story constructionist. . . . But I had to put somebody's name up, and he was on salary with us.

"You see, I'm the guy that made a picture called *The Playhouse*. I played all the parts. With double exposures, I'm the whole orchestra, I'm the people in the boxes, in the audience, on the stage. I bought a ticket from myself—I'm the ticket-taker taking a ticket from myself. So on the program we put the cast of characters: they're all Keaton. I was deliberately kidding most of the guys in motion pictures, especially a guy by the name of Ince. At the front of his pictures it would say, 'THOMAS H. INCE PRESENTS *Hemstitching on the Mexican Border*. WRITTEN BY THOMAS H. INCE. DIRECTED BY THOMAS H. INCE. EDITED BY THOMAS H. INCE. THIS IS A THOMAS H. INCE PRODUCTION.'

"So when I made *The Playhouse,* I used that. Written by Keaton . . . directed by Keaton . . . costumes by Keaton . . . and everyone on the cast list was Keaton. Which got a belly laugh from audiences. They laughed like hell at that. Later on, we'd have done it to Zanuck and Mervyn Le Roy and a few people like that.

Having kidded things like that, I hesitated to put my own name on as a director and writer."

Steamboat Bill, Jr. was Keaton's last independently produced film. As a whole, it does not have the sustained quality of the usual Keaton product, but the last part of the film is unforgettable. It eclipses for sheer panache anything he ever did. Appropriately, it is a cyclone sequence.

Keaton plays the collegiate and foppish son of a tough Mississippi steamboat captain, Steamboat Bill Canfield (Ernest Torrence). A feud with the owner of a spanking-new riverboat leads to Canfield being thrown in jail.

Buster goes to the rescue through a fantastic rainstorm, carrying with him a loaf of bread filled with such useful escape tools as screwdriver, files, and wrenches. But his father, who wants to disown him, will have nothing to do with him. Buster explains to the jailer, "I'll just wait around till he's famished."

When the jailer's back is turned, he tries to indicate with some splendid mime exactly what the bread contains. Steamboat Bill fails to understand, and thinks his son has gone crazy.

"I know what it is," says Buster in a title. "You're ashamed of my baking."

The loaf, which has been soaked by the rain, begins to sag alarmingly. Suddenly, the tools burst out and clatter to the floor. Buster is thrown into jail himself.

Now, Keaton and his gag men had planned to make escape possible by leading up to a gigantic flood. The rainstorm had already been introduced, the river had been established. But Harry Brand had told producer Joe Schenck that a flood scene could wreck the comedy's box-office chances. Recent floods had caused a number of deaths.

Schenck saw the point, and insisted that the scene be changed. Buster compromised with a hurricane—and a hundred thousand dollars' worth of street sets were adapted for another thirty-five thousand.

This scene is the swan song of Keaton's faithful unit, and one of the most astonishing special-effect sequences ever attempted.[1] The location for all exteriors was on the Sacramento River, right opposite Sacramento. A crane, a hundred and twenty feet high, was set on a barge and used to tear up the breakaway buildings, and to hurl Buster around, apparently airborne.

The sequence begins with a shot of a car. Its driver is cranking the starting handle. It is already raining; suddenly the hood shoots up, like a sail, and the car vanishes down the street, dragging the owner still clinging to the starting handle. Then the pier collapses. Complete houses are battered to pieces by the tremendous wind.

"I took a pretty good beating," said Keaton. "We had six of those Liberty motor babies, and working in front of those wind machines is really tough. We drove a truck past one of them—and the machine blew it off the bank and into the river. Just one machine!"

Buster dashes for safety into a hospital. The entire building is lifted by the wind, leaving only the floor—and a startled Buster, sitting up in one of the beds.

Then occurs probably the most celebrated Keaton moment: the front of a

[1] *Harry Langdon's* Tramp, Tramp, Tramp (1926; *Harry Edwards*) *has a brilliantly staged cyclone scene, but it does not approach the spectacle of this one.*

house falls in a complete section on top of him. But he remains standing, the attic window fitting neatly around him.

Checking with the New York Weather Bureau, Keaton was told that the previous year seven hundred and ninety-six people had died in windstorms, and only thirty-six in floods.

Then Keaton made what he called "the biggest mistake of my life" when he abandoned independent production with United Artists, persuaded by Schenck to move into M-G-M. He quickly fell foul of studio production methods. Thalberg refused to accept that the Keaton method was efficient. He insisted that comedies should be written—and Keaton was mortified when it took eight months to finish a scenario. Attempting to secure some scenes carefully scripted for the New York streets, with the instructions that "no one in New York knows this character exists," Keaton caused a traffic jam for three blocks in all directions. He was mobbed again trying to shoot other scripted scenes at the Battery.

Thalberg conceded defeat, and *The Cameraman* (1928) proceeded smoothly under the direction of Ed Sedgwick, with whom Keaton worked extremely well. The picture was a triumphant success.[2]

But Keaton's unit had been split up. Gabourie became head of M-G-M's technical department. Dev Jennings became a process cameraman. The gag men were replaced by regular scenarists. When talkies arrived, M-G-M tried to build up Jimmy Durante at Keaton's expense. Disaster followed disaster. Keaton's drinking increased. His wife divorced him. He managed to offend Louis B. Mayer, who fired him.

He struggled to make pictures in Mexico, France, and England, but all were unsuccessful. In 1935 he underwent two cures for alcoholism, and he did not touch drink again for five years. M-G-M re-employed him, but not as a comedian. Instead of his former salary of three thousand dollars a week, he now earned a hundred dollars a week as a gag man, working with Abbott and Costello, the Marx Brothers, Red Skelton, and most of the comedy stars on the M-G-M lot.

It was a period of humiliation and frustration. To reduce a man who had been one of the three acknowledged masters of screen comedy to a gag man is a comment on the blindness of Hollywood producers.

To become a great comedian was never a conscious ambition of Buster Keaton. He made pictures the best way he knew how. He was fascinated both by the medium itself and the challenge of elaborate effects.

His greatness was due to a combination of factors; his approach was ideal for silent comedy. He had a unique screen personality. He had real acting skill, with the sense of timing and of movement that this implies. He was a film director of brilliance, who knew exactly where to put the camera. He also had an intuitive sense of cutting, he was mechanically very ingenious, he had qualities of resourcefulness, authority, and foresight. And he had a degree of personal courage which, had it been displayed under conditions of war, would have won him national honors.

But greatness would still be lacking were it not for one added quality: a capacity for tremendous hard work, a complete dedication to motion pictures

[2] *In 1953, an M-G-M executive told Keaton and Blesh that the projection print of* The Cameraman *had worn out. "It's been our training picture. Ever since 1928 we've made each new comedian study it."*

which, fused with the other remarkable elements, made Buster Keaton a master film maker.

One final episode illustrates both his courage in dealing with problems and his genius for solving them. He described the shooting of the underwater sequence in *The Navigator:*

"First of all, we thought we'd use that big tank down at Riverside. If we built it up, we could get five or six feet more water in the deep end. So they went down and built it up, put the water in—and the added weight of water forced the bottom of the swimming pool out. Crumbled it like it was a cracker. So we had to rebuild their swimming pool.

"Next thing, we tested over at Catalina, and we found there was a milk in the water—the mating season of the fish around the island causes that. The moment you touch the bottom it rises up with the mud, rises up and blacks out your scene on you.

"Lake Tahoe is the clearest water in the world, and it's always cold because it's up a mile high, and that's an awful big lake. So we went up to Tahoe. I'm actually working in around twenty feet of water in that scene.

"You imagine: we built this camera box for two cameras, a little bigger than this table square, with a big iron passage up to the top with a ladder on the inside. It holds two cameras and two cameramen. It was built of planks and sealed good so there was no leakage. But it's wood, and there has to be added weight. Well, I added about a thousand pounds to it. Now we find that the inside's got to be kept at the same temperature as the water outside. So we hang a thermometer out there so the cameraman looking through the glass can read it. And one on the inside.

"First thing in the morning, and the night before, we have to put ice in there, and then add more to make sure to keep the temperature of the camera box the same as the water on the outside, so it won't fog up the glass. Either one side or the other will fog on you, see. The difference was that when two bodies are in there, the body heat means we have to add more ice immediately. So as you put the cameramen in, you roll more ice in.

"So there's the whole outfit, and me with that deep-sea diving suit down there—and the cameraman says, 'I'm too close. I want to be back further.'

"I moved that camera box. I moved it. That's how much you can lift when you're down around fifteen to twenty feet deep. The box must have weighed fourteen hundred pounds, something like that, with two cameras, two cameramen, about three hundred pounds of ice, another thousand pounds of weight—and I picked it up and moved it. I was one month shooting that scene. I could only stay down there about thirty minutes at a time, because the cold water goes through to your kidneys. After about a half hour you begin to go numb. You want to get up and get out of there."

44 / CHAPLIN

Chaplin's *My Autobiography,* published in 1965, and *A Countess from Hong Kong,* released in 1967, led to a great many revivals, not only of his films, but also of the bitter controversies, rumors, and resentments that have shadowed his career since his first motion-picture appearances fifty years earlier.

Within the Hollywood community, Chaplin is still an explosive topic. In 1966, the American Society of Cinematographers made a film about the contribution of the cameraman to the technical advances of the industry, and flatly rejected any Chaplin extract.

"You'd be astonished how they hate Charlie in Hollywood," wrote one of the men associated with the film. "They laughed at everything of Charlie's, but nixed it. I'll admit it does not show any progress in cinematography, but what's wrong with the sort of comedy Charlie can give you? I think he got a lousy deal in this country. I'm ashamed of the way the Truman Administration brought those charges against him when he left the United States on a vacation. Of course, he was asking for trouble. He was pretty arrogant, and pushed people around a bit. But I believe in liberty and justice for all—and he did not get the justice he was entitled to. I've never thought he was a Communist, or even a Commie sympathizer. But what an entertainer he is! This, in the final analysis, is all that counts."[1]

A less tolerant opinion was expressed by an otherwise rational, and greatly respected, Hollywood production executive, who has worked in motion pictures for almost as long as Chaplin himself: "So he's a great actor. So does that give him the right to sneak out of the country? We Americans gave him a home . . . gave him a career. He made many fortunes out of us, and what does he do in return? Nothing. Does he become a citizen of the United States? He doesn't. He just sneaks away and then turns around and insults us. He has no loyalty to anyone; and I hope for his sake he never returns to America."[2]

Researching into the silent era, I talked to several people who either worked with Chaplin or who knew him well at the height of his success. Ordinarily, I avoided the name, feeling that everything that could be written on Chaplin had already been said. But without any prompting, Chaplin soon became the topic of conversation. And several unusual facets of his character and his work were revealed.

Minta Durfee followed Virginia Kirtely as Chaplin's leading lady at Keystone in 1914. Invited to Europe, to celebrate her fiftieth year in pictures in 1963, she brought a tape from Hollywood. It was a conversation she had recorded with another Keystone veteran, Chester Conklin.

Conklin said that he liked working with Chaplin, but that at first he didn't fit in at Keystone. "He was a character comedian. He had to work slow. We got all of our comedy out of fast movement, and Charlie couldn't do that."

Conklin then described one of the most important moments in the history of film comedy, the moment in which the character of the tramp was crystallized. Chaplin's autobiography describes how Sennett told him to get into a comedy make-up, and he details the delighted reactions as he improvised on the hotel lobby set. But Chaplin himself had evidently forgotten one other vital moment. Said Conklin:

[1] *Private source.*
[2] *Private source.*

In the earliest days of the tramp character, with Frank Williams, who later developed travel-ing matte, and Henry "Pathé" Lehrman; 1914.

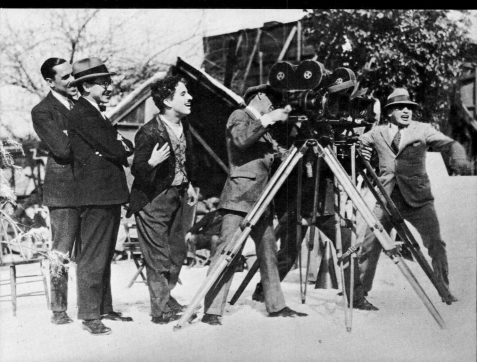

The Gold Rush (1925); Henri d'Abbadie d'Arrast, Eddie Manson, Chaplin, Rollie Totherah, Chuck Reisner.

"I remember one rainy morning, Roscoe Arbuckle, Ford Sterling, and myself were sitting in the dressing room playing pinochle. Charlie wandered in and went up to the make-up bench. In those days we used crepe hair a lot. Charlie held up various pieces of this crepe hair under his nose, then looked at himself in the mirror. Finally, he found a piece that he liked, and he stuck it on there with spirit gum, went over and got Roscoe Arbuckle's hat and his pants, my coat (a cutaway, we called it in those days; now it's called a morning coat), and he took his own cane and went out on the set. This was a hotel set, built for Mabel Normand's picture, *Mabel's Strange Predicament* (1914), and Charlie went out into the lobby and started clowning around doing the drunk act he'd done on vaudeville. He'd get his foot stuck in the cuspidor and couldn't get it out—all that kind of thing. Everyone had gathered around and was laughing. Sennett stood back of the crowd and watched. Finally, he went up to Charlie and said, 'Listen, do what you've been doing when we shoot this picture with Mabel and Chester.' Well, of course, it wound up that he stole the picture from us."

Minta Durfee first saw Chaplin when she went out to dinner one night with Mack Sennett and some other Keystone people, and they ended up at the local Sullivan and Considine theater. "He was wearing a silk hat, kind of a little jacket with cuffs on strings so he could lose them, and a cane." Sennett had apparently seen Chaplin quite frequently and liked his act. Some time after he had been signed to Keystone, to replace Ford Sterling, Miss Durfee was cast opposite him in *Cruel, Cruel Love*.

"I was sitting on his knee, in the middle of a funny love scene, when the boys decided to initiate Charlie. They had filled the tarpaulin that covered the set with water and right in the middle of the scene they let it down. Well, of course, we were both drenched. Charlie hated water, and he threatened to walk right out on everybody. But he soon came back. He was a pretty good guy about that. And later on, he and my husband [Roscoe Arbuckle] did one of the most difficult things an actor can do: in the last scene of *Rounders* they lay in a boat, pretending to be dead drunk, while it slowly sank in the middle of Echo Park Lake. For a man who hates water, that was pretty good."

Eddie Sutherland, director of *Behind the Front* and *We're in the Navy Now,* worked as Chaplin's assistant on *A Woman of Paris* and *The Gold Rush,* and took a four-hundred-dollar cut in salary to do so.

"Chaplin taught me more than I can say. On *A Woman of Paris* I questioned a moment in the picture—I thought it was too much of a coincidence. Edna Purviance has been seduced by the boy, Carl Miller, in reel one, then she meets him again, accidentally, in reel five.

" 'Do you think it's convenient?' asked Charlie.

" 'Not particularly,' I replied.

" 'Good,' said Charlie. 'I don't mind coincidence—life is coincidence—but I *hate* convenience.'

"In the same picture, there was a scene where the boy died. Lydia Knott played the mother, and Charlie wanted her to give a reaction of complete shock. As the Sûreté asked her all the usual questions—'What's his name, how old was he?'— he asked her for a totally dead nonreaction. He wanted the audience to supply the emotion, not the actress. I can't tell you how many times we shot it. She kept playing it as a sweet, smiling, courageous old lady. She was a very fine person, and very determined, so it was tough going. Charlie took it maybe fifty times. Then he told me to take over. I shot it about thirty times. Finally the old lady got so angry that she swore at us. "All right," she snapped. "If that's the way you want it. But it's not the way I am." And she went through the scene in such a temper that we got it. I would say we shot that scene more than a hundred times. It took nearly a week to get that one reaction. Lydia Knott was the only player I ever knew to argue with Chaplin."

"It took us weeks to cook up the routine in *The Gold Rush*, when Chaplin eats his boots. The shoelaces were made of licorice; so were the shoes. The nails were some kind of candy. We had something like twenty pairs of boots made by a confectioner, and we shot and shot that scene, too. Charlie ate it as if it were the most sumptuous meal served at the Astor. He knew that an audience liked a character to play against himself; if the character was shabby, he should act in a very genteel manner.

"Some people got sore at Charlie because they said he took their ideas as his own. This is unfair. While we were working out *The Gold Rush*, he got the idea of the cabin being blown away by the wind. Then I said, 'Hey, how would it be if it gets to the edge of a cliff and teeters?'

" 'No, no, no,' said Charlie. 'Too obvious, too obvious.' So I dropped it. We went on with the story line, and one day Charlie dashed in excitedly and said, 'I've got it! The house is blown to the edge of a cliff, and it balances on the edge and they think it's going over . . .'

"Now I know that Charlie didn't steal that from me. I planted it in his mind. He probably didn't hear it consciously. But subconsciously it stuck there.

"When I started work with Charlie, I asked everyone who knew him about his characteristics. I found he was such a complex person that to simplify him and to sum him up was impossible.

"When he was in front of the camera, I would be behind it. But I wasn't directing Chaplin. He pretty well knew whether it was good or bad. He'd say, 'How was that?' I'd say, 'Well, I don't think that went too well,' and he'd agree. 'Let's do it again.' Of course he did everything five thousand times. "We'll shoot this over," he would say at rushes. "I can do it better. We'll only be one day behind schedule." That put him one day behind schedule every day. But Charlie had the patience of Job. A real perfectionist. With this basis of working, it took us about a year and a half to shoot *A Woman of Paris*. I left *The Gold Rush* after eighteen months, and he was about two thirds through. But of course he didn't shoot all the time. We'd shoot for three or four days, then lay off for a couple of weeks and re-think, rehearse, and rarefy the scene.

"I found out early in my career with Charlie that if you said no at the inception of an idea, the idea died, because he's a very sensitive man. I tried to keep an idea boiling. On *A Woman of Paris* he came in all steamed up. He'd dreamed up an idea during the night; the whole thing was going to end on a leper colony. Edna Purviance would see the light and go off and nurse little lepers.

"Instead of saying no immediately, I suggested that we investigate the idea. He investigated this one for two or three days—and it was a dog. Finally, he said, "What's the matter? You don't like this, do you?"

"I said, 'Frankly, I don't, Charlie.'

" 'Well, you're wrong,' he said, and went off for three days. It was never

Chaplin directing Tom Wilson in Sunnyside *(1919).*

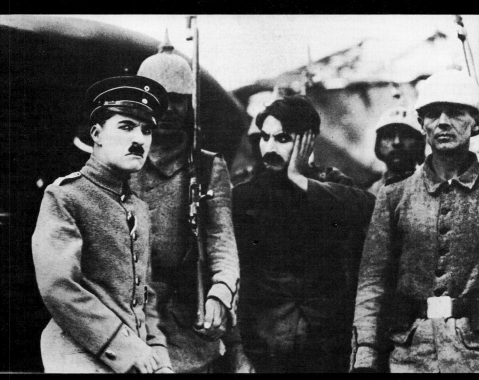

Shoulder Arms (1918).

Checking make-up on location for The Gold Rush.

The mechanics of a gag; property men on the roof push snow on Chaplin. A location scene for The Gold Rush.

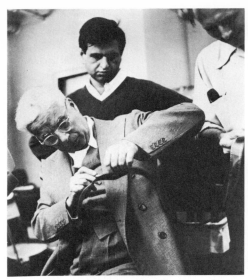

Throughout his career, Chaplin not only supervised every stage of production, but also did much of the work himself.

mentioned again. In later life, I don't think Charlie had people to say no to him, which was a pity.

"I remember my days with Chaplin with great affection. He's a guy I love personally, and whose work I admire greatly. And he was always just great with me."[3]

Chaplin's ideas were generally conceived in the classic silent-comedy tradition, at story conferences. Other ideas came to him from visual springboards. The most celebrated scene in *A Woman of Paris* suggests Menjou's relationship with Edna Purviance by showing him taking a handkerchief from a drawer in her room. A property man had accidentally left a dress collar in a drawer, and that was how Chaplin hit upon the idea.

The idea of a Yukon picture came to him at Pickfair. Mary Pickford had given Douglas Fairbanks a set of three-dimensional stereoscopic cards. When Chaplin found Fairbanks with a library of these photographs, he spent an afternoon examining them. A number dealt with the days of 1898, and so the basic idea for *The Gold Rush* was born.

According to many who knew him, Chaplin could find a particle of quality in the poorest picture. He enjoyed seeing films, and he always expressed this enjoyment. He would spring to the defense of any film or of any director who was being harshly criticized, for he knew how difficult it was to make a picture.

"I loved going to see his movies with him," said Dagmar Godowsky. "He used to laugh till he cried—then he would nudge me and say, "Wait till you see what's going to happen now!' When it happened he was convulsed. I think I enjoyed watching Charlie watching Charlie more than the movie."[4]

[3] *From tapes recorded by the author, New York, Dec. 1964, and the Oral History Research Office, Columbia, New York, Feb. 1959.*
[4] *Dagmar Godowsky:* First Person Plural (*New York: Viking Press; 1958*), *p. 76.*

"Much has been written about Chaplin's gifts as a talker," says Agnes de Mille in her book *Dance to the Piper,* "his virtuosity of improvisation, which made every parlor stunt a work of art, but has anyone paid him his due as a courteous, enkindling listener?

"My God, what an audience Chaplin was! Singers sang as at a premiere. Folks talked with a wit they had never suspected—even Margaret and I, even as kids, he sat giving us, the children, his whole undivided interest and doing for us in a corner his incredible imitations of disagreeable wives, nagging relatives, French actresses, and so on. Yes, and by heaven, getting us to do them. I have never been so dazzling since."[5]

Astonishingly, a generation has grown up since the war which has never seen Charlie Chaplin. Copyright strictures, implemented by Chaplin and his agents, have forced a number of films out of circulation. Others are obtainable on eight-millimeter, poor print quality effectively deadening the comic sparkle.

Chaplin meant a great deal to the audiences of the silent era. Without any question, he was the most beloved personality of the entertainment world. He could not make films fast enough. One comedian, Billy West, duplicated Chaplin's make-up and costume, and made a series of comedies. The press was hostile to such plagiarism; *Photoplay* printed his name in lower case: billy west. Chaplin,

[5] *Agnes de Mille:* Dance to the Piper (*Boston: Little, Brown & Co., 1952*), *p. 10.*

The Circus (1927).

however, was unperturbed. Seeing the Billy West unit at work in the streets, he paused long enough to say to West: "You're a damned good imitator."[6]

However great their affection for Chaplin, audiences of all ages bewailed the long delays between his pictures. In 1920, *Photoplay* addressed an editorial to "A genius on vacation: Charlie! We have no part in your quarrels; we have no will to meddle in your business. But all of us . . . are imploring, because we are doleful and bewildered in a doleful and bewildered world. Give us again those magic hours of philosophic forgetfulness that you once set out so charitably, like beacons of a kindly neighbor.

"We are not commanding nor advising nor even criticizing; we speak because we need you—because you have made this turbulent God's marble a better place to live on—because since you have been out of sorts the world has gone lame and happiness has moved away. Come back, Charlie!"[7]

Watching Chaplin Direct / 1966

Gloria Swanson's chauffeur-driven car drew up at the gates of Pinewood studios. The sergeant on duty saluted smartly.

"Good afternoon, Miss Swanson," he said, and gave directions to the chauffeur. Miss Swanson sighed with relief. "Thank heaven for that," she said. "I thought I was going to have to play a *Sunset Boulevard* scene to get in."

Miss Swanson was visiting Pinewood studios to meet Charles Chaplin and to watch him direct Marlon Brando and Sophia Loren in *A Countess from Hong Kong*. She wanted the visit to be informal, and had not spoken to Chaplin. "Let's just arrive and see what happens," she had said. The last time she had seen Chaplin at work on a set was at the Essanay Company, in 1915. The film was *His New Job*.

"A lot of people think I was in that. I can remember that one morning Chaplin was on the set, and he wanted someone to do a bit. I was chosen from a group of extras. After the twelfth rehearsal of being whacked on the behind, he said I wouldn't do. I was delighted, being a tight-laced young lady without a sense of humor. The scene was in a doctor's office; as I bent over to pick up my purse, he kicked me in the *derrière*. Once I failed to please him, that was that. I didn't do anything in the picture. It's interesting to wonder what might have happened to my career if he'd liked me."

Miss Swanson's arrival delighted the veterans of Pinewood studios. One man, strolling up the corridor, did an astonished double take as she walked past. In the commissary, star-struck waitresses took turns to serve her, and to request autographs.

The Chaplin set was closed: POSITIVELY NO ADMITTANCE. A producer from another Pinewood picture offered to go inside. He emerged a few moments later. "Okay," he said. "Mr. Chaplin's just finished shooting. He said he'd be very happy to see you."

The set was crowded with seated, inactive technicians. It was quiet and orderly, but with an air of expectation, like the moments before a boxing match. The ringside spectators turned and stared as Gloria Swanson entered. From the lighted

---

[6] *Ben Berk, unit manager with Billy West, to author, New York, Dec. 1964.*
[7] Photoplay, *April 1920, p. 27.*

area of the otherwise dark, hangar-like stage, a stout figure appeared, in a gray hat, a gray jacket and green-tinted glasses. He grinned that unmistakable Chaplin grin, and held out his arms.

"Fifty years!" cried Gloria Swanson. They embraced.

"Do you remember when you kicked me twelve times in the *derrière,* and then threw me out?" she asked. "Back in 1915, at Essanay?"

"Ah, yes," replied Chaplin. "Well, I always thought you'd make a better *dramatic* actress . . ." Chaplin took her by the arm and introduced her to Sophia Loren, who was wearing a spectacular white evening dress, and curlers.

I stared at Chaplin, mesmerized. Here, at last, was the greatest single figure of motion-picture history. He was clearly preoccupied with the problems of his picture, but he seemed delighted to meet this old friend. He chatted easily, short American *a*'s and some West Coast vernacular breaking through his soft English voice. When he gave a hilarious impression of his three-year-old child reacting to the assistant's yell of *"Quiet!"* ("Let's go home, Daddy," said the child, tugging at his father's sleeve), the irrepressible Charlie broke through the polite exterior of the busy director.

The name of Allan Dwan cropped up in the conversation, and the fact that he was soon to make another picture, at nearly eighty.

"Allan Dwan . . ." said Chaplin, nostalgically. "Eighty! Well, you know, I'm pushing eighty myself. Four years to go . . ."

Chaplin had last met Miss Swanson seven years before in the south of France; was she still living there?

"No—New York."

"Oh. Not Los Angeles?"

"No . . . I couldn't live there. It's too empty. I need the theater. Besides, all those high-risers . . ."

Chaplin nodded in vehement agreement. "Yes, and those monoxide fumes! We are very comfortable in Switzerland, you know. It's nothing pretentious. The life is quite simple. But it's comfortable. Very comfortable."

They recalled *His New Job* with amusement, and established that despite the claims of film historians, Gloria Swanson had not appeared in it.[8]

Finally, Chaplin had to leave to go on the set. Miss Swanson perched on a ladder to get a better view over the obstructing lights. Sophia Loren, devastating in her low-cut white dress, was joined by Marlon Brando in a blue dressing gown, looking furious. A wave of tension followed him as he shuffled from behind the camera onto the set.

Chaplin seemed oblivious. As he directed Loren, and then Brando, I scribbled down the directions verbatim. He tried to work out a way in which Loren could walk over to Brando, holding a glass. He paid no attention to dialogue. I heard him give only one dialogue direction. He may have written the words, but he could not remember them. "So-and-so-and-so-and-so etcetera," would be his delivery of an average line.

The associate producer, Jerry Epstein, paced behind him, reading the correct lines from a script. The set was a cabin of a luxury liner; at one point, Chaplin stood by the cabin door and looked across at Epstein.

[8] *James Card ran* His New Job *to Miss Swanson at Eastman House, Rochester, New York, in May 1966—and there she was, playing a tiny part as a stenographer.*

"This walk lays an egg," he said, and laughed. Then he stalked back to his director's chair, beneath the camera, and shouted, "Go over there, make up your mind, take it."

The action did not proceed smoothly. Brando, sullen, kept saying, "All right, all right." He did not seem to be listening as Chaplin instructed him again. Finally, Chaplin got up and walked back onto the set.

"You go, open the door, 'Excuse me-so-and-so-and-so-and-so.' " He paused, and gave a classical, balletic Chaplin gesture. "All right, you're here . . . come to the door . . . say, 'I'm etcetera, etcetera.' "

Brando came in and did a tolerably good, if lifeless, scene, ignoring the Chaplinesque gesture; at the end he uttered, 'Oh, no!'

Chaplin interjected a long drawn-out, "O-o-oh, n-o-o-o!" Then he hurried in to make adjustments. "We'll have to do the same choreography." He went through the moves, ignoring the dialogue, and then turned to the director of photography, Arthur Ibbetson.

"I think that will be the first close-up till we get it natural and sincere," he said, crossing his chest with his arm to indicate the limit of the close-up.

He stood by and watched a run-through of the scene. Then he said, "I think that's all right," and took his hat off, revealing a shock of pure white hair.

Gloria Swanson leaned forward: "You can see why actors find him difficult," she whispered. "This is a simple scene, and he's making much ado about nothing."

A publicity man, Harry Mendelsohn, said he had just come from America to take over on the picture, and was amazed to find, on his second day, both Chaplin *and* Gloria Swanson.

"He's still the greatest," he said. "He's the best actor and actress in the picture."

Life photographer Alfred Eisenstaedt introduced himself, and told Miss Swanson that he had photographed her at the Palace Hotel, Vienna, in 1938. "I am finishing a book, and your picture is *that* big in it!" Miss Swanson whispered a reply, and grew silent as Chaplin began directing.

Having worked out a bit of business for Brando, Chaplin did it himself, combining Chaplinesque grace with the suggestive vulgarity of the music hall. He picked up an imaginary glass of Alka-Seltzer and drained the contents, leaning his head right back. Then he gave a funny belch, and laughed at his audience— the rows of technicians, who laughed back. Brando gave no visible reaction. Chaplin did it again; he took the nonexistent glass, drank deeply, and burped. It didn't quite work. "We'll put that on sound," he said, gesturing vaguely off set.

Then, still thinking out the scene, he walked up and down, clenched fist held at forehead in classical style.

When Brando tried the scene, he used a real glass with no contents, and took a short draft. Chaplin sprang forward.

"No—you're going to take longer to do that, you know." The old professional advising the young apprentice. And he demonstrated the whole gesture, going all the way back, swallowing the Alka-Seltzer, and belching at the end of it. Brando followed most of Chaplin's instructions, but he then achieved two startlingly realistic belches which effectively killed the comedy.

Rumors about Brando's temperamental behavior were circulating widely at this stage of the production. Later, press reports indicated that all was harmonious.

But at this point, it was clear that Brando was expected to imitate Chaplin rather than to develop his own performance. For such a great dramatic actor, such direction must have been bewildering.

For the onlooker, however, such direction was miraculous. It was as exciting as watching a Chaplin film no one knew existed; first he played the Brando role, then he skipped over and did the Loren part. One was aggressively masculine, the other provocative and feminine, yet both remained pure Chaplin. It is a real loss to the cinema that Chaplin refused to allow a film to be made about the production.

The publicity men had by now alerted a photographer to take stills of Chaplin and Miss Swanson together. But Miss Swanson was just leaving for an urgent appointment in London. She was genuinely disappointed at losing the chance of a commemorative still. "Why didn't you do it *then?*" she asked.

In the car, driving back to London, Miss Swanson reflected on the meeting. "Well, wasn't *that* a nostalgic time for me. To walk on that set and be greeted with open arms! He looked as fit as a fiddle. He was bouncing in and out of his chair. Frankly, he didn't look a day older than when I'd last seen him, seven years ago. Did you notice that he isn't as articulate with words as he is in pantomime, when showing people what he wants? What an artist. I suppose he is the most creative man it is possible to meet."

45 / *THE SILENT FILM IN EUROPE*

Before World War I, England and France produced more films than any other country. The war gave supremacy to America. The shattered European industries took time to recover. Germany, affected not only by defeat, but by crippling postwar economic crises, recovered surprisingly swiftly, for the entertainment industry was financed by men like Krupp, together with prominent bankers, secure in the knowledge that in a time of crisis, entertainment will always flourish.

Germany, and particularly her foremost director, Ernst Lubitsch, presented films of high quality very soon after the war, and while the output could scarcely rival Hollywood's, American producers grew anxious.

"This 'German Invasion' fright is the oldest and silliest of alarms," said Adolph Zukor in 1921. "One would think that the Germans had some magical recipe for making great pictures. A European might just as sensibly, after seeing *Birth of a Nation, Miracle Man,* or *Four Horsemen,* fall into a panic and believe that every American film was of equal caliber."[1] When Mr. Zukor made this pronouncement, he was leaving for Europe, to negotiate with the most famous star of German films, Pola Negri.

Producers decided that if you can't lick the Germans, get them to join you. They built up strong European interests, exchanges, and studios and lay in wait for talent. As soon as a promising director or star appeared, representatives from these branch offices enticed them to Hollywood with irresistible offers of fame and fortune.

In America, meanwhile, they did all they could to stem the flow of German productions. Actors' Equity came out against them; in an already overcrowded market, they declared, such imports could lead to further reductions in output and more layoffs. Labor generally opposed the importations on the grounds that they encouraged the low wages of Germany by showing a preference for low-cost big pictures. The American Legion entered the dispute on the grounds of outraged patriotism.

But America controlled eighty per cent of world distribution. "It is a humiliating thing to confess that we are frightened by a film menace from any nation," said James Quirk. "The motion picture is *our* art, and fright over rivalry seems like a confession that we have been beaten on our ground."[2]

The Cabinet of Dr. Caligari was refused a showing in Los Angeles, after protests from the American Legion, Actors' Equity, and the Motion Picture Directors Association, although it was screened when the fuss had died down. German pictures were morbid and pessimistic because, general opinion asserted, the Germans liked horror and suffering on the screen—not to sympathize with the sufferer but to enjoy watching the sufferings.

Nevertheless, Adolph Zukor attracted Pola Negri to Paramount, and Mary Pickford imported Ernst Lubitsch. The most alarming rivals were safely, if not happily, integrated.

To make certain that Germany was suitably immobilized, another Pola Negri director, the Russian Dmitri Buchowetski, was brought over.

Attention swung to Scandinavia. Before the war, in 1913, a Danish director, Benjamin Christensen, made a feature film called *The Mysterious X.* Technically,

[1] *Quoted in* Photoplay, *July 1921, p. 55.*
[2] *Ibid., p. 56.*

this was an astonishing piece of work. Christensen was obsessed with light; the visual effects he and his cameraman, Emil Dinesen, coaxed from shadows and chiaroscuro were far ahead of practically anyone else at the time. Not only was the lighting remarkable; Christensen intuitively understood the whole grammar of film. His cutting was remarkably sophisticated, and he knew how to *develop* scenes instead of merely recording them.

Night of Revenge, in 1915, was even better. The story, of a convict who returns after a long-term sentence to seek his child, was brilliantly handled. Had the story itself been of greater stature, *Night of Revenge* would have been one of the cinema's classics.

Haxan, or *Witchcraft Through the Ages,* was completed, after much research, in 1920. This remarkable achievement opens tamely enough with a long series of engravings. Then follows a series of sharply etched episodes depicting the power of witches in the Middle Ages. Some scenes are unbearable; fifty years has not dulled their impact. When released, the film shocked and amazed everyone who saw it. Christensen was brought to America, where he made a number of bizarre films; *Mockery* with Lon Chaney, *Devil's Circus* with Norma Shearer. None of his American films are known to survive.[3]

Sweden, respected then as now for the artistic quality of its productions, lost the cream of its talent to America; Victor Sjöstrom (known in America as Seastrom): Einar Hansen; Lars Hanson; Sven Gade, another Dane; and later Mauritz Stiller and Garbo. From Hungary, Alexander Korda and his wife, Maria Corda, were signed by Richard Rowland, together with a number of writers. Germany lost another clutch of valuable directors and stars; Paul Leni, Lothar Mendes, and later, F. W. Murnau.

When *Variety* shook Hollywood, Universal succeeded in signing its director, E. A. Dupont. They parted company after an allegedly disastrous first film, *Love Me and the World Is Mine.*

Apparently immune to Hollywood's lures were film makers in Italy.

Italy's great days were before World War I. The Italian cinema produced two vital contributions to the medium: the spectacular picture and the naturalistic drama. The spectaculars, born of Italian mammoth, open-air theatrical extravaganzas, triggered off the Griffith epics. Many of them were grotesque and banal, with innumerable extras running from innumerable disasters, racing around and around the camera waving their hands in the air. *Quo Vadis?* (1912, Enrico Guazzoni), was the most important of the early spectaculars; huge sets, enormous crowds, and a sophisticated filmic treatment gave the film a unique impact. However, *Cabiria,* made in 1913, was the greatest example of its type. In what has been described as "an attempt to achieve the third dimension," director Giovanni Pastrone moved the camera, very gently and very smoothly, in long tracking shots.

---

[3] *John Gillett informed me that the Danish Film Museum had a copy of* Seven Footprints to Satan, *a comedy with Creighton Hale and Thelma Todd, photographed by Sol Polito, and I saw it in Copenhagen, in August 1967. It was a beautifully shot, sharply cut, haunted-house comedy, clearly owing its existence to the success of* The Cat and the Canary. *Very exciting, and full of surprises, the picture again demonstrates Christensen's obsession with light. Much of it is reminiscent of* The Mysterious X, *and his fascination for the occult and the bizarre is still very strong. The supporting cast of monsters are disturbingly convincing. When the whole thing turns out to be a joke, Christensen has the last laugh. For once, the monsters do not remove their disguises. They sit down to a banquet, happily chatting; clearly well-adjusted monsters.*

Bernard Partridge cartoon from Punch; *ironically, the camera is an American Bell and Howell.*

Marco de Gastyne's La Vie Merveilleuse de Jeanne d'Arc (1928). *Cameraman Brun, using Bell and Howell.*

Cabiria used artificial light very effectively, and while the editing tended merely to link shots which were complete in themselves, Pastrone often cut in powerful close-ups, ·such as an outstretched hand of a high priest during the Moloch sacrifices. The burning of the Roman fleet was surprisingly realistic, although done with models. The location scenes, in the Alps, represented another extraordinary achievement. Besides the large number of extras needed for Hannibal's army, the company even shipped up elephants to ensure authenticity.

Julius Caesar (1914) does not eclipse *Cabiria,* but it proves that Pastrone was not the only innovator in Italy at the time. The picture was so impressive that when it was released in America, in 1922, it was mistaken by critics for a contemporary film. Enrico Guazzoni placed his columns of Roman troops in bold, exciting compositions, much as Eisenstein was to do ten years later. He displayed a knowledge of history, an advanced sense of choreography, and a real understanding of cinema. One shot of Guazzoni's soldiers on the march has more impact than anything in *Fall of the Roman Empire.*

After the war, the Italians held little sway over world markets, and however good some of their films were, they could offer no competition to the Americans. A number of Hollywood productions were made in Italy: *The White Sister* and *Romola* by Henry King, *The Eternal City* by George Fitzmaurice, *Nero* by J. Gordon Edwards, and the legendary *Ben-Hur.*

"I thought the Italian technicians as good as any we had in the States," said Henry King. "When I returned in 1949 to do *Prince of Foxes,* I only took department heads with me because I knew the excellence of the Italian technicians;

The Nibelungen Saga (1923–4) *in production at UFA's Neubabelsberg studios, under the direction of Fritz Lang. Carl Hoffman at camera. See p. 509 for final result.*

I used again many of the same people I had used in *The White Sister* and *Romola*."

Arthur Miller, cameraman on *Eternal City,* was horrified by Italian laboratories, however. "Their idea of quality and mine were a little different. Their handling of film and their results were anything but up-to-date. Their actresses wore Theda Bara make-up and to them any negative I shot should be like theirs. We got some pretty bad rushes."

Charles Rosher, who made *Santo Ilario* (Henry Kolker) in Rome, was amused by the studio protocol in Italy.

"It was amazing to see how the Italians worked. The director, with mustache and beard, would stride in in the morning and everyone on the set would stand up and give him the bow. *"Bonjorno, signor . . . bonjorno."* And the director walked straight up to the camera, picked it up, placed it where he wanted it, and then started placing the actors."

Italy had also been responsible for a number of naturalistic dramas, the most famous of which was *Assunta Spina* (1914: Gustavo Serena). The acting, perfectly restrained, was a welcome contrast to the operatic, emphasized representation which remained so popular in Italy for so long. Francesca Bertini, generally cast as a vamp, played a working-class girl humanly and convincingly in *Assunta Spina,* and the atmosphere was captured as realistically as in the later neo-realist films.

At the end of the twenties, the Italians made several last attempts to capture the international market with films like *The Last Days of Pompeii.* Smothered by bureaucracy, the Italian cinema was itself to lie buried for several years before Mussolini unearthed it and brought it back from the dead. But by then the silent cinema was history itself.

The English films of this period form the basis for the illusions that surround the silent era. English films, with few exceptions, were crudely photographed; the direction and acting were on the level of cheap revue, they exploited so-called stars, who generally had little more than a glimmer of histrionic talent, and they were exceedingly boring.

The silent-film industry in Britain never advanced beyond the atmosphere of the barns and glass houses in which it began. It never outgrew the boyish amateurism of those early days when a strip of film with pictures on it was hailed as a miracle. The film industry's chiefs never regarded the cinema as having any more potential than a slightly superior fairground entertainment. To them, the word "arty" was the ultimate in invective. No producer thought in terms of artistry, and none of them ever dreamed that it was necessary for a director to be an artist.

Many of Hollywood's finest technicians came from the British Isles: Chaplin, Herbert Brenon, Rex Ingram, Charles Rosher, Albert E. Smith, J. Stuart Blackton, Charles Brabin, Donald Crisp, Edmund Goulding, Frank Lloyd, Tom Terriss, Wilfred Noy, Charles Bryant . . . Imagine what might have happened had these men stayed to consolidate the English film industry.

Famous Players' abortive attempt to start a studio was followed by the arrival of a number of directors—Tourneur, Millarde, Neilan—who came to England to shoot exteriors. American technicians were constantly being hired by British producers to try to raise the quality of their products. Harley Knoles went over quite early, as did Harold Shaw, who founded the London Film Company; his assistant in later years was Jo Sternberg. Writer Denison Clift became a director in England. Toward the end of the silent days, British International Pictures was formed to attract the cream of foreign technicians, among them E. A. Dupont, Richard Eichberg, Geze von Bolvary, Arthur Robison, Charles Rosher, Charles van Enger. . . . But somehow nothing these men did in England could be compared to their work in their own country.

"One of the worst arguments for British films in the past has been—the British film," the English fan magazine *Picturegoer* remarked with surprising candor. "That painful fact must be perfectly obvious to any but a blind and bigoted patriot. In spite of the far too large percentage of rubbish that emanates from the other side of the herring pond, one of the best arguments for the American film is, quite often, the American film."

The American film industry had grown to become the third most powerful industry in the country. Britain, which had led the world in the beginning of the cinema, saw its industry heavily reduced by World War I. Postwar slumps, and the ever-increasing flood of American pictures, ensured that the British film industry could never rise above its status as a fringe activity. The government clamped colossal import rates on American films and, toward the end of the silent period, introduced the Quota Act—which forced exhibitors to screen a certain number of British films. While this assisted the industry economically, it did not improve its chances of an artistic renaissance.

E. Temple Thurston, author of *The City of Beautiful Nonsense,* several of whose stories were filmed in England by Cecil Hepworth, gave an indication of the state of English pictures in a *Motion Picture Classic* interview in 1926:

"The American films are so infinitely superior to the British that I don't wonder at the state of things here and the poverty in English film circles. English producers [meaning directors] never really studied the thing. In the main they are made up of cheap photographers. Not one that I can think of has the faintest conception of what a story is, let alone of how to tell it when he has it. All they want to put on is pretty pictures.

"I might compare the English film producer with a taxi driver. The only viewpoint in life that he has—and it is perfectly right and normal for *him*—is a fare, a paying passenger. The British producer has his eye only on fares. And the English author's attitude is equally culpable; his is one of lucrative indifference.

"He knows that it won't affect the sales on the production of his work and doesn't as a rule even go to see its production—possibly because he might be ashamed of it."

Not surprisingly, the British film people developed a painful inferiority complex, and when an American film enjoyed a smash success it twisted the knife in their wound. *The Big Parade* was panned by the English critics: "The film tells how America won the war," they sneered. James Quirk, editor of *Photoplay,* received letters of apology from English fans, apologizing for the stupidity of their critics.

"English picture criticism," said Quirk, "is on a par with English pictures. They just do not know how to make pictures. And they just won't learn. There are no more beautiful places in the world than in England to make pictures.

Their producers have a great opportunity. The motion picture is universal and international, and we would welcome English pictures as well as German pictures."[4]

Herbert Wilcox's *Nell Gwyn,* with Dorothy Gish, was the first film from England to meet with approval from American audiences, and that was not released until 1926.

Alfred Hitchcock, who had gained his experience as art and assistant director with George Fitzmaurice, and other visiting American crews, was the first top-line British director, together with Anthony Asquith, whose *Cottage on Dartmoor* is still an impressive production.

England's most celebrated film maker, Cecil Hepworth, was not appreciated by American audiences. *"Comin' Thro the Rye,"* said *Photoplay,* "is thirty years behind American films. You'll enjoy it better if you stay at home. It just gives one a desire to shoot everybody that had a hand in its making."[5]

It is a tragedy that this period of film making, glittering with achievement elsewhere, should have remained as dour and fog-enshrouded as it did in England.

In France, the cinema during the silent era gained the status of a fine art. The work of its finest practitioners has thus been well documented. Perhaps too much attention has been paid to René Clair and Jacques Feyder, and not enough to Raymond Bernard, whose *Miracle of the Wolves* and *The Chess Player* were imaginative and powerful historical dramas, or to Marco de Gastyne, whose *Merveilleuse Vie de Jeanne d'Arc* contains sweeping spectacle worthy of the best of Eisenstein.

After the Revolution, Russian émigrés poured into France—among them the best part of the Russian film industry. They set out to make Russian pictures in exile, with Russian players and Russian technicians. *Michael Strogoff,* directed by Viatcheslav Tourjansky, is one of the finest examples, starring Ivan Mosjoukine, Natalie Kovanko, Chakatouny, and Prince N. Kougouchef. *Casanova* is another, directed by Alexandre Volkoff, assisted by Anatole Litvak, starring Mosjoukine and Natalie Lissenko.

The French cinema has not disappeared to the extent of the American. The Cinémathèque Française has amassed enormous quantities of film; all that is required now is finance enough to catalogue and preserve it.

There is more interest now in the cinema of the past in France than anywhere else in the world. The country which first recognized the motion picture as a fine art has already learned to appreciate its old masters.

Some, like Jacques Feyder, Max Linder, have died. But others, René Clair, Marcel l'Herbier, Jean Renoir, are still alive and still active. But the greatest French film maker of all is a man little known outside France. In Paris, a cinema is named after him, books by him and about him are available. Elsewhere, he has been forgotten.

His name is Abel Gance.

[4] Photoplay, *Aug. 1927, p. 27.*
[5] Photoplay, *March 1925, p. 106.*

46 / ABEL GANCE

This book is dedicated to Abel Gance not because he had a blemish-free record of sparkling successes, but because, with his silent productions, *J'accuse, La Roue,* and *Napoléon,* he made a fuller use of the medium than anyone before or since.

Abel Gance is one of the giants of the cinema. Some historians hail him as the D. W. Griffith of Europe, others dismiss him as the De Mille of France. Both realize his importance, neither fully comprehend his talents.

His *Napoléon* is a masterpiece in the original sense of the word; containing every conceivable technique of cinema, it has served as a masterwork for the motion picture in Europe ever since. The young directors of the French Nouvelle Vague were profoundly influenced by a version revived in Paris in the late fifties. Many of their experiments, and particularly their unrestrained use of the hand-held camera, have their origins in Gance's work.

The motion-picture industry, in France as elsewhere, was alarmed by Gance's monumental talents, and frightened by his revolutionary ideas. They determined to control him, and to limit the length of his artistic leash. Unfortunately for all of us, they succeeded.

Gance still has the spark of genius, but it is a long time since it was set ablaze.

He has made many pronouncements about the cinema, and he has written a great deal. But his style is rich and romantic, his poetic metaphors, brilliant in themselves, are mistaken for pomposity, particularly in translation.

He is naturally embittered by the system which has crippled him, and his writings seldom underplay the importance of his contributions. Thus, many have dismissed him as a pompous has-been nursing a grudge against commercialism.

To meet him is to realize the preposterous inaccuracy of that description. Gance has retained his youthful enthusiasm; his strong sense of humor affects all he says, until he begins to talk about the future, about his plans. Then a single-minded determination rules out other emotions. One can easily appreciate how he achieved greatness. Although not very strong physically, he has an iron will. He is very productive and is still capable of extremely hard work. As a person, he is warm and considerate—with one endearing quirk, unusual for a film maker and former actor. As soon as a camera is produced, he becomes self-conscious and his expression assumes the anxiety of someone facing a firing squad.

Gance is an impressive-looking man. His face is proud, sensitive, delicately etched, with an aquiline nose and a majestic crown of white hair swept arrogantly back. He looks rather like a medieval saint, although his mischievous grin quickly dispels any such resemblance.

Gance lives in Paris—at Boulogne-sur-Seine, in a bright, beautifully decorated modern apartment. Behind his desk, the walls are plastered with paintings, photographs, newspaper clippings, and what he calls his "static explosions"—quotations from philosophers which he uses "to recharge my batteries":

"For those with a mission to accomplish, bodily existence will last as long as necessary."—Brahma Putra.

"*Malheureux*—all that you want you shall have."—Plato.

There is a magnificent triptych in a frame—a close-up of Dieudonné, framed by cavalry . . . there are stills of Gance himself as Saint-Just, of the Brienne pillow fight, with the screen split up into nine separate shots, a photograph of D. W. Griffith raising his hat and shaking hands with a shy-looking Gance, a tiny

Abel Gance and D. W. Griffith, Mamaroneck, New York, 1921.

a Folie du Docteur Tube *(1915).*

portrait of Schweitzer clipped from a newspaper, another newspaper portrait of the writer Celine, a signed portrait of Charles Pathé, a faded, yellow photograph of the beautiful Ida Danis, a painting of Mme. Gance, and many pictures of his daughter Clarisse, taken at his country home at Châteauneuf-sur-Grasse.

One wall consists entirely of books, tightly packed and ranging from classical works and *Les Grands Auteurs du Cinéma* to *My Wonderful World of Slapstick* by Buster Keaton.

Gance spent a great deal of time answering the telephone—an old-fashioned Paris model which was also used as a paperweight.

"If Edgar Allan Poe had not written "The Pit and the Pendulum." he would have written "The Telephone," he said.

As he talked about his life in the cinema, dusk fell, and the light in his study seemed to heighten the strange, almost mystical quality that Gance undeniably has. At one point, he produced the two-volume scenario for *Victoire de Samothrace,* carefully typed in both black and red, which he wrote for Sarah Bernhardt in 1914. He had illustrated the front page with a magazine photograph of the *Winged Victory* in the Louvre. He felt the play had lost nothing with the years. . . .

The career of Abel Gance provides a fascinating contrast to the careers of the American directors. In many ways, he is their complete antithesis, yet he shares their most important attribute—a genuine love for motion pictures.

A brilliant and erudite mind, Gance is one of the few who have succeeded in putting a literary background to visual use. He sees the cinema not as a single art, but as a pantheon of all the arts. He is a true master, in the sense of a da Vinci—a man who has enabled artists to progress their own work with the help of his innovations.

It is difficult to convey with full impact the extent of the tragedies, setbacks, and frustrations that this man has been forced to endure.

"My greatest mistake," he said, "was ever to have compromised. My greatest achievement has been to survive."

Born in Paris on October 25, 1889, Abel Gance's early life was hampered by his father's insistence on an "honorable career." His father was a doctor; his attitude to the arts mirrored that of many Victorians, involved in what they considered more essential work, for whom painting, writing, and acting were not occupations so much as immoral frivolity.

Young Abel Gance was a brilliant student. He disliked boarding school intensely, however, and as an antidote to the dismal routine, he immersed himself in literature and poetry and learned the works of his favorite authors by heart. He was invariably top in every subject, but his precocity was not held against him. The other boys felt rather that his intellectual accomplishments were part of his complex and highly engaging personality, and he was very popular. He returned this popularity in an action characteristic of the future film maker: he produced a class newspaper.

The *Journal de la Classe* was good value for a sou: serials, stories and articles were illustrated, on exercise-book paper, with colored drawings. Another creative activity Gance enjoyed enormously was acting, and he often staged impromptu plays. He was especially fond of tragedy.

But while he dreamed of literature, poetry, and the theater, his father determined to make a lawyer out of him. After passing his Baccalaureat, Gance tried vainly to convince his father of his true ambitions—and, without telling him, put his name down for the Conservatoire. He narrowly failed his entrance exam.

Thoroughly disheartened, he gave in to his father's demands and became an articled clerk in a solicitor's office, where, at the age of seventeen, he was assigned to divorce cases. Gance says this was one of the most depressing periods of his life; whenever he could manage it, he played truant and spent hours at the Bibliothèque Nationale, reading Racine, Rimbaud, Omar Khayyam, Edgar Allan Poe, Novalis, Nietzsche. . . .

He never quite lost sight of the theater, for he regularly read stage journals. An agency advertisement in one of these papers, for the Théâtre du Parc, Brussels, raised his hopes; he pleaded illness, took a day off, and was signed up at three hundred francs a month. Life began again. He lived out the last days at the solicitor's office in a much happier frame of mind—carefully preserving his secret in case his parents should discover it.

When the date for the Brussels opening drew near, and it was too late to change anything, he felt safe in telling his mother. She was upset, but she understood. However, he dared not tell his father; he dared not even bid him farewell. This was the beginning of a rift that was to widen, to the distress of both father and son; years later when *Napoléon* was honored by being shown at the Paris Opéra—*Le Miracle des Loups* (1924) was the first film premiered at the Opéra— the elderly doctor used to make an elaborate detour to avoid seeing his son's name shamelessly emblazoned for all to see: "NAPOLEON VU PAR ABEL GANCE."

The Brussels season of 1907-8 was very rewarding. He acted continually, he made many valuable friends, including Blaise Cendrars and Victor Francen, and he wrote his first scenario for the cinema, *Mireille,* which he sold to Léonce Perret.

Returning to Paris with renewed confidence, he decided to continue acting for a while longer before he achieved his ultimate ambition: to write for the theater. But life in Paris was considerably less easy than in Brussels. Work was far from plentiful, and he was offered few important parts. His financial position rapidly became crucial. His friends—Cendrars, Guillaume Apollinaire, Séverin-Mars, Riciotto Canudo, Chagall, Pierre Magnier—helped as much as they could. At their meeting place, the Café Napolitain, they would make a daily collection for the most impoverished member of their group. Gance frequently benefited from their generosity. Nevertheless, he was forced to cut down even on essentials, and his health began to trouble him.

In 1909, he played his first screen role, in Léonce Perret's *Molière*. With good reason, he regarded the cinema somewhat scornfully, and thought its products puerile; what interest he had was purely mercenary. These were primitive years, and even D. W. Griffith, a struggling actor in New York, had expressed similar opinions about this pale imitation of the theater.

"I suppose, first of all, I was surprised by the cinema," said Gance. "I had seen the Lumière films when I was younger, and right then I was fascinated by the moving image. But when I saw the early efforts of the silent cinema I felt they were infantile and stupid—much like traveling shows, they were merely spectacles and of no artistic value. That discouraged me. I felt that they provided little but the simplest amusement—the most elementary pleasure. I had to wait until I had seen my first Mack Sennett before I could say to myself: 'Aha! This is more interesting than I thought!'

"At that time, when I was poor, I was doing little parts for films as an actor—at the Gaumont studios, or at Lux—and I was equally disillusioned when I discovered what little importance was given to the actors working there. This attitude was so childish that I became seriously discouraged, but while I was reflecting on it, I suddenly thought, 'Well, now, if *I* were doing it, I'd set about it quite differently. For one thing, I would set up the shots in a different way . . .' This was the time of *The Assassination of the Duke of Guise,* of the first, simple films of that sort, a time when our great players, like Sarah Bernhardt and Mounet-Sully, were being made to look idiotic.

" 'This is very strange,' I thought. 'They're very good on the stage, yet they're very bad in the cinema.'

"Laboratory processes were often very bad, too, but these difficulties were slowly being overcome.

"When I began writing scenarios, I decided to sell them to Gaumont. I wrote a dozen or so small scenarios—four or five pages—and sold them for fifty to a hundred francs. That was a bargain, believe me. You could eat for three days on fifty francs, that was all."

Gance's health was now causing him real anxiety, and he submitted to a medical examination. The doctor diagnosed a disease which, in those days, was equivalent to a death sentence: tuberculosis. He made it clear that he would have to stop work. To his mother, he admitted that the young man had only a few months to live.

Half-starved, with financial demands crowding in on him, such news might well have caused collapse then and there, but with a tremendous effort of will, Gance forced himself to undergo a self-imposed respiratory treatment—away from the grimy city air, in a town called Vittel, where he had secured an acting job. To their astonishment, doctors were forced to admit that he had conquered the disease.

His other anxieties, however, remained unchecked. To earn money as quickly as possible, he wrote some more scenarios.

"I wrote all sorts of little stories, but they were very much cinema stories. Some of these scripts were shot by directors like Albert Capellani and Louis Feuillade, and some of them turned out quite well. I regained a little confidence. Then I had an idea for a film which I wanted to make myself."

With a group of friends, among whom was the celebrated actor Edouard de Max, he formed a production company called Le Film Français.

"I shot the first film at a studio called 'Alterego.' At Alterego I made films which were so bad they could never be released—due to faults on the production side and at the laboratory."

His first production was *La Digue (ou pour sauver la Hollande)*, made in 1911, which introduced Pierre Renoir, brother of another future director, Jean Renoir. Set in the Holland of 1600, it was not entirely filmed in the then customary long shot, but contained several medium close shots.

La Masque d'Horreur, with Edouard de Max, was an unusual Grand Guignol production which was released, but in bad condition, due to a laboratory defect—

intermittent softness of the image where the celluloid touched the wooden frame of the developing drum.

Nevertheless, it sold well, and aroused the interest of Film d'Art.

But a small success could not offset the failures. Gance returned to the theater, where money again became a problem. "My poverty is indecent," he wrote in his diary. "I can understand now why hunger is called the best general of revolutions."

Despite his poverty, Gance's enthusiasm was afire over his great dramatic work, *Victoire de Samothrace*. At last he was achieving his ambition of writing for the theater. Setting the style for his future chefs d'oeuvres, this tragedy was intended to last for five hours. Emile Fabre, of the Théâtre Français, said he would play it on condition that an act was cut out. Gance refused to compromise. Eventually, Edouard de Max persuaded Sarah Bernhardt to read it.

She cabled Gance her enthusiasm. He was elated; he felt the privations he had undergone to write it were now fully justified. In the light of this supreme triumph all his failures and frustrations seemed worthwhile.

Four days later, war broke out. General mobilization was followed by the closing of many theaters. Gance was drafted, but he failed his medical and was discharged. Most of his friends left for the army, and he found Paris increasingly depressing. He retreated to the Vendée, and drowned his despair in concentrated study.

After a few months, he felt strong enough to face Paris, and, the supreme compliment of Bernhardt's approbation still in his mind, he sent a scenario to Film d'Art.

Film d'Art—or rather its dynamic new director, Louis Nalpas—wrote back and asked him to drop by.

"This scenario for *L'Infirmière*," said Nalpas, when they met, "is very good. We will buy it for three hundred francs."

The amount was considerably more than Gance had ever received from Gaumont or Pathé. He asked if he could watch the shooting; Nalpas agreed, and told him that the direction was being assigned to Henri Pouctal.

After his own experience at directing, Gance watched with a new, professional interest.

"I wanted to ask Pouctal why he was doing it as he was . . . I wanted to make suggestions, but I didn't dare. He was quite an old man, with a mustache, who was something of an authoritarian. He might well have sent me packing; after all, I was only the insignificant little writer.

"That evening I saw Nalpas.

" 'I have been watching Pouctal shooting,' I said. 'I think he could do better.'

"He listened to my criticisms and suggestions with interest and then said, 'M. Gance, if you have another scenario, and if it's a bargain, I'll try and get you a little money to shoot it yourself.' "

L'Infirmière was completed; Gance had given Pouctal one or two ideas, and the film was a success, although, Gance added, Pouctal slipped back to his old ways afterward.

Nalpas liked the next scenario—*Les Morts Reviennent-ils?* was its original title —and he gave Gance five thousand francs to cover everything—his fee, film stock, sets, costumes, and actors.

"It's not much," said Gance, feeling somewhat alarmed.

"We haven't got enough money," replied Nalpas. "It's all I can do for you."

Gance completed the film, finally titled *Un Drame au Château d'Acre,* in five days flat.

"There were some very curious scenes in this film," said Gance. "In the Palais de Madrid, here in Paris, there is an enormous mirror. I took a shot of an actor in this mirror so that on the screen one couldn't actually see that it was a reflection. Another actor goes up to this reflection—I think he was trying to kill him— and suddenly realizes he is dealing with a reflection. By this time, the other actor has quietly left the set. This had an element of surprise about it, and I liked it very much.

"When I had finished this film, Nalpas said, 'That's great! Just look at him— this young M. Gance who can make a film in five days for only five thousand francs!'

"After that, the other directors were a little envious of me."

Nalpas was so delighted with the modest success of this film that he gave his new director carte blanche for his next production. As future producers were to learn to their cost, giving carte blanche to Abel Gance was equivalent to touching dynamite with a lighted match.

The film that caused the explosion on this occasion was *La Folie du Docteur Tube,* a black comedy which carried Méliès fantasy into the realm of the avant-garde. Historians have sometimes called it the first experimental production, a foretaste of *The Cabinet of Dr. Caligari.* Apart from the similarity of the mad doctor, the film was actually a self-indulgent romp with camera tricks rather than a serious excursion into psychology. Gance and his new cameraman, the brilliant Léonce-Henry Burel, used distorting mirrors to create startling effects.

Nalpas and the other executives of Film d'Art were infuriated by what seemed to them a criminal waste of money. It was wartime; the public needed entertainment, diversion—not unsettling experiments such as this. The company refused to show it.

Gance was ordered to toe the line. Normal stories and normal treatments: "Don't take your camera too close," warned Nalpas. "You know you're supposed to show the whole of your actors, so you can see their gestures."

The close-up, by 1915, was a common feature of American productions. Wartime France, however, received their overseas pictures late, often as much as a year late, and the more conservative producers were not always aware of the latest trends. This was the cinema's formative period; as with a child, one year saw enormous changes.

Gance was deeply discouraged, and while he complied with his employers' instructions to turn out straightforward melodramas, his faith in the cinema had been dealt a shattering blow.

"I hardly recognize myself," he wrote in his diary, "struggling to live by making pictures for concierges. The cinema, this alphabet for eyes tired of thinking, wastefully devours my most precious possession."

When Nalpas set up a production, he did it for the minimum possible expense.

"He got the actors for next to nothing," said Gance. "And the studio, at Neuilly, had only the most basic form of equipment. The props were always the same—a palm tree in a big flowerpot, and two inkwells. They used to say, 'Be careful with those inkwells. If you use one in one scene, you must use the other in the next.' I pointed out that they were both identical, and they ought to get another, different one.

"It was the same story with the door. I suggested they change its color once in a while. The palm trees, in the flowerpots, too; we used to keep moving them on and off the set. It was all great fun, a sort of Commedia dell'Arte.

"*L'Enigme de Dix Heures* was a very good thriller. The film was based on a very simple story which could easily have been true. You know that people can be electrocuted by telephone. Well, that was the basis of the film. The murderer (Aurele Sydney) wanted to get rid of a number of important people. He would say: 'Tomorrow at ten p.m. you will be dead.'

"They would put guards on the person threatened. There would be a guard at the window, a guard on the ground floor, and so on. At ten p.m. there would be a telephone call, and the man would be dead. This went on until even the chief of police had been killed.

"It was a well-constructed plot, because the audience had to wait until the very end before they discovered how the murders were being carried out. The film was quite advanced for its time, and was a success even in England, where Aurele Sydney went on to make the *Ultus* series. It was on the strength of his performance in *L'Enigme de Dix Heures* that he was selected.

"Little by little, I made progress with my understanding of camerawork. My understanding of optics kept pace with the technical advances in cinematography. The quality of the photographic image was getting better and better, and they were now beginning to supervise the developing of film, but still we saw just the negative. We could only afford to develop the film, we didn't have enough funds to print all of it; we selected the shots for printing by viewing the negative."

La Folie du Docteur Tube apart, Gance's films were commercially successful. But he never had enough time; Nalpas needed more and more pictures. One day, Nalpas ordered him to select four actors, catch a train the next morning, and return as quickly as possible with two completed films.

"But I haven't even got the scenarios," protested Gance.

"Never mind. You can do them on the train."

So Gance wrote the scenarios for two full-length feature films on the way to Cassis.

"I had to work it out so that the two films could be shot at the same time. Now, let's see: did I have four or three actors? Was this one dead already in this film? Could he go on playing in the other? I had great fun. As soon as the train arrived, we started shooting. The first scene was scene forty-eight of *Barberousse* and scene fifty-two of *Gaz Mortels*—both together. Quite a business! But it gave me a great facility. I really had to exert myself—it was like doing one's Latin and Greek at the same time. . . .

"The psychology was always very rudimentary. Good and bad—these were the elements of the story, and I could, therefore, make the films quickly, without putting myself to impossible lengths. The actors used to play their parts very seriously, but I knew the spirit in which the script had been written!

"I tried several innovations in *Barberousse*. There was a tracking shot on a motorcycle, but I had used short tracking shots much earlier than this. In the earlier films, I had made use of a sort of tricycle, which we built ourselves. The trouble was that it wasn't very stable. We couldn't secure the camera properly and the tripod, on the tricycle, kept bouncing about. The final effect was not very pleasing on the eye. It was only later, when they introduced the rubber tire, that we managed to build a steady tricycle.

"The motorcycle shot was quite difficult to do. We put the camera in the sidecar to secure a really big close-up of the driver as he looked over his shoulder. But the camera was hardly the most convenient size—it was the old wooden Pathé studio model, with the magazine on top."

Both *Les Gaz Mortels* and *Barberousse* illustrate Gance's capabilities at this stage of his development—1916—and prove conclusively that his eyes were still not fully opened to the potential of the cinema.

Les Gaz Mortels is extremely well photographed, by Burel and Dubois, and sharply and professionally edited, but the performances are ludicrous, even by the circus-tent standards of 1916. Not even the naturalistic exterior backgrounds persuaded him to soften the outrageous gesturing of his players. The treatment, although as straightforward as any serial, is not without interest. There is a vividly staged poison-gas panic at a remote country factory (the film, despite its title, has nothing to do with the war), and a suspense-filled sequence of a venomous snake crawling toward a sleeping child. . . .

But basically, *Les Gaz Mortels* is a cheap little thriller which most directors of the time could have handled with ease.

Barberousse is much more intriguing. The story, if anything, is even more absurd, but the controlling hand now begins to shape and mold the material. This was clearly a film Gance enjoyed making more than *Les Gaz Mortels,* for all the technical effects find their way into it.

Barberousse is a bandit, garbed in an eyepatch and an outlandish flowing beard, like some Gilbert and Sullivan pirate, who organizes a forest maquis to terrorize the area and thus to boost sales of *La Grand Gazette,* a newspaper of which he happens to be the owner.

For all its ridiculous narrative, *Barberousse* is irresistible. Gance pops in his cinematic ideas with flamboyance, and while the film was obviously intended to be taken seriously, the element of parody cannot be ignored.

The most outrageous episode is one in which the hero's wife, Odette Triveley, goes shooting in the forest and finds herself pursued by creeping bushes. This Birnam Wood idea is intercut with the asphyxiation of the police chief by poisoned cigar. The intercutting is effective, but the creeping-bushes scene is so hilarious that the suspense dissolves in laughter.

"Drama always contains an element of comedy," said Gance. "In a thriller, if improbable events are well done, you say, 'Well, that's not exactly probable, but it's well put over, so all right!' Everyone took their parts seriously enough, but I had my little bit of fun. I didn't take films all that seriously. I remember how we came to shoot that scene—it wasn't influenced by *Macbeth,* because I hadn't seen it yet. We were at a place called Saucy-les-Pins, where the Mistral blows so strongly that, in one part of the forest, the trees are permanently bent over. They gave me the feeling of the whole forest being on the march. I felt that if I could have movable trees in among the other trees, we could create this feeling on film. Men would move the trees while hidden from sight, and I would move the camera to increase the movement.

"Unfortunately, we were never able to set the shot up properly, because when

I brought the camera back to move it, and angle it to follow the shape of the trees, I found myself too far from the actors to be able to control them. But if it had worked, it would have been very good. The audience would have seen first the trees upright—the camera being at an angle. Then, as we tilted the camera back to normal, the trees would have appeared to lean over. Then we would have moved in closer, and taken the trees in actual movement—the whole forest would have been on the move.

"Finally, I settled for single bushes on the move, but it was still very difficult, because I had no idea at the time how I was going to use the sequence within the framework of my story!"

Another unusual effect, which appears throughout the picture, is the horizontal wipe—acting as a sort of curtain for the end of scenes.

"Burel had the habit of putting his hand over the lens at the end of an N.G. take," said Gance. "I thought about this and realized that if he covered the lens completely, he would black out the entire picture. I told him that if he did this, I would cut the camera while the lens was covered—his hand would come in from the side, and we would thus have a wipe. Then we started sliding a piece of black paper across the lens. When it was covered, we would cut to the next scene. Later, we started wiping the paper across the lens, linking two scenes with a continuous movement. Then we began using two pieces of paper, coming together like elevator doors, and finally we used an iris diaphragm for fades, and dispensed with the wipes."

Barberousse features a number of close-ups, including one enormous one: Odette is about to drink poisoned tea, and to heighten the impact, Gance cuts to a huge close-up of her lips as she raises the cup. Then he cuts to a close-up of the jangling telephone bell, interrupting her.

He also uses low-angled close-ups, which were very unusual at that time. Placing the camera low, looking up at the face, produces a very dramatic effect, but such shots came into common use only after the German experiments of the twenties.

Most prophetic of all the effects in the film is a triptych. When Odette telephones the newspaper office, her call is intercepted by the bandit's accomplice, standing aloft on a telephone pole. Odette, the interceptor, and the person receiving the call are shown on the screen at once.

These embellishments of technique enraged Gance's conservative employers. A cable arrived before the end of production, insisting on the company's immediate return.

"Impossible to continue under these conditions. What are you doing? Letter follows."

The letter was a mass of objections. Nalpas took particular exception to the close-ups.

"What are these huge pictures supposed to mean? They'll show up all the faults in the face. You'll have people panicking in the cinema. They'll make for the exits!"

This time, Gance refused to submit. There was no money to pay the actors, but he persuaded them to work for nothing to finish the picture.

"I had a lot of trouble over the scenes Nalpas disliked," said Gance. "He didn't want to accept my innovations at all. I kept pointing out that I had done something new and unusual, but it made no difference. In the end, the public applauded the film. You know, people in the cinema don't notice technicalities. It's only you and I who do that. If a film interests someone, he won't care whether he's looking at a close-up or not. My audience probably didn't notice anything unusual —they just enjoyed the picture. Today, of course, the audience is more on the watch for such things, but for years nobody thought for a moment about technical styles.

"Of course, the people who run the business have been pretty stupid from the very earliest days. They have always been scared of audience reaction. I used to say, 'Let's try them, let's at least see what they say.' It was only in that way that I ever made any progress at all. But what a struggle! Look at my white hair. . . .

"Nalpas objected to my innovations for exactly the same reason that people disapprove of new ideas today. What now appears the simplest of things may once have seemed the most incredible of inventions.

"We used to get orders from Pathé. We were told that if the camera cut off the actors below the knee, then the film would be rejected. The whole body had to be in the frame. Pathé himself, of course, was too preoccupied with the superstructure of the business to worry about these filmic niceties. It was Ferdinand Zecca who supervised the films themselves.

"It was I who raised the first dissenting voice, who sowed the seeds of revolt. As one or two of my films succeeded, they began to accept my ideas—and then they began to copy me. Gradually, I realized the inanity of the sort of thing I was making. I pulled myself up short and said, 'Why are people making films which are about nothing but events, when they have at their disposal such a marvelous medium for psychological stories? They go on making films about people chasing each other, killing each other, or trying to commit suicide, but why not films which show feelings instead of just action?'

"I spent two or three days with Nalpas, pointing out to him that the cinema was in a rut, that unless we looked for some new formula, we would go on forever making the same sort of film.

" 'But, M. Gance,' he said. 'What you want to do can't be done at Pathé. Don't try your luck too hard.'

" 'But,' I said, 'we can't just go on with films about murder and spies—all this facile rubbish. We need to create something more interesting.'

" 'You can't do it. You'd need too many subtitles.'

" 'No, no, no. We'll do it with a minimum of subtitles. We'll make real dramas about real feelings. That's the sort of thing that will catch the public's imagination.'

"Nalpas was an intelligent man, but he was bound up with a firm which was difficult to run. In those days, they virtually bought films by length. It didn't matter whether the film was good or bad, only the length mattered, and only that decided the price. Pathé was the firm who bought from Nalpas, and that was whom he had to satisfy.

"In the end, Nalpas relented. 'Look,' he said, 'I'll let you have a try. Here's forty-five thousand francs. Go and make a film.'

"I went away, and in a night or two I wrote the script for the first—*Le Droit à la Vie.*"

Nalpas thought it was interesting enough to give the go ahead. The film was melodrama with strong psychological overtones, retaining nevertheless the basis of a thriller. A financier, suffering from an incurable illness, falls in love with a young girl, who marries him knowing he has only a short time to live. She consents to this sacrifice in order to obtain his fortune and, later, to marry her lover. But the lover has made his own fortune, in America, and when he returns, tensions mount, culminating in the attempted murder of the financier. A *crime passionel* charge is cleared by the wounded financier, who unites the two lovers before he eventually dies.

Le Droit à la Vie was the first film in which a close-up of Abel Gance appeared at the front, giving greater prominence to the director than to the actors. This was later to become a personal trademark of all Gance silent films; later he reverted to a signature. It was also the first in which he used his technique of isolating the player.

"I tried to suppress the inessential details in an important scene by hanging black velvet behind the actors. In the films in which I did that, no one notices the absence of décor—all they see is the actor. This was really a very good idea, although I know the present generation does not support me. The eye is not distracted by a chandelier, or by the corner of a window."

Le Droit à la Vie so successfully proved Gance's theory about the value of psychological dramas that he was given a far higher budget to make another.

"I was going to make a film called *Combien?*, but it never came to anything, because the idea was a little too similar to *Le Droit à la Vie*. I was going to use the same actor in it—Paul Vermoyal, who was very interesting, and who reminded me physically of Artaud. (Antonin Artaud played Marat in *Napoléon*.) He was to play a character who never said anything but 'Combien?'—'How much?' He spoke very little, and when he did, it was always this one word—even for women. He was practically dumb, but that one word was to have made him a fortune."

Gance's next film was *Mater Dolorosa*, featuring Emmy Lynn, the wife of a prominent film director, Henry Roussell, who had agreed to the role out of admiration for Gance. *Mater Dolorosa* achieved enormous success. It told the story of Dr. Gilles Berliac, a specialist in child health, who is more interested in his work than in his wife, Marthe. She has an affair with the husband's brother, Claude, which culminates in her attempted suicide. While trying to stop her, Claude is fatally wounded; before he dies, he manages to write a suicide note, but suspicions, nevertheless, are aroused and the discovery of a compromising letter from Marthe forces the doctor to remove their child.

"Tell me the man to whom you wrote this letter," he demands, "or your silence will be proof that Pierre is not my son."

The anguished mother has no clue to the child's whereabouts. Even when the child falls ill, the doctor refuses further news. The mother, desperate, is willing to tell him anything in return for reassurance about her son. The doctor is so moved by her despair that he forgives her, and reunites her with her child, who has completely recovered.

Mater Dolorosa has been quoted as being France's biggest money-maker for the season 1917-18. It made no further strides forward cinematically than *Barberousse*, but it was a far more worthwhile production. The melodrama was intense, but directed with what can only be described as a pure nobility—enriched by Burel's striking photography.

La Dixième Symphonie (1918) brought this style, and Gance's experiments in the realm of psychological melodrama, to fulfillment. With this finely controlled production, for which a special score was composed by Michel-Maurice Levy, Abel Gance proved himself the equal of any director in the world.

Despite the inevitably melodramatic plot, *La Dixième Symphonie* is remarkably sophisticated marital drama. The performances are no longer subject to elaborate gesturing; emotions are conveyed through facial expressions. The characters are convincing, strong and full of humor. The story is gripping and the drama is well constructed.

The inspiration for the picture came from a quotation by Berlioz: "I am about to start a great symphony in which my great sufferings will be portrayed."

Eve Dinant (Emmy Lynn) marries Enric Damor, a composer (Séverin-Mars), who is a widower with one child, Claire, of marriageable age (Mlle. Nizan). Eve has not told Damor of her past, for while attempting to free herself from a former lover, Frederic Ryce (Jean Toulout), she accidentally killed his sister. Since that day, Ryce has blackmailed her; when he begins courting Claire, Eve tries to stop the marriage, but she cannot produce a satisfactory reason. Damor is deeply hurt, and accuses her of being in love with Ryce herself. Paradoxically, he thanks Eve for the pain she has caused him:

"Suffering either kills or creates," he tells her. "I have just found the subject for my next symphony."

Eve is ready to sacrifice her own happiness and return to Ryce, if he will only leave Claire alone. Eventually, Damor discovers the truth and forgives his wife.

Melodrama is a misleading description for films such as this: the word implies a plot in which characterization and motivation are sacrificed to action—the very trend Gance despised. The word epitomizes *Les Gaz Mortels* and *Barberousse,* but it does not begin to do justice to the quality of *La Dixième Symphonie.*

The story is highly dramatic, played in a highly dramatic style, but the visuals are used to create character, to describe thoughts, to provide metaphors, and not merely to depict incidents.

The opening of Part I crystallizes the situation with bold close-ups of Eve's agonized face, her smoking pistol, the dead body, and a sinister hand, its fingers outstretched, descending upon a tiny bird.

"I shall say nothing," says Ryce, "if you agree to go on with our life."

When Eve, sickened by a last look at the dead woman, tries to leave, Ryce kisses her hand, and in a large close-up, the symbolic fist loosens its grip and the tiny bird falls from it, lifeless.

An ardent suitor, an elderly marquis (André Le Faur) provides the comic relief for this demanding drama. Some of the humor is rather heavy-handed, but a duel scene, restoring the comic figure's dignity, is most effective.

"I may be clumsy," says the marquis to Ryce, "but my honor must not be."

The protagonists fire, and a bird falls at the marquis' feet.

"Marquis," grins Ryce, "I believe you shot this bird by mistake."

"True," replies the marquis. "I mistook the target . . ."

The character of the marquis was evidence of Gance's belief, summed up in a subtitle: "Comedy passes through the most tragic of human dramas."

The sequence of the first performance of the Tenth Symphony requires the accompanying score to be entirely successful. But it retains great quality even when silent. Burel's stark cross-lighting illumines the audience dramatically, and Gance slowly dissolves between close-ups of each enraptured face. The mood of the music is evoked by a dancer (Ariane Hugon of the Opéra), who appears allegorically framed by a vignette. The motifs surrounding the vignette are hand-tinted in Pathécolor and the dances are staged exterior, divorcing them completely from the atmosphere of the soirée.

With *La Dixième Symphonie,* Gance proved himself a sensitive, brilliantly imaginative director. He proved, too, that he had fully exploited the existing techniques of the cinema. In order to make further progress, he would now have to advance the art itself.

The war was still on. Gance had been called before seven recruiting boards and rejected on medical grounds each time. "They used my carcass like a tennis ball," he said.

He was constantly hearing of the death of close friends. Sickened by the incessant waste of human life, Gance formulated in his mind the idea for *J'accuse.* Before he had had a chance to develop it further, the military authorities finally mobilized him into the Cinematograph Section.

"What a preposterous business *that* was!" said Gance. "It was dangerous in the front line—a lot of cameramen had been killed—so we did all we could to keep out of harm's way. One day, Pierre Marcel, who was a captain, the head of the section, and who had been very kind to me, came up and said, 'Gance, you never have anything to do. You just sit there.'

"I was doing my best to hide in a corner and to disappear altogether. 'Well, you'd better give me something to do,' I said.

"He thought awhile. 'All right,' he said. 'You can make a film about animals at war.'

"Well, that was fine, because what do animals do in time of war? Like me, they hide. So I thought about the subject, and I went on thinking about it for several weeks. Animals! A difficult subject. What animals were there? The mascots that airmen took up with them . . . the cats and dogs left at home. But if a dog has been left by his owner, all he does is bark. And a barking dog hardly makes an interesting shot. Then there were the horses in wartime. But I could hardly stand in front of these just to take a picture. It wouldn't be the most sensible of positions. And anyway, the horses were not in the front line merely to provide shots for the cinema. So one way or another I always found an answer. After a few weeks of this, during which time I had discovered nothing about animals in wartime, I received an order from HQ transferring me to the École Militaire.

"Every day, thirty of us were paraded, and officers asked us our civilian occupation. If you said you were a butcher, they'd send you off to be a butcher at the front. The same with a musician: 'Fine. The soldiers like to listen to music.' Then they asked me what my job was.

" 'I'm a playwright.'

" 'A playwright? Ah. Well—yes. You stay here until tomorrow.'

"For two or three weeks they could find nothing for me to do. Then, one day, they decided they'd had enough of me and I was sent to the Transport Corps. On the first day, they discovered I could speak German, so they decided I wasn't as simple as the others.

" 'Right; get yourself four men, go to the Gare de l'Est and start unloading ammunition trucks.'

"So I got my four men and set off, but on the way one of them said, 'Look, I'd like to drop in on my sister on the way.' And another said, 'I'll see you on the bridge at the Gare de l'Est in an hour.' A third spun me a story about his brother having arrived the day before. . . . So by the time I got to the station, I was all alone. The trucks were there, full of dud shells waiting to be unloaded. I waited and waited. Eventually, one of the men turned up. 'What are we going to do?' I said. 'It's already ten o'clock and we have to finish the job by midday.' Perhaps the others would arrive?

"We decided to do the work ourselves. My companion had a sort of lifting apparatus with which he raised the shells and swung them out of the truck. Then we threw them on the ground. Eventually, an officer arrived and saw this. 'Good God!' he shouted. 'What's this idiot doing?' Apparently, there was a certain amount of cordite in every shell, and one shell in twenty was still live. We could have blown up the whole station. After that, we treated the shells with great care. By midday we had unloaded only half the cargo. Then the others rolled up, dead drunk, having stopped off in every little bistro on the way . . . even the one with the sick sister.

"So my mission was a failure, and I was transferred from Transport to the poison gas factory at Aubervillers. That was wretched. Every day two or three people died; they would take the bodies away at night so as not to scare the others. Everybody who worked there became yellow, from the chemicals. We had to wear masks. My health wasn't very good, and I thought that this was the end. Had I been well, I wouldn't have minded. But I had the beginnings of tuberculosis. Every two weeks there was an inspection committee. I shall always remember the first one, because I owe my life to it. The committee was worried that everyone would die. As they didn't want this to happen, they decided to exchange people with the École Militaire.

"I was lucky. I met a major, who said, 'You look pretty dispirited. What's your usual job?' I told him I was a playwright, that I had written a long play which Sarah Bernhardt was going to do. The major looked at me and said, 'Very well. Go back to what you were doing before the war. You are dismissed.' I wanted to embrace him, but I could hardly do that with people standing around. He saved my life."

Film d'Art offered Gance the artistic directorship of their company. He began work on a film called *Ecce Homo*, hoping meanwhile to locate a sponsor for *J'accuse*. After a few scenes had been shot for *Ecce Homo*, Film d'Art announced that there was no money to continue. The production was heavily in debt, so he decided to write a letter to Charles Pathé, in which he described his disappointments and his hopes. M. Pathé replied with a historic cable: "WILL SETTLE DEBT—MAKE J'ACCUSE."

Gance asked for permission to return to the front to secure the battle scenes. He was re-mobilized into the Cinematograph Section. Now his enthusiasm returned. Alongside American and French troops, he took part in the battle of St. Mihiel, shooting material which he incorporated into the main battle sequence of *J'accuse*.

"The conditions in which we filmed were profoundly moving. There were great numbers of soldiers coming to the Midi on eight-day passes—a little breather after four years at the front. By that time, I was shooting in the Midi, so I asked the local HQ if I could borrow two thousand soldiers. I wanted to shoot the sequence of the Return of the Dead. These men had come straight from the Front—from Verdun—and they were due back eight days later. They played the dead knowing that in all probability they'd be dead themselves before long. Within a few weeks of their return, eighty per cent had been killed."

The opening of *J'accuse* shows a great mass of soldiers who come together and form the letters of the title. While Gance was filming this scene—with the soldiers in a valley and the cameras on a hill—a general approached him and asked him what he was doing.

"I told him I was drawing the soldiers up into the letters of a word.

" 'What word?' he asked.

" 'You'll see soon enough,' I said. The word began to grow as the troops formed up. 'J . . . a . . . c . . . c . . . u . . . s . . . e . . .' The general was stunned. But already it was too late. Who was I accusing? I was accusing the war, I was accusing men, I was accusing universal stupidity.

"Obeying a whistle, the men all knelt down, still in the form of the word, and then stood up again.

" 'You know, M. Gance,' said the general, General Vincent. 'This is most moving. But we are still at war. So what can I do?'

" 'You must try and stop the war,' I said.

J'accuse was released shortly after the armistice was signed. It caused a sensation wherever it was shown. A Prague newspaper wrote: "If this film had been shown in every country and in every town in the world in 1913, then perhaps there would have been no war." Such a view has been expressed about many antiwar films, from *The Big Parade* and *All Quiet* onward, but *J'accuse* was the first major pacifist picture in the cinema's history—and among the first big films to deal with World War I.

"*J'accuse* was intended to show that if war did not serve some purpose, then it was a terrible waste. If it *had* to be waged, then a man's death must achieve something. If a husband returned to find his wife had gone off with another man, or that his son had squandered the family savings, it would be terrible for him to have to die for this. Everybody who saw the film understood and felt this, too. The film was a great success in England. The man who ran Pathé Ltd. in London sent me a telegram to say that in one big English town, women were fainting and having to be carried out of the cinema." Because it followed so closely on the end of the war, *J'accuse* had a significance which it has lost today.

Because of its obsession with infidelity, *J'accuse,* some historians have declared, was not the pacifist statement it purported to be.

"I'm not interested in politics. I never have been. But I *am* against war, because war is foolish. Ten or twenty years afterward, one reflects that millions have died and all for nothing. One has found friends among one's old enemies, and enemies among one's friends. To wage war for nothing is totally illogical. People who get killed are never asked how they feel about going to war. In the old-fashioned sort of war, people were paid to fight and they fought because they wanted to. This was when war was considered a noble occupation. But now to tell a man, 'Tomorrow you're off to the front, where you'll be killed . . . there's no alternative.' I'm afraid I don't consider that a normal attitude. One doesn't have the right to play with people's lives. People's lives are sacred."

Seen today, *J'accuse* is unexpectedly powerful. Creativity bursts out of its every scene. The picture bristles with ideas; like the force of a shock-troop assault, it carries you along with its narrative, throws you into its objective, and leaves you at the end shaken and sobered.

Despite its length of nearly three hours, *J'accuse* is consistently exciting, and is as inventive and as impressive as anything produced up to that time—1919—with only *Intolerance* taking precedent, although some American critics considered its artistic merit greater than that of any Griffith production.

"The Most Romantic Tragedy of Modern Times," as it was described in its publicity, *J'accuse* is basically a triangle story. Edith (Marise Dauvray) is married to François Laurin (Severin-Mars), a strange mixture of violence and tenderness. Jean Diaz (Romuald Joubé), a poet, also loves Edith. François, aroused by jealousy, returns on leave and sends his wife to his parents. She is captured and deported by the enemy. Jean Diaz becomes a lieutenant in the very battalion in which François is a sergeant. At first, there is great tension between the two men, but when Jean takes François' place on a dangerous mission, the two become reconciled, and they resign themselves to Edith's fate. Discharged, Jean returns home to find his mother dying . . . and Edith returns from captivity, with a child.

François comes home on leave and both Jean and Edith attempt to conceal the child's identity. Again, François' jealousy is aroused, and he accuses Jean. A deadly fight between them is interrupted when Edith finally tells the truth. The two men, bound by vengeance, return to the front; Jean has rejoined as a private under François.

During a tremendous onslaught, François receives wounds from which he dies. Jean is so shell-shocked that he is driven insane. Escaping back to Edith, he conceives the weird idea of posting letters to the villagers, inviting them to Edith's house to hear news of their dead. When they arrive, he begins his terrifying description of how, on the battlefield, the dead rose up to march in procession through the countryside—a frightening invasion into the conscience of the living. As the shattered, maimed figures of the dead choke the country roads, the villagers disperse in horror.

When Jean returns to his home, he discovers some poems, entitled *Les Pacifiques,* which he wrote before the war—poems in praise of peace. Amazed at the mind that could have conceived such rubbish, he tears them up. And turning toward the sun, to which one of his poems was dedicated, he curses its impartiality.

To illustrate this difficult point, Gance employs startling stylized imagery: he dissolves from the lush landscape, over which the sun blazes, to the stark battleground, with the sun in the same position. On a title appears this poem:

> My name is Jean Diaz, but I have changed my Muse!
> My dulcet name of yesterday has become 'J'accuse!'
> And I accuse you, Sun,
> Of having given light to this appalling age.
> Silently, placidly, without reproach,
> Like a hideous face with tongue cut out,
> From your heights of blue, sadistically contorted,
> You watch indifferently to the very end!

The sun sets, and the sunbeam, which had been pouring light into Diaz's room, gradually fades. When the light dies, so does Diaz himself.

As with a great painting, the way the artist treats his subject is more important than the subject itself. The story of *J'accuse* is compelling, but the film's continuing value is entirely due to the richness and freedom of its treatment.

Again, Gance employs the visual metaphor. When François first appears, he throws the carcass of a deer across the kitchen table; it is dripping blood. Grabbing his dog, he thrusts its head against the body, tries to make it lick the blood. When Edith turns from her window seat and catches sight of her husband, she flinches—and we flinch with her. From that moment on, we see François as she sees him.

When François surprises Jean Diaz and Edith together, he raises a shotgun. Looking down the barrel, we see it is aimed directly at the couple. On a reverse angle, François fires—and a bird falls dead at the feet of the startled Diaz.

Such unexpected twists of melodrama are interlaced with delicate touches, several of which are understated in order to take the audience by surprise.

A group of children are playing in the street—the sort of scene used by most directors as atmosphere. A small girl patters up, and she smiles with uncomprehending innocence as she says: "War has started."

The shock provided by the gentle subtlety of this scene takes the audience off guard, and carries far more impact than the conventional drum-rolling dramatics.

The general mobilization scenes, fast-cut close shots of swirling, cheering crowds, is excitingly staged in the style to be perfected in *Napoléon*. The scene has similarities with the mobilization sequence in Rex Ingram's *Four Horsemen of the Apocalypse,* but since *J'accuse* was not shown in America until 1921, the similarities may be coincidental.

However, Gance's influence on other directors, particularly those in Russia, is illustrated in a beautifully evocative sequence which follows the title:

> In all the houses in the village, the humble moments of parting
> were played out in all their touching details.

Gance concentrates on close-ups of hands: hands packing kit, lifting hat from hook, lighting candle, drinking farewell toast, holding the hands of a baby. . . .

The extremes of the dramatic situations are often made human and realistic by flashes of humor. When Diaz joins François' battalion as a lieutenant, Gance is faced with the problem of presenting the antipathy visually—without resorting to long-held close-ups of glaring faces, which were a cliché even then. We see some soldiers lounging around. An NCO calls out, "Our new lieutenant—Jean Diaz," and the men scramble to their feet. All except for Sergeant François Laurin, who lies full-length on the ground. Lieutenant Diaz stands shyly among the men, while François insolently pulls out his pipe and begins smoking.

When the two men become reconciled, there is a hilarious scene which takes place in the midst of battle. François and Jean sit in a shellhole, talking about Edith. Shells explode around them, but they are blissfully unaware of any interruption. "No more ammunition!" yells a soldier. "Couldn't care less," replies François, and continues: "Do you remember when she—" A man is shot, and he falls violently, his boots landing on François' shoulder. François takes no notice, and carries on with his reminiscences.

When the main battle scene begins, François receives the full force of an explosion. He rolls over and over in the dust, and then, finding himself in one piece, anxiously searches for something—his pipe.

Gance's facility for the realistic staging of action scenes had not yet reached the standard he was to attain in *Napoléon*. Some of the early scenes of the front are slightly unconvincing: a shellhole and some barbed wire are not enough to suggest acres of devastation. The preliminary assault scenes are thrown away in a single, symbolic shot—the action staged on the skyline, in silhouette. But toward the end, the atmosphere crystallizes, the soldiers are obviously real soldiers, who know how to hold their rifles, how to operate machine guns, how to move with heavy equipment. The feeling of the First World War is captured with the veracity of a newsreel, although no newsreel could impart the emotional power of the sequence just before the battle:

"Everyone knows the battalion is lost, but no one says anything—they just write their last letters."

Superb shots of resigned men; Gance links each close-up with a slow dissolve. The faces themselves are moving: they are faces one seldom sees in feature films, the faces of real soldiers, chosen not for any quality of the picturesque, but simply because they were there, on leave, when Gance was shooting.

Interspersed with the close-ups are titles containing quotations from actual letters from soldiers: "If these letters reach anyone, I hope they will find fruit in an honest heart—that they will find someone who will realize the appalling crime of those responsible for this war."

"The majority of quotations were from letters written by my friend, the writer, Drouot, who was killed during the war, and from those of another friend, who was also killed." (Of ten close friends, Gance lost nine.)

The main battle is impressionistic: rapid cutting, later developed in *La Roue* and used in so many Russian silents that this innovation of Abel Gance became known as "Russian cutting," is much in evidence at the beginning. The opening sets the pattern for every subsequent over-the-top scene: the officer looking at his watch . . . the men, tensed, waiting . . . big close-up of the watch as it reaches zero hour . . . the men pouring over the top of the trench. . . .

The actual battle is chaotic—a complete muddle, as most battles are, but filmically a most impressive muddle, with wild tracking shots, fast cutting, smoke, blurred images, explosions . . . and in *Birth of a Nation* style, the daylight fighting gives way to a night battle, with men moving through the blackness, punctuated by blinding flashes from artillery and star shells.

The climactic sequence of the Return of the Dead is an allegorical scene of unique and bizarre power. In the book of the film, published by *La Lampe Merveilleuse,* Paris, in 1922, Gance gave the hero's speech in full:

"I was on sentry duty on the battlefield," cried Jean Diaz. "All your dead were there, all your cherished dead. Then a miracle happened; a soldier near me slowly rose to his feet under the moon. I started to run, terrified, but suddenly the dead man spoke. I heard him say, 'Comrades, we must know if we have been of any use! Let us go and judge whether the people are worthy of us, of our sacrifice! Rise up! Rise up, all of you!' And the dead obeyed. I ran in front of them to forewarn you. They're on the march! They're coming! They will be here soon and you will have to answer for yourselves! They will return to their resting places with joy if their sacrifice has been to some purpose."

An extreme long shot of a battlefield is superimposed with a heavy, stormy sky. As far as the eye can see, lie dead bodies. (The scene was shot on a wide beach.)

As the dead rise up, Gance splits the screen across the middle and contrasts the Parade of the Dead with the Victory Parade through the Arc de Triomphe.

The relentless march through the countryside is shown in every possible way, with superimpositions, tracks, and varying-shaped masks—all tinted a funereal purple. The courage required to execute such a boldly experimental sequence in these uncertain, formative years of the cinema surpasses everything except the achievement. *J'accuse* certainly justified the description of "a miracle film."

In *La Dixième Symphonie* the composer tells his wife that suffering either kills or creates. Following *J'accuse,* Gance was to endure a period fraught with the deepest suffering—a period in which he was to create the monumental *La Roue.*

Gance had fallen in love with Ida Danis, who had been a secretary at Film d'Art. Following an amicable divorce settlement with his wife, Mathilde, Gance and Ida were living in Paris when the great influenza epidemic struck them both. Again, Gance managed to save himself, and he thought he had succeeded in saving Ida. But while convalescing in Nice, a routine medical check-up revealed that she had developed an extreme case of consumption. She was not expected to recover.

Under no circumstances, said the doctors, was she to be moved from this climate. Gance wondered how he could prolong their stay in Nice without arousing her suspicions, for at this stage she did not realize the gravity of her condition. He had already planned *La Roue;* now he decided to center the action around the big marshaling yards at Nice.

The fact of Ida's illness was agonizing enough, but Séverin-Mars, Gance's close friend, who had appeared in *La Dixième Symphonie* and *J'accuse,* and who had been cast as Sisif in *La Roue,* was also seriously ill, although able to work.

The making of *La Roue* was a constant act of heroism on Gance's part. Besides his deep anxiety about the two people closest to him, he encountered innumerable problems of production. Roger Lion, in a contemporary account, graphically evoked the atmosphere of the location:

"Imagine a sunlit plain at the foot of a mountain. On this plain, countless railway lines converge toward a huge building which houses fifty powerful locomotives. In this striking setting, amidst the lines, a mechanic's house has been erected, complete in every detail. The electric light, specially fitted up for the filming, is produced by two generators, mounted on a special train. The railway cuts the scene in two—the interior of the house is separated from the cameramen working on the lines. Every member of the company is in constant danger from the incessant passage of trains, so to avoid accidents, a watchman keeps constant lookout and rings a heavy bell every time a 'Hundred Tonner' bears down.

"Even at night, filming goes on in this fantastic house amidst the rails. One would need the artistry of Gustav Doré to depict the violent explosions of light on the monsters which thunder past.

"Gance is busy overcoming all the technical obstacles, and we fellow technicians are the only ones who know the thousand pitfalls and crises which constantly threaten the director's progress."

Gabriel de Gravone, who played Elie, expressed his admiration in another contemporary article:

"I have often expressed a strong desire to work with Gance. Now my desire has been fulfilled. What actor wouldn't want to make pictures with this innovator, this marvelous director, this perfectionist, who obtains the most impressive lighting one can get in photography—and does it all with simple means, which are available to every director. Indicating, thinking, playing, living each role with each player. He is not merely the author of the scenario, the cutter, the chief mechanic, the electrician, the cameraman—he is everything: the heart and soul of the film. During the shooting of the scenes, he invariably repeats the same words: 'Human, simple, great intensity.' Everything is contained in those three words."

Halfway through production, Ida realized there was little hope, and she realized, too, that there had been no improvement. The doctors thought, however, that there might be a chance if she was taken to the rarefied air of the Alps.

Gance altered the scenario, staged a train wreck for which Sisif was blamed, and had him transferred to a funicular railway in the mountains.

"We have to go to St. Gervais, I would say to myself. At St. Gervais, there would be snow. So I wrote in a snow sequence. Everything was changed to fit in with circumstances. Everybody knew that Ida was ill, and they were all very kind.

"Séverin-Mars did not, however, know about his complaint—which was something to do with the heart. He was a man who had too much unused energy. The whole drama of his life was physiological, and was bound up in this fund of energy. When he made a film, he would give too much, so that he became theatrical—he would use his energy uneconomically. Sometimes he didn't even understand what he was doing. But he would listen carefully to me, because there was only one copy of the scenario and I had that. No one else ever had a chance to read it. When we shot, they had little idea what the picture was all about. I merely explained as the need arose. Even I didn't know all that much about it, because while I wrote the first part before we started shooting, I wrote the second half as we moved from place to place."

While filming in the mountains, an avalanche overwhelmed the unit; only a small flag, carried by cameraman Brun on his pack, enabled rescuers to locate them. Shortly afterward, a storm trapped the company in a mountain hut, imprisoning them for three days and three nights, until provisions, and men, were practically exhausted.

The mountain air could not save Ida. Gance's diary tragically records that *La Roue,* begun on the first day of her illness, was finished on the day of her death:

"9 April 1921 at 1 p.m.: forty centuries of love
9 April at 4 p.m.: I finish cutting *La Roue*
12 April: I leave for New York to escape from myself."

Gance spent five months in America, but he was unable to escape further pain. In July, he was informed of the death of Séverin-Mars: "I cried like a child."

During his stay, Gance read the reports of the commission which examined foreign films to be shown in America—alert for subversion, pacifism, and so on.

"Their criticism of *J'accuse* was not very favorable. The film had been with Pathé for a year and a half, and no one had been able to sell it. So I decided to try and launch it myself."

War films were now regarded as box-office poison. The public wanted to forget; the mood in America had changed significantly.

Dr. Hugo Riesenfeld arranged for a gala presentation of *J'accuse* at the Ritz-Carlton, presented by Mark Klaw, of Klaw and Erlanger. Among the audience was the one man in the world who Gance hoped would like the film—D. W. Griffith. At the end of the show, to his horror, he saw Griffith, together with the Gish sisters, leave their seats and walk out without a word. Deaf to the applause and the praise from others, Gance returned to the Astor Hotel, deeply depressed.

"It was an error to invite the aristocracy of New York. They were so moved by the picture that when they got home they reacted, and were suddenly seized by doubts. You know, money is such a powerful force. . . . The film might well have suffered had it not been for Griffith."

Later, Griffith telephoned him and explained why he and Lillian and Dorothy Gish had walked out: "We were too moved to speak. Yesterday, we canceled shooting on *Orphans of the Storm* because your film had overwhelmed us so."

Griffith invited Gance to his Mamaroneck studio, and promised to telephone Chaplin, Pickford, and Fairbanks to persuade them to distribute the film through United Artists.

"I did not like America. After the showing of *J'accuse,* I went out for a drink with Valentino and Nazimova. He asked me to find him a job in France. 'I can't stand the atmosphere here,' he said. 'Your film is marvelous, and I would do anything for you, but I must get away from here.'

"I told him that I could do very little for him. He was doing well in America and he should stay. 'I'm fed up with this place,' he said. 'There's a terrible feel about it all. It's so artificial. I want to get back to Europe.' Nazimova agreed with him. For people with a certain sort of spirit, success means nothing. Such people would rather spend three years in a place they feel at home in, than have ten thousand people cheering them in the street. I told Valentino I had my own difficulties in Europe, so he asked me to stay and make a film there. But I didn't like the feel of the place any more than he did.

"Later on, Metro made a very generous offer—three thousand dollars per week for the first year, four thousand dollars for the second. I was rather poor then, but I refused. Quite rightly, because the majority of European directors who went to America either died there or came back here, to France. René Clair came back, so did Feyder and Duvivier. For my part, I could never work happily with Americans because of their formula methods of shooting. To make a film you must be independent."

Gance admired certain American stars—particularly Lillian Gish, who visited him twice during trips to Europe. He was also impressed by Nazimova, but felt she lacked good direction, and by Betty Compson, Fanny Ward, and particularly, Mae Murray.

"Griffith was the giant—the only giant—of the cinema. I thought highly of Ince, too. And De Mille for *The Cheat.* Beyond that—who? Von Stroheim, Lubitsch, von Sternberg—these people all came from Europe. I don't classify them as American directors."

Gance left America in the summer of 1921 and returned to France, and to his responsibilities on *La Roue.* The final cut ran to thirty-two reels, split into three

Shooting La Roue *on Mont Blanc, 1920.*

episodes to be presented at three consecutive screenings. Pathé eventually asked for a version of twelve reels, which could be more easily distributed. It is this version that has survived.

"There is the cinema before and after *La Roue*," said Jean Cocteau, "as there is painting before and after Picasso."

This revolutionary, overwhelmingly imaginative work would have required the combined talents of scores of other film makers to achieve the pictorial, directorial, and editorial effects that Gance achieved with his small crew.

The film advanced the cinema further than any other single work since *The Birth of a Nation*. The Moscow Academy held a complete print of thirty-two reels, which was shown to the new Soviet film makers.

"All their great directors came to Paris at about the same time," said Gance. "Eisenstein, Dovzhenko, Ekk, and Pudovkin—and all of them told me that they had learned their craft by studying *La Roue* at the Moscow Academy. That gave me a great deal of pleasure."

The story of *La Roue* is rather similar to that of *J'accuse:* two men, one a tough old mechanic, Sisif (Severin-Mars), the other his son Elie, not a poet this time but a violinmaker (Gabriel de Gravone), are in love with the same girl— Norma (Ivy Close), whom Sisif rescued from a crash when a baby. The background, instead of the mud and smoke of war, is the grime and soot of the railway yards.

Elie and Norma are brought up by Sisif as brother and sister, but when a company engineer appears on the scene, courting Norma, Sisif is obsessively jealous. Confessing his plight to the engineer, M. de Hersan (Pierre Magnier), Sisif reveals the extent of his desperation. Pathetically, he complains of Norma's indifference: "She can't see my suffering under my layer of soot." That night he decides to kill himself, but he is saved by the rapid action of his fireman, who stops the train inches from his body. De Hersan becomes extremely persistent, and Sisif realizes he will have to submit.

Sisif drives the train that carries his daughter to her marriage. He is in despair —and decides to wreck the train. His faithful old fireman is too busy swigging alcohol to care about the unusual speed, but when he realizes the danger, he takes control and averts the accident.

Elie finds out that Norma is not in fact his sister, and he accuses his father: "What reasons have you for keeping this secret?"

Norma's marriage is a failure. De Hersan, portrayed as a vain, dissolute, and extremely unpleasant character, is now revealed as a sensitive and considerate man. (Gance was fond of apparently black-and-white characters slowly emerging as a likable shade of gray.) Norma's unhappiness hurts him deeply.

An accident with a steam valve blinds Sisif. He recovers partial sight, but he realizes his life on the railways is coming to an end. He decides to destroy his engine. His fireman, left behind, alerts the signalman—but he is fatalistic. There are no passengers—"He's the only one who'll get hurt." But Sisif survives even this.

He is discharged and reduced to driving a funicular railway in the mountains. Elie goes with him, and continues his work from their châlet. A famous violinist uses one of his instruments at a recital in a fashionable resort hotel; Elie attends, and sees Norma in the audience, with her husband. He dare not approach her;

instead he sends a violin with a love letter concealed inside. He knows she will never discover it, but he contents himself with the knowledge that "my declaration of love will be near her heart whenever she plays my violin."

De Hersan discovers the violin. During a quarrel, he breaks it and finds the love letter. A tremendous fight on the mountainside culminates with Elie falling over a cliff. He hasn't died, however; he is clinging to the root of a tree, suspended above an abyss, when Norma finds him.

"I love you!" he cries, biting his sleeve in a desperate effort to prevent himself from letting go. A sequence of frenetic, rapid cutting, in which Elie remembers his past life with Norma, reaches a climax and Elie falls.

When Sisif realizes what has happened, he cries out to Norma: "He's dead because of you!"

Sisif goes blind, and his châlet in the mountains becomes a squalid hovel, neglected, damp, and miserable. Norma moves in quietly and cleans and paints and polishes. From the deepest grief, their life together achieves contentment.

One spring evening, the local people invite Norma to the yearly farandole. Sisif sits in the window with a model of an engine. Norma joins the rondel dance. Sisif's engine falls to the ground. He does not stoop to pick it up, for he has died, quietly and painlessly. The shadow of a cloud, like Sisif's soul, lightly caresses the circling dancers. . . . Norma has become part of the human wheel. Sisif leaves his life as a sunbeam fades from a window at dusk. His soul caresses Norma. . . .

La Roue's most important innovation was its introduction of rapid cutting. Rapid cutting is a complex editing process, which has nothing but brevity in common with the fast cutting already used by Griffith in *Intolerance* and by Gance himself in *J'accuse.*

Rapid cutting is an art in itself. Basically, the style takes the form of sustained sequences in which strong images are intercut rhythmically at great speed. The impact is intensely dramatic and since rapid-cut shots range from two feet to one frame, the impact is also physical. For the flashing light from the screen activates the optic nerve and excites the brain. If the images are strong enough, if the rhythm is powerful enough, it is almost impossible to resist the effect of such cutting.

Today, the style is out of fashion, partly because few can remember it (and even fewer can actually do it), and partly because rapid cutting is a technique impressionistic, almost abstract, and essentially of the *silent* screen.

The Russians were particularly fond of the technique; so many Russian silents used so much elaborate rapid cutting that the method became known as "Russian montage." The French continued to use it occasionally, and it was very popular in the English documentary movement of the thirties. American directors and editors, however, ignored the technique. They felt that it aroused the audience to an awareness of the mechanics of film making. The Hollywood aim was to perfect technique and thus render it imperceptible.

The death of Elie, in *La Roue,* could not be cut faster. Gance starts by intercutting three frames of Elie's horrified face as he begins to lose his hold on the cliff's edge, with six of Norma. The speed increases to three of Norma and two of Elie, until a frenetic climax is reached, one frame of Elie, screaming,

Ivy Close as Norma in La Roue. *(Ivy Close is the mother of English director Ronald Neame.)*

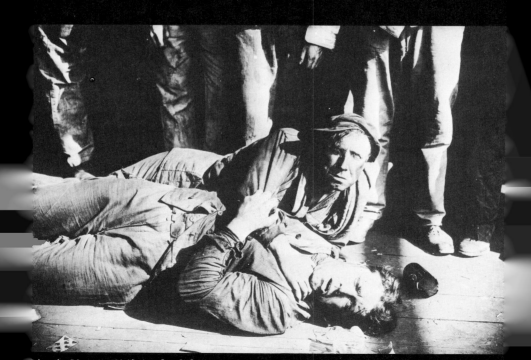

Séverin-Mars as Sisif, in the fight scene from La Roue.

intercut with one frame of Norma. The sequence is given a final punctuation of three frames of Elie, taken from a different setup, before we see his hand slip and his body fall.

When Sisif decides to wreck the train, taking Norma to be married, a rapid-cut sequence combines close-ups of pounding pistons, flashing rails, shuddering gauges, and belching smoke with shots of the strained face of Sisif and the anxious face of Norma.

The cutting of this sequence is precise, but the final, fantastically powerful result achieved its impact through patient trial and error, and not through any simple mathematical calculation. Some shots are half the length of others, but the number of frames follow no exact formula. Frequently, a shot sets up its own rhythm, and the length of the subsequent images alters. Bardèche and Brasillach, in their *History of the Film,* claim that Gance followed the rhythm of Latin verse. While there can be no doubt that his fascination with poetry inspired rapid cutting ("film is the poetry of light"), the only rhythm he followed was the one dictated in the cutting room.

Few directors were able to calculate their sequences of rapid cutting in advance. They developed them in the cutting room; shots of conventional lengths were chopped into fragments and reassembled by the editor. Often, rapid cutting was used as a last resort—a rescue operation for vital scenes ruined by uninspired direction.

Gance, however, knew what he wanted from the start. The sequence of rapid cutting in which Sisif is reliving the crash was written in the script:

"On the original scenario, I wrote: 'Image 1—ten frames, image 2—nine frames, image 3—eight frames,' and so on right down to one frame. I thought that the eye would be quicker than the brain—that it would transmit to the brain the message of the images. I didn't intend to startle; it just seemed the right way to do it."

Another unforgettable quality of *La Roue* was its authentic atmosphere. The idea of building a set among the tracks was inspired; instead of a painted backcloth providing the only view, real trains thunder by, real smoke drifts past Sisif's little house. The châlet set loses this appeal: a backdrop of the Alps reveals it as an interior construction. (Gance had no studio for *La Roue,* only the use of a large hall, and this apparent disadvantage, keeping him outside for most of the picture, greatly enriched the atmosphere. The châlet set is well designed, but the backdrop, standing out among all the realism, irritates unnecessarily.)

The drama of *La Roue* reaches a head-splitting intensity—without Gance's customary injection of humor. There are some amusing moments: Norma, as a tiny girl, feeding Elie from a milk bottle, and trying to drink from it herself; and the canteen fight scene, as hilarious as any of John Ford's Irish brawls. But such moments are too infrequent to contrast with the overall mood.

However, with the anguish Gance was experiencing, the appearance of any humor is little short of miraculous.

The canteen fight scene seems to be an attempt to outdo *The Spoilers:* Sisif, informed that a railwayman has attacked Norma, advances menacingly on the unfortunate man. A tremendous fight begins, with Sisif pushing his opponent onto a hot stove, from which he recoils energetically. Splendid, swirling close-ups and beautifully paced cut-ins, often with Cinemascope-ratio masking, conceal the fact that the punching is somewhat ineffectual. Fight scenes in silent films invariably suffered from protagonists pulling punches too obviously; on sound films, a crisp *smack,* as fist meets chin, enlivens the most ineptly staged struggle.

During the fight, a close-up shows a hand reaching for a bottle. A by-stander delightedly urges the fighters on. The hand grasps the bottle, but it is the by-stander who gets showered with glass. Sisif eventually gains the upper hand and looms over his cowering victim; but suddenly he notices the clock: the time is five fifty-nine.

"Your train's at seven minutes after six," he says, railwayman to the last—and lets his victim go.

As with *J'accuse,* the elements are coerced into co-starring: the wind scatters Elie's papers, motivating his discovery of the Livre de Famille, with Norma's birth certificate missing . . . thunderstorms heighten the overpowering desolation and despair of Sisif and Elie in the mountains . . . clouds join in the final sequence of the farandole, and over the human wheel provide ethereal steam.

The richness of the picture is infinite. Gance shows objects which no one had previously considered worth showing; rails, gauges, signals, and the mechanisms which operate them, details of locomotives presented not in a dry, documentary style, but poetically, as an integral part of a sequence, as essential stages in the creation of a mood or of a thought.

Gance continues his technique, evolved for *Le Droit à la Vie,* of isolating a close-up, superbly molded with lights, against a totally neutral background. The lack of background is not disturbing; the close-up achieves a striking, three-dimensional impression—it seems to leap out of the screen.

The intelligence of the direction is demonstrated in such difficult scenes as the blinding of Sisif. Gance plays this convincingly, by showing Sisif repairing a valve on his engine with a screwdriver. Inside the cab, Sisif's fireman is reading a book; it is boring him, and he begins to doze off. His hand is resting on the pressure lever, and as he falls asleep, he inadvertently moves the lever. Sisif receives a blast of scalding steam full in the face. Other railwaymen rush to his rescue and pull him away. Gance cuts to a reaction of the fireman, who has been awakened by the noise. He presses his knuckles against his teeth, in an agony of suspense, but as he realizes the full extent of his carelessness, his anguish makes him distraught. Gance seldom uses a close-up merely to register one expression: still holding on to this one, he shows the fireman standing helplessly, as overwhelming compassion fills his face.

The only mediocre effect in the entire film is a propensity for superimposed close-ups of Norma. These are supposed to represent the obsessiveness of Elie and Sisif in their mountain loneliness. But Elie reacts, horrified, to the superimposition; esthetically, this is most offensive. Had Elie reacted as though to a vision of his imagination, the scene might have been effective. As it is, he throws up his arms as though warding off the Hound of the Baskervilles. The effect was old-fashioned, even for 1920.

La Roue itself, however, is still ahead of its time. Melodrama in the grand style, performed by a great actor, Séverin-Mars, exquisitely photographed by Burel, with Bujard, Duverger, and Brun, it is a film of true genius. Capping one climax with another, even stronger, Gance hurtled the cinema from a timorous infancy into full-blooded maturity, with a rich life of endless possibility ahead of it. The

Russians succeeded in developing it further along the lines set by *La Roue,* but the full potential of the cinema, as suggested by this astonishing film, has not yet been realized.

Abel Gance himself was to carry the cinema as far as it was ever to go with his monumental *Napoléon.*

As a rest cure, and as a challenge, Gance followed *La Roue* not with another world-shaking epic, but with a tiny comedy called *Au Secours!*

"Max Linder and I were great friends," recalled Gance, "and one evening we were in Paris, dining together, and I was telling him—no, wait a minute—*he* was telling *me* the story of a haunted house. I said I thought it would make a fine little film.

" 'But we don't have the means,' he pointed out.

" 'Nevertheless,' I told him, 'I would be very willing to make it with you.'

" 'Well,' he said, 'it would be difficult. It would cost a great deal—'

" 'It won't cost a thing,' I retorted. 'We'll do it in less than a week.' You can do anything in Paris! So finally we shot it all in six days, just for the fun of it. It wasn't too bad a film."

Au Secours!, co-starring Jean Toulout and Gina Palerme, and photographed by Specht, was unfortunately never released, because of complications with Linder's American distributors. *Au Secours!* is a piece of Grand Guignol; it is rather scrappy, and lacks Gance's usual cinematic fire. Nevertheless it has some delightful moments. Trapped in the haunted château, Max holds the door against the advance of a Ghastly Thing. But his strength is unavailing against the might on the other side. The door is finally forced open, and a diminutive duckling waddles between Max's legs. . . . Slumped dejectedly on the stairs, Max is electrified by the sight of two enormous skeleton's legs descending on either side of him. He leaps up—and discovers a gigantic apparition, at least twenty feet high, gazing down at him. Galvanized into action, Max races off, pursued by the tall, thin specter—and a tiny, fat little ghost who toddles after them to watch the fun.

The visual resources of the cinema have never been stretched further than in *Napoléon vu par Abel Gance.* The picture is an encyclopedia of cinematic effects —a pyrotechnical display of what the silent film was capable of in the hands of a genius.

Few of the experiments have been carried further, even by Gance himself. He admits he has made no progress since this picture was completed. On its release, *Napoléon* played in its original three-screen form in only eight cities in Europe; M-G-M paid four hundred fifty thousand dollars and then showed it complete only in London. They never released the full version in America, being unwilling to risk a Polyvision revolution on top of the talkie upheaval.

The definitive version of *Napoléon* is as extinct as the original ten-hour *Greed.* Many different copies have been pieced together, some of them such travesties that the picture's reputation has suffered. The National Film Theatre, in their "Real Avant-Garde" season, presented what they took in all good faith to be a definitive print, and it turned out a roughly assembled melange of out-takes, superimposition experiments, and rushes. One sequence began with a super-imposition of two images, lasting at least fifty feet; this was followed by the same basic shots, with the addition of one more layer, then another—and another, and so on until about twelve layers had been superimposed on top of each other.

Originally, the complex superimposition was used as a title background, but this copy, from the Cinémathèque Française, presented it as an intentional effect. A large proportion of the audience walked out before the end, baffled that such integrally fine material could have been so appallingly put together.

Two years later, the National Film Theatre again presented a Cinémathèque Française print—but this version had been lovingly pieced together by Mlle. Epstein from six different copies. Some vital scenes were missing, some titles were in the wrong place, but its seventeen reels gave the most comprehensive picture of *Napoléon* since the original presentation. Of course, the amazing triple-screen sequences were missing, and the climax of the film, the Entry into Italy, was a baffling jumble of shots taken from various portions of the triptychs.

The effect of the sudden transition to Cinerama must have been electrifying for those lucky enough to have seen it. Gance describes the premiere, at the Paris Opéra, on April 7, 1927, as "unprecedented, unbelievable. There were four Polyvision sections: the storm in the convention and the storm at sea, which I called Les Deux Tempêtes, the Return to Corsica, Le Bal des Victimes, and the Entry into Italy. Sometimes I used the full width of the screen for one picture, sometimes I split it up into a central action, with two framing scenes. At the end of the film, the left-hand screen went red, the right-hand screen went blue, and over this tricolor I superimposed a huge eagle! The audience was on its feet at the end, cheering.

"De Gaulle was in the audience, as a young captain. Malraux told me he stood up and waved his great, long arms in the air and shouted 'Bravo, tremendous, magnificent!' He has never forgotten the film."

Gance began work on the scenario for *Napoléon* with the intention of dividing Bonaparte's life into six separate films. The first one was to be split into three: The Youth of Bonaparte, Bonaparte and the French Revolution, and The Italian Campaign. The second film was to be "From Arcole to Marengo"; the third, "From 18th Brumaire (second month of the French Republic) to Austerlitz"; the fourth, "From Austerlitz to the Hundred Days"; the fifth, "Waterloo," and the sixth, "Saint Helena."

Not unexpectedly, Gance quickly encountered difficulties of finance.

"I couldn't find the money in France. [Pathé had retired.] In fact, I found it by the purest luck—a story which is worth telling.

"I knew a Russian named Wengeroff, who had dealings in all sorts of things, in the cinema, in the coal business, in railway engines, in everything. When he couldn't sell a film he would be trying to sell an engine. I had no thoughts of actually setting up Napoleon at that time, but I had a synopsis divided up into six films—the whole of Napoleon's life in six films.

"Wengeroff must have been worried about something, because he got up about four o'clock in the morning and went to talk to Hugo Stinnes, one of the biggest German financiers, about a sale of coal. He took my synopsis in his brief case, not to show to Stinnes, but simply because I had told him that he might find people in Germany interested in such a project.

"Stinnes, who was tired, told him that the deal wasn't really of any interest to him. 'But come back in a week,' he said, 'and I'll see what I can do.'

"And so, a week later, Wengeroff returned to see Stinnes. It appears that when he left the first time, he had accidentally dropped the synopsis of *Napoléon*.

Stinnes told him: 'I'm not interested in the coal deal, but the other day you dropped a sheaf of papers as you left. Now that *does* interest me.'"

Gance immediately began the impossibly difficult task of casting Napoleon as a boy, Napoleon as a young man, and the hundreds of main and incidental characters.

He selected Vladimir Roudenko, a Russian boy, for the part of Napoleon as a child. For Napoleon as a young man, he tested René Fauchois, Pierre Bonardi, Jean Bastia, Edmond van Daële, and even the German director who was eventually to make the Saint Helena scenario, Lupu Pick. He seriously considered Ivan Mosjoukine, the hawk-faced Russian. Another strong possibility was his friend, Albert Dieudonné, who had previously appeared in *Dr. Tube, Le Fou de la Falaise, L'Heroïsme de Paddy,* and *Le Periscope.*

Since those days, Dieudonné had put on a great deal of weight—too much for the young Napoleon. Determined to play the role, he began an intensive slimming course.

"One evening, I met him at Pathé and he told me he would come down to Fontainebleau for an audition and would read Napoleon's address to the troops in Italy. I said he could come if he wanted to. I was writing the scenario in one of the wings of the château. I had the keys of the building, and I could go wherever I wanted. This helped me to get the feel of Napoleonic times, to live there, even to sleep there with my wife.

"The caretaker, who was at the gate, saw Dieudonné arrive. It was eight o'clock and already dark. He called out, 'Who's there?'

"Dieudonné called back, 'Don't you know Bonaparte, you fool?' The caretaker was dumbfounded. Dieudonné was in full uniform, and completely convincing.

"'It can't be,' the caretaker mumbled.

"'Are you asleep, are you dreaming or something, that you can't see me?' Dieudonné went on. The caretaker took to his heels and came rushing up to d'Esparbès, the curator. D'Esparbès was just getting into bed. He was just a little man, but very, very intelligent, and obsessed by the story of Napoleon.

"'Bonaparte is at the g-g-gate,' stuttered the caretaker.

"D'Esparbès went to investigate. The caretaker's story had impressed him to some extent, and when he got to the gate he was stunned. He was positive for just a few moments that it really was Bonaparte. He just stood there.

"Then Dieudonné called out, 'D'Esparbès, what's the matter? Aren't you going to let me in?' Then he realized what was happening. But he had been so taken in, this man who loved Bonaparte so much, that his eyes were full of tears.

"Dieudonné was taken to the great hall, the Salle des Glaces, where I suddenly came across him. He was lit by candlelight, and he looked absolutely perfect.

"He launched into his address: 'Soldiers, you are naked and ill-fed. The state owes you everything, and can give you nothing. . . .' and so on. He spoke with such power and conviction that d'Esparbès and I were amazed. Afterward, I went up to him and told him he had got the part."[1]

The making of *Napoléon* has been well documented: Jean Arroy, assigned to the unit as a *stagiaire,* or person under instruction, wrote an account of the filming in a book called *En Tournant "Napoléon" avec Abel Gance* (La Renaissance du

---

[1] *Dieudonné's version of the story indicates that it was a practical joke between him and d'Esparbès.*

Abel Gance in New York, 1921.

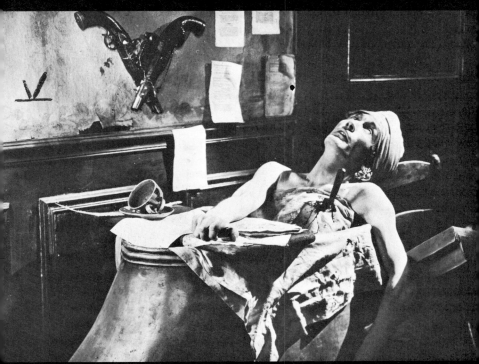

Antonin Artaud as Marat in Napoléon.

Livre, Paris, 1927) and Gance himself published the scenario in book form, *Napoléon vu par Abel Gance* (Librairie Plon, 1927).

The one element to which every account draws attention is the astonishing personal magnetism of the director. The demanding and exhausting task of coping with large crowds drew from Gance a superhuman energy, and a power of oratory which, in other circumstances, could have assured him an immediate dictatorship.

"There is a really extraordinary enthusiasm in this man," wrote Jean Arroy. "An enthusiasm which annihilates all inertia, all caution, all fatigue—which overthrows every material obstacle imprisoning the dream."

"The actors took their roles very seriously," said Émile Vuillermoz. "Their costumes gave them a mind and a soul. The personal magnetism of Abel Gance, this great manipulator of men, electrified this mass, which had been so suddenly transformed into a sort of emotional conductor. These humble men and women instinctively rediscovered their ancestral instincts. They felt themselves swept away by a surge of enthusiasm much stronger than their will power. Gance directed their emotions as a conductor directs his instrumentalists. All that shrieking, gesticulating hubbub belonged to him."

In so many historical epics, the period atmosphere is destroyed by the lack of vigor of bored extras; in *Napoléon,* not one extra of the thousands that pour across the screen betrays the fact that he is acting a part. Gance achieved, with this film, the ultimate in reconstruction; he re-created the period not merely through costumes and sets, but through a metamorphosis of those taking part. While they were shooting, they were hypnotized into the eighteenth century. As Arroy wrote, at the end of production: "The return: modern Paris seems dull and gloomy. Our lives lack purpose. We have been thrown abruptly into a later century. . . ."

Gance explained his attitude toward directing actors:

"The best aspects of the cinema are, first, things; a flower, for instance. A flower is always good. Then come animals. These, too, are always good. Then there are people, but people who do not realize they are being used as actors. Lastly, there are actors. These have to unlearn all that they have learned. They must be stripped of their mannerisms—if necessary, one must get angry with them. They must no longer 'look like,' they must *be*. The better known an actor, the more difficult he becomes. This is because he has succeeded through using certain formulas. These formulas are acceptable only when they are good actors— Jeanne Moreau, Belmondo, or Gabin—because they always remain true to themselves. That's good.

"I always spoke a lot before shooting. I would tell the actors, and extras, everything I had been thinking. 'Don't think that because you are only an extra you will not be seen. You will be seen, because my camera will search you out. It is therefore imperative that you do exactly as I say. If you do not, you will have to be cut out of the film.' And because these people were simple, they were very good at imitating. I would tell them, 'Don't exaggerate! Think of what you are supposed to be, of the period you are supposed to be in. You are no longer in nineteen twenty-six, you are in the Fourth Year of the Republic. . . . Try to project yourself into the period, into the feel of the times.' I would feel a certain contact with these extras.

"Émile Vuillermoz, the great music critic, wrote a review at that time in which he said, 'I am sure that M. Gance, with his extras, could successfully storm the Élysée Palace if he wanted to.' "

The shooting of *Napoléon* began at Billancourt Studios on January 17, 1925, with the interiors of Napoleon's school, the military academy of Brienne.

The exteriors for the famous snowball fight were shot at Briançon. Historian René Jeanne, who played one of the masters, recalled that the combatants were recruited from local schoolboys, aged eight to twelve. Gance was trying various technical experiments, and the shooting took several days.

"The children were warm enough in the heat of battle, but they froze in the intervals between takes. A lot of them had to go to bed, and their parents sent a delegation to ask for their boys back before they caught flu or bronchitis."

" 'I only have a few more scenes to shoot. It will all be over soon," promised Gance with his most angelic smile. And having got everyone together again, he yelled, 'Action!'

"The next day, needless to say, they hadn't finished and the parents came over to see if the promise was going to be kept. But Gance had assembled a band from the garrison, and the battle began again, more furious than ever, to the beating of drums and the calls of bugles. And this time the parents joined the boys in shouting "Vive Abel Gance!"

"For three days more, the young combatants continued throwing snowballs and delightedly falling about in the snow, with their thin jackets and open shoes. The charm of dynamite!"

Most directors could cover a similar scene in two or three setups and be finished by lunchtime. But this snowball fight had significance; Gance was using it as the first of Napoleon's victories, demonstrating his natural aptitude for leadership.

Determining to lose the rigidity of current technique, Gance allied his rapid cutting to another, equally significant innovation: the hand-held camera.

To Gance, a tripod was a set of crutches, supporting a lame imagination. His aim was to free the camera, to hurl it into the middle of the action, to force the audience from mere spectators into participants—into active combatants.

The snowball fight, tragically missing from the surviving thirty-five-millimeter versions, which include only the build-up to the climactic onslaught, is a wild series of furious tracks, intercut rhythmically with static close-ups of the young commander. The camera is completely subjective, and becomes one of the struggling mass. Snowballs are thrown at you, little boys appear to punch you on the nose, and as the racing, swirling mass loses control, the boyish face of Napoleon breaks into a smile of victory. The cutting reaches a frenetic climax in which the face appears for one frame in every four.

"I found myself becoming bored with the stationary camera," said Gance, "and I wanted to be completely free. The cameramen never refused to do what I asked of them, but they were not particularly pleased at the idea of having to hold the camera. At that time there were no lightweight cameras, and hand-holding was very tiring. Eventually, we invented a sort of cuirasse which, strapped to the chest, supported the camera.

"Also, I made an underwater camera, encased in a sort of metal cage. I put the camera in the water at the level of the waves and shot like that. As a result, you can see enormous waves; the picture is not that seen by a person looking at the waves, but rather that of one wave seen by another. It makes a very pretty effect."

In his desire to achieve fluidity of movement through the complete liberation of the camera, Gance's work was paralleled by the German studios. Technicians like Murnau, Freund, Pommer, Dupont, Lang were putting the camera on wheels. But Gance put it on wings. He strapped it to the back of a horse, for rapid inserts in the chase across Corsica; he suspended it from overhead wires, like a miniature cable car; he mounted it on a huge pendulum, to achieve the vertigo-inducing storm in the convention; he attached gyroscopic heads to it so that cameramen could walk around and achieve complicated maneuvers with it. But he did not, as many historians have asserted, actually throw it about. "That would have been very expensive."

The company's arrival in Corsica, a veritable invasion by an army of technicians, players, and workmen, was greeted with a hysterical welcome. The Corsicans went mad. Napoleon was once again in their midst; their nostalgic dreams were coming true before their eyes. Every time Albert Dieudonné went out, several hundred Corsicans escorted him; no one on the island would accept money from the Little Corporal. Elections took place while the company was on the island, and the Republican Municipal Council was replaced by a Bonapartist majority.

An authentic Corsican bandit, Romanetti, invited Gance to his hideout. Few directors have been provided with such fervent cooperation.

The unit was able to film in every one of the places where the action occurred; they even shot in Napoleon's house. An obstacle here was the plaque commemorating Napoleon's birth, placed right over the door. Unable to ignore it, Gance exploited it. He inserts a title, declaring that every scene in Corsica was reconstructed where it happened, and cuts to a long shot of the house, and slowly mixes ivy leaves over the plaque. The long shot of Napoleon's house was an achievement which only those tourists who have vainly tried to fit it in their camera viewfinder could possibly appreciate. The house is a few feet away from a wall, and no ordinary lens can accommodate the entire building.

Gance, and director of photography Jules Kruger, solved the problem with deceptive simplicity—by inventing a special wide-angle lens.

"There is one thing in particular that few people realize," said Gance, "partly because I have made so little use of it. That is that it was I who invented the Brachyscope. The Brachyscope was a lens of 14mm. focal length. It was a simple thing to invent, but no one had bothered to do it, until I came along. It was like a telescope used the wrong way round."

Only in recent years has a 14.5mm. lens been made available. Gance's 14mm. lens was not perfect—the edges were diffused and the verticals were thrown off balance by the inevitable wide-angle distortion—but it was efficient, and overcame a number of similar problems throughout the picture.

The company returned to Billancourt—and the first major disaster struck. Hugo Stinnes, who had formed the Westi Company (WEngeroff-STInnes) to finance *Napoléon,* died.

"We had no more money to carry on. He died at the very moment we needed his money most. The bankers immediately froze his assets. For six months we could do nothing. I had to tell my actors that we couldn't go on with the film.

They were all very generous and told me that when I had found the means to start the film again, they would return. To find the money in France seemed impossible.

"One day, I met a very able, very intelligent young Russian named Grinieff, who was the director of a steel combine. He told me, 'M. Gance, you have a studio' (I was paying for Billancourt), 'now I would like to take over the financial side of things, no matter how much it is going to cost, if you will continue with the film.'

"But, he went on, there was one little thing. He was making a film with Raymond Bernard, who had directed *Le Miracle des Loups*. Grinieff said that he was worried, and that he didn't know what to do. I told him that Bernard was a good friend of mine, that if he had promised to finish the film with Bernard, then he should do so. Afterward, we might arrange something, but I couldn't steal somebody else's work from him—not from a sensitive, charming man like Bernard.

"Bernard heard about this and came to see me. He told me to go on with my film, that it was most important that I finish it and get it shown. He was making the sort of generous gesture one never finds in this profession."

Gance resumed production with Grinieff, who formed a French company, called Société Générale de Film.

After shooting the storm at sea, which included some impressive studio tank work, Gance began the big "Marseillaise" sequence.

"We played the 'Marseillaise' over to the crowd of a thousand extras again and again. The extras were strikers from the Renault factory, who had come for the extra's fee. But by the time we had finished, they were so enthusiastic they were all ready to leave their cars and work in the cinema! There was one extra who, through no fault of his own, was left out of some sequences by one of my assistant directors. This young man arrived one morning and the assistant director told him, 'No, absolutely *no!* M. Gance has no use for you.' Of course, this wasn't true. But as it happens, the Seine runs through Billancourt and the young man threw himself in and had to be fished out."

The Marseillaise sequence is one of feverish excitement, in which rapid cutting, swirling tracks, and huge close-ups of strikingly contrasted faces make one's blood race—even without the music. (In the sound remake, Gance post-synchronized the song over these shots and played it through his Perspective Sound invention, which was nothing less than stereophony.)

To capture the pulsating rhythm of the song, Gance strapped a camera to the chest of Alexandre Koubitzky, a Russian tenor who was playing Danton. It seems a brilliant idea, but only a small section of the shot found its way into the final cut.

"Obviously, I took a great many shots which aren't in the film. In those days, I was trying to find the best ways of getting the best results. With so many innovations, there were bound to be a few failures. There were many scenes which were very interesting in themselves, but which I had to exclude because they would have broken up the rhythm of the film. The whole film is cut to a rhythm; there isn't a moment without this rhythm. But many shots, particularly close-ups made with a hand-held camera, were too jerky and had to be discarded.

Abel Gance directing Vladimir Roudenko, as the young Napoleon, at Billancourt studios 1925.

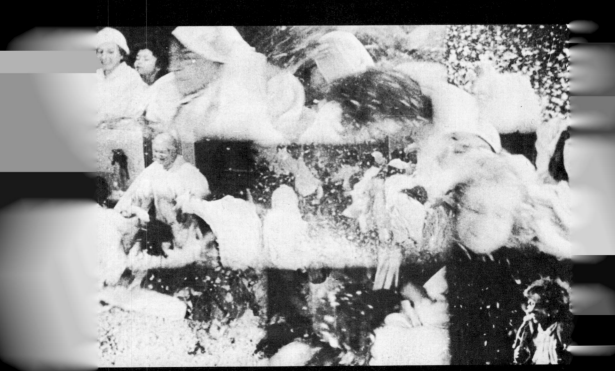

The first appearance of Polyvision: nine separate exposures for the climax of the pillow figh n Napoléon. (Frame enlargement.)

The Debrie cameras—one mounted on top of the other—for the three-screen sequence of Napoléon.

"I shot to a high ratio. Film wasn't expensive in those days. I never did much in the way of rehearsals. I found that if a rehearsal was good, the shot would be bad. This was particularly so with the difficult scenes. The first time would be the best. Afterward, the actors would be imitating the part. The first time there would be an element of veracity, of conviction in their actions, in their movements."

As full impetus was reached, a second major disaster occurred. The armorer, an experienced man who looked after arms and explosives, took a day off, and a less experienced man was taken on.

"I was shooting a scene in a cellar, with Nicolai Koline (as Tristan Fleuri) and Annabella (as Violine). Koline, who was supposed to be in a fever, was saying, 'It would be wonderful to fight with Bonaparte,' and Annabella was looking up at the grille, through which we were shooting. Studio rain was pouring on us, and we were protected by umbrellas. We had English rifles all around the camera, and these were firing in through the grille in such a way that their barrels appeared in frame. We used magnesium in the lights. Instead of making it up into separate packets, this new fellow put a whole kilo [a little more than two pounds] of magnesium at my feet.

"At a signal, the soldiers fired their guns. The shot was simulated by a plug of paper—and a piece of burning paper fell on the magnesium. There was a tremendous explosion. Tremendous! That stuff burns at two thousand degrees. There were seven of us, and we were all set ablaze. I tore off my jacket and protected my face as best I could. We were all blinded. Georges Lampin, right beside me, was seriously burned.

"In those days, we had a special ointment for use on burns. We had a bottle with us. I shouted to everybody to use this ointment as quickly as possible. We tore off our clothes and rubbed it all over ourselves. But it wasn't powerful enough. Somebody shouted, 'Come on, we'll have to get you all to the hospital as quickly as we can.'

"I looked around. Where was a car that could take us? Damia, the great singer, who played La Marseillaise, had brought her car, so we all climbed in and went to the local chemist. On the drive, a journalist did all he could for us. From the chemist we went to a surgeon, who took one look at us and immediately treated us with Lambrin. That's a kind of wax. You light it, like a candle, and cover the wounds with it without bothering to clean them first. We were so badly burned that Dolange, the helpful journalist, suddenly became sick. I felt perfectly all right until, after a while, the pain began. And you can never imagine how bad that pain was. I went home with bandages all over me, and there I took a tall glass of cognac—and I don't usually drink—to try to lessen the intense pain. I walked up and down in absolute agony.

"But the Lambrin saved me in the end. Without that, I should have been covered in scars. At the end of a month, it had all healed and I was better. Although, while it was healing, I could see through the wax all the black, charred flesh.

"Georges Lampin took longer to heal. But less than eight days after the incident I was back on the set, together with my bandages, directing the 'Cordeliers' sequence—the Marseillaise."

Gance said at the time that one can't stage battle scenes without having to put up with real accidents and real wounds, however much one deplored them.

"For me, the cinema is not just pictures. It is something great, mysterious and sublime, for which one should not spare any effort and for which one should not fail to risk one's life if the need arises."

The Battle of Toulon took forty days to shoot, forty days in which the army of extras struggled up to their shoulders in cold, muddy water, in which they withstood driving rain from overhead pipes, supplied by firemen with motor pumps in the studio courtyard, in which they shivered in the blast of heavy airplane propellers, set up to simulate the gale that was blowing on the night Toulon was fought. It is a further tribute to Gance's powers of leadership, and the excellence of his assistants, among whom were such full-fledged directors as Viatcheslav Tourjansky (Alexandre Volkoff had worked on the Brienne scenes), that the extras worked uncomplainingly through the day, and sometimes through the night and on Sundays.

"If Gance had asked us to go to the end of the world," said one of the extras, "no one would have protested. Everybody would have followed him—that's how great his magnetic power is."

The daylight assaults and cannon fusillades were shot at Toulon itself, but the main battle takes place at night. This battle is so elaborately staged that to think of it being shot inside a studio seems absurd. Great vistas of marching troops, charging infantry, and exploding cannon shells are intercut, with swirling, hand-held shots of cursing soldiers, soaked through, hauling heavy guns, then grappling with the enemy in close-combat fighting, soldier drowning soldier as the raging torrents pour down the hillside.

The fighting is of unparalleled ferocity, but contrasted with the bitter cruelty of the carnage are flashes of humor, the sort of incident which may seem trifling, but which gives a greater significance to the tragedy.

A soldier, floundering in the mud, is astounded when a drum slithers past him. It sidles through the darkness under its own power, until a drunken sergeant sits on it to take a swig from his flask. He leaps off in baffled amazement as the drum stands up: inside it is a tiny drummer boy, taking refuge from the rain and the shells.

Toulon's spectacular panoramas are brought to life by this skillful use of individual cut-ins; a battle scene may be impressive, but emotional impact will be lacking if its participants are shown only en masse. A meaningful shot of one human being will give significance to the rest. Gance uses many such shots: after a musket volley, a soldier is shown struggling to reload in the wind and rain . . . an officer whose leg is trapped under the heavy body of his horse, struggling to escape . . . a disembodied hand writhing in mud . . . a cannon passing over the leg of a wounded soldier . . . men standing up to their chests in water, waiting, while their sergeant tells them: 'You can't smoke, but you can sit down' . . . and, above all, the rain-splattered face of Bonaparte, in his element in the thick of battle—the light of triumph in his eyes.

The action sequences are the most startling elements of *Napoléon,* but the romance between Napoleon and Josephine is also brilliantly handled. Le Bal des Victimes, held to mark the end of the Terror, is attended by many exquisite women. Napoleon sizes each of them up, but remains only tolerably attentive as they are presented to the community. Josephine de Beauharnais, however, produces a swift and decisive reaction. He strides out of the crowd to meet her.

After the dance, he plays chess with Josephine's lover, General Hoche. "Be careful," he says, "or I shall take your Queen." Hoche, an admirer of Bonaparte, acknowledges defeat. Josephine sits by the chessboard, wafting her fan seductively across her face as she gazes at Napoleon.

"Tell me, General," she says. "What weapon do you fear most?"

"Fans, madame."

Later, Josephine comes to thank Bonaparte for granting her son permission to retain the épée of his late father. Bonaparte clears the room of his general staff. He picks up a cushion and places it politely on a seat. But it is a footstool—Josephine is unable to sit down. Slightly flustered, Napoleon puts it back on the floor, and then stands, awkwardly fumbling with the gold tassel on his tricolor sash. He says hello to Josephine's dog, trying to make friends by tickling it under the chin. That does not succeed in breaking the icy atmosphere, however, and there is another awkward pause, Josephine's small son is still in evidence, so Napoleon takes him to the back of the room and gives him a pile of books to keep him quiet. He returns to Josephine. She is nervously playing with the folds of her skirt. Napoleon slaps her hand. "Stop that!" he laughs, and pulls up a chair next to her. The ice is broken, but now Napoleon is pensive. The small boy looks up from his books, grinning. Josephine at last says something: "When you are silent, you are irresistible." A title: Two hours later. The general staff is still waiting outside the door. . . .

After this romantic episode, Napoleon is seen in an iris mask, expressing ardent passion in a ludicrously theatrical manner. The iris fades in, and Talma is revealed—Napoleon's favorite actor—hearing him after his instructions in the art of love.

The scenes of Napoleon and Josephine alone are filmed in discreet, heavily gauzed long shot; these scenes are very delicate and very beautiful.

Napoleon forgets his wedding. The wedding party gathers in the notary's office, and they wait there for hours before someone is dispatched to Bonaparte's house. There, the general is stretched out on the floor, surrounded by maps, absorbed in working out his Italian campaign.

"But, General, it's your wedding!"

Bonaparte leaps up, grabs his sword belt, hat, and sash, and races out.

He marches in to the notary's office without even a glance at Josephine. The notary is asleep. He bangs his fist on the desk. The notary comes to with a start. He begins reading the lengthy marriage contract.

"Leave that out, please," orders Napoleon.

"Do you take this—"

"*Yes!*" snaps Napoleon. The marriage is over. Josephine is looking extremely anxious. Napoleon pauses, and looks at her tenderly for the first time.

The wedding night: Napoleon holds Josephine at arm's length, delaying the embrace, while he gazes into her eyes, smiling. At last, they draw together in a passionate kiss, while layer upon layer of gauze falls before the lens, finally obscuring them both in a luminous haze—a most imaginative visual metaphor for the transports of love.

The Campaign in Italy sequence introduced Abel Gance's most astonishing innovation—the triptychs.

This triptych process, given the name Polyvision by Émile Vuillermoz, formed the climax of *Napoléon,* and the climax, too, of Abel Gance's love affair with the cinema. Basically, Polyvision is Cinerama. As such, it was thirty years ahead of its time. But it was Cinerama used creatively. Gance did not enlarge the screen simply to stun the audience with a larger picture. As well as gigantic panoramas, Gance split the screen into three, into one central action and two framing actions. In this way, he orchestrated the cinema.

Gance explained that Polyvision gave a new dimension to the experience of viewing. A simple example, he said, would be to make a Polyvision film of the making of a film. The final production would be contained on the central screen. The two framing screens would show the hilarious and agonizing incidents that go into the making of a picture.

How did Gance invent Polyvision?

"I had so many extras at Nice that I couldn't fit them all into one frame!"

So determined was he to outdo himself, and everybody else, with the climax of *Napoléon,* that he filmed it not only in Polyvision, but in 3D and color as well.

"The triptych cameras were built for me by André Debrie. They arrived early in the morning on the very day we were to shoot—we had two thousand soldiers for one day only. So without even waiting for tests, we mounted the Debrie cameras one on top of the other, and Jules Kruger started shooting with the synchronized motors.

"I had another camera, operated by Burel, taking the same scenes as the triptychs, but in color and 3D.

"To see the rushes, I had to wear those red-and-green spectacles. The 3D effects were very good, and very pronounced. I remember one scene where soldiers were waving their pistols in the air with excitement, and the pistols seemed to come right out into the audience. I felt, however, that if the audience saw this effect they would be seduced by it, and they would be less interested in the content of the film. And I didn't want that at all.

"I only had one roll of color—and I felt it was too late in the film to introduce this. Also, the 3D effect did not encourage the same feeling for rhythm in the audience. I felt that if it fascinated the eye, it would fail to do the same for the mind and the heart.

"Now, the triptychs. This is a most important point for the history of the cinema. We did not see the triptychs on the big screen because we only had one projector, and we really needed three. I could only tell from the rushes whether each individual shot was acceptable or not.

"We had no editing machines. We would cut it by eye. [Night and day for seven months Gance edited this film. His eyesight was irreparably damaged.] I would hold one scene up to the light, and put the other ones beside it. I could see that they would match together well enough. After a while, I got three Pathé projectors, and I set them up side by side and ran the first triptych in the little room in which I did my cutting.

"That was really one of the greatest moments of my life. I cannot describe the pleasure it gave me. It was magnificent. Afterwards, I ran the color and 3D roll, and decided finally against them. That was the only time I ever had

Triptychs from **Napoléon.** *The triptych screen was used panoramically . . .*

. . and in separate images . . .

anything to do with color and 3D. The process was quite advanced in those days. No one has ever discovered that color roll. I think it was Burel who said that it must be in existence somewhere, because no one would destroy a thing like that. But where is it? It could be at the Cinémathèque without Langlois knowing about it. He has so much stuff there. In any event, it is most important for the history of the cinema that somebody finds that roll."

Gance intended the Polyvision process to be used only for the last two reels—the Entry into Italy. But when he was cutting, and he saw the exciting material for the *"double tempête"* of the Convention, he decided to convert that to triptych—three shots side by side. He did the same with the Bal des Victimes. But only at the end of the film did the panoramic Cinerama effect appear.

The *double tempête* is an astonishing sequence even on one screen. On three it must have been overwhelming. Gance intercuts shots of Napoleon, caught in a storm off Corsica in an open boat, with the gathering storm between Girondist and Jacobin in the Convention. The inspiration for this superb idea came from Victor Hugo: "To be a member of the Convention," he wrote, "is like being a wave of the ocean."

As the tension in the Convention increases, the close-ups of Robespierre, Danton, Marat begin to waver. The crowd starts to seethe with anger and the camera lurches over them. The whole scene begins to sway. Cut to Napoleon's boat, lurching through the waves. Back to the Convention: the swaying is more pronounced as the assembly becomes riotous. Napoleon's boat is lifted by the enormous waves, and then dropped into a trough. Back to the Convention: the camera sees the crowd fighting and struggling from a very high angle on the roof. Suddenly it hurtles toward them, over their heads and past in a pendulum motion. Back swings the pendulum and down again . . . at the pitch of Napoleon's boat.

"The actors were terrified that the camera would fall on them. Their cringing improved the scene considerably."

The existing prints of *Napoléon* jumble all three screens of Polyvision into a single melange, making nonsense of Gance's original idea and stretching the scenes to three times the length that they should be.

It is doubtful whether the film has ever been seen as it was originally presented.

"The premiere of *Napoléon* at the Opéra was unprecedented, unbelievable. The triptychs were shown on a screen a hundred feet wide. The audience was on its feet at the end, cheering. I met a banker outside who told me a woman had thrown her arms around him and said, 'It's too beautiful for words! I have to kiss somebody!'

"Two hours before the projection I had a row with the conductor. I'd realized that the lights on the musicians' stands were spreading onto the screen. I insisted they put a cover over the orchestra. The conductor was furious, but they finally did so. Some of the music didn't fit—which was a pity—but the eye conquered."

The next morning, the press was full of astonished praise. One man who was profoundly impressed was Henri Chretien, inventor of the Cinemascope lens. In 1953, Professor Chretien wrote to Abel Gance: "It was your film *Napoléon* which gave me the idea of applying this panoramic technique, after suitable conversions, to a camera which I had conceived for military purposes."

The complete version of *Napoléon* was shown in eight European cities only.

"Metro-Goldwyn-Mayer bought it for a very great sum, just to lock it away. They said to themselves, 'If we put out these triptychs, we'll cause a revolution, and we'll complicate the whole structure of the business. We'll have to use three projectors and three cameras each time we shoot. . . . No, let's put an end to it before it starts.' "

M-G-M, already alarmed by the talkie revolution, decided against equipping even a first-run theater for Polyvision. Their publicity campaign for *Napoléon* was lamentable. No explanations were made; they just sneaked it out. The triptychs were contained on a single reel. Instead of the screen bursting into a new dimension, the climax was suddenly reduced to miniature proportions, three tiny pictures appearing side by side on the main screen. Exhibitors were baffled and infuriated.

"Brother exhibitors," declared a theater owner from Newark, Ohio, "stay away from this one, it's terrible. The worst bunch of junk I have run in four years. It's a British film, released by M-G-M. No stars, no actors, no directing. Amateur cameramen, and some kid must have done the cutting. Four and five blocks of some scenes. I screened it in two towns and even the children couldn't stand it. Take my advice and don't even use this."

A Nevada exhibitor called it "A Gaumont production to stay away from. A life history of Napoleon, with a lot of battle scenes, riots, insurrections and whatnot, done in the usual 'old-country' style. Doubtless a great subject, and is probably considered a great production somewhere, but we can't see it."

A Princeton, Missouri, exhibitor gave a clue to the disaster: "Eight reels of the nearest to nothing we have ever had on our screen." Eight reels! The commercial version in Europe ran to seventeen reels. The exhibitors' report could well be applied to some of the existing versions of *Napoléon,* distorted and disjointed, the gaps filled with out-takes and rejected montages, the rhythm destroyed, the narrative fractured; Abel Gance's masterpiece reduced to a tedious display of historical charades.

Abel Gance produced two short Polyvision experiments in 1928, *Cristaux* and *Marines,* but *Napoléon* marked the end of his silent-film career, and the end of his reign as Europe's revolutionary master film maker.

The producers took over on his next film, the talkie *Fin du Monde.* He disclaimed responsibility for it. The producers tied his hands and clipped his wings; Gance was to be a danger no longer. The genius at large was finally in captivity.

Abel Gance suffered in France as Erich von Stroheim suffered in America. Gance was able to continue working for some years longer, but not for a moment could he re-create his past glories.

"I made those films with my eyes shut," he explained, sadly.

Von Stroheim's reputation rests on some masterly films of the twenties. Gance's reputation rests on some cheap, uninteresting productions of the thirties.

Gance and von Stroheim were close friends.

"He was very kind, and a very fine man. But you know, I'm not like him. I'm not tough enough or sharp enough in a profession in which the struggle for life is so intense, that one is always being pushed in the back by the up-and-coming generation. *Quel metier!*

"The forest without the rain—that would be wonderful . . ."

In spite of all his setbacks, Gance remains enthusiastic about Polyvision.

"To get the public enthusiastic, you have to get the same feeling into your camerawork—poetry, exaltation . . . but above all poetry. That's why Polyvision is so important to me. The theme, the story one is telling, is on the central screen. The story is prose, and the wings, the side screens, are poetry. That's what I call cinema. I must admit that from the first moment I saw Polyvision, the normal cinema had no further interest for me. I was convinced that Polyvision would be the cinema's new language.

"People are very slow to learn. Charles Villon, the painter, who died a little while ago, said that it is one's first seventy years which are the most difficult in France. Corbusier said the same; he said it takes fifty years to make friends and thirty years more for your friends to recognize your talent."

47 / *THE TALKING PICTURE*

"**We** talk," said *Photoplay*, "of the worth, the service, the entertaining power, the community value, the recreative force, the educational influence, the civilizing and commercial possibilities of the motion picture. And everyone has, singularly enough, neglected to mention its rarest and subtlest beauty:

"Silence.

"In its silence it more nearly approximates nature than any arts save painting and sculpture. The greatest processes of the universe are those of silence. All growth is silent. The deepest love is most eloquent in that transcendent silence of the communion of souls.

"The value of silence in art is its stimulation to the imagination, and the imaginative quality is art's highest appeal. The really excellent motion picture, the really great photoplay, are never mere photography. Continually, they cause the beholder to hear things which they suggest—the murmurs of a summer night, the pounding of the surf, the sigh of the wind in the trees, the babel of crowded streets, the whisperings of love.

"The 'talking picture' will be made practical, but it will never supersede the motion picture without sound. It will lack the subtlety and suggestion of vision— that vision which, deprived of voice to ears of flesh, intones undisturbed the symphonies of the soul."[1]

At the time James Quirk was writing this eloquent hymn to the beauty of the silent picture, the talking picture had become a practical proposition. But silents were doing excellent business commercially. Not until the industry faced one of its periodic slumps were certain of its promoters forced to search for novelty. This novelty successfully revived the industry, but it killed an art.

Historic legend has it that when Thomas Alva Edison returned from his visit to the Paris Exposition of 1889, his assistant, W. K. L. Dickson, ushered him into the darkened attic of his new photographic building and projected a motion picture onto a screen. The picture showed Mr. Dickson raising his hat and smiling —and talking.

Dickson himself described this amazing moment in his book, published in 1895. He is quoted, guardedly, by Terry Ramsaye. Gordon Hendricks, in *The Edison Motion Picture Myth*, recalls, equally guardedly, Dickson's later account, in 1928:

"The subject of film was: self entering through door, advancing and speaking —'welcome home again, hope you had a good time and now like the show'— or something to this effect—raising and lowering my hands and counting one to ten at each gesture to prove synchronization."[2]

Talking pictures have as long a history as motion pictures themselves. Among historians, the subject is dynamite; there are as many unsubstantiated claims for the inventor of the first talking picture as there are for the inventor of the first moving picture. But whoever successfully obtained results first, one thing is certain: talking pictures existed years before *The Jazz Singer* shook the industry and precipitated the collapse of the silent film.

In 1901, a German professor of physics, Professor Rühmer, fascinated by the process and the possibilities of recording sound, employed the "singing-flame"

[1] Photoplay, *May 1921, p. 19.*
[2] *Gordon Hendricks:* The Edison Motion Picture Myth (*Berkeley: Univ. of California Press, 1961*), *p. 89*

method of Tyndall, Koenig, and Helmholtz to record sound waves on film. He was not concerned with motion pictures. He was anxious to analyze these waves, and film gave him the opportunity.

The optical sound track obsessed Eugene Lauste, and in 1906 he took out patents for his system, which incorporated an arc and vibrating wires.

The possibilities of the gramophone were at this time being investigated, with more fruitful results commercially.

Arthur Kingston was a veteran of the talking picture, later to become a distinguished inventor; he was responsible for the development of plastic lenses and for the Marconi Flying Spot fast-pull-down telecine machine. He had the benefit of a bilingual education. He was at school in London with Eugene Lauste's son, Henri. When he left school, his mother, who was French, took him to Paris to learn a trade.

"I landed in a firm named Matelot and Gentilhomme in 1907, who were making talking films for Pathé. I spent some time at the bench, working on the synchronizing machines and the amplifying arrangement. There were no electronic amplifiers then, of course; these were pneumatic. I had done a fair amount of photography as an amateur, and my boss took me under his wing, and taught me to develop films, to print and to perforate.

"I happened to like that work, and when he saw I wasn't letting him down he increased my responsibility. Quite a few of the talking machines were installed in fairgrounds, and if one went wrong, he used to send me off to repair it. I remember going to Brittany, and living with the fairground people for two or three days in their caravans while I repaired the machine.

"A year after this I was sent off to install a municipal theater, all on my own. I was seventeen. I took brand-new Pathé equipment packed in cases. The theater was in Bolbec, fifteen miles from Le Havre; it was lit by gas, and I had to arrange with the local power station to bring cables over for my supply. Then I wired the place, set up the machine and erected the operating box—a fireproof booth with shutters which you could open and close in case of emergency. I operated, myself, at opening night, and everything went so well that the delighted proprietor came up to the box with drinks during the intermission.

"In those days we synchronized the disc with the projector. We would take a ready-made disc, and artists would mime to it while we photographed them. The synchronization was a complicated and very clever device, completely automatic. We got perfect lip synch—provided the artist miming the record was doing his job properly.

"A lot of people ask about the volume of sound: how could you hear anything in a big cinema with just a gramophone? It was quite simple. It wasn't just sound coming out of a horn. Not having electronic equipment, we made pneumatic sound boxes, which worked on the valve principle. The amplification was terrific. If you cut something off suddenly, like a tap in the bathroom, you sometimes get a terrific bang. Well, the same applies with air. If you open and close a valve that way you get terrific amplification. The air pressure came from a one-horsepower compressor pump, which pumped air through slits in the sound box. The sound volume was on a level with the sound you get today with electrical amplification.

"Pathé's closest competitors, Gaumonts, had what they called the Chronophone.

This used a similar system of amplification, except that it involved acetylene gas.

"After a while, this miming to discs began to bore my boss, and he wanted to try some direct recording. So we made a gravity-fed recording device, and I made an electric cutter which I still have to this day, and we started experimenting. We made microphonic relay amplifiers—one microphone feeding another, feeding another—and the results we got were so much better than the acoustic method that we went straight from miming to direct electric recordings. So we were doing electric recordings in France on talking pictures in 1909. The quality of sound was so good that my boss got a contract from the French Columbia company, to make discs of the Garde Republicain."

Arthur Kingston returned to England, worked in laboratories and as a cameraman, and in 1919 his links with the talking picture were renewed.

"I became associated with one Grindell Matthews, who was experimenting with sound on film. First of all, I made a rotary printer for them. Then Grindell Matthews said, 'Kingston, look, would you like to stay with us?'

" 'Well,' I said, 'yes, I don't mind at all. I'm far more interested in this class of work than in camerawork, really.' I soon found out that they'd been having difficulties. They knew so little about sound that they put the sound recording gadget by the gate, and they got a blob of light. Once I got the right sort of camera, a Newman, things got cracking. I took pictures of Ernest Shackleton before he left on the last expedition of his in 1922. I took three hundred feet, and of all he said there were only three or four words we couldn't quite get. I remember distinctly Sir Ernest saying at the start: 'This expedition, made possible by the generosity of my old friend John Rowett, is going to be most interesting. We have approximately three thousand miles of coastline to cover. What we are to discover lies on the knees of the gods.'

"We were really much more advanced than anybody else at that date. We were still messing about with selenium cells when the first Fleming valves started coming over. We began making amplifiers. Our sound got better and better. We were practically there. But about fifteen thousand pounds had been spent on experimental work, and Grindell Matthews wanted another ten thousand. The money was not forthcoming. He folded up."

The date was 1922. In Germany, Tobis-Klangfilm had been developed in 1921, and this provided the basis for the later American sound-on-film systems.

In 1924, Dr. Lee De Forest announced his De Forest Phonofilms. James Quirk wrote: "Talking pictures are perfected, says Dr. Lee De Forest. So is castor oil."[3]

"My talking pictures have not yet been perfected," Dr. De Forest retorted. "I have never said they were. But I will make this prediction; within a year from now we will have perfected talking pictures to a point where the voices will be recorded with such clarity that it will be impossible to distinguish between the actual human voice as spoken by a person present and the voice of the same person recorded on film."[4]

At the same time, the Bell Telephone Company was experimenting with the old system of synchronous sound-on-disc for motion pictures. A number of test films were made, and offered to various film companies, none of whom were attracted by the system. Sam Warner, of Warner Brothers, was given a private

3 Photoplay, *March 1924, p. 27.*
4 Photoplay, *July 1924, p. 78.*

demonstration late in 1925. Since his company was facing financial crises, he and his brothers decided to take the plunge.

Western Electric merged with the Bell Telephone Company, Warners signed an agreement with them, and a Vitaphone production unit started work at the Flatbush studios. The studios were not soundproofed. They had been the headquarters of the old Vitagraph Company, which Warners had acquired in 1925. They were glass-roofed studios, designed for silent pictures. Apart from traffic noise, the hiss of the Kliegs, and the odd background noise, the crew had to chase pigeons from the glass roof with bamboo poles.

They moved to the Metropolitan Opera House, assuming that it would be ideal. But again, traffic roar, the clanging of trolley cars, and other noises forced the unit to shoot at night. And at night, blasting operations began on a subway extension, directly beneath.

However, the test program was finally completed. It consisted of a series of musical items. The Warner Brothers did not want talking pictures; Vitaphone was intended for music and effects alone. It would enable the music of a first-run theater to reach the tiniest movie house, and thus audiences all over the country would hear the best music and the finest playing. The sole concession to the spoken word was an introductory speech by Will Hays.

The "Vitaphone Prelude" was followed by a feature film, *Don Juan* (Alan Crosland) with John Barrymore, accompanied by orchestral music and certain sound effects. This first public demonstration of Vitaphone took place on August 6, 1926. Next morning, *Variety* came out with a special edition devoted to Vitaphone.

The Warner Theatre run was a carefully controlled affair. In a special seat, equipped with a telephone and signal buttons, sat Western Electric engineer Stanley Watkins.

"One night," recalled Mr. Watkins, "when we had been running for a couple of weeks, Will Hays opened his mouth and out came the tones of a banjo. After that I stayed close to the theatre for quite a while and I reckoned that I saw the main picture, *Don Juan,* about ninety times with very few breaks. We were very particular about the level of the sound."[5]

When other theaters of the Warner chain were equipped for Vitaphone, the sound quality frequently suffered from a lack of control.

James Quirk announced in an editorial that he had gone to see Syd Chaplin's *The Better 'Ole* but had been forced to walk out because the Vitaphone short showing with it was so excruciating. He had stood in line to see another picture—a silent. "My feet," he said, "are not as sensitive as my ears."[6]

This was the time the joke about the parrot went into circulation—"a canary that's taken up Vitaphone."

For many moviegoers, their first Vitaphone experience was a baptism of fire. Squawks and howls, unmonitored and of a seemingly endless variety, wrecked any of the wonder that the process might have had. Accustomed to a fair-sized orchestra beneath the screen, audiences could see no reason for transferring the music to tinny speakers beside and behind the screen.

It was over a year before Vitaphone was to deliver its knockout blow to the

[5] *Stanley Watkins in tape, recorded by John Huntley for the British Film Institute, 1961.*
[6] Photoplay, *April 1927, p. 78.*

silent picture; up to now no other Hollywood producer would take the process seriously. It was a flash in the pan, they said, and it would die out. Only the Movietone men, working at Fox on their sound-on-film process, acknowledged the importance of the sound film.

Finally, to convince producers and theater owners, who objected to the high cost of sound installation, Warners decided to make a feature film which would fully exploit the potential of Vitaphone. They signed Al Jolson, who, while sensationally successful on the stage, had never managed to make it in the movies; his style depended on his voice. Without his songs, he felt, he lost his appeal— and it was this lack of confidence in himself as a silent actor that had caused him to run away from Griffith's Mamaroneck studios in 1923. He was to have made *His Darker Self,* a blackface comedy eventually completed by Lloyd Hamilton.

The Jazz Singer, a sentimental Jewish story from the stage play by Samson Raphaelson, was planned as a silent picture with titles—but with moments in which the Vitaphone score burst into full song. Alfred A. Cohn's scenario was a trifle uncertain how to cope with this novelty. The shooting script read:

SCENE 353 FULL SHOT STAGE FROM FRONT

The chorus is lined up looking towards entrance at which Jack is expected. The orchestra is playing the introduction to his song as he enters. He speaks the few lines which serve as an intro-duction to his song and then begins singing it.
NOTE: The rendition of the song will have to be governed entirely by the Vitaphone routine decided upon. The scenes herewith are only those necessary to carrying on the story. In all scenes before he exits, the voice of Jack is heard in volume according to the distance from him.

"Jolson was to sing, but there was to be no dialogue," recalled Stanley Watkins. "However, Jolson was an irrepressible fellow and when the picture was being made he insisted on ad-libbing in a couple of places. Sam Warner managed to persuade his brothers to leave the scenes in. Then, October 6, 1927, came the premiere. The contrast between those little bits of speaking and the rest of the film, silent with background music and titles, was decisive. It produced such a re-action that the rest of the movie industry had to give up the cold war."

The ad-libbing, remembered as one immortal line, "You ain't heard nothin' yet!" is quite extensive, and was obviously encouraged by director Alan Crosland. A scene in which Al talks to his mother (Eugenie Besserer) while seated at the piano is a lengthy piece of ad-libbed nonsense which becomes quite hilarious. "I'll take you up to the Bronx where you'll meet your friends, the Goldbergs, the Friebergs, and all the other bergs."

The film itself is full-blooded Jewish schmaltz—sometimes overpowering, but always entertaining, and well shot by Hal Mohr. Jolson has a potent film presence, even when he is not singing and even though he is no actor in the conventional sense. That *The Jazz Singer* was a sensation is common knowledge even to those unfamiliar with film history. But *Photoplay,* unhappy with the idea of sound, tucked their review of the picture into the back pages:

"Al Jolson with Vitaphone noises. Jolson is no movie actor. Without his Broad-way reputation he wouldn't rate as a minor player. The only interest in the picture is his six songs. The story is a fairly good tear-jerker about a Jewish boy who prefers jazz to the songs of his race. In the end, he returns to the fold and sings "Kol Nidre" on the Day of Atonement. It's the best scene in the film."[7]

[7] Photoplay, *March 1927, p. 144.*

"Producers now realized that it was a case of sound or sink," said Stanley Watkins. "And after a decent interval while they tried unsuccessfully to make sound equipment themselves, they came to us at Western Electric for contracts. By the end of 1928 about sixteen sound stages had been built, equipped and were working, and theaters throughout the country were being wired for sound.

"One major development, unnoticed by the public, was the change from sound-on-disc to sound-on-film. We could have started with sound on film (Western Electric had been working on it in 1916) and from the start it was pretty obvious that this would be the answer. At the time, however, discs were really better. Their processing was a well-known art of forty years' standing, whereas no one had processed sound-on-film commercially. There was an interval of several years, during which theaters had to have both disc and film equipment, before the change to s.o.f. was complete."

In 1928, the least impressive sound film attracted more interest than the finest of the silents. At this time, the artistic gulf between them was not so pronounced because there were no all-talking pictures until *The Lights of New York;* the offering was a silent picture with either a Vitaphone accompaniment and a couple of talking sequences, or a routine silent at the end of which the theater orchestra ceased and a talkie scene took over. Other "sound" films, like *Lilac Time,* were big silent productions with no talking but with music and sound effects, and often some Technicolor thrown in.

It was a period of charlatanism in showmanship and cynicism in artistry; silent productions, caught short by the fetish for Vitaphone, hurriedly added a few lines at the end and rushed out some talkie ballyhoo. Exhibitors, attempting to combat a slump in moviegoing, surrounded the pictures with vaudeville acts and personal appearance spots—a policy which raised an outcry from those moviegoers who loathed vaudeville. The business of seeing a film was an expensive, lengthy and uncertain venture, harassed by the mess of pottage the exhibitor chose to display on his stage.

"I have a brickbat for these Vitaphone and vaudeville theaters," wrote a fan from Washington state, "If they can't give good movies when they have the Vitaphone, then I suggest they leave the Vitaphone out."[8]

James Quirk warned producers that ear entertainment in motion-picture houses was not as essential as eye entertainment—yet. He pointed out, with due credit to the talking picture already made, that as motion-picture productions they were of inferior quality. "This is not criticism. Every year the technique of pictures brings new developments. The two-year-old picture, while it may retain its full emotional value, is technically as belated as women's fashions of equal age."

Quirk felt it would be regrettable if, in the effort to perfect sound technique, there should be any retardment of motion-picture art. The sound film would come into its own, with time, study and experimentation. But if there was a frantic rush to add sound to every picture produced, the result would be a surfeit of mediocrity.

"To expect a good director of motion pictures to make fine sound pictures today is like asking the first violinist of an orchestra to play his own instrument with one hand and the drums and traps with the other."[9]

The role of a director at this transitional stage was one of the most unenviable

[8] Photoplay, *March 1928, p. 114.*
[9] Photoplay, *Oct. 1928, p. 28.*

New York City, 1926.

in the history of the business. He could scarcely have been working under greater stress. Apart from his own insecurity, he was dealing with players whose very existence in the business was threatened.

These were the days when everything was ruled by King Mike. The man in the monitor room held dictatorial control. In these early talkie days, the cameras were enclosed in soundproof booths. Recording onto disc was a matter of several cameras turning at once. Lighting reached an all-time low because the cameraman had to light for all these cameras. A new position—Director of Photography—was instituted so that one experienced cameraman could supervise the team of operators.

This transitional period lasted for a comparatively short time—a couple of years at the outside, but it was enough to dislocate the smooth running of the whole industry. Casualties were enormous; stars, directors and title writers were the worst hit. Laboratories found themselves forced to completely re-equip in order to survive. Musicians found themselves high and dry. The Musicians' Union managed to persuade some theaters to retain their orchestras until alternative jobs could be found in vaudeville houses and the silent theaters still surviving. At the Strand Theatre, New York, the eighteen musicians played for sixteen minutes a day at full salary.

Fortunately, the gloomy picture was counterbalanced by the fact that some directors, especially those with stage experience, took to talking pictures smoothly and happily. Many old stars' careers were given a tremendous fillip and new stars were created who were of enormous appeal. One of the greatest films ever made, *All Quiet on the Western Front* (Lewis Milestone), which had begun as a silent, was transformed into a talkie and given new stature; it had all the quality of a silent with few of the defects of the talkie, apart from some awkward delivery from actors unaccustomed to speaking dialogue.

The addition of sound certainly brought a new dimension to motion-picture production, and opened out tremendous new horizons for inventive film making. It added so much that it changed the basis of motion-picture production. Instead of a gentle grafting, the arrival of sound acted as a brutal transplanting; the cinema was ripped out of the silent era by the roots, and transplanted into new soil— richer, but unfamiliar. Unable to adjust to the new conditions, some of the roots withered and died, and much strength was lost.

Had the talkies been delayed just a few years, to give the onrush of silent-film technique time to reach its limits and settle down, had it been possible to use sound with discretion and discernment, instead of plastering dialogue thick over every inch of every picture, we might today be seeing commercial films of a far higher artistic and technical level. Silent films of 1928 were so fluid, so astonishingly beautiful, and so adept at telling a story in pictures, with relatively few titles, that it seems tragic to have cut the technique off in its prime. Occasionally, one can see sound films which carry on the basic silent treatment—Lubitsch's *The Man I Killed* is a fine example— but these gradually died out to be replaced by slick dialogue pictures, in themselves often brilliant, but following new methods of narration.

> *I cannot talk—I cannot sing*
> *Nor screech nor moan nor anything*
> *Possessing all these fatal strictures*
> *What chance have I in motion pictures?*[1]

"The public wants theaters to differentiate more sharply between spoken dialogue and distracting incidental noises. Now that the novelty is wearing off, mechanical imperfections are beginning to jar."[2] That was 1929, and the whole world was talking talkies.

"Some of us are bitterly disappointed in the talkies so far. Some of us are going haywire and screaming that they have kicked all quiet films out of the back door. Neither is true nor just." James Quirk sensibly pointed out that talkies were getting fat on their novelty; they needed a lot of development, technically and on the human side. But they were here to stay and nothing could stop the flood. "It's up to us to sit tight, cross our fingers, and let the scientists tinker."[3]

The rival companies took ads competing for their respective sound systems. Fox Movietone, pushing out a series of shorts, tried to outdo the Vitaphone features

---

[1] Photoplay, *Jan. 1929, p. 47.*
[2] *Ibid., p. 8.*
[3] Photoplay, *Oct. 1928, p. 28.*

and splashed "These Talking Shorts are Really Features" across a full-page spread; "Elaborately Produced at Fox Movietone City." These shorts consisted of Chic Sale comedies and *Napoleon's Barber,* directed by John Ford.

"We hope that they make a lot more talkies like this one," said *Photoplay,* of Ford's first talking film, "and then—goody, goody!—maybe they won't make any more! Now wouldn't that be just dandy? It is all very crude and unreal. The characters, as usual, seem to speak from their vest pockets. There is but one real consolation—it is only a two-reel picture."[4]

Fox Movietone, moviegoers were told, was more than sound—it was "Life Itself" . . . the only *perfected* talking film because the sound waves were photographed right on the celluloid "and you therefore hear ONLY absolutely life like sounds."[5]

Vitaphone headed their ad (a few pages away): "At last 'PICTURES that TALK like LIVING PEOPLE!' "

"Do not confuse Vitaphone with mere 'sound effects.' Vitaphone is the ONE proved successful talking picture—exclusive product of Warner Bros. Remember this—if it's not Warner Bros. Vitaphone, it's NOT the real, life-like talking pictures."[6]

Audiences did not care as much as was thought. The furor was dying down, and the public were accepting talkies for their integral entertainment rather than for their novelty value.

Letters, pouring in at the rate of three to five thousand a month, gave *Photoplay* a good cross-section of public opinion.

"These letters indicate that the public is not so sure they will continue to be satisfied with full-length, all-dialogue entertainment. Nine out of ten say they would rather have a first-rate silent picture than a second-rate talking picture. They complain of the mediocre photography and static quality of acting in the talking versions. They are unanimous in their praise of talk and sound in newsreels, and there seems to be a definite acceptance of two reel talking pictures when combined with a silent feature. There are many who say they will not attend any more talking pictures because of the strain."[7] Even Thomas A. Edison, as late as 1930, said, "Without improvements people will tire of talkies. Talking is no substitute for the good acting we had in silent pictures."

Catering for the theaters still unequipped with sound, many talkies were released in silent versions, with titles. Sometimes completely new versions were made, as with *Interference* (Lothar Mendes); the chief of Paramount's sound department, Roy Pomeroy, reshot the whole picture, carefully re-creating Mendes' original, with dialogue.

Clive Brook, star of *Interference,* remembered an episode in connection with the talkie version. His mother, in London, went to the Plaza to see her son's first talking picture. An episode in which an anonymously written postcard arrived, to be torn up by Brook, with the words, "Another one of those damn postcards," suddenly went awry. The needle stuck in the groove—and Brook continued with the scene, kissing his wife, but repeating "Another one of those damn postcards. . . . Another one of those damn postcards. . . ."

4 Photoplay, *Jan. 1929, p. 93.*
5 *Ibid., p. 11.*
6 *Ibid., p. 14.*
7 Photoplay, *March 1929, p. 23.*

Talking pictures released as silents, with titles replacing the dialogue, were disastrous. *The Drake Case* (Edward Laemmle), with Gladys Brockwell, did well as a talkie, but the silent version looked like an Edison drama of 1903. Long, long takes, with the players mouthing paragraphs of unexplained dialogue, then a title to tell you what you have seen and what you should have heard. Static and completely uncinematic pictures like these, taken at their face value as silent pictures, accelerated the death of the medium.

For in the United States, by April 1929, there were only sixteen hundred theaters equipped with sound, and people coming to the city and seeing their first talkies were quick to voice their opinions. One fan welcomed the talkies as "a panacea." She felt that films had been obscuring their plot in a wealth of elaboration and technical effects and, at last, talkies were focussing the attention on the characters and on the plot. "They're as good as an evening at the spoken stage."[8] One can hardly argue with that.

Another fan felt that as the silent film had improved homes, dress and health by its influence, so the talkie would improve speech and articulation. "The movies are urging us up out of vulgarity. They are bringing to the people culture, a virtue considered before impossible to obtain."[9]

More theaters were equipped, sound quality improved—and so did the attitude of the letters. By mid-1929, ninety per cent were in favor of good talkies . . . and, for all practical purposes, the silent film was extinct. M-G-M, terrified that Garbo's husky voice would sound ruinous through the speakers, continued to star her in silents; *The Kiss* (Jacques Feyder) made in 1929, was her last silent before the sensational *Anna Christie* sent the signwriters scurrying for their largest letters, to emblazon GARBO TALKS! on theater marquees.

Films as expensive and potentially popular as *Anna Christie* had to be distributed as widely as possible; consequently foreign versions were required. The entire film was reshot, with a different cast and a different director—but on the same sets. Garbo could do the German version easily enough—but the rest of the cast had to be replaced. Jacques Feyder, who had directed her in *The Kiss,* took over from Clarence Brown.

Some of John Barrymore's Warner Brothers successes were remade for the South American market by Antonio Moreno, who was Spanish. And Ramon Novarro, a Mexican, directed Spanish versions.

The trouble was that Hollywood soon discovered an irritating flaw to all this; there were as many Spanish dialects as Spanish speaking areas. French, German and Italian language versions ran into similar objections; audiences and renters frequently complained that the films, though in the right language, were still unintelligible.

The problem was partially solved by the Dunning process, which supplied a background matte and enabled the films to be remade abroad, with foreign actors. This method was neither economical nor artistically desirable; it was eventually replaced by subtitles, and the post-synchronizing or dubbing process.

Some big silent films were reissued with sound; *The Big Parade* was quite successful, and the battle scenes were helped considerably with shellfire and machine-gun effects. *Ben-Hur* was not so well received, and critics made glib observations

[8] Photoplay, *April 1929, p. 10.*
[9] Photoplay, *May 1929, p. 8.*

about the actors' exaggerated gestures "taking the place of words."

An interesting aspect to the arrival of the talkie was how *slow* the action seemed after silent pictures. Characters appeared to float across the screen—there was a suggestion of slow motion. Cameras and projectors were now synchronized at twenty-four frames per second, a standard arrived at quite fortuitously when the Western Electric engineers took the average speed at which silent films were projected.

The most celebrated talkie tragedy was that of John Gilbert. Put under contract, with terms highly beneficial to himself, he refused to be bought out when his recorded voice proved inadequate. An unfortunate tendency of early recording was its habit of raising voices by an octave or two; the best results came from booming baritones. Tenor voices, such as Gilbert's, sometimes recorded as a high-pitched squeak, suggestive more of Mickey Mouse than Don Juan. Gilbert's normal speaking voice was a pleasant tenor, which was eventually recorded properly, too late to save his foundering career, in *Queen Christina*. Louise Brooks considered his demise was a deliberate act of sabotage

"Gilbert had a well-trained actor's voice. *Redemption* was made by Fred Niblo. It was pretty good. They previewed it and Quirk gave it a good review. So they shelved it. John was terribly unpopular with producers—he was such a ham, and he was always making a fuss. So when they found that the organization was stuck with the guy, they figured all they had to do was give him a couple of bad pictures.

"The plot thickens with *His Glorious Night*. The title alone shows that it was twenty years out of date. They got Lionel Barrymore to direct it: 'You make that picture and make it *lousy.*' And he certainly did. Then they put out the bad publicity."

As John Gilbert stepped off the boat on his return from Europe, his first words were: "How's my picture? What do the critics think of my picture?" His friends had a task as wretched as breaking the news of a bereavement. They had to tell him he had failed.

Gilbert received a fatal injection of discouragement. Chaplin announced a proposal to make a number of silent films—he called them non-talkies—with such notable casualties of the sound film as Gilbert. Nothing came of it. Despite the continued support of thousands of fans, Gilbert's career was doomed.

Directors suffered in greater numbers but with less publicity. Their first talkie was their testing ground. If they appeared to fumble, if they seemed insecure, their careers were finished, for the whole structure of the industry had changed. Instead of yelling "camera!" directors now shouted "interlock!" New words were being added to the film-term vocabulary: "barney" for the covers that muffled the noise of the camera on exteriors, named after a comic-strip character (Barney Google), because the completely covered camera looked like Barney's racehorse; "blimp" for the more compact padded cover which fitted around the camera, so called because it looked like a blimp, or airship.

Metro-Goldwyn-Mayer hoisted a "silence" balloon to warn aircraft that they were shooting sound; on the string were tied red flags. Under an agreement between the Department of Commerce, the California Aircraft Operators Association and movie producers, aviators avoided these marked locations by twenty-five hundred feet; for months, passing planes had wrecked open-air sequences.

The early talkies were often dull and lifeless, not only because they were poorly made, but because of the material of the screen itself. The surface had to be pierced to allow sound through; at first a meshed material was tried, with lamentable results. Eventually, a fireproof oilcloth surface was developed which was treated to ensure maximum brilliance, and punctured with tiny holes to admit the sound.

The theater felt itself threatened as never before, but George Jean Nathan restored morale with one of his inimitable remarks: "The day that sees men waiting at the stage door for an electric phonograph to come out will see the day that the talkies will triumph over the theater."

Chaplin, last-ditch supporter of the silent film, said: "A good talking picture is inferior to a good stage play, while a good silent picture is superior to a good stage play."

"One of the revelations of the talkies," said the New York *Evening Post,* "is the fact that the most beautiful nose in the world isn't much of an asset to an actress if she talks through it."

"The picture shows," said the Carolina *Buccaneeer,* "have gone from bad to voice."

David Belasco, with an eye on his threatened theater receipts, thought that talkies were a great mistake. "If I were younger and had plenty of money, I would go into the production of silent pictures. That is the great field for the right man today. Good silent pictures would sweep the country."

But Mary Pickford, in *The New York Times Magazine,* summed up the whole situation:

"It would have been more logical if silent pictures had grown out of the talkie instead of the other way round."

Additions and Corrections

Identification of Frontispiece and Chapter-Opening Photographs

Frontispiece: Mary Pickford and director Maurice Tourneur (1917).

Introduction: Joseph Ruttenbert (1916).

p. 65: George Fitzmaurice directing *The Eternal City* on location in Rome; Arthur Miller at camera.

p. 76: The Battle of Bunker Hill from Griffith's *America* (1924).

p. 94: Allan Dwan, center; Arthur Rosson, his assistant, at right; Santa Barbara (1913).

p. 136: Clarence Brown and Greta Garbo with the phonograph which replaced the orchestra on their set (1928).

p. 154: Edward Sloman, in white helmet, directing *The Foreign Legion* (1928); Jackson Rose at camera.

p. 164: William Wellman and Harry Perry during the making of *Wings* (1927).

p. 178: *The Ten Commandments* (1923).

p. 189: Von Sternberg directing *The Drag Net* (1928); Hal Rosson left of camera.

p. 211: Harry Fischbeck.

p. 222: Charlea Rosher, Mary Pickford and the first Mitchell camera to be used on production: *The Love Light* (released 1921: photo 1920).

p. 237: *The Hunchback of Notre Dame* (1923)—a full-size set combined with a hanging miniature; the border is just below the row of statues.

p. 269: Donald Ogden Stewart.

p. 279: Editor William Nolan.

p. 301: The assembly room of the Goldwyn studios (Margaret Booth is not in the picture).

p. 312: *Captain Blood* (1924).

p. 325: *The Sheik* (1921); George Melford directing (straw hat); William Marshall at camera.

p. 328: *Trail of '98* (1928).

p. 337: Ruth Dickey, sister of Paul (*Robin Hood*) Dickey.

p. 343: Lillian Gish in *The Wind*.

p. 355: Greta Garbo in the unreleased Dmitri Buchowetski version of *Love* (1928), reshot by Edmund Goulding.

p. 429: A Selznick supervised production, *Forgotten Faces* (1928). Extreme left: assistant director Russ Myers, cameraman J. Roy Hunt, uk, Wm Powell, uk, Victor Schertzinger, director, Clive Brook, script girl, Orville Beckett with cigarette.

p. 446: Reginald Denny, ZaSu Pitts, Otis Harlan in *What Happened to Jones?* (1925).

p. 457: Harold Lloyd, John Aasen in *Why Worry?* (1923).

p. 495: Chaplin in *City Lights* (1931).

p. 517: Albert Dieudonné as Napoleon.

Text Emendations

Explanatory note: I used to think that for a book of film history to contain a single error was shocking enough to dismiss it out of hand. I was determined that *The Parade's Gone By . . .* should never be so disfigured. How naive I was! Writers forced to depend upon existing historical studies are condemned to perpetuate mistakes; and press agentry was always mendacious, so it is fatal to believe anything which emanates from a publicity department. The importance of film history was a concept few took seriously in the picture business, and any ruse was legitimate which encouraged people to pay for tickets.

So mistakes have occurred, and I am glad of this opportunity to atone. I include them here together with additional information. I am profoundly grateful to those who took the trouble to write to me with these additions and corrections. Due to printing problems, the first edition contained typographical errors which were corrected in the two subsequent editions. My list applies to this new reprint, which is identical to the third edition. It contains many points which have already been absorbed into the English and American paperbacks.

Kevin Brownlow
London 1975

p. 7, top caption: *Add* Edwin S. Porter directing.

p. 10, l. 11: Jack Spears in *Films in Review* (June-July 1970) categorically denies that the film was a collection of stock shots. I defer to him.

p. 18, l. 27: Was it Trotsky? Some historians say he was in the U.S.A. only in 1917.

p. 26, l. 1: This information, acquired from Arthur Miller, who had talked with Alder, is at variance with Miller's account in *One Reel a Week,* p. 118.

p. 30: Robert Florey's *Hollywood Années Zero* (Seghers) deals with the beginnings of Hollywood in a much more detailed and authoritative fashion.

p. 30, l. 40: Fred Balshofer represented Kessel and Baumann.

p. 36, l. 10: *Dust of Desire* was the working title for *Song of Love.*

p. 45, lower caption: Karl Brown's book *Adventures with D. W. Griffith* reveals that after all there *was* an art director on *Intolerance*—Walter L. Hall.

p. 47, l. 2: *For* Maclay *read* Mackley.

p. 56, l. 25: *For* flour barrel *read* wooden chest.

p. 67, l. 10: Van Dyke's press agent cooked this one up. See *Van Dyke and the Mythical City, Hollywood* by Robert Cannom (Culver City: Murray & Gee, 1948) for biographical details.

p. 78, last line: Chaplin has now been presented with an Oscar, so this is out of date (applies also to p. 496).

p. 82, paragraph 3: *The Sorrows of Satan* was high drama.

p. 96, l. 12: For filmography see *Allan Dwan, the Last Pioneer* by Peter Bogdanovich (Studio Vista). It doesn't run to 1400.

p. 113, l. 30: Not until his very last appearance in *Stella Dallas* does Douglas Fairbanks, Jr., sport a moustache.

p. 133, l. 4: Mary Pickford's maid was from Alsace Lorraine, but the more common spelling of her name was Bodamère.

pp. 140, 141, 212: *For* van der Broek *read* van den Broek.

p. 142, l. 20: Floyd Mueller says he did one or two Tourneur films earlier.

p. 144, l. 16: Charles van Enger, who photographed *Last of the Mohicans,* says he used panchromatic stock on exteriors.

p. 152, l. 34: *Butterfly* (1924) was about a girl studying the violin.

p. 156, l. 8: *Shattered Idols* has since decomposed, but I'm glad to say several other Sloman pictures have since been rediscovered, including *His People.*

p. 170, caption: *For* Café de Paris *read* Folies Bergère.

p. 176, l. 42: A Wellmanesque exaggeration! Harry Perry calculates that the largest number of planes in the air at any one time was eighteen.

p. 194, l. 20: *Children of Divorce* came after *Salvation Hunters.*

p. 195, l. 35: *For* on the jaw *read* in the stomach.

p. 196, l. 25: Robert Florey says that Lodijenski was a general in the Russian gendarmerie and not the army, and had therefore not been near the front. He worked in pictures, but as owner of a flourishing restaurant. His similarity to the Jannings character was purely coincidental.

p. 198, l. 44: Except *The Blue Angel!*

p. 213, l. 4: This refers, of course, to black-and-white.

p. 220, l. 8: *Paths of Glory* was the working title for *The Restless Spirit* (1913).

p. 224, l. 6: *For* 1913 *read* 1914.

p. 225, lower picture: I have since examined the original and discovered that it is photomontage; Rosher took the picture of General Villa, and stuck himself on the right-hand side, then rephotographed the result.

p. 228, top caption: *Add* Art director: Harry Oliver.

p. 231, lower caption: Rochus Gliese was *the* art director.

p. 234, l. 42: *For* Geze *read* Geza.

p. 241, lower caption: *For* Gareth Hughes *read* Ramon Novarro.

p. 254, l. 24: It was Fairbanks' profile.

p. 264, paragraph 3: Louise Brooks points out that many Southern white actors would not play with Negroes.

p. 266, l. 9: Art direction by Ben Carré.

p. 270, Scenario chapter: I have omitted the vital contribution of Richard V. Spencer, of the New York Motion Picture Company, and of Thomas H. Ince, who structured the whole company around the scenario, and Spencer's successor C. Gardner Sullivan.

p. 294, l. 40: Ray wrote his thoughts in a diary.

p. 302: Margaret Booth's brother was the actor Elmer Booth.

p. 311: *For* Tavaris *read* Tavares *throughout.*

p. 315, paragraph 3: Lloyd did occasionally use a double for climbing—such as Harvey Parry.

p. 318, top picture: The men jumping are Earl Montgomery and Joe Rock.

p. 319, caption: Another photomontage. *For* Hutchinson *read* Hutchison.

p. 321, top caption and elsewhere: *For* Omer *read* Ormer.

p. 327, caption: This is Haakon Froelich.

p. 369, l. 18: *For* Panka *read* Pancha.

p. 384, last paragraph: Two of J. Gordon Edwards films have been found—*Drag Harlan* and *The Silent Command*.

p. 389, l. 22 and 36: *For* Metro *read* Goldwyn.

l. 23: J. J. Cohn says he was production manager. He adds that Bowes made a second trip to Europe without Cohn—and that's when he signed with the Italians.

p. 393, l. 21: *For* Sylvano *read* Silvano.

p. 396: A. Arnold Gillespie writes that the only MGM man aboard the stricken ship was himself—"doubling as assistant director, special effects impresario, etc.", and he made a watery exit. He recalls that only six boats were produced in Anzio and that shipbuilder Tito Neri worked 24 hours a day with Gillespie and 300 workmen to produce the seven majestic-looking galleys that appear in the film.

p. 402, l. 37: Gillespie says that the political battles are overplayed here.

p. 403, paragraph 4/5: Gillespie says that "break-in" rehearsals for the chariot race were held in Rome, but not one inch of the race proper was shot until the new circus was built in Culver City. There were injuries to the horses, he said, but the figure of "100 lost" is a gross exaggeration.

p. 405, l. 36: *Add* Horace Jackson. Gillespie was his assistant, and he regards him as the true hero of this episode.

p. 411, l. 46: *For* Ferdinand Pinney Earle *read* Christy Cabanne.

l. 47: *For* against the design *read* against Ferdinand Pinney Earle's design.

p. 412, last line: *For* sighed *read* sighted.

p. 417, paragraph 4: This occurred on *Merry-go-Round*.

p. 434, paragraph 4: *For* rhinoceroses *read* hippopotamuses. Cooper says a street was named after him, but no statue was raised. *The Four Feathers* was a silent.

p. 497, lower caption: *For* Totherah *read* Totheroh.

p. 524, l. 25: Burel says the cameraman was not he but Wentzel.

p. 556, last line: The Cordeliers sequence was complete by this time.

p. 559, l. 16: Juan Arroy says it was Toulon, not Nice.

p. 562, last line: Since writing the book, I have reconstructed *Napoleon*—as much of it as exists—and I have quizzed Gance closely about the length of the original. He said it was shown in four screenings of 2,500 meters each (which would be 10,000 m altogether, roughly 30,000 ft). The premiere was a specially cut version to fit into one evening, and it lasted three and a half hours. The whole of France received the 10,000 m serialised version, which evidently made a lot of money. I have since discovered that the print shown in London was a shortened version.

p. 570, paragraph 6: This is not exactly verbatim; the original dialogue goes, "We are going to move up to the Bronx . . . and a whole lot of people you know. The Ginsbergs, the Guttenbergs and the Goldbergs and a whole lot of Bergs. I don't know 'em all."

p. 573, l. 5: Lewis Milestone assures me that *All Quiet* was a talkie from the outset.

Chapter 48, p. 580 has been dropped. It was written, oddly enough, before the rest of the book, in the early sixties, when the cinema had sunk into a slough of despond. From the mid-sixties, the cinema effected a miraculous recovery—and this chapter was thus rendered obsolete.

Index

A NOTE ON THE TYPE: The text of this book was set in Garamond, *a modern rendering of the type first cut in the sixteenth century by* CLAUDE GARAMOND *(1510-1561). He was a pupil of Geoffroy Troy and is believed to have based his letters on the Venetian models, although he introduced a number of important differences, and· it is to him we owe the letter which we know as Old Style. He gave to his letters a certain elegance and a feeling of movement which won for their creator an immediate reputation and the patronage of the French King, Francis I.*

Printed by Halliday Lithograph Corporation, West Hanover, Massachusetts

Typography by Herb Migdoll